The Kanner Aliyah

The Kanner Aliyah

A NOVEL
BY

MARK GORDON

GROUNDHOG PRESS
TORONTO

Published by:

Groundhog Press
Box 189, Station Z,
Toronto M5N 2Z4

Canadian Cataloguing in Publication Data

Gordon, Mark, 1942–
   The Kanner aliyah

ISBN 0-9690127-0-5

I. Title.

PS8563.0635K35   C813'.5'4   C79-094808-7
PR9199.3.G665K35

Manufactured in Canada by Webcom Limited.

Aliyah is the Hebrew word for "a going up".

It also means immigration to Israel.

Contents

Part One

Part Two

Part Three

Part Four

PART ONE

CHAPTER 1

Kibbutz One Sun

The sun mixed with manure stench and dust began to sicken him. He could feel it in the pit of his stomach, the nausea building, spreading into his fingertips, into his brain. The skin on his fingers was soft, too soft, soft and easily cut by the rims of the buckets he was carrying. The sharp edges of the pails dug into the fingers on both hands. The galvanized metal had cut through the soft pads. It drew blood just as viciously as any animal.

Martin despised his hands for being soft, for being so easily cut. He hated the exhaustion he felt in his chest, in his shoulders, in his legs, in his feet. The others were working steadily. A few of the immigrants from Rumania were slacking off, one guy stopping to wipe the mist from his glasses, the sweat from his forehead. And he stopped too often, standing for a minute, two, three, as if he were caught in the middle of his own dream or a snapshot, his handkerchief moving slowly across his forehead as if it were a lazy white moth, just barely moving. It seemed that almost everyone else was moving quickly through the banana fields on sturdy sun-burnt legs, muscled legs with spring and energy, speedily, their hands calloused and brown, uncut. Their hands and bodies almost one with the galvanized buckets filled with manure, with the broad blank leaves of the banana trees, with the sun that poured from its yellow hole in the blue sky. Not a cloud in the sky. Not a single puff of white, not one solitary ball of fluff. Metallic expanse of blue, and a single, solitary object, yellow, blazing, one eye unblinking.

The sun of Israel, the sun of the one-sunned kibbutz ruled the sky. The name of the place in fact was "One Sun" in Hebrew. It was near Afula, halfway on the road to somewhere else. The kibbutz was a couple of miles from where the bus stopped. Martin remembered a few days ago getting off the bus. He was walking up the sun-baked highway on leather shoes. Ordinary street shoes worn in Toronto. Thin-soled shoes that made his feet feel each pebble dig and the heat from the highway. It was told that this country got so hot in the summer you could fry eggs on the pavement. This was not just a way of saying things, a convenient metaphor, but here on this long strand of sand, rock, heat, this patch of land at the Mediterranean's far eastern tip, this was the truth. An egg placed on the pavement would actually sizzle, the mucous fluid turning to white, the yellow jelly in the centre slowly hardening, hardening, hardening.

And Martin wanted to harden in this sun, to go black as the shit he was carrying, black as the energetic Algerian Jews, black as any *Sephardi* from Aden or Iraq. He wanted the muscles to harden in his arms, in his forearms, in his shoulders, in his stomach, in his legs. He wanted to become long and hard and invincible as a rod of iron no sun could melt or sizzle, no sharp-edged bucket could cut.

Yet the job in the banana field cut deeply into his softness. It made his legs ache and wobble. The two buckets pulled his shoulders toward the shit-strewn field. His tongue lost its wetness. His saliva dried up like a patch of desert. His tongue almost seemed like a foreign object in his mouth. It felt like a piece of felt cleaving to the roof of his mouth, sticking to his cheeks. For the first couple of hours he was keeping up with the other men. He almost believed for a fast dizzy whirling second that he could keep pace with the fastest among them. That was before the buckets' edges began to slice through his skin seeking blood. That was before the sun's sick heat entered his brain and stomach, and it seemed like a piece of the sun had gotten deep inside his gut, and was just lying there like a piece of bad food sending a sickish feeling into his throat, a dizziness into his head.

As a kid he had known times, situations like this, when he would just give up. Just go up to the person in charge, the supervisor or teacher, and just tell them he couldn't do it. Just couldn't, couldn't, couldn't. And then he would leave the other kids and just go sit under a tree dreaming, a shadowy tree with long cooling black branches. Just sit there alone. It was different now. He wasn't a kid anymore. He was nineteen and he had to do it. And he didn't want to go whining to any boss-man or go to the sidelines or watch anybody brought in as a substitute. His muscles had to grow, his fingers had to toughen up, that was all there was to it.

Martin kept his eyes on one kibbutznik in particular. He was young and tall, muscles shivered on his chest, danced up and down his sturdy legs. He somehow didn't look as black as most, not as black as the shorter immigrants from Morocco or Algeria, yet he moved swiftly and lightly, effortlessly, it appeared, up and down the long black field between the banana trees. And he floated like a deer as if the terribly blue sky was just a roof over his head, and the sun was in its allotted hole in the sky just as it should be. There was no one working any faster than this boy. Martin could not detect a single droplet of sweat on his forehead. Martin took him as his model, as the perfect example of how one should work and trample and dance between the green-bladed banana stalks on this shit-strewn field. He was the real thing: a *sabru*, born and raised at "One Sun" in the dormitories where all the boys and girls lived together like a huge conclave of brothers and sisters, taking showers together unashamed and unabashed to look at each other's naked parts, with boy-eyes running freely down tits and nipples into crotch hair, and girl-eyes used to watching the dangling dingles of their brothers, and the two sacks swinging in the soapy rains.

What would it have been like to grow up in one of those long dorms? The boys and girls sleeping side by side, so close they could hear each other breathe, and hear each other murmur in the night, dream-secrets tumbling and bubbling out, floating among all the siblings. And night fears if there were any, shrieks and fears heard by all up and down the creaky long house. If there were any. If there were any night-after-night terrible wakings with monsters caught in the throat, shadows stalking the sleepers. If there were such things in the long halls of beds near beds, and girl tooth-brushes nudging boy toothbrushes. If it happened in such places.

These children, even little kiddies three and four years old, only saw their parents alone for about a half hour each day. They might spot them in the huge plate-crackling dining room among a hundred others or between the vines in the grape fields or among the drooping oranges, but alone behind closed doors for only thirty minutes or so. No, Martin decided, it was not a place where the kiddies clung to Mommy's apron strings or the boys rode around all day long in Daddy's car. There were not hours and hours of talking with Daddy, and Daddy taking them (each boy like this tall dancing worker) upon his knee for hours and hours, night after night, reading them poetry, and running his hands through their curly locks. It just wasn't set up that way.

Martin wanted to work as fast, as magically, as gracefully, as blank-eyed, as tearlessly as this young *sabra*.

And somehow he was able to make it through those first few days at Kibbutz One Sun. The blood dried and hardened in the crevices of his fingers. His bones ached, his muscles seized, but slowly, slowly he could feel his body getting used to the work, to the shit-fragrance, to the sun and its relentless outpouring of gamma rays, and ultra violet, and searing white bullets. His speed in the shit and sun and dust slowly, notch by notch, increased. Muscles started to harden under his skin, oblong, elliptical, long oval dynamos of flesh. On his arms, in his thighs, on his back. Even his stomach began to ever so slightly ripple. Slowly he could feel a springiness above his feet. The energy built and he grinned to himself, almost unable to believe that the shit had not buried him, and the steel had not cut through to the bone, and the sun had not turned him into a puddle of sweat and tears and defeat on the ground. He was actually doing it. The first few days he could not look that blue-eyed sabra in the face. He kept his eyes on the shit, on the green, almost motionless leaves. Now he was actually saying hello to him in Hebrew, smiling at him, talking with him in English. With great effort and concentration his speed revved and revved, built and grew. He outdistanced and outworked the Rumanians and the Russians and the Bulgarians first. He actually, to his disbelief, came near and finally overtook the black-faced Algerians, some of them anyway. There remained one or two now who still outfoxed him, outdanced him, outworked him in the acres of shit and bananas and sun and sweat. But he came close, so very close, just a hairsbreadth away from beating that sabra boy at his own game.

In the shower house after work, after most of the others had gone to supper, when the place was dank and empty, the mirrors casting back not a single reflection but his own, Martin strode up and down, peering into the horizons of wide glass. He pulled in his stomach, and eyed his chest cage, the muscles beginning to appear above the buds of faint red. He flexed his arms day by day, gazing in semi-amazement, almost dreamily, at the wonder of those bulging orbs. And he had the feeling there was no stopping him now. The process had begun, the hardening of his body, the blackening of his flesh. He gazed at other men from time to time, the hardest among them, the real workers, the young powerful ones, and compared himself to them. And when he regarded his chest, his thighs, his forearms, he had another picture in his mind, another strong, remembered image with which to compare his progress: it was his father's body, a body he was very familiar with, having seen it morning after morning when he was a child, his father in the bathroom in the mornings swishing a blue hot washcloth on the back of his neck. The steam rose from the sink and mingled with the hair on his father's chest, mingled with his admiring gaze. It was a compact body, the body of his Dad. The chest loomed above powerful thighs. The shoulders, a little hunched, were nevertheless strong to Martin's little boy's eyes: they looked like they could support the whole house if necessary, and even the whole damn world, just like Atlas the wonder man. His arm muscles seemed enormously large, especially when his father flexed them, and asked him:

"Well, Martin, what d'ya think—not bad for an old man?"

A grin would roll across Martin's face, an uncontrollable snicker that filled his belly with warm tingling feelings, which made him a little dizzy.

"I'm going to have muscles like that some day," Martin would say.

And his father would tousle his hair with steam-warm hands. And grip the back of his neck, and squeeze.

"Sure you will, Martin. You're a chip off the old block."

His father would grin, showing the bright edges of his teeth, a nick in his cheek, a scar that looked like a dimple. And his father's face would get serious again, his eyes almost dreamy in the morning bathroom among the fragrances of Old Spice and shaving cream.

Was he as strong as his father this very moment?—Martin wondered from time to time on the kibbutz. Was he getting closer? Would he be able to beat him in an arm wrestle this very moment if called upon, and encouraged, and challenged to do so? It was not going to be long before Martin had his answer. One of these days he would travel back to Tel Aviv, perhaps for a visit to his parents' apartment, and he would shake his father's hand, gripping it, squeezing, even crunching a bit, as he had never gripped it before. These contests had been going on for a long time, in fact as long as Martin could remember. It seemed that he had locked hand to hand, arm to arm with his powerful father even at three years old. And his father never faked or gave up or pretended to lose. For years and years Martin's hand went down swiftly, quite swiftly, to the table top. Never once in all those years did he ever really believe that he had the faintest chance of forcing his father's arm to the table, down to the table, and beaten.

Yes, he strode in front of the mirrors in the evening, gauging his progress, wondering, just wondering if . . . How different his body was beginning to look compared to his years at McGill. How white the flesh was then, how pale and soft. Now every inch seemed to be building in weight as well as strength. He wasn't walking clumsily anymore, or dreamily carrying books through the hallways of a university, hiding a weak pale body beneath winter sweaters.

And to his amazement a couple of the kibbutzniks, tall powerful men, were beginning to notice the change in him. They had glanced at him as he carried the long irrigation pipes through the mucky fields. They had seen him empty sack after sack of potatoes onto the conveyor belt. They had asked him if he wanted to sort, whether he needed a rest. But Martin refused, shaking his head, half-grinning. He jumped at the bags, the hundredweight sacks, never slowing down for a minute, grabbing them, swivelling, dumping, dumping, faster and faster, with sweat rolling down his cheeks, soaking his armpits. He just ate up the sound of the potatoes rattling as they fell. Bumping and falling together like tiny rumbles of thunder. Potato dust flying. Burlap bags flung to one side. Older women, their heads kerchiefed, their skin toughened by the sun, sorted. He wanted to burrow and dig and claw his way through every sack in the room, grabbing them, till not a sack was left to be emptied. He just wanted to see that conveyor belt jam-packed with potatoes he had emptied, and the hands of the sorters flicking at their jobs faster and faster. He wanted to lift those bags, to some day feel them light as feathers, like pillows he could toss around.

Yes, the kibbutzniks began to notice him. One evening he walked into the dining room with a white T shirt tightly wrapping his chest, his brown muscles bulging out the thin cotton sleeves, his legs springy, his face brown and grinning, his eyes clear and black, his teeth shining whitely, wreathed by brown skin. He strode into supper amid the clatter of plates, the murmur of talk, jokes, stories rumbling and buzzing up and down the long tables. And Aaron, who was six foot three and weighed well over two hundred pounds, all muscle and sinew, Aaron, his working companion and boss in the irrigation fields, strode up to meet him, slapped him on his shoulder. Aaron slung a hairy arm around his back, his fingers beating lightly against one shoulder, and Aaron guided him over to a table. He said in a loud voice to his sabra friends, a voice that could be heard down the length of the table:

"*Chaverim*," he grinned, "what do you think of this man from Canada? And he works, you should see. There's no carrying this one."

And the men looked up smiling. They nodded their approval and agreement, still forking up sour cream and lettuce and tomatoes and forkfuls of chicken, they looked up, and one or two gave him a friendly wink.

Martin's whole body tingled, almost shivered. He was proud, proud, proud, there was just no other word for it. He hadn't fallen and seeped into the ground, he hadn't run back to his parents' apartment in Tel Aviv. And he felt that he deserved this acclaim, this evening in which he starred in the huge communal dining room. And the skin that was cut on his fingers during the first week, and the nausea he endured in his gut, and the inability to move his aching legs in the morning, all this seemed worthwhile now. It was a part of his life he never wanted to forget or toss in the garbage or sweep under the rug. There were other things that had happened to him in his boyish life, things that embarrassed him, times, so many times, when he had given up or never even tried. He remembered lasting at a Jewish camp for only two weeks. He thought, too, about never trying to get a job. This was his very first, in fact. But this evening he wanted to savour, to remember, to dream about, as the days swept by, just to recall Aaron's voice in the dining room, the surprising words that came out, all the sabras, all of them, nodding their heads in accord. Who would disagree with Aaron anyway? He supervised one of the toughest jobs on the kibbutz. He was excellent in sports. He took part in planning activities, had his hand into the economic intricacies of kibbutz living. For Martin he was the voice of just about everything the community stood for: hard work, and fellowship, and not giving up, and shouldering a rifle if need be. That evening Kibbutz One Sun had spoken in his favour, in fact it almost seemed to Martin that an ancient voice of prophetic Israel had murmured and uttered and laughed from the rocks and sand, saying: "This is a man. He's a man. He's a man. Not a boy, but a man, a real man."

And yet there was another area more intangible, harder to grasp, difficult to nail down, another something he wanted to do. The black kibbutz sky popped with a million stars one evening, almost as bright and near as the stars at sea, the stars that hung over the S.S. Atlantic, the swimming-pooled, cocktail-lounged, ping-pong-playing, dancing ship that sailed him to Israel. How close they were at sea. One morning he walked on deck. He saw a huge orb, a bright shining light in the distance. He thought for sure it was a lighthouse, and somehow the S.S. Atlantic was swerving toward some port, some little dot of an island in the Mediterranean. And that bright star that dazzled the sky was Venus, the great planet of love and poetry, of those feelings so difficult to express.

The cool darkness swept across the picnic tables outside the dining room at the kibbutz. The moonlight and starlight lit up Aaron's face. Martin noticed for the first time that there was just perhaps a faint pudginess to Aaron's cheeks, and a slight billowing hardly detectable, a slight protuberance of his belly beneath his T shirt. His eyebrows looked bushy that evening. They seemed almost to resemble, together with the sunken sockets of his eyes, two questioning eyes on an animal wondering and curious and wanting to know what made this boy from Canada tick. This college-educated boy who worked so well.

"Well, *chaver*," Aaron said, putting a hand, a furry hand on his shoulder, "would you like to become a kibbutznik?"

The thought had whizzed and spun through Martin's head on more than one occasion. He dreamed from time to time of marrying a dark-skinned sabra girl with a bosom firm as a watermelon, and settling down among the rooster crows, the pig grunts, the trickling waters in the irrigation fields. He'd considered for fleeting dreamy moments living his life among cattle hides, plump green grapes, and the clatter of a thousand plates and knives and forks in the huge dining room. He would not be the first to do it. Thousands of Americans and Canadians and Australians and South Africans had done it before him. They had left the huge white cities, the tall buildings, the red lights, and settled like tired animals, just fell down and settled on a kibbutz.

"I'm not sure," Martin murmured. "I really like it here, but there's other things I'm interested in."

"You mean your school?" Aaron asked, his bushy eyebrows slightly jumping.

"Yes, and writing. I want to write."

"Well, chaver, you can write here. A lot of our Hebrew poets and novelists live on kibbutzim, you know."

"Yes . . . " Martin considered.

"What did you take in university anyway?" Aaron asked.

"English," Martin almost whispered. "English Literature."

Aaron snickered. He chuckled, and his whole moonlit face, white and slightly pudgy, and his starlit eyes twinkled.

"You know what we call that?"

"What?" Martin sighed.

"A moon subject."

"A moon subject?"

"Yes, a moon subject."

"You mean faraway," Martin offered.

"Yes, and not very useful, chaver. What has literature got to do with anything? Economics, yes. Engineering. Accountancy. Life is practical, Martin. We don't live on the moon."

"And what do you think life is?" Martin asked, feeling the anger starting to burn and rise in his throat. "Do you believe it's all cows and oranges and muck?"

Martin was angry, but as soon as he started he regretted the attack. It twisted in his throat. It left his stomach feeling cold. Aaron, just a little surprised, his voice just slightly hurt and aching, answered:

"Well, chaver, that is our lives. That is what it means to live on a kibbutz. Yes, you have it right."

And the conversation somehow dwindled, evaporated, came to an end on that cool evening when all the bright stars in the universe and the pale face of the moon shone their lights upon them. "A moon subject." It was a phrase that stuck in Martin's mind for years and years. It was not something easily rubbed out or forgotten. Not something easily ignored. It was like a thin piece of straw that somehow lodged in his cortex. And above his head night after night for years and years to come, there was a huge pale orb to bear Aaron's phrase witness.

No, Martin thought, lying on his cot in one of the cottages set aside for the *ulpan* students, new immigrants like himself, who were studying Hebrew and working on the kibbutz at the same time, no, Martin dreamed, life couldn't just be the building of muscles, the gathering of grapes, the irrigation of ditches. Not for him anyway. There were too many other urges rolling and murmuring inside him. Things he had to do, to experience, to feel, and finally someday to write about, to capture and examine and express with a pen and paper. Sure, it was important to conquer the flesh's sphere, to not remain chicken-soft forever, to pull in his gut so that he could keep up with the fastest and bravest. But he had done this in just about three months, and the kibbutzniks attested in chorus to his accomplishment. Already in his cot, the stars twinkling outside, the summer trees barely whispering, already he could feel just a little bored and restless with the days passing. Just a little sleepy with the prospect of tying up his workboots each morning and joining the others on the work wagon going to the fields, or jumping into the jeep with Aaron. The hundreds of purple plums he had plucked off trees, the thousands of seedless green grapes, the tons of potatoes he had dumped onto the conveyor belt, the miles of irrigation pipe he had laid among the potatoes and among the tall stalks of corn—they all seemed now to sway and moan and almost groan in his dark head. Fruit, vegetables, chicken shit. It all mixed in his heart endlessly, almost drearily. And dreary the prospect of waking each morning to do and redo these things.

And the learning of the Hebrew language, he had let it slide, and fall by the wayside. In fact somehow he had gotten out of attending Hebrew school with the other members of the *ulpan*. He worked a full shift, nine hours like anyone else, and spoke little Hebrew. It seemed a dark wearisome language full of gutturals that stuck in his throat, squiggly lines that ran into each other on the page. In Hebrew school as a young boy he had the same attitude, learning just enough to read his *maftir* at his bar mitzvah. Even then it was all by memory. He had no idea what he was singing out in the cavernous hall of the synagogue. No idea until years later that what he had sung out were the ten commandments, the nut and crunch of Mosaic law.

And finally it came to another issue, one that touched him deepest in the evenings lying in his cot alone. It burrowed into his crotch, burned and tingled. There was no ignoring this one either, or burying it beneath the corn. He was nineteen, and except for two whores in Mexico two years ago, he had never entered a woman's body. He had gone through petting and kissing and licking and pawing like just about anyone else, and excitement till he came in his jeans. But never the full impact of what he imagined must be a wonderful thing and an inspiration and perhaps a solution to some of his problems, to his pin-and-needle restlessness—namely the experience of having a woman of his very own, a body he could enter night after night, just sink his pain and yearning into, and feel and ram and slide and poke and come out thankfully soft and subdued.

On the kibbutz he saw women, sabras and immigrants, sleek ones from Canada and the U.S.A., but somehow he never got to the point of talking to them, holding their hands, patting their hair, or squeezing softly their soft breasts.

Tel Aviv with its circular Dizengoff where the cars danced and putted, where the women high-stepped it, Tel Aviv with its outdoor cafes, and free living, and girls, a variety of them, began to spin into his mind. Tel Aviv with the Mediterranean lapping at its city shoreline, with its possibilities of meeting someone female who might find him interesting, even attractive, perhaps slightly exciting in his own intense poetic way, began to light up the dark spaces in his brain. And he hadn't seen his parents in about three months. They had, in fact, not communicated except for a letter or two. He wondered how his father's business efforts were going in this jabbering, talkative, black-skinned country. His father always seemed to make his way somehow, whether it was in his hometown, anglo-dominated Halifax, or in the heart of Montreal, or among the wheeler-dealers on Bay Street in Toronto. His father with his financial finesse, his acquaintance with all the turns and spins of numbers, his ex-accountant, stock-broking, financial-consulting father had always danced a path between the opposition, coming up with a deal that sucked in the loot. He had fallen a few times from high places, his invincible father. He went from millionaire to broke a couple of times, he took a faltering turn and nose-dived into nothingness, but he always seemed able to pick himself up and replenish the empty coffers. He always got his "second wind", as he was fond of calling it. No matter how hard he was running or fighting or sliding backward, that second wind dashed into his lungs, flushing his face with new vigor. Martin could not imagine that Tel Aviv would be any exception.

Yet his father's reason for leaving Toronto, the real scoop, the honest-to-goodness facts, escaped him. He didn't delve into it too deeply, as if fearing to discover something he couldn't understand or fully accept. It was fishy, the whole thing, and no matter how much Martin blocked what had really gone on in Toronto the clean and beautiful, there were a few things he couldn't get out of his mind. *Lash*, the local scandal sheet in old Toronto, had reported—just about the time his father disappeared from Bay Street and flew to the promised land—that Mr. Kanner was probably at the bottom of the St. Lawrence. Martin remembered that this terribly upset his mother. But sure enough, when they disembarked from the S.S. Atlantic, his mother, his sister, and himself, there his father stood alive and well as ever, his face blackened by the sun, his teeth even brighter, and his smile that day glittered triumphantly.

"What were you worried about, Dahlia?" his father grinned. "Christ, you know damn well I've got nine lives."

And his mother purred on his father's shoulder, and perhaps a tear or two dampened her cheeks. Martin's heart had also taken a leap and bolt in his chest when he spotted his father from the ship's deck. A grin shone out from Martin's face, a wide stretched grin, which he was sure his father spotted among the crowd of faces peering down. And Martin thought to himself with a slight tingling of pride: fuck, there's no killing that guy. That day his father reminded him of Humphrey Bogart or Victor Mature, some tough nut of a man who always somehow, through spit and hail, smoke and jungle, comes up grinning and very much alive.

Yet, there was a strong yearning in Martin to settle like a bug in the crotch of an orange tree, to marry a girl and love her and fuck her and laugh with her and work with her and cry on her shoulder among the grapes, the cattle moans, the roistering of the cocks. It seemed a simple life. Just keep picking those oranges and laying down those yards of aluminum pipes. Just keep eating his sour cream and tomatoes until his heart became a weak mushy thing, until the end of his days when finally no breath could be drawn, no eye would blink, then darkness, darkness, a thankful sleep.

It was an effort to think about boarding that bus once again for Tel Aviv, and rattling and roaring back to his parents' apartment. But he had to do it. There were too many blank spaces, too many urges fluttering just beneath the skin. Perhaps he would take a trip down to the Negev, to Massada, and the Dead Sea. He had heard much about it at the kibbutz. The wonder of Lot's wife, her body turned into a pillar of salt, tall and motionless, still standing after all these worn centuries. The wonder of a sea that supported no life, just tons of potassium and other chemical mutations. A huge black deadness in the centre of this lean country. And the slightly thrilling thought of being close to the border where the Palestinian terrorists often roamed late at night, their eyes masked by darkness, their mouths breathing hidden fire, their hands fingering and refingering the muzzles on cool-nosed guns.

A short visit to Tel Aviv, just to let his parents know that he was still alive, to let them see the amazing transfiguration of his body. To stand before them, his skin dark, almost musky, his chest expanded, his muscles bulging. But not to stay too long.

Finally, he boarded the bus after getting a leave of absence from the kibbutz authorities.

CHAPTER 2

The Arm Wrestle

"How is business going?" he asked his father in the living room of the small apartment.

"This is a tough country, Martin. Everyone has a mind of their own. You know what Ben Gurion said to Kennedy once? He said, 'President Kennedy, you are the president of one hundred and sixty-five million people, but I am the president of three million presidents.' And that, Martin, is close to the truth. Toronto and Montreal were child's play in comparison. Then, to complicate things, it's a backward place in many respects. For Chrissakes the ultra-religionists actually dictate laws to the *Mapai*. And the *Histadrut*, representing the wage earners, is altogether too powerful. It's just very difficult to get a foothold."

His father sighed, just enough to be heard, and he looked toward the floor. Martin saw just a few signs of aging, even weakness, in his eyes. Things he had never really noticed before. His eyes were just not as black and fiery and darting through space. A few grey hairs were beginning to appear above his ears. A few more wrinkles near the corners of his eyes.

"And how did you like the kibbutz?" his father smiled.

"It was tough at the beginning. My bloody hands were raw. I guess I did it, though. It's a good life."

"But it's not a place you can stay forever, right?"

"Well..."

"I know what you're thinking, Martin," his father gleamed. "I've known you long enough. It's good to experience hard work. But there are other things in life."

His father reached out a hand and squeezed Martin's arm on one of the biceps he had become proud of. Martin flexed his arm.

"Not bad for a young guy," Martin grinned.

"Not bad at all," his father laughed. "I guess you're feeling pretty tough these days. Stand up, let's take a good look at you."

Martin got up from the sofa. He stood before his father, his stomach pulled in, his chest expanded, his neck almost taut. And his father's dark wondering eyes fell upon his body. The gaze travelled along the hardened muscles in Martin's thigh, to his arm, his shoulders.

"A regular Greek god," his father smiled.

"Dahlia!" his father shouted. "Come in here for a second. Have you taken a good look at this boy of yours?"

And his mother swung into the room, her face just slightly flushed from making the beds, and dusting, and bending, and looking for lost things on the floor.

"Dahlia, give his arm a squeeze. I tell you, he's catching up on the old man."

His mother reached out a hand, her fingernails polished red, and she just lightly felt the muscle in his arm.

"Wow!" she almost whistled. "The girls won't be safe now."

"Dad," Martin said excitedly, his lungs filling with heat, his blood rushing faster, a dizzy feeling in his head. "Dad, I think I can take you in an arm wrestle."

"Martin," his father sighed, "I know you're feeling your oats, but I haven't been exactly standing still either. I've been swimming every morning at the 'Y' and walking to work."

And his father flexed his arm.

"There's still a little power left," he grinned.

And like the old days, the muscle in his arm expanded. It was thick and round and hard. It was a muscle he had used in the slums of Halifax, down on Water Street when he was a young boy. A muscle that grew from carrying sacks of potatoes for his father, controlling a bicycle weighed down with groceries, delivering meat and vegetables through the icy streets. It was a muscle that had swung Martin's arm down again and again for years and years. It had never lost a single match, never shown a sign of weakness. It was the muscle behind his father's fist, and that fist had never lost a fight in the Halifax slums or anywhere else for that matter. It was a muscle that had sent men to the hospital with broken jaws. It was a muscle that had carried Martin from midnight till dawn, night after night, when Martin was two years old and everyone was deathly afraid he was going to die of bronchitis. It was a muscle that raised a boulder one night and crunched the head of an attacking dog, one night when his father and mother were returning from a dance. It was a muscle that no man in the Jewish community of Halifax or anywhere else, no man except Martin's grandfather, his father's father, had ever twisted and slammed to a table.

Martin felt every inch of his flesh tingle with excitement. He remembered the sacks of potatoes dumped on the conveyor belt, and the deep cuts in his fingers, and the aching in his shoulders, and the nausea caught in his throat. Martin breathed deeply to feel every ounce, every speck of muscle he had put together so carefully and maniacally at Kibbutz One Sun. The muscles shivered in his back, in his legs. How he wanted, desired, burned and almost choked with excitement to put his father's arm down, to beat him, to just fucking beat him, to just squelch once and for all that muscle in his father's right arm.

"C'mon Dad," Martin said, his words almost shooting forth, mixed with the dryness in his mouth, the excitement, "I think I'm going to take you today."

"Well, Martin"—his father's voice was now serious—"don't be disappointed if you don't. I just don't believe you're there yet. You're close but . . . "

"We'll see," Martin interrupted, feeling the blood in his brain clang loudly, his blood zipping up and down his legs, buzzing in his chest, excitement caught in his throat. "Mom, you stay and watch. I want somebody here as a witness."

"O.K.," his father groaned, rising from the sofa. "Let's go to the dining-room table."

It was a slow plod and walk to the table for Martin, his body and brain racing to get there, but somehow the whole motion taking place slowly as if he were marking time, his legs moving, his heart racing, his brain alive and trembling, but each movement slowly taken. He could hear his father's shoes behind him creaking on the fake wood floor. He could smell the Old Spice and faint perspiration of his father a foot or so behind him. It was not merely a déjà vu, this feeling in Martin that he had wound this trail before, hundreds of times. To the dining-room table, the mahogany black shiny dining-room table, where the faces could be seen reflected back, almost every feature identifiable in the polished wood surface his mother's rubbing had created. Soft cloths and polish. The faces at a hundred thousand meals and discussions and arguments and arm wrestles were hidden in such mahogany reflections. They were all sealed there, thought Martin, ready perhaps to be revealed on judgement day. And this event recorded by some celestial or sub terra observer. And if he failed, if his sinew and muscle and blood vessels trembled, folded, snapped, it would be the same old weary recording that someone up there, and something inside Martin, would have to view again.

And now he was facing his father, both of them seated, just a corner of mahogany surface separating their knees. How familiar was the thick hand of his father, the palms always rose in hue as if the heat of this man lived and beat close to the surface. He had never noticed that rosy complexion on the palms of anyone else, no other man or woman, or artful picture painted. And he knew as soon as he grasped his father's right hand with his own, he would feel once again, as so many times before, the faint perspiration that beaded near the surface on such occasions. For this too was exciting for his father. It was never a nonchalant exercise, merely a game. Martin could see the light rise in his black eyes, now fully black and alive before him. He could see the lips on his father, more mobile, more alive, more expressive. Only a big business deal in the offing could move his face to reach for, but never quite attain this same aliveness, expectation, and sense of wonderment. Only when his hand shook and squeezed the hand of his own father, only then did he smile as broadly, his eyes twinkling.

Martin gripped his father's hand. This was the moment he was waiting for, the moment he had dreamed about at Kibbutz One Sun. This was the supreme test. It meant even more in a way than being paraded through the dining room by Aaron. It was the final test. And when he thought of the possibility of his blackened arm and hand being slammed to the table, a tired weary sensation built in his gut. He had to do it. When again would he ever be in this shape? The muscles toned from months of steady work. When again would he be so bloody close, just a breath away from doing it?

They started off square and even, no one getting the edge. Both arms straight, no one testing the other, just a fair edging and planing of arm against arm, muscle to muscle, eye to eye. His mother stood about two feet away from the table. She held a yellow dust-cloth almost limply in her hand. She too had borne witness to the struggle for years. And suddenly she blurted out:

"C'mon, Martin, you can do it this time. I know you can."

And this sudden encouragement, which Martin never remembered hearing before, sent a jolt of blood through his body he'd never quite felt before. The energy rose to a height he had never experienced. He had to do it, now, or never.

"Are you ready?" he almost spat.

"Yes," his father responded.

The full weight of their two arms and gnarled hands locked together, pressed, heaved. Not an arm moved in either direction. They were locked vertically together. Fuck, the guy was still strong, Martin's heart and brain hissed.

"Come on, Martin," his mother almost shouted this time. "C'mon, Martin, do it!"

And Martin put his full weight, every ounce of muscle and nerve and excitement and pain and yearning into it. And his father's arm, almost to his disbelief, began just slightly to give. Another jolt of blood flashed through him, spun and trembled and waterfalled straight up his back. Now or never, his heart banged. And his father's arm unbelievably, inexplicably, went down, down, down, down, flat and beaten beneath his hand.

"Oh shit," Martin whispered, "I did it."

His mother rushed around the table and hugged him closely.

"I knew you could do it!" she almost yelled. "I'm so proud of you, Martin."

And his mother kissed him on the cheek.

It was a long time before Martin could raise his eyes from the table to look into his father's face. Never before had he seen that look in his father's eyes. It was the look of a lamb being carried. It was surprised, unable to explain. The eyes soft and brown, puppy-dog eyes.

"Martin," his father said, placing a warm rose perspiring hand on his shoulder, "I didn't think you had it in you. I honestly didn't."

Martin's face trembled. It tried to smile. It didn't know what to do. A grin hung on the brim of his lips, a tear caught in his throat.

Martin was stunned. He couldn't quite believe that it was over, so swiftly brought to a conclusion. The trembling, the waiting, the excitement, the slow building, building, building, and then the sudden end, the climax, with a rush of blood, his father's hand after nineteen years finally beneath his own hand on the table. Would there be any next contest in the skin's domain? A fist fight perhaps, or a wrestling match? Martin doubted it. No, that was it, the arm wrestle was the contest of muscle, and the mahogany table the battlefield.

Everything in the apartment was queerly quiet for the rest of the afternoon. His mother went about her business, cooking the evening meal: cabbage soup and chicken. His father retired to the sofa, a business paper in his hand, the paper rustling, his eyes half hidden. Martin paced up and down. In the streets of Tel Aviv the busy active people raced back and forth, into short squat office buildings, into kiosks to buy little glasses of mitz tapuzim (orange juice) or Israeli pop, or carrot juice, or any mouthful of liquid that would cut through the dryness in the throat. The heat in Tel Aviv hung like a limp cloud over the city. It was always wet. And to Martin there never seemed enough liquid to drink in little glasses and bottles. The throat continued dry, sandy and dry, stretched and yearning to be wetted, to be smoothed, for the pain and the dryness to be waterfalled away.

As he paced in the weirdly quiet living room, he wondered what to do next. The kibbutz seemed even farther away than before. He remembered the boredom, the routine, and it seemed even duller.

The rocks of Massada, the cliffs of Sodom and Gomorrah kept edging into his mind. His mother and father had driven through the area, but did not stop. His father had commented about the sheets of rock, the treeless slabs of heat and sun. "It's so dry," his father said, "so rocky, without shade or water, there's only one word for it: it's obscene."

Martin decided to go. Swiftly he decided, when a particular shaft of blood darted into his brain, he decided. There was no turning back. Before he knew it, he was getting off the bus in the twilight near a lone kiosk, in the wastes and rocks and cliffs, in the darkness falling, he alighted somewhere near Sodom and Gomorrah.

CHAPTER 3

On the Road to Massada

The darkness fell so weirdly, at such a peculiar angle, carving the cliffs with cheeks of purple, that there was in him, momentarily, a temptation to retreat, to go back to the safety of the city or the kibbutz. But wasn't this part of being a poet, a young visionary and seer, nineteen years old, didn't he owe it to himself to nudge and nibble at these shivery feelings? He thought of Dostoyevsky, his back lanes in St. Petersburg, his Raskolnikov Russian soul, undaunted by cats in back alleys and whores with hearts of gold. And Kafka, his shimmering castles hung halfway between the stratosphere and mountain peaks. The lanes so dark and unknown, he lost the feeling of the presence of his own Czechoslovakian foot. And D. H. Lawrence chasing plumed serpents and feathery gods through the jungles of Mexico, or the badlands anyway. They hadn't flinched when they entered their own personal bottomlands. Fuck, thought Martin, this has got to be one of the deepest ditches in the universe. The earthly counterpart of the black hole in outer space.

There was no looking back. What weird dead shadows curled their wantonness toward heaven? Near these cliffs King Herod, bejewelled and bedecked with glittery crown and spear, in 70 A.D. or thereabouts, hunted into a rock by the Roman legions, stood his ground. The Roman hordes advanced with stomp of boot and clang of shield and "Long live the Emperor" on their lips . . advanced. Each haunted, hunted Jew in turn drove a knife or wooden fork through his heart, so that nothing would remain for the goyim to gloat over, no live beating heart for the *vilders* to crush. Only King Herod stood alive, his Jewish heart singing victoriously as the man-worshippers entered his sanctuary. It took three spears to kill him. One for the torah of Moses. One for the lion of Judah, David's lineage. And one for all the power and might and wisdom and cunning erect King Herod had culled from his father.

And near these rocks slim David the future king slithered, just a breath and whinny away from Saul's imperious spear. David and Jonathan allied, clasping hands, their friendship glowing. Saul bellowing. Saul stumbling through darkness. But David, the lithe shepherd boy, harp and wisdom and courage in hand, outsmarted the very darkness itself, dodged the deadly coral snakes and the snapping-tailed scorpions.

The heavy, dark, aching tradition of *do it*, do it at any cost, do it and write it and sing it and dance it, until the wives get angry with the antics, do it for the Lord, and for prophecy—all this in darkness; this tradition of courage and lion-heartedness hung on Martin's head. Even the shivery tingle of fear felt like a deserved mantle across his neck. So what if he couldn't see his feet. So what if it all ended—unconscious in ninety seconds, dead in two minutes at the end of a snake's fang. This was a risk he had to take. Where else could the gutsy muse, and the unearthly enlightenment, come from? He was going to slide to the very bottom of this ditch, this mineshaft, this obscene place, if need be.

And from some passers-by drinking mitz tapuzims and colas in the kiosk, Martin heard some rumours about the locale that tingled shivers into his root of roots. It was, indeed, one of the lowest inhabited places in the world, thousands of feet below sea level, matching the unmatchable Death Valley in the U.S.A. The temperature the next day was going to soar to one hundred and twenty-seven degrees. The sun would bake its eggs on the highway, sear any piece of flesh that would dare stand before its unblinking eye. King or poet or god-man alike would melt before its hot-faced presence. It was not a respecter of persons. The snakes in this area, Martin was told, were the most insidious, the most instantly killing of any place in the entire world. Ninety seconds—that was all—and poof: unconsciousness, death. There was no serum available, no hospitals close enough. Only stretchers waiting to carry the victim home to his loved ones. The scorpions might not kill, if one were lucky, but their venom would jump through the bloodstream, and finally strike the heart with a stroke so sudden, exquisite, pure and painful, no man could ever forget it. And the guerillas roamed the rocks, the twilight, matching wits with Israelis in jeeps. They had been known to toss bombs through windows of touring buses. Kaboom, crash—twenty bodies lying bloodied and torn on the floor. Snakes, scorpions, madmen, they danced and wriggled in the twilight just outside the kiosk.

The soldiers served at Sodom and Massada only for a year, a year at the most, before they were given a new assignment. The sun, the fear, the snakes, the loneliness of rock and salt and sand would drive any man crazy if he attempted to stay longer. He would wind up in the Dead Sea, bootless, shirtless, and stark raving mad, his belly bloated with angst and heat.

At the kiosk each tourist was asked to take a salt tablet, and a supply with him on his journey to the Dead Sea, to Massada, and on to Ein Gedi. The sweat poured out so fast in this grassless land no human organism could replace the salt fast enough. And the terror of heat prostration stalked each living soul. Sizzle and sizzle into the blood and brain. The salt getting baked, sucked out. Then a stumbling, a faintness, a weakness. A final tossing backward or forward ... black-out. It sometimes took weeks to nurse the sun-tormented victim back to his proper senses. Weeks to unglue the fried synapses in his brain.

Martin had no definite idea where the kiosk was situated, only that it was nestled, half-buried in twilight and rock, at the foot of a cliff. What was towering above? Was it the pillar of salt, or the ashen remains of Sodom and Gomorrah? How those fools gamboled among the forbidden cheeks and crevices of each other four thousand years ago. How it found disfavour in Jehovah's eyes. It must have become a sour tinge in His mouth, a pain in the neck, to watch, day in, day out, these men with men, women with women, performing their unseemly acts. Ah, the cleansing power of the Lord's anger, finally it fell from His abused black eyes, from His sensitive mouth and angry teeth. Cleansing fire. Absolving brimstone. The whole bloody city of buggeroos wiped out in a single flash of Lordly wrath. No more would they gambol and creak and moan and perform their unnatural acts. No, thought Martin, Jehovah had not yanked a rib from Adam's chest for nothing. He had not fathered in the beginning Eve—she and her offspring, the breasted kind—to be mocked in this way. Sodom and Gomorrah flashed into nothingness with all the speed and finality of Hiroshima beneath the weight of the atoms splitting. In Sodom, too, the bugaboo eyes must have melted in their sockets. Not a bone left standing. Only ash and marrow and weeping and gnashing of teeth, and the terror of the inevitable blackness covering everything.

Sodomy, Sodomy, Sodomy, he thought. What a musical word. And Gomorrah, so filled with soft poetic rhythm. What beautiful words for acts defiled. I want more of Gomorrah, he sang under his breath. It did have a ring to it: Gomorrah, the beautiful. A ring, a slant, and a rhythm, like guerilla or goat—a beautiful word, yet tainted forever.

The twilight nursed the rocks, the rocks covered the sand, the sand swallowed the water, the water lay stagnant and unalive at the bottom of the Dead Sea. Lonely was this place, Martin mused. And he didn't quite know fully why he had travelled to this empty ditch in this lean forsaken country. Here, he was sure, he would find no members of the breasted kind. He might spot one, her skirt uplifted, as she mounted Massada. But he was expecting nothing more. Not in the twilight below Gomorrah. Yet maybe he could write a poem or an Odyssey of sorts about these travels in the twilight zone. If he couldn't get inspired here with a million snakes hissing beneath rocks, the scorpions clapping their tails, the terrorists padding along the roads, the bible just a breath and whistle away, where else, pray tell, would the tunnels of darkness in his brain and soul be vented? Yet he felt no rush for pen and paper. Rock, rock, rock, snake, hiss —that was all that rumbled inside his brain. But he would tuck all this away, the tons of obscene rock, the bullets of the sun, the lapping of dead waves, tuck it away for future reference, to be converted, perhaps, decades hence, into his first lonely epic.

Lonely—that was exactly how he was beginning to feel in the tiny kiosk below the cliffs of Sodomy. There was no place to curl up and go to sleep. There were no buses at this hour leaving, going back or forward. He had been warned by some of the people in the kiosk not to walk these roads at night. A guerilla could be lurking. And if the guerilla didn't finish him off, then a dutiful Israeli marine might mistake his stumbling shadow for an enemy, and shoot to kill, asking the questions later, apologizing much later. It was not the place to walk a lonely shadow on crackling pebbles, either forward or backward, or even to stand in one spot shivering.

The loneliness began to crowd in on him, the doubt of what to do, of where to stay. A slight terror of the darkness outside began to nibble at his brain. Just as this was happening, he struck up an acquaintance with two other travellers from distant lands: Rick, a brown-skinned lean Jewish boy from England; and Jan, a blond-haired tall blue-eyed boy from the Netherlands. They too were beginning to itch and feel the prong in their behinds, the desire to move on. Especially Rick. His black eyes flashed with excitement and anxiety. His skin stretched tighter on his face as he spoke.

"What the hell," he said, "we can't hang our asses around here all night. I'm game for walking to Massada. It's cool tonight. We might get a ride. It's only a few miles down the road."

"Sure, why not?" Jan added. "These roads are well patrolled. And if we carry a light, we shall be quite safe."

"Of course," Rick agreed. "I don't believe half the stories anyway. I think they're old wives' tales just passed around to give the tourists their thrills. Guerillas are just as scared of the dark as anyone else. And snakes go to sleep at night. Are you with us, Martin?"

"Sure," Martin answered, almost too quickly. "Why not? It's only a few miles down the road. We can get there in a couple of hours."

"Well, let's set out," Jan smiled. "But if we do hear anything suspicious, just lie down by the side of the road. Don't make noises."

"Yes," Rick added, "I'd rather take my chances with the snakes than walk into an Israeli patrol."

They set out together. Which would he rather do, Martin wondered to himself, die by snake-bite or bullet-head? Well, it was decided, lie down in a ditch without a breath. This he would do also. But not near rocks—no, in an ordinary ditch, flat and sandy. For he had often heard that beneath the rocks the snakes slithered and slept.

As they were about to leave, a laggard and hanger-on, three days' growth of beard fuzzing his cheeks, a guy named Paul, a French Jew, decided to join them. Martin noticed immediately a strange cobweb of sleep that hung on his mouth. A brown sheepishness in his eyes. Yet he seemed the kind of inoffensive person, innocuous, quite harmless-looking, who could hide a stiletto in his boot, and he might fumble and get to it in the nick of time, piercing the darkness and the terrors and the oblique shadows, and rip, if aroused, his own stupor.

They set out, each for his own dark personal reason. At times, the others seemed naked in Martin's eyes. They were all travelling the same road together, each matching wits with snakes and darkness, bullets and fear, each trying to get a foothold in the shifting sand, each razor-keen to stumble and claw and tread the path to Massada; yet the others, to Martin, seemed just a little naked. If he himself did not have his acquaintance with words, the possibility of etching a few square inches of all this some day on paper, would he be walking now this crazy lean road? In fact, would he bother to breathe at all, to eat, to sleep, to continue anything? Those words he was just beginning to manipulate, were his clothing, his shield, and they were slowly becoming his reason for doing anything. Why the hell would he be here at all, if there was not the chance of telling himself and others about it some day, of just making a speck of sense or nonsense out of it? It was really difficult to figure out why the others were doing it. Was it just to feel the movement of darkness around their waists? A fill-in for standing still. Perhaps Jan was a philosopher. Rick, an adventurer. And Paul, a Shakespearian fool, tagging along for the laughs, yet suffering with the rest.

The four of them set off on the pebbled road to Massada. Rick led the way, Jan keeping pace. Lean Rick, his skinny face determined, kept always a heel-length, just a breath in front of Jan. The union jack shone on the back of his knapsack—those fields of glory: Richard the Lion-Hearted, Andrew of Scotland, the highland fling, and breezy kilts. He was Jewish, Rick was, but he had the spirit of Sir Edmund Hillary implanted in one of his thigh muscles. He sprinted ahead.

"Boys!" he yelled over a rushing shoulder. "If we don't get a ride, who cares? We can walk to Massada. Just let everyone keep pace."

"Sure," said Jan, flushed with Rick's vigor, "it is entirely possible. I had a good look at the map before we left."

Paul and Martin walked in back, saying little. Martin was determined to keep up with the others. So it began. Boots on pebbles, foot in front of foot, crunching and crackling the dark swirling miles. The darkness fell. The moon rose. It was a lean white thing in the sky. Martin had never seen it so bright. It almost appeared mechanical, a huge reflector aimed from outer space. It cast an eerie light on the cliffs, on the road, on the sparse underbrush. It lit up the four faces, each one a bright target. Ping. Ping. Ping. Ping. FOUR

YOUNG TRAVELLERS FOUND DEAD ON ROAD TO MASSADA
—the headlines could read the next day, thought Martin.

Paul began mumbling something. It started as just a murmur. In fact, Martin wasn't quite sure if he was speaking or humming a tune, or merely yawning. He knew, however, that they would finally form themselves into sentences, these barely audible moans. Martin realized he would eventually have to listen to what Paul was saying. Out it came, finally.

"I think that guy's an idiot."

" . . . What?" asked Martin, his ears blocked.

"That fuckin' Englishman," he hissed.

Martin cleared his throat.

"What are you talking about?"

"The limey," he whispered and hissed in the moonlight.

"Oh, Rick."

"Yeah, Rick the prick. We shouldn't have left the kiosk."

Martin kept his mouth shut, just kept putting down one foot in front of the other. Onward. Onward. And Paul began to lag behind, a foot, a yard, farther behind. Martin stumbled back toward him. Paul was sitting on the sand, one shoe off.

"What's the matter?" Martin asked.

"My feet are sore. I got a pebble in my sock. And I'm tired."

And the inevitable shout Martin knew was going to come, came wheeling back at them.

"Where are you bloody guys?" yelled Rick.

"Paul's having problems," Martin replied.

Something muffled, a phrase came trembling back down the road. Martin was not sure what it was. Perhaps just a crackling of pebbles. But it sounded like, "These Frenchmen, damn them."

Paul looked like a hump of tired, dirty laundry sitting by the roadside. Only his teeth faintly glowed. His head was bent, his hands fingering a filthy blue sock. He seemed to be massaging the sock, trying to smooth out each wrinkle. Slowly he kneaded it. He repeated the process with the other blue covering. And began on his feet. Each toe in turn. Finally Rick and Jan stood beside Martin.

"What's the matter anyway?" Rick asked.

There was no answer coming from Paul. The webs grew thickly around his tongue, blocked the passage from his voice box, settled and grew in his chest.

"Paul's got sore feet," Martin answered.

"Sore feet!" Rick spat. "Did he cut himself?"

"Uh, no," Martin murmured. "It's the pebbles. He got some in his sock."

"Well, what's he going to do? He can't sit here all night."

Silence. Long, dead silence.

"What do you want to do, Paul?" Martin finally asked. "Can you walk now?"

"No, they're too sore. I can't go another foot."

"Fucking typical," spat Rick. "Well, I'm not standing around here for anyone. I'm walking to Massada, and I'm not going to stop until I get there. Who's going with me?"

"Rick, listen," Jan said. "We give him a few minutes rest. Maybe he'll feel better. We can all go on together."

Martin was relieved by the sound of Jan's reasoning voice among the rocks and the whisper of underbrush. He wanted to continue with Jan and Rick. Somehow he felt obligated to remain behind with Paul, if Paul refused to get to his feet. Rick was turning disagreeable, but it seemed a worse fate to spend the evening in a ditch with Paul, forced to watch him pat his feet.

"A few minutes, and that's all," hissed Rick. "These guys are all the same. I had my fill of them in Greece."

The wind hissed. Paul hissed under his breath, and he continued to massage his toes. Jan stood loose-limbed, half gazing downward at Paul, then turning occasionally to look down the black road that led to Massada.

"If we can't get to Massada tonight," Jan said, "we can stop at the Dead Sea. It is half the distance."

"If this fellow will get off his ass, I know we can make it," hissed Rick, his face twisted, his eyes glaring.

Rick occasionally glanced at Paul. The foot massage seemed to thoroughly disgust him. The skin on his face stretched tighter as the slow, wind-blown minutes passed. Finally, words emptied from his tight mouth.

"Well, what are you going to do?" he asked Paul.

"I'm going to sit here."

"Sit here all night, you fool?"

"Yes. It was insanity to leave the kiosk."

"O.K., that's it," Rick almost shrieked, "I'm leaving. I'm not stop-

ping until I get to Massada. And I don't care if I have to do it
alone."

Jan's considered voice rang in the night-black silence that followed.

"Martin, stay here with Paul. It is not safe for anyone to be alone.
I will go on with Rick. You won't be here long, I'm sure."

Martin felt that he had no other choice. Jan, the voice of reason,
had spoken. And it was reasonable, the only thing to do, given the
given situation. It left him with an empty feeling in his gut. He
preferred to be on the move with the others, yet he kept thinking of
Paul sitting in a ditch all night long, lonely as a vulture on a desert
tree, kneading his toes. It seemed that if no one kept Paul company,
he was capable of falling asleep, and not remembering to wake up.
The next afternoon, all that would be found would be a sack of fried
flesh, sockless and dirty-toed. A fleeting thought whipped through
his mind. What if Jan stayed with Paul? Yet the idea of a forced
march with Rick—spit and hiss, and crackling underbrush—left him
feeling even emptier. If he had a choice, if he could arrange it as he
wanted it, he would walk on with Jan, leaving Rick and Paul to
murder each other.

"Enough talk. Let's go," and Rick was off down the road a
hundred yards before Jan began to move.

"We'll meet up," Jan said. "If you get a ride, look for us along the
roadside."

And Jan took off down the road, seeking Rick's shadow.

Martin stood still, a little bewildered.

The entire desert seemed to hiss and moan and creak with unknown sounds. The stars, bright as cleansed teeth, stood in their
ancient courses. Crazy thoughts whirled through Martin's mind.
How many of those stars were dead, he wondered. He was told that
the light was no guarantee that any of those white gems still existed.
What a strange thought. The light reaching his eyes, but the source
dead. He picked out a particular star. Did King David ever stand in
this exact inch of sand, composing a psalm, his eyes fixed on the
self-same star? Perhaps the whole world had shifted in those thousands of years, and he was really standing where a pyramid used to
be. There was no end to the whirring of his thoughts. They kept
pace fast and furiously with Paul's moans. He groaned like a

wounded dog. The sound passed through Martin's ears, then up the road, then down to the Dead Sea. Who could say where it ended? On Paul's death-bed it perhaps would return after circling the globe three or four weary times, finally return and join his death rattle.

"How are your feet?" Martin asked.

"They are ruined," Paul sighed. "I have never felt anything like it. They are completely useless."

"Oh, come on Paul, that's a little melodramatic, don't you think?"

"No," Paul groaned. "I don't want to ever walk again. I am finished."

Martin was not quite sure what was happening. Was Paul trying to be funny—a subtle French sense of humour which Martin just couldn't understand, or did it just lose its gist and punch in translation? Or was the guy bonkers, completely off his lid? Yet Martin realized that if he voiced some of his own thoughts, they too would be regarded with suspicion by a sane observer, if such a thing existed.

"Why do you feel this way?" Martin asked, half curious and half wanting to hear the sound of voices.

"It is the moon," grimaced Paul. "It is too bright out here. It is this fucking country. I've been here too long. Too many Ricks, too much sand, too many impossible pebbles. It is life itself. I can't stand it any more."

"I wish I could say something to make you feel better," Martin said faintly, shifting from foot to foot.

"Merde, that's all that can be said."

The silence and the shit slowly closed in once again. Paul's mouth fell shut. Martin searched the black gaping road backward and forward, praying under his breath that he would see the two golden globes of headlights coming in their direction. But the blackness stretched on to the end of the world, to the end of time.

"How long have you been here?" Martin asked.

"Too long, my friend."

"Where are you going next? Do you have any plans?"

"Anywhere. I must get out of this place. It has been nothing but pain. I will go, perhaps, to India. Or I will sit here forever. It is the same to me."

The conversation with Paul as usual trailed off into nothingness and merde. And Martin began to see him as a vegetable, a huge watermelon that somehow could utter fragments of intelligence. Occasionally a flash of anger jolted through Martin's system. He was tempted to kick the unmoving vegetable that sat in front of him, just to see if real blood would come out. It was not an anger he could clutch for very long. It sickened him, and the violence he felt made him jittery, as if suddenly his foot might involuntarily strike out, and slam into Paul's expressionless face.

"Why did you come here?" Martin finally asked.

"To find an answer."

"To what?"

"To life, my friend," Paul sighed. "I want to know who I am. Do you know who you are?"

"No," Martin admitted.

"Well, my friend, it is a very important question. But I have found a wall, and the wall keeps growing higher. I am tired of climbing it. I give up. You see, I give up. I will sit here and let it grow."

For a minute a light flashed in Paul's eyes. A twinkling like a sudden bright noise in the desert. Then dead. It was happening all the time, this sudden spurt across his face, then a blankness, cold as a stone. And Martin got sucked in each time. He expected the aliveness to continue. It surprised him to see how quickly it died.

"Why don't you sit down?" Paul groaned. "You are making me nervous."

This very idea had been nibbling at Martin's mind: to sit down in the swirling darkness, in the snake-infested night. His legs were getting tired. Just the effort of standing still, listening to Paul, watching for cars along the road. Long pulses of weariness moved up and down his legs. His back was beginning to faintly ache. Slowly, his knees folded. He slipped to the ground.

Just as he felt the stones against his backside, a whir and a roar and lights came through the darkness from up the road, the direction Jan and Rick had travelled. It sounded like a thousand vulture wings clapping together, loud in the desert stillness. He got to his feet again. The lights grew brighter.

"The marines are here, boys," Rick shouted from the jeep. "Get that Frenchman off his ass!"

"Merde," hissed Paul, slowly pulling his socks on.

"It is good to see you," Jan shouted.

An Israeli soldier sat behind the wheel, his teeth just faintly glimmering through a half-smile.

"C'mon Paul," Martin whispered.

With the four travellers safely tucked inside the jeep, a vehicle of the Israeli army, a khaki-colored jeep of the Jewish state, the soldier with furry arms and large hands swivelled the black wheel, pirouetted and danced the jeep around in a circle, the wheels crunching pebbles, snakes, scorpions, anything in its path.

"Fuck, we've got it made now," Rick laughed. "This guy can take us to the Dead Sea. There's a sanitarium there. Lots of empty beds, he says. They use it in the winter for old ladies. They come to bathe their arthritis in the hot springs."

"Yes," Jan smiled, "we will get a good night's rest."

"Chaverim," the soldier interjected, "you should not travel these roads by night. There have been many shootings. We can't be responsible for the tourists. Yet it would be very bad for us, if you got hurt. Chaverim, we have enough problems down here. Please use your common sense."

The voice of the Israeli soldier was quiet and controlled, but it seemed to encase the jeep, still the motors as he spoke, and it seemed to twirl around the edges of the desert. It was a still voice that shut every mouth in the jeep, including Rick's. On to the Dead Sea with four wheels spinning, the jeep roared. It cut a clean path through Sodom and Gomorrah, and the sand.

"Have the terrorists been active?" Rick asked, his voice less shrill, almost calm.

"Yes, they are always on the alert. But we know their ways down here."

"Then, they are disorganized?"

"Sometimes yes, sometimes no," the soldier said, half smiling. "You cannot count on anything. We can't go to sleep."

"But there must be a pattern they follow," Rick persisted.

"Yes, the pattern of the wind."

The soldier chuckled to himself. Martin couldn't unglue his eyes from the khaki uniform, the gun in its holster. A Jewish marine, he kept thinking.

"Are you students?" the soldier asked.

"Yes," Rick answered for the group, "students of life."

"Are you going to settle in *Eretz*?"

"I can only speak for myself," Rick said. "I am going back to England. Maybe I'll come back some day."

"Yes . . . " the soldier mused, "I've heard that before. How do they treat the *Yehudim* in your country?"

"The same as they always have," Rick smiled. "We go more or less unnoticed. We are quite civilized, nothing like the krauts or Polacks."

"That is good," the soldier said, tight-lipped. "I want to travel some day to England or America. But this is my country. We have fought for it. And some day even you might have to come here."

"I doubt it," Rick answered.

"Don't feel too safe, chaver, that is a fault of the *Yehudim*. The yids in Germany felt safe. They thought everyone loved them. Here we know how we stand. I like it that way. You see a snake, you shoot it. That's it."

Jan, the gentile boy, his head leaning to one side, seemed to be listening intently to the conversation. It was as if nobody was taking his presence into account. Martin kept a half eye on him, interested in his reaction. It was like looking at his own life in reverse. How many cars and buses he had travelled in, where he was the only Jew, listening to conversations centered around the gentile world. Yes, Martin thought, this was a sure-fire way for a Christian to get some inkling of what it felt like to be a Jew in the diaspora. He tried to imagine the thoughts going through Jan's mind. The conversations were very open here in Israel. There was no reason to hide or disguise one's Jewishness.

"Are you all Yehudim?" the soldier finally asked.

"I am not," Jan answered. "I am Dutch."

"That is a fine country," mused the soldier. "We have much respect for you here in Israel. You and the Danes. You were not animals during the holocaust. I hope you enjoy your stay here."

"Thank you," Jan answered, his voice with just the very slightest tremble to it. "I have found your country remarkable. It is amazing what you have done in such a short time."

"Have you been on the kibbutz?" the soldier asked.

"Yes, I spent a month in Galilee."

"Ah, the Galil," the soldier smiled, tapping the wheel, his face broadening into a smile. "It is very different from here. Tiberias, how I would like to be there now. How clean the water is, and the trees. That is my home, very near the lake. We have a small farm there. As soon as my two years are up, I am going back to help my father. He is getting old. You see, I am not a soldier, only by necessity. I have seen Tel Aviv and Jerusalem, but I will go back to the farm."

"Well," Jan said, his voice rich with thought, "that is what holds your country together, the kibbutzim and the farms."

"Yes," said the soldier, "we do what we have to with our guns, but we don't enjoy it. Do you know where we learned our farming? From those Arabs we have to shoot. They are good farmers, no matter what propaganda you have heard."

The Arabs, Martin mused. He had seen a few in their white robes, a few with thick black hair, eyes hot and brown from generations of living amid sand dunes and sun, their faces swarthy. A few he had noticed on the bus to Afula sitting on their watermelons, perched on the green curvature of fruit, a gold watch glinting on their wrists, and one with a bejewelled dagger, rubies or fake rubies, bright red gems glittering, and the white-toothed smiling Arab very proud of the dagger tucked into his belt. They had a look about them, those Arabs. Yes, the same dark skins of the *Sephardi* Jews, yes, definitely brothers and common offspring of Abraham—yet a difference that Martin found very difficult to pinpoint. Perhaps the secret rested in the kilt-like robes. He had seen no Jews dressed this way. Perhaps in the fringed keffiehs. Perhaps the difference came to the way they perched, one knee on a ripe watermelon.

Yes, the Arabs, and there was a difference. Their faces, to Martin, seemed just somewhat rounder, smoother, softer. The sun, the round blistering sun had not scarred their faces in exactly the same way. Perhaps not at all. But it had done something too. It was as if the centuries of sand dunes and heat, sand flies and watermelon feasts had rounded their faces, making their eyes just a touch sleepier than their Jewish brethren.

Martin had seen an amazing thing one evening at Kibbutz One Sun. An Arab who was passing near the kibbutz had been invited to eat in the communal dining room and to stay the evening. Martin remembered sitting across from Vladimir, a Russian Jew who had recently immigrated to Israel. He was a stocky man in his late twenties. He said little, laughed even less. He worked hard, but did not seem to take much joy in what he was doing. It was surprising to Martin when he began shouting and yelling, his face blistered red with anger.

"That Arab!" he shouted. "That piece of dirt, what is he doing here? He should not be here."

It was loud enough for the Arab to hear. It was angry and shrill enough for almost everyone in the dining room to hear. The chatter suddenly ceased. The roar and din of cutlery striking stopped. A quiet cloud of interest and hushed suspense descended on the dining room. Across from Vladimir sat Yacov. Yacov was in his early fifties, lean and almost pinch-faced, wiry and muscular, without an ounce of excess fat. Through his rimless round glasses he stared stone-eyed at Vladimir. Yacov had fought against the Germans, and had been decorated for bravery by the Red Army in which he had served. If at this point his eyes had been bayonets, they would've drilled deep holes through Vladimir's skull.

Vladimir ignored him, and paid no attention to the heavy silence that wrapped the tables. His voice got louder, cursing the Arab for his dirtiness, for his very presence, for his very existence. The more he shouted, the redder his face got, and his fists curled into angry knots which he shook in the Arab's direction.

"Get him out of here!" he yelled. "I won't eat in the same room with him."

Yacov, very slowly, with a great deal of intent and concentration, rose to his feet, his short wiry body just beginning to tremble. His body looked like a tuning fork ashudder with constricted anger. Vladimir ignored him.

"Chaver," Yacov suddenly said, his voice sharp, but not strained, "he has every right to eat with us. He is our guest."

"I will not eat with him!" stocky Vladimir yelled. "He is dirt."

Yacov slowly moved around the table, each step uncoiling like a tense spring. He stood in front of Vladimir.

"I will not eat with you," Yacov spat.

Vladimir's flushed face looked just a little surprised. He picked up a knife from the table, and he began playing with it, fondling it, as he returned Yacov's strong gaze. Fuck, thought Martin, somebody's going to get killed. He had visions of Vladimir going completely berserk and driving the knife through Yacov's leathery neck. Yacov kept one eye fixed on Vladimir's hand, the one holding the knife. He reached out and lifted Vladimir's plate, his plate filled with chicken and celery and tomatoes and sour cream, he lifted the plate from under Vladimir's nose, he lifted it with both hands and threw it on the floor. The porcelain cracked in two.

Vladimir just for a second, the tiniest of seconds, raised the knife just a little higher. Then he looked around the dining room. Hundreds of dagger-filled eyes stared back at him. Vladimir got up from his chair and left the dining room. Everyone sighed a breath of relief. The chatter and jokes slowly began once again, and the Arab visitor finished his meal in peace.

"We want peace with the Arabs," Aaron told Martin later that evening. "We are a socialist kibbutz. And we believe they are our brothers. There are madmen in Israel like anywhere else. They would kill every one of them. But the Arabs are fine people. They have a tradition as rich as our own."

"What was wrong with Vladimir?" Martin asked.

"He is a strange one," Aaron said meditatively. "He got out of Russia, and swung the other way. He's a fascist, a Jewish fascist. It's as simple as that. We have our crazies in this country, believe me."

"I couldn't believe what Yacov did."

"Oh, he's tough," Aaron smiled. "He fought three wars in his life. Against the Germans, and against the Arabs in '48 and '56. He's eaten enough war to last him six lifetimes. We don't want any more harsh feelings. We want peace as soon as possible. Yacov spoke for every one of us tonight. He had to do it. If he hadn't, someone else would have."

The jeep roared over the top of a hill, and descended toward the Dead Sea. There it sat, the Dead Sea, its dark waves lapping the shore. How black and impenetrable this sea looked. There was no seeing to the bottom of it, Martin thought. And the silence in the jeep, the sleepiness lay equally black and heavy and opaque. What was this whole trip about? Off at twilight, now the Dead Sea, to-morrow the sun, tomorrow the snakes, on to Ein Gedi. And there were hundreds of travellers zipping between Haifa and Eilat, Jeru-salem and Tel Aviv, through the mountains and the bypasses, up and down, back and forth, taking pictures, real or in the mind, of stone cliffs, monuments, dead seas, red seas, apples and oranges, tawdry women and muscled men. Minds and cameras clicking,

clicking, clicking. Across the world they marched and ran, dawdled and spun, men and women looking and seeking from Katmandu to the wastes of Australia. What was it all about—Martin wondered— the ceaseless movement, the endless search? It disturbed him that he didn't know what exactly he was looking for, or what exactly he was doing in the jeep, or what exactly the others were expecting. The soldier, yes. He had a job, something he had to do, something he was told to do. And there was no way out. The kibbutzniks performed their jobs, the businessmen, the secretaries, the teachers. They were doing such and such for so much pay to acquire this and that. But what exactly was he doing here at the Dead Sea, the waves hiding potassium and other chemical gunk? The moonlight beating weirdly on the water. Long white limbs. A spooky white-ness that seemed to have little meaning. The sea without meaning, and the silence, and the sanitarium for old ladies with arthritis.

Nobody had told him to come to the Dead Sea, no one had di-rected him to the pillar of salt and the ashen remains of Sodom and Gomorrah. He would not receive a cent for his trouble. And curiosity, mere curiosity didn't seem a very adequate explanation. Yet he felt he was looking for something, some explanation to a question, and he didn't quite know what the question was. It swirled somewhere in his gut, this question that he should be ask-ing. It made him move in this direction and that.

Was Paul right? *Who are you?* Was that the question, the impor-tant question that dawdled and spun inside him? And did the an-swer contain the explanation for why he was here at midnight this particular evening, at this particular deadest of seas? And who the hell was he anyway, and what in God's name was he looking for? What did he know about himself: why he said this instead of that, why he travelled in such a direction and not in its opposite? Was it all a haphazard thing like a million ping-pong balls shot into space by some madman? Could he just as well have been in India at this moment? Why here? Why not the Khyber Pass, or for that matter Toronto? Was there just a speck of explanation for the directions his body and mind and heart and soul moved in?

And he began to imagine himself as the only fish in the Dead Sea, the only gilled being that somehow was able to flourish amid the killing chemicals. It drove him a little crazy, this thought. Was there just one tiny scaled swimmer, just one in that black of blackest seas?

And by the time the jeep came to a stop he just wanted to find a place to go to sleep, to hear no more motors roaring, or pebbles crackling. To hear no more arguments and hissings between Paul and Rick, to see no more limbs of moonlight, just to sleep, to drown in a quiet blackness for a few hours. He just wanted his mind to shut off, and shut up for a few painless hours.

What did he sleep on, that night in the empty sanitarium beside the Dead Sea? He just couldn't remember. It was a cot, perhaps, a cot flimsy as a hammock where the wrinkled ladies stretched their heavy limbs winter after winter. On the same cot where hundreds of poor arthritic beings had lain, humming to themselves and gossiping to each other. Or was it the floor he lay upon, the splintered planks creaking under his restlessness?

The sky was black that evening, and he went to sleep wearing his jeans and a T shirt.

The sun rose, an orange orb, fiery and determined, it rose over the Dead Sea the next morning. It was already beginning to get hot, the heat sliding over boulders and sand, between the crevices and fissures of prehistoric rock. Martin kept waking, then drifting back into unconsciousness. The others slept as the sun ascended over the sanitarium. By eleven o'clock everyone was up except Paul. He continued to sleep with the flap of his knapsack pulled around his ears.

There seemed not a breath of cool air anywhere.

"Do you see any cars on the road?" Rick asked.

"No, it looks quite deserted," Jan answered. "There is a bus about a half-mile down the road, it looks stuck in the sand. It hasn't moved for the last hour."

Rick walked to the window and glanced up and down the dusty dirt road.

"Yes, I see it. I doubt if they're going to get it going. I'm going to start for Massada."

Jan visibly winced, a frown playing on his usually smooth forehead.

"It is not advisable to expose yourself to this heat," he said. "It will be 130 Fahrenheit today. Why don't you wait and see what happens with the bus? In the meantime we can go for a swim and cool ourselves a bit."

"No," Rick replied swiftly, "I want to be on my way. I'll take a canteen of fresh water and another salt pill."

"It is dangerous to do that alone," Jan protested. "What if you are overcome? There will be nobody to help you."

"I want to see if I can do it. I'll take my chances."

Rick's tone closed the door on any further exchanges between them. He seemed determined. Mad dogs and Englishmen, Martin thought to himself. A few minutes later, Rick was walking down the road alone, his knapsack hugging his shoulders, the union jack shining its crosses, red wedges, and blue horizons.

"He is crazy," Jan whispered to Martin as they made their way to the shoreline of the Dead Sea. "He's not even wearing a hat."

"Perhaps he'll get a ride."

"For his sake, he had better."

And Rick, walking sprightly along as if he were highstepping it around the Picadilly in London, disappeared, a dot on the road. The waves of heat and sun and dust engulfed him.

They got undressed, leaving their jeans and T shirts, socks and shoes and underwear draped over rocks. Jan made light conversation, offering points of information about this body of water they were about to step into. Martin had his reservations about this noon-hour skinny dip in this chemically clogged sea. It seemed, however, the thing to do. How could one pass by this miraculously buoyant sea without seeing its amazing effects on one's body? He had heard reports about how it lifted and supported one's weighty tissues and fibres, bones and muscles, lifted and cradled those that relaxed in its black arms. A man, he had heard, could lie on his back for hours reading a newspaper. There was no danger of sinking. Absolutely no risk of ending up at the bottom and slowly becoming a long-limbed salt crystal.

"You must not try to swim in this water," Jan said quite seriously. "It is not advisable to splash around and get these chemicals in your eyes. Just float on your back or stomach. I'm sure it will be enjoyable, and cool us down."

How lean and long Jan's body looked, accented by his blond hair. Few Jews, Martin mused, were composed in this way. Although he was not short, his own body seemed squat, almost blocky in comparison. Jan seemed constructed of long sinews, as if from his neck to his feet one continuous lithe muscle vibrated. It was a Hans Brinker body, ready to sprint across miles of ice. It was a boyish body, one finger forever in a dyke.

It was a queer sensation, lying suspended in the black arms of the Dead Sea. Martin could feel the salt clinging to his skin; a fine layer was building over his pores, each opening in his body. He felt the contact of chemical against flesh between his legs. It stung in the crack of his ass.

"Isn't this wonderful?" Jan asked, his eyelids shut as he floated on his back.

"Yes," Martin agreed.

"I could stay here all day," Jan smiled. "Rick doesn't know what he is missing. And Paul, what has become of him?"

"He's still sleeping," Martin said dreamily, allowing his eyelids to shut, and the water to support him, and the sun to bathe his naked body.

"They should be down here," Jan purred. "After all, this is a once-in-a-lifetime experience. There is only one sea like this on the entire planet. This is the kind of story we'll be telling our grandchildren someday."

And Jan's purring voice, golden as the sunlight, life-supporting, buoyant as the Dead Sea, sent images curling through Martin's mind. He saw himself as an old man, mellow and greying, sitting in a rocking chair surrounded by chubby grandchildren.

"Did you really swim in the Dead Sea?" a little girl was asking.

"Oh yes, it was many years ago. But it's a memory I cannot forget. We went swimming without any clothes on, you know. A Dutch boy was with me."

"You swam in your skinnies, Grandpa?"

"Yes, honey, it was such a good feeling too. It was so darn hot that day. We were so tired and thirsty. Yes, it was a beautiful swim. Well, we floated actually. And you couldn't sink even if you tried."

"Boy, that must've been fun, Grandpa."

"Yes, my dear, it was a lot of fun. You know, it only lasted a half hour. It happened more than fifty years ago, but I can remember it like yesterday. The sun, the chemicals, the Dutch boy. I wonder if he remembers. I wonder if he's still alive, in fact."

Martin smiled to himself as this future conversation formed in his mind.

"Martin," Jan asked quizzically, "why does Rick treat Paul so meanly? I must tell you I was surprised. They are both Jews, after all."

Martin cleared his throat, trying to think of some logical explanation.

"I guess their personalities just don't mesh."

"I liked Rick when I first met him," Jan said thoughtfully, "but his treatment of Paul wasn't at all fair. Paul has some problem. Perhaps some pain in his life. Did he tell you anything about it when you were alone?"

"Not really. Just that he was tired and fed up with Israel."

"Yes," Jan said, his voice golden-soft like butter and toast, "I guess we all get tired from time to time."

Martin had no desire to move now. He was just getting used to the cool ripples under his armpits, the cool tingling sensation beneath his back. Yes, he could stay here all day with the sun melting on the rivulets of water, melting in the hairs on his chest.

Just a hundred yards away the burning dusty road waited, the road baked and cracked, the rocks sun-split, dry as bones, dead for centuries. He wasn't looking forward to putting his clothes on once again, his ripped work boots, his dust-covered jeans.

"We must go soon," Jan finally hummed across the ripples. "We have a chance of getting a ride on that bus. Maybe if we help push it, the driver will take us to Massada."

At some point during this trip to the world's ditch and bottom-lands, a bug entered Martin's system, and swam up his ducts with all the ferocity of an avenging angel. It sank its claws eventually into the pit of his stomach, attacked his liver and spleen, seized upon his gall bladder. Had it been lurking, this bug of dysentery and diarrhea, in the chemical lingerings of the Dead Sea? He could have picked it up anywhere in those travels along the road to Massada and Ein Gedi, in some pool or glass of water or bowl of wrath below the cliffs of Sodom and Gomorrah. They drank water on the shore of the Dead Sea, Jan and Martin. For a pipe hung from the rocks and issued forth a constant outpouring of fresh saltless water. The women used it, the old arthritic women, and each swimmer of the Dead Sea used it to wash away the film of salt that clogged the pores. Martin's entire body felt stretched and taut with crystals of salt when he emerged from his swim.

The two young men, still naked, took a shower beneath this pipe, and having no towels, they raced up and down the shore together like the famous goats in the bible, frolicking and drying themselves with the rush of wind and sun against their gamboling nude bodies. It was a free, free, free sensation, two beings alone at the bottom, the rock-bottom of the universe, naked as Adam and Eve before they ate those naughty apples, two animals running and laughing and giggling up and down the pebbly sands.

Jan's long lithe legs served him well, and even at an easy gallop he could out-zig and out-zag Martin, and outdistance him. His flesh of flesh swung between his legs, as did Martin's, and the whole sky blinked and winked and laughed and clapped at the antics laid before it. The royal sun shuddered, and the bullets, though hot that morning, never entered their skulls, and they both passed from sea to shore and eventually to the bus without a hair on their heads harmed. Yet somewhere along the way a bug entered Martin's bloodstream, an unprovoked avenger started its growth unbeknownst to him, began its mutations and sick culture in the pit of his being.

And as Jan so reasonably and wisely predicted, they did finally help push that bus from its sandy moorings, and the driver, thankful, and not wishing to leave them stranded, invited them to ride in his bus as far as Massada. And although Paul slept through the whole thing on his cot in the sanitarium, he too received a seat of welcome among the tourists. Martin was happy to finally see women, for there they sat, some with binoculars in their laps. O how he wished they had used those binoculars a half hour earlier, how he hoped they had spied his naked body prancing along the beach.

What a blessing and good feeling to be finally seated on this cushioned vehicle, among the women with their handkerchiefs dabbing sweat from their foreheads, among the faint fragrances of their perfumes. It was as if he hadn't seen a real live woman in twenty years, and now each movement, each quiver of their flesh, however slight, tingled its way down his spine. A few nuns were seated on the bus. Even they in their black habits and white-rimmed bonnets, their faces ovals of shaded light, even they succored his sun-rocked heart, his sand-blistered feet.

The motor of the bus, the rocking and trembling of its frame brought hope to his heart that just around the next twisted corner something in his life would click into place, something unforeseen and unexpected, a new meaning that would fill him with an understanding and joy that he had never experienced before. Vehicles had had that effect on him from time immemorial, from rides in the country with his mother and father along the wave-beaten shores of Nova Scotia. Trains too, especially trains, with their twelve wheels churning sparks and whistles up the long singing tracks. And jets — the rides he had taken from McGill at Christmas breaks to his parents' apartment in Toronto. And boats like the little fishing boats at Digby N.S., as they rocked over waves, their decks smelling of salt-spray and codfish. How many fast, joyous, sometimes terror-stricken rides he had taken with his father to visit places like Springhill, N.S. with its hidden manna of black compressed trees, its buried gases that blew up from time to time, and trapped whole families of miners . . air exhausted . . faces gone white . . . sleep.

His father spun the wheel with an expert and daring hand. He wove between the traffic, and on occasion Martin's heart jolted inside him, the whole beating lump jumped into his throat when his father headed straight for an oncoming car. But he was swift in those days, his father, with the reflexes of a cornered cat, and always just in the nick of time and by the grace of his steady nerves, he swung them both back into the right lane.

It was almost as good in the bus as resting and floating in the Dead Sea. Just to be carried forward without any effort or thought, to be floated along on tires of heated air with all the other hopeful travellers.

The windows were all tossed open from the front seats to the very back, everyone just trying to catch a thread of fresh breeze, everyone with mouth ajar, and sweat-beaded foreheads. There was little breeze to be had, and the sun flashed mercilessly off the rocks, the sun encompassed each metal strut on the bus's roof and side. Sweat and sweat, heat, the smell of dust and perfume mixing with the rich odors from armpits and the body's secret parts. Hands flailed and floated handkerchiefs, trying to soak up the beads of heat. It was almost painful to the eyes to look outside at the rocks, for at high noon and later the light was so bright it flashed through eyes into the brain, and it was as if the brain could not adjust quickly enough to the shafts and spikes of sun. As the heat rose, Martin began to think about Rick and his fate along the road to Massada. Jan, too, was anxiously darting glances through his window. He had told the driver about their friend and his lonely trek, and the driver had promised to keep a sharp lookout.

"I hope he found shade somewhere," Jan finally said. "There are a few large rocks. I hope he had the sense to sit down."

"I wouldn't like to be out there myself," Martin replied.

Paul yawned, his mouth still cobwebbed with sleep and dreams. It seemed, however, that the conversation had seeped into his semi-conscious stupor.

"Foolish," he yawned, "you do not fight a bull with a sword. The cape, that is the important weapon."

The cape, Martin thought. He tried to seize the full meaning of Paul's yawning philosophy. Perhaps this guy was in possession of some truth, something significant despite his heavy eyelids that looked glued to his cheeks. But the more he plunged into what Paul had to say, the darker it became. He would just get to a certain point —it looked, by golly, it appeared to be a revelation, and just as his mind was about to digest it, it evaporated. It was a bit like cotton candy, this soul searching of Paul's. It melted so quickly on the tongue. He got suckered in, Martin did, again and again with Paul's dreamy observations. And yet as soon as he got close to the essence and the core, it was gone, just a thread of a taste lingered.

Paul slumped back into sleep, half-snoring, wheezing through his nose. As the miles began to spin and rock past, Jan and Martin craned their necks toward the windows, trying to get a glimpse of Rick somewhere on the road. Martin could feel the tension building in the back of his neck. They didn't want to miss him, to somehow not notice him, to lose him under some rock, or just not see him because of the flashes of sun and blistering heat. It was like a vigil. A keen eye was necessary, and a wide-awake brain. Where the fuck was this offspring of Judah, this mad Englishman? Just a slight anger gnawed in Martin's throat.

"Perhaps he got picked up by someone else," Martin offered.

"That would be best for him," Jan smiled, catching the fragrance of Martin's hopefulness. "He's been out there much too long already."

"When we get to Massada he might even be there to greet us."

"Yes, it is possible."

Martin had a picture in his mind of Rick triumphant on the steps of a kiosk in Massada. It was a face in an old movie, blackened and beaten by the sun, yet stretched with the excitement of victory. Black eyes flashing. White teeth grinning. "What took you so long?" he heard Rick in his daydream asking with a smirk stretching his lips apart.

But wait, just wait, not so fast: a bedraggled shape began to take form up the road. It had something loose and white draped over the top of its head. The bus slowed, the doors creaked open, and Rick pulled himself up the steps. He wobbled from side to side, drunk with heat, as he made his way down the aisle. His eyes were not flashing the least little bit. They had gone soft and mushy. His face was not black. It had an odd hue to it. The tan was still there, but beneath the blackened layer of skin the tissue was a pale ghostly white.

On his head a handkerchief loosely perched, wrinkled, a sweat-drenched handkerchief. It somehow looked pathetic, this thin white attempt at staving off the heat, this crumpled head-covering. A *shmatah*, that was all it was, a loose *shmatah*, the kind the women wore in the markets of Tel Aviv, the Yemenite women selling their oranges and herbs. And a picture shot through Martin's brain: his grandfather at baseball games with a wrinkled hanky covering his bald head.

Rick's knees buckled beneath him a couple of times before he dropped into his seat. His eyelids immediately closed. There was not a word proceeding from his fast-talking mouth. Not a syllable. The sun of Israel had drilled its fury into his skull.

"Are you alright?" Jan asked, his face wrinkled with concern.

"It was bloody awful," Rick groaned. "I just can't believe how I feel. Do you have some water?"

Jan passed him his canteen.

"Drink this slowly. If you drink it too quickly or if you take too much, you'll bloat your stomach."

Rick moved the canteen toward his lips, jerkily at first, his hand shaking, his fingers trembling, almost unable to direct its movement. His lips quivered. They looked loose now, his clever lips, and he had a hard time trying to wrap them around the spout. "Slowly," Jan again warned, as he tried to steady the canteen in Rick's hands. Rick moved a hand to let Jan get a better grip, and then replaced his hand on top of Jan's. "Lean your head back," Jan ordered quietly and calmly, "let me do it for you."

"Thank you," Rick murmured just faintly below his breath.

Jan's body now leaned over Rick. Trickles of water slipped from between Rick's lips, dribbled down his chin.

Rick was slumped in the seat now, almost lying down, as Jan tended to him, Jan with a careful steady eye on just how much water came out of the canteen, withdrawing it when he felt Rick was taking too much in.

Paul in the meantime had unglued his eyelids, was in fact almost wide-awake, and he looked just a little fascinated at what was happening across the aisle.

"The worst hasn't hit him yet," Paul said. "This is only the beginning. He's got heat prostration. I've seen it before. A guy in Spain."

"Yes," Martin agreed, "I remember getting sunstroke once."

And Martin remembered the afternoon when he was thirteen, just after his bar-mitzvah, on a visit to his aunt and uncle's summer home near Fredericton. He had taken a rowboat out on the lake, not a thread of cloth covering his head. He couldn't stop rowing that day. Not a cloud in the sky—the sun flashed and drilled into his scalp. His hands became sore and raw from handling the oars. Yet he kept going. It took two days to recover. Paul was right: a forecast of gloom, but right. An older cousin, a big freckled girl named Beatrice, took care of him in much the same way Jan was tending to Rick.

"Rick, they will look after you at the kiosk in Massada," Paul said softly.

"Yes, you'll be able to rest," Martin added.

Rick let a few muffled sounds issue from his lips, hard to make out, muffled and bubbly, low and suffering, muted and mixed in the dryness of his parched throat. It could have been anything, but it sounded just faintly, ever so faintly like, "Thank you, fellows."

The three of them now leaned and hovered over Rick's crumpled form.

"Better move back," Jan said, "he needs as much air as he can get."

Rick slipped off into sleep or unconsciousness, his body jerking suddenly, twisting from side to side as if someone were beating him.

Then his limbs went still again, without a tremble, not a sign of life, just a bare trace of breathing.

The bus continued rumbling forward toward Massada, crackling pebbles under its relentless wheels, and a tiny stony silence filled the bus. After Rick's fall into the pit of weakness, the tentacles of heat gripping him, the trip to Massada and on to Ein Gedi became, for Martin, dreamy, smothered, and enveloped by more heat and sun. He could not still his mind any more, nor look at anything and feel much respite. There was a vague sensation of unease that had entered his own body. Who stayed where, who went with whom was very difficult to remember. At Massada he saw Rick stretched out on the stone floor of the canteen, a nurse and soldier hovering over his limp body. The nurse taking his pulse, the soldier trying to prop open his eyelids, to get a better look at the heat-tormented pupils. That was the last he saw of Rick, the very last.

And he lost track of Paul and Jan. He could not really say who climbed Massada, Herod's fortress, now an army lookout. Martin did not. He had an old wobbly dizziness in the pit of his being when it came to heights. He took no joy in looking from a pinnacle down a thousand feet to the swirling stones below. It was an old reluctance that caught in his throat and bothered him from time to time. In his father's office when he was three or four or five years old, he used to stand on a radiator and look down six floors at the buses and cars on Barrington Street. They rushed past, shiny roofs in the five o'clock twilight, and at times his chubby legs swayed, wobbled, a watery feeling in his knees, and terror-stricken, he clutched at the venetian blinds.

Massada—the climb to those dizzy heroic heights. Massada—the cherished remembrance of Herod's last stand against the Romans, Massada with its mass suicidal protest, Massada the modern armed fortress with its guns, its multifarious artillery, with its weapons poked out, long, silent and deadly, its rifles and bazookas, its machine-guns and howitzers—he just didn't climb to this Massada: the only historic and heroic point of interest on the whole trip that he omitted. And yet a guilt gnawed inside him. Had he missed the whole point of this trip by not steeling his nerves and making the climb? Massada—it was on everyone's lips, a tone of reverence and awe, respect, and each time he heard the word spoken he could sense a thrill of adoration skipping through the speaker's blood. Yes, it was not a slight omission. Yet he could not get up the steam and stamina, courage and commitment to haul his weary ass and dizzy mind up the long rock path to Herod's cranny.

He consoled himself by thinking of Rick and Paul, for he was sure somehow that neither one of them, the sprightly English Jew, nor the sleepy Frenchman, neither one of them, he was almost certain, made the climb to the desert fortress. It was a little ironic when he thought about it on the bus heading to Ein Gedi. Out of the group of four desert wanderers, only Jan, he was convinced, only Jan the Dutch goy climbed that ancient rocky path, only he stood where Herod had planted his determined feet two millenia ago, only he, the blond-haired blue-eyed Dutch boy, surveyed from Massada the long stretch of desert below, only he had a machine-gun view of what a marvellous natural fortress this Massada really was.

And yet he thought, fuck it, fuck it, fuck it. So what? He was a poet, was he not? What thrill could he really experience by nudging the heroic ghosts of the past, by viewing with pride the firepower of these modern Jewish brothers, how well they commanded and controlled this stretch of god-forsaken heat and rock. Fuck it, and to hell with his guilty feelings. And if he wasn't going to join the army and shoulder a rifle, and kill his share of the enemy terrorists, or be killed, what was the use of standing in that cave of rock, Massada? What would be the meaning of the wild flappings of his heart and brain? What did it really mean to any of the tourists?

He doubted, he really doubted deep in his heart that he would ever don a khaki Israeli uniform and a brown beret. The closest he had ever come to killing anything, he recalled, was with a slingshot and U-nails when he was a young boy of nine or ten playing in the woods near his home. Had he ever really hit a bluejay or sparrow or a scraggly starling? He doubted it. The U-nails slashed through branches and leaves, the birds jumped and leaped and squawked to one another, but he never found a dead bird at the bottom of a tree, or saw his U-nail implanted in a fragile skull. He had fired a rifle perhaps a dozen times at most during his nineteen years. And this was during his year in cadets in junior high school. Target practise with a .22 had been part of the training in the basement of the armoury. He didn't do badly either, hitting the bull's-eye, performing the feat of getting the bullets to collect on the cardboard, close together, knotted together as the instructor had ordered. He gave it a try for a few Saturday mornings in the basement of the armoury, but it soon bored him, this exercise in marksmanship. It was an optional part of his cadet training, and he soon dropped it, and used his Saturday mornings instead to fly aeroplanes with rubber-band motors, to sail kites, or to get a game of baseball together.

The bus creaked and swayed its way toward Ein Gedi. Martin was pushing forward to another sight, another point of interest, yet his mind felt encased, his heart wondering why he was going forward. Why Ein Gedi? He knew little about it: a slight biblical acquaintance with the words. His thoughts continued creaking and rumbling around in circles. He thought of the soldiers who died in '48 and '56 fighting for this lean country, this homeland. He saw their bodies on desert sand. Their blood trickling out and hardening on hot sun-baked stones. He saw the Arabs, too, lying side by side with the Jews. Egyptian Arabs and Russian Jews. Arabs from Jordan, and Jews from Aden. Bodies and bones and pale faces. Why was he heading for Ein Gedi, why not back to Tel Aviv? It seemed just the last spot he had to see on this trip, and then he could tuck the whole area away forever, knowing he had done it. He had done it. Yet he had missed the climb to Massada. And along the way he had lost his three companions.

Rumble of wheels, and thoughts he could not stifle. What if that Israeli soldier was right, the one who had given them the lift to the Dead Sea? What if he went back to Canada and something happened, another purge, another final solution to the Jewish problem, and he had to come back to Israel begging admittance, his very existence depending upon it? How would he feel then, knowing that he had done nothing to secure the country, had never shed an ounce of blood? Would he fight then? Would he kill his share of the enemy?

Visions forced themselves into his mind. Stormtroopers marching up Sherbrooke Street in Montreal. Swastikas draped over the library at McGill. Trains leaving for some Auschwitz in the north Quebec woods. Schweinhund Jew shouted in perfect English, and Juif echoing all night long from the top of Mount Royal.

He looked around the bus for just anything that he could look upon that might quiet these swirlings in his brain. Across the aisle he saw a young couple murmuring and cooing to each other in

French. He could feel the warmth rising from their two bodies. Her hands looked delicate, her fingers soothing. She had wriggled her fingers inside his half-open shirt, and slowly, slowly, slowly, she was rubbing his chest. He leaned back, his eyelids shut. A smile flickered across his lips. That was the only place Martin wanted to be at the moment, in the French boy's shoes with a girl of his own. Someone with long cool sensitive fingers. A girl to nibble at his ears. A girl with long hair, perfumed and soft, long soft hair he could bury his face in.

"French girls are like that," Martin heard a voice saying. It came from the stranger sitting beside him.

"They are?" Martin's voice was more surprised that the stranger had spoken than at his bit of information.

"Oh yes, very caring, very tender."

"I haven't seen that too much before," Martin murmured.

"You should visit my country," he said with a French accent. "It is a country of lovers. Very different from England and Germany and the others. My friend, we live for love. This Israel of ours—much too coarse. They are men when it comes to war, but mere children in matters of the heart."

"They don't seem to put much emphasis on it, do they?"

"No, it is a struggle here. Love does not grow in such harshness. Love, it takes time, it takes joy, it takes easiness and relaxation. How can you have it here? It is much too serious. War, making money, trying to get by. Love, it takes centuries of cultivation."

Martin cast his eyes across the aisle again. He yearned to experience what the stranger was talking about. Enough rocks and heat and guns and snakes, he had experienced enough of these things. No, he probably would never experience shooting and killing, bazookas and flares. But "love"—that was within his reach, something he wanted to feel, to know about, to write about.

"You are not a fighter, I can see that," the stranger said.

Martin did not reply. His thoughts were still fixed on the French girl's hands, how they moved so slowly, intently and with concentration, how they lingered on her boyfriend's chest.

"I do not mean," the stranger added, "that you cannot take care of yourself. Correct me if I'm wrong, but it would not surprise me to find out that you are an artist of some kind. A painter, perhaps."

A thrill, a feeling of pride shot through Martin's heart. He had never been told this before, not by a complete stranger. Did it show, Martin wondered. Was there something in his eyes, his expression?

"I'm not an artist really," Martin murmured. "I've really not done anything. But I'd like to write some day."

"It's a long struggle, my friend. I want you to know that. I was a painter, oh I wanted to paint great pictures. I just couldn't do it. There was something I was missing. But I keep very close to art, even today. I own a gallery in France. I am very interested in the young painters."

The stranger, a man in his fifties dressed in a light summer suit, reached into his jacket, looking for something. Martin thought it was perhaps a picture of his gallery, or an old crumpled photo of one of his paintings. It was neither, however. The stranger withdrew from his jacket a flask.

"Will you join me in a schnapps? We will toast your success."

"Sure," Martin grinned.

The stranger unscrewed the red cap, and wiped the lip of the bottle with his sleeve.

"Here, drink. You look tired."

"Thank you," Martin said, and he took a swig of the brown burning liquid, and passed the bottle back.

"I drink to your future," the stranger smiled. "You must learn many things. Patience, and care. But you must learn how to feel. That is very important."

They passed the bottle back and forth a couple of times, and the stranger grew silent, letting his eyelids shut, and finally going to sleep. Martin was just as glad. It was getting a little difficult to carry on this conversation with this man so much older and more experienced than himself. The brown liquid, the sharp taste of whiskey lingered in the back of Martin's throat. The bus moved forward to Ein Gedi, the stranger wheezing in his sleep, the girl asleep on her boyfriend's shoulder. Martin allowed his eyes to close. The miles of rock and desert and sun no longer interested him. He had seen enough, and he fell into a half-slumber, his mind just a little dizzy from the whiskey, his stomach warm. "It would not surprise me if you were an artist." Those words echoed in his mind, and a faint smile hovered on his lips.

Where along the way to the pools of Ein Gedi did the bug enter him, the microbe of dysentery, the insidious avenger? Did he pick it up while drinking with the stranger, from the lip, perhaps, of the whiskey bottle? His mother often warned him when he was a young chubby boy to beware of strangers lest they carry him away in dark vehicles. He could never figure out way back then what a stranger would want with him, a little chubby boy, a dark-eyed little cherub. But he was careful not to speak to any men dressed in rags or enter any vehicles except his dad's, or his relatives', or people he knew real well.

Somewhere along that sunny and primrose path, that rocky road to Ein Gedi the clawed avenger hooked into his intestines. It began its subtle workings. He was unaware, completely unaware that any sick germ had entered his entrails. He was walking, talking, breathing, going forward as usual, smiling and brooding, drinking and observing, climbing and scrambling, yet all along a culture had taken root inside him. There was no sign that anything was amiss, not one sign in those two days of wanderings. His body was tanned. It looked perfectly healthy. He felt no gnawings or tremors of warning in his gut. Yet it had begun. Somewhere near Massada, or the Dead Sea, or the pools of ancient Ein Gedi, the bug that would bring him to his knees had entered, settled, and begun its sick growth inside him.

Ein Gedi was even more of a dream, sometimes a nightmare. He didn't get much sleep at the youth hostel after he had heard that the dank cement barracks were infested and overrun with rats. There were gaping holes in the cardboard-supported walls to attest to their night-time burrowings. He awoke several times. He believed he could see the red eyes of a rat near the foot of his bed staring brazenly back at him. They rattled through his sleep, slithered along the edges of his pillow. Rats, desert rats. At every turn, at every shift of desert breeze during this whole long trip a new fright had formed, but the rats seemed the closest, close enough to nibble at his cheek. His father was once locked up by a bunch of Jew-hating little boys in a warehouse near the harbour. They had tied him with ropes. His father was only nine years old, and the ropes gnawed and burned at his wrists and ankles as he struggled to free himself. For hours he was locked in the darkness, and he swore he could feel rats slithering over his legs. He shouted for help again and again, his throat raw with anger and fear. And finally Grandpa Kanner with a fine

psychic fatherly intuition came hunting for him, walked to exactly
the right warehouse, and freed his imprisoned son.

Martin was not tied up with ropes, nor was he any longer a boy, a
chubby boy of nine or ten, but the old story burned into his brain. It
was as if every story his father had ever told him, and there were
many: stories filled with struggles, adventures, close escapes, fights
and beatings, stories of his father's waterfront boyhood—it was as if
every story had been stored in the recesses of his mind, and on such
occasions as the night at the youth hostel at Ein Gedi, the locked tale
would surge to the surface with all the strength of its original
intensity.

The night was sleepless with tossings and turnings, with the other
travellers snoring, groaning, dreaming, each of them in their private
night-time worlds. How many, Martin wondered, didn't get a wink
of sleep that night? How many had old stories, ancient fears burning
in their restless heads? He often wondered about such things: what
others thought, what went on in their heads. Was there any similarity, any slight resemblance to his own brain's meanderings? It was
difficult, very difficult to find these things out. How could he tell
another person what went through his mind that evening? It just
seemed a little too dark and embarrassing to share and compare
with another human being. Perhaps it was just fear, raw senseless
fear without any meaning. What would there be to talk about? He
couldn't exactly say: "Hey, listen, I thought the rats were going to
get me last night. I didn't get any sleep. Were you really asleep? Did
those holes in the walls bother you?" No, for the time being, he
would have to keep all such shivers and broodings to himself.

The pools of Ein Gedi surge up from deep beneath the ground,
from hidden springs of icy water. Up the mountainside there are five
pools, each a gem of freshness in the desert heat. Each invites with
its tantalizing cool ripples. No wonder these pools are mentioned in
the bible, and the eyes of beautiful women are compared to them.
No wonder the goats of Ein Gedi are portrayed with hidden vigor in
their limbs, frolicking little beasts. What a miraculous occurrence:
fresh water, clean cool icy life-supporting water in the midst of the
inferno.

Martin climbed that mountainside, the tree-hung paths, enjoying
every branch, every leaf. He hadn't seen a tree in days. The foliage
was almost thick. At each pool along the climb he took off his jeans

and T shirt. He jumped in, wearing only his underwear. He tasted the water, he rolled it in his mouth, he let it shimmer under his chin and roll down his back. He swam: crawled, backstroked and duck-dived. Five times on the way up and five times on the way down, he threw off his clothes and dove in. He enjoyed each pool, each caress of coolness over his hot hide. Yet it was momentary, so momentary, this respite and relaxation. An aerial view would show Sodom and Gomorrah baked and cracked by heat, the hot pebbled road to Massada, the black illusion of the Dead Sea, the sun-blistered fortress of Massada, and over Ein Gedi, five glistening gems of light. And those glistening small pools, only five of them, would make the whole desert stretch look even hotter and dryer and more forbidding.

But he swam in them, savored them, tasted them, clung to them, knowing all the while that they were only temporary joys; they were dreams. Real, but dreams. It was almost as if they didn't exist. For when he came down the mountain, the sun drilled into his back just as hot and furiously, and within an hour he was just as tormented and dry as before he climbed to the top. They disappeared, they lay in their cool slumbers, they were no longer with him. Only the memory remained, like so many other things about this trip. Jan and Paul and Rick were gone forever. He was sure he would never see them again. Jan with his long legs and thoughtfulness. Rick screeching. Paul yawning. They disappeared from his life. Like the pools of Ein Gedi, they seemed to be part of a dream, a memory, but no longer touching him. It was as if they never really existed— just a fragment of a dream, a shudder and rush of light behind his eyelids.

The bus trip back to Tel Aviv was uneventful, as if his whole being were marking time, half-asleep, remembering what had happened in those two days, wondering where to go, what to do; and there was a feeling inside him that he had walked and talked and slept, had grown frightened, had met people, seen events, thought thoughts—but now it was all locked away. He tried to focus his attention on the future. Perhaps he would go back to the kibbutz, and try that communal farming life once again. At least it was something that he knew. He had gone through the trials of hardening his body. He had learned the various jobs. If he could only get into it, into their way of thinking and feeling and living; it was not a bad life after all, among the real moans of cattle, the summertime succulence of grapes and oranges and plums. If he could only give up all these things he thought he had to do: writing and learning and experiencing and taking trips to out-of-the-way places. Why couldn't he just be satisfied, as they seemed to be? They went about their business. They married and had children. They ate day in and day out in the huge communal dining room. They smiled at one another, argued, but they didn't seem to hold grudges for too long. They persisted year after year, doing their communal jobs. They even took holidays on occasion. There were hundreds of kibbutz-niks, thousands of them, sprinkled inside farms from the Lebanon border to the shores of Eilat. They lived out their lives, their simple lives. They made love and drank wine, fought in the wars when necessary. They even put on plays from time to time. Why couldn't he just do it? Just smother all those other urges when they came to the surface. Cover them over like burying seeds in the ground. Why couldn't he just take a giant step forward and exist like a normal human being? He could, perhaps, even write on the kibbutz. Certainly there must be a few stories hovering under stalks of corn, a few tales hiding away in the neglected corners of the communal kitchen.

During the slumberful trip on the bus, he decided to go back to the kibbutz and try it again.

CHAPTER 4

Dysentery

The first day or two back went smoothly. A reunion with old familiar faces, and a routine he knew. Nothing had changed. They still ate bread and jam, drank tea at four o'clock break in the afternoon. The cutlery and plates clattered as usual in the dining room. Chatter and jokes and stories circled the tables. He worked in the chicken pens. The manure had collected beneath the wire-mesh cages into thick hard slabs. He dug in his shovel again and again, thankful that his hands still retained the old calluses. It was a tough job. The smell of chicken shit almost choked him at times. The manure clung to his jeans, to his hands, lingered in his throat well after he had put down his shovel for the day. But he endured, as he had endured the biting teeth of the buckets in the banana fields. He slung his share of shit as fast and determined as anyone else.

No, nothing had changed. The swimming pool was just as jammed and noisy after work as it had always been. The sun rose over the plum trees and the grape vines, and went down again. The moon was just as bright as ever in the cloudless black sky. The cattle groaned. The cocks crowed. Work. Eat. Sleep. Talk. Aaron had not changed, nor Yacov, nor the eager students at the ulpan. A few Rumanians were slacking off as usual. The Algerians were working their asses off. The sabras led the way, exuding the least amount of sweat, with hardly a wrinkle crossing their foreheads. Life went on as usual, as it had for the last twenty years at Kibbutz One Sun, more or less the same. A certain number of plums had to be picked, a certain number of turkeys slaughtered. The pipes went down on schedule in the dry fields.

Martin worked, ate, slept, talked, along with the three hundred other inhabitants. It was a life not too different from that led by the cattle and the sheep and the chickens. All needs were provided for: a place to sleep, enough to eat, shade when necessary. People grew old and died. Others were born. The bug he had picked up near Massada had not yet reared its ugly head inside him. His body was functioning as it should. The food was going down his throat properly. His eyelids shut at night, and he went to sleep. His hands and feet worked in unison, his mind in a reasonable harmony, his heart pumped blood and oxygen to his brain. He finished his nine hours of work without incident or complication.

On the third morning he felt a little weak and wobbly when he got up and put on his jeans and work boots. He paid it little attention. He sat on the work-wagon going to the fields with everyone else. He dangled his feet over the side. The wheels jogged and jumped them out to their work locations. Martin had just a faint, an ever so faint feeling of weakness in his stomach. This he had experienced before on many occasions. He had a long history of nervous stomach. During his first year at McGill he missed his final exams. His stomach churned and heaved before those final tests. Daggers of pain shot through his intestines. He was sure he had appendicitis, and was deathly afraid the tiny vessel would suddenly burst inside him, ending all his worries. The doctor was called several times at two or three in the morning. He took his temperature, performed a rectal examination, but each time found nothing. After a battery of x-rays, tests, injections and consultations at Mount Sinai Hospital, the verdict was made known to him: nervous stomach caused by anxiety.

Such tremors as he now felt on the work wagon, rumbles of his gut, and twinges of his belly were not at all unusual. An unimportant minor nerve was probably agitated in the infinity of his ganglia, or in a hidden recess of his brain. So he continued dangling his feet with everyone else and paid it little attention.

But the bug was at work, deep in his gut, growing now by leaps and bounds. It split and divided as fast as a smashed atom. It sent out tentacles to the north, to the south, to the east, to the west, to every corner of his flesh. It split, divided, reunited, split again, spread and spread, leaving not a single inch of intestine unpolluted. And it struck with full force, suddenly, without warning.

Martin put in three hours planting beans. There was absolutely no indication that anything was going wrong inside him. In fact, he was enjoying the work. There were two girls working with him. He hollowed out the holes with his spade, being careful to make the hole neither too deep nor too shallow. For he knew that if the hole was too deep, the tiny bean would rot and never get its fragile shoots above ground. And if it were too shallow, the water from the irrigation pipes would either drown it or swish it away along the surface. Pop. Pop. Pop. The tiny beans fell into their warm hiding places. The girls smiled. He smiled back. There was no reason to be unhappy. It was eight o'clock in the morning. The morning air was fresh, his body was not getting tired. He was doing his job exactly as he had been instructed. The sabra girls who smiled at him did so with beautifully curved red lips and extraordinarily white teeth. It must be all that fruit they eat, Martin speculated. And he eyed them as they bent over to pop in their beans. How tight their shorts were. What marvellously rounded bums and shapely legs. What fine Israeli tans. Would it be all that bad to marry one of them, to settle down, and pop beans for the rest of his life?

The call for breakfast rang out across the fields. A long wooden table had been set up at the side of the road. It so happened that on that particular morning Aaron and his work team were busy laying pipes in an adjoining field. They gathered around the table, laughing and joking with one another, their faces tanned and alive with hunger. Martin moved slowly to his seat, just a slight shakiness in his knees. The table was loaded with food. Huge bowls of shemenet, an Israeli version of yogurt. Bowls of tomatoes, onions, green peppers, ready to be sliced and mixed with the shemenet into a huge early-morning salad. Knives clanged, bowls clattered.

Martin noticed that he was sweating just a little more than usual; not excessively—it was not pouring down—but his forehead felt just the slightest bit damper, and the beads of sweat were just a little cool to the touch. He ignored this and began to eat. And he ignored the fact that his appetite was not at all voracious as it usually was after three hours of early-morning work. He ate slowly, just nibbling at his food.

Just before the bug struck for the first time, he had the odd sensation that he was sitting above the table, sort of floating in space. The chaverim looked distant, their faces vague. The clang of cutlery and laughter seemed miles away, and the noise just barely filtered through to his brain. And just before the bug hit, he began to feel uneasy, restless, jittery. He felt tied to his chair, almost imprisoned at the breakfast table. It was not half over, the eating and the jokes and the chatter, not half complete when he arose. Why was he getting up? He didn't know exactly, but he couldn't sit another moment, or listen to one more word, or look at one more sliced tomato soaked in its shemenet bath. As he swivelled from his chair, the bug hit him for the first time. That wily bug, that multi-fanged avenger.

His legs buckled beneath him suddenly, almost without warning. Down he went, down on one knee. His stomach upheaved and churned. But he did not vomit. His whole body was soaked with sweat, cold pebbles of sweat, cold, cold as death. He was down, down, down on his knees, weak and helpless. For a few minutes, no one seemed to notice his condition. Then he heard a voice, a distant voice through the clouds and cotton that filled his ears. His eyes, out of focus, just barely discerned a form hovering over him. He could just faintly feel a hand on his back.

And from a distance, a canyon away, a galaxy away, years and years away, a thin voice was speaking.

"Chaver, what is the problem?"

It was Aaron, his voice filled with concern.

Martin moved his lips to answer, but no words came out. His tongue stuck around the sentence, the vague sentence in his mind. His throat locked on forming the necessary movements to speak. "You must lie down, chaver," Aaron's voice trembled. "You look white as a sheet." The vague hand, the light loose fingers gently pushed and guided him backwards. He could just barely feel the back of his head touch the ground. His eyelids closed and fluttered open. Miles above him he could see a circle of cloudy faces hovering. The noise died down, the clatter of cutlery and the laughter.

"Move back, chaverim, give him some air," the butterfly-light and distant voice of Aaron commanded.

Aaron bent over him. Martin could just barely feel a furry sensation against his ear. It was Aaron's lips whispering encouragement.

"Just rest, Martin, don't try to move or speak. Relax, just try to relax, perhaps this will pass in a few minutes."

He did as he was told. He let his arms and legs go completely limp. He allowed his fingers to uncurl and his mouth to hang open. He was completely at the mercy of the universe. The sun had him now, the blue sky had him, Aaron had him, the tanned sabra girls, Yacov. The ground had him, and the twigs of straw. He could not defend himself. He was defenceless as a worm. Any spear of heat could go right through him, and nail him forever to his resting place. Any tremble of anger from any lip could utterly destroy him.

He was a baby once again, dying of bronchitis. What a good thing to have had a daddy who carried him all night long in the cradle of his arms, who cooed and whispered encouragement into his ears. What a good thing to have had a soft-lipped, caring daddy.

Now he was in the arms of the slightest breeze that winnowed across the field.

What a good thing that people cared about his life, that they were concerned about the sweat that encased him, about his tongue that couldn't move, about his throat that was frozen. For if they didn't care, they could crush him so easily beneath their feet. He was at their mercy, completely at their mercy. He wouldn't be able to raise a single finger in his own defence. What a good secure feeling to know that Aaron existed with his huge furry hands and wide shoulders. He was a kind furry man. He wouldn't let a hair on his head be harmed.

He didn't last long on the kibbutz, after the bug began its work inside him. He tried to hang on, to do the work expected of him. But it was useless. The bug was winning. Even after eating a small serving of shemenet, he broke out into a sweat, his entire body buckled, and he ran again and again to the outhouse. The antidote for dysentery was almost as bad as the disease. They gave him huge chalky sulphur pills to swallow, pills so large he was frightened at times that they would lodge halfway down his throat.

Martin was tired from sweating and shitting and weakening and eating his chalk-white pills. He was also weary of everything about the kibbutz. He was fed up and disenchanted. He didn't want to look another plum in the eye. He was sick of the slabs of chicken shit, of planting beans.

A change he needed. A rest. It was almost September, and the idea of going to university occurred to him. Not a full-time course, just a chance to hang around those easy walls and grasses once again. It would be a slow life. He had heard about the Hebrew University. Its reputation spanned the seas. Yerushalaim, the holy of holies; he suddenly had an intense desire to see the ancient city, the mysterious spiritual Jerusalem. And if I forget thee, O Jerusalem, let my tongue cleave to the roof of my mouth.

He felt he just had to slow down, or a bug even worse than his present tormentor would enter him, attack him, and destroy him completely.

Even Aaron agreed.

"Kibbutz life is not for everyone," he said. "You want to be a writer. Jerusalem is the place to go. You can come back some day. You'll always be welcome."

"I feel like I'm quitting," Martin half-moaned.

"No, you did not get this dysentery on purpose. Massada is very bad for it. The drinking water can't be trusted. Martin, I believe you need a rest. Go to the university. Get into your books."

"Moon subjects?" Martin grinned.

"They have their place," Aaron smiled, placing a furry hand on his shoulder.

That was the end of it, the finish, the last go-round. The bus swirled him down the dusty road past Afula. It carried him back to Tel Aviv. The fields passed before his eyes, all blending into one another. Corn fields, apple orchards. They were a huge mist of green-yellow vegetation.

*   *   *

He walked slowly up the steps to his parents' apartment. How different from his first visit when his body was taut and tanned and muscled for the first time. He was sick now, weak, beaten, his shoulders bent. His head was bowed.

"Welcome back," his father grinned in the living room. "How are you feeling? We read in your letter that you got dysentery."

"I'm not too bad."

"You should take it easy for a while. Decide what you want to do."

"I'd like to go back to university, perhaps in Jerusalem."

"As a full-time student?"

"Yes."

"I'm sorry, Martin. I'm taking a hell of a beating. There's no way I can afford the tuition."

"What if I just sat in on classes?"

"Perhaps. How much do you think you would need?"

"About fifty lira a week."

"Could you get a place to stay for that? And not starve yourself to death?"

"Yes, I think I could manage."

"O.K., fifty lira a week. But Martin, I want you to realize that I can't guarantee how long it's going to last. Business is slow. I just can't get going. Everyone's cautious, everyone's hedging their bets. I have a total of about two and a half clients. My bank account's dwindling. I'll send the money as long as I possibly can. But don't expect it to be a permanent arrangement."

The conversation ended. Martin felt a noose tightening around his neck as he sat and smoked in the living room. His heart was beating too fast, the breath was catching in his throat. He just had to leave with his first fifty lira, say goodbye and head for the trains.

CHAPTER 5

Jerusalem Rains

The apartment building in Jerusalem, across a valley from the Hebrew University, was a modern structure, and it fit in nicely with the long flat buildings of the university complex. There were three of these apartment buildings in a row, each supported in front by long spindly legs of concrete. They looked weird to Martin at times, almost surrealistic. They reminded him of old ladies, thin and brittle great-aunts. He moved into one of them in the ancient of ancient cities. He didn't really have a room. A section of the living room was curtained off, and this was his place, impermanent, cold and rugless, without a picture on the wall. This was his doorless cubicle of the apartment which he shared with two sabra boys and a young boy of eighteen from Cleveland, Ohio.

He had to begin anew. It was a cold task, a hard proposition, this beginning again without a close friend, without the faintest idea of what the future had in store for him. He spent days wandering around the campus when he first arrived in the city. The slabs of pink-grey stone, the small newly-planted trees, the hundred glass windows of the library, all these looked alien to him. The bare hills, the Judaean hills, the valleys, the underbrush, the sparse vegetation— it all looked cold, distant, hard to grasp, hard to fathom, difficult to warm up to, stony, silent, mysterious, secretive.

The Judaean hills. He was finally in the Judaean hills where prophets of old wandered, shaking their beards and fingers at the faithless. Here Jeremiah lamented the downfall of the whoring wayward town. Jeremiah—friendless, outcast, with only stones to hug, bare cold Jerusalem stones.

Beginning anew. He had to try to make his way through the cracks and openings, narrow streets, laneways and byways of the old spiritual place, this Jerusalem. When he first arrived, he met an old man from India in the library who wore a tam on his bald head, who kept adjusting his false teeth. This old guy offered him candies, and took him on a dark sabbath evening through the almost empty streets to look for wine and cheese and bread. This old Indian library attendant was very concerned about Martin's welfare. In Martin's room, having drunk some wine, nibbled some cheese, and chewed some bread, the old guy stretched out on Martin's bed.

"Do you believe in God?" he asked.

"No," Martin shook his head.

"If I gave you a book, the greatest book you ever read, and I gave it to you in a brown cover without any writing on it, what's the first thing you would ask?"

"Who wrote it?" Martin answered.

"Well, young man," he said, "go to that window. Raise your head. Look. Just look at those stars, those galaxies, those lights. Just think of the amazing order, harmony, beauty to that whole creation. Doesn't it make you want to ask, 'Who is the author?'"

"You have a point," Martin agreed.

"Be sincere! Don't say things if you don't mean them. We are trying to be sincere tonight. We're having an enjoyable evening. We are partaking of God's gifts—wine and cheese and the beauty of His creation. This is no time for insincerity, or wobbly-kneed condescensions. Come here and sit beside me."

Oh boy, thought Martin, what does this guy want? He knew somewhere inside himself what he wanted, but he couldn't actually believe it was happening. In a daze, an almost half-slumber, his head buzzing with wine, his throat still tasting cheese, he sauntered over to the bed and sat down. The old Indian library attendant, the philosopher and faggot, placed a bony hand on Martin's knee. He rocked his knee back and forth.

"Just relax. Why are you so tense?" the old man almost hissed. "You must learn to enjoy life, to give in to your feelings."

Martin had no answer, or anything he really wanted to say. He kept a sharp eye on the bony fingers that clutched his knee, the long fingers that squeezed, then relaxed their grip.

"You are so young," the old man sighed. "What a waste. If I were only your age and knew what I know today—that would be paradise. We learn too slowly. By the time we really know, it's almost too late. That's sad, my boy, very sad. It's no laughing matter. It's part of the tragedy of this existence."

The old man withdrew a hanky from his pocket and wiped the corners of his eyes. His eyes were large and grey. They looked weak, almost colorless.

"Why don't you talk to me? Don't sit there like a lump. I thought you were a good conversationalist. Ach, you're disappointing, my boy, thoroughly disappointing."

Martin cleared his throat.

"I'm sorry," Martin sighed.

The old man laughed, folds of wrinkled flesh stretched along his neck.

"You are weak, my boy. How do you do in school anyway?"

"Quite well," Martin answered.

"I bet you're a sluggard. You have to work for every mark you get, don't you?"

"No," Martin shook his head. "I pick things up quite quickly."

"Well, you don't project that. Not at all. I'm sorry to say this to you. I don't like being critical. You just seem slow."

"I guess I just have to live with that," Martin grinned, a sarcastic gleam in his eye.

"Can't you be sincere? Isn't there a speck of truth in your whole body? Well, I can see this is going nowhere. I'm going to go home. My wife will be wondering where I've gotten to. You must come to visit us some day. I have a son about your age. A couple of years younger, perhaps. You know where to find me."

He left. He went home with a quarter-bottle of wine, a little cheese, and a chunk of Sabbath *challah*. Martin took the blanket off the bed. He went to the balcony, and under God's great luminous harmonious stars he shook the blanket again and again, making sure that every speck of lint or grime, every fallen hair the old man had left behind flew down the black valley. He went to sleep uneasily, just wondering if the Indian queer, the old married philosopher was perhaps lurking under the balcony, near the spindly-legged supports. Was he waiting there for Martin to doze off, waiting his chance to sneak back in and smother Martin's sleeping face with a thousand old Indian kisses? And for some reason, although he was tense and uneasy and restless, a half-grin hovered around his lips, and it did not take long for sleep to come, unconsciousness, the happy relief of a dreamless night in bed.

Cold and frightening it was to begin from scratch, from point zero, from nowhere, from nothingness. His plans in this country had come to nothing. He had not written, and he had not met a soft understanding girl to share his suffering with.

Professor Tufeen he had run across, a lonely Rumanian professor of philosophy. He had a tragic vision of the universe—how everything was sliding into murk, how another holocaust was inevitable, and another, and another. The professor invited Martin to his room at a small pension in the bare hills near the campus. Martin was amazed that a grown man of forty-five, a professor to boot, could live in such a sparse lean room. What did he have to show for his life? Nothing much, Martin mused. A tea kettle gleaming, and the glint on the tea kettle, on the chrome, made the room look somewhat smaller, darker, colder. A small bookshelf, a few choice books. A narrow window with a frayed curtain. Professor Tufeen offered Martin some plum brandy imported from his dark Balkan homeland, a brandy that curled under the tongue and tickled the tonsils with its sweetness and its alcoholic bubbles. Professor Tufeen gradually became drunk, and he too, like the Indian library attendant, stretched out on his narrow cot-bed, his eyelids heavy with tragedy and weariness.

"Don't you think people will grow to understand one another?" Martin asked.

"I see little hope. There is nothing to convince me that these times are any less forboding than the late thirties. And now we have the power to blow ourselves to smithereens. Life is tragedy. You can afford to be optimistic. You are young. But don't be fooled—you, too, will learn."

Martin read him a poem.

"Yes," Professor Tufeen commented, "you have talent. There is no doubt about that. But I have seen many young men with talent. And I've seen them put bullets through their heads. You must work at it. Try to survive."

Shivers ran up and down Martin's spine in the dark, secluded room. Shadows seemed to crawl along the walls, spider-like, creepy shadows, and the air seemed cool, and the cool tentacles of wind were able to jab through Martin's skin, and seize his heart, and grow faint crystals of ice on his bones. Oh fuck, Martin thought, life just can't be this bleak and dark and hopeless. It just can't all end in a room such as this with nothing for companionship but a gleaming chrome kettle. There had to be something else, just something more to hope for, to clutch, to even love. Martin's back began to ache as he sat on the stiff-backed wooden chair. Professor Tufeen drank glass after glass of plum brandy. His speech became slurred, his eyelids fluttered up and down, opened and shut; he snored.

And Martin knew in a secluded haunt of his psyche that Professor Tufeen was a queer as well as a philosopher. But he could do nothing to help him. It was a route he just couldn't take, no matter how much brandy was pumped down his throat. The professor awoke with a snort.

"I must've dozed off. Forgive me. It is no way to treat a guest. And a poet."

"I should be going soon. It's late."

"You can stay here the night if you wish."

"No. Thank you. It's only a short walk to my place."

"O.K., I understand," the professor groaned. "We can be friends anyway. Share another glass of brandy with me."

They drank again two tiny glasses of brandy. Martin was grateful that Professor Tufeen was no longer in a philosophic mood. He had heard enough about the essential evil that inhabited mankind. Goodness, the professor had said, was not natural to man. That was a great error in perception. Mankind was basically evil. There was a root of darkness in everyone that could not be washed away, or plucked out. Martin was grateful for the stillness on Professor Tufeen's lips. He had heard enough of his tragic outlook.

The evening ended. Professor Tufeen went to sleep on his cot, a glass of brandy still clutched in one hand, and balanced on his chest. Martin quietly let himself out the door. It was a lonely, cold, shadowy walk back to his apartment. Evil fingers curled from the branches of trees, the wind squealed malevolent laughter. The stars looked icy cold. The stars. The stars. Millions of them overhead, cold and uncaring.

As the days passed, days of September, October and November, the rains fell on Jerusalem, the winter rains. They splattered in the valley, turning the ground into muck. Big, huge drops fell across the city from Herzl Mountain to King David's tomb, dark and forboding drops. The Jerusalem rains, the fall downpours and drizzles and mists matched Martin's mood. How he longed to meet a girl. It seemed a long time since he had held one in his arms. He lay on his cot, the rains driving through the valley, he lay on his back dreaming. He could almost feel the softness of breasts in his palms, nipples erect and excited. He could almost smell the soft fragrance of hair. It seemed years ago, it was only months in fact, when he danced with that Maltese girl aboard the S.S. Atlantic on the way to this lonely land. She was only fifteen, but her body was warm, her lips willing. He remembered how they had parted beneath the gentle pressure of his tongue. She had freckles, and blue-grey eyes, this young little girl from Malta. She was natural and sweet and warm. She never clipped the hairs in her armpits. And this made her seem more exciting to him, more daring, even more animal. And he even enjoyed the faint odor and aroma that he could detect rising from her armpits. His mother laughed, and his sister chuckled, because she never bothered to clip those hairs. They teased him about it from the Straits of Gibraltar all the way down the narrow throat of the Mediterranean. But he clung to her, danced with her, held her and kissed her. He shut his ears to his mother's jibes and his sister's teasings. What did they really know about love anyway?—with their lipstick and mascara and shaved underarms.

At Malta she disembarked with the rest of her family: a couple of moustachioed men, a couple of old women who had never in their entire lives touched a blade to their bodies. He liked hair on women. It stirred him, the feel of hair on legs, in armpits. It made them somehow more real, more tangible. She disappeared into her Maltese homeland. Gone her freckles, gone her warm lingering kisses.

He remembered her lovingly as he stretched out on the cot. The rains splattered and dripped and slashed against the windowpanes. The need to find a girlfriend was beginning to bang in his brain, knock at his heart. He would go crazy without one, he would surely die of loneliness, and all they would find in his bare curtained room would be a damp blotch of yearning on the floor. It seemed years ago, what had happened on the S.S. Atlantic. And what a slim, short-lived memory to cling to.

He remembered his old girlfriend Cheryl in Montreal, a soft bunny of a Jewish girl who lived in Outremont with her beak-nosed mommy and her dad the butcher. Oh how he clung to her on Friday and Saturday nights, kissing her, fondling her, feeling her secret wet parts. How many times he came in his jeans listening to Tchaikovsky in Cheryl's Jewish home. He never entered her body, he never dared. How he yearned to go inside her. She, too, was a memory, soft-haired and vague, a distant aroma that was so faint now it gave him little satisfaction.

And one by one, all the girls he had ever kissed and touched from early childhood to his cold present aching situation flocked through his mind. Gentile girls with blue eyes and blond hair. Gone, they were all gone, swallowed and devoured by the march of events and time. It seemed that he didn't have any past, anything real to cling to. He had to go forward, to start again from nothing. And it was ridiculous, he thought, to be almost twenty and still almost a virgin. At seventeen, while screwing away a summer in Arizona, he had taken a trip to Nogales, Mexico. There, he got laid for the very first time. Twice in a row, on two Saturday nights, one following the other. But they were whores, after all, paid for, and somehow they didn't seem to really count. Drunk he had plunged into them, drunk he had come.

The need grew in his bones. It gnawed at him, up and down his spine. How could life be real without a soft-skinned friend? Books were just books, ink on white paper. Men were men, professors were professors, studying was studying, writing was writing, rain was rain, mud was mud, but all this conglomerate of activity and people—what did it all come to without a woman to hold and love and kiss and fondle?

Then he discovered Gila. She lived next door to him, the very next apartment—under his nose for two months, yet he had missed her. He had overlooked the possibility, or had just not seen her. She was dark-skinned; her eyes were black and alive; her cheeks dimpled when she smiled. And she was the real thing—a sabra through and through. Israel was carved into her bones, *Eretz* Yisroel etched into her marrow. Four generations of her family had lived in this country, soaking in the sun, decade after decade. And before that, they had lived for centuries in Iraq, only a few hot borders away. She was a black grape nurtured and raised and honed to her own perfection in the Middle East. She was three years older than Martin.

She got into him slowly, into his brain waves and heart murmurs, slowly, with her almost innocent smile, her white white teeth, her contrasting dark skin, her black boyish haircut. She told him one evening about her brother.

"He was killed about a year ago," she said. "Near Tiberias. He was working in the fields. On a tractor. They shot him from the Golan Heights."

"I'm sorry," Martin sighed, bowing his head.

"That is part of life here in Eretz. We accept it."

"It's a hell of a life."

"From your point of view, yes," Gila said, trying to smile. "You boys from Canada and America don't understand us. You are spoiled."

"Do you believe you are better?" Martin asked.

"We don't live in our heads over here. We have little time for writing and thinking. There are enemies. We have to work and fight. We want to keep this country."

"Were you in the army?"

"Of course," she chuckled, "who doesn't go to the army?"

"What did you do?"

"I worked with the paratroopers. I helped to sew the parachutes for them."

"I hope you did a good job," Martin grinned, remembering his fear of heights.

"Why don't you join?" she suddenly said.

"The paratroopers?"

"Why not? They're the best soldiers in the country. Not everyone can jump."

"Well, I have this thing about high places," Martin admitted.

"Oh, you silly Canadian boy," she chuckled.

And as she smiled, she leaned her head to one side. Light was dancing in her black eyes. Spit was tingling on her lips. Martin bent over her and kissed her. She responded warmly, and threw her arms around his back.

"You find that funny, don't you?" Martin said, drawing away.

"You are funny," she smiled. "What do you do? Do you write your poems all day long?"

"I go to classes."

"Yes, you would make a good professor. *So serious.*"

She pursed her lips together on the "so serious", drawing it out, mocking him and chuckling at the same time, light again dancing in her eyes.

That night in bed alone in his apartment, Gila's face swam and bobbed behind his closed eyes. A thousand parachutes snapped and fluttered open, plummeting on their assigned targets. It was never enough, he thought: arm wrestles, dysentery, trips to the desert. Did he now have to shoulder a rifle? Jump from a plane, prove and prove his manhood, give of his own blood, and take a few drops, a few vital breaths from the enemy? Aw hell, he felt, maybe he could just let it be. Words were his weapons, poems his parachutes, and perhaps Gila was one of his assigned targets. He wanted to screech every doubt and yearning out on paper. They just had to sparkle and flash and explode, those words, to make up for the jumps he would never take, to atone in his own way for Gila's brother.

Yet the way the words came out on paper never seemed to satisfy. They looked clumsy lying on white sheets. They were just not as deadly and keen as bullets, nor did they flash as bright as flares, or roar like bazookas. There was turmoil inside him, a gnawing, a red bruised sore on his stomach's lining. He just wanted to get every speck of that feeling on paper, to nail it down.

He wrote, and wrote, and wrote. Love poems. Poems about Gila. Poems about tractors, and bullets, and bodies of brothers dead in furrows. Poems about the valley and the mud, and the cold Jerusalem rains. Very few he kept, very, very few. As they came out, he looked at them in disgust, filled with dissatisfaction—they left so much unsaid. He didn't know the nature of the sore in his stomach. He crumpled sheet after sheet with a fist that was angry, with a fist that yearned to slam a hole through the plaster walls of his room.

Gila didn't satisfy him either. A friend in Montreal had told him that Israeli girls were warm and loving, easy and free with their bodies. One evening Gila revealed a startling truth to him.

"You're only the second boy I've ever kissed."

"What!" Martin gasped. "You're kidding."

"No, it's the truth. Why are you so surprised?"

"I thought . . . "

"I know what you thought. I've heard those stories about us. They're just stories."

"Do you know something?" Martin asked. "I've had girlfriends since I've been six years old."

"Have you ever slept with a woman?"

"Of course," Martin snapped back as if it were old hat. The two whores in Nogales whirled through his brain.

"Many times?"

"Yes."

"And I suppose you want to sleep with me."

"Well, why not?"

"I'm not going to sleep with anyone until I get married. Besides, I'm afraid of getting pregnant."

"You can take precautions."

"Oh, you boys are all the same. Is that all you have on your mind?"

"Lovemaking is supposed to be beautiful," Martin added.

But his voice was tired and weary, full of sand and gravel, just too weak and thin to press the point. The rains came down on Jerusalem and engulfed his brain. Gila didn't really satisfy him. She was sweet and young and black-skinned, but he just couldn't get that close to her, nor she to him. They kissed and kissed and fondled each other from chin to toe, from hairline to ankle-bone, with jut of tongue, and lips wet and warm, yet he couldn't get inside her. Not just her body, but inside this person Gila. She was a plaything, soft and squeezable, lovable and giggly. He went to her room often, she came to his. They clutched and grasped for one another, struggled to get close, struggled with their bodies and in conversations, but there was a limit to the feeling they were letting out for one another.

She was the girl in the next apartment whom he happened to notice one day, who smiled at him kindly, who invited him to taste her lips. He had tasted. He had talked. But there was a huge gaping vacuum inside him that Gila with her smiles, no matter how warm, was just not filling.

And he did not have the energy to ram himself inside her. Nor did he have the energy to campaign for her virgin body, to convince her to let him inside her. He tried for a while to cajole, argue, to get her to part her legs. But he soon gave up. It just wasn't worth the strain. He gave up completely, and resigned himself to nights of kissing and petting and talking. Were Israeli girls really free and easy, warm and loving? That was how all the stories went. Was she the exception?—the only twenty-three-year-old virgin sabra girl in all the land, the only one that existed from the borders of Lebanon down to Eilat?

The rains continued in Jerusalem that first winter. They were long and sorrowful strings of wetness. They were the huge drops of his dissatisfaction falling on the mountaintops, in the valley, on the trees. They pinged his forehead, ran down the back of his neck. They soaked his socks and twisted the leather on his shoes.

CHAPTER 6

Through the Eyes of Jesse

He attended classes at the Hebrew University, his body seated in large lecture halls, his body present at cozy seminars, but his mind wandered. His gaze often drifted towards the window, looking towards the tops of trees just barely discernible on Herzl Mountain. Something was being said by the professor or one of the students, some point of criticism or information. Words and sentences issued from their mouths, but he was separated from their meaning. They could've been uttering pig Latin, and it would have had just as much significance. During these dreamy months, he met Peter Stoneman, a tall Canadian boy from Toronto. Martin could not stop marvelling at how handsome Peter was. He was over six foot three with black wavy hair, white spotless teeth, and a smile that was filled with vigor —but not just vigor—with cleverness, but with warmth as well.

Beside him, Martin felt ill-formed, rough. How different the two faces were: Martin with his broken nose, the half-moon birth scar still visible on his right check. His lips just a little too loose and thick. His teeth not perfectly straight. He remembered his father calling him a Greek god. This was a joke when he compared his body and face with Peter Stoneman's.

Peter seemed to walk in a different world, not just a realm distinct from Martin's, but somewhere inaccessible to most other beings. Yet in Peter there seemed to be doubts lurking. He listened carefully to what Martin had to say about this poet and that, this philosopher and the other, as if he really believed that Martin had a way of seeing into books and ideas that was somehow more filled and charged with significance than his own.

"Martin, I have a good friend I would like you to meet," Peter Stoneman told him one day. "I believe the two of you have a lot in common."

Peter's voice was filled with near-reverence when he spoke of this friend. Martin sensed immediately that this wasn't just anybody that he was going to be introduced to, but someone very close to Peter's life, someone very important to him.

And Martin felt complimented that Peter had chosen him to meet this friend.

In Jerusalem there were many restaurants that served tachina and hummus, shish-kabob and pita, falafel, and all the Arab-Israeli hot dishes. But in the heart of Jerusalem, just off King George Road, there was a large restaurant that specialized in old Yiddish cooking: sweet and sour cabbage soup, shnitzel, chopped liver, all the warm sour sweet dishes Martin remembered his mother and grandmothers cooking when he was a child. In fact, his mother's specialty still was cabbage borsht.

It was a rainy night in Jerusalem. Peter Stoneman and Martin sat at one of the tables at the Warsaw Restaurant. The matronly waitresses, faces flushed, rotund hips swaying, fluttered from table to table carrying bowls of beet soup and plates filled with shnitzel. Martin relaxed in his chair. It was good to be in this place that smelled of chicken fat and chopped liver, that reminded him of his nannies' kitchens. The cuffs of his trousers were still wet and frayed. His hair was still dripping from walking with Peter in the downpour. Between the clink of glasses and the smacking of lips, he could hear the million drops of rain pinging on the roof overhead.

"I think he might be here tonight," Peter whispered across the table.

"I would really like to meet him."

"I just have the feeling," Peter added, "that you two are going to get along very well."

There was a slight buzzing of excitement in Martin's stomach, an expectation and hope that tingled along his spine. Peter had told him so much about Jesse: his linguistic abilities, the depth and power of his mind, his experience and knowledge and sensitivity. And Martin was just a little high-strung and nervous, ever so slightly fearing that he would not measure up to Jesse's standards, or that somehow the two of them would not get along. This would be ruinous. Peter had such faith in his friend, such belief and adoration. It shone from Peter's eyes when he spoke of him, and light danced on his wide handsome forehead.

A short, wiry, elastic-legged man finally appeared, almost out of nowhere, when Martin was least expecting it. He reached out a long-fingered hand and gripped Peter's shoulder.

"Shalom, my friend," he smiled. "Good weather for ducks."

"Ah, shalom, Jesse. I'm really glad you could make it."

Peter's face danced with light as Jesse took a seat at the table. His handsome face was glowing, every feature alive, his black eyes blacker yet softer, his mouth soft and sensual.

"Jesse," Peter said, "I would like you to meet my good friend Martin Kanner."

Jesse extended a hand across the table.

"So you're the fellow Peter's been talking about," Jesse grinned. "I'm glad we could all finally get together."

"It's good to meet you," Martin smiled back. His voice was a little stiff, just slightly tense.

Martin was fascinated by Jesse's face. It had a hypnotic quality about it that drew Martin's gaze. He had never seen a face quite like it anywhere. It was not any particular feature, but the combination of his wide forehead, the high cheekbones, the eyes sunk deep in the skull but glimmering, the scraggly forks of beard hanging from a delicate but chiseled chin. It was more than this, though. Something Martin couldn't put his finger on, an elusive quality that wasn't determined by flesh and bone, color and bloodbeat. It was something in the way Jesse's face caught the light. It made his face look transparent, as if the light were traveling through his cheekbones, his forehead, and somehow coming out the other side.

Martin realized that he was staring. It was not polite, it was not the proper thing to do, but his gaze kept leaping from his plate, back again and again to Jesse.

"I understand that you're quite an authority on Nietzsche," Jesse smiled, licking the corner of his lips.

"Not really," Martin blushed, "I've read a few of his books."

"And Peter tells me that you write."

"Yes," Martin nodded.

"You're quite prolific, in fact."

"It kind of comes in spurts," Martin smiled.

"He's being modest," Peter added. "He writes very well. He's very consistent."

"You must show me some of your work," Jesse beamed. "I dabble a little myself. Mostly essays."

The talk circled the table between steaming bowls of soup and plates of bread-coated shnitzel. Martin felt wrapped and warm, sitting at the table with Peter and Jesse. He could no longer feel his rain-wet socks. The waitresses kept circling the dining room, the restaurant was quite crowded, but Martin's attention was almost completely centred on the small round table, and his two friends. He sank into his chair dreamily, a little weary and tired, but he let his legs stretch out, and his fists uncurl. That evening the food tasted particularly good. He could taste every strand of tomato-soaked cabbage, the meat with a slight lemony tang. After the meal, he drew the smoke from his cigarette to the very bottom of his lungs. He allowed it to linger as it travelled back up his throat, and he expelled it gently in long easy furrows.

The conversation began to travel more and more between Jesse and Martin. Peter had grown quiet, almost heavy and serious. Martin could sense Peter's mind turning over and over, and he could feel that he was growing just a little restless. He had not been excluded from the conversation. It was as if he had decided to drop out for the time being.

"You're quiet this evening, Peter," Jesse commented.

"I enjoy listening to the both of you," Peter smiled. "And I've got something on my mind."

"What does she look like?" Jesse quipped, his hazel-brown eyes flickering.

"That's the problem."

"You're kidding. A guy like you not getting enough. That's ridiculous."

"Well," Peter sighed, "It's the truth."

A small smile quivered on Peter's lips. It *was* hard to imagine, Martin thought. But Peter wasn't kidding. His eyes looked heavy, and his head leaned to one side.

"That's not the real problem either," Peter added. "I can get enough, but it's all the same shit. You know, very superficial."

"I understand," Jesse sighed in a deep, almost gravelly voice.

Suddenly, Martin found himself thinking about Lisa, an American girl who lived in one of the rooms in Gila's apartment. She was about twenty-six or so. How many times Martin had dreamed about her full breasts, her strong ample womanly thighs. She had a hazy, blue-eyed, sensual smile. Martin himself had wanted to make a pass at her on several different occasions, but he never got up the courage to do it. She was too much for him. His tongue got all twisted together when he talked to her, the blood buzzed crazily in his brain, his palms became wet with sweat. He had had the same experience a couple of times in his young life. Someone that really stirred him, usually older and more mature, someone attractive and well built and very, very womanly. And on all occasions he ended up biting his tongue, not making a single move. And he wound up with Lisa on his mind, at nights alone in bed, Lisa burning behind his eyelids.

But Peter, a guy like Peter, certainly he could handle her, and his tongue would not become twisted and useless from excitement and yearning.

"I know somebody," Martin suddenly blurted. "You might like her, Peter. She lives in the apartment next to me."

"Really?" Peter smiled. "Is she a student?"

"Yes, I think she's taking fine arts. She's about twenty-six, and boy, is she ever built."

"Does she have a mind to go along with it? I can't stand any more of these mindless bodies."

"She's quite intelligent."

Peter laughed. He covered his mouth with his hand.

"No, I'm not kidding," Martin smiled and blushed. "She's really quite sensitive."

"You don't have anything to lose," Jesse added. "Why don't you let Martin introduce you?"

"Why not?" Peter agreed.

"I'll tell her about you," Martin said softly. "She hasn't got a boyfriend as far as I know."

So it was settled. And this added to Martin's enjoyment, his feeling of well-being at the Warsaw Restaurant on that first evening he met Jesse. He had never brought two people together before. He had never even tried. In fact, the idea had never occurred to him. But the ideas were flowing that evening at the old Warsaw. He liked the idea of playing the matchmaker. What if it worked?—he thought. That would be terrific. And he honestly believed these two great specimens of man and woman, Peter and Lisa, would hit it off, click, and perhaps even fall in love.

Peter again grew silent, almost morose. It was a strange sight: such an extraordinarily handsome face, every feature carved to exquisite proportion, a strong jaw-line, high manly forehead, deep brown sensitive eyes, white flashing teeth—it was strange and incongruous to see a face like Peter's wrinkled and buckled with sorrow. Martin reviewed his own struggles with Gila, with practically all the girls he ever knew. Peter was right, there was something superficial about them. He was glad that Peter had revealed this gnawing sore in his gut. For at times, Martin had felt there was something disastrously and uniquely wrong with him. Now, it was somehow easier to take, knowing that Peter was going through the same doubts, the same struggle and anguish.

Peter cupped his mouth, letting out a half-sigh, half-yawn.

"Fellows, I really feel tired tonight. I think I'll go home and get some rest."

Good-nights were exchanged. The "goodbyes" and "see you agains" were quiet, reserved, almost solemn. Even Jesse's glimmering hazel eyes had lost their usual resilience. Peter left the Warsaw, stepping quietly and swiftly between the waitresses and the tables. He pulled the collar of his raincoat well up over his ears.

"He's had a hard time with women," Jesse confided, whispering across the table.

"He can't find anybody serious?" Martin asked.

"They use him," Jesse twinkled. "He's a sex object to most of them. He's a male beauty queen. He's just too fucking good-looking. They don't look for anything else in him, and it's beginning to get on his nerves."

"Hmm," Martin sighed, plunging deep into thought. "I don't think I've ever seen that before. It's weird, isn't it?"

"The guy's got everything going for him. Maybe too much. He's got looks, brains. He's talented, sensitive, warm. That can scare a girl, you know. They get him for his body, and after it's over, that's it. Kaput."

On the "kaput", Jesse blew a breath across the table, as if he were mimicking a strong wind blowing the last lonely leaf off an autumn tree.

"I hope he finds somebody," Martin groaned. "Lisa could be right for him. She really could."

Jesse's gaze fell to the table. He grew silent, and seemed to be contemplating his long bony fingers. His knuckles were pronounced, knobs of bone and flesh thinly covered by pale, white skin.

Martin regretted that Peter was feeling low, but he was glad that he had left the Warsaw. He really wanted to be alone with Jesse, this man of twenty-eight who fascinated him. His ideas seemed to twirl around in long spirals and circles. At times, there was no telling what was the beginning or ending of a certain train of thought. He didn't think in a straight line at all. Jesse slowly began to speak again. He talked about the women in his life, just touching on the subject. Then, he connected this bit of conversation with ideas on ballet, and then, almost magically, interwove ballet and women with his ideas on art and writing and Zen Buddhism. When he spoke, Martin got the feeling that every ounce of air and energy in the universe was connected. It was only the unenlightened who couldn't see this.

At McGill, Martin had hung around with a group of iconoclasts. Nietzsche, D. H. Lawrence and Catullus were among the writers they idolized. Everything that got in the way of zest and greatness and tragic heroics had to be smashed. They had no liking for weak-kneed socialism, or vague Oriental philosophies, or a common good for all mankind. They drew their inspiration from the great Canadian poet, Jake Manning. What Manning said was gospel. This Nietzschean predilection for struggle and celebration and superhuman effort had rubbed off on Martin. Most of mankind were bugs, insecure and insignificant, only great passionate men were worth considering. A poet had to become great, he had to raise himself above the rabble, the oceans of riff-raff that opened their maws for his soaring soul.

Martin still carried these ideas in his head, clutched them to his heart. They were worlds apart from what Jesse was expressing. Mountains separated his high-flying, tight-lipped Nietzscheanism from Jesse's open-ended, loose, flowing, oriental, "all is connected", "all is worthwhile" philosophy. An argument began between Jesse and Martin.

"Who suffers?" Jesse asked.

"Great men. They suffer for their ideas. They're crucified."

"What about the shoemaker down the street?"

"You can't compare a shoemaker to Byron or Napoleon."

"They are both flesh," Jesse snapped back. "They both have a heart and brains and feelings."

"Yes, but a great man climbs much higher. He has a longer way to fall."

"What great men have you known?" Jesse asked sarcastically.

Martin grew silent. What great men did he know? Was Jake Manning an ubermensch, a superman, the real thing? He had struggled a long time to get his poems accepted. He had fought against a tight-assed Wasp puritanism. When he was a student, he had predicted Hitler's rise to power, he had prophesied the persecution of the Jews. His fellow students were enraged. They gathered together, flocked to his room, and filled his bed with garbage. Was Jake Manning, truly, the archetypal great man? A Canadian Byron? A Montreal Nietzsche? He certainly had suffered during the lean years before his life-affirming, sensual poetry had been accepted. But another picture of Jake Manning flashed through Martin's mind. He was at a blackboard teaching a course on creative writing. He was still brown from his vacation in Hydra. He even had a slight potbelly. And it was rumoured that he was beginning to become an economic success. His books were selling wildly, his teaching job was paying, and he had invested very wisely and judiciously in real estate.

"That's the problem," Martin finally answered. "There are hardly any great men left. The system grinds them down."

"Well," Jesse sighed, "I will tell you one thing, Martin, about greatness and suffering. Here's what I really believe. A young girl who is not invited to the prom because she has pimples suffers just as much as your beloved Nietzsche."

Shit, Martin thought, this Jesse had a way of putting things that jabbed into his brain and heart like a hot poker. He could see it so clearly. A young girl in a white cashmere dress. Her face covered with little red blemishes. It's a pretty face, but the blemishes hang around the lips in clusters. They are red and sore and shiny. It is two hours before the prom, the last big event of the high school year. All her friends are going, all the boys and girls for blocks around. She is sitting by the phone, still hoping, still praying that, perhaps, at the very last moment, it will ring, and someone will ask her to the dance. As the minutes fly past, the tears slowly collect in the corners of her eyes. Pain shoots through her chest. The tears flow into the corners of her mouth, salty and spiced with remorse.

Martin had no answer, no quick, easy way to overturn Jesse's point. It had been made solidly. He could see exactly what Jesse was driving at. Jesse's entire perception of human beings, their relationships, was different from anything he had been exposed to before. It did not end at the human condition, but he had a way of talking about trees and wind, songs and animals, books and women that attracted Martin, drew his heart and mind, his feelings and thoughts. And there seemed no end to the subjects they talked about. The time went by quickly. Before they knew it, almost everyone had left the Warsaw. Only the waitresses remained, scurrying back and forth to clean up the last crumbs of the evening. It was just about closing time. Two customers remained at the Warsaw, Jesse leaning back in his chair, stroking his beard, talking, talking, talking, and Martin hunched over, leaning forward, intent on each word that dropped from Jesse's mouth. Finally, they made a move to leave.

It was warm outside, a particularly warm evening for winter in Jerusalem. The rains had cleansed the streets of dust and grime, and left behind a fragrance of flowers, a fragrance that revived and rejuvenated Martin. It was as if the whole city had been renewed by the downpour, and he was seeing it, this Jerusalem, for the first time. The way it was meant to be seen. He was seeing it through Jesse's eyes. It was a softer place now; it had nooks and crannies, shades of purple, grey and black he had never noticed before.

"I love this city," Jesse sighed. His mouth curled around the words. He spoke them softly like a kiss.

"It's beautiful," Martin agreed. He was being swirled into Jesse's enthusiasm.

"It's the oldest and youngest city in the world. Smell it. Smell it. Just look at it. It's a woman."

And Jesse, to Martin's amazement, began to skip and dance down King George Rd. His hands and arms flew loosely out behind him. He looked like a satyr, a young boy, a ballerina. Martin began to laugh. It bubbled up from inside him. It seemed months and months since he had had a real good laugh. It seemed a long time since he had been this happy. He ran after Jesse, leaping occasionally, touching the branches of trees with the tips of his fingers. He caught up to Jesse. He was still laughing. Jesse's face in the moonlight looked smooth and white, soft and defined. He had an old face. It was almost the face of a Cro-Magnon man. And it was the face of a monkey. In the Warsaw, that was what Jesse had told him: that if he ever came back to this life for a second go-round, he would want to come back as a spider monkey. But he already looked like a spider monkey, Martin thought, with his long loose arms and legs, his wrinkled forehead, his skinny torso.

"It's ours, all ours," Jesse sang out.

He spread his arms out, as if to embrace all the buildings, trees, monuments. In Martin's imagination, the stars and the moon were dropping into Jesse's outstretched arms.

"This is my town, Martin."

As they walked and talked and skipped along, Martin began to believe that Jerusalem was Jesse's. The city, after three months, had suddenly come alive. Martin was no longer feeling the endless muddy walks through the valley to the university. He was no longer feeling the angular, cold shapes of the apartment buildings. They glowed, now, softly. Even the Knesset, the main building that housed the offices of government, even the Knesset looked a soft amber in the moonlight. It was a hunched miracle of yellow-pink brick. Each pebble danced with life and vitality. The windows shone.

Jesse flung a long sinewy arm around Martin's back, embracing him, drawing him close.

"Why the hell would I ever want to leave this place?" Jesse asked rhetorically. "I can't understand it—all these American kids coming and going, flying here, flying there. Not getting anywhere. It's right here under their noses—everything."

"How long have you lived here?" Martin almost whispered, as if to talk too loudly would break the magic of the mood.

"Thirteen wonderful years," Jesse beamed. "It grows on you, Martin. It becomes your skin."

"Where were you before?"

"I grew up in Bulgaria. I lived in France. They were O.K. But Jerusalem is my place. I'll probably live here forever."

A city becoming your skin. Forever. What a feeling that must be, Martin thought. He had never experienced it. In Halifax, he had moved with his family from street to street every three or four years. Then to Montreal, Toronto, Tel Aviv. He was just getting a glimmer of what Jesse was talking about. It seemed that he was content, almost satisfied: as if his feet had grown down into the pavement, and the earth beneath the pavement had become part of his bones.

Martin yearned to grasp every single element of Jesse's feeling for Jerusalem. He wanted to clothe himself as Jesse had with the pink building stones, the long lean cypresses, the fragrances, musty and holy, ancient and sacred, of this city. For a split-second, he almost found himself wanting to be Jesse, to be as loose, as seemingly serene, to be a master of ten languages, to be able to spit and curl out German, Hebrew, French, English, Slavic dialects, to be able to mix all the ancient tongues into collages and beautiful cadent constructions. He was tired of thinking in a straight line, fed up with it. It was choking him—even his efforts to write. How strained the poems were coming out, like brick and mortar, bullets and firepower. He wanted to be swallowed by Jerusalem, the holy of holies, the serene of serenes, to be devoured by the sensual limbs of this womanly city, not crunched, not broken by it, just immersed as in a warm, cozy bathtub.

Bathe me, Jerusalem sky, he was thinking. Bathe me with your bricks and soft black awnings. With your dark Yemenite women in bright red shmatahs. Drown me in your valleys, in your mud, even in your slime. His brain was leaping in circles as he walked beside Jesse, as they floated down King George Rd. They were two free spirits, Martin was thinking. What harm could befall them as long as they were this light-footed, as long as their nostrils flared to pick up the aromas of each bush, flower, alleyway? Let it all come: shishkabob on a stick, burnt by charcoal, herring in vats of vinegar, black bloated olive smells, and even the choking stench of urine. Let it all surround them, pour down their throats. He wanted everything that evening. He wanted his hands to be miles long, he wanted to emulate his childhood comic-book hero, Plastic Man, for his fingertips to touch Mount Zion, Mount Herzl, the sleeping rabbis in *Mea She'arim*, and for it all to be done simultaneously. He wanted to be a disembodied breath travelling down each lung that lived in this city, to seep into each pore of cement and ground.

And Jesse was happy too, particularly happy to have met Martin. He felt ten years younger, eighteen once again. Martin's enthusiasm for his ideas, for his city, for his way of life buoyed him, gave him new hope. For it had been a long struggle of a winter for Jesse. Things had lost their freshness. It was as if he had been travelling in a circle he had travelled many times before.

Martin didn't realize that he was giving anything to Jesse. This feeling was beginning to weigh him down, it was beginning to grow in his throat. Finally, he had to speak about it, share it with his new friend.

"Jesse, I really enjoy talking with you. This is hard to say, it's a little embarrassing. But I don't know what you get from me."

Jesse for a second, before he caught himself, was startled by Martin's directness. He doesn't hold anything back, Jesse thought. But it was refreshing—this straightness, almost bluntness, this onslaught of feeling that had been pouring out of him the whole evening.

"It's difficult to express, Martin. You make me feel like a kid again. This world is filled with old men, tired and pooped out."

Martin tossed an arm around Jesse's shoulder.

"I hope when I'm your age I'm still as free."

Martin could see clearly the image that Jesse had of him. A young kid. A young writer. Full of vim and vigour. Martin almost believed it himself. But Jesse had not seen him buckled and broken at Kibbutz One Sun. And Jesse had not seen the dreamy days and lonely nights he had spent lying on his cot. But he wasn't going to disillusion Jesse by bringing up these things. In fact, Martin began to believe that he could leave them behind, become just that side that Jesse was seeing: young, vital, life-affirming. No tears on his cheeks or sighs lingering in his throat.

"You shouldn't put yourself down," Jesse added. "You're young, talented, you have everything going for you."

"But I haven't lived. I haven't even suffered, not real suffering."

Jesse laughed. He stroked his beard and laughed.

"Do the trees suffer?"

They walked and talked their way along, turned a corner, and started down a side street towards Jesse's one-room apartment. Martin, without realizing it, was marching along now with his fists clenched, his fingers gnarled together, his hands formed into two knots. Jesse's eyes, large and observant, had picked this up. He told Martin about it. He told him that he was tensing up, that he was curling his fists, and that it was a vicious circle: the more he curled his fists, the tenser he would become. Martin let them unfurl, let his fingers hang loosely by his side. And it was true, he did begin to feel easier and lighter once again. He noticed that Jesse's hands were never knotted. His fingers looked light as butterflies, loose as the wind.

Down they travelled into the centre of the night, into the core of the darkness, where the street lamps only twinkled miles apart. The night was never going to end. It stretched its long tentacles of moist fragrance all the way to Haifa. It was two or three in the morning—who could tell any more? The night was a glove. They were two hands, Jesse and Martin, squeezed into the same mitten. The moments, moist and full, lingered. They grew, they developed, they swelled, until each moment of blackness encompassed the city, and it sent out a million spokes and ripples of feeling.

Jesse was Martin's guide on the streets he had walked and talked to for thirteen years. What better guide could he find in all of Eretz? What uniformed, paid-for servant could know this city like the wrinkles of his own skin? They came to a valley, a cheek and crevice of darkness that stretched and meandered below them.

"Martin, do you know what valley that is?"

"Uh-uh," Martin shook his dark head.

"That's the Valley of the Cross."

In Jesse's voice there was reverence now, a heavy, rich, Bulgarian-Jewish, thick-throated reverence, almost awe, and in his voice lingered the sweet vapours of nostalgia. His voice sounded two thousand years old. It was rabbinical and priestly. The voice of a grandmother humming and praying over Sabbath candles.

"From that valley, Martin, they cut Christ's cross. They cut it from a tree that used to grow there. Just down there. Can you believe that?"

Martin's head was flooded with images. He could see the crippled tree. Zzz-zzz, the saws scraping. Or chop chop, the centurion hatchets slicing through the sap-moist limbs of a tree. The whole valley buzzing with activity, clamor of voices, plans for the great day of the crucifixion. Shields flung to one side in excitement. Sequins of armor shimmering.

"So close," Martin sighed.

"Yes, that valley is the beginning of the Via Dolorosa."

Jesse curled his lips around the words—Via Dolorosa. It sounded to Martin like the most beautiful phrase he had ever heard in his life. It flowed like a viaduct of ancient Rome. It was rose, a blood red rose, and it swam in sorrow. It oozed dolor and pain. Via Dolorosa. It was the name of the most beautiful, soothing woman who ever lived. It had the texture of Madonna, but more, more shades and contours, turns and spins. It had the magnificence of the name Michelangelo, but more—less angular, softer, more caressing.

Via Dolorosa. Via Dolorosa. Via Dolorosa. It repeated in Martin's mind, the soft night-time wheels of a train, an endless black vehicle. Via Dolorosa. The way of tears, the way of sorrow, the way of the rose. Colorful, rosy, on the move, sweeping, caressing, crying, sighing, sleeping, awaking, loving, dying.

What better name could they ever have found for the magic soft route of the Saviour?

It befitted his suffering and strength so well. It fitted like a perfectly adjusted crown of thorns. There He walked, his forehead sprouting petals of rose blood. The Jewish boys running at him, the vulgar Romans charging and plucking strands from his beard. Kill that nobody Jew from Galilee, that impostor, that carpenter's son. Scourge him with whip and salt, with tongue-lash and spit. Humble him. Bring him to his knees. How dare he call the great Jehovah abba? Abba! he called him abba! Can you imagine—abba, daddy? He called the Lord daddy. Crucify him! Hang him from a tree.

"He walked," Jesse continued, "from here, this very spot, to the Mount of Olives."

Jesse stretched out a loose-fingered hand towards the valley below. They both stood in the darkness. They were silent. Even the mad whirl of thoughts had slowed down in Martin's head. How long did they stand like this? Was it seconds or hours? The tick-tock of watches and clocks had lost all meaning. They stood silently, eyes and limbs wrapped in darkness. Tears formed in Martin's eyes, inexplicable globes of salt and sorrow. It was strange. What did he know about this Christ, man-god of the gentiles? What possible connection could he have to Jesus, the star of Christmas?

He had seen a lot of Christmases in Halifax when he was a young boy, when he felt cheated to see the lights up and down the street, and his house dark without a tree, without the comfort of a red-nosed Santa sliding down the chimney. He celebrated Chanukah with his family. But it was never the same. A Chanukah bush could never replace the soft sprigs of a tall spruce. Chanukah *gelt* could never replace the mounds of red-green sparkling presents. And the eight candles in their gold menorah could never substitute for the Christmas carols he knew so well, the splendor and triumph of "Come Let Us Adore Him". It was comforting, though, when his father told him that Jesus was Jewish, and all this fuss and bother was being made over a Jewish boy. That was comforting. He couldn't understand it at the time; in fact, he still didn't, but it was a comfort, almost a joy to realize that Jesus Christ was a descendant of King David.

He had cried when he was four and five and six years old over this Jesus, this Son of God. He had yearned for a Christmas tree, he had wanted so badly to be like his friends. And he remembered another time when he had shed tears over this Jewish messiah whom the gentiles loved dearly. He was nine years old at the time. Some of his Protestant school friends had found a crucifix and rosary lying in the gutter. Perhaps a young Catholic schoolboy had dropped it on his way home from Mass. The Protestant boys picked it up. They began to laugh and jeer. They spat on it, soaking the silver body with goo. They flung it back into the gutter and ran home, still laughing. How could they do this to their own God, Martin had wondered. His young boy's mind just couldn't understand. And strangely, very strangely, he had felt that his friends had spit on him, soaked him with their goo and slime. Jesus was Jewish, Martin Kanner was Jewish. They had spit on this poor Jewish man.

Martin picked it up from the gutter, wiping away the spit on the sleeves of his coat. He rubbed and rubbed and rubbed. It took a long time before every speck of slime had been rubbed off. Still, he wasn't certain. Had he missed any? Was there goo still clinging in the cracks between the beads?

When he got home and told the story to his father, his father explained the strife and warfare between Catholics and Protestants.

"They almost hate each other as much as they hate Jews," his father sighed. "It's been going on for centuries."

"Dad, may I keep this crucifix?" Martin asked.

"Sure," his dad replied. "I see no harm in it. Just don't mention it to your grandparents. I don't think they would understand."

He was very happy to own this crucifix. He had seen them before from a distance, but never this close, not in the palm of his own hand. He ran his finger along the bumps and crevices of that skinny silver body. He wanted to keep him warm, this Jesus, so he placed him in a drawer of his bureau, deep down among his socks and underwear. He never wanted his Jesus to be spat on, or laughed at again. And at nights, alone in his room, when everyone was asleep in the house, he would take the crucifix from its hiding place. He would hold it up to the light, shake it, and watch the beads twirl. It was a magic thing, this crucifix. He knew, he was almost certain, that he was the only Jewish boy in all of Halifax, maybe the entire world, who had a rosary and crucifix of his very own.

They walked to Jesse's apartment together. It was a small one-room apartment with a kitchenette, just across the highway from the Valley of the Cross. They entered in a hush of darkness at about two o'clock in the morning. Jesse switched on a small table lamp which shed a quiet glow.

A note was resting on Jesse's pillow. He picked it up and began to read. His curved, sensual lips twitched with pleasure, a wrinkled grin played around the corners of his mouth. He held the piece of paper lightly in his fingers, reading and rereading. He held it carefully, delicately, as if it were a snowflake, as if it might melt or suddenly fly away. It gave Martin another opportunity to look at his face, unobserved. Certain hidden lines kept making their appearance: strong crevices, almost gouges near his lips. The years had done it, Martin thought, the rough years of living and loving and suffering. His own face was baby-smooth in comparison, no wrinkles of experience. What an interesting face. Martin remembered, two years before, being paraded through the B-47 Club in Nogales, just after he had made love to his whore. She held him by the hand, grinning, chuckling. "Look at baby face," she chortled to her sister whores, "baby face with the big prick." The two intervening years had not produced any suffering, sensual lines around his mouth. He was beginning to fear that his face was going to remain babyish and smooth forever.

Jesse handed Martin the note.

"Take a look at this," he smiled. "I'll make us some coffee."

It was a love note, and Martin was a little surprised at Jesse's openness. He devoured the words with his eyes.

Wow! Wow! Wow!—it read—You were so good last night, Jesse. It's ten o'clock and you've been gone for two hours, but I can still feel you between my legs. I never knew it could be that way. You should see me. I just took a look in the mirror. My eyes are shining. My complexion is out of this world. Don't laugh! Even my tits look bigger. I'm going to have a great day. I know it! Darling, you're the best lover I've ever had. Keep well, I'll get in touch. Love, Darlene.

Martin felt waves of warmth crawl up his legs. The back of his neck tingled. Pictures of Darlene shot through his mind. She was parading through the empty apartment thrusting out her tits in front of the mirror, sighing and remembering. She was aglow from head to foot. Martin felt an erection begin to stir beneath his jeans. He sat down on the edge of Jesse's bed.

Jesse was making the coffee, doing it very slowly in a hush, taking tiny steps around the kitchenette. He looked over at Martin, a grin stretching his lips.

"She's a sweet girl," he sighed. "I had to teach her everything. Quick. Quick. Quick. That's all she was thinking; you know—let's get it over with, have an orgasm and call it a day. I had to slow everything right down. But she caught on. By the way, do you have a girlfriend, Martin?"

"Yes," Martin blushed, "she lives over by the university."

"That's good," Jesse smiled. "Well, anyway, you know the kind of thing I'm talking about."

"Sure," Martin lied.

Martin had no plans of telling Jesse his troubles with Gila, definitely not. It just wouldn't sound right. Oh yes, Jesse, I have this sabra girlfriend and she's a virgin. I've been going with her three months and nothing's happened. Martin decided to keep this to himself. He was going to let Jesse imagine whatever he wanted to imagine.

"Ah, girls," Jesse cooed, "what the hell would we do without them? Each one's a different universe. Books, cities, travel, ideas— that's all O.K. But a woman, Martin, is a realm, a thousand nooks and crannies to explore."

Martin nodded his head in agreement, smiling. He was smiling as if he knew exactly what Jesse was talking about. But it was completely new to him, fresh and interesting and exciting. How he wished to have Jesse's perception and enthusiasm for women. His own view was flat, one-dimensional, colorless in comparison. When Jesse talked, the entire apartment filled with the fragrance and body of Darlene. She was everywhere. Gila, he thought, why can't you be Darlene? Martin, he thought, why can't you be as sensitive and woman-appreciating as Jesse?

Jesse walked across the room carrying two cups of coffee, perfectly balanced, not a drop slipping over the lips. His feet moved lightly, slower than a dance. They knew exactly where they were going. He took a seat in the armchair beside the bed.

For a few minutes he just sat there, not saying a word, with his cup held lightly between the tips of his fingers. He held the cup gently. The cup could have been the most precious jewel in the world, the way he held it. His eyes dreamed forward and inward at the same time. Martin took a sip of his coffee, slowly, being careful not to slurp or smack his lips. He didn't know exactly the meditative space Jesse had dropped into, but he didn't want to do anything to disturb it.

"And there are boys," he finally said.

Martin was not absolutely sure that he had heard correctly.

"Yes, it might surprise you, Martin, but I do appreciate the male body. It is just as exquisite, perhaps purer. I've had a few boys as lovers."

Jesse's eyes glimmered over his coffee cup. A faint smile hovered on his lips. His cheekbones glowed softly in the hushed light of the room. Martin was surprised, but not shocked. Jesse's voice had not been harsh. And Martin sat silently on the bed, the coffee cup warming his hands. No words were surging up his throat. He wanted to sit there, listen, just listen for the time being.

"I don't do it that often," Jesse continued, "but there have been periods. A certain boy will catch my attention. Maybe it's the way his hair catches the light. Perhaps the curve of his lips. To put it simply, I start to desire him."

Jesse began to talk about the different guys he had gone to bed with. Most of them were young, in their late teens or very early twenties. Most of them were sabras, dancers, guys who were studying acting or ballet in Jerusalem. He described the flat, muscled feeling of chest against chest, and what it was like to slip his long loose fingers around their pricks. His voice filled the room. Softly he spoke. He savoured each word, mouthing it, rolling it from cheek to cheek; he made each phrase sound like smoke and incense, light and holy, delicate as sunlight on muslin curtains.

For quick, intense flashes of seconds, Martin worried that Jesse wanted to go to bed with him. Yet he was consoled by the fact that he didn't resemble these young ballet dancers Jesse was describing. But his mind began ticking and humming. What was it like to run a hand down the length of a male body, to grip the genitals, to come inside some plump boy's ass? He imagined Jesse and himself lying together on the very bed he was sitting on. Without a thread of clothes on. He couldn't help wondering, imagining. He found himself for seconds, just quick seconds, wanting to try, to try it out just once. But a feeling of fear and disgust gnawed away at his stomach.

"I get the best of both worlds," Jesse smiled. "I don't believe I'll ever be able to settle just for one."

A sentence was choking in Martin's throat. Words trying to take form, to come out.

"You make it sound beautiful," Martin whispered, "but I don't think I could ever do it."

"Not everyone can," Jesse smiled. "For me, love is an art. It includes men and women. Skin is sensual, the most alive thing in the world."

Jesse plunged into himself again. Jesse and the coffee cup, and the hushed glow of the room.

The night stretched backwards and forwards in Martin's mind. It was filled with stars and revelations, feelings he had never experienced before. He felt that on this evening his young life had turned a corner. His bones and skin and mind and heart had been marching, oozing, plodding in this direction for months. The journey had started months ago on Kibbutz One Sun. Forward he had been creeping, inching his way to something new. It was there, just beyond his fingertips. Beckoning. Beckoning. Closer, closer he approached. Now, with Jesse's help, he had turned the corner. He had the strong feeling that he would never see life in the old way again. Not after Jesse's dance on King George Road, not after his own bubbling laughter, not after Jesse's flow of words, his openness, his soft contours, his descriptions of the fuzzless boys he had kissed and nuzzled in this very same room.

"What are you dreaming about?" Jesse asked.

"Everything. So much has happened tonight. I'm so glad that Peter introduced us."

"You look different."

"Really?"

"No, I'm not kidding," Jesse grinned. "You looked pretty downtrodden and tired when I first saw you at the Warsaw."

"How do I look now?" Martin asked excitedly. He wanted his thoughts confirmed.

"Hopeful."

"I feel so alive!" Martin exclaimed. "I don't even feel sleepy."

"Let's walk to the university," Jesse suggested. "We'll be able to watch the sun come up."

Martin had become so entranced by Jesse's voice and words that he had not noticed the first faint glimmerings of light squeezing through the curtained windows.

It was a brand-new day when they emerged from Jesse's room, his cozy cave beside the Valley of the Cross. The sun had not yet risen above the Judaean hills, but its light already was beginning to touch the tips of the cypress trees.

Not a car was moving along the narrow, hilly highway to the Hebrew University. Not a person was stirring, not a single door opened or shut on the row of small homes that huddled along the curved highway. Martin sucked deeply on the fresh morning air. He gulped it into his lungs. He felt new strength, even new hope surge into his legs and muscles and bones.

"What a beautiful day!" Martin shouted, skipping on the grass in front of Jesse's house.

"Oh, to be young again," Jesse smiled.

They started up the curved highway together, skipping and talking, throwing stones, laughing like two kids. Martin felt grand that morning, as if he and Jesse were two modern-day prophets, as if everything belonged to them, every ancient rock, every cypress, every bird chirping. Who in all Jerusalem was singing with life and strength and vigor as they were at this very minute? The rabbis, the doctors, the politicians, the teachers—they all slept and dreamed, huddled in warm beds. They didn't own Jerusalem. They didn't love it in its first morning awakening, the curved highway wakening, just coming alive, the cypresses taking their first breaths of the day.

As they walked together, the red sun, fiery and ablaze, triumphant and alive, rose above the tops of the hills. It shot forth spokes and wheels and flashes of red light. Everything was drenched in its blood-red vigor. Each bone in their faces, each pebble, each inch of pavement. Why couldn't life always be this way, Martin wondered: as strong as the trill in the throat of a cock awakening?

They sat down together on a stone wall, dangling their feet, Jesse still talking as if in the bottom of his throat he had a well of words that would never dry up. An inexhaustible spring, triumphant as the red rising sun.

"I am very big, you know," Jesse was saying, "about nine inches long. It's not the only thing. You gotta know how to use what you got. But I'm sensitive too, and when I go in I can feel every little tremor of her cunt. You probably find that hard to believe. But there are fine little crevices inside—you just gotta learn how to feel those rivulets. And they love when I bang against the opening of their wombs. That's where the length really helps."

Jesse was very graphic, detailed, and complete in his descriptions of lovemaking, smiling as he talked, licking his lips, rubbing his cool early-morning hands together. Martin did not feel obliged to comment, or question, or add to Jesse's remarks. He just kept both ears open. He allowed the streams of words to enter him, his inner ear, his brain, his bones and the marrow of his bones. He felt warm and hard between his legs as he listened; his heart beat wildly, his mouth watered. How it made him yearn even more for a woman of his own, a real complete woman, a sensual soft woman. But the only woman he knew with any intimacy was Gila, and he could foresee no hope of getting inside her to try to feel all those rivulets and creases Jesse was describing, to see if he too could bang and nudge the opening of her womb.

One thought kept nudging at his brain, screeching to be admitted and examined and considered. It was a fantasy. It was the dream of Jesse becoming a woman, his woman. Everything would be almost the same. This woman would have Jesse's mind, his sensitivity, his vigor and intelligence. But she would be a woman. He knew, oh he knew so well that it would be love, real love, the kind they sang about in songs. It wouldn't be partial and half-assed and tormenting as it was with Gila.

Martin felt torn: here was Jesse on one side who showed him everything he wished to know, who excited his mind and sent waves of feeling surging through his body. But he was a man, a fucking man with cock and balls. And there was Gila on the other side, whom he had very little in common with. How shallow their conversations were in comparison. He knew it wasn't working out right: something was definitely wrong. But where, where, where in the entire world, in Jerusalem, or Tel Aviv, or on the desert roads, or in the mountains, or down by the sea, where could he find a woman like his new friend Jesse? Mountains separated these two people: Jesse and Gila. Gila—black-haired, soft and kitteny, with her giggles, and her stories about dead brothers, and her parachute-sewing hands. And Jesse, with his mind and vigor, intelligence and sensitivity. Martin felt hung between them. Hung on a wire and sagging. Hung and dissatisfied, hung and tired. Miles and miles stretched between them. O Gila, he thought, have you any idea of what happened to me tonight?

Jesse and Martin walked to the university together. They had breakfast at the cafeteria. The flow of words between them never stopped. It was ten o'clock in the morning when they decided to break it up, to go their separate ways. They promised to meet each other the next day. Martin knew it was the beginning of a long friendship.

He walked across the valley to his spindly-legged apartment building. A thousand ideas and words and feelings spun through him. The night and morning had finally ended. He went to sleep almost immediately, and he slept and slept without a dream.

CHAPTER 7

The Match

Martin stood in the doorway of Lisa's small room. Everything looked a little topsy-turvy—half-used boxes of tampax at the foot of the bed, a purse sprawled open on the floor revealing its contents of mascara, lipstick, compacts, loose change, half-spent booklets of matches. Books were flung around, on tops of tables, under the bed, on the bed, large wide volumes with glossy covers photographically describing the life and work of Picasso, Chagall, Matisse, etc. Small paperbacks: Camus' *Stranger*, Sartre's *Words*, Genet's *Our Lady of the Flowers*, half-devoured books smudged with fingerprints, chocolate, and orange stain.

Lisa was tunneling through a pile of debris in one corner, looking for a tea bag. She had found some already, but they were ordinary tea bags, and she had some jasmine-scented tea that she wanted Martin to try. His eyes were fixed and burning on her marvellously round ass. It was tightly wrapped in short white shorts. Her back was wide, her shoulders broad, and her breasts swung back and forth like bells. If he only had the courage, Martin was dreaming, to leap across the room and hug her from behind, cupping her breasts at the exact same time.

It was still a half hour before Gila was due back from work. The apartment was empty, the time seemed right. What a wide-backed, swinging, horsey ride Lisa would make, if he could only get up the courage to forget his puppy love for Gila, to forget that Lisa was six years older, in her first year of M.A. studies, analysing the masters, modern and ancient, if he could only forget about Peter and his promise, if he could only suddenly become a lover, strong and determined, unabashed, just surprise her suddenly with his passion and ardor, switch on all her humming glands, suddenly and surprisingly, love her, love her, make her his own.

"I know it's here somewhere," she said. "Just when I want something badly it never seems to be around."

Oh Lisa, I'd like to fuck you, Martin was thinking.

"I know what you mean," Martin chirped.

"I want you to try this stuff. It's from Nepal. I think it's Nepal anyway. A friend of mine gave it to me."

I'd like to try your stuff, Martin was thinking, his mind flapping wildly. Your hair-covered stuff, jasmine-drenched and juicy. Your bell-swinging stuff, hard and enticing. Your round-bellied stuff from the sweat-holes of America. Your old musty stuff, experienced and bloody. His throat sang love songs and warbles and cries of lust, but not a single note could be heard.

We could ride into the future together, Lisa, with your volumes of Picasso and old Matisse, with your tampax and chewing gum. I'm sure your broad shoulders would support me, Lisa, and I'd find no end to the mystery in the debris of your rooms.

"Would you like one?" Lisa asked.

She held up a half-empty plastic container of pills, shaking the container, rattling the contents.

"What are they?"

"My little head-trips. When I get too tired. When I get sick of all this fucking mess. Tranquillizers, my dear."

"Do you really take those things?" Martin asked a little incredulously.

"Not recently. But sometimes. When life gives me a pain in the ass."

"Have you ever been in love, Lisa?" Martin was surprised by his own question, how it popped out so suddenly.

"Ha, ha," Lisa chortled. "You're sweet, Martin. Innocent but sweet."

Her eyes went dreamy blue, hazy and sensual, blending with the slight scattering of freckles along the bridge of her nose.

"I've had a few love affairs," she sighed, "and hate affairs, and affairs, and affairs—and you know what? After that, I had a few more affairs. What about yourself?"

"I guess so."

"You don't know for sure?" She laughed, tossing back her head, letting the long tresses of her brown hair swing behind her. "What about Gila? You make a cute couple. Don't tell me she's a virgin."

"Yep," Martin sighed, shaking his head up and down.

"That's too bad," Lisa cooed, smiling and biting at the tips of her hair.

"Lisa," Martin said quietly. "I have a good friend I'd like you to meet. He's a student. He's a great guy."

"What's he studying?" Lisa asked dreamily.

"Philosophy. Literature. He's very intelligent and extremely handsome."

Lisa laughed. She let her head fall forward, and chortled.

"He sounds too good to be true."

"Would you like to meet him?" Martin asked excitedly, his face getting red.

"How could I pass up such an opportunity?" Lisa drawled. "I haven't had a blind date in years. What the hell. How old is he?"

"Just about your age. Maybe a little younger, but not much,"

"Your age?" Lisa frowned.

"No, older."

"Much?"

"Yep, he's about four or five years older."

"What does he look like?"

"I told you, he's really good-looking."

"Describe him to me. Get me interested."

"O.K.," Martin grinned. "He's about six foot three. Black hair, brown eyes. But you gotta see him for yourself. You'll really be surprised."

"If he's so good-looking, why hasn't he got a girlfriend?"

"He can't find anybody with any brains."

Lisa laughed again, leaning against her bed. The laughter came out in streams, chortles and giggles circling the room. Her round, full breasts bobbed and stretched. Martin wanted her more than ever. He wanted to slip his hand down the front of her white shorts, to kiss each inch of her soft freckly skin. But it was too late now, too damn late. He had spoken on Peter's behalf and that was it.

"You're too much, Martin. Much too much," she laughed. "If this works, I'll give you a big kiss."

"Can you give it to me now? And maybe I won't have to speak to Peter," Martin grinned.

"And break up your beautiful thing with Gila? Martin, you behave yourself. When can I meet him?"

Martin sighed, a breath taken with much sadness and regret.

"This week. I've already told him about you."

"You don't waste any time, do you?"

Martin smiled. His stomach tingled warmly. He was frustrated, but he smiled.

As the steam was twirling to the ceiling, Lisa prepared two cups of jasmine tea. A few minutes later, Gila came home from work. Her cheeks were flushed, red and aglow from walking down the hill to the apartment building. She came into Lisa's room smiling.

"Here's the sweetheart of Jerusalem," Lisa sang out. "I'll put on another cup of tea."

Lisa got up from her chair, walked over to Gila, put one hand around her back, and with the other patted her short black hair.

"How's this guy been treating you anyway?" Lisa laughed.

Gila blushed, the color running up her neck.

"Come here, Martin," Lisa said. "I want to take a picture of you two."

Martin got up slowly from his chair, trying to smile.

"Come right over here where the light's good."

Lisa grabbed him by the hand and drew him forward. She placed his hand around Gila's shoulder and pushed them together, shoulder to shoulder.

"Just watch where your hand is going," Lisa laughed.

She ran to the end of her bed, throwing boxes this way and that, until she came up with a small camera.

"Now, I want you two love-birds to smile."

Gila beamed, and Martin smiled. The kettle was beginning to bubble almost ferociously. Then it boiled, whistling to be unplugged. Lisa snapped two or three pictures, the flashes flooding the room with light. A bright penny of light stayed in Martin's brain each time for a minute. They were two kids, he kept thinking: he and Gila, two lost kids in the lowlands of Jerusalem, clinging to each other, hoping that love, the real thing with capital letters, would blossom forth. Yet they were forlorn, babies, and lost. Why, Martin thought, would Lisa want a picture of something so intangible, something so fragile? Martin knew it was going to pass, like winter changing into spring, blossoms falling in mud, mud drying into the hard cakes of summer. Pass it would, this childish attempt at romance and feeling. He knew it with an ache in his belly.

What did they know, these two lost souls, Gila and Martin, hidden away night after night in a room, a brick room, a frozen room, dreaming and faraway as their fingers touched?

"Maybe I'll meet you one day," Gila once said, "on a ship going across the Atlantic. You'll be a famous writer by then. I wonder if you'll even remember me."

Martin had a vivid image of this ship wandering through oceans of ice and salt. He saw himself greying and using a cane. But Gila had not changed. She wore the same black pixy haircut, boyish and sweet. Her sabra eyes still glittered without too much pain. Her face was still flushed, red and healthy from walking home on chill Jerusalem evenings. He wanted to talk to her, to tell her about the miles he had travelled, the books he had written, the suffering and joys he had experienced. But it was so difficult, forty years hence, to speak to her. Just as it was now. She listened, she nodded, she smiled and she joked, but he wondered if she had heard a word he was saying. He was not talking about how furrows were deep near the Golan Heights, nor was he talking about the boredom of being a typist, he was talking about important things: how the solar system swung through his brain, how love was an effort and a struggle, a slow inching forward year by year, so slow that it drove a person mad; drove him to ask if he was going forward at all, or was everything a never-ending circle, the exact same circle every time, and was he walking the exact same circumference, bored to death with the sameness and unreality of the whole thing?

Oh yes, aboard that ship, in the autumn of his years, he was saying important things to Gila, his old friend from bygone Jerusalem days. But was she hearing even one word with any meaning? Or were her ears inescapably tuned to the click-clack of typewriters at her place of work, tuned and riveted to a different rhythm?

Flash. Flash of light behind his eyes as Lisa snapped her camera—two bright coins of light and pain.

Somewhere, he was thinking, there would be a record in fine white dots and black of what occurred in his twentieth year. A record, indelible, if the ice and snow and heat didn't melt and freeze it and turn it into slush. If a crow didn't snatch it from the garbage. If the incinerator didn't burn it. If the changing seasons didn't devour it, down to its last slight chemical film.

Martin was hoping that Lisa and Peter's love would be different.

Perhaps they could get into each other, deeply and for all eternity, their love growing each year like the rings on a giant redwood tree. And people years and years hence could note some look, some gaze in their eyes, just as surely as counting growth rings on a tree, and they would be able to see a wonderful development, a union of two souls that really worked and grew, that bore fruit. He knew it was vicarious, this wish for Lisa and Peter, but he wanted to see it happen just once between two people he knew, two souls he had brought together. He wanted it to be real between them, not just a play of grey dots and white, not just a flash of two bright coins. Not just a sudden inspiration.

A few days later he was sitting in the cafeteria with Peter Stoneman in the basement of the Hebrew University.

"I told her," Martin smiled.

"How did she take it?" Peter asked.

"She was interested. I think she's had some bad experiences."

"In relationships?"

"Yes."

"What makes you think that?" Peter asked, a smile crossing his handsome brown face.

"Just the way she talks. She seems tired."

"I know how she feels. I know exactly how she feels," Peter said, his face becoming serious.

Did Peter too, Martin wondered, hide half-devoured containers of tranquillizers in his room? It was possible. But Peter seemed a little more controlled. He had shown Martin a bit of his writing one day. It was the story of an archer, a Zen initiate trying to hit a target. It was almost an essay, this story, with cool straight lines that never wavered into tears or excessive laughter. It was a little bony and wooden, almost straitlaced, this story. Martin couldn't even remember if the archer finally succeeded. Perhaps, in Peter's mind, it was not important. He described the way his arm came back without sweat or effort, without a clanging in the brain. The end of the story tailed off, a blossom falling into a canyon of abstract observations.

They sat together sipping at the dregs of their second coffees. By some wonderful telepathic coincidence, Martin spotted Lisa with a platter in her hand, curving her way along the counter at the far end of the dining room.

"She's here," he said excitedly.

"That's great," Peter smiled.

"I'll go get her," Martin whispered.

Martin guided Lisa back to the table, and introduced them. He sat back and watched them talk to each other. There was nothing more he could do. Now it was up to the stars and the moon, to the chemicals flowing through them. He had prepared the way the best he could. It was a bit like getting a kite to sail two thousand feet above a town and then snipping the string. They were on their own now. He could no longer be responsible.

A relationship between them began very quickly. A few days, about a week, after he introduced them, Lisa decided to move out of her room. She decided to go and live with Peter. They really did feel something for each other, and Martin was glad. It would take months and months to determine how the whole thing would turn out, what course it would take. An echo from the bible kept floating through Martin's mind. "Who can know the human heart?"—all its pathways and byways, all its hairpin curves and greasy spins. It was beyond him now. The match had been made.

CHAPTER 8

Spring Days

He was beginning to make friends in Jerusalem, a fine network was developing, people he knew, mostly displaced Americans and Europeans, students and artistic types who hung around Jerusalem in the year Eichmann was put on trial and finally hanged.

His friendship with Jesse continued to grow, his friendship with Peter Stoneman.

At the university he met Professor Townley, an American Jew who taught courses in modern poetry. He was a tall, wide, bear-soft man in his early fifties. And Professor Townley was a poet. Although not published, he had spent many years of his life fidgeting with words and phrases, images and metaphors, juxtaposing them, joining and breaking them, casting them together into odd and interesting assemblies. Martin was very anxious to show him some of his poems, moonlit poems about Gila and the muddy valley.

Professor Townley was outgoing and friendly and took an interest in him. Martin was excited and happy when he invited him down to his basement apartment on Bialik Street. A date was set for a Saturday afternoon. Martin was to bring his poems, and the professor would give him an honest opinion.

On Saturday afternoon he stood before the grey wooden door, the paint peeling, and the wood scarred from years of rain and summer heat. He brushed back the loose strands of hair that had fallen over his forehead, straightened out the collection of papers in his hand. He tried to catch his breath. He had been walking quickly down Bialik Street, wanting to get there in time. He didn't want to huff and puff down the basement stairs, didn't want the excitement to wheeze out of his mouth. He had made a special effort to rewrite the scribbled poems in a handwriting that was even and legible. They looked almost neat, the next best thing to a typewritten job.

He knocked evenly: bang, bang, bang; and he waited patiently for Mr. Townley to answer.

Mr. Townley answered the door with a soft-faced welcoming smile. He was dressed in a housecoat, long and grey with black dots.

"Good to see you, Martin. Glad you could come. I hope you brought your poems with you."

"Thank you," Martin smiled, happy to be received so warmly. "Yes, I brought some poetry."

"It's a little dark down here. It'll probably take a few minutes before your eyes adjust."

Mr. Townley led the way down the carpeted staircase to his cozy underground apartment. This was a warm place, Martin kept thinking, the warmest apartment he had entered so far in Jerusalem. The floor was covered with various rugs: an old faded bearskin, and a wall-to-wall mellow orange rug that also showed signs of wear and tear down through the years. It was a little bald in spots, tattered at the edges, but warm to look at.

"I hope you can see," Mr. Townley smiled.

"There's quite a contrast. The sun's so bright outside."

Jerusalem was already beginning to heat up in late April. But Mr. Townley's cave and burrow, his underground hideaway was cool, just a little dank. Both atmospheres were hitting Martin at the same time: the warmth of the surroundings, with carpets and pillows, knickknacks and pictures, photos and books; and a slight dank feeling from the concrete underlying the floor coverings.

"Have a seat. Can I make you a coffee?"

"That would be fine," Martin smiled.

Professor Townley left the room. It gave Martin a chance to settle down into a cushioned armchair, just to sink as far as he could into the cushions, to allow the large arms to surround him. He was a little nervous about showing the professor his poems. What if they were just too wild and frazzled? What if he saw them that way? He rarely reworked a poem, carving it and shaping it like a precious jewel. He had tried this a few times, but it never worked. Sometimes he would cut the thing into a bony nothingness. No, these poems came out under pressure, surging up. What if he saw them as just wild yappings, uncivilized, uncouth, adolescent spewings? What if he thought that any high-strung college student could pour forth such lava and heat?

"I'm going to look them over carefully," Mr. Townley said, as he came back to the room with two cups of coffee. "I want to be absolutely frank with you. Do you know, Martin, a person could waste years of his life if there's no substance to build on."

Martin's hands were shaking slightly as he handed over the loose batch of papers. It felt like he was handing over his heart and brain. He wanted to be a writer very badly. A long time ago—or it seemed a long time—when he was seventeen, he had made this fateful decision. He had told a good friend, a young talented poet:

"I don't want to be a professional: a doctor or a lawyer. I just don't want to do it."

"Don't worry, Martin. That's a good decision. You can be a writer. There's nothing to stop you."

He knew inside him that this bug to write had been gnawing away from that day onward. Scraps and scraps of paper he had scribbled up, long poems and short, sad and happy. Poems and poems and poems he had written, read to people. Bunches of white scrawl-covered papers he had thrown in the garbage.

Mr. Townley's opinion was very important to him. He was excited that he was going to hear it absolutely straight. No condescension or patronizing or making him feel good. He was going to hear it straight from his new friend's gut and heart. He wanted Mr. Townley's words to go straight into his bloodstream, into his marrow-bone, into his brain's deepest cavity. If it was all shit, and hopeless, he wanted to hear it that Saturday afternoon late in April. Mr. Townley had sensed this: it was a crossroad, a decision-making time. And Martin had made up his mind. If Mr. Townley gave the go-ahead, that would be it. All or nothing from that time onward. Through muck and grief and dry spells. Through doubt and fear, his pen would never stop moving. His future, it seemed, now rested in Mr. Townley's hands. Ten scraps of scribbled paper.

"I'm going to go into the next room," Mr. Townley whispered. "I want to give these my full attention."

A cat jumped from the floor onto the arm of Martin's chair. A large, muscular angora tomcat with hazel-orange blazing eyes. He nudged his arm, leaned against it, pushed his whole weight against it.

"Oh, I'm sorry," Mr. Townley smiled. "I forgot to introduce you to Moog. Moog, I would like you to meet Martin. He's a friend."

The angora purred, half-growled in his throat.

"I'll let you become acquainted," Mr. Townley smiled, and he left the room.

Moog looked directly into Martin's eyes, his black pupils dilating. "Who are you?" Moog seemed to be asking. "What are you doing here?"

"I'm Martin Kanner. A friend of your master."

"Are you going to be here long?" Moog murmured in his orange fur-covered throat.

"I just got here."

"You can't stay the night. I hope you realize that. I don't like upheaval."

"Well, Moog, I have my own home, you know. A room anyway."

"Are you another one of these writers?" Moog purred and snickered. "I've seen a lot of your type here before. You never have much money."

"Yes," Martin answered wearily.

Moog had grown tired of the conversation. He scraped his claws along the arm of the chair, stretching, arching his back. Martin felt relieved when he finally leaped off the chair, looked once back over his shoulder, and sauntered off to the kitchen.

The minutes dripped past slowly, evenly, five, ten, fifteen slow, slow minutes. Papers rattled in the adjoining room, ten papers filled with emotion and ink and hope and yearning. He was glad that some of the poems talked about his feelings for Gila. He wanted Professor Townley to realize from the beginning that he was a lover of women, not men. For he had heard it rumoured that Mr. Townley, a bachelor his entire life, was gay. Not that it mattered to Martin. He was entitled to his personal likes and dislikes, but Martin didn't wish to lead him astray or have any hassles or misinterpretations, as he had experienced with the Indian library attendant and the lonely Rumanian philosopher.

Martin kept wondering how many of his new friend's lovers had sat in the very cushioned chair he was now occupying. How many had sat there bare-assed or with just a towel draped across their nakedness, exhausted after a bout of homosexual encounter, or anticipating a night of man-to-man lovemaking? It made him queasy, the thought of two male bodies scraping together, sweaty chest to sweaty chest, penis rubbing penis. He was propositioned once, he remembered, in Arizona when he was seventeen. He never saw the other guy. But the guy had followed him into a washroom. Martin was sitting on a toilet seat in his own small cubicle minding his own business. He heard a scratching noise on the floor. A white note was being slipped under the partition. He picked it up, his hands trembling, and read: "Do you want a blow job?" Hurriedly, he had done up his pants, pulled the zipper, and buckled the belt. He rushed away, not even looking back. He didn't want to see the guy's face, the contorted lips, and the eyes ablaze with lust.

Mr. Townley was entitled to fulfill his desire with men if he wanted, if it did not make him queazy or blow his brain to smithereens, but Martin was doubtful that he would ever follow the path of gay fulfillment. He looked around the apartment for signs of the professor's preference in matters of the heart and body. There was nothing outlandish about it, no indication at all that his new friend and mentor had lived with men, or loved them on weekends. What was he expecting to find, he wondered. Would he suddenly see a pair of red silk panties? A scarf of mauve? A bottle of ass lubricant?

Slowly the minutes passed. Mr. Townley must have been examining the poems from every possible angle. Reading and rereading them. Not allowing a single image to pass unnoticed. The poems themselves had been written quickly, with his blood aflame and his brain frazzled. Now they were being regarded by a careful, cautious, knowledgeable man. He wasn't going to make a spur-of-the-moment decision. Not a fast, sleazy criticism. It was going to be done right, with his thirty-five years of experience, his fifty years of life brought to bear. His grey, calm eyes were drilling into the sheets of paper, into Martin's life and hope for the future. He was bathing those words determinedly with wisdom and foresight.

Martin was not exactly on trial, but he was waiting for a verdict just as Adolph Eichmann waited that same year. They caught the pale, lean-faced man in Argentina. Now he was surrounded by barb-wire during the long days of the trial. Barb-wire fence, so nobody could slip through and knife him in the heart before justice was carried out. A lot of people had lost parents and children when Eichmann and his cohorts stalked Europe. The barb-wire was not just a prop.

Everyone was crying blood that year. Blood and revenge. Martin saw the whole thing as a never-ending circle of death, revenge, more death, more revenge. What if Israel, he thought, could spare this man's life? As an example? As a symbol of letting the blood-war stop? They could say: "Look here, you fucking bloody terrible world, this man exterminated thousands of our people, but we are stopping the flow, right here in Jerusalem, city of David and Jesus Christ. That's it. No more. He can go back to Argentina. Look here, you murderous blood-lustful world, no more, no more, do you understand, no fucking more."

Images of Eichmann flowed through his brain as he waited for Mr. Townley to reappear with his poems. What went on behind the glint of his glasses when a hundred bulbs flashed, the photographers relaying his picture to the newspapers all over the world? London, Tokyo, Delhi, New York. Adolph Eichmann, the beast of Belsen, captured! The madman of Auschwitz now in Israeli hands. Such a newspaper photo Martin's mother described, and its fate in Toronto, just a month before she came to Israel. She showed it to Mrs. Fontano, an Italian housekeeper who helped her out a couple of days a week. Mrs. Fontano looked for a minute. Her eyes became two spikes of anger. She ripped the picture to shreds with her fingernails digging, clawing. "Killer!" she shouted. "Crazy! I hate, I hate, I hate!" she screamed. His mother finally settled her down, embracing her, patting the back of her frenzied head. Mrs. Fontano described the war years when she was a girl of twelve, what it was like in Florence, how her parents hid Jews in their basement amid olives and bottles of wine.

What a twist of history! Did he feel it in his casual business suit, his white shirt and conservative tie? Only twenty short years after the attempt at the final solution, these inferior people had formed a state, a police force, an army, a network of spies, a dragnet that sent its tentacles into the four corners of the earth. In South America they seized him and brought him back.

Martin did not feel completely connected to what was happening in Jerusalem that year. The hubbub, the uproar, the frenzied conversations, the arguments. He had heard the stories of the gas chambers, the ovens, the mass graves a hundred times. He had heard the figure 6,000,000 so often it was burned into his brain. He had seen the tattoos on arms, and photos of rake-skinny bodies, nothing but skin clinging to bones. Yet, when they finally caught one of the perpetrators, one of the crime masters, and he saw his picture close up—the whole thing seemed like a dream. Eichmann's face looked puzzled. He had a nervous tic. He did not look anything like the beast of Belsen. In fact, Adolph Eichmann looked Jewish to him. He couldn't get this out of his head. Now, he looked Jewish, like an uncle or delicatessen owner. In a few months Eichmann would feel the noose of the final solution around his own withered neck.

Mr. Townley came into the room, smiling. Martin didn't say a word. He leaned slightly forward in his armchair.

"I like them, Martin. In fact, they're quite good."

Martin let a sigh issue from his mouth and slumped back into the chair.

"You look surprised," Mr. Townley smiled.

"Then you think I should continue?" Martin asked

"Yes. But just remember it's a long haul. Don't get discouraged." They talked about poetry, the elusive muse, how Mr. Townley had chased it down through the years, how he had moved from the States to Puerto Rico, and finally to Israel fifteen years ago.

On one of the walls hung a picture, a framed photo that Mr. Townley had preserved from his thirteen-year stay in Puerto Rico. The picture fascinated Martin. He got up from his chair to take a closer look at it. The sun played through the leaves of tropical trees, white dots and black shadows. Mr. Townley had a smile on his face. A black boy of about three years old sat on the professor's shoulders, his chubby legs hugged around Mr. Townley's neck, and his hands gripped the professor's forehead.

"He adopted me," Mr. Townley smiled. "Do you know, Martin, his parents wanted me to adopt him legally and take him back to the States with me."

"He's really cute."

"Yes, I almost did it too."

A dreamy sigh of nostalgia had entered Mr. Townley's voice, and Martin could visualize him walking beneath the sun in Puerto Rico, in short pants and a white T shirt. The birds coo-cooed, red-feathered birds with tufts of turquoise.

*　*　*

And Jerusalem became a nostalgic dream that April, with courses at the university beginning to end, to trail off into the cold business of examinations. Martin wrote poems and read poems, he talked with Jesse night after night wandering the empty streets.

They went to the market together around midnight, eating shish-kabob and hummus and tachina together.

The midnight streets, the empty streets of Jerusalem sometimes had a peculiar fragrance clinging to them.

"What does that smell like?" Jesse asked, his eyes twinkling.

"I don't know," Martin lied.

"You do so. It smells like 'come', doesn't it? Just like everyone was making love up in the trees. We call them the sperm trees."

"Aw, come on, Jesse."

"Of course that's not their real name, but those are the sperm trees."

Martin couldn't deny it. He had smelled semen before on the tips of his fingers, the rich sickening fragrance.

Gila, Mr. Townley, Peter Stoneman, Jesse, Lisa, they all weaved in and out of his life, those sunny days in late April, dreamy days in Jerusalem. But nothing extraordinary was happening in the city of eternal peace, the magic floating city that sat in the cleft of the hills of Judaea, and rested in the palm of God's hand. Nothing was changing quickly, and Martin floated through his days, kissing Gila occasionally, talking to Mr. Townley, to Jesse, and sometimes imagining that he could talk to the wind as Zarathustra had done centuries before him. "Do not spit and spew against the wind." He remembered that commandment well.

He tried to float along like a blossom or a ray of sun, trying his best not to examine too closely the course and direction of his existence. Why couldn't he just bathe himself in these windy, sunny spring days forever?

Near the end of April he received a letter from his parents, asking him to return to Tel Aviv. They had something important to discuss with him. On a Monday morning Martin packed his suitcase and headed for the bus terminal.

PART TWO

CHAPTER 9

Allenby Street

He had taken that bus ride on several weekends to visit his parents in Tel Aviv, that shuttle ride from Jerusalem to Tel Aviv. It was a long curved ride down the hills. He had seen the burnt-out trucks on the side of the road, left there to commemorate the War of Independence. Every May the people came from up and down the lean country to place wreaths on the broken vehicles. In May the wreaths were fresh, green sprigs of leaves, red and yellow flowers. By the time April rolled around once again, the winter rains had turned them into frail brown corpses. Withered and dry.

Down from Jerusalem, the dreamy, fragrant, holy city, he once again was bouncing. Down to Tel Aviv, the workaday city, the steaming hot metropolis where all was business, people rushing in and out of office buildings. Often he had told Jesse and Mr. Townley that there was a tremendous contrast between these two cities. He saw it so clearly. They were poles. They were stark psychic polarities. Once he had recognized this, he couldn't stop telling people about it. Don't you see it, he wanted to know. Jerusalem the spiritual. Jerusalem the dream. Tel Aviv the practical, the almost deadly computer heart of the country. Yes, they saw it, they agreed. But did they see it like he saw it?—the gulf between them—how far the mind and heart had to stretch to accommodate both of them. Was it humanly possible to do it? To be at peace with a Jerusalem and a Tel Aviv floating through his psyche?

Someone should write about it, he often said. It could be the theme of an entire book.

"Maybe you'll do it some day," Mr. Townley said.

Maybe. Maybe. Maybe, Martin thought. He knew it was there, this stark duality. Jerusalem of the sleeping rabbis. Tel Aviv with its outdoor cafes filled with chic perfumed women. King David's Jerusalem. Tel Aviv a nothing during biblical days.

Flip, flop, back and forth, systole, diastole of the blood. Jerusalem. Tel Aviv. Dream, reality. Spirit, flesh. It was there, just as certain as Jerusalem in a cleft of the cool Judaean hills, and Tel Aviv a steaming hiss of cars and pavement. Maybe. Maybe. But what the fuck did it really mean? It was real. They were different. Everyone could see it. But why did it bother him so much? Why did it fascinate him?

In the centre of Tel Aviv, just off Allenby Street, his father rented his office. Here he was trying to introduce computer accounting to this backward nation. He was having a tough time—this Martin knew. He had the old skills he had developed in Montreal and Toronto. But this country resisted him. This hot lean country. Something resisted. Like the Dead Sea resisting life. Like the Negev resisting trees. Like the rocks resisting water.

The temperature rose as the bus rolled him to Tel Aviv once again. He began to sweat once they hit the flat ride toward the busy outskirts. Handkerchiefs came out. Deodorants. Perfume. Anything to wipe away or mask the drops of heat.

He left the bus terminal and walked up Allenby Street towards his father's office. The sun flashed off kiosks, cars, windshields, even the pavement. It pierced through his eyes, through his skull into his brain. There was no hiding from it. He tried to dodge it, to skip from the shade of awnings over small stores to the shade of tall buildings. But it was always waiting to wrap its searing arms around his neck. Dark and tanned were the faces that passed him, marching, rushing through their daily routines. What was it like during a war? —Martin often wondered. These were peaceful years, but what was it like when the sirens wailed, when the command to mobilize screamed through the streets?

The whole bloody country must move like a single war camp, Martin often thought. Moving out, striking, surprising. Moving out suddenly without warning. Very few laggards. He remembered his father talking to him about the elements of business when he was a teenager.

"They're clever," his father said, describing his competitors. "They're educated and refined. But you know, Marty old boy, they always forget one thing—the element of surprise. There's no preparing for that one."

His father would grin, recalling some coup, some sudden stroke of financial wizardry on the stock market.

There was a back entrance to his father's office up a rickety wooden staircase. The wooden planks, peeled and worn, squeaked under his weight. The toilet at the top of the staircase didn't work properly. He could smell the stench of urine, the heavy odor mixing with the heat of noon hour. His father's office on the second floor was small and cramped. It was an ill-lit cranny in an older building, hidden away. How different from the old days on Bay Street, just three short years ago, when his father and Danny Berlman, his partner, were flying high. They sold stocks on helium and other commodities. Then the offices were resplendent with mahogany furniture, swivel chairs, wall-to-wall broadloom.

"They love us here on Bay Street," his father was fond of saying. "Danny and I are the fair-haired lads. Marty, we got this town in the palm of our hands."

"Your dad ain't just whistling Dixie," Danny smiled.

Danny's face glowed, brown from a recent vacation in Florida. It was a handsome face.

During those flushed days when business was good, he would go with his father and Danny Berlman down to the Imperial Hotel for a haircut and a facial massage. The three of them were treated like kings. The blond, shapely manicurists jumped and bent to attend to their fingernails. The barbers massaged their scalps and faces. The phone rang out, often. *Mr. Kanner wanted on the telephone.* And his father, still wearing a plastic bib, sauntered back and forth from the barber's chair to the telephone. *Sell it .. Buy it .. Forget it .. Maybe next week .. Something's got to give .. Get the engineers working on it .. We need a brochure for this one, the best. I'll do the writing myself, if I have to.*

They were on the upswing in those days, Danny Berlman and his dad. Before things crashed, before some roof caved in, before something went rotten and sour. Martin never understood it completely, but the bottom fell out, and somewhere along the way Danny Berlman, handsome and forty-seven, dropped dead of a heart attack.

Martin tried to stop breathing momentarily as he passed the washroom at the top of the stairs. But the urine stench seeped down his throat into his lungs. It clung to the pores of his skin.

His father was sitting alone in the room at a small wooden desk piled high with papers. He was staring out into space, his eyes fixed on something only he could see.

"Hi Dad," Martin smiled.

"Oh Martin, it's you." His father shook his head as if it were an effort to fully remember who this person was who was standing before him. "You got our letter?"

"Yes."

"Martin, I have some bad news. You'll have to give up your room in Jerusalem. Things are terrible here. I can't carry you any more."

"Are they really that bad?"

"Nothing's moving. I haven't got two clients to rub together."

His father's head bent forward. Had he been sitting there day after day, week after week, waiting for the telephone to ring? He twirled his fingers absentmindedly in front of him. The fingertips were red and raw.

"What's wrong with your hands?" Martin asked.

"Nerves."

"They look really sore."

"Yeah, they're bealing. I never thought I'd see the bloody day. I used to have nerves of steel. You remember."

Yes, Martin remembered. His father's assured grin in every situation, whether it was weaving in and out of traffic, or settling down Danny Berlman when things got rough in Toronto.

"This country makes you into a mule. They want to reduce everyone to their same level. Talent doesn't mean a thing."

"I wish I could help in some way."

"Martin, I want to lay this straight. You have to come to Tel Aviv and stay with us. And it wouldn't hurt if you got yourself a job."

His father's eyes grew dark and heavy. They brooded over the smoke-filled room.

"Maybe I can teach English."

"Yes. English. Just get some work. You know what I had to do? I had to wire my father for money. Enough for a car. This country's so fucking poor, a simple means of transportation is a luxury. I needed that car, Martin. My back's in bad shape. I'm told it's Marie Strumpell's disease."

"Christ," Martin whispered.

"It can be serious," his father continued. "I've gotta keep that spine straight. If it bends, I'm in real trouble. I work out at the 'Y'. Swimming helps a bit."

A line from T.S. Eliot kept whirring through Martin's head. A haunting line. "This is the way the world ends, not with a bang but a whimper." It seemed to Martin that his father was locked into his cramped office, stuck in this country. The black phone sat on his desk. When would it ring into life?

"How's Mom and Debrah?" Martin asked.

"They're holding up, I guess. They don't belong here. But they're getting by the best they can. You can imagine, Martin, what it must be like for them. You have your books and writing. That's pretty much the same the world over. But their whole world has changed."

"Where are they now?"

"They went out to get some hamburgers for lunch."

His father's head slumped forward, his eyes half-shut.

"The whole thing's ridiculous," his father added. "Do you know what they have to do? They cover the toilet seat with paper towels every time they use it. Afraid of getting some disease. And frankly I don't blame them."

Yes, it was ridiculous, Martin thought. He found it hard to believe, this transformation in his father. Was this the same man he knew as a child, always on the move, his jet-black hair glistening, his eyes tunnels of black light?

Martin walked over to a dusty window. He could see up the alleyway to Allenby Street. People moving. Talking. Gesturing. Nothing done slowly from the rising of the sun to the end of day. He caught sight of two women. They could've been sisters. They walked slowly, clutching paper bags. It was his mother and sister.

"There they are," Martin announced.

"Good. I'm starved."

His mother entered the room wiping sweat from her forehead. Debrah trailed behind. Martin kissed his mother on the cheek. He could feel his lips sliding over the perspiration. She smelled of lipstick.

"It's horrible out there today, Jake. If it gets any hotter, I'm going to melt."

"Take a chair, Dahlia. Relax. Did you get enough so Martin can have lunch with us?"

"Yes, I'm not too hungry. The heat's making me sick."

"The toilet really stinks today," Debrah added.

"O.K., O.K., enough complaints," his father snapped. "Let's just have a half-hour of peace. Martin's going to look for a job. At least that's settled."

"That's good," his mother smiled. "Martin, Debrah's going to work next week. She's got a job as a typist."

"Great," Martin said absentmindedly.

Deep down he didn't give a shit, but it was great, it had to be great, everything looked so bloody awful that something just had to be great. They sat in the small office eating hamburgers and drinking coffees. The Kanner family, Martin kept thinking. Here was the Kanner family in Israel. It looked haphazard, the whole thing. Wax paper and hamburgers. The four of them huddled together with sweat oozing out, with the stench of pee wafting in from the wash room. Refugees, he kept thinking. A small refugee family above the wastes of Tel Aviv.

That same day Martin put an ad in the newspaper. He advertised himself as a teacher of English poetry and the modern novel. For private lessons. It would be an easy thing to teach, and he was hoping that a woman would answer the ad, a sensitive poetry-loving woman.

In the afternoon, he walked down Allenby Street looking for a job. Danny Berlman, his father's ex-partner who died in his youthful brown body, swam through Martin's memory. Danny Berlman, high-strung and nervous. He remembered Mrs. Berlman too, her body also brown from trips to Florida, and if she didn't go to Florida she tanned herself with sunlamps. Her skin remained brown in the middle of Toronto winters. Brown she walked through the snow-piled streets down to slushy Eglinton, and into boutiques. Brown she glided through her apartment in the Valhalla hi-rise, one of the poshest buildings in Toronto at the beginning of the sixties. It was just a floor below his parents' roost, high above Eglinton, at the edge of Forest Hill. Tanned brown, fingers manicured, hair formed by permanents, she walked across a white shag rug in her living room, glided into the bathroom, a place of huge mirrors, gilt-framed. What did they do all day, Martin often wondered, Mrs. Berlman and his mother and a million other wives of rich men? They played the horses—this he knew; each one had a favorite bookie, and they placed bets on baseball, hockey, football games. It was part of their lives, just as important as gin rummy games in the afternoon, and trips to the hairdressers. At the Valhalla a bookie lived just down the hall from his parents. He had five phones in his apartment. At least that was the rumor. Martin never saw the phones face to face, nor did he see the mysterious man who spent his days dialling, dialling, or waiting for the phones to sound—a report from Hialeah, or Woodbine, or wherever a race was taking place. Martin read in a book once (he forgot the title) about people betting on birds, two birds on a fence: which scraggly warbler would take off first into the sky? They laid all their excitement and hopes on a flimsy warbly body.

Danny Berlman died the summer Martin spent in Tucson. Martin was flying off to Nogales where he got the clap—the first body he ever entered, and the snaggle-toothed bug seized him. During that summer in the hot southwest of the U.S.A., between his visits to the B-47 Club just south of the border, inside the lip of Mexico, between those visits and the lazy summer courses he was taking at the university, between his rides on a newly-acquired motor scooter and reading John Steinbeck and E. E. Cummings for the first time, the phone rang and a message was delivered to him—Toronto calling for Martin Kanner. Emotion had clogged his father's throat. His mother had to be the one who gave him the news.

"Danny Berlman died," she said. "A heart attack."

That was the meat of the conversation. Nothing else remained to be said. When Martin hung up the receiver, tears welled to his eyes. They surprised him, these tears for Danny Berlman. What was Danny to him, beyond a mere acquaintance? They surprised him. They were unplanned. They came from a black river inside him. They sprang up. But he was glad when they came. He just wanted to cry and cry and cry, to let his tears gush forth, to release something blocked inside him. Tears, tears, tears for Danny Berlman so handsome and young, so fragile and brown, so married and jittery, so attached to his father's endeavours and the swinging up-and-down bob of the stock market.

Danny Berlman said to Martin once:

"Martin, don't take your studies too seriously. Please be level-headed. I had a brother. He was an idealist just like you. It killed him. He lasted to forty. That's awful young to die."

What killed Danny Berlman? An argument filled with bile, recriminations, guilt, accusations raged in Toronto, in Forest Hill, on Bay Street, but especially in the Valhalla hi-rise, the poshest new apartment building of the golden ghetto. Mrs. Berlman did it, he heard voices saying. She wanted too much, too fast. She was never satisfied with rugs and sofas and trips. She wanted more, more, more. She gave her jittery husband no peace. She drove him to his fragile final breaking point. Other voices growled against his father. Among them, Mrs. Berlman's voice. Jake Kanner killed him. Jake Kanner with his crazy schemes, his brochures, his stock-market fantasies. Danny couldn't take the pace, he couldn't follow that wild, careening, crazy trail. Jake Kanner shook his thin-skinned heart until the walls broke with blood, and the flimsy organ collapsed, gave up, surrendered, knelt and died in the vault of his sun-tanned chest.

Martin walked down Allenby Street, half-looking for a job, half-asleep, dreaming about bygone days and the handsome brown corpse of his father's partner.

And yes, his mother's life had changed. No more canasta games at three o'clock in the afternoon, or calls to her bookie, or walks with Mrs. Berlman down Bathurst Street. She spent her days in his father's office, the cramped cubicle wreathed with pee-stench, helping out with odds and ends of papers, with short and long letters that needed typing. She spent her time sitting there and talking and keeping his father company during these down days.

Down Allenby Street he dragged himself. Where in this hissing city could he find employment? Up what dark staircase would he have to crawl with his meagre talents held out in upturned palms? Shots of sun through his hair. Spikes of light through his eyes. Light. Sharp, penetrating light that flashed from the Mediterranean.

A fantasy formed in his mind. A wild uncontrollable root had started to grow beneath the city. It was the root of a huge black prehistoric tree. It splintered through concrete, lamp-posts, glass. It toppled buildings from Tel Aviv to New York City. No bomb, or fire, or chemical could stop it. Its leaves devoured people. Snaffle, and they were gone. Whole populations devoured until there was hardly a living soul left on planet earth.

Presidents were gulped, swallowed, gone. Businessmen. Soldiers. Women. Children. Gone, swallowed, devoured. Miraculously, he was saved. For some mysterious unknown reason, he was the last man on earth, walking down Allenby Street. Miraculously, the tree bore delicious, life-sustaining food. The fruit hung from the branches, all colors, shapes, and textures. He ate and ate. He had to forget about his loneliness. The fruit had a million subtle ways of tingling his taste buds. It filled his stomach as it was never filled before. It satisfied his hunger completely.

Then he saw across the street the most miraculous thing of all. One other person had been saved, a woman, the most beautiful creature he had ever laid eyes upon. She sat on a splintered concrete block, she was chewing with beautiful, curved lips the insides of a soft, red fruit. Her eyes sparkled blue and black. Her eyes contained all colors, all promises. Love oozed from her slightest glance. Her body was a curved mystery. His eyes were lost and dazed from their travelling from her slim neck to her firm breasts to the power and strength and loveliness of her thighs. He was not wearing a stitch, neither was she. And the temperature on this devastated, rearranged planet was perfect. The sun no longer scorched, but soothed every inch of his body.

"I love you, I love you, I love you," he said, walking across the street.

Her eyes brightened. Her lips opened. He could see the tip of her tongue. The most beautiful sight he had seen in his life. And the tongue formed words that bathed his being in peace.

"Oh, I love you, too," she smiled. "I love you, last man on planet earth."

Down to the sea they strolled together, naked and alive. They bathed and loved and cooed to one another forever. No end. The first intensity of their first touch and kiss never slackened. No boredom crept into their hearts or minds. The fruit of their love like the fruit on the tree had infinite joys and subtleties.

Allenby Street hissed back into his head—the cars, the fumes of gas, the heat, the people marching to work, back from work. He was standing under an awning, the sweat oozing down his sides. The magic tree had evaporated. Across the street he saw a woman in a red skirt bending over a baby carriage. She wore a thin red scarf on her head to protect her from the sun. He could hear the baby screeching. Its small mouth curled into a slot of rage. Why aren't you naked, woman? Why aren't you alone? Why are you fastened to that baby carriage? And why do I stand frozen in the shadow of this awning? Why, Martin thought, should he move? He could look for work tomorrow. The offices would remain. The desks. The pencils. The teachers. The pupils. He just didn't have it in him that first day back in Tel Aviv to track down employment, wherever it might be hiding.

CHAPTER 10

The First Pupil

For three days he walked up and down Allenby Street looking for work. Certainly, he thought, there must be a hole in the wall, a rickety language school that needed his services. He dreaded going back to his father's office empty-handed. Yet he wasted time. After an early-morning surge of knocking at doors, talking to secretaries and principals, filling out application forms, he slowed down. He found himself in book stores, standing, dreaming. Up to the ceiling the books were piled, row on row. The great ones. The masters. Just to have a single volume, no matter how slim, along those rows of dust and venerability—that was all he wanted. He bought very little. He just stood there dreamily, the names sailing through his head. What gorgeous names. Melville, Whitman, Joyce. A magic parade of names. He would take a book down, his fingers trembling, open it at random, read a paragraph. The words washed over him, the power, the assembly, the beauty of images and metaphors. Just to be able to string words together, to create beauty out of nothingness—he ached to do it. What occupation could compare with it? What could be more honourable? To make the dust sing, the sky fill with birds. To take nothing, to take blankness and pain, to make the pebbles cry. This was the only challenge. He knew he could be a doctor or a lawyer or a professor. He had the brains. But what a dull life— scissors and scalpels, ink and contracts, papers and criticisms.

He got drunk inside those bookstores. He got so dizzy with words, their beauty and power, he no longer knew where he was, or how many hours were skipping past. He was Ishmael dumped into the sea, he was Ahab stalking the deck, spear in hand; he was the whale spewing water skyward, a fount spurting through the hole in a black forehead. He was a child sitting in Whitman's grass. He was Stephen Dedalus. He, too, was the unforged voice of his race.

And he found himself at other times down by the sea. He stood there scanning the blue horizon, the entrance to the Mediterranean. Not a dot of black could he see, not a single vessel, not even a row-boat. He remembered the wharves in Halifax, the stench of fish being processed, the black-grey sea gulls, how they dove and squawked over the loose intestines of gutted fish being flushed back out into the harbour. When he was nine and ten years old he bicycled down there often on Saturday mornings, a fishing rod slung loosely across the handlebars. He saw the Queen Mary at her berth, a huge groaning ship caked with salt and seaweed.

He found himself standing in front of kiosks watching the dark men and kerchiefed women straining carrots, chopping them, mush-ing them, mixing them into drinks. Watching the goo being spread inside pita to make falafels. He found himself thinking of Jerusalem, of Jesse and Mr. Townley, Gila and Peter, Lisa and the Judaean hills. He had disappeared. He had to go back one of these weekends to pick up a few belongings he had left behind, to let them know that he was still alive. He found himself again down by the Mediterra-nean looking at the sea gulls. They were white and slim in this part of the world, nothing like the huge grey shrieking carcasses that flew over Halifax harbour. Here they seemed to fly much higher, as if they were pieces of cloud that had broken loose.

On the afternoon of his third day of job-hunting he returned to his father's office. The bottoms of his feet ached and burned from walking. His handkerchief was soaked with sweat. He could almost wring it out. His father had a small smile hovering around his tight mouth.

"A Miss Laver wants you to call her. She gave me her number at work."

It didn't register. Why would anyone leave a message for him in a city where he knew nobody? He had forgotten about the ad in the newspaper.

"What's it about?"

His father smiled knowingly. It was an old smile that had passed between them before.

"Your first pupil," he grinned.

Martin didn't want to smile. But it was hard to control. To smile, to let it come out, would be to acknowledge that his father knew exactly what was going on in his mind. The smile forced itself at the corners of his mouth. He wanted to keep this private, between Miss Laver and himself. But it was useless; the old smile asserted itself, curled the edges of his lips.

"Here's the telephone number," his father said, handing him a slip of paper. "Just try to come home tonight, Martin."

He didn't want to look at his father's face any longer, or try to make a reply. As quickly as he could, he swivelled around and left the office.

He thrust the piece of paper into his pocket. It seemed to burn against his thigh as he went searching for a telephone booth, a place where he could close the glass doors, shut out the coughing and hacking of cars for a few minutes. There was no way he was going to use his father's telephone. He needed a private space, just a little breathing room. No, he wasn't going to speak to Miss Laver with his father grinning in the background.

A simple piece of white paper with a name, and a telephone number. It was a slim thing to pin a lot of hopes to. But already his mind was whirling with possibilities. Who was this Miss Laver? What did she look like? Did she really want him to teach her about the dark mysteries of modern poetry, Baudelaire, and the untameable Arthur Rimbaud?

It was exciting—not knowing what was going to happen, who she was, what she really wanted. His fingers trembled as he closed the doors on the telephone booth, the rubber smacking together, sealing out the insistent yak of Hebrew. His mouth went a little dry, his throat parched as he dialled the number.

"Hello," the soft voice, a little high in pitch, answered.

"Hello," he half-choked, "may I speak with Miss Laver, please?"

"Miss Laver speaking."

"Miss Laver," he said very formally, almost in a dignified professorial tone, "this is Martin Kanner calling. I believe you answered my ad in the newspaper."

"Oh yes, Mr. Kanner," the voice chirped, high and friendly, "you teach poetry, I understand."

"Yes, that's correct," he answered, his voice still seizing in his throat.

"What are your credentials? Not that I doubt you. I'm just curious."

"I have three years of university. And I'm a writer."

"Oh, you write," she chirped. "I would much rather take lessons from a creative person."

"Sure," Martin agreed, his voice loosening up just the slightest bit. "Can you come by this evening? Or is that too short a notice?"

"No, that's fine. I can prepare the lesson this afternoon."

"Good, Mr. Kanner. I'm really looking forward to it."

She gave him the address, very detailed instructions on how to get to her apartment. And she set the time for eight o'clock. He hung up the receiver, and let out a long loose sigh of relief. If the sigh were a sparrow or a feather, it would have gone through the doors of the telephone booth, skipped down Allenby Street, and flown straight up over the blue waters of Tel Aviv beach.

Now, there were a few more lines added to the slip of paper. It burned hotly in his pocket. Her apartment was on the top floor, a rooftop roost above Tel Aviv. It was on Sholom Aleichem Street, just up the hill from the Four Seasons Hotel and a block away from the El Al building, that wonderful modern structure of concrete and glass that curved like a giant bow. He remembered her voice. It was an English accent, no, not exactly English, but an accent that seemed more British than American. Who was this Miss Laver, this name and address that clung to his sweaty leg?

He had to prepare his lesson fast. He didn't want to do a sloppy job. He wanted to give a lesson that compared with anything that he had received in Montreal or Jerusalem. He wanted to give all the facts, but at the same time to live up to Miss Laver's expectations. It had to be zesty, even affirmative, the kind of lesson only a young dark-eyed poet could give. He wanted it to fly and swirl and dive and yelp like one of those slim-winged seagulls that soared over the blue stillness of the Mediterranean.

He took a bus back to his parents' apartment in Ramat Aviv. He was excited and happy. A smile flickered across his face. Nothing bothered him any more. His mind was fixed on eight o'clock, his mind centered on preparing his first lesson in modern poetry. He overlooked the clanging in the streets, the dust in the suburb of Ramat Aviv. He had no room of his own in this apartment. He slept on the sofa in the living room. But he preferred it this way. It gave the idea that he was only visiting, that this wasn't his home any more, not really his permanent place of residence. His books stood in the bookcase, his clothes hung in the hall closet, and maybe they would continue to do so for a month, six months or a year. But this was no longer his home. He was a man visiting, a son who was passing through.

At first, he did nothing about preparing the lesson. He stalked and paced through the empty apartment. He filled his lungs with great gulps of oxygen, blowing it out in long sighs. He wandered into the bathroom, smiled at his tanned face in the mirror. Smiled, so that he could see a row of white teeth flashing, and note the contrast against his brownness. Would she find him attractive, this Miss Laver, whoever she was? He ran his fingers through his hair. He winked at himself. And he laughed.

Out to the seventh-storey balcony he ambled. He cast his eye over the roofs of buildings in the direction of downtown Tel Aviv about two miles away. Down there, over there, on a roof in that direction she lived—a place he would travel to that evening. He let out a long breath mixed with a smile. He aimed it towards the heart of the city.

He prepared the lesson slowly, meticulously, cramming it with every important bit of information he had culled and gleaned over the last four years. How the movement had begun in France, how Baudelaire had seized on the magnificent inspiration of converting ugliness into beauty. How he made old women, whores and garbage sing and dance like the daffodils of former epochs. How he gave birth to the Flowers of Evil, the title alone worth ten thousand volumes of lesser souls. How Arthur Rimbaud sailed through the cataracts of the new-born psyche in boats drunken and wild. How he gave up the whole business of writing when he was only nineteen, nineteen, only nineteen, gave it up to run guns in North Africa until gangrene seized him, stopped him in his fast-moving tracks. Martin wanted to dwell on this theme during his first lesson. How wrinkles, ulcers, boils, crooked backs, twisted fingers—how it all became beauty under the inspired pens of these French geniuses.

At supper he sat at the dining-room table with his parents and Debrah. They sat over steaming bowls of cabbage soup, a dish that had become his mother's specialty in Israel. She never cooked it this well, Martin thought, never in Toronto or Halifax. She had finally gotten the balance between sweet and sour.

"Are you ready for your first lesson?" his mother smiled.

"Yes," Martin said almost somberly.

"Professor Kanner," Debrah chirped.

"Leave the poor guy alone," his father grinned.

Debrah sniffed the air.

"You're wearing a lot of something. Is that part of the lesson, Martin?"

Martin blushed. He spooned an extra-large piece of meat into his mouth, chewing it.

"I hope you remember to get paid," his father added half-seriously.

"Of course. What do you think I'm doing this for—for laughs?"

"Just a reminder," his father sighed.

Martin finished his soup quickly. The conversation was choking in his throat.

"I'd better be going," he said.

"We were only joking," his mother smiled.

"Yeah, I know. I just need some fresh air."

"Good luck, Martin," his mother smiled again.

"Good luck," his father echoed.

He collected his scribblers together hurriedly and left.

It was a warmish June night in Tel Aviv. The darkness had masked the searing heat of the day. The sidewalk still retained a warmth, and he could feel it seeping through the soles of his shoes. A few small trees were in blossom, delicate white blossoms etched with veins of red. He drew breaths deep inside him. The fragrance of the blossoms mixed with the aroma of Old Spice. He had sprinkled his father's cologne generously around his neck and chest.

He was glad to be outside, away from the dining-room table, away from his mother's chirpy comments and his father's cleverness. Now, he could breathe freely.

He examined the directions on the sweat-stained slip of paper. Miss Laver, who are you?—he kept wondering. Why you, why did you answer my ad in the newspaper? As he rode downtown on the almost empty bus, he saw Miss Laver in his mind. She wore a gown of white silk. She was almost six feet tall with a bosom that squeezed and rushed over the edges of her deep-plunging neckline. She changed shapes and dresses very quickly. Her height grew and decreased. One moment she was fat, then skinny. It was a wild parade of images and fantasies.

He saw Canal Street in Nogales once again. It was there two years

ago that he lost his virginity. A couple of Saturday nights, and it was
gone. But did it really count, he wondered, a body he had paid for,
two dollars for the body, and two dollars for the room? His only
experience of having a woman open her legs for him. The only time
he had ever entered that dark, wet passageway, and unloaded his
sperm inside. He was drunk, he remembered, from mixing stale
Mexican beer with the hot spikes of tequila. He was so drunk he
wobbled. His first whore, his first Saturday night in Nogales, was a
dark-skinned thing. Her face was pock-marked, but she had been
aggressive, almost pulling him out of his chair. Drunk he stumbled
down the rolling hallway to her room. He was surprised at how
quickly she got out of her clothes, how quickly she jumped on the
bed and spread her legs.

Three days later, the thing he feared most happened. It happened
with such precision, such dispassionate regularity that he could
hardly believe it was really happening. It ached when he tried to piss
in the morning, it burned up to his gut. A doctor in Tucson confirmed his fears. He had gotten the clap on his very first try. But this
was a knowledgeable doctor, who drove one needle into his ass, one
long stinger filled with penicillin. The disease was squelched.

"You gotta be careful down there," the doctor frowned. "Eighty
per cent of those whores are infected. Look, take my advice, if you
have to go down again, wear a safe. It's the only protection."

And he had to go down again. He just had to. How could he live
with such a disastrous first experience? He would never survive the
winter back in Montreal with that memory moving through the cells
of his brain. So he dragged his seventeen-year-old clap-cured carcass
down to Canal Street once again. He found another whore with
creamier skin, a softer mouth, and a twinkle in her eyes. She helped
him into a safe, laughing at his size. She did a lot to restore his
confidence. Perhaps she knew he had taken a beating the week
before.

"You're big," she laughed, "and such a baby face. It's funny, I see
lots of men down here. Football players over six feet tall. You can't
tell the size of the prick by the height."

He was drunk again that week, but the doctor's idea proved itself,
in his case anyway. He never contracted through the safe's thin skin
the stinging bug of gonorrhea.

Martin got off the bus at the corner of Allenby Street and Sholom

Aleichem. The excitement was beginning to build in his chest. His heart pounded under his thin summer jersey. Did he know enough about Baudelaire and Rimbaud to pass the test, to give a successful first lesson? He still had a half hour to go. He walked down to the sea-shore, clutching the scribblers, the notes he had prepared. The Four Seasons Hotel glowed. Finely-dressed people walked in and out of the front doors. Tourists with money. Businessmen. Jet-setters. They came to Tel Aviv with their wallets bulging, ate in the dining room of the finest hotel, ate their T-bone steaks and seafood platters as they did back home in New York City or San Francisco. His father used to be one of these men, suave, confident, even magnetic. His mother used to be one of these women, her neck adorned with pearls, her shoulders shawled with a light mink fur.

He drank in the lights of the hotel that evening. His eyes burrowed out to sea. Through the darkness he stared. And what did it all mean? How small and insignificant he felt standing in the darkness clutching his scribblers. The sea stretched to the end of all darknesses. Lines from Ecclesiastes rolled through his head. All is vanity, saith the preacher. He thought of books again. A book had to devour and encompass all this, the lights, the darkness, the sea. A book had to compete with the thousand lights of the Four Seasons Hotel, or it was nothing. A book had to contain the darkness of the Mediterranean on such a promising June evening. It had to be the soft flesh on oysters, but not merely soft. It had to be the hard shell, the gold key-chains, the women in pearls.

He felt so small and insignificant standing beside the Four Seasons Hotel, ablaze with lights, laughter tinkling out the open windows. He was merely a speck of salt dancing on the moonlit waves in front of him. He wanted to shriek like the gulls his tininess. He saw his wail curve from his mouth, spin and somersault over the waves—out to sea, past Malta, Sicily, Spain, through the narrow corridor of Gibraltar into the surly Atlantic.

He clenched his fists together. Well, Miss Laver, here I come, ready or not.

CHAPTER 11

In Josephine's Hands

Was she mies? Mies was a horrible thing for a Jewish girl to be. She could be brainless, but not mies. She could be penniless, one-legged, an orphan, but a mies Jewish girl was a horror. The word mies, meaning ugly in Yiddish, reminded Martin of a poor forlorn mouse with a tattered ear, one eye, and a limp.

Martin looked at her as they sat at the small coffee table together. Was Josephine Laver mies? Did she have the curse which made his mother and sister shudder? He gazed at her again and again. Her tiny mouth that looked like it could cry, even moan, at a moment's notice. Her eyes that had a popping quality about them. Did she somehow escape? Two minutes ago he had watched her take her contact lenses out. They were bothering her eyes, burning them. They had been worn all day, too long. She just had to pop them out and slip them into her felt-lined case.

Mies or not mies, Josephine had already startled him with the keenness of her observations, her amazing psychic ability. After he had delivered his lesson quite successfully, she made her first acute comment.

"You look worn out," she said.

It was so true, so true, so true. How happy he was that she recognized this. How delighted he was that she was not fooled by the polish he had applied to the lesson, that she was not deceived by the clean clothes he was wearing, nor the cologne, nor his combed hair.

"I am," he sighed. "I've been looking for work."

Josephine's eyes drilled into his forehead. They seemed to be battling with the tangle of thoughts and emotions inside him. Look below the surface, please do, he kept thinking. Discover all the things I yearn for.

"I know something about you already," she said.

"You do?"

"Yes, Martin. Let me tell you about your family. Your father is a very lonely man. He's never had close friends. And your mother, she's quite a submissive woman."

Martin was surprised. These were things he knew, of course. But he never dragged them up, never said to himself: Look here, Martin, your father's a loner, and your mother his lonely appendage.

"I never thought about it before," he said, "but when I think about it, I believe you're right."

He was thinking particularly about his father. He was a lonely man. Josephine was absolutely correct. A sadness filled Martin. A heavy weight in his chest. And guilt. He felt just a little responsible for his father's loneliness.

"Well," Josephine added, "he at least has you."

"But I can't stay with him forever."

Josephine didn't reply. She was beginning to look better to Martin as the minutes passed. So what if the whole world considered her slightly mies? So what if the Jewish women hung out their windows as she passed in the street, mumbling under their breaths: Oh poor soul, so mies. She had a small springy body. He was even beginning to admire the little lines of suffering around the corners of her mouth. The wrinkles, just a few in the corners of her eyes, that indicated that she had gone through some wear and tear in her twenty-eight years upon the earth.

There was even a sense of mystery about her: this executive secretary, a top-paid woman in Tel Aviv, who worked atop the El Al building. This South-African Jewish woman, much older and more experienced than himself.

"I was married once," she said. "It wasn't a happy experience, Martin. The guy was Catholic, and a sadist. Not that there's any relationship, of course."

"Did he beat you?" Martin asked, just a little shocked.

"Yes," Josephine replied, lowering her eyes. "He beat me with a strap. It was the only way he could get aroused. You know what I mean—sexually."

She twirled the word "sexually" around her small mouth, as if it were a buttercup she was tasting, but did not wish to swallow.

"That's awful," Martin groaned.

He could feel the strap slapping against Josephine's small naked back. He could almost feel it on his own back. The red welts rising, sore and bruised.

Josephine began to giggle. She laughed, trying to cover her mouth.

"What's so funny?"

"Well, he finally wanted a divorce. But you know what he wanted to do?"

"No, what?"

"Well, he wanted to become a priest. So you know what he told me to do? He said I had to go and talk with the bishop. I had to tell him that we never made love during the marriage. Otherwise, no divorce."

She started giggling again.

"Did you do it?"

"Of course I did," she laughed. "It wasn't true, but I would've done anything to get rid of him."

She was twenty-eight, but she began to look like a little girl. Martin wanted to reach out a hand and pat her on her small head.

The conversation flowed between them very easily. Josephine told him a little about her life in South Africa. She was very proud of one story in particular. How she had hitch-hiked and walked from Cape Town up into the heart of dark Africa, all by herself. She travelled one thousand miles north alone, without a gun or knife. Martin visualized her springy legs moving through the jungles. He saw her dodging leopards and natives.

She was beginning to look more desirable as each moment passed, as each story tumbled from her mouth. They talked on and on, until two or three in the morning. How he wanted to make love to her. He just wanted to take her small whipped body in his arms. Her courageous little body. He reached out and lightly touched her fingers.

"Martin," she said, "do you want to make love with me?"

It was so simple, the way she put it. But the small question made his mind reel and his heart thump.

"Yes," he managed to choke up from the darkness swirling in his gut.

"O.K. then," she smiled, "let's get undressed."

Wow. Wow. Wow. Martin's mind convulsed. His blood was leaping for joy. His fingers shook. So this was how it came about, so

simple and straightforward. He admired her for her straightfor-
wardness, for not beating around the bush. He admired her for the
lashes she had taken on her back, for her travels into the darknesses
of Africa. Her eyes looked beautiful now, her grey myopic eyes
beneath her glasses.

Josephine didn't waste any time getting undressed. Before he
knew it, she had snapped off the lamps, taken off her dress, brassiere, panties, and slipped into a blue nightie. Martin lingered over
getting undressed. He didn't want to rush it. This was his first time
with a woman who was doing it because she liked him, wanted him.
He tried to erase the whores in Nogales from his mind. He wanted
tiny, well-built, round-breasted Josephine with her small, crying,
giggling mouth to be his very first woman. And she was, really, if he
didn't count those two wayward ladies in the B-47 Club.

Slowly, he slipped out of his underwear. He was naked now, with
the moonlight illuminating his body, the moonlight that came over
the rooftops and slipped into Josephine's apartment. He could see
Josephine lying on top of her bed, a single bed with just barely
enough room for two people. She rested there calmly, eyeing him.

"Oh, hurry up, Martin. I'm cold and I want you."

A warm feeling surged up through his belly to his chest and
shoulders.

He was not drunk this time, he was not stumbling, nor was the
floor rolling beneath his feet. He was excited, warm and hard. He
wanted to slow everything down, just to feel what was happening to
him. He wanted to feel everything, even the coolness of the tiles
under his feet as he walked across the room towards her bed.

"Come here," she laughed. "I think you're teasing me."

As he approached the edge of the bed, Josephine wrapped her
small arms around him, squeezed him, pulled him, and tumbled him
down on top of her. He was surprised at how quickly she was doing
everything. It was a little too quickly, but there was something about
her directness that excited him. He was just a little scared this very
first time. But he knew, now, that Josephine would help him inside,
straight into her warm, wet opening.

She wrapped her fingers around his penis, rubbed, and fondled it.
Her breathing was coming in little hoarse gasps. Then, she did
something that startled him, surprised him a little, but he enjoyed it.

She spat in the palm of her hand, and rubbed her spit-wet slippery palm over the tip of his cock. It was an excruciatingly tingly feeling. In his years of petting and doing "everything but", no girl had ever done this. He admired her for it. It was creative.

The texture of her skin surprised him. It was the skin of a much younger woman, almost elastic and new. And the size of her breasts surprised him too. He fondled them beneath her blue nightie. They were rounder, heavier than he expected. Her nipples were rougher, larger, more pebbly. His head was dizzy now, drunk and dizzy from touching her, slipping his hand between her legs, running his forefinger along the wet warmth. He was drunk now, his mind reeling from Josephine's wet palm rubbing the very tip of his cock.

"Come inside me, Martin," she groaned, her voice hoarse and her breath gasping.

Just as he expected, she didn't wait until he fumbled around in the darkness, prodded and poked. She wrapped her hand around him, spread her legs, and directed him inside. She was wet and warm, wide-open and waiting. He slipped inside, deep inside without any trouble. It wasn't a tight squeeze at all. And he wanted to do it slowly. He just wanted to make this first time last. He tried his best not to come immediately. Josephine was getting more and more excited, breathing hoarsely, gasping, wrapping her springy legs around his back. He couldn't keep his eyes closed. He wanted to see her head tossing back and forth on the pillow, her moonlit face grimacing with pleasure. She knocked against him, squeezed against him, and the excitement was building between his legs, shuddering, building, tingling, getting hotter. And just about the time Josephine moaned and groaned and gasped the loudest, he came and shot and filled her with his sperm.

They lay beside each other. Josephine was cooing.

"Oh, that was so nice," she said.

Martin felt happy and warm. He wanted to tell her, he just yearned to tell her the truth.

"Josephine, I want to tell you something," he whispered. His eyes were slightly burning.

"It sounds serious," she smiled.

"I've never made love before. Not really. You're the first woman."

"You're kidding," she said.

"No, it's the truth. Why are you surprised?"

"You just did it so naturally. If you hadn't told me, Martin, I wouldn't have guessed."

"Really?" He was surprised now. "I just did what I thought people do."

"Well, let me tell you something. I've been with a few men. It's not a thing that comes easily."

Martin had never realized this—that there could be any difficulty with pumping up and down. What could be difficult about it?—he wondered.

"I want to tell you something else," she giggled. "You're big, you know."

The whore in Nogales, the one who paraded him around, flashed through his head.

"Have you ever been told that before?" she asked.

Now he wanted to tell her the whole truth. He didn't want to keep it to himself. So he told her the story of the B-47 Club, and the two whores. He told her about getting gonorrhea, about the doctor, about the shot of penicillin.

"Really," she said, smiling. "What a bad experience. It's a good thing you went back the second time. That could've ruined your whole sex life."

"My poor baby," she cooed and whispered into his ear, and drew his head down between her breasts, squishing his ears and hair and cheeks against the soft flesh.

"But you're really the first, Josephine," he sighed. "That's how I want to remember it."

"Of course I am," she chirped.

They lay in the moonlight together. The cool winds were flowing over the rooftops, through the open door, caressing their bodies. He began to feel lonely, a crazy feeling, lying beside Josephine and experiencing their loneliness. He had the same feeling he had experienced with Gila. They were two small kids, lost and alone, clinging to each other on a Tel Aviv rooftop. The stars—he couldn't help thinking about them, blanketing the city, the world. Galaxy and galaxy, pinpoints of light, curving forever in Einstein's infinity. No end to the whole thing. Impossible for the mind to grasp.

He thought about his own parents in their bed in Ramat Aviv. Did they ever feel what he was feeling this evening? What would they think about Josephine, his very first woman? What would they think about the whole course his life was taking? It was useless, now, to even try to describe the people he knew. How could he really tell them about Jesse, Mr. Townley, Peter?

It seemed that his world was drifting apart from theirs, faster and faster, like one galaxy shifting from another. When did it all begin? —he wondered. Was it that fateful decision in university? To set aside any desire to be a professional. Or did it begin even earlier? He remembered high school, drifting along, yet getting very good marks. Then something started to happen. It started with music, he remembered. He was shocked and abashed by what he was beginning to hear come from the radio. It was a guy named Elvis Presley. He was singing Heartbreak Hotel. And there was a hotel, and the hotel was broken, and the heart was smashed. It wasn't only him— this he knew. He had friends, too, who were swallowed by this new music. It swept over them. It was as if one year they were all still listening to Eddy Fisher singing O Mein Papa, or Bing Crosby crooning about the Bells of St. Mary's, and all of a sudden, one summer or fall, crazy, wild music with equally crazy words assaulted them; not only attacked them, but entered them. Became as close to them as their own heart-beats.

No, he was not alone. Nor was Josephine. They were not the only people feeling this weird loneliness. Together, yet not together. And how could he really set himself straight, start to make money? He grew up with money. He saw what money did to Danny Berlman. How could buying a car really get him excited? He had three cars to drive when he was sixteen years old. He burnt out the motor on one. Wrecked the transmission on another. Only his mother's green Oldsmobile did he leave undamaged.

Elvis Presley was a lightning stroke. Before him, Martin lived a different way. But Elvis didn't do it—this he knew. Elvis was singing for all of them, Martin and his friends. When he sang Jailhouse Rock, they knew the jail he was talking about. They all knew the cement and mortar. They were all behind bars. And the music they were hearing, and the music inside them was wild and fantastic. It was shaking their prisons, trembling the rocks. And they knew those rocks were going to fall down. Down. Down. Down.

How could he say to his parents: Look, I found Josephine, and I feel warmly towards her. I don't know if I love her. I don't even know what the word means. She's twenty-eight and a little mies. She's divorced and all the way from South Africa, but I love the way she spits in her palm. How could he share this with them? And this was very important to him. What did he have to share with them any more? If he had gone into one of the professions, he might have been able to talk about the ups and downs of business with his father. If he married a woman like his mother, the two women would be able to talk as Debrah and his mother talked. What would his mother talk to Josephine about? Or his father? What would his father talk to Jesse about?

It was beginning to dawn on him that he was living in a very different world from that occupied by his parents.

And when Elvis sang, "You ain't nothing but a hound dog," he was talking about a feeling in the blood. They were dogs that had broken their leashes, dogs with noses that were quivering, hound dogs in the forests and jungles, sniffing, sniffing, padding along on stone-torn feet. It was not a small little crack between the tunes his parents loved and the music he first heard in grade ten. It was an opening larger than the Grand Canyon. Everyone said, kids will be kids, and kids will revolt. But the hole in their hearts was not a tiny crack. It was a hotel and a world and a galaxy, and the whole bloody universe splitting apart.

They went to sleep for three hours, Josephine and Martin. He woke up at seven in the morning with Josephine's tiny hand wrapped around his cock. This time she just let him lie there on his back. She did the whole thing herself, rubbing him, kissing him, flicking her tongue inside his mouth. She got on top of him, and rubbed his penis between her legs, up and down her warm wet slit of skin. She was smiling. She licked her lips with the tip of her tongue. Her eyes looked dazed and drunk in her head.

She opened up wider and wider, sitting down on him, sliding all the way down his shaft. She rode him wildly, her head tossing back and forth, tiny drops of saliva at the corners of her mouth. She plunged again and again, trying to swallow each inch of his taut skin. His eyes were open. He was watching. It was almost like watching a movie. He was not exactly consumed in the act. He was watching.

She came two or three times in little starts and fits before he was fully awake, before the sperm started tingling up, heating up, and finally she pulled and squeezed a stream from inside him. He was smiling.

It was a strange thing to watch her get dressed for work just a half hour after she made love with him. His sperm was probably still gooey and wet deep inside her. The two things seemed worlds apart —how she looked on top of him, and how she looked now, applying a black ointment to the tips of her eyelashes. Getting ready for her no-nonsense job. Straightening her skirt. Combing her hair.

His mind flashed back and forth. Josephine typing. Josephine naked. Josephine groaning. Josephine politely answering the telephone at work.

"What are you going to do today?" she asked.

"Oh, I'll look for a job," he said dreamily, half-heartedly, without too much conviction.

"You can stay in bed if you want. I don't mind."

"No," he groaned, "I gotta find some work."

"Will you be back tonight?"

"Do you want me to come back?"

"Yes . . . just a second, I'll get you a key. You can let yourself in if you come back early. Just make yourself at home. Take a look at my books, you might find something interesting."

Josephine rummaged around in her purse, and found a worn brown key. She gave it to him, smiling.

"Well, I better be off," she chirped. "See you tonight."

"See you tonight," he echoed.

He wandered around the apartment for an hour or so, taking books off the shelf, opening them at random, reading a paragraph here and there. He remembered that he didn't get paid for his lesson. How could he ever ask for it? He knew very well that the lesson was the first and the last he would ever give to her.

That day he decided not to check in at his father's office. What, after all, did he have to report? He had found no job. He rode the bus up Allenby Street. Did the people going to work know how he had spent the night? Did Josephine's groaning rides shine through his eyes? Did her gasps and moans cling to his skin? He felt different, just a little different. It was as if a stone had dissipated inside him, one stone among many. It had turned into sperm the night before. It was not bothering him any longer. He felt lighter.

He was half-dazed by the sunlight when he got off the bus. Half-dazed, dreamy, feeling a little lighter than the day before, he walked into language schools asking for work. He kept it up for about a half hour before he quit. Was he really a person?—he wondered. Or was it all a dream? Was he really a shaft of sunlight, a filament of salt-spray beating against the beach? He didn't feel like a teacher. It was difficult to take his job-hunting seriously. His father's face floated behind his eyes. His father's fingers with the skin peeling. His father's hunched back.

He was sitting in Josephine's apartment when she got back from work.

"Guess what?" she smiled.

"What?" he said absentmindedly.

"I got a call from your father today."

"You're kidding," he grinned. "What did he want?"

"He was worried about you."

"Shit, I should've told them something."

"It's O.K.," she chirped, "I calmed him down. I assured him that you were in very good hands."

"How did he take that?"

"He apologized for bothering me at work. Your parents really love you, Martin."

Martin didn't reply. His eyes were fixed on Josephine's tiny hands. The nails were long, curved at the tips. Her skin was very white. Little blue veins, a network, shone through. Were those good hands, he wondered. Was he, indeed, in good hands?

Later that night he discovered that Josephine had a very good imagination, and a sense of humour. She told him about a fantasy that had taken root in her mind about two years ago. The fantasy was centered around a real person, a government official, a man in his late forties whom she claimed to love. Josephine had lovers regularly, a variety: artists and businessmen, young and old, tall and short. But this one man she really cared for, she couldn't seduce. She wanted to kidnap him, tie him up, take him to one of the bomb shelters in Tel Aviv, lock him up until he gave in and made love to her. Everything was planned thoroughly—where she would get water to keep him alive, what she would feed him, how she would keep the bomb shelter neither too hot nor too cold, too light nor too dark. She didn't care how long it would take. Even if it took three months, it would be worth it. As she spoke, it sounded very real to Martin—

as if she was actually capable of doing it. There was one hitch, something that Josephine had not considered. It seemed very obvious to Martin. Finally he smiled and blurted it out.

"Everything's perfect," he grinned. "You've thought of everything, but where's the poor guy going to shit?"

Josephine was startled and taken aback. She sucked on her cigarette, drawing at it deeply, as if she could drag the smoke down to her feet. She began to laugh and cough at the same time.

"It would get putrid in there, wouldn't it?"

"Yuck," Martin frowned, bunching up his nose.

"Double yuck," she giggled.

Did this woman really work at a typewriter all day long?—he wondered. How could she take it?

"Can you imagine what it would smell like in there?" he asked.

She let her eyes roll to the ceiling, her contact lenses glimmering.

"My plan is ruined," she sobbed. "It's full of shit. It's really full of shit."

"It stinks," he agreed.

The next evening around suppertime he returned to his parents' apartment. He didn't want to go back, but he had to pick up a change of clothes and a toothbrush. And he felt that he had to stand in front of his parents in the flesh once again to prove that he was still alive.

His father was sitting on the living-room sofa, a knowing grin around his mouth, his eyes slightly worried.

"You should've called us earlier," he said. "Your mother was worried."

"I'm sorry," Martin mumbled.

"Well, it's good to have you back."

Martin felt a stone thicken in his throat.

"I'm not staying long. I'm going back to Josephine's."

He said it with determination.

His father tapped his fingers on his knee.

"What are you eating?" he asked.

"Food. I eat at Josephine's."

"You can't do that forever," his father's eyes narrowed. He looked annoyed.

"Why not?" Martin asked, his throat stretched like a string on a taut bow.

"She'll run out of food," his mother chimed in, smiling.

He didn't find it funny.

"Look," he said, "I love Josephine and she loves me."

His mother and father laughed in chorus. Anger choked in his throat.

"What do you know about love?" his father glowered.

"Puppy-love," his mother chimed in again.

"It takes a long time," his father sighed, "to learn how to love a person. It's not just a matter of jumping in and out of bed. So you're having a good time. But don't mix it up with love. She's having a good time, that's obvious. You're acting as her stud."

Martin's eyes burned. He resented his father's analysis of the situation. He resented the word "stud", that one word in particular. He saw a black horse, mouth foaming, hooves kicking. The word caught in his throat.

"I'm leaving," Martin spat at them. "Don't be surprised if you don't hear from me."

He was angry. Their heads recoiled at his last remark. It was a threat, and he was glad he had made it. He was sick of both of them. His mother with her dyed-red hair, the black roots showing. He was sick of his father with his knowing smiles. He was sick of the apartment.

"Martin, I want to say only one more thing to you. We're telling you this for your own good. Listen, take it from your old man. Believe me, I've been around. I've had a few broads in my day. There's some women you just can't satisfy. They'll wear you out, and then toss you out. This Josephine sounds like one of them."

Martin laughed, a cold calculated laugh, the stream of his laughter aimed directly at his father's face.

"She'll have to go a long way before that happens. And besides, you don't even know her. How can you size a person up that way?"

His father lowered his eyes.

"O.K., O.K., let's just forget it. Go over to Josephine's, have a good time. But for heaven's sakes, Martin, make sure you get enough to eat."

Sure. Sure. Sure, he kept thinking. I'll get enough to eat. I'll empty the fridge. I'll eat her plants. And if I'm still hungry I'll eat the bed, the bedsprings and the mattress. What was this mania about food?—

he wondered. He left the apartment, not looking back. What was it all about?—his father's concern about getting worn out. The thought had never entered his mind. He found it hard to imagine his father ever encountering this problem. But he must've, somewhere along the line. How could a woman wear him out?

He was still angry as he rode the bus back downtown. The whole conversation clanged in his mind. He didn't like to be compared to a horse. This wasn't the way he wanted it: Josephine, himself, and his father commenting. It wasn't any business of his father's. He was no longer a child. "Stud", the word swept through his brain, a giant black stud flying in from the Mediterranean, mouth white and foaming. He was not a horse, and his father was not going to turn him into a horse. Did his father know about the conversations he shared with Josephine, conversations about books and ideas, conversations about Buddhism and psychic phenomena? What did his father ever talk to his mother about? Certainly not ideas—this Martin knew. About business perhaps, the bare essentials. Did his father ever make love out on a roof-top as he did with Josephine? Did his father in all of his existence ever talk to a woman for more than an hour at one stretch?

Josephine was watering one of her small plants when he arrived back at the apartment.

"How did your day go?" she asked, pouring water liberally into the dry ground.

"I just had an argument with my parents." He was agitated, and paced up and down.

"I hope it wasn't because of me," she frowned, picking off a dead leaf with her long-nailed fingertips.

"Ach," he said in disgust, "they wanted me to move back in with them."

"You know something, Martin, I get the feeling that your father doesn't trust me. He thinks I'm a femme fatale."

She gave a slight wiggle to her backside, round and wrapped in white shorts. He noticed for the first time she was wearing high-heeled shoes. He liked the combination. The high heels rounded and stretched the calves of her legs. A soft inch of her bum squeezed through her short shorts on either side. Yes, short pants and high heels, very appealing, but not exactly fatal.

Martin slipped up behind her, pressing himself against her backside, hooking his left arm around her shoulder. He squeezed her breast. He massaged her crotch with the fingertips of his right hand.

"You are deadly, aren't you?" he whispered in her ear.

"Like a snake," she chuckled, and hissed air through her teeth. "I'm going to send you back without an ounce of flesh left on your bones."

"Good," he whispered, his breath hot against her ear, "send me back in a little box."

She placed the vase of water on a bookshelf. She reached a hand around and rubbed his jean-covered crotch.

They made love again and again as the days passed, whenever they got the opportunity, first thing in the morning or late at night. But Martin noticed something that really bothered him. He was beginning to feel less and less at each session. In fact, he developed a slight pain in his side—a twinge just after he came.

It bothered him that he was not feeling enough. It was O.K., but it was not lovemaking as he imagined it. Jesse had described the process with such glowing words. Those rivulets and tiny creases. But he had not felt those creases inside her. It shocked him that the lovemaking was going downhill, slowly becoming less exciting, less interesting. Jesse had assured him that each time should be different, fuller, more alive. Exactly the opposite was taking place with Josephine. She didn't seem to notice this: at least, she didn't talk about it if she did.

One evening around eleven o'clock, he got into bed and turned his face to the wall. He just didn't feel like making love that night. A cold, solitary feeling had entered his chest. It weighed heavy on him, a chunk of ice. Josephine came from the bathroom wearing a nightie, her shoulders dabbed with perfume.

"What's wrong with you?" she asked. "You've been acting strange lately."

"I just want to be alone." He choked the words up. They were words that somehow managed to dislodge themselves from the cold block inside him.

Josephine suddenly lost her temper with an intensity that surprised him. She stamped her feet on the floor.

"This isn't a hotel, you know."

She picked his socks up off the floor and tossed them at him.

"You better go!" she snapped. "Now, *I* want to be alone."

He decided to go. It was an effort to pull himself off the bed, to go through the slow mechanical effort of putting on his socks. The whole process of dressing bored him. He was determined, however, to leave. A struggle was going on in his mind. He knew very well there was only one place to go at eleven o'clock in the evening, and that, of course, was back to Ramat Aviv. He wanted neither, really: Josephine, or his parents. The thought of having his own room flashed through his mind. Slowly, he got dressed. Ramat Aviv and Josephine—the sharks on one side, a tornado on the other.

He got fully dressed without darting one glance at Josephine.

"Where are you going to go this time of night?" she asked.

She seemed a little surprised, almost hurt, that he was making no effort to apologize, that he was actually going to leave. He was making no attempt to stay.

"That's my problem, isn't it?" he said coldly.

"I think it's stupid, myself," she hissed, "walking out at this hour."

"Well, who told me to leave?" he spat. "I just want to be alone."

"The buses aren't even running," she said, pointing towards the window.

"I'll walk. I'll walk. Just leave me alone."

"Oh c'mon, Martin. Things can't be that bad."

She walked over to the bed where he was now sitting fully clothed. She placed her small hands around his head, and drew him towards her, squeezing his face into the round softness of her belly. He could feel the soft skin breathing beneath the nightie. The fragrance of her perfumes wreathed him, circled his head, travelled up his nose.

"Yeah," he sighed, "I guess they're not that bad."

She smiled and lifted his chin, bending down so that their eyes met. Her hazel-grey eyes and his brown weary sockets. Her eyes were glimmering in an unusual manner. They were stung and burning with just the slightest hint of tears. His eyes began to burn. The block of coldness inside him was slowly beginning to melt.

"I love you, Josephine," he whispered.

It made him feel good to say it. "Love"—it was such a powerful word. He couldn't figure out what it really meant, those four squiggly letters. It was a word he had seen in hundreds of books, a word he had heard pouring out from a thousand radios. It was the word on a million lips. And it was a word that puzzled him more than any other. Yet it made him feel good to utter it—this most powerful, richest, fullest, most hopeful of all words. Just to say it to another human being. Just to whisper it to Josephine. It tingled in his head and stomach. He remembered a while back being frustrated by it, not knowing its meaning, not knowing how a person in love was supposed to feel. "It's a lousy word," he had told Josephine. "It's too abstract, too vague. They should cut it out of every diction-ary in the world." He had a vision of a million scissors snippety-snipping from Japan to New York.

And now, just to utter that word made him feel less lonely. It made him feel like a person, a full person with blood and brain-waves, guts and genitals, with everything beating in unison inside him. Did he love her? He honestly didn't know. Did he love his own parents? Did he love anything?

"I love you too," she echoed back at him, her eyes still stung with tears.

It was a word he loved to hear—whether it was true or not. As it slipped from Josephine's lips, the last splinter of ice melted inside him. He slipped his hands into her nightie, cupping her full, droop-ing breasts in his palms. Where else was he supposed to be in the entire world? He wanted to make love slowly, to run his hand slowly down her side, to feel the soft flesh of her inner thighs with the very tips of his fingers. Slowly and quietly and calmly he wanted to do it that evening.

And they made love once again with their eyes still stung with sorrow and tears, as if they realized that sometime in the future, in a month perhaps, or in a year, their friendship was going to end. They made love gently that evening without snatching or grabbing at each other. It was one of the few times he felt almost satisfied, warm and cozy, snuggling against her. It was as if they both had melted into the wetness of their own eyes. That evening—one rare occasion—he went to sleep without that aching sensation, that sharp pain in his stomach.

CHAPTER 12

Country of Miracles

The arguments between them didn't cease. They kept cropping up. It was like the painful experience of walking barefoot in the dark and having an unexpected tack shoot through the tender flesh. He had to have time away from her, even if it meant sleeping on the sofa in his parents' living room. He alternated between the two places, and Josephine put up with it. His parents put up with it. Martin put up with it. It was a compromise for everyone concerned, certainly not a perfect, or near-perfect state, and deep in Martin's brain a clanging continued—a declaration of bolts and motors, cogs and wheels, that perfection and peace and calm had to exist, somewhere. That winter he searched for it in books. He devoured paperbacks, one after another, looking, reading. The answer could be in the next purchased volume. On page 353, paragraph 4, in two lines, the answer hiding. A key to his dissatisfaction, a formula, a phrase that summed up his anxiety.

He finally found work just off Allenby Street, in the Kadimah School of Languages. Kadimah—the name held promise. Forward, it meant in Hebrew, a word used when the army thrust ahead. The work came easily to him, almost too easily, as if the ability to teach had grown from childhood, part of his jawline, intimate as his teeth. Later that winter he switched to Berlitz, a more structured schedule, the famous Berlitz; and he realized that these schools dotted the globe—the backlands of Tokyo harboured them, the frenzied mazes of New York, outpost cities from Korea to Mozambique. It was easy going, the work. He prepared very little, thought about his work less and less. It became a mechanical opening and shutting of his mouth, the bare essentials of Shakespeare's language chopping the stale classroom air. The only thing that gave him a problem, other than the sheer boredom, was his temper. The kids, some nine and ten-year-old groups, got on his nerves. Chewing gum, whispering, yakking, scraping their desks. He didn't like the job of teacher cum babysitter. Nor did he like laying down the law. Instead, he exploded from time to time. He laid his hands on the scribblers of a particularly bothersome student, and threw them across the room. Or he grabbed a pencil, snapping it mercilessly in two. The students looked shocked at times at his behaviour. Martin too was surprised at some of his own storm and stress tactics. Was he going just a little berserk?—he wondered. Was he going just a little too far? But it broke the boredom, it at least got the blood rushing through his body once again, his scalp tingling during a semi-enraged outburst.

Often in the mornings, he hung around the Ramat Aviv apartment. His mother usually didn't go down to the office until noon-hour. She padded around from kitchen to bedroom in her slippers and nightie. She was still an attractive woman, often receiving the compliment from strangers that she and Debrah could pass for sisters. Her skin was still smooth—only a few wrinkles at the corners of her hazel-brown eyes. She was slightly plump, certainly not fat, and she was still proud of her round-breasted figure.

On one such morning, Martin was sitting in the living room, reading, dreaming over a recently acquired novel. He heard a screech coming from the kitchen. He jumped up and ran to his mother, out of breath. She was clutching her finger, a grimace of pain crumpling her face.

"Oh shit!" she cried. "I'm so stupid. I burnt my finger."

"It's O.K.," he reassured. "I know what to do. I just read about it the other day."

He rushed her from the kitchen through the dining room to the washroom. He turned on the cold water full blast, testing it, until he could almost feel an iciness in the stream pouring forth.

"Put it under there, Mom. Believe me, it'll help. It'll take all the pain away."

Obediently, she edged her finger towards the stream pouring from the faucet.

"Don't be afraid. Put it right under."

"It's pouring so fast," she half-protested.

"Never mind. Honest, you'll see, it'll work."

Martin was excited. He wanted to see the cold water perform its soothing service.

"How does it feel?" he asked, after she had plunged her finger into the downpour, and left it there a few minutes.

She withdrew her finger, held it up, waved it in the air, eyed it.

"It's amazing," she smiled. "It really feels better."

"You won't have any redness or scar either," he declared proudly.

"I always thought butter was supposed to work," she said dreamily, her young middle-aged eyes mistily gazing at him.

"Nope, it's the worst thing. It keeps the heat in, Mom. The only thing that really works is cold water. It's funny, you know. I just read about it two days ago. An article in Time."

He wanted to show her the article, but especially the photo, the very dramatic photo that accompanied it. In fact, it was not the words that convinced him of this method of healing burns, but the picture, a picture that had engraved itself on his brain. It was a photo he would carry around inside his skull for years to come.

He went on a search throughout the apartment—the living room, his sister's bedroom, his parents' bedroom. He finally found the magazine on a night-table beside his parents' bed.

"Here it is," he almost shouted. "Just take a look at this picture, Mom. You won't believe it."

And it was a dramatic, convincing photo. There was no doubt about it. It showed a woman's arm. Above the elbow the skin was twisted and scarred, the flesh looked like pieces of rubber tied together. Below the elbow, the skin was smooth, untouched, perfectly normal. The contrast was vividly stark.

"See, Mom," Martin explained, "she had her arm burned when she was a little girl. A maid plunged her arm into a bucket of ice-cold water. But it didn't go all the way. Isn't that just an unbelievable difference?"

"Poor child," his mother sighed. "What a shame. Thank you, Martin. My finger feels so much better. I must tell Dad about it."

She placed an arm around his shoulder, crushing him to her. She smacked a kiss off his cheek with her well-formed, still-beautiful, warm lips.

A warm feeling tingled in his stomach and chest for the rest of the day. He was just happy to have done something right, exactly right. There were no ifs, ands, or buts about it, as his mother was fond of saying. No fence-sitting or wavering. No doubt or hesitation. The act, though simple, was right on target, dead-centre, through the bull's eye.

If only all of life, he dreamed, were that straightforward. It would be like teaching without any boredom or anger. Writing without strain. A burn—cold water; no scar or pain. Streamlined and simple. Without agitation or nightmares.

It was in the kitchen again, the small kitchen in Ramat Aviv, that the next turn of fate, the next twist of events took place. Martin was just finishing the last of his noon-hour meal, a fruit salad that his mother had prepared, chock-full of grapes, apples, oranges, all sliced so that their tingling essences could be tasted. He was nibbling on a green grape. His mother was standing by the stove in her blue nightie.

"Oh Martin," she gasped.

Out of the corner of his eye he saw her knees buckling, her hand go to her forehead. He jumped up. She grabbed his shoulder, and hung her full weight on him.

"What's wrong, Mom?"

"Just let me sit down. I feel so weak."

He eased her down gently, supporting her, holding out the chair. She brushed the beads of perspiration from her forehead. A smile kept flickering across her face, curling the corners of her mouth. It surprised him.

"Mom, why are you smiling?" he asked, mystified. The smile was so inconsistent with the rest of what was happening.

"I feel so funny inside."

For no good reason, he too began to smile. His insides tingled. His mother somehow was communicating her feeling to him. It was as if his stomach was floating, his stomach turning over in free space, lighter than it was supposed to feel. And his blood was rushing up and down his legs, doing dizzy spins and turns, for no good reason, without explanation.

"Now you're doing it," she said.

He laughed. He just couldn't help it. It forced its way up, and out his mouth.

"I don't know what I'm laughing about. I just got this crazy feeling."

"It's O.K., Martin," his mother said softly.

She was reassuring him. Even this was strange. Something strong was happening in the kitchen, but he had no idea what it was. Not knowing, yet feeling it so deeply inside him, made the experience even stronger.

"Mom, I think you should go see a doctor."

He was thinking about his grandmother, his mother's mother, how she had taken a stroke just two months after his bar-mitzvah. She had been preparing the Passover meal, dishes that took long hours to cook. It struck her suddenly, as she was walking from her bedroom to the kitchen. In the dark hallway, it hit her without warning. Down she went. The stroke paralysed her entire left side. It took away her power of speech. It left her bed-ridden. Now, almost nine years later, she was still in the same condition, living in Halifax with his Aunt Ida.

These diseases, he knew, ran in families. Heart attacks, ulcers, cancer. They were passed on from mother to daughter, father to son, travelling down through the generations via a contorted gene. They rested in the gene pool, in the blood. Suddenly, they struck without warning. There was no way he wanted to see his attractive, soft-cheeked mother in the same condition as his grandmother. He had seen her close up. She had lived in their house in Halifax for a couple of years, after her devastating stroke. Close up he had seen her, almost too close, her food dribbling out of the corner of her paralysed mouth. She cradled her left arm as if it were a baby. When she became angry, frustrated at not being able to communicate, unintelligible grunts and roars issued from her mouth. He gazed at his mother. Yes, she was still beautiful. A rose hue to her cheeks, a natural rosiness. She reminded him a little of Betty Grable and other stars of the forties.

As he sat there at the table with his mother, keeping her company, waiting for her to recover from the weak turn, he remembered how she used to take him to the movies when he was six years old. The first movies he ever saw. She was a "movie nut". It was a phrase she herself used to describe her fascination with the huge figures who floated and loved and hated their ways across those pebbly screens. They were his very first movies, and he sat beside his mother in the darkness that smelled of popcorn and freshly unwrapped chocolate bars. His mother's smells mingled with the fragrances that surrounded them. He remembered them well: thick red lipstick, perfumes, mascara, and the odor of various sprays to keep her hair from flying around wildly in the wind.

It was a cozy, warm, dark world in those old movie houses. No blast of winter rain could get at them. No ice or hail. Except when watching horror films, which sent chills of fear running up his spine, he was happy in those old theatres. In fact, they were probably the happiest moments of his childhood. How he hated to see the films end. How he hated to go back into the streets where the horns of cars blasted, and people argued.

Outside, school waited—a place he hated to go to, a place where he was teased for being overweight, or teased because of his name, or teased just for any old reason. How he dreaded going to the cold, dank showers after gym. How he dreaded and feared getting undressed in front of his tormentors. Every stitch of clothing had to come off; not a thread could remain. He had to stand fully naked before them, without a place to hide his chubbiness.

But the Armview Theatre, and the Capitol, and the Paramount—that was a different story. They were places where he could relax, finally just sink into the plush cushions, just chew on his popcorn and watch with his mother the wonderful parade of people on those huge screens. Clark Gable, a handsome man with his bushy eyebrows and big ears. Debbie Reynolds, oh how beautiful and delicate she looked dancing with Gene Kelly, singing and skipping her way down a rain-soaked street. The rain pinging her umbrella, her pink umbrella, rain rolling off the canopy she twirled in her tiny hands.

"All good things must come to an end, Martin," his mother used to say, as if she knew how much it pained him to leave the darkness, to go back into the glare of the foyer, and then the coldness of the streets. He knew they had to end. Saturday afternoons ended, movies ended, THE END in huge white letters always appeared on the screen. He knew very well he couldn't sit forever in the darkness. He knew very well that on Monday school would be waiting for him, waiting with its shrieks at recess, and its towels snapping in the shower-room.

He gazed at his mother across the kitchen table. How he hoped, almost prayed, that nothing would happen to her heart, that nothing would attack or burst that fragile organ.

*　*　*

Dahlia Kanner sat in the doctor's waiting room. She was leafing through a Home and Gardens magazine, but the greenness of gardens and the whiteness of the houses merged as the pages flicked beneath her fingernails. She just couldn't concentrate, nor read a single word. Was this really happening to her?—she wondered. Was she really sitting in Dr. Goodman's foyer awaiting the results of a pregnancy test?

She rubbed a forefinger along her eyebrows, erasing the tiny ridges of perspiration which kept emerging.

It was not a thing to smile about, her possible condition. She was forty-two, a young forty-two, a well-preserved forty-two, but nevertheless she could still feel her age, especially in this country with its relentless heat waves. Giving birth to Martin had almost killed her. Debrah's birth was easier. But then the doctors had examined her very carefully with all their lights and instruments and tests, and informed her that she would not have any more children. For eighteen years she went her merry way with Jake, taking the doctors at their word, trusting them, never even considering that she should be taking precautions. As the years rolled by, she became convinced that the doctors were correct, that she was, in fact, barren. Now something tingled inside her, a feeling that she recognized, an old familiar feeling that made her smile. Perhaps she was imagining the whole thing: just the power of suggestion—one of Jake's favorite expressions. Nothing was final until the test results came back. Dr. Goodman was an excellent obstetrician, one of the best in all Israel, but he could be wrong.

Finally the young Yemenite nurse came to the door of the waiting room and motioned her into Dr. Goodman's office.

Dr. Goodman was smiling. He walked up to her, placed a large warm hand on her shoulder.

"Mrs. Kanner, I congratulate you. You are going to be a mommy once again."

Her legs went weak suddenly, her head dizzy.

"Oh, my God!" she gasped. "It can't be."

"Please, Mrs. Kanner, sit down, just relax. We are going to have a nice little talk together, just you and me."

He tightened his warm grip on her shoulder, easing her down gently into an awaiting chair. It seemed that his large hand was encompassing every bit of her shoulder.

"I know what my husband's going to say. I just know it. He's going to make me have an abortion."

"Don't you worry," Doctor Goodman cooed, pouting his lips in an exaggerated way as if he were speaking to a small child. "I'll speak to your husband. You just leave that to me. Now, young lady, I want to have a serious talk with you."

He looked directly into her face with his large brown eyes. He has a gentle face, she kept thinking, a gentle middle-aged face. She liked him. He was funny and serious and warm, all at the same time.

"But I'm too old to have a baby," she sighed.

"Nonsense. Do you know, Mrs. Kanner, that just two weeks ago, I had a patient of forty-eight who became a proud mommy? And just think, you don't have an ordinary baby inside you. You are going to give birth to a sabra."

Dahlia smiled. She hadn't thought of that. Yes, it would be a real sabra.

"Doesn't that make you feel proud?" he asked, running the back of his fingers down her cheek.

How warm his hand felt. How gentle he was.

"Yes, a little bit," she smiled through her tears.

"Of course it does. Now, you know what I want you to do. I want you to call Mr. Kanner, right this minute on my telephone, and tell him the good news."

Dahlia lowered her head. She shook it just noticeably back and forth.

"It's not a good time," she sighed, pressing her right foot into the carpet.

"It's always a good time," he smiled. "I've never seen a bad time. Dahlia, if I might have permission to use your first name, Dahlia, it's a blessing. It always turns out for the best. Tell me the number, and I'll dial it for you. If he has any doubts, you let me speak to him."

Dahlia Kanner knew her husband well. As soon as she told him, the words shot from his mouth. Fast and hard. She had heard that kind of reflex action before. It was a quick, almost surprising one line or two, without a chance for thought to take place.

"You must have an abortion, Dahlia. That's obvious. It's dangerous at your age." Jake spat out the words, his neck reddening, his fists clenched.

At this point Dahlia began to quiver. It began with a tiny rippling of the flesh near her shoulders. Tremors flitted across her neck. She opened her mouth to say something, but no words came out. She stood there shaking, the receiver in her hand.

"Dahlia, please let me have the phone," Dr. Goodman said, taking the receiver from her limp hand. "Hello, Mr. Kanner, this is Dr. Goodman speaking."

Jake's voice lost its cutting edge. It mellowed into a warm, buttery flow.

"Oh, hello, doctor. We have a bit of a problem, it seems."

"Not at all, Mr. Kanner," Dr. Goodman said in a very rich, full, deep voice. "I understand that you are worried about your good wife's health. Mr. Kanner, let me speak to you as one man to another. There are absolutely no grounds for worry. Dahlia is a perfectly healthy woman. Believe me. I've examined her thoroughly. There is no reason why she can't bear a child. Not only that, Mr. Kanner, but I believe she will absolutely glow with health during her pregnancy."

Jake cleared his throat. The furrows lining his forehead were showing signs of gradual fading. He was impressed by the voice he had heard speaking on the other end of the line. Dr. Goodman sounded like his kind of man. The voice was definite, without hesitation or doubt, yet warm, filled with consideration and feeling. He despised fence-sitters, and weak-kneed hesitaters. On the other hand, overly cool analysts sent shivers of disgust, almost hatred through his body. He considered himself decisive, yet warm—at least that was how he wished to see himself, and wanted others to perceive him.

"Doctor, did she tell you about the difficult time with Martin? I wouldn't like her to go through something like that again."

"Yes, Mr. Kanner," Dr. Goodman smiled, "I understand your concern. But a great deal has changed in the last twenty years. I am going to see to it personally that your lovely wife will be fully prepared for the birth. I will show her myself some very simple exercises that she can practise at home. Not only that, Mr. Kanner, but I give you my word that I will be able to predict not only the sex and weight of the baby, but the exact half-hour in which it will be born. How does that sound?"

It sounded very impressive to Jake Kanner. This man was talking his language. In fact, he had used a phrase that he himself used very often, but had heard come from very few lips down through the years. It was a neglected, forgotten phrase. How many people in this cold computerized world ever thought of giving their word? Contracts they would give. Legalities. Bonds. But not "their word". When Jake Kanner first started out in accountancy, he gave his word to clients again and again. And he was very proud of the fact that he stood behind it with the full force of his being. To him, in those days, it was a matter of honour to keep his word. Part of a personal code he had developed. He looked upon his word as something sacred, just as dear to him as his right hand, just as important to him as his wife and children.

"Dr. Goodman," Jake answered, "I'm going to hold you to your word. You know why—because you sound like a man capable of delivering the goods."

Dr. Goodman smiled broadly, his eyes twinkling on his end of the line. Jake had broken out into a grin on his end. Dahlia was smiling to herself, still quivering, but smiling. The tears glistened in the corners of her eyes. Yes, Dr. Goodman thought, he liked this man he had just heard speak. He decided right then and there to do his damnedest to deliver the goods. He was already beginning to feel a warmer connection than usual, with this Kanner family. Jake's forthrightness, Dr. Goodman thought, matched the loveliness of his wife.

"Good," he said. "It is settled. I am looking forward to meeting you, Mr. Kanner, perhaps in the papa's waiting room."

At this he chuckled. Jake Kanner chuckled. Dahlia wiped the last remaining tears from her eyes. The conversation ended with good feelings all around. It was settled. All systems were "go" for the birth of Dahlia's third child.

*   *   *

On the same afternoon, Martin was sitting on the living-room sofa in Ramat Aviv, dreaming, reading, gazing at the blue sky beyond the balcony. It was a lazy afternoon, not a thing unusual about it. He had experienced a thousand that were exactly the same. Blue sky. Green grass. Dust in the parking lot below. A book in his hand, the same paragraph unread. He had started it approximately six times. In the middle, before he could complete it, tuck it away, his mind wandered like a feather being blown off the balcony, drifting, dreaming, floating into a limitless space.

A dull afternoon. He had forgotten about his mother's weak turn, forgotten completely that she had made an appointment to see a doctor.

It was only four o'clock, and it surprised him to hear a key turn in the front door. He was too listless to move. In came his mother, father, and Debrah. All three were beaming. His father looked just a little sheepish, but his black eyes darted with vigor.

"Don't get up, Martin," his mother smiled. "Just stay where you are. We have some news for you."

"Mommy's pregnant," Debrah blurted out. "She's going to have a baby."

"What?" It was as if he hadn't heard correctly. The words had come forth, but they hadn't made any logical connections in his mind.

"Martin," his father grinned, his eyes flashing, "your mother's going to have a baby."

Martin was shocked. This time he understood. Surprised he was, amazed. He couldn't believe it. Blood rushed to his head. A smile stretched at his lips.

"You should see your face, Martin," Debrah laughed, her voice almost squeaky with excitement.

"But . . . is it safe, Mom? How could you be? I thought the doctors told you . . . "

"You tell him, Jake," his mother smiled, wiping sweat from her forehead with the back of her hand. "Tell him about your talk with Dr. Goodman."

His father beamed. Martin hadn't seen this much life in his face for a long time. He almost looked like the old Jake Kanner, the one who flew so high on Bay Street, the one who defied the R.C.M.P. in Nova Scotia, the one who lifted him up in his arms at Sunnyside, gave him a toy rifle, and let him shoot the ducks.

"Well," his father said very deliberately, "first things first. There is no worry, Martin, about your mother's health. I've been assured of that by one of the best doctors in the country."

"But . . . "

"Her age is no problem. Women eight and nine years older are bearing children."

"But she had such a tough time with me," he finally managed to say.

"That was years ago, Martin," his father reassured. "R. D. Mc-Taggart, the old coot who delivered you, was a butcher compared to the doctors of today."

He had heard the story of his own birth so often that it seemed like a part of his memory. How his mother sweated and strained in labour for two days. How old R.D. finally hauled him out with the forceps, catching him on the cheek, leaving a half-moon, deep, red scar. The scar had whitened and shallowed out during the years, but the half-moon of indented flesh was still visible.

"But . . . how . . ?"

His father grinned.

"That is one of the mysteries of life," his father said. "Who knows? Maybe the heat changed your mother's hormones. And besides, this is a country of miracles, isn't it? We see miracles everywhere. The desert everyone said wouldn't bloom. The kibbutzim."

Martin was still seated. He was not able to move. He was still stunned. The three of them stood before him, above him, all three grinning, their eyes flashing with new life.

"Martin," his mother said, "when we told you, your face went through every emotion in the book."

"It did?"

"Happiness. Shock. Disbelief."

The three of them grinned down at him. It was amazing, the news he had just heard. He could feel what all three of them were feeling. It was a twisting, rolling, powerful spring inside him, rushing waters of feeling, a force in the blood that felt so strong he knew it could move rocks. Yes, that was what they were all feeling. It was like a man who has a dream. He dreams that he is bald, not a hair on his head. The dream is absolutely, totally real to him. He believes it completely. There is no question about it. Tragedy has struck. He has gone bald. How sad he feels. How old. How worn out. How without hope. There is no way to grow a new head of hair. He awakes. He slowly realizes that he has been dreaming. Hesitantly, he moves his hand towards his head. He feels it. It's there, all there, his precious hair. It was only a dream. He is overjoyed. And for that afternoon, the Kanner family was in the mood for celebrating, for laughing and talking, for reminiscing. His father's business trials were temporarily forgotten. The tight economic situation was pushed aside.

"Who knows?" Jake smiled later that afternoon, gazing over the balcony. "This could change my luck completely."

"Sure it could," Martin agreed. "It makes me feel that anything's possible."

The four of them sat on the balcony together on light-weight beach chairs. His father was wearing a pair of blue shorts that rose above his knobby knees. The sun flashed off his face, a red full blazing sun, sinking over the Tel Aviv skyline. Jake Kanner's face was beginning to look lean again, brown, almost healthy. His black eyes stared ahead, contemplating, and Martin sensed a new rush of feeling inside his father, fresh hope for the future. Perhaps he would get this computer-accounting business off the ground. He seemed to have an endless capacity for going down—hitting the rocks, broke, without a cent—and rising once again. A new unexpected charge from somewhere would enter him, and lift him up once more.

That afternoon he could see a resemblance between his father and Moshe Dayan, the general and tank commander. The one referred to by the Arabs as the black devil, or the Jewish scourge. In an expensive restaurant in Tel Aviv, Jake Kanner had been introduced to Moshe. They got along well, his father had told Martin. They dealt with two completely different areas of existence, but they were both fighters, his father said proudly.

"And he's quite a lady's man," his father grinned, rubbing sunlight with clenched fists from the corners of his eyes. "Well, let's call a spade a spade, he's a well-known philanderer."

"Gets around, does he?" Martin added.

His father nodded, smiling, bobbing a slippered sockless foot up and down.

"Well, what are we going to call this son of ours?" Jake asked, his eyes flashing.

"Who says it's going to be a boy? It's going to be a girl, isn't it, Mom?" Debrah half-grinned and pouted, touching her mother's elbow.

"Of course it is."

"O.K.," Jake laughed. "You pick out some girl-names and we'll pick out some boy-names. How does that sound?"

"O.K.," Debrah sighed, "but I'm sure it's going to be a girl."

His father suggested a few names he had been mulling over, biblical names, names suitable for a bona-fide sabra. He began the naming seriously, suggesting things like Gideon and Joshua.

"Gideon sounds too giddy," Debrah teased.

"How about Samson?" his father came back. "Or Brutus?"

"Brutus," everyone laughed in chorus.

"It sounds like a dog," his mother said.

The names were hitting Martin all wrong. They were just too harsh, too sharp. He knew the kind of name he wanted. It had to be soft, more musical, but have a hidden strength about it. Excitement began to froth inside him. What if he could find the name that would please everyone? A name his brother would bear for the rest of his life. He wanted to be attached to this new baby in some intimate way. But the name itself was not in his head, only the tone and rhythm of it. He ambled over to the bookshelf, looking at the rows of authors' names. What if he could find an appropriate name among the men he loved dearly, among the writers he idolized? William, no, too simple. Ernest, no, not Ernest, it was too moralistic. Herman, no definitely not Herman, it was just too Germanic. The minutes rolled by as his eyes wandered back and forth like a flashlight moving across the covers, trying not to miss anything.

He came upon a name that stopped him, a last name, not a writer he particularly adored, but a writer nevertheless. Lawrence Durrell. Just make a slight change—the "u" to an "a". Darrell. It had that musical quality he was looking for, that soft lilt at the end. Perhaps a little too soft. That was his only misgiving. But what name was perfect? A person could grow into a name, somehow try to fit it— wear it without too much suffering. And hear it without too great a jolt to the system.

Martin was a little surprised. As soon as the name slipped off his lips, just two or three seconds later, it was accepted by the others. Even Debrah liked it. That would be the new baby's name, a name he had picked, and now all he had to do was hope that his mother carried inside her a boy.

CHAPTER 13

The Birth

They walked together along the street that overlooked Tel Aviv beach. It was one of the rare times they left the apartment together, walked in public together, were seen by the eyes of the world, by the black penetrating eyes of the city.

Josephine walked with spring in her legs, a scissory two-step on high heels. The shoes gave her just a little bit of extra height. Barefoot, she just barely nudged five feet. It gave her that extra zip, that extra clickety-click which she felt she needed. They stopped, gazing out at the waves. The sun sparkled a bright yellow path all the way to the horizon. The water seemed to seethe, alive and trembling under the sun's outpouring.

"That's wonderful news, Martin. I bet your mother's really happy. You know, it's almost like Sarah all over again. And I bet your dad's proud as punch."

"Yeah, he's pretty pleased."

Josephine gazed out into the waves, the sparkling effervescence.

"You know, Martin, I can't have kids. There's something wrong inside."

"Do you want them?" Martin asked, a hint of surprise in his voice. It was somehow difficult to imagine Josephine, tiny, springy Josephine carrying a baby.

"Sometimes." Her voice was cloudy, not distinct; the word melted into the intense blue of the sky.

"I would like to bring a little girl into the world," she continued. "You know, just somebody I could love. She wouldn't be messed up either. I'd teach her right from the beginning."

Josephine drew on her cigarette with determination. Her small mouth gripped the tip, almost crunched it. She tilted her head and expelled the smoke towards the sky.

"What would you teach her?" Martin smiled, thrusting both hands into his pockets.

"Love," Josephine declared. "That's the most important lesson, isn't it? How to love. I'd let her see me do it. I wouldn't want her to have any embarrassment about her body. I'd read to her. All the best love poems. I'd read her Song of Songs every night."

Yes, Martin thought, the Song of Solomon was one of Josephine's favorites. She had introduced him to it, curling her mouth around the images. She identified with the black and comely sister, the outcast, the Shulamite. "And I command ye, O daughters of Jerusalem, not to wake my love before he stirs."

"You need a husband, don't you?"

Josephine laughed a little nervously, sardonically.

"No. I could do it alone. You know, Martin, this story about your parents has really inspired me. I can have an operation if I want, get my baby ducts opened up."

She gazed out at the trembling blue and whiteness of the Mediterranean. She stamped her right heel against the pavement. The leather snapped. Josephine looked determined.

"I think I'm going to do just that. Yes, that's what I'm going to do. I've decided. I'm going to make an appointment to go into the hospital and have it done."

"Are you sure that's what you want to do?"

"Sure, I'm sure. I'm feeling more sure every minute. This will sound stupid, but I feel I have a responsibility to bring an intelligent human being into the world. Christ, just look around. All kinds of people without a sensitive bone in their bodies. Martin, it's people like you and me that should be having children."

It almost sounded good to Martin—for a minute to contemplate it. But it was really the last thing that he wanted to do. He had a strong image of himself holding a warm bottle, slurping the milk into a tiny awaiting mouth. The mouth curled and gasping, crying and sucking, all at the same time. He could see himself baby-sitting night after night, rocking a cradle, holding a tiny fragile body in his arms, trembling lest he drop it.

"I'm going to wait awhile," he grinned. There was a bite to his grin, an almost too-obvious sarcasm.

"You are kind of young," Josephine admitted, "but did you ever think of it this way?—you're old enough to be the father of that baby your mother's going to have."

Yes, he had thought of it. It was perfectly obvious to him, perfectly true. It came to him as a weird thought sometimes, a perverted train of reverie that he tried his best to dismiss from his mind. Late at night the thought had nudged its way into his half-slumbering head. Had he taken a sleepwalk one evening into his parents' room and somehow... but he dismissed this ridiculous tangle of nonsense inside him. It was his mother and father's doing, as it should be, according to what was right and moral—their baby, their doing, their autumnal inspiration.

"Yes," he answered vaguely, then snapped back. "But it's their business, not mine. I've got a lot of things to do before I start thinking of that."

"Will you come to see me in the hospital?" Josephine asked.

"Sure."

The reply slipped too quickly from his lips, too easily. What else could he answer? Here was the woman he was sleeping with, eating with. It wouldn't be right not to visit her in the hospital. Yet he was not at all sure.

That evening before she went to bed, Josephine stood in front of the washroom mirror. The glass reflected back her shoulders, the tops of her breasts just above the nipples. But that wasn't what she wanted to look at. She nipped out to the kitchen and carried in a chair. She climbed up. Now she was looking down at her belly and her breasts. Her face was no longer visible. "Shit," she muttered under her breath, "I wish I had a full-length mirror." This would have to do: the reflected image of her breasts, her stomach, her legs above the knees. She protruded her belly, sticking it out as far as she could. She tried to visualize herself nine months pregnant. She smiled to herself, then frowned. Did she look pregnant or just simply bloated like one of the starving people in India? How beautiful, she dreamed, how sensual and lovely, glowing and satisfied, a woman looked carrying her first child. A live thing growing. The tiny hands and feet already formed, even the eyelashes flickering.

She had watched them for years on buses, on park benches, crossing the street. How stately and fruitful they carried themselves, so proud and content with the round sack of life inside them. It was true—that was when a woman reached the peak of her beauty. Not a superficial attractiveness, the lure of an eighteen-year-old model or beauty queen, but a full, womanly, motherly, life-giving beauty. It shone from their damp eyes, from the new glow in their cheeks.

Even the chubbiness of their arms was attractive, not only attractive but sensual. She would never tell anybody, not even Martin, but at certain times she had gotten excited just gazing at one, and felt a tingle and slight dampness between her legs. She smiled again as this suspect feeling coursed through her.

Her own condition—it was unnatural: the tangle of tubes inside her, the blocked passageway. It was almost cruel. Certainly unfair. She was being prevented from experiencing one of the richest things. To bear a child. To have the sperm unite with the ova, a new life springing up inside her, growing, being fed from her own blood-stream, and finally issuing from her loins. Tomorrow she would make the appointment. She had delayed long enough.

Martin stretched out on the cot in Josephine's livingroom-bed-room. He always got into bed first. It gave him a chance to think, dream, to float and relax before Josephine joined him. He was thinking of her baby ducts, the clogged tubes that wound their way up to her womb. He had never given them too much thought before. On their first night together, he had questioned Josephine about prophylactics. "Don't worry," she smiled, "I can't have babies." It had been a relief to him. No worry about safes or diaphragms. As the days went by, he didn't give the thing a second thought. He just took it for granted. Josephine couldn't have babies and that was that. But that day out near Tel Aviv beach, the whole matter had taken a new twist. He almost regretted telling her about his mother. Her reaction surprised him, so quick and decisive, with hardly a second thought.

His head was almost dizzy now, thinking, visualizing the doctor's scissors and scalpel at work, cutting, trimming, opening the fibres of flesh, making a path to her hungry womb. But she would have to have this baby with someone else. Certainly she couldn't be thinking of making him into a father. He wondered about it. Was she plan-ning something? Even scheming? No, it was ridiculous. She knew damn well he was only twenty-one, with no means of supporting anybody, not a single book of writing to his name. No definite plans for the future. Certainly she realized he was just floating along, trying to find his way, to figure things out. What he was clutching, she certainly knew, was as flimsy as a straw in a hurricane—the hope that some day he would get a feeling about life, just an inkling of what was going on, and then, almost miraculously, by the edge of his teeth, scribble it down on paper.

Josephine came dancing into the room, her arms above her head, imitating a ballerina.

"Oh Martin, I feel so good tonight. The best I've felt in years. Do you know why?"

Martin gazed at the ceiling, fixing his eyes on one particular crack in the plaster.

"Not really," he fibbed.

"Oh, you do so. It's the best decision I've ever made. Martin, I learned something today. A woman isn't really a woman until she has a child. It sounds old-fashioned, but it's true."

Martin didn't answer. How did he know if it were true or not? He didn't have a womb inside him, nor any yearning for a seed to travel up his innards. What could he say?

"Don't look so glum," she laughed. It was a high-pitched whinny, almost shrill. "I'm not going to run out and have the operation and make you a daddy tomorrow."

She came over and sat beside him on the bed. She placed a small hand on his forehead.

"I need to do it, Martin. Even if I don't have a child. Just to know that it's possible, that my insides are untangled. You understand, don't you?"

"Yes, I think so," he sighed.

Did he understand? Wombs and ducts, vaginas and seeds, stomachs billowing, babies being born one a minute all over the blasted earth.

"Martin, will you come to see me in the hospital?"

"Yes."

"Do you promise?"

"Yes, I promise," he said wearily, a tired, heavy sensation in his chest.

"What will you bring me?" she asked, cuddling up beside him, her eyes glimmering like a little girl's, her face gazing expectantly into his.

"Flowers?" he asked.

"Yes, flowers. Please, no chocolates, Martin. I'm still on my diet."

"No, no chocolates," he promised.

"Martin? I want you to bring me roses, red roses. O.K?"

"O.K., Josephine. Let's go to sleep."

He was happy when she agreed. It was one of the few evenings he didn't feel like making love. He just felt too tired, vague, half-asleep, uninspired.

It was cool that evening in Tel Aviv. Before they went to sleep, Josephine asked him to turn on the electric heater beside the bed. It was a long coil, protected by a wire mesh, that rested on the floor. In the middle of the night Martin awoke, slipped from Josephine's grip, and walked to the washroom. In bare feet he padded along the cool tiles of the floor. On the way back he could hardly see a thing, still blinded by the bright glare from the washroom lights. Suddenly, he heard a cracking sound beneath his left foot. Fuck it, he thought, he had stepped on the heater. Josephine didn't awake. He pulled the plug out of the wall. He checked his foot. No, no blood, but he was sure the element on the heater was cracked beyond repair. What a loud snapping noise it had made! In the morning he would have to apologize, apologize sincerely and profusely. What a clumsy, stupid thing to do. He felt very bad about the heater. In the morning he would really have to apologize, and maybe offer to buy a new one. He didn't know where he would get the money. But he had to offer, in the morning, in the morning. Apologize in the morning, his mind yawned as he drifted off to sleep.

*   *   *

His mother billowed inch by inch, even her face looked larger, moon-soft, moon-big. The baby, his baby brother, was growing inside her, wrestling against the walls of her womb. Struggling, fighting, curling hands into fists. She could feel him kicking, the feet nudging against her, tickling, stretching her. She asked Martin to place a hand on her tummy, to feel the tremor, the kick, the flung foot. Hesitantly, he reached out the tips of his fingers to touch.

"Don't be afraid, Martin. It won't bite you." His mother guided his hands with sweaty fingertips. "Did you feel it?"

He had just barely touched her billowing tummy through the sheer fabric of the nightie. He wasn't sure. Had there been a tiny ripple of flesh beneath the soft pad of his fingers? It made him feel squeamish inside to touch this life-beat. It made his knees water, his head dizzy, as if he were standing on a cliff, a little too close to the edge. It was too real, too close. He had a similar feeling about listening to a person's heartbeat. The thump-thumps were just too charged with blood, too deafening. How fragile it seemed to him when he got his ear or finger this close to a live, pulsating thing. He felt as if it could burst without warning, suddenly explode, the heart splitting its sack of thin-walled flesh, the womb and ambiotic fluid breaking suddenly its confines.

"It makes me feel funny inside . . . " he admitted, "to touch it."

His mother smiled. It was a large, warm, benevolent smile which wrinkled the corners of her eyes. Even the wrinkles looked beautiful. They were essential too. Josephine was absolutely right. There was something about a pregnant woman, a beauty as old as the apple tree in the Garden of Eden. He thought at the beginning it was going to look ugly. A big stomach hanging out, a woman puking over a toilet every morning. Yet his mother did puke every morning, the sweat popping out on her forehead. Even this was beautiful, and necessary. It tingled his stomach. Warm tentacles moved up through his chest.

A month after she made her decision, Josephine went into the hospital to get her innards untangled. A day passed, two days, three. He knew she was going to be there for a week, but he didn't make any move to use a telephone, to call the hospital's front desk, to enquire about the room number or visiting hours. It was unfair, he thought. The doctors' knives had twisted inside her. She had come out of the heavy cloud of the anesthetics. Slowly, with a stone of reluctance growing in his chest, he began to realize that he was not going to make the promised visit. No young man of twenty-one with a beard barely fuzzing his cheeks would walk to the front desk carrying a bouquet of red roses. There would be no Martin Kanner asking the nurses directions to her room.

He didn't want to look like a father in front of all the nurses with their starched white hats, their black bands that indicated their position in the hospital hierarchy. But she wasn't having a baby, his mind clanged. The right side of his mind answered: Yes, but she's twenty-eight, too old, it would look ridiculous. The left side: Yes, but can't she pass for a little younger? The right: They're going to see you as too young, a fuzzless boy with a bouquet of crinkling cellophane, with shaky fingers. The left: You owe it to her, Martin. You ate her food, entered her body, read her books, told her you love her. The right: But she's mies, just too forlorn and ragged-eared. It went on and on, the clanging dialogue in his brain. He went to sleep in the afternoons to forget the squabble. The days passed. Four, five. His last chance. Six, seven. It was too late. He had slept through Josephine's trial, the time she needed him most.

She was out of the hospital and back home by now. Her innards were slowly healing. He knew she was back home convalescing, thinking about the bouquet she never received. How could he ever walk up that staircase again on Sholom Aleichem Street? How could he possibly ever ignore his guilt, and knock at that old familiar door of that rooftop apartment? With tears of anger, frustration, guilt in his eyes, he decided to forget her. It was all a dream—from beginning to end. A mirage, an illusion. It never happened. No ad was ever placed in the Jerusalem Post. No Miss Laver ever answered. He never lived with any twenty-eight-year old woman. There was no operation, no promise of roses. There was no hospital he should've gone to. He had done nothing wrong, nothing lowly or obscene.

You liar!—his guts screamed. You fake! You phony! You with buttery words of love smeared all over your lips. You folded when she needed you most. You went into hiding, you cracked and buckled. How can you look at yourself in the mirror? She was waiting all alone in the hospital. Hardly a single visitor. Her seared tummy ached. Martin will come today, I know he will. Alone, she waited with no father or mother, sister or brother to visit her. You, her best friend, her closest friend in all of Israel, for you the poor girl waited. He probably had something to do, her mind reasoned, he'll come tomorrow. Ha! You prick! She was absolutely wrong that time, dead wrong.

He groaned in his sleep, whined, cried out. The accusing voices rose and fell. Waves cracking against rock. He dreamed. He was six years old again walking along Macdonald Street. He was carrying an ice cream, a strawberry ice cream home from the corner store. Watch out! Watch out, Martin, there's a dog across the street, a burly black German shepherd. Watch out for your bare arm, Martin, your soft chubby arm. The dream was merciful. It didn't make him feel the teeth snapping through the flesh again. It spared him that pain of fifteen years ago. But the dream continued. He had a ragged doll in his hand. How tired he felt walking up the alleyway to his house. He was crying. Sobbing. The doll smelled like strawberry ice cream. There were teeth marks all over the rubber flesh. One ear chewed off. The stuffing hanging out of the legs. He threw it away before he entered the house. It landed among the huge, veined, green leaves of the cabbage weeds. It disappeared in the long grass.

He never breathed a word to his parents about Josephine's operation. Night after night he slept in the Ramat Aviv apartment. During the day he read books, gobbling them up one after another, obsessively. He left the apartment for two or three hours a day. He performed his duties at Berlitz, received his meagre pay every two weeks. When he left the apartment the glare of the sun bothered his eyes. The voices of people joking and gossiping pierced through his ears. The world outside looked ugly. Huge slabs of concrete. Sunshot windowpanes. Tires squealing around corners, brake-linings whining. Horns honking. Dark swarthy faces. People in stores smelling of marinated herring. What an ugly place the world outside the pages of books was. It had no order or harmony. No rhythm. Not a speck of gentle loveliness. How sharp and brutal it was, compared to the lilting lines he bathed his eyes in. How was it possible to make any sense out of it? Sirens screeching. People dying of heart attacks and old age. Men arguing with one another, shaking their fists, spitting curses in each other's faces. He didn't want to be part of it. He wanted it to disappear completely.

He clung to the novels he was reading. If only they could replace the world. If only he could live forever on Steinbeck's Cannery Row, or take an eternal Passage to India.

"Martin, aren't you seeing Josephine any more?" his mother asked one evening as the family sat together around the dining-room table, eating the last crumbs of supper.

"No." He shook his head.

"Is it all over?" she asked.

"Yeah. It's all over."

"But you were so close."

Martin coughed, a lump in his throat.

"Dahlia," his father commanded, "leave him alone. He has his reasons. Maybe he got tired of her. Those things happen, you know."

His mother bit down on her words. Martin let out a long sigh which seemed to circle the table, rise to the ceiling, dissipate in the cigarette smoke.

"I'll just have to find someone else," he grinned.

The grin was not convincing. It was a stretched curve of flesh that he forced to appear. His face felt tight as plastic, not quite real, a mask he was wearing. It was an awful feeling. He could actually feel that he was wearing his own face.

"Sure," his father grunted, "there are plenty of fish in the sea. Just play the field for a while, Martin. There's lots of time before you have to get serious. I'd give my eye-teeth to be your age again."

If only his father knew what he was going through. Would he really hand over his eye-teeth?

* * *

The day they had all been waiting for finally arrived. Martin's mother had passed through the dangerous eighth month. Why it was dangerous, this dark eighth month, Martin did not understand completely. The baby could be born upside down, or lopsided, or without oxygen—he wasn't sure what the problem was exactly; but a baby born on the black eighth month could endanger the mother's life as well as its own. They had all gone through the tense misgivings of that month together, shuddering together, hoping that the water would not decide to burst prematurely. Martin was relieved when the last day of that month dawned. He could finally heave a sigh of relief. One more obstacle had been passed, a narrow creaky passage navigated.

Dr. Goodman had been gentle with Dahlia Kanner, talking to her in a warm soft voice as his bony yet gentle hands parted her legs, showed her the exercises that would guarantee a straightforward birth. There were long talks between them in Dr. Goodman's office, his gravelly-soft voice, word by word, building her confidence.

"Just stretch yourself, Dahlia, as far as you will go. Then relax, let everything relax. Stretch, relax. That's it, dear, you're getting it."

Under Dr. Goodman's warm knowing glance, Dahlia stretched her body as she had never stretched it before in her life. So much depended on it. This she knew. What a horrible two days of pain and anguish she had experienced with Martin. What a burden, now, on Jake it would be, if she could not deliver this baby easily, without worrying him. And she wanted to do it for herself and Dr. Goodman. So many people would be let down if it were another messy affair. And she knew damn well that in this day and age they would never use the forceps, instead they would slice an opening through her soft tummy to let the baby out. It was too much to contemplate. The scarred flesh. The stitches. The unnecessary pain. She was going to believe Dr. Goodman, have complete faith in him down to the very last minute. Stretch and relax, yes, stretch until every fibre in her body stretched and yearned to meet the walls. And then relax, yes, as Dr. Goodman instructed, completely relax until she was nothing more than a ball of fluff. Relax so much that a breath from Dr. Goodman could blow her across the room.

"I think I'm getting the idea," she said hesitantly, her well-formed lips lingering on each word.

"Sure you are, Dahlia. You're doing wonderfully. Let me tell you something, you're better than some of these young sabra girls. Your whole heart's in this, isn't it?"

Dahlia smiled, allowing her eyelids to shut, not answering, letting her smile answer.

What a wonderful doctor he was. She told Jake about their sessions together, about the exercises that were making her feel so good. She was amazed. Here she was, forty-two and pregnant, in this strange country, without a close friend or relative to confide in, yet her body and her mind felt wonderfully at ease. She felt younger than she had for years, a little chubbier, perhaps, around the upper arms, but how smooth and toned her skin looked. How much spring and strength she was beginning to feel in her legs. Jake Kanner listened attentively to Dahlia's glowing, enthusiastic descriptions of Dr. Goodman. He had never met the man, but it seemed that he already knew him and he was looking forward to the time when they could meet face to face. Jokingly, when the family had been gathered together in the living room, in fact on several light-hearted occasions, he had said:

"I tell you, Martin, I think your mother's got something going with that guy."

"Oh Jake," Dahlia gasped, her eyelids fluttering.

"See, Martin. She's blushing. Just think, I get her pregnant after eighteen years, no mean feat, and she runs off with her obstetrician. That would make quite a story, wouldn't it?"

Martin's face rippled with amusement. Debrah giggled, sitting very close to her mother, her hand reaching out from time to time to gently cup her mother's tummy. It would make quite a story. But it was unthinkable—this Martin knew. His mother had always seemed inextricably attached to his father. They had their ups and downs, squabbles and jealousies, but to Martin it always seemed that they were attached just as securely as the moon was locked in its orbit around the earth. He always had the feeling that if his father ever left his mother, she would fly off into space wildly, careening without an anchor, and finally crash. But the opposite also seemed true. What could Jake do without Dahlia? She had listened day after day for almost twenty-five years to his stories, to his ambitions, to his angers and even his lusts. Martin himself had heard these stories until he knew each line before it dropped from his father's mouth. His mother was a vast unwavering ear, an ocean of listening, a universe of assent. Into her Jake poured every speck of worry, every whoop of egotism, and Dahlia had kept nodding, approving, listening.

The hopeful, magic day had finally arrived, and by some quirk of fate, already it had an extra meaning, an extra jolt of excitement. It was a Saturday morning, the Sabbath, the hushed day in Israel when all the corrugated doors fell from Haifa to Eilat, closing everything down. A quiet descended on the noisy streets, a sleepy hush throughout the country. It was the day that no business could be enacted, no drinks drunk, no wild carousing permitted in bars and hotels. The business world came to a stand-still. But giving birth, that was different, it was necessary and allowed. In the Jewish tradition there was a specialness attached to a Sabbath baby. It was as if he had a head-start right from the beginning. Martin didn't understand what exactly it meant, but a child born on a Saturday, on Jehovah's day of rest, when He stepped aside from tossing darkness and light, planets and stars, into the void, when He stepped back, gave a sigh of relief, wiped His magnificent brow, on that day a new-born baby was somehow imbued with a special aura of holiness.

So be it, Martin thought. Let this baby be born on the magic, hushed Sabbath, in the country of his forefathers, from a mother barren for eighteen years, to a father who resembled Moshe Dayan, to a brother who took two days to come into the world, as if he knew already in that dark hiding-place that the world was not a place for him to leap into, not a place to jump wildly at: a place to have reservations about. Martin had cowered in the darkness for two days; this he could never forget. It was a story he knew as well as his own name. How his mother shook and trembled, cried out. Was he imagining it, or could he actually feel on this Sabbath morning in the waiting room, what it was like in that dark, warm cave? How he smashed and smashed with his tiny fists, striking out, pounding, hitting, fighting and fighting with no results. Left fist. Right. Smash. Bang. How constricted it was beginning to feel in there. How he just had to smash his way through. Then, suddenly, something big reached in, a huge powerful thing twisted him around so that his head would face the entry. Wow! What power! In a second, he was turned completely around, a full one hundred and eighty degrees. Turned, as if he were nothing more than a tiny grain, shifted all the way around.

The rest he could not remember, or even imagine as vividly. But it must have been a red-hot, searing pain when the teeth of the forceps locked on his tender cheek, locked resolutely and with force. Terrific pain and agony as he was hauled through the too-narrow passage, the constricted walls of flesh, yanked into the glare of the operating room. His head was pressed by the narrow, agonizing squeeze into a dome of red soreness.

He prayed in the waiting room that this birth would in no way resemble his own. Let it be smooth, he kept thinking, smooth and simple and straightforward. Let his mother's exercises, her confidence in Dr. Goodman, now bear fruit. Let him now keep all his promises, his wonderful predictions. His mother had been very excited. Dr. Goodman had pressed his ear to her belly, not just once but several times—his ear and the stethoscope, the magic stethoscope that could listen to even a breath below the hundredfold layers of flesh. After careful, attentive, experienced listening he had predicted this Saturday morning, had predicted the birth of a boy, and had predicted the time of arrival down to the last half hour. Martin glanced at his father's watch. If Dr. Goodman was correct, if he knew what he was talking about, if he had not just babbled and bleated like the old women selling spices and silk in the open-air market, then Darrell Kanner, his baby brother, should slip into the world in about twenty minutes.

It was quiet in the waiting room that Saturday morning, a large room set aside near the back of the hospital, curtained with water-falling white muslin, as if the room were designed for quiet intakings of breath and thought. The sabbath stillness nudged at the room, the room dripped back into the Saturday hush. It was as if the room was set up to be a sabbath of its own, not a place to jabber and argue, nor to joke wildly, a place to seep into one's own stillness.

Jake Kanner sat with one leg slung over the other, a coolness in his sun-darkened face, yet his molars continually ground together beneath his ears. A tiny, controlled mincing of his teeth against each other, slowly, inevitably grinding away at any problem.

Debrah sat in her own stillness. Rarely was she ever quite that still, her eyes aimed at her lap, her whole being turned inward.

Martin paced the waiting room, trying to hush the click of leather against the tile floor. Occasionally, he glanced at his father, but Jake averted his eyes, avoided meeting Martin's directly.

Martin found himself standing by the window that looked upon the hospital garden. The sun was shining on the grass this March day, stroking it, weaving in and out of the grass, and gliding over small heaps of cut grass which had already yellowed. Through the heaps of hay he was amazed to see a legion of cats playing. At first he rubbed his eyes. It looked like something out of a dream: cats by the dozen, old grey disheveled beasts, small tongue-licked kittens. But no, it was real, these cats in the hospital garden. They were sliding through the grass, enjoying the sun. How simply they moved. When they got tired they merely flopped down, took a rest, napped. It looked like generations of these fluffy, nonchalant beings had been born in this very place. Died in this place. Gamboled here beside the waiting room. They had seen it all through the green slits of sidelong glances—all, every type: the pacers, the chewers, the grinders, the criers, the laughers; those that nibbled on their shirt collars; those that took innumerable walks to the washroom to relieve their bladders. The waiters they had seen, the expectant papas, and brothers, sisters and aunts, *zeydes* and *bubahs*. They were laughing to themselves. Oh, how they worry, these folks with hairless skins.

The cats were talking to Martin, whispering. "Can't you take it easy, silly boy? The world doesn't hang on the vigor of your pacing, no, not for a second. It goes on and on and on through an infinity of Saturdays. Don't you realize, quirky lad, we have played here from the beginning of time? Danced here, slept, fornicated, given birth, died." They giggled at him. They were so right, Martin thought.

What was his worry going to accomplish? It was beyond him, just as
surely as the sun's rising was beyond him, it was out there happening, and if he paced until the tiles were worn thin, until the hospital
disappeared, it would still be beyond his control.

* * *

Dahlia Kanner had trusted Dr. Goodman completely, so much, in
fact, that she decided to give birth without the help of anesthetics. It
made sense to her. How could she help bring this baby into the
world if her limbs were numb, and her tongue thick with artificial
sleep? How could she stretch, push, relax, urge the new life forward
unless every muscle toned through months of exercises in Dr. Goodman's office, unless every fibre was aware, willing, ready to do its
utmost? She had been afraid of the pain, but she decided to take
part in the birth of this child.

Now, it was happening. "Push, Dahlia, stretch, push, remember
your exercises." Dr. Goodman's gentle, soft, penetrating voice filtered down at her through his mask. Not a single drop of anesthetic
had been leaked into her veins. The delivery room was more real to
her than her own kitchen: the lights, the faces hovering above her,
the table, the flat, hard table beneath her buttocks. And there was
pain, but she didn't care any more, she concentrated on pushing,
stretching, relaxing, taking those gentle periods of utter surrender,
before she pushed again, expelling with every muscle that ran along
her legs, that rippled on her tummy. She was determined. This was
one time, maybe the only time, but one time at least when she had
decided that she was going to do it come hell or high water. Crazy
thoughts from the past nudged at her mind. Her mother's paralysis,
the frozen left side, the words that would no longer come from her
mouth. But no, it was no time for thoughts like that. Stretch, Dahlia,
an inner voice commanded, you can do it, she whispered to herself,
stretch as if you were reaching for the morning star, for the most
gorgeous gem in the universe. Now relax, Dahlia, Dahlia Kanner,
relax, let yourself melt, let yourself become as light as a breath, just
one eensy-teensy breath.

"Dahlia," Dr. Goodman whispered excitedly into her ear, "you're
almost there, dear. Just a few more times."

And she could feel it between her legs, the pressure building,
growing, approaching a climax. Oh yes, it just had to give. She knew
it had to, her whole insides were stretched to the breaking point.

Tighter and tighter it felt. How tight could it get without splitting her apart? She didn't want to be left in two split pieces on the table. Is there enough room?—she wanted to cry out to Dr. Goodman. But no, that was a waste of time now, she had to concentrate, push one last, final time.

Then it happened, it happened, it happened. An unbelievable feeling between her legs, in her vagina, a shudder that rushed into her stomach, up to her head, an explosion, and all she saw behind her closed eyelids were bright red lights flashing. An explosion! And then, thank God, oh merciful God, a relief of pressure, of stretching, and even a relief of intense pain.

"It's a boy," announced Dr. Goodman. "You did it, Dahlia, not a scratch on him. Not a mark. Oh, you should be so proud of yourself, Mrs. Kanner. Come on, let's see you smile."

Dahlia was crying with tears of relief. But she smiled, smiled and cried at the same time. What an explosion, she thought to herself, remembering back one minute to the moment of birth. Never in her entire life had she felt anything like it—that shudder of feeling that wrapped every inch of her body. No, there was nothing in the world to compare with it. It was as if every orgasm she had ever experienced had come to focus in that single moment. And still that was not, she felt, an adequate way to describe it.

"Dahlia," Dr. Goodman whispered, "take one little look at your son. We'll bring him down to you later. I think you should rest now. We'll give you something to help you get some sleep. O.K.?"

"Yes," she whispered back.

Now she could have something, just a small something to help her drift off, just for a few hours, drift into the quiet pool that she deserved. She just got a single glance at her new baby before they whisked him away, and Dr. Goodman was so right: there was no redness to his skin, no scar or mark, just a smooth covering of flesh. She felt the needle sliding and stinging into her leg. Her eyelids fell silently. Sleep, that was all she wanted to do now—a well-deserved rest. She had done it, and she was happy.

CHAPTER 14

A Short Journey

It was impossible, this life he was leading in Tel Aviv. How narrow
and confined it had become, a dark rut he walked in, from Berlitz to
the apartment in Ramat Aviv. He hadn't seen Josephine in months,
not since she entered the hospital. He wasn't at all sure he was ever
going to see her again.

There was an excitement when his baby brother was a new fresh
thing, a thrill on the day of his birth when Dr. Goodman came
directly from the operating room. His hands had been freshly
washed, smelling of disinfectant and soap. The long-awaited meeting
took place between the two men: Dr. Goodman and Jake Kanner.

"Perfect," he enunciated, extending a cleansed hand towards Martin's father. "It went perfect, my dear Mr. Kanner. What a brave
little lady your wife is. You should be very proud of her."

"We are," Jake managed to murmur, a little surprised at Dr.
Goodman's enthusiasm for Dahlia's courage.

He had never thought about her in that way. Quite the opposite,
in fact. It surprised Martin, too, to find out that his mother had gone
through the birth without a single drop of anesthetic. Was this his
mother Dr. Goodman was talking about? Perhaps there was some
mistake. But no, it was Dahlia Kanner, and she had given birth
without anything to kill the pain.

The news sounded almost too good to be true. The baby in
perfect health, delivered as promised, his mother resting, also in
perfect condition. No mess, no fuss, no forceps or hysterics. All
done according to schedule and plan.

There was a basic similarity between the two faces: Jake Kanner's
and Dr. Goodman's. They were both faces of men who looked like
they could be dropped into the middle of a strange forest, and left
with nothing but their instincts and cunning to survive. Both, some-

how, would find their way out. And if they didn't, Martin mused, they would grow the skins of beasts, become immune to cold and heat. They would learn to eat raw berries and fish, lie down at night under a covering of darkness and stars. Grow their teeth longer if they had to.

And there was a difference. His father's eyes shifted faster in their orbits. They were blacker, more penetrating for fast intense seconds, but they didn't have the steady warmth which flowed from Dr. Goodman's. Dr. Goodman seemed to inhabit his face with greater ease, not tightening and relaxing the muscles as quickly.

"Wait a few minutes," Dr. Goodman suggested, "then you can go down and take a look at the new baby."

Before Dr. Goodman left, he and Jake shook hands once again. Jake grasped the hand, pumped it, let his fingers linger. It was as if he wanted to thank him in this way, to transmit his gratitude through the heat in his palms.

"We are grateful," Jake said in a soft subdued voice. "We are grateful for everything you have done. You know, Dr. Goodman, it's a good thing you're a married man. If you weren't, I might wake up one morning . . . "

Dr. Goodman chuckled, shaking Jake's hand more vigorously, looking directly into his eyes. The sentence was left unfinished. Dr. Goodman placed an arm around Jake's shoulder, squeezing it. Jake beamed. He almost looked small now, even fragile, standing beside the doctor.

It was exciting too when Jake, Debrah and Martin walked together down the long waxed glossy hallway to the place where the newly-born babies rested in their cribs. They marched together, the blood singing inside them. It was as if a battle had just been fought, the final conflict of a long war, and their side had won. Victoriously, they marched along, nothing to worry about now, the war over, a sweet tingle buzzing inside them.

Martin pressed close to the window to get a good look at his new brother, the soft bundle of blanket and flesh. Smooth and new, he yawned and cried. A small bundle of flesh just beginning, starting, crying.

And it had been exciting to hear his mother describe what she felt in the delivery room. Rarely had he seen her face that animated by excitement, the sentences emerging quickly, spontaneously, as she hit upon words to describe it.

It had all happened months ago, and it was over. Martin slipped back into the routine of his life in Tel Aviv. In Jerusalem he had made friends easily, people he had gotten close to, but Tel Aviv was a harder place. He had made no close friends except for Josephine. Day after day he took the bus into the core of the city, taught his classes, but it was all a tremendous effort. At times he felt like a robot, just wound up by a force beyond his control, and set going. To the bus he creaked his way, to the school, back again. The whole process was becoming unbearable. What was he doing it for? Just to survive? Just to fill in time? He began to question his very presence in Israel. Certainly things had been better, or could be better, back in Canada. But how was he going to get back, to cross three thousand miles of European continent, and then four thousand more of surly brine?

Neil, an English Jew who also taught at Berlitz, a lean-faced wiry person who wore glasses and maintained a palish complexion under the cloudless sky, Neil was planning to putt-putt back to England in June. Why couldn't Martin, he suggested, travel with him, share car expenses, and then, once in England, look for work aboard one of the merchant vessels that were heading towards New York or Montreal? Why not, indeed, Martin wondered. The only hitch was money, and a gnawing doubt inside him whether he could travel those foreign roads all the way to England without conflict with Neil; and if it turned out that he had to travel alone, would he be able to cross the borders of all those countries, sleep in flophouse after flophouse, eat bowl after bowl of mush, travel through all the lands that jabbered their own strange tongues, do this without losing his bearings, without cringing, fearing, even going a little mad?

What seemed to most people not a great Herculean task, but a straightforward journey with a friend from Tel Aviv to London, then on a boat across the foaming sea—this, to Martin, was not something so simple as rubbing lint off his sleeve. No, not simple at all. Thousands of students did this sort of thing every year, made a semi-adventure out of it, as they tasted and sniffed the air and sensibility of each slice of European earth that bore a different name, spoke a distinct language, smelled of its own vegetables and sweat. It bugged him that he couldn't even contemplate such a trek with ease. Just the worry of two countries in a row boggled his mind, the unknown factors, the hidden ways of life, the impressions hitting him just too fast. He knew very well what could easily happen. Too many flashes of light and noise, from the left, from the right, from dead centre, the ache rising through his feet, his nose assaulted, his ears jammed, and finally his mind swinging wildly this way and that like an unhinged door—a bar door in an old movie during a fight, cracked and swinging, splintered and flung into the street.

It could happen: his mind seizing in the middle of the trip, knocking first, then locking, an unoiled motor that refused to function. But he could try, give it a try, even if he knew from the very outset that there was very little chance of ever making it to England.

From his wages at Berlitz he saved a small amount each payday, knowing very well that he would never leave Israel with enough in his pocket to set his mind at ease. The sum he wanted would have to be enough to ensure a complete paid passage on trains and boats all the way to Canada. This was impossible. It would take him at least a year, maybe two, to save such a sum from the deflated Israeli lira. For every three lira, he would receive one honest-to-goodness American dollar with a picture of Washington smiling contentedly, or one Canadian equivalent with the profile of Elizabeth, stately and cool.

The trip began to materialize, a thing growing of itself, a fungus taking root at the base of a tree. He realized almost from the very inception that the endeavor was doomed. A canoe he was building, knowing all along the bark would poop out halfway across the lake, just quietly bubble and sink to its watery rest. Yet he proceeded, the process continued, a plan that was shaping up with very little involvement on his part. Did his parents really believe it when they exchanged what could've been the last goodbyes for many a year, did they really expect him to disappear from their lives? Or did they harbour doubts? Could they really see him working his way across Italy, the Alps, France, and whatever other country happened to block his passage?

The trip was topsy-turvy from beginning to end; it resembled the hodge-podge tumble of buildings in Istanbul, and the young Turks running and walking through the streets in army uniforms, some so poor they wore cardboard shoes. Neil's Volkswagen was placed on the Turkish boat in Haifa.

The first night aboard, Neil leaped from the upper bunk, jumped past Martin, ran to switch on a light.

"Goddammit!" he cursed. "Something's eating me up."

Sure enough, his back had been chewed by something. Red welts and blood speckled his skin. Martin couldn't stop scratching. Neil lunged at his bed, grabbing with his fingernails, pressing something, inspecting it with his lips curled into a sour loop of disgust.

"This is fuckin' ridiculous. The place is infested with bedbugs."

"Oh shit!" Martin gasped, leaping from the lower bunk as if his sheets had suddenly burst into flame.

"We paid our fuckin' money for this crap!?" Neil shouted. "Let's go. C'mon, I'm going down and report this to the captain!"

They never met the captain that morning at one o'clock. Instead, a bleary-eyed steward listened to their complaints.

"Don't you have some way of cleaning up that room?" Neil demanded.

"Yes sir, we do. A bomba. A smoke bomb. It goes phoot! A big explosion, kills every one of those pests. Does the whole thing very queekly, sir."

"Can you do it? Now?"

"Oh, no sir," the steward protested, his brown brow wrinkled, his black eyes bleary with sleep and dismay. "That can only be done when we reach Istanbul. You want a bomb to go off in your room?"

"Istanbul!" Neil shrieked, his pale face flaming with exasperation. "Don't you understand, man?—that's where we get off. What good's that going to do? Fuck, we'll be eaten alive by that time."

The steward began to snicker, a hidden truncated giggle flickering at the corners of his mouth. Martin began to get angry. Everything up to this point, he could with effort stomach and bear, but the smirk on the steward's sleepy face aggravated him, and sent billows of rage flaming through his chest.

"What's so fucking funny?" Martin shouted, clenching his fists. "You clean that fuckin' room up right now! You understand?"

Neil seemed surprised at Martin's outburst. It came so suddenly, without warning. The contrast between Martin's silence and this unexpected belligerence made him feel uneasy.

"Take it easy," he whispered.

"Why should I take it easy?" Martin snapped back. "I'm not going to stand here and take this bullshit from this monkey."

If such a feat were possible, Martin would have liked at this point to swipe both the steward and Neil simultaneously with the back of his hand.

But the anger brought results. The steward began to apologize, and Martin was pleased that he had not vented his burning bile in vain. He was glad that he had inside him a flame that was not easily brushed aside, a flame he did not wish to let out too often, for it tensed his body for hours afterwards; but nevertheless he was pleased that he could call upon it when necessary, and more important, that it brought about the desired results.

"Yes gentlemen, of course, you are right," the steward's voice half-whined and trembled. "Why don't you sleep in the large dormitory? There is no one sleeping there. And I promise, gentlemen, you can be sure, there are no bugs. O.K? Is that good idea?"

"Very good. Very good. Fuckin' tremendous," Neil hissed. "I just want to get back to sleep."

Down the hallway to the dorm Neil muttered under his breath, communicating more with himself than with Martin. "A bomb in Istanbul, what a bunch of fuckin' idiots!"

It was a pleasant surprise to both of them when they discovered that the dorm was free of the vicious vermin. The steward was right, and they had the whole wide room to themselves. It was a puzzle, though, to Martin: a thing he mulled over for many months, even years to come—how was it possible for their original cramped room, just down the hall from the dorm, to be overrun with bedbugs, and this neighboring abode fresh and clean without a hint of the pests? Was it possible that they had imagined the whole thing? But no, he had seen the welts on Neil's back and felt the red lumps on his own. Yet he still doubted. Could the imagination raise such mirages of itching on the skin, could worry and fear draw blood?

* * *

Around the same time, in June of 1963, Britta Lystrom was travelling in the opposite direction. By boat and train, by car, and by foot, she had picked her way through France, Germany, Italy. A photo-story of Israel lingered in her mind. It was many months ago that she had read about kibbutz life in Stockholm, her hometown. Turkey was the very last country on her route before she would set foot in the biblical land, a place she knew very little about, an image she tried to reconstruct from stories she had heard in Sunday school. Was it really a land of milk and honey with long stretches of desert, with those wonderful communal farms growing like flowers? The people in the photos had fascinated her: sweat dripping from their dark foreheads, rifles slung nonchalantly over their shoulders.

They could've been in Istanbul at the same time, in different youth hostels, perhaps. It was possible that they could've almost bumped into one another at the Grand Bazaar, Martin apologizing and allowing the blond stranger to cross in front of him.

Instead of meeting Britta in Istanbul, Martin had a short conversation with a Norwegian boy. The dormitory was empty except for the two of them. The others, including Neil, had left early in the morning. They wanted to gaze once again at the wonders of the city: the chairless Blue Mosque, which leaked a holy hush of tile heavenward; the Grand Bazaar, where genuine leather jackets still smelling of ranches and cattle were sold for a measly ten American dollars; womanless coffee houses, where hundreds of men crammed together elbow to elbow, tilting back their sour black brine; street-corners where frenzied young men, espousing some intense political affection, raised their Turkish tongues to the sky, shouted in the face of the four winds, gleefully, angrily, burning newspapers to display their displeasure.

For three days Martin tagged along—down to the Bosporus to dart an eye at the cascading foam, into a mosque to once again hear a tour-guide describe bloodletting of the fifteenth century. He had gone with them, one nonentity amid the bands of student travellers roaming the streets. Among them the young Germans had the reputation of being very determined travellers—they, however, were put down for their fastidious complaints about toilet facilities. Everyone agreed, down to the last weary traveller, that the best voyagers in all Europe, in all the world, in fact, were the Australians. They maneuvered from country to country without a slip of anger on their tongues. They were certainly, it was agreed, the elite. No one could keep up with them, not even the Germans. There was much discussion centering around the reason for their prowess. How could they stay on the road, often for years, and make the route look like a jaunt to the corner store? It was concluded that the Aussies realized they lived at the tilt-end of the globe, and some day they would have to return and grow old there. This was their one chance at globe-trotting, and they made the best of it.

On the fourth morning Martin decided to remain in the youth hostel. The streets no longer enticed him. In fact, he was quite weary of the city, its jumble of buildings. The Norwegian boy looked equally blasted, stretched out on his cot, a pair of cowboy boots hugging his feet. He reminded Martin of his Dutch friend, Jan, his

Dead Sea swimming companion. He had the same long limbs loosely worn.

"Where are you coming from?" Martin asked hesitantly, not wishing to intrude on the hush that wreathed him.

At first he didn't reply, just a vague grunt emanated from his lips, a hard-to-hear acknowledgement that was muffled by the vast silence of the dormitory. Martin was ready to give the whole thing up, to forget he had asked a question. Finally, words swelled on his lips.

"I am returning from India."

"Oh, India."

"A monastery."

The Norwegian tossed his head as if his eyes were trying to avoid a bright light.

"Yes," he continued, "I lived there with the monks for quite a few months. I'm a philosophy student, but I can't think straight any more."

Martin stood by the cot, rocking his weight from one foot to the other. The Norwegian's lips no longer moved.

"Where are you going now?" Martin asked.

"Home. Back home. I'm not going to do anything when I get back. Just think. It's going to take me years to straighten things out. All we are taught in school, it's just not true. There's a big black canyon underneath it. That's what happened. Those monks opened it up, the hole, and everything I believed, everything I thought I was, fell into it."

Yes, mused Martin, that was how he appeared—swallowed by something, still breathing, but completely devoured. Wasn't he, too, feeling a little devoured, consumed yet still functioning in the guts of this Turkish delight?

Martin slowly edged away from the cot. What was this dark emptiness they both felt, the underside of what was taught in high school and university? The world was not at all straightforward or reasonable. It was a geometry problem that never seemed to arrive at the Q.E.D., the final three letters of victory and respite. That which was to be proved. The lines kept curving, making the problem more complex, more difficult to grasp. A miasma of angles, circles, spaces to be interlocked and understood.

The swallows, according to one of his teachers, always returned to Capistrano. Each spring they winged their way back to the pinched crannies of rock and straw. Instinct, she exclaimed, with her glasses sliding down her pinched nose. Wasn't instinct a wonderful thing? She never told them a dark cavern loomed beneath their wings, a place where one could forget how to fly, how to speak, how to do anything except cling for dear life to a cot, trying to be still, trying not to let the mind splinter.

The trip continued with Neil's Volkswagen putting across the Greek-Turkish border. In Istanbul two Jewish girls had hitched a ride with them. They sat in the back seat crammed together, plump hip sliding against plump hip, heads together whispering. Martin found less and less to say to Neil. The feeling was mutual, and a stony silence filled the front of the Volkswagen. An invisible barrier separated the front of the car from the back. It reminded Martin of the tradition of Orthodox synagogues, the ladies separated from the men, as if the former might in some way taint the latter. A block of silence in front. Chit-chat in back.

It was a dark, cloudy day, with the skies threatening to open, but only managing to spit odd drops. That afternoon they circled Mount Olympus, and Martin was not impressed by Zeus' mythical playground. Nothing seemed to distinguish this vague hump of rock, except the stories he had read about it. It was an ordinary mountain in every respect, and as far as Martin was concerned, it could've stood in Nova Scotia and not been out of place.

The silence in front grew. The chit-chat in back degenerated into giggles, reminding Martin of an old blind date with two girls and a fraternity brother. To hell with it, he thought. Let my mouth be stone, my tongue as uninspired as a boulder. The silence seeped into his bones, into the frame of the Volkswagen. Underneath, a tension sizzled, almost a hatred which he couldn't understand.

It was a relief when they finally reached Saloniki, and he could untangle his legs from the cramped front seat. He decided there and then to go his own way. The girls were going to travel all the way to England with Neil. Martin couldn't take another mile of it. It was too much: the giggles in back, the silence in front. No, he decided, he would rather part company in Saloniki, and go the rest of the way alone. Neil didn't argue with him, in fact he seemed relieved.

That was the last Martin saw of him. Sometime the next day Neil and the girls rattled out of town.

The sun shone in Saloniki. It sparkled off the water, giving the whole place a soft dreamy tone, as if in this northern Greek town summer always reigned. A wispy aquamarine melting into a golden sea-washed sun. The hostel was smaller than the one in Istanbul, just a little more bearable. Slowly, his money was dwindling, dollar by dollar. He had started with a slim sum—with a meagre seventy-five. There was no need to worry yet, but he knew very well that soon his pockets would be empty. It was not something he wanted to think about. He had never encountered this problem before, never in his entire life been absolutely penniless. Nothing in his pockets but the cloth they were made from, and a few spent matches. Where would he find work in this Greek fantasy of the north? Where would he sleep if he no longer had the half-dollar to pay for a room in the hostel? What would he eat and drink?

He counted his money again and again, figuring and refiguring the cost of the room, and the bare minimum to put enough in his stomach to survive. For the time being no decision would have to be made. He had enough to coast along on. Why not regard the whole thing as a holiday, until his money reached that dangerous point of no return? There would be time enough then for decisions: where to swing his carcass, in which direction.

With a few casual acquaintances he visited the dank wine cellars. It was a cool place to sit drinking retzina, smoking cigarettes, avoiding the mid-day glare of sun and water. In the underground cavern the Greeks were very friendly, sending wine to their table, packages of cigarettes. Why they received this benevolent treatment, Martin couldn't understand. But he smiled at his benefactors, beamed as his fellow wanderers beamed, surprised and glad that the Greeks lived up to their reputation for hospitality.

Underneath the hot inspired tingles of retzina, and the carnival tones of Greek music, reality nibbled. His money was slowly evaporating.

A couple of Greek boys with whom he had made friends invited him to travel with them to a Greek village in the north. Why not, he thought. Another side-trip. A wedding was scheduled for the afternoon, a classic Greek wedding under sun and sea-spray. And it was inspiring: fife and drum, the couple emerging from the small church, friends of the bride and groom sprinkling wine in their path. It was a perfect sun-splashed wedding, the bride in a long white gown, the lacy hem rustling against the stones. The groom flushed with pride, his black eyes classic and near perfect. It was a thing to rave about, to write poems about, to enter, to become part of, to imbibe, to use as a brilliant wand and with this wand to wave away the outside world: the roads to northern Europe awaiting his decision; the long lean tracks to dark Yugoslavia, and the hustle of Deutschland. Wave it away for the afternoon, the fact that soon he would have to decide.

But the truth attacked his mind. He was not a Greek villager, nor did he play the fife and drum. He was not a bride or black shiny groom, nor even a wine-sprinkling attendant. He was on the road now, alone. The black mysteries of the Baltic beckoning. The Black Forest whispering for his soul. O come penniless waif into the hinterlands. Do you dare to travel north, do you dare leave the sun behind, the fife and drum, the classic beauty, and the village softness? Do you dare turn northward without a friend?

Back in Saloniki he counted his money again. Had he allowed the whole unreasonable farce to go too far? Did he have enough money to return to Israel? He had been away for three weeks, and already the decision was upon him. Was this whole venture for real, or a holiday from beginning to end? A summer joke his insides shared with each other?

Were the last goodbyes to his parents all part of a melancholy play, everyone realizing that it would be a short one-acter? Everyone thinking: after all, that seventy-five dollars isn't going to last forever. Did his parents think to themselves—when he gets hungry, he'll come home. He had run away once as a child. He left with a bagful of cookies, pedalling his bike for the outskirts of the city. Stopping. Nibbling at the cookies. Getting hungrier as his small supply resolved itself into crumbs. "Don't worry," his parents had reassured one another, "when he gets hungry, he'll come home." Was this merely a re-run of a tattered dusty reel?

He was beginning to feel hungry once again. Food was still entering his mouth and dropping into his gut, but an emptiness filled him. When he thought of heading north, all he could visualize was a blank patchwork of cool countries. A tangle of languages. A glut of costumes, the colors merging. How could he jump on a train and ride into this bleak unknown? Was there anything reasonable about this thought? It would be simpler to turn into a coyote, or a fir tree. The decision was making itself. There were not a thousand equal doors open, and he soon realized there were not even two. One and one only. Back he would have to go, his bag of tricks empty.

Thank God for trains, he thought, and the straight tracks they travelled. All he would have to do was plunk down his money, buy a ticket for Istanbul. The wheels would do the rest. The tracks. The conductor unseen, but steady at the throttle. Through light and dark the wheels would carry him: a straight unwavering path from point A to B. They, the tracks, would certainly not jostle him into the woods. Into the cushioned chair he would sink, knowing the next miles would spin without surprises. Just sit, and drift off, watch the trees click by the window, the sun clicking on and off through the branches. Dream and sit and take it easy. The tracks knew exactly where they were going. The long glint of steel contained not a single doubt.

We are going to Istanbul, they sang. We are straight and we are narrow, held together by ties of oak. Parallel and equidistant, nailed to limbs of ancient forests. If only, he wished, his own future were laid out as clearly before him. If only the route he was supposed to take was always going forward to better things. Trees grew from little seeds. Straight and tall they sought the sky. Branches they grew, and a crown of leaves. They didn't travel in dark confusing circles. They grew to a stately height, matured, and eventually died. Bears did not spend their days chasing their tails, or getting lost in circles of their own blindness. Was there anything straight about his life's journey?—he wondered. He could not see any progress. Had he advanced one inch in his chosen art? Had he found love or understanding? Did he understand anything, or had the black hole completely swallowed him?

As the train rolled forward he searched the passing trees for an answer. It scared him. A tree, a passing tree, a presence he was passing forever. He had seen it, yes it existed on the route from Saloniki to Istanbul. But he would never see it again. Friends, old friends in Montreal passed through his mind. Childhood acquaintances in Halifax. He had known people, loved them in his own way, and he had moved on, following his parents. When he was a child, he had protested their moves from street to street. Every three years or so they moved into a new house, into a new section of town. Each time, his friends were erased just as surely as a wet rag doing its allotted job on a blackboard. The slate was wiped clean, and the task of starting anew began again.

Who did he know in Canada? At least in Israel he could count on Josephine still being alive and well on Sholom Aleichem Street. Jesse in Jerusalem. Mr. Townley. He could count on a good meal of cabbage soup when he returned to Ramat Aviv. It would be a surprise like the return of the prodigal. A reunion, a thrill, festivities, a celebration, even if it was short-lived.

In Istanbul he once again counted his money. He tried not to overlook one penny. He compared what he had in his pockets with the price of a boat ticket. He was short. Hungry, and short. Briefly, panic seized him. He looked through his suitcase. Was there something there to sell, something worth ten Turkish dollars? Then he found it with a chuckle in his throat. He knew immediately that it would sell in the Grand Bazaar. Certainly the Turks would snap it up. It was a green corduroy jacket. Not the cheap variety often worn by students. It was a jacket he had purchased with a good chunk of his father's money during his first year at university. It was a jacket, streamlined and trim, bought at Morgan's in Montreal. Yes, it was still there—the Morgan's tag inside the collar.

This time he was right on target. At the first stall he tried, the Turkish salesman held it up to the dust-flecked light. He twirled it a couple of time, his eyes smiling to themselves. There was not even an attempt at haggling.

"You want ten dollars, my friend," the Turk smiled, wiping saliva from the corners of his lips. "Ten dollars you got. Here!"

He snapped the bills towards Martin. With a click of his thumb and forefinger he curled the money into Martin's awaiting hand.

"That's a very good jacket," Martin frowned.

The Turk grinned, his black eyes flashing.

"I know, my friend." He was still grinning, but a sweet sadness filled his voice—the sadness of an overgrown forest past its prime. "I have not seen one like it."

"I bought it from a very good store in Canada."

"Canada" rolled out of Martin's mouth with the rush of a waterfall. It pounced upon the stale air of the Grand Bazaar. What was he trying to do?—Martin wondered to himself. Buy the jacket back again? But the Turk seemed to care.

"You must need the money badly," he said. He was already folding the jacket gently. "I'm going to give this the special treatment. It goes off to the cleaners in the morning."

"Well I've got to go," Martin mumbled. He had run out of things to talk about.

"Au revoir, my friend," the Turk gently smiled. "Ah yes," he sighed, "a beautiful piece of material."

Martin turned in a single motion, and shuffled along the dusty concrete. The sun was shining brightly when he left the huge concourse. Suddenly, he felt happy once again. In his pocket rested the sum he needed. It was not a great accomplishment—to sell a jacket in the Grand Bazaar; but his chest tingled with pride. It was a mixed feeling. Not just the fact that he had obtained the money for the boat trip. He didn't know why exactly, but he was happy that the Turk had seen the jacket for what it was.

*   *   *

Martin leaned on the rail of the boat, salt-spray whipping his cheeks. The tons of water and brine rolled through his mind. He was thinking of his new friend, Steven Goldman, an American boy from Cincinnati. He had met him on the ship the first day out of Istanbul. He too was a poet. Martin was delighted. Finally, he had discovered a fellow-spirit, one who fiddled with the magic of words. A metaphor-slinger and image-maker. He was travelling to Israel for the first time.

Here was someone he could talk with, someone he could share Baudelaire with, Nietzsche, D. H. Lawrence, and all the towering spirits of blood and freedom. But Steven Goldman was a different sort of poet. Most modern poetry he dismissed as crude, heavy-handed, vulgar, unrhythmical, without one line of pure lyricism.

"It must be pure, crystal-clear," his voice lilted. "Just listen to this."

He opened a book of Elizabethan poets, courtly balladeers, and proceeded to read a poem by Thomas Campion. As he read, his round-cheeked, brown face became transformed before Martin's very eyes. As each line rolled from the tip of his delighted tongue, and as his lips curled around each celestial image, an aura of light seemed to encase him. A mellow hue rose from his shoulders, touched the tips of his well-formed ears, caressed the strands of his black wavy hair. He looked cherubic, as if he were reading from the edge of a cloud.

"But it's so vague," Martin protested, scraping back his chair.

"Vague?" Steven grimaced, annoyed at Martin's criticism. "You're not listening with your soul. Man, you know what I believe—our ears have become polluted. It's gotta have 'cunt' in it or 'balls'. This is beauty. Can't you hear it?"

Steven began reading again. Martin strained his ears to hear what his new friend wanted him to appreciate. For a second he could perceive it. A fine pure note. But it was too tiny, too difficult for Martin to drown in. How did he do it?—Martin wondered. How could Steven sink into this note, this poem, this poet? He wore the whole poem from head to foot, and at times Martin believed that he could rest there forever.

"It's just not my kind of stuff," Martin shrugged.

Steven closed the book gently. He allowed it to rest in his lap, his fingertips lightly caressing the cover.

"It's not going to come to you overnight. You gotta get used to it. But when you finally do, man, it's the greatest poetry ever written."

The sea swirled below him. Martin frowned as he thought over their conversation of the day before. There was a beauty to it, Martin had to admit. The lutes and the moon. The faces of beautiful, almost intangible women summoned forth beneath the poet's pen. Women who seemed to be born and raised on the dark side of the moon where no taint of sweating flesh could ever reach them. It scared him a bit, Steven's complete adoration. It mystified him. Steven looked normal in every respect. He had a handsome face, quick keen black eyes, a trim, somewhat muscular body. Even his speech was quite regular. Nothing forced or stilted about it. Yet it seemed that something inside him, perhaps his very heart, was composed of a perfectly constructed sonnet.

Suddenly, Martin heard a rush of feet behind him. It was Steven, out of breath, panting, his face flushed.

"Aw, shit!"

"What's wrong?" Martin asked, thinking at first that Steven was sick—perhaps a sudden attack of sea-sickness.

"Fuckin' shit," he spat over the side of the rail, and clutched at his chest.

"Are you O.K?"

"Just give me a second," he wheezed. "Just let me catch my breath."

Steven allowed his head to drop forward. He shook it back and forth.

"Keep this under your hat," he half-wheezed and whispered. "I think our captain's a queer."

"Really?" There was a shocked surprise to Martin's voice. After all, Steven was not talking about one of the waiters, nor a lowly steward, not even a lieutenant, but the captain, the chief of the whole blasted ship. "The captain?"

"Yeah, the fuckin' captain," Steven wheezed, and choked on his own words. "I think he's gay."

Steven tried to catch his breath.

"I noticed something funny yesterday," he continued in a whisper. "He was just looking at me in this strange way. You know what I mean. Well, I didn't think about it too much. I just thought I was imagining it. But holy Jesus, I wasn't."

"What happened?" Martin asked, his mind whirling with curiosity.

"Just give me a moment," Steven frowned.

Martin stared at the rolling waves. Wave on wave, a relentless onward push. Tons and tons of meaningless water. Rolling, seething, ending up on distant beaches. He saw the captain's face reflected back at him, a bobbing Turkish face on the crest of each wave. The black eyes gazing upward—the curled black moustache, perfectly twisted and combed, pointed at each tip. The face was whining something towards him. It was jumbled with the crash of foam. "Have mercy on me, stranger. I am just human. Please don't kick me for my sins."

Steven finally got a grip on himself.

"I still can't believe it. Our own captain," he muttered. "Anyway, today I went to take a leak. Just a few minutes ago. And the fuckin' captain followed me in. I was standing there minding my own business. Trying to take a piss. Shit, I looked over my shoulder, and there he was. He was staring at my cock. I mean right at it."

"Holy fuck!" Martin gasped.

Suddenly, he could feel laughter building in his chest. He wanted to laugh, to let it come out of his mouth. But it wasn't the right time, and he was just a little afraid of getting Steven angry at him. The laugh that he needed to release so much burned in his throat.

"His eyes were glued to it!" Steven whispered.

Unbelievably, Steven began to giggle. The giggles began almost like chirps—a chipmunk running through the leaves in the woods. Martin laughed, buckled over with the rolling billows inside him.

"Oh fuck," Martin choked. "I don't feel safe. You know what I mean. If the captain himself ... "

Steven's face turned quickly serious once more. His cheeks were no longer mellow and cherubic. They looked like two round stones side by side.

"A guy like that's dangerous," Steven proclaimed in a gravelly undertone.

Steven fished into his back pocket, searching for something. He took out an eight-inch hunting knife, its blade snuggled into a leather sheath. He withdrew it, the blade flashing clean and bright under the sea sun. He held it in front of him, twirling it, his eyes mesmerized by the curve of steel. Martin's eyes fastened on the steely sharp glint.

"If he tries anything," Steven hissed, his mouth curved with anger, "he'll get a stomach full of this. I don't mind queers, if they mind their own business."

Would Steven actually do it, Martin asked himself. Use the knife, plunge it into those tender layers of stomach? Martin searched Steven's face for an answer. For a second his eyes looked absolutely serious, keen, sharp, black and murderous. Then they changed, as if they were laughing at everything, as if it were all a joke, an act, a shriek of bravado.

This was the first time that Martin had seen Steven's knife. It was not something that he himself would travel with. In fact, he had never owned a real weapon in his entire life—nothing more lethal than a fishing rod.

"Do you think the crew knows about it?" Martin asked vaguely, wispily, as if the question were part of the sea-spray attacking his face.

"Ach," Steven spat in disgust, "the whole pack of them are probably fruits. I'll be glad to get off this heap of tin."

"What are you going to do in Israel?"

Martin was dreaming into the waves again. He was trying to imagine the life of the dolphins. A few hours ago, a school of them had been following the boat, leaping their silver-black bodies under the sun. What was it like, he wondered, to live without these human traumas?—to be nothing more than black skin on wet water, joyously whinnying, chirping to your friends in porpoise language; to feel the belly and back coated with silky water. But they must have their problems too, Martin mused: enemies lurking, a driving need to find food. But what a difference there was between people and these fish, their brothers and fellow creatures. It was ridiculous—the separation, the gulf of thought and feeling between them: captains chasing passengers around washrooms, poets wielding knives. This kind of thing, outlandish in every respect, he was sure the dolphins did not have to worry about. If, at that moment, he could've had one wish fulfilled, he would no longer be standing at the rail with Steven Goldman, no, he would be miles away, leaping from a wave, his mouth a chattering, foamy thing, his back arched, his belly cooled. Leap and leap, see nothing but green water, yellow sun; dance with a shiver of his tail, float, dive, become a slippery torpedo of flesh.

Steven slipped the knife back into its leather jacket. Delicately, his anger subsiding, he snapped the ring shut over the handle. Between his thumb and forefinger he revolved it affectionately. Then he raised it to his nose, closing his eyes dreamily, sniffing.

"It's real leather. Here, smell it," Steven said, the words rich and full in his throat. Steven floated the leather sheath under Martin's nose.

Martin sniffed at it.

"No, c'mon," Steven complained, "take a real good whiff. There's nothing richer than the smell of real leather."

Almost dutifully, Martin drew a full breath through his nostrils.

"It does smell good," Martin agreed.

He was not just trying to make Steven feel good. The rich aroma had entered him. Steven was absolutely right—there was a faraway, mysterious odour to the material. It contained for Martin memories of forests and lakes, early-morning fires in a wood stove. It was one of those distant, but inside fragrances. Miles away, years past, yet close as the fingertips. It made him think of Nova Scotia, summer holidays in cabins along the south shore—a place where he gathered periwinkles with his gentile friend, Jim Cogswell. The smell of the leather had the same full odour of mussels cracked against rock, the tender insides used for bait. Mussels, seaweed, salt-spray. Jim Cogswell running up and down the piles of rock, lean and agile, young and fair-skinned.

"What am I going to do in Israel?" Steven said, remembering Martin's question. His eyes gazed over the waves towards the horizon. Out there Israel was waiting, and soon they would be there, Steven for the first time, Martin already a veteran. After one more spin of the earth, another revolution of the horizon, they would step into the promised land.

"I'm going to give kibbutz life a try. If I really like it, I might stay. Who knows—maybe I'll find a wife and settle down. Were you ever on one?"

"Yes," Martin's head bobbed. An invisible string seemed to be jerking his chin up and down.

"How did you like it?"

Again his head began bobbing.

"Fine."

He wanted to say more, but only the one word trickled from his mouth. He wanted to be enthusiastic for Steven's sake. Two years ago he, too, had travelled for the first time to the land of his forefathers. With hopes and dreams, plans and energy, he had thrown himself into the new venture. He didn't want to ruin the experience for Steven.

"You'll enjoy it," he managed to say. Then his voice caught the original hopefulness he had felt. "Yeah, it's really great. A lot of hard work. The one I was on had a swimming pool. In the evenings it's really good. You can just sit around eating grapes. Once in a while you get wine."

Then, he suddenly changed the subject.

"I wonder if we'll see the captain at supper tonight."

Steven grinned. His eyes leaped with black light.

"Sure. He'll be there with bells on. I'm going to give him the evil eye. You know, just make him a little jittery. Just for the hell of it."

Martin smiled to himself. He could see the captain lifting a cup of after-supper tea, surrounded by chief officers and certain honored guests. The captain's table was buzzing gaily, rich women chortling. Two tables away, where the tourists sat, Steven Goldman was screwing his eyes into daggers. The captain couldn't help but see it. His hands were beginning to shake, the tea-cup rattling on its fine china saucer.

That evening after supper Steven asked him for his parents' address in Tel Aviv. Maybe they would be able to get together again in Israel. Martin had written out the address for other travellers, but nobody had ever used it. He never really thought that he would see Steven Goldman again. Once again he was going through the politeness of exchanging addresses. Steven tucked it neatly into his wallet.

This time, as it turned out, he had not given it in vain.

CHAPTER 15

The Fleishers and The Pearls

Two days before Martin returned, Britta Lystrom got off the boat in Haifa. The customs officer glanced quickly through her passport, and stamped it.

"Welcome to Israel," he grinned. "Where do you think you'll be going?"

"I want to find a kibbutz."

"Good, I'm sure you will like it. But dear, go to one in the Galil."

"The Galil?"

"Oh, I'm sorry. Galilee. You know, the famous sea. It's north. I'm sure you wouldn't like the desert," he frowned, screwing up his mouth. "Too much sand. You'd get your pretty hair all filled with it. Ach!"

Britta couldn't help giggling, her lower lip trembling. The man was making such funny faces.

"How is the life in Stockholm?" he asked.

"Good," she answered, not knowing how to reply to such a vast question. She looked back over her shoulder, and noticed that the line was lengthening, and the man in back of her was getting restless, letting long sighs stream from his mouth. "I guess I'd better go through."

"You see what kind of job I've got," he said, his voice self-mockingly somber. "I see them, I check them through. Before I can say Ben Gurion they're gone. And such as you, I don't see too often."

He sighed again, handing back her passport.

"Miss, promise me something."

"Yes."

"Don't let this awful heat ruin your skin—such a milky complexion."

He screwed his lips into a whisper, pouting over his last sentence.

"I promise," she said, blushing, lowering her head.

As she walked through the luggage depot, her heart was skipping lightly. She was wondering if all Israeli men were that comical. How young he had made her feel, as if she were seven years old, as if he was a store owner, and she was trying to decide between a lime and cherry lollipop. What a funny feeling in her stomach. So this was Israel, she thought. It was like none of the other countries. But what was different?—she wondered. Everywhere she looked, she saw something that amused her: two ladies on a bench, each with a bottle of smelling salts to their noses; an old man in a skull cap standing at attention in front of an Israeli flag, his head leaning to one side as if he were listening to music only he could hear.

I must remember that piece of advice, she thought. I'll look for a kibbutz in the north. She had never been to a desert, but the thought of living among sand dunes made her throat feel dry.

*   *   *

Martin sat in the kitchen, back in Ramat Aviv once again, alone with his mother on a Monday morning.

"I'm so glad you're back, Martin. For your father's sake. I never thought I'd see the day that man would cry. While you were away, we sat around in the evenings out on the balcony. Everything was fine until your name was mentioned. That was it. Your father's eyes would fill with tears. Martin, he loves you very much. We all do."

Martin's head hung forward, his gaze fixed on the white flecks on the green tile floor.

"I've never seen him cry for any reason," she added.

It was true. His father had often mentioned this fact. Proudly, he had proclaimed it to Martin. "You know something," he would say, "the last time I cried I was ten years old." These stories about his father's tears made him feel uneasy. The relationship had always been close, for as long as he could remember. When he was only ten years old, ages ago in Halifax, he and his father used to sit at the dining-room table. As the night darkened, they sat together under the glow of the chandelier, talking, whispering. There seemed no limit to the things they had to say to each other. His father talked about politics. Even at that young age, he told him about Karl Marx and Das Kapital. He explained the difference between capitalism and socialism. He answered every question that popped into Martin's mind. Why did people fight wars? Why were the colored people laughed at?

The answers, Martin never questioned or doubted. How could a single word of untruth fall from his father's lips? What man in the entire world knew as much as his father? Had any man ever read as many books? Could there exist a man as fair anywhere?

Everything about his father fascinated him. Even the way he signed his name. He had a way of looping the J and running it very close to the K in Kanner. It made his signature look mysterious. The letters had so many loops and curves to them. Martin used to practise signing his father's signature. He wanted to imitate it exactly —not to miss a single curve of the J. He wanted to get it so perfect that even his father would be fooled. One day he was practising this endlessly fascinating game down at his father's office. He had covered a whole sheet of paper with the signature. His Uncle Simon, his father's younger brother and business partner, appeared suddenly over his left shoulder.

"What are you doing?" he asked.

"Oh, just trying to sign Dad's name," Martin whispered, blushing a little. "Doesn't it look just like his?"

There was an excitement in Martin's voice as he showed the sheet of paper to his uncle. He was sure Uncle Simon would agree that there was an amazing similarity.

"Do you think that's a good idea?" his uncle asked, his voice a little tense.

Martin didn't understand the question.

"What?" he asked, his voice and mind in a daze.

"Martin, I want to tell you something. Let's keep it between us, O.K? You've got to learn to sign your own name. Do you understand what I'm saying?"

Martin was surprised at the words he heard tumbling down at him. He didn't know if he understood.

"I don't think you should keep doing this," he added.

What was wrong with it? It was his own father's signature, a wonderful, distinct curve of letters and spaces; even the dot looked like a shimmering bead of blackness. How could he stop doing it?

How could he stop until he was able to duplicate it perfectly, without a single speck of loop or curve out of place? But the short
conversation with Uncle Simon stuck inside his head. When he least
expected it, his uncle's words came rushing into his mind—at school
in the playground, at supper. Didn't he have a right to do it? His
very own father, his very own signature. Didn't it belong to him?

The story about his father crying made him feel guilty. Nobody
had made him cry before, nobody but his father's own parents.

"I'm going to Jerusalem again," he said to his mother.

She stood at the sink peeling potatoes, making sure she carved out
every brown dot of potato-eye.

"Can you get work? We don't have the money, Martin."

"I'm sure I can," he said in a high-pitched voice. He was trying to
reassure himself with the determination in his own words. "I've got
all this teaching experience."

She held a potato under the rushing water, massaging every speck
of dirt from the white surface.

"That's fine then. You can visit us on weekends. At least you
won't be thousands of miles away. Martin, we worry about you."

"I know," he said.

His voice was tired. His mother had told him this hundreds of
times. He had always answered with the same two words. I know. I
know. I know. How could he help but know? It was a fact. It was
just as sure as the days of the week. Tuesday always followed
Monday. They worried about him. He knew it—just as well as he
knew his name. He just had to get back to the clean, high, hilly air
of Jerusalem. There were no two ways about it.

* * *

Before he left for Jerusalem, he wanted to see Josephine. Would
she even talk to him?—he wondered as he climbed the familiar
staircase on Sholom Aleichem Street. There had been no contact
with her since she entered the hospital. Hesitantly, he reached up a
hand to knock at the door. Still there was time to forget it. He could
sneak quietly back down the stairs. The air slumped in his chest. Be
a man, his mind clanged.

He knocked gently at the door. Perhaps the apartment was empty,
and his thumps were floating through the ghostly still air. But he
heard the familiar, scissory footsteps moving towards the door.

"Oh Martin, it's you," Josephine smiled, opening the door. "It's so good to see you again. Come in. Tell me what you've been doing."

Martin blushed and smiled sheepishly. He was relieved. There was not a speck of anger or condemnation in her voice. Not a hint of rancor, or hate. It was just like the old days, as if the hospital episode had never happened.

They sat down at the small coffee-table in the living room. It felt good to be seated in this room he knew so well, to be surrounded by familiar furnishings. What a relief after the miles of completely foreign soil he had crossed; after the craziness of Istanbul. No, he decided he would not even mention the hospital, nor the operation. It was best to forget it.

Josephine reached a hand across the table and floated it down on top of his hand.

"Tell me, what have you been doing with yourself? I've had nobody to talk to. Just the same old boring conversations. Have you been writing?"

She seemed excited to see him. It made him feel warm inside, his stomach glowing.

"I took a trip," he smiled, "just a short trip to Turkey and Greece."

Josephine's eyes began to sparkle. The contact lenses made her eyes look like two bright dots of light.

"That's wonderful, Martin. Oh, you can't imagine how boring my life is. Work, work, work. And the people I'm surrounded by are so dull . . . with very few exceptions."

She began to laugh to herself, her nose bunching into wrinkles of amusement.

"What's so funny?" Martin asked curiously.

Josephine buckled over into a tight little knot of gaiety.

"Sometimes I think life's a farce. Here's what I mean. I met this real nice girl down at work. Somebody I could talk to. She's sweet, intelligent. To make it short, she's not a bloody bore. We became real good friends, and Martin, guess what? She's gay. A real little lesbian."

Josephine went off into another fit of laughter.

"You're kidding. How did you find out?"

Abruptly, the laughter ceased, and Josephine's face became serious.

"It didn't take me long to put two and two together. You know what the little hussy started doing? Every time I went to the wash-room, old Claudia followed after me."

For a split-second, the Turkish captain shot through Martin's mind.

"Did she ever try anything?" Martin asked, unable to keep a smirkish grin from stretching his lips apart.

"No," Josephine sighed, flicking a match across a booklet, igniting the tip of her cigarette. "I caught on before it went too far. It's just too bad, though. It ruined a perfectly good friendship."

"That is too bad."

Martin let a long sigh stream out, commiserating with Josephine's loneliness.

"Well," she groaned, "that's the way it goes. Dull people, and the exciting ones are gay."

"I'm not gay . . . I guess that makes me pretty dull."

Josephine's glance darted directly between his legs. He couldn't help but notice. She ran the tip of her tongue along her lower lip. Martin could feel an aching, tingling sensation begin to leap in his genitals. Slowly, the whole area began to burn. It was almost two months since he had slept with her. It would be almost like the first time, he kept thinking. She was almost a stranger once again.

"No," she smiled, "no one could accuse you of either. That's why I like you, Martin. You should know that by now."

"I'm glad you don't hold a grudge."

He reached out and gripped her shoulder. He could feel her tiny body trembling slightly.

"I really wasn't expecting you to come to the hospital, if that's what you mean. In fact, it would've surprised me if you had."

Martin was glad that it was coming out into the open. Her words surprised and relieved him.

"It was a pretty rotten thing to do," he said, his voice thickly laden with guilt.

"Let's just forget it. It's water under the bridge. A lot of shit flows under that bridge, don't you agree?"

Josephine's smile flashed once again. Martin's face relaxed. His whole body was beginning to tremble and throb, wanting to hold her naked body.

"A hell of a lot of shit," he laughed.

She slipped a hand between his knees.

"Well, Mr. Kanner, shall we celebrate this reunion in bed?"

Where else?—he thought. What better place in the whole bloody world?

He felt free entering her body. There seemed, now, to be no strings attached to their friendship. If she forgave him about the hospital, how could he ever offend her again? It seemed that she was just accepting the friendship for what it was—a chance to talk together, to have a few laughs, to satisfy each other's sexual needs. There was no more illusion between them about "real love" or having children together, or getting married, or staying together forever.

The Tel Aviv summer wind trembled through the apartment, winnowed among the creases of their naked forms. The night-time summer breeze that carried a fresh fragrance from the Mediterranean. No commitments. No promises. He felt free with her now, as if they were both slim skiffs of summer wind gliding together over the rooftops.

The next day was Saturday. They could wake up slowly together, just let the sun drip in through the windows. Josephine didn't have to rush off to work. No noisy reminders rose from the streets below. No jackhammers splitting their way through concrete, or heavy buses lumbering around corners. It was the sabbath. The stores and markets were finally still.

They could almost pretend that this one day had no beginning and no end. It stretched its lazy arms around them like a dream.

How easily and freely she had forgiven him about breaking his promise to bring roses. It seemed that he could talk to her about anything now, as if he were talking to a boyfriend. But with even greater freedom. He could bring up subjects that were too embarrassing to share with another guy. Jerusalem was on his mind, and with the thought of going back, he remembered Gila. What better person could he find than Josephine to talk about that subject with? Josephine with her limitless experience. But he had to begin very slowly, delicately, feel his way along.

After making love with her, he perched himself on an elbow, his hand supporting his chin.

"Josephine," he whispered, "I've gotta go back to Jerusalem. Except for yourself, there's nothing here for me. I just realized the other day that I've been in Tel Aviv nearly a year, and I haven't made one male friend."

Josephine propped a pillow behind her back. Her eyes looked misty without glasses or contacts.

"Were you close to anyone in Jerusalem?"

"Quite a few people. You remember me telling you about this guy Jesse."

Josephine took an extra long drag on her cigarette.

"The Zen Buddhist?"

"Yes, that's the one. But not only him. It seemed so easy to meet people there. I don't know why exactly. Maybe it's the atmosphere. Maybe it's easier-going or something. You're the only person I've gotten to know in Tel Aviv."

"Aren't I enough?" Josephine grinned. It was a mischievous, knowing smile.

Martin groaned.

"I understand," she said. "You need stimulation. You are a writer, after all. I keep forgetting. Sometimes I just think of you as a teacher. I guess for that, Tel Aviv would be as good as any other place. But there's something else on your mind, isn't there?"

Martin frowned with surprise. Sometimes he felt that Josephine could read his thoughts as easily as glancing through a newspaper. She did this sort of thing often, but it always surprised him.

"I don't know if I should talk to you about it."

"It's about a girl, isn't it?" Josephine said, rolling the tip of her cigarette between her lips.

"Yes," he admitted, hesitantly.

"Well, I'm not naive, Martin. I never thought I was the only woman in your life. Now, out with it."

Josephine was staring intently at him. She was sitting completely upright.

"Come on," she encouraged, "let's hear it. Is it that little virgin you've told me about? Let's hear the whole gruesome thing."

She was smiling now, almost gaily, her cheeks flushed with curiosity. Martin shook his head back and forth, his gaze aimed at the white sheets. He didn't want to meet her sparkling hazel eyes. He clicked his tongue inside his mouth.

"Aw, it's just embarrassing to talk about, that's all."

He paused, dragging deeply on his cigarette, trying to draw courage through the heavy smoke into his lungs.

"I want to sleep with her," he finally said.

"So, sleep with her, what's the problem?"

"I tried once," he continued. "It was impossible. You know what I mean. It was just too tight."

Josephine bent forward laughing, her tiny nose bunching into wrinkles. What a good sport she was, he thought. Listening to all this without getting jealous or angry.

"Face it, Martin," she giggled, "you're not exactly built the right way to go around deflowering young maidens. I pity that little innocent thing. What's her name? I forgot."

"Gila," Martin said. The word came out like a drop of glistening spit.

"Gila," Josephine repeated. "Poor little Gila."

Josephine tilted back her head, blowing a chain of smoke toward the ceiling.

"Well," she sighed, "you should be able to do it. If she's not impossibly small. And she's probably scared too. That doesn't help. All tensed up. First of all, you've got to try to make her relax. Don't jump right into it. You know what I mean? Be very tender with her, go very slowly, lots of foreplay. Talk to her gently, softly into her ear. Another thing, which you should know of course—use some sort of lubricant. A gel of some kind. Not anything harsh. Something they use for babies like vaseline. Work it all around her with the tips of your fingers. Don't be afraid to put a lot on. Work it inside a bit. And put a lot on yourself. Then, the rest's up to you. You have to be very tender and firm at the same time."

Josephine began to laugh again, choking a little on a stream of smoke that went down the wrong way.

"Martin, I won't be able to be there with you. It's something only you can do. Right?"

"Right."

Martin shook his head up and down. Tender and firm, he kept thinking. Lots of vaseline. Josephine really made it sound possible. He still had his doubts, however. Gila was so darn small, and tense, and afraid. But he was hoping she had changed during his absence. Maybe, he thought, she had gotten over her fear of becoming pregnant.

Josephine whistled under her breath.

"I must be crazy telling you all this. Here you are, running off to Jerusalem, and I'm giving you advice about some other woman. Just merrily going along cutting my own throat. Oh well ... " Josephine sighed, "I guess that's life. My life anyway. But Martin, the least you can do is come to visit me when you're in Tel Aviv. You can let me know how it went with Gila. Do you promise to do that? We don't have to stop being friends. You're not in love with her, are you?"

"I don't think so. She's a friend, that's all."

Josephine ground the tip of her cigarette into the ashtray.

"I'm going to miss you. But if you have to go, you have to go."

"Josephine?"

"What now?" she half-laughed and frowned.

"I'd like some of my friends to meet you. Would that be O.K.?"

"As friend friends? Or as lovers?"

"It doesn't matter. You know that. Whatever you want."

Josephine smiled to herself. She stretched her arms above her head. She reminded him of a kitten stretching in the sunlight.

"Sure," she purred, "feel free to give them my address. I'm kind of curious about the kind of guys you hang around with."

She stretched again.

"When do you think you're leaving?"

"In a couple of days."

She reached out, lifted his hand, and placed it on her thigh.

"Let's make the best of it," she yawned and smiled. "I'm feeling horny again, what about you?"

Her words more than anything aroused him, and he could feel the blood pulsing between his legs. Slowly, he slipped his hand under her nightie.

What kind of friends were they?—he kept wondering, his mind active throughout the lovemaking. Were they friend-friends or lovers, or just a couple of lunatics discussing things that he never believed a man and woman could talk about together? He felt very close to her after the conversation, as if they were two guys who had compared notes on women. And he felt distant. It didn't seem to matter when he stepped out of her life, whether it was the next day, or in two months. And it didn't seem to matter when he came back. Josephine would always be there on Sholom Aleichem Street. She'd always be there with a cup of tea waiting for him. Whenever he came back she'd be willing to fold back the sheets, and share her tired body with him.

* * *

So this was the kibbutz on a sabbath, Steven Goldman thought to himself. Kibbutz Ruach Chadash, it was called: New Spirit. Even the chickens were still that Saturday morning at ten o'clock. He wandered down to the tennis courts. Was he the only person awake?—he wondered. Quiet now were the conveyor belts in the fruit-processing building. It was not a religious kibbutz, no services would be held this Saturday morning, but he felt a pin could drop from heaven and he would hear it ping in the grass. He saw a cow grazing in a field behind the courts. One lone cow swishing its tail silently. It reminded him of a corner of a Chagall painting. The large brown suffering eyes, the heavy thick-skinned shoulders. Put two angels in the sky, a church steeple, he dreamed, and voilà—Marc Chagall.

He felt sleepy and a little bored.

What a change from the rushing, chattering madness of Istanbul.

A dirt road led from the tennis courts to an apple orchard. Why not take it? He was sure that he would find only more stillness, and the green fruit beginning to grow, just beginning their summertime journey to ripeness. What could he lose? He took his knife from his back pocket, withdrew it from its sheath. He stood before a small tree, held the knife by its steely tip, tossed it, and to his amazement the knife thunked home into the bark, deep into the tree, and vibrated with the force of its entry.

Sleepily, half in a dream, he yanked it away, wiped the flat of the blade against his bare leg. It felt good—the cool steel against his skin. He continued walking among the trees, each one looking like an exact replica of the other . . . into the orchard, into the greenness, into the stillness.

Under a distant tree he saw something that made his heart thump crazily. This can't be real, he thought, rubbing his eyes with knotted fists.

What was she doing there? He hid himself behind a tree, and tried to calm himself. Luckily, her head was bent over a book. She had not seen him. He looked again. Yes, it was real: a young, beautiful, blond-haired girl dressed entirely in white. Since his arrival in Israel two weeks ago, he had seen hundreds of women—bustling around the port at Haifa, selling their wares at the market; secretaries rushing in and out of office buildings in Tel Aviv, intent on what they were doing. He glanced at them. They at him. They passed each other. But he hadn't seen anything like this girl who was sitting no more than a hundred yards away. Her hair was so bright under the rays of the sun, it looked almost silver, then white, then golden again.

He stood there trying to build up the courage to approach her. Take it easy, he said to himself. It's only a girl. Just remember that. You're a guy, and she's a girl, and fate somehow has put you together in the middle of this empty orchard. True, she's the most beautiful girl you've seen in weeks, perhaps years. Maybe she's the most perfect girl you've ever laid eyes on. But remember, she's still a girl. See—she has skin on her bones, shoes on her feet, hair on her head.

He had an intense desire to reach for his knife, to bring it out and just toss it in the air. It would relax him: to see it somersault, twist, and spin above his head. He repressed the thought. Again and again, he cleared his throat, testing to see if he would be able to talk to her without choking or stuttering. Slowly, he edged towards her. He was almost standing above her before she looked up from her book.

"Oh my God," she said, "I didn't see you there."

Her eyes grew large and surprised.

"I'm sorry," Steven said a bit stiffly. "I didn't want to startle you."

"You're an American," she said, her eyes brightening.

"Yes, my name's Jacob. Well, it's not really Jacob, my real name is Steven. But I wanted to use something more biblical here in Israel. Do you think Jacob's O.K?"

"It sounds fine to me," she smiled. "Wasn't he the one who wrestled with the angel? And he hurt the angel's thigh . . . Or did the angel hurt his thigh? I'm afraid I don't know my bible very well. My name's Britta."

"How come I haven't seen you at the ulpan?" Steven asked, slipping down to sit beside her on the grass.

"I just got here yesterday," Britta said. She wriggled her legs, as if to make room for him to sit beside her.

"Where are you from?" Jacob asked. "You're not German, are you?"

"That's fairly close. No, I'm from Sweden."

Jacob felt a little sheepish, almost silly, about asking the next question. It was a difficult one to form in his throat, for his lips to curve around, for his voice to utter without it coming out sounding completely ridiculous. It was a question he burned to ask, yet he suspected, almost knew, what the answer would be.

"Are you Jewish?" When the question finally emerged, it sounded embarrassingly innocent in the stillness of the orchard. But still he wanted an answer, to hear it come from her own lips.

"No," she shook her head, allowing her eyelashes to fall over the bright blue of her eyes.

"I didn't think so," he laughed. "It was a stupid question, wasn't it?"

"Well, not really. You can never really be sure. I've seen some blond girls who were Jewish. Back in Stockholm. They even had blue eyes."

Steven let a deep breath flow from his throat. He lowered his head, and chuckled to himself.

"It was still a crazy question. What are you reading anyway?"

"Oh, it's nothing much."

She hid the cover in her lap.

"Is it a novel?"

"No, it's an oriental book. Very popular nowadays in Sweden. It's kind of funny really. You've probably heard about it—The Perfumed Garden."

"Oh yes," Steven smiled. "The Perfumed Garden. It's the rage back home too."

Then he paused, thinking... "Isn't it funny?" he continued. "All over the world we're reading the same books at the same time. I meet you here, and what are you reading—maybe the same book I read a couple of weeks ago in Cincinnati. Doesn't it just blow your mind a bit?"

Britta was trying to sense what Jacob meant. Yes, she thought, it was rather peculiar, this thing about books, and people meeting in strange countries. It did rock her mind a bit.

They talked to each other for the rest of the morning, and walked together back to the dining room. Jacob didn't want to leave her alone for a second. He didn't want to appear pushy, or over-anxious, but he wanted to keep her by his side, close to him.

* * *

The lights of Tel Aviv flickered below him. Martin Kanner stood on the balcony in the darkness in Ramat Aviv. What was it all about?—these millions of families that lived in the houses and apartments his gaze surveyed. Families like his own. Out there—the Rubins, the Goldsteins, the Fleishers, all huddled together in their separate cubicles of concrete and wood and stone. As far as his eye could see, the houses of Tel Aviv glowed—a thousand fireflies flickering in a black forest; touching each other for a second, missing each other, passing on.

He drew in a deep breath, trying to sniff from the almost dank summer fragrance a message and a meaning. What if there was no meaning? What if every ounce of meaning came to nothing more than the sniff he had just taken, nothing more than the fleck of dust he had drawn through his nostrils: the full meaning in that fragrance of distant lilac, and the salt-tinged breath of the sea?

Why should there be any meanings? Why should his mind yearn for them? Ants didn't seek any message in the bodies of fallen foes. They went about their business, lumbering around all day and all night with huge dead carcasses on their backs. They lived out their days in hills, complex yet orderly. Be thou as the ant. Wasn't that a bit of biblical advice his heart was churning up?

The Goldsteins, the Fleishers, the Rubins, the Pearls, there they lived and abided. He could scan them all at will from his seventh-storey perch. From the Kanner balcony, he could see them: slamming screendoors, charcoaling pig and beef in their backyards, wiping the curse of hayfever from their noses, reading novels at midnight in dimly-lit bedrooms.

His head was becoming dizzy with reverie, imagining himself as invisible, walking an invisible tightrope into every home his eye could see. Ah yes, the Fleishers having stew tonight, the *bubah* Fleisher sitting in a corner of the kitchen knitting a pair of socks. The mama Fleisher in the bathroom applying eye-shadow to her tired eyes. Oh yes, the Pearls playing scrabble, father Pearl winning as usual, placing an extraordinarily potent word on a triple-word square. Grandpa Pearl sucking on a rye and ginger.

His head was beginning to swirl, and the flickering lights below began to merge into one another, a fuzzy wash of yellow-amber fireflies.

He heard footsteps behind him. The clap-clap of rubber beach sandals slapping against wood. A familiar fragrance joined him on the balcony. A familiar voice, soft and still as the darkness in Ramat Aviv, began to speak.

"Quite a view from up here, isn't it?" his father said to him at the balcony rail, standing so close Martin could feel warmth radiating from his side.

"Yeah, you can almost see to Allenby Street."

His father stood beside him, his mouth now still, just a slow even breathing slipping in and out of the slight opening between his lips.

"Do you ever wonder what it's all about?" Martin asked.

His father placed an arm around his shoulder, and rocked him slightly back and forth. The grip was strong, and loose.

"I don't think about it much any more. I guess it's a young man's question. Don't get me wrong. I'm not saying I know what it means. I just don't ask the questions I used to. But there are a lot of things I used to do . . . I used to read, think, dream. I used to get hot about a lot of issues—political, social, even artistic. I guess that kind of thing has gone by the boards."

His father sighed. He seemed to be reconsidering.

"I don't know, Martin. Maybe it's a dormant stage for me. Things change. People change. Everything turns into its opposite. The pendulum swings as far as it will go in one direction and then comes back again. But one thing I know, it always swings back—in economics, in politics, in our personal lives."

Martin felt a heavy weight in his chest. The ideas he was hearing, he had heard before. The tone of voice was a little different. But the thoughts had a familiar ring to them.

"Have you given up?"

As soon as the question emerged, he knew it was harsh. It was almost like kicking somebody when they were lying on the ground.

"Perhaps," his father groaned, "or maybe I've just grown more cautious over the years."

His father shuffled from one foot to the other. He tightened his grip around Martin's shoulder.

"Your mother tells me you're going back to Jerusalem. I guess you'll be teaching there."

"Yes, I think I'll be able to get a job. But you know, Dad, the only thing I want to do is write. There's nothing else. It's the only thing that really interests me. I don't know if I'll ever be able to do it."

His father reached for a package of cigarettes in his shirt pocket. It was a soft package of Philip Morris, twenty loose unfiltered cigarettes.

"Would you like one of these?"

Martin hesitated. His own brand was a lot milder. Once in a while when the mood hit him, he would accept a Philip Morris from his father. That evening he wanted to savour the strong taste, the thick British aroma, to draw it down, to hold the fragrance inside him.

"Sure."

His father tapped the bottom of the box lightly, expertly, with his forefinger. Two cigarettes slipped past the opening.

"You've taken on quite a challenge, Martin. In a way, I envy you. But you must realize that an artist's life isn't an easy one. Very few make it. It can break a person. And an artist, a real artist is never satisfied. When one thing's finished, it's on to the next."

Martin dragged the heavy smoke to the bottom of his chest. He allowed it to linger there, to fill him, to dwell in all the passageways.

"I've decided, though," he said with determination. "It's writing or nothing. I've just got to figure out how it's done. There's got to be a way. Just like anything else. I've just got to find it, that's all."

His father squeezed his shoulder, the heat of his palm filtering through Martin's jersey, through the light cotton mesh, the heat penetrating the skin.

"Martin, do you remember something I've always told you? And I'm not just saying this to make you feel good. I believe it with all my heart. Martin, whatever you set your mind to, you can do. That's how much confidence I have in you. Anything. As long as you really want it."

Yes, he had heard it before. But did his father realize what he was saying? Writing was not the same as becoming a lawyer, or a doctor, or an accountant. There wasn't a set of books he could study, an examination he could write. There was just life. People, houses, emotions. Somehow, a writer had to transform that frenzy of activity and feeling into books. How could he set his mind to such a thing, and make it happen?

What was it all about?—Jake Kanner wondered, standing on the balcony beside his son. How did the wash of time and events manage to place him in this country? Things were simpler in the beginning. He was brought up near the waterfront, among the rats, and colored people, and the poor Jews who had just arrived from Russia and eastern Europe. "Kike, get the little kike." It was a shrill thin voice he had often heard on the way to Hebrew school or back again. Learn to fight, his father had told him. His inner voice agreed. Build the fists until they were knotted like cords of steel. Build the muscles, the courage, the stamina. Get the reflexes working so fast that his body could swivel as suddenly as a stroke of lightning. Smash any mouth that uttered an insult.

It was straightforward in those days—what he had to do. Fight when necessary, never show a tremble of fear. And above all, learn some skill, take a profession, and move with the rest of the small community uptown. Make money, lots of it, leave the rats behind, the drunken weekend sailors, the whores, the reek of homebrew booze. Never become anybody's bumboy, and never allow his own son, when he had one, to experience the hell he had grown up in.

He chuckled to himself remembering an incident in high school. He had become a quiet, serious student by the time he was fifteen, happy to have discovered a talent for numbers, how they worked and flowed, how they could be manipulated. Near the end of his final year, he was sitting in class one day near the back, his head bent over a text. The teacher was amusing the class with some anecdote from his personal life. Everyone was chuckling, giggling, jabbering to one another. Jake continued to read, allowing the information to seep into his brains, holding it there until he was sure it was fully assimilated. He didn't have time to go over things twice. Suddenly, he heard a voice.

"Jakey, vy are you so quiet?" the blue-eyed teacher twanged in a mock Yiddish accent. "Cat got your tongue?"

His blood began to slowly simmer. But he didn't look up. His eyes were fixed on the lines in the textbook, but he was only seeing black meaningless squibbles. Blood and anger began to pulse on the tips of his shoulders. Footsteps—he could hear them like a shuffle of wind—they slowly, inevitably proceeded down the aisle in his direction.

"Jakey, vat's the matter with you, so serious?" the teacher twanged, mocking him in front of the entire class.

That dumb goy is asking for it, Jake thought, his gaze still penetrating the page in front of him. The teacher stood above him. Still,

Jake did not look up. His body, now, was trembling with the intensity of his anger and embarrassment.

The teacher floated a pencil down, jabbing it lightly through his thick black hair. As soon as the lead tip touched his scalp, Jake exploded. The teacher was in mid-sentence:

"Jakey, you think you're solving ... "

Those were the last words the teacher uttered that afternoon. When the tip of the pencil hit his scalp, Jake reared from his seat, a click of anger and hate uncoiling in his right shoulder. His fist smashed against the point of his teacher's chin. That was it. One blow, exactly aimed and delivered. Back he went, out flat, his arms flailing uselessly, his back crashing amid desks and screeching students.

The teacher was in the hospital for a couple of months. When he came back, his jaw was still wired up. Jake was expelled. It was the last time he ever entered a place of learning as a student. He did the rest on his own, taking correspondence courses until he finally accumulated enough credits to get his degree as a chartered public accountant.

For the first years of his married life, things went as planned. Slowly, with dedication and hard work, he built up a practice in Halifax. Year by year, his earnings increased, his stature in the community. He moved his small family from house to house, each one in a more desirable area of the city. In those years, there were no wild imaginings about the millions of dollars to be made on the stock market. His practice was firmly established. He and his staff serviced the accounts for about three hundred clients.

The question Martin had just asked him was perfectly valid. "Do you ever wonder what it's all about?" He grimaced to himself. There was a time when the answer was clear.

Jake tapped another cigarette from the package.

"Just don't be too idealistic, Martin," he suddenly said. "Just remember the world doesn't owe you a living. You have to have a place to stay, enough to eat."

The crickets were chirping in the parking lot below them. They seemed to be calling to one another, singing, harmonizing. Martin had watched a number of houses grow dark, the lights in every room go out. It was quickly approaching midnight, and the following morning was the beginning of another work week. The Fleishers were bedding down, rolling back the sheets, as they had rolled them back each night for years. The Pearls were resting in bed, the lights out, listening to some music on the radio. The Rubins, the Goldsteins, the Swartzes, all of them slowly going off to bed, overcome by sleepiness, yawning, stretching, brushing their teeth, gargling, then finally dousing the lights one by one, in the kitchen, in the living room, the upper bedrooms.

Dahlia Kanner was still puttering around in the kitchen. She had brushed her teeth, put on her nightie.

"Jake," she shouted, "don't talk all night. You gotta get up early tomorrow."

Debrah Kanner was drifting slowly off to sleep in her bedroom. Darrell was lying in his crib protected from insects and dirt by a fine cotton mesh. He was sleeping quietly with a thumb lodged in his mouth.

"Dahlia," Jake shouted back, "you go to bed. I won't be long. I'm going to stay out here and talk with Martin for a while."

A muffled O.K. floated back from the kitchen, followed by a few more words. The end of the sentence was unintelligible. The words were lost in passage, or spoken so quietly in his mother's throat that they had no chance of reaching the balcony.

When Jake finished his cigarette, he balanced the butt between his forefinger and thumb, and flicked it over the balcony rail. It shot forward about twenty feet, and described a long glowing arc in the darkness. Jake snickered and clucked his tongue.

"Don't know what I'm thinking about. That's not a very clever thing to do."

Martin laughed in his throat. "Well, it's all concrete down there. There's nothing much to burn."

Jake shuffled from foot to foot, and slowly loosened his grip on Martin's shoulder. "Wouldn't that be a hell of mess, though?—if it landed in somebody's apartment."

Jake chuckled to himself again. "I can just read the headlines. Middle-aged arsonist nabbed in Ramat Aviv."

His father moved back, easing himself into a beach chair. He sat down as if his body were fragile, each bone delicate. Martin could feel the pain in his father's back. It was something he had described to him frequently—how the discs in his spine felt fused together, rigid instead of supple, how the ache travelled from his ankles up his legs, through his shoulders, and finally knotted in his neck. The base of the skull at the back, he described as rock-hard. Swimming at the "Y" seemed the only thing that gave him any relief. And he refused to mask the pain with pills.

Before Martin sat down, he glanced once again at the houses below him. Only a few lights were still shining.

"You know, Martin, I've been through a lot in my life. I've seen things right from the bottom to the top . . . Yep. I often think of writing a book myself. I have really been through it."

Jake chuckled and sighed to himself.

"You wouldn't believe the half of it. The rounders, the pimps, the whores. The suckers, the wheeler-dealers. The phony politicians. The cowards. The punch-drunk ex-fighters. There wouldn't be a hell of a lot missing, I'll tell you that much."

Martin knew it was true. His own life in comparison seemed uneventful, protected, almost dull. He had grown up in a middle-class neighbourhood. Gone to school, and university. Only in the last year or so had he started to live. But what a lot of catching up he had to do. Would he ever catch up?—he wondered. It seemed impossible. How could he ever duplicate a childhood near the waterfront? Wasn't that whole period lost to him?

"Perhaps we could work together on something," Martin suggested. "I'd really like to write the story of your life."

"Yes," his father sighed, "you'd just have to get a feeling for it—from the inside. But you know, Martin, I have the feeling that's a story that's never going to get written."

There was a sadness in his father's voice. A wispy, throaty feeling of nostalgia. The tone of his voice floated over the balcony-rail, joined the crickets in their night-time chirpings. There was a longing in his voice to see the jumble and glitter and harshness of his life set to words. Ordered into something that had beauty, something he could look at and say: yes, that makes sense. That's why that happened. Yes, it's so clear now, just like a vein of gold in quartz.

"Martin, I'll say it again. I envy you. Not that I have any regrets, mind you. But you have everything in front of you . . . "

His father leaned back in his chair. He tilted his head, allowing his gaze to survey the dark star-sprinkled sky.

"You asked me what it was all about. In all these years, there's only one conclusion I've come to. A person has to live every minute of every day—to the hilt. Without that enthusiasm for life, for work, for love—there's nothing, absolutely nothing. You have to live like there's no tomorrow. From the moment you open your eyes in the morning, until you go to sleep at night . . . and it doesn't even end there. I've sometimes had a problem I really believed I couldn't solve. Do you know something? I would go to sleep not even thinking about it, and by golly, in the morning I had the answer. Our minds never stop working. If I could put it in one word, I would say 'zest', that's what it's all about."

His father folded his hands in front of him. He rested them on his stomach, his hands rising and falling just perceptibly with each breath.

"That's why I'm going back to Jerusalem," Martin said. There was a bite and determination to his words. "I felt it there—what you're talking about."

Martin paused. "But I believe even suffering's got to be part of it."

"Yes, suffering," his father mused. "That's an art too, Martin. Don't confuse it with self-pity. And don't search for it. Just look at those stars. Look at the life beating and pulsing all around us."

That evening Martin believed that part of the answer had tumbled from his father's mouth. Rarely had he heard him voice such positive opinions. He couldn't stop thinking about it. Was his father's life really charged with enthusiasm from morning to night? He felt dark, vague areas in his own days. Hours of sleepiness, boredom. Hours where there wasn't a speck of zest, not a hint of enthusiasm.

His father always appeared thoroughly involved in his work. This, he thought, was the key. Day-by-day total involvement in work that he loved. Why couldn't he feel the same enthusiasm for writing? He wanted the words to flow from his pen daily, words charged with fragrance, words so rich in texture he could smell them, taste them, touch them. Words as real as the concrete, the dust, the sweat on his father's forehead. Words like the pimps and whores his father had mentioned, words that were beautiful, wild, real as any deal swung on the stock market. Words that were discoveries. Exciting as finding uranium in the backyard.

Who could argue with what had just poured from his father's mouth? Zest. Enthusiasm. Didn't D. H. Lawrence, William Blake, Walt Whitman support the same vision? His father's words seemed to beat in harmony with nearly all the "greats" who had ever touched ink to paper.

And common sense told him—what else could be the message?

Each moment a live, vibrating breath. Every second glowing, as if the seconds of each day were Roman candles shot skyward, bursting, flowering. Reds, greens. Colors. Noise. Beauty. The heart so seized with excitement it could hardly manage its next beat.

His father placed a hand on Martin's knee, rocking it back and forth.

"Well, Martin, are you ready to call it quits? Tomorrow's another day."

"Yes," Martin agreed. "I'm leaving tomorrow."

"Are you O.K. for money?"

"I have a few dollars."

His father bent his head slightly. He thrust a hand into his pocket. "Here, take this. Let's just call it support of the arts."

His father opened the fingers on his right hand, and slipped fifty lira into it.

"What will you do? Stay with friends until you find work?" his father asked.

"Yes, I'll get by."

He was thinking of Gila. Perhaps he could stay with her. But he was sure that Jesse or Mr. Townley could put him up for a while.

Jake moved his hand slowly from Martin's knee to the back of his neck. He squeezed the loose flesh between his fingers, massaging with fingers that were strong and warm.

"If you need anything, let us know. Don't forget—we're still your parents."

Martin nodded. It wasn't necessary to reply.

PART THREE

CHAPTER 16

Going Up to Jerusalem

It was a bright Sunday morning around eight o'clock. In the center of Tel Aviv people were beginning to bustle around, walking to work. Secretaries, store owners, businessmen, teachers. The sabbath was over for another week, that one day of respite, that quiet sleepy day.

It was a fresh morning, almost cool. It would be a couple of hours before the sun delivered its full, hot rays to the city. Martin wanted to leave early, to board the bus for Jerusalem. He wanted to begin the trip in high spirits without sweat clinging to his armpits. He wanted to begin it hopefully, a young bird in the early morning chirping. Singing. Wrestling with a worm. He wanted to begin with enthusiasm as if his body were part of the clean, blue sky.

The buses trembled and shuddered at the station, shooting blue smoke and fine films of gas from their exhausts. The bus to Jerusalem was crowded. Rabbis, soldiers, Arabs in keffiehs and white robes. Martin searched around for a seat. At first, it appeared that every available seat had been taken. Then he spotted one halfway down the aisle. A young soldier was sitting beside the window, the seat next to him was vacant. Martin hauled his suitcase down the aisle, stopped, heaved it over his head, jammed it in until it rested securely in the rack.

The bus smelled of marinated herring and olives. Mixed with these aromas, the smell of exhaust and sweat. On the other side of the aisle, two Chasidic rabbis sat in long black coats. They chatted to one another, their earlocks swinging back and forth. Between them they shared a bag of sunflower seeds, expertly opening the hard skins with their teeth, devouring the seeds, spitting out the shells. All this was done with their mouths. They only raised their hands to slip another seed between their teeth.

At the back door an Arab stood, one leg bent and a foot on top of a watermelon. A dagger was hooked into the belt of his robe, a curved dagger sheathed in a bejewelled case.

The soldier sitting beside Martin leaned his head against the windowpane. He looked extremely tired. His face was drawn and pale with exhaustion. It was a lean, chiseled face. He looked no more than eighteen years old.

These were the people of this country, Martin kept thinking. In two years he had learned little about them or the strange guttural language they spoke. Only a few words of Hebrew had seeped into his skull. It was almost like listening to the chirp of birds, or the cry of gulls. Once in a while he could pick out the odd phrase, a familiar greeting or exclamation. Otherwise the chatter was meaningless. From the slap of the bus's wheels he could understand as much, or from the frame rattling, or the clicking of sunflower seeds as the shells broke against teeth and mixed with saliva.

For the most part his friends were Europeans and Americans; Gila was the only exception. Josephine from Johannesburg. Mr. Townley from New York. Jesse from Bulgaria and Paris. Peter Stoneman from Toronto. Lisa from Chicago.

The bus rattled down the single-lane highway. They crossed the flatlands very quickly. Irrigated fields whipped past the windows. Small farmhouses, kibbutzim.

Martin felt something on his left shoulder. He was almost afraid to glance over. It was the soldier's head. During his sleep his head had swung from its windowpane rest, and had fallen on Martin's shoulder. It was not a comfortable feeling for Martin: this stranger sleeping like a small, weary child on his shoulder. He was tempted to nudge him, to say something, to wake him. But how tired he looked. Why be embarrassed?—Martin thought. Who was noticing anyway? And the young man looked so innocent with his eyelashes trembling. Just for a second Martin felt a rivulet of pride course through his body. Wasn't it an honour to have his shoulder so used by an Israeli soldier? Sleep, he kept thinking, have a good sleep, my shoulder is strong enough to support you. Rest from all the watches you have kept, the nights that shudder with cocked rifles. Rest from the scorpions, and the desert sun.

Martin glanced around the bus. Everyone on it was just as innocent, he kept thinking, when sleep relaxed their faces. When sleep allowed their lips to part. Everyone in the beginning was a baby just like his brother Darrell. Under all the scarred, wrinkled, semi-scorched skins, a small baby hid. A gurgly innocent thing. A help-less bundle of flesh that hid no evil in its heart.

They hit a bump and the soldier stirred. He opened his eyes for a second.

"I am sorry," he murmured, still half-asleep.

"That's O.K.," Martin managed to reply in Hebrew.

His eyelids fell shut again. For a second he had jerked his head as if he were going to move it away. It was a quick, momentary motion. But he didn't do it. His head continued to rock and press against Martin. He was back to sleep again, gurgling in his throat, wispy snores issuing from his nose.

A few Hebrew words had sunk into Martin's heart. They had a biblical ring and beat to them, an old desert power. He was startled by their economy and force. One such word was "ruach". It meant wind, breath, spirit. All three meanings wrapped into a single vibra-tion of sound. Wind, the wind that blew from the Judaean hills, and that same wind was the spirit, the holy spirit, the spirit of freedom, joy, poetry and love. And again it was tied down to the breath in his mouth and his lungs. Breath, a holy life-giving breath, wind, spirit—all one inside his throat.

It was only a matter of letting it out, transforming it into those blue squiggles on white paper. "Ruach", to make the page dance and sing, cry, moan, whisper, laugh, die and be born again. Ruach—the spirit and high pure wind of Nietzsche's dream. Wind that bathed the prophets in their anguish. Breath, the breath of God inside Jeremiah when he lay for three hundred days in dung. It was out there and inside. The breath that Jehovah blew between the stars was the same wind inside his lungs. The spirit that grew shiny planets from black murk was the gurgly sound, the very same emanating from the spent soldier lying on his shoulder.

The soldier continued to sleep. His head rocked back and forth as dreams crossed his weary rest. Occasionally he mumbled a message deep from his insides, only intelligible to his unconscious. A mes-sage, a warning perhaps, an instruction, a hope, a memory, a wish, a word of love, mumbled on Martin's shoulder.

Martin began to think about Chaim, his sister's boyfriend. He too was a young soldier doing his two years in the Israeli army. He was dark-skinned, a lean, muscular Yemenite with bright blue eyes. Martin was fascinated by some of his stories. How they camped in the desert. Often in the morning a young soldier would discover a scorpion on his bare arm.

"It's not a hard thing," Chaim said in broken English. "The scorpion. You just have to get him off. You know, with your fingers. What's the word? . . Debrah, you know."

"Flick him off," Debrah said excitedly, her brown eyes burning and full of life.

"Yeah, yes. That's it. Very simple thing. Just flick him off. Then maybe," Chaim began to grin, "stomp him with a boot. Grind him in."

Chaim began to laugh. His white teeth flashed in startling contrast to his almost black skin.

Martin tried his best to imagine the situation: how one could possibly flick a scorpion from the skin without bungling it. Without the tail suddenly and vigorously snapping over the head to deliver its full load of poison into the bloodstream. Just flick him off. How was it possible? Chaim made the motion look so effortless and cool, as if he were talking about removing a bread crumb.

Sleep, soldier, Martin thought. You need your rest. It's the least I can do for you: offer my tired shoulder, let you sleep undisturbed until the bus rattles into Jerusalem. What deserts had the young soldier camped in? How many poisonous snakes had he dodged in the Negev?

Up the snake-curved highway the bus began its ascent. Another Hebrew word jostled and burned inside Martin's mind. It too flowed, danced, curved. It was double, intricate, complex, orderly. It wedded idea to blood, spirit to flesh. This word, the word in his mind, was a double entity like Jesse's yin and yang.

Aliyah—going up, it meant. Going up physically in the bus to Jerusalem, going up spiritually to a higher plane. When a Jew in the synagogue was called forward to walk up the steps of the altar and read from the sacred sheepskin torah—this was an aliyah. When a Jew heard the call to go to Israel, land of his fathers, this was an aliyah. And when a Jew heard himself beckoned to Jerusalem, this too was an aliyah.

Up to Jerusalem in a bus full of rabbis and olives. Up to the city that was supposed to sit in God's palm, in a cleft of the Judaean hills.

Once again Martin was going up to the city of his fathers, to the place that smelled of sperm trees on summer nights. Two years before, his whole family had been called to Israel by an old goat-horn in the blood. Now they had no words to read from. No law. No torah. They had to read the message, now, from the rocks, from the sun-splashed highway, from the bones of soldiers who died in '48 and '56. They had to read what they could from the rusted tanks that littered the roadside up to Jerusalem.

Left there, stranded, burnt-out, useless, a commemoration of that war in 1948.

This was the trouble, Martin kept thinking. How well was he reading from the rocks? And reading wasn't enough. He had to make sense out of the whole thing. At his bar-mitzvah he had read the holy words. Hebrew he was reading, word upon strange word. But he had no idea what they were saying. He sang it all out on the day he was supposed to become a man, and join the whole community. He did his best. He got through the ordeal. But he had no idea of what he had spun over the heads of the congregation.

Now, it was even more difficult. Stones were the words; hills, highways, sunsets, people, buses, movements. From this, from these bare clues he had to learn something—discover himself amid the turmoil. What was it? Who was he? Where was he going? Why was he on the bus that day? What was he doing in this country? He couldn't answer a single question to his satisfaction. But how could he continue to live without making some sense out of the whole thing?

The bus rocked around a curve, hundreds of feet, now, above the flatlands. The soldier awoke for a second.

"Yerushalaim," he breathed.

Jerusalem, that was all that issued from his mouth, a whimper, as if the word was the name of his wife or girlfriend. It was as if he had breathed forth Shoshannah, Rebecca, or Ruth. Yerushalaim, that was all he said, and his eyes closed once again.

Martin smiled to himself. He glanced out the window past the soldier. He looked down to the valley below. It almost made him dizzy, his knees turning to water, his heart a fumbling butterfly. Down, the hills plunged.

For two thousand years, he mused, this land belonged to strangers. It was passed like a tired old cow from landlord to landlord. The cow grew sad-eyed and its belly sagged. How it detested the feel of strange hands on its udders. It yearned for its proper owner. And the Jews looked back over their shoulders. From Warsaw they gazed. From Odessa. From Dachau. From Auschwitz they leaned. How was the old cow doing?—the beloved pet and family milk-giver. How was she aging? And they heard reports that saddened them. The flowers no longer bloomed—an ear was tattered. The sands grew over the cities—the pet had developed a sore on the leg.

Martin gazed out the window at the burnt-out, rusted tanks. He knew the story well—how Jerusalem was cut off during the war, how there was an attempt to starve its inhabitants into submission. Up and down the lean highway the Jews fought. They were not the same people who had bowed their heads in chambers of remorse, and sucked in their last breaths, death mixed with gas.

The bus rocked over a bump. The soldier woke again.

"Are we there?" he murmured.

"No, not yet, chaver," Martin sighed.

The soldier yawned, and slumped back down, almost nestled into Martin's armpit. For a second Martin was tempted to place an arm around his shoulder, to draw him close like a small child, to cradle him. To say: some day the wars are going to end. Just rest, soldier.

He wished that such an act would not evoke hostile stares. He wished that the rabbis would understand, that the soldier would understand, that he himself could do it without a sneering voice harshly rasping in his ear:

"Have you gone crazy, Martin?" the inner voice nagged. "Have you turned fruity? Have you gone queer on us?"

What a relief if he only could do it. Just let the soldier know completely that he understood how hot the sun flashed above Massada. Let him know that his own mind and body were equally tired. That his own face was equally pale and drawn.

The bus heaved and nudged up the last steep incline toward the city. Already the air was noticeably cooler. Martin had not set foot in the city for almost a year. He had recently corresponded with Gila; luckily, just before she changed apartments.

A smile hovered around his lips as the bus lunged and groaned its way towards the last hill. He felt exhilarated. This had always been his feeling when arriving in Jerusalem. The air was not only cooler, but cleaner, purer. It seemed to supply more oxygen to his brain. He could hear music inside him as the first buildings appeared over the brow of the last hill. What was the song? Did it have words or did the lullaby change each time he entered the ancient capital? Perhaps it had elements of Beethoven's Ninth, a chorus singing triumphant odes of joy.

To enter Jerusalem, Martin thought, was like coming to a different country. It was unlike anything else in Israel. Haifa, Tel Aviv, the Negev were all somehow related. They all bustled and bristled in their own ways. Jerusalem sang and dreamed. It spread its skirts of cool air, and the air riveleted among its buildings, its valleys, its cypress trees. The air travelled down the mountains and the hills. It seemed to give hope to the workers and soldiers, businessmen and housewives who lived in the flatlands and deserts below.

It sang a song to them: above you I make a garden of flowers and prayers, with my skirts I make it, with my cobbled streets. I make you a song of fine silk and pink stones. I devise a dream of vine-yards, grapes and gold. Some day you can lay down your pens and diapers, your drills and guns, when you are tired, when your throat has filled with dust, you can come unto me.

Martin filled his lungs with the high, mountain air. It was rushing through the open windows of the bus. It was dispelling the stench of gas and herring, sweat and sleep. Everyone on the bus perked up as the bus devoured the last hill. The rabbis shook dust off their coats, put away their seeds. The Arab tucked his watermelon under his arm, his face, too, smiling and refreshed. The weary soldier revived. He sat bolt upright in his seat.

"Ah, Yerushalaim," he said with enthusiasm. He put his fingers to his lips and blew a kiss out the window. "I am so glad to see you again."

He turned to Martin and asked in broken English:

"How do you like our Jerusalem?"

Martin smiled. His blood was tingling in his chest and forehead. The old song lilted in his veins.

"It's the most beautiful city in Israel," he grinned, sniffing the air.

"Yes," the soldier sighed.

The bus rolled into the city. Martin was thinking about Gila, Jesse, Peter, Mr. Townley. What would it be like to see them again? Had they changed in the last year? Had he been transformed in some noticeable way? He wanted to surprise all of them with his sudden reappearance. Only Gila knew for sure that he was coming back. But he had not told her the exact day of his arrival.

He walked down the steps of the bus breathing deeply. His legs felt springy and energetic. The suitcase felt light. He wanted to breathe and breathe and breathe great gulps of air. Pure air. Clean air. High mountain air, the freshest, coolest air in the whole country.

CHAPTER 17

Gila

On the evening of his arrival Martin found himself in Gila's new room. It was a peculiarly cool evening for late June in Jerusalem. It was almost chilly enough to wear a sweater inside. Gila's room smelled of concrete and fresh paint. The building had been recently constructed.

"Well, writer-boy, how has your life been this last year?" Gila asked.

She sat curled up on her bed, clutching a pillow. Martin sat beside her leaning against the wall. The room was decorated in bright yellows and reds. A couple of miniature dolls sat on her bureau. She didn't give him a chance to answer, but followed the first question with another.

"Have you made any new friends? I know the girls in Tel Aviv. Oo-la-la, so pretty. I bet you met some on the Dizengoff."

Martin felt himself blushing. He still didn't answer. His gaze dreamed forward at Gila. She looked almost the same, as if her life in the last year had continued as the year before. Weekdays at the office perched over a typewriter, pecking out with increasing speed the letters her boss needed. She wore her black hair in the same way, cut into bangs across the forehead, boyishly short at the back. Her black eyes sparkled and danced as they had previously. She still looked like a virgin to him. Yet he was seeing her differently when he leaned back against the wall, took a deep breath and relaxed. Was this a change in Gila, or something he was unable to see before?

Her whole body looked rounder, softer, more vulnerable. He could see it beneath her pixyish grin. Beneath the sparkle in her black sabra eyes. An area of softness. A place that could bleed and weep, suffer and cry out. It was something he had overlooked during his first year in Jerusalem.

"No, I didn't make too many friends," he replied, squirming his back into a more comfortable position against the wall.

"You mean you were all alone?" Gila asked in disbelief. Her brown eyes grew larger. She looked almost disappointed.

Martin had never been good at lying. It made him feel uneasy, as if the lie were a dark area he had allowed to settle in his heart. He was almost afraid to do it. It seemed that a lie once rooted could grow just like a weed. It could flower, develop, be joined by others. If one got started, then two, three, four, what could prevent the darkness from taking over his entire being? It would be possible for his whole person to be so filled with this poison that he would no longer be able to distinguish what was true and what was false. He didn't want one to get started with Gila.

"I met one girl," he said softly, hesitantly, pulling at the bedspread with his fingers. "An older girl from South Africa. We were good friends."

"From South Africa!" Gila exclaimed, her black eyes widening. "Was she a dancer?"

It seemed a strange question. Martin smiled, then frowned.

"No," he shook his head. "Why do you ask that?"

Gila's face wrinkled with giggles. She hugged the pillow to her, forced it between her legs.

"Oh, it's stupid. I saw a belly dancer once in Tel Aviv. She was from South Africa. Isn't that silly? How could she be the same one?"

Gila patted the pillow.

"So, don't just sit there like a log. Tell me about this older woman."

Gila drew out the word "older", and sucked in her cheeks at the same time. It made her face look gaunt, and mockingly serious.

"What's there to tell?" Martin shrugged. "We were close friends. We talked a lot about poetry and books. Stuff like that."

Gila rubbed her cheek against the pillow. She began to blush. The color ran up her neck into her cheeks.

"Did you sleep with her?" Gila asked.

"Oh, Gila, come on," Martin gasped.

He was a little embarrassed, but happy that she had asked the question. The question, it seemed, had been sitting on the bed with them. Like an invisible person it had been sitting there, leering. Now it was out in the open.

"Yes," he whispered, bowing his head. "But what about you? You haven't told me anything about yourself."

"Are you trying to change the subject?" Gila blushed.

Martin could see her body trembling. She looked like she was cold and unable to get warm. The light sweater wasn't helping, nor the pillow.

"Are your teeth chattering?" Martin asked.

"Yes, this house gets so cold. We've had quite a few of these nights. But I guess it'll soon be summer. Then we'll be saying that it's too hot."

Martin bunched more of the bedspread beneath his hand.

"You didn't answer my question," he said.

"Oh, you know my life. It's not exciting like yours. I go to work. Come home at night. See a few of my friends."

"Have you been to Tiberias to see your parents?"

Martin could hear her teeth clicking together. Suddenly, he wanted to put his arm around her, just to warm her up. She looked lonely to him. Even a little frightened. He hadn't noticed this in her the year before, when she was living in the apartment with Lisa and her Israeli girlfriend, Esther. Now, she shared this apartment with nobody but the landlord, Moshe.

"Not so often as before," she shivered. "It's a long trip "

Martin moved closer to her, and put his arm around her.

"*Mah pitom?* What's that for?" she asked, drawing away, but not completely out of his embrace.

"You look so cold."

She moved closer to him, and let her head fall on his chest. Her teeth chattered more violently than before. Her whole body shook under his arm.

"What's wrong with you, Gila?" Martin asked. His voice sounded worried. "Are you sick?"

"It's O.K. It'll go away."

Gila looked like a small fragile thing, still shivering and clutching her pillow, nestling against Martin. With Esther gone—who did she have in this city to cling to? Martin could see her walking home at night over the bare stones, chill wind biting at her ankles and calves.

"How is Esther?" Martin finally asked.

Gila squirmed around in his embrace.

"I think she's O.K. I don't see her too much any more. You know what happened to her? Something terrible," Gila giggled. "She got married."

"Really? That was kind of sudden, wasn't it?"

Gila pushed herself away from Martin, and sat upright once again.

"She married a doctor. Well, a student really. He's going to be a doctor."

A heaviness seeped into Gila's voice. It hung over their heads.

Martin could hear the wind blowing outside. It rustled through the cypress trees, and just slightly rattled the windowpanes.

"Have *you* had any romances?" Martin asked.

Gila slipped a corner of the pillow between her teeth. She bit down on it. For a second or so it stilled her teeth, the insistent clicking.

"There is a man," she said dreamily. "He's a lot older than I am. One of my bosses down at work."

"How old is he?" Martin asked. Gila's tone had emphasized his age.

"About forty-two."

"Forty-two," Martin repeated as if the answer had given him a small electrical shock.

Forty-two seemed ancient to him. His own mother was forty-two, and his father only three years older.

"Yes, forty-two. That's not so old."

"What do you see in him?" Martin asked.

Gila let the edge of the pillow slip out of her mouth. She hugged it to her as if it were a giant ragdoll.

She began to smile to herself. She was no longer giggling. The smile was gentle and soft.

"Well, he's not much to look at. He's going a little bald, and he wears glasses. I guess it's the way he touches me. It's hard to explain. He just caresses me on the chest. Not even on my breasts, but between them. I know it sounds silly, but it makes me feel so warm and protected. I can just lie there and let him do it for hours."

Gila sighed to herself. She leaned her head against the wall, letting her eyelids shut.

"Have you slept with him?" Martin asked. There was just a touch of anger and jealousy in his voice. He felt cheated. He knew he had no right to, after telling her about Josephine. But the feeling was there. It was mixed with a feeling of disgust. A vivid picture of the boss's hand hung in his mind. The flesh was wrinkled from its forty-two years. The hand was bony. It was massaging Gila's fresh young skin. The contact made him feel sick to his stomach. Gila's skin—young, alive, glowing, without a hint of wrinkles or flab. The boss's skin—scarred by the weather, wrinkled with age It sickened him to imagine them naked together: the boss flabby, bald-headed, near-sighted, hovering over Gila, wheezing in his middle-aged throat.

"No, I wouldn't let him. He wanted to," Gila said, avoiding Martin's stare. "I wanted to sometimes. I guess I was just scared. But he's a gentle man. He never forced me, not once."

Martin felt like letting out a long sigh of relief, but he pressed his lips together and prevented it from coming out.

"I'm glad you didn't," Martin said.

"Why?" Gila asked sarcastically. "Because you want to?"

Martin began to blush. He lowered his head. The embarrassment rolled through his body in waves. His neck got hotter, his cheeks, his forehead. He could feel sweat beading on the palms of his hands.

"Don't you think he's kind of old?" Martin asked, putting a bite into the question.

"I don't want to talk about him," Gila said angrily. She pushed the pillow away from herself, and threw it on the floor. "Anyway I don't see him too much any more."

A sudden switch of emotion occurred inside Martin. Gila's loneliness once again flooded him.

"You don't?" There was a tone of regret in his voice.

"He's married," Gila spat. "It's not very safe for him. And I start feeling guilty when I think about his wife and kids."

Gila began to shake again. Martin couldn't tell if she was cold once again, or trembling with anger. He wanted to put his arm around her shoulder, but he was afraid she would throw it off just as quickly as she had thrown the pillow. The walls of the small room began to close in on him. He wanted to make peace with her, but he didn't know exactly how to do it.

"I'm sorry, Gila," he finally said, whispering the words from his chest. "It's your business. I don't have any right to say anything."

Gila let her head drop forward.

"Gila? Do you want to go for a walk? I think it's still light out."

"Yes," Gila nodded, "I want to go out for a while. I get tired of this room . . . Martin, I have an idea. Let's go up to Herzl Mountain. There's a good view from there. You can see all of Jerusalem. Have you ever been up there?"

Martin shook his head back and forth.

"Is it far?"

"No, silly. You don't even know where Herzl Mountain is? Come on, I'll show you."

Gila jumped off the bed, grabbed his hand, pulling him up.

The sun hung low in the sky, bright and fiery, large as a harvest moon, but robbed of its usual heat. Gila's apartment was not far from her old one, near the university on the outskirts of Jerusalem. The Warsaw Restaurant was a couple of miles away.

The streets were almost empty. Once in a while they would spot a housewife going home to her suburban apartment, carrying a netted bag filled with groceries: *challah*, olives, herring and tomatoes.

Couldn't they get along without anyone?—Martin wondered. Just Gila and himself like two pioneers in the desert, clinging to one another, warming one another, holding hands, subduing the cool shafts of early evening wind? Could they build a little world together on the outskirts of Jerusalem, and people it with their dreams? Eat challah together for the rest of their lives? He gazed at Gila. Could she somehow satisfy him? Could she get along without Esther and her parents, could he survive without Josephine and his parents? Wasn't it worth a try?—to see if it could be done.

Yet he felt lonely as they walked together towards Herzl Mountain. It was an old feeling: one he used to get as a child when he wandered the empty schoolyards and fields with his dog Blackie. It was as if they were the only two people in the entire city, in the whole world. Only they were real: Gila and Martin. The others were imitations, made of cardboard, composed of cotton and sawdust, going through the motions of life, but not completely real. And this feeling would change suddenly. No, it was Gila and himself who were imitating life, imitating lovers, trying to be in love, to be real, alive; but it wasn't working, no matter how tightly he squeezed her hand. They were only two bits of straw blown by the wind. Nothing more substantial than that—blown helter-skelter, here and there, this way and that; swirled from the apartment, blown along the road and up the mountain.

How he wished that they were self-contained, a universe of two with not a need outside their mutual embrace. It would solve so many problems. He could just come to rest against her thighs and breasts. They could just blot out the world with their kisses, hang a blanket over the whole sky, just get under together and be happy and content. This too, he did as a child when he was nine or ten with a girlfriend in Queensland, the vacation area down the coast from Halifax. There too, the wind blew, driving chill salt-spray up the winding south-shore road. He and his new girlfriend built a tent together out of blankets, hung it between two lawn chairs. The blankets were well draped, securely tucked in at the bottom. Not a gust of chill breeze was able to enter, not a shaft of unwanted light. They crawled in together. They held hands, kissed until their mouths and tongues became weary and sore. He wanted to stay inside it forever and ever and ever. He wanted to live happily ever after, just as Sleeping Beauty did, and Snow White, and Hansel and Gretel. There they would live, just the two of them, surrounded by the warmth and comfort of blankets. Just drink cokes, chew on potato chips. No longer would he have to deal with the harsh reality of going to school. No longer would he have to make friends back in Halifax.

He gazed at Gila, searched her face for an answer: her black eyes, her round cheeks, her black hair. How long could he love, hug, kiss and talk with this person before he got bored? It had happened before when he was younger, just a teenager. Everything in the beginning appeared exciting and new, fresh. Surely, he had thought, his new love would be endless. And then, the disappointment would set in—the let-down, the sameness, the utter boredom with his girlfriend's voice, face, whispers and kisses. She slowly would become as uninteresting as a rubber doll. She still spoke, but he had heard the words a thousand times before. It was an old recording with worn sounds emanating from her lips. Her body was no longer exciting to touch, nor her lips. Rubbery. It had all become rubbery, flat, dull, repetitious.

"There's Herzl Mountain," Gila said excitedly, pointing it out to Martin.

"It's not very high," Martin answered, shuffling along, looking at the pebbles on the highway, kicking at them occasionally, watching them spin into the ditch beside the road.

"What do you expect?" Gila asked, a little annoyed. "It's not Switzerland."

Martin gazed at the hill in front of him, Herzl Mountain on the outskirts of Jerusalem, named for that first Zionist who dreamed long ago of carrying the Jews back to Israel. It definitely wasn't a mountain. It was given that grand title, but it was no higher than any of the other hills surrounding the city, and it wasn't a high hill at that.

Herzl Mountain was almost deserted that evening, only an attendant or two walking the gravel paths, picking up loose papers, tending to the flowers. The flowers were well cared for. Those who planted them seemed to be saying: look, even here on this lean, bare rock that not so long ago felt the sting of bullets and blood, even here we can grow petunias, pansies, roses, red tiny subtle flowers. Look, the flowers said, as their delicate heads tossed in the breeze, see, we are flowers, just as in any other country of the world. Look at us, gaze at and appreciate the fine fibres along our petals, the slim stems alive and pulsing with sap. Touch us, we are real, smell us, we can be cut and placed in vases, just as they do in Germany, France, Czechoslovakia.

The flowers eased Martin's mind, this display of delicate beauty on the sides of the gaunt hill. Surely Herzl, the bearded visionary with black gaping eyes, would have appreciated this monument. He would've bent his tired back, cupped a blue-petalled pansy in his hand, touched his nose to the fragrance.

Gila bent down and sniffed at a red-yellow bunch. Martin followed her example, bending his stiff, chilly legs, crouching, paying tribute to those who had spent their hours planting, watering, taking care of these fragile things. It seemed very important to him to learn how to appreciate them, and all other small, inoffensive spurts of life: plants, flowers, grass. He remembered Jesse, his friend. He certainly had a love for soft, tiny things. Things that were red in color, or yellow, things that were like certain women. From Jesse and Josephine he had begun to see a dark emptiness inside him: a roaring, ferocious area. In that space no flowers grew, no fragrances wafted. Instead, storms lashed out, lightning-strokes, hail, hurricanes. It was filled with screams, shouts, hysterical laughter.

Why not start from this minute onward, Martin said to himself, here on Herzl Mountain with Gila, why not begin to turn over a new leaf, start to notice the tiny inoffensive beauty that surrounded him? Why not begin with these very flowers he was cupping in his hand, drawing towards his nose? And wasn't Gila part of it? Didn't she have a subtle sweetness that he had overlooked, trampled upon, ignored? He gazed again at her face. He wanted very much to see her, the real Gila, the Gila beneath the sabra, the Gila who was hiding beneath the tanned skin, the sparkling eyes.

They walked together up the side of the hill, each one silent, floating along in their own thoughts and dreams. Martin took Gila's hand; he squeezed it as if he wanted to tell her about his new resolution. Her hand felt tiny in his, lost inside his palm and long fingers. She didn't squeeze back.

"Come on," Gila said, "I want to show you something up there."

Gila was pointing to the top of the hill. It was only a hundred yards away, the stone-studded brow of Herzl Mountain. It looked black, angular, impenetrable against the startling blue of the sky. It was a hill that had stood in the same spot since the days of the prophets. It had seen the coming and going of David, Solomon, Jeremiah, and Jesus Christ. They had fought beneath its visage, written beneath it, sung, loved, committed sins. For all those centuries the hill had endured, its pebbles getting rounder perhaps, its peak getting slightly worn. But it had stood. Armies marched over it, angels sent by God, messiahs.

Gila ran up the hill, her sandals spurting out tiny pebbles behind her. Martin was curious and followed closely.

She finally stopped, and stood silently in front of a huge black slab of rock. On the rock was engraved Herzl's name, and the dates of his birth and death. There were a number of other slabs with the names of other members of his family.

Gila pointed to a few gravel plots beside the huge rocks. They were empty, without flowers, monuments or words.

"Do you know what those are?" Gila asked.

Martin shook his head.

"Those are for the other people in Herzl's family. When they die they'll be brought up here and buried beside him."

The idea sent shivers down Martin's back, cool tingles that swept from his neck down to his ankles. Looking into those empty gravel plots was like looking into an eyeless socket. And they seemed almost alive, like animals, or huge eerie spirits, waiting, just waiting for the bodies they would eventually swallow.

"It's a horrible idea," Martin blurted.

"*Mah pitom?* What's wrong? Shouldn't his family be buried with him? What's wrong with that? He was a great man."

Martin screwed up his face. The expression was a mixture of horror and disgust.

"But they're just sitting there. Waiting. It's death-worship, that's what it is. All these stones praising death."

Gila looked puzzled.

"You talk so crazy sometimes," she said. "I don't understand what you're saying. It's just a cemetery, that's all."

Martin was angry. His chest ached. He was angry with the huge, black stones, with the empty gravel plots, with Gila, with the cold wind sliding up his trousers. He felt an intense desire to smash everything, to blow up the rocks, the graves, to leave only the flowers, the bright red-petalled flowers untouched.

He turned his back on the tombs, and walked away alone. The pebbles crackled beneath his footsteps. Glancing back over his shoulder, he could see Gila still standing in front of the graves. Her shoulders were hunched, rounded. She looked smaller than before, lonelier, more vulnerable. It seemed that the wind could suddenly snatch her away, fling her skyward into a void where nobody would ever find her. Gila dreamed in front of the stones, the words, the gravel plots. She almost felt like crying. It would be a relief to feel her eyes fill with tears. But she knew that this wasn't going to happen, not here, not at this time.

Martin walked with determination towards the edge of the hill, where the sun could be seen setting. She could stand there forever, he thought to himself, just stand there, hunched and weary, tired and lonely, just stare at the blackness of the stones, and dream. He wasn't going to go back and pull her along by the hand. Nor was he going to apologize. It *was* death-worship, he kept thinking, ancestor-worship, with everyone walking up the cold mountain to stand before the lifeless stones. Why didn't they stop at Herzl? Why did they have to bring in the whole family, wife and brothers, cousins and aunts? Who could tell where the thing would end? Death-worship, that was what it was, he said to himself with conviction.

Nietzsche had warned against such things: a monstrous fascination with the black pit that swallowed everything. Death the king, and head of the family, death the final judge and lover. He didn't want to be sucked into it, nor did he wish to idolize this dead prophet of Zionism.

A quote from Einstein rumbled inside his head. He gazed at the red fiery ball of setting sun. It was blood-red, hanging above the horizon. Bright as an unripe cherry. Dazzling as blood. It looked curiously cold, this fiery mass, curiously unreal that evening. His father had first told him of Einstein's immortal words.

"I believe in internationalism," his father had said once, back in Halifax. "The Jews were living that way in every country on the globe. They were a people without a country, but they had something more valuable—freedom. All this ended, of course, with Hitler. But Martin, do you know what Einstein had to say about Zionism? He said it so well. He expressed my own thoughts to a T. 'Israel,' he said, 'is a necessary evil.' It was a backward step, Martin, not only for the Jews, but for the entire world."

A necessary evil, Martin kept thinking as he stared at the globe of blood before him, the sun in its early-evening death. Surely Einstein was right. How could it be good? How could any country be good?—huddled inside borders, cursing the inhabitants of the next country, lusting after their fields. Poking out their guns, knocking holes in buildings. Japs cursing Yanks. Yanks laughing at krauts. Everyone despising kikes. His head began to swirl, and the wind seemed to be tugging at the sun, trying to pull it down, but the bright blood-red orb was not descending quickly that evening. It stood defiant, a drop of blood in front of him. Martin's thoughts swirled with the wars of history, this country and that rising to power, trampling on neighbours, gaining dominion, and eventually falling apart at the seams. How succinctly and with wisdom bushy-browed Einstein had put it. His white locks must have been in a flurry of inspiration that day: Israel, he said to himself, obviously necessary, but an evil.

The splash of orange-red sunset flooded his eyes. He looked back again. Gila was a vague bent outline against the rock-face of Herzl Mountain. She merged with the rocks. She was swallowed by them. Slowly, she turned, and walked towards him. Her head was bent. She raised it suddenly, smiling once again.

"What are you looking at?" she shouted.

"The sunset," he shouted back.

His words echoed through the hills. They sounded like heavy stones falling, heavy, strained, almost lifeless. His throat felt stretched. It was an effort to form any word in his throat. His throat was stretched and dry.

"Oh, it's so beautiful tonight," she chirped, standing beside him.

"Yes, this is life," he said, "not those stones and graves."

There was a finality in the tone of his voice, a professorial statement of fact. He wanted to seize Gila by the shoulders, to shake her, to turn her head into the sun. He wanted her head to spin as his head was spinning, for her to feel the thoughts that stampeded through his mind. If only, he thought, they could exchange brains and hearts for a few minutes or hours. Perhaps then, they could understand each other better.

The sun held on, giving up bits of sky grudgingly, refusing to die and be swallowed by night. Blood-red and defiant it hung above the horizon. It summoned up a legion of images that evening. It was the bleeding arm of a child, the arm freshly bitten by a dog or torn by shrapnel. It was the vagina of a young girl before she grew hair to cover the sore. A drop of blood it was, and the ruby at the center of a crown. It was the hooked, bloody eye of a fish, a poor perch he had caught when he was a child. The sky seemed to be weeping that evening huge drops of blood; crying for all the soldiers blown apart in wars.

It slowly descended. The chill wind picked up on Herzl Mountain. Martin began to shiver. Gila hugged her sweater around her shoulders and arms. Martin glanced around. Nobody could be seen, not a soul stirring, not even a tiny animal slithering over the stones.

They were the last people standing on Herzl Mountain, the very last—two sets of eyes watching the sun go down.

"It's getting cold up here," Gila gulped.

Martin was shivering. He began to feel sorry for Gila once again, and sorry for himself. What a cold bloody world they both lived in. Were they not surrounded by death? On all sides? The cool dogs of death leering at them from the shadows. Darkness was falling on Herzl Mountain, on Gila and Martin, a blackness that the sun could no longer hold off. Surely Herzl was groaning in his grave to see the flowers all extinguished.

He put his arm around her shoulder. She didn't protest this time, or draw away.

"Let's go back," he whispered, "and get the heater going in your room."

Gila nodded on his shoulder. No words came out of her mouth, not even a sigh. Her chin pressed against his arm, up and down it moved in agreement.

* * *

In Gila's room the gas heater sputtered blue-yellow flames. The stone floor and the walls were cool to the touch. Was this the right time, he wondered, to take her in his arms, to try to enter her body? It was not going to be easy, he thought, no, not easy as it had been with Josephine. It wouldn't be a matter of riding into her, gliding, floating, travelling upwards. She did not have Josephine's knowing hands that could guide him to the exact spot, nor Josephine's experience to make everything appear fluid and natural. The burden was on him now, squarely on his shoulders. He would have to show the way, to do it gently, kindly, with sensitivity and warmth.

There was another problem that gnawed at him. She was not barren as Josephine had originally been. She had no idea, he was sure, about diaphragms. The responsibility rested with him. Before he left Tel Aviv he had purchased a package of safes. It was up to him to get one on, to make sure it was fitted properly and did not break.

Gila was standing in front of the gas burner warming her hands. Her eyes looked soft and dreamy as if she were becoming a part of the blue-yellow warmth she stood above.

"Do you have any place to stay tonight?" she asked. Her voice sounded soft and faraway, gentle and a little vague, as if the words were floating up from sleep, from the middle of a dream.

"Not really," he answered.

Gila smiled. Her face looked soft above the light cast by the flames.

"Would you like to stay here? Moshe's away on holidays. He won't be back tonight."

Martin felt relieved, and tiny fingers of warmth began to massage his chest and the inside of his stomach.

"Yes," he whispered back at her. It was barely audible, this reply. It was gently spoken, softly uttered, a whisper, a sigh.

He was very happy that she had asked him, that he didn't have to manipulate the question himself, to sneak it into the conversation. He liked the way she had said it, with an openness that surprised him a little, and the question sent ripples of warmth through his chest. He got up from the bed-sofa and walked over to her, wrapping his arms around her. How much he wanted to love her, to feel "the real thing" as he imagined it should be felt: two beings melting into each other, becoming one, totally immersed in each other's warmth.

"Let's go to bed," he whispered in her ear, "it'll be warmer under the covers."

Gila nodded silently, pressing against him, nestling, cuddling, trying to make herself tinier so that she could lose herself in Martin's arms.

The idea excited him. He had never been so completely alone with her before. Nobody in the apartment except the two of them. No voices seeping in from adjoining rooms.

The blood began pulsing, beating, throbbing in his groin as he began to undress her—slipping her black jersey over her head. She held her arms straight over her head like a child.

She was not playing a game with him any more, he kept thinking. He could see it in her eyes, a brown dreaminess, a giving in. He could feel it in the softness of her flesh, a surrender. And he was sure he could detect a tremor of desire on her lips.

How soft and malleable she was becoming as he unzipped her brown slacks. She seemed to be melting, turning into butter beneath his fingertips.

How careful he would have to be with her now, careful not to hurt her, to cause her pain, to stretch her too far.

He was totally responsible for her now, for making sure no sperm entered her and united with her eggs.

They got into bed together, both of them naked and clinging to each other, trying to warm up the room, the city, the world. And suddenly, for a few minutes his desire waned. Why not just embrace, hug, offer each other warmth and friendship and let it go at that?—Martin thought. Did he have to make love with her, to go through with the whole thing as Josephine had instructed? He had slept with a woman, he had made Josephine happy; what else did he have to prove? He held her tightly, the full length of his naked body against hers. He rocked with her back and forth. Why not just sway this way until they both fell asleep?

"Gila," he whispered, "do you want me to sleep with you?"

A tiny reply came back. It was tearful, caught in her throat, choked upward.

"Please, Martin, do it, just do it."

It surprised him, these words, their tone, a plea floating up from inside her belly.

He was no longer hard. Her words did not excite him, but now, there was no backing out of it.

"O.K.," he said, "just a second."

He got out of bed, his toes curling as his feet hit the cold tile floor. It was a chilly walk across the room to the chair where his jeans were draped. Perhaps she would change her mind, he thought, by the time he got back. He fished into a pocket among loose change and keys, until he found the small cardboard package. He clutched the package inside a clenched fist. Shivering with the cool air licking at his armpits and legs, he scampered back to the bed.

Gila was waiting with the covers raised.

"Hurry," she whispered, "it's getting cold in here."

He hugged her once again, bundling her up in his arms, with the package still tucked inside his right hand. He was still soft. For a minute or two desire would return, and a throbbing would begin between his legs. Then he would think about her, this person he was lying naked with, this Gila. He would think about her tiny home beside Lake Tiberias, her brother dead two years. He would think about her life in Jerusalem, how lonely it was, now that Esther was married. Again he would become soft, without a speck of desire.

How could he do it?—he wondered—plunge into this young sabra girl, stretch her apart, force himself inside her? How could he cause one drop of blood to trickle down her leg? He didn't want to hear her cry out in pain. Hadn't she experienced enough pain in the last two years?

Gila reached down and began to massage him with a tiny hand.

"Don't you want to do it?" she asked.

There were tears in her voice. A tiny, faraway cry.

"Yes. Sure," he whispered.

It took a few minutes, but he managed to get the safe on. It felt like a piece of cellophane wrapped around him, a film of plastic that would separate his bare skin from hers. But he had to wear it. There was no way around it—this he knew.

"Try it, Martin, please," she whispered.

He heaved out a sigh as he rolled on top of her.

She was even tighter than he imagined she would be, closed, impenetrable. He had forgotten everything Josephine had told him. It was going too fast. There wasn't any lubricant. He had no idea how gentle he was being, nor how firm. He pressed and pressed and pressed against the small, tight opening. He was afraid if he jabbed too hard the tissue would suddenly split, a jagged tear in her flesh.

"Do you have any vaseline?" he asked.

He tried to relax as she got out of bed and made the chilly journey to the bathroom. At least she had some, he thought to himself. He was going soft inside the safe. The plastic film wrinkled as he lost his erection.

When she returned with the small jar, he scooped out the jelly, and smeared it on her. He anointed the safe with it. Jelly everywhere. A mass of oozing vaseline between her legs, on the safe, on his thighs, on the sheets, on the tips of his fingers. It was dripping and oozing everywhere, it seemed. A mass of greasy lubricant.

It was still difficult to get inside her. He could feel sweat on her shoulders.

"Is it hurting?" he asked.

"Yes," she moaned. "But just do it. Please don't stop now."

Into the mass of jelly he pushed himself, forced himself, with Gila moaning occasionally with pain. Once she cried out, and he stopped completely, ready to give up.

"Go on, please, I'm sorry," she groaned.

This time he pushed harder, almost ramming himself inside. Something seemed to give beneath his weight, to loosen, to part to allow him to enter, completely to enter. He was amazed at how soft she felt inside, once he was completely in. Josephine was rough by comparison. Inside, Gila felt soft as a pouch of tears, a quiet, soft, dark place. What a different place, he thought, thinking about Josephine, how her muscles clamped around him, squeezed him, almost scraped him. He felt almost the exact opposite with Gila—a soft, tearful, dark place where there was no pull of gravity, no weight, just a giving in, a complete melting.

He came very quickly, too quickly to give Gila any pleasure, if she could've felt any after the scraping and pushing and tearing. It was all over suddenly, finished. His sperm spurted into the tip of the safe, and it was over, the air smelling of sweat and vaseline.

That evening they went to sleep quickly without too many words between them. They were both thankful when their eyelids grew heavy, and sleep began to coat their tongues. Outside, the stars wheeled and stood still in their ancient courses. They sparkled white and cool above Herzl Mountain. Above the graves and sleeping flowers they glinted. In *Mea She'arim* the rabbis slept beside their wives and helpmates. Somewhere in Jerusalem Jesse slept, and Peter Stoneman. In Tel Aviv, Jake and Dahlia Kanner slept. Above them all the darkness stretched as it had since the beginning of time, a blanket of blackness sprinkled with cool, white gems.

On the outskirts of Jerusalem, near Herzl Mountain and the university, Gila and Martin slept. They slept on wrinkled sheets, sheets smeared with vaseline. Below their bodies a few drops of blood dried.

CHAPTER 18

Peter's Room

His relationship with Gila didn't end suddenly. There was no explosive argument between them. He made love to her a few more times, but each time she cried out in pain, struggled, pushed him away at the same time as she drew him near. She was no longer a virgin, but the scraping and pushing continued. Each time he would finally slip inside and find that same dark, warm place. It always seemed filled with tears, so soft he could hardly feel it against him.

They drifted apart slowly. After a few days, he came to a decision —to leave completely, to end it once and for all. He wanted to strike out on his own, to get a room, to move from the outskirts to the center of the city, where Peter Stoneman and Jesse were living.

"I think we better end it, Gila," he told her one evening. "It'll be better for both of us."

He was glad when she didn't argue with him. She nodded her head. He could feel tears beneath her eyes, tears in his own throat and chest. But it couldn't continue—both of them weeping together, clinging to one another in the outskirts of Jerusalem. There was something impossible about the whole thing.

"I wish you luck, Martin, with everything."

He kissed her on the forehead, on the cheeks, as if she were a first cousin or a sister. He no longer felt desire for her. It was replaced by a feeling of tenderness. How he wished he could save her from loneliness, that she could somehow save him, that the journey they were on could magically end in each other's arms. But it was impossible.

The next morning he left with his suitcase, early in the morning before she went to work. Once again he kissed her on her cheeks, and they wished each other well.

It was only eight o'clock when he closed the front door of the

apartment. The sun felt bright and cool against his face, and as he
stepped into it, a surge of freedom rippled through him. Again he
was making a fresh start as he had so many times before—he was
leaving everything behind, walking into the brightness of a new
morning. Stepping out he was, alone and free, stepping out into the
cool morning breath of Jerusalem.

A tear hung inside him. The tear was called Gila, Josephine,
Martin. But he couldn't think about it, this sadness that lingered.

He had no definite idea of where he was going, only that he
wanted to take the bus to the center of the city. Inside his wallet, he
had Peter Stoneman's address. It was written on a worn piece of
paper, and he had carried it with him for a long time. Peter Stoneman could've moved three times, but he was going to give the
address a try anyway. He unfolded the crumpled piece of paper as
he waited for the bus. He leaned one leg against his suitcase.
Twenty-nine Rehov ha Neviim, he read in his own scrawled handwriting. After Rehov ha Neviim there was an English translation—
Street of the Prophets. He knew the street was in the downtown
area, this Street of the Prophets where his old friend, he hoped, was
still living. He knew it was somewhere near Zion Square, near the
heart and core of Jerusalem where the chestnut-vendors stood, and
the falafel-sellers hung out.

The bus whisked him past the outlying hills, the low flat buildings
of the university, and the open-air market. His suitcase jostled in the
aisle beside him. A quiet music played in his heart and brain. The
notes seemed composed of early-morning sunlight dancing on the
pink stones of Jerusalem. The city was an old familiar friend. It was
a place he could get close to as Jesse had done. It was a city with
soft contours, shades, ripples of light on old stone, that he could
caress with his eyes. Tel Aviv in comparison was jarring to his
senses, as if on every corner a jackhammer bit into concrete.

The music filled him, bathed him. The notes were composed of
the faces of his old friends—Peter Stoneman with his wide forehead,
Jesse with his elusive, intangible complexion. It was a music filled
with familiar smells—chestnuts roasted on Zion Square, falafels, pita,
and an indistinct aroma that only Jerusalem contained.

What could he call that fragrance that rose from the downtown
streets? There was no name he could think to give it. It was musk,
snuffed candles, oranges, concrete, dust, sunlight, Yemenite women,

chestnuts, lilacs—all mixed together in such delicate proportions that it produced the fragrance he knew so well. He was sure he would recognize it anywhere, but he was equally positive he would only encounter it here, in the old Judaean hills. If he went away for fifty years, and returned a hobbling old man, he was absolutely positive that he would instantly recognize it again.

On Zion Square he stood with his suitcase and dreamed into the faces that passed him. The mouths uttered Hebrew, English, German, French, Yiddish, and a troupe of other languages. They mixed together in the sunlight. Sabras passed him, Moroccans, Yemenites, South Africans, Californians, Texans, Russians, all walking much more loosely than the hordes of intent people in Tel Aviv. Many walked as Jesse recommended: with fingers loose and knees bent.

He stood on Zion Square watching it all, drinking it in with his eyes, trying not to miss anything. The music played inside him. How he wanted to get this music down on paper, these smells and shades of light. But he knew that he didn't have the power to do it justice. He had tried before on several occasions. The poems came out too tight, too partial, too harsh and incomplete.

He walked up to a fruit stand, stood there with his suitcase beside him, his eyes dreaming and wavering above the wooden trays. Green grapes, purple ones, red cherries, apples, watermelons, oranges, pears, the owner with dark hands popping orders into brown bags, his fingers flicking back and forth above the fruit.

A few cars whizzed through the streets, circled Zion Square. He looked across the street and saw a familiar sight. It was a blind man, overweight, cheeks puffed out, forehead reddish in complexion, a white cane poking out in front of him. He often walked around the square. He was there that day, doing something he was noted for. The cars on Zion Square seemed to annoy him. As he crossed the street, a car came a little too close to him. Without warning, with an incredible speed and accuracy, he lashed out with his white cane smacking the hood of the car. The snapping noise sent a shiver through Martin. He had seen it happen before, the same blind man with his ferocious cane. But he couldn't quite get used to it—how violently he lashed out, and cracked the metal with his full weight behind it. Martin shuddered just for a second, trying to control it, trying not to twist his face into a full, contorted grimace.

From the vendor, Martin bought an apple. Absentmindedly, he

stood in front of the fruit stand chewing it. The apple tasted okay, but he noticed an odd sensation along the side of his tongue. It was a slippery, cool feeling, something he had never experienced before. The piece of apple slid along. He finished it, trying not to think about this strange feeling in his mouth.

* * *

Peter Stoneman sat crosslegged on the floor in front of a low coffee table. The table was covered with a piece of rich-looking purple material. Martin glanced at his friend, then around the room. He liked this place at twenty-nine Rehov ha Neviim. The sunlight filtered through the trees in the backyard, dappling the room with soft early-morning shadows. A couple of candles stood in wine bottles on the table. They had been allowed to melt and drip over the lips of the bottles.

"A lot of colors in those candles," Martin commented.

"Yes, you can buy them down on the square."

Peter had a calm, faraway expression on his face.

Martin let his eyes travel around the room again as he sat on the floor opposite Peter. He noticed a large painting on one of the walls. It was a print of Picasso's Boy with Pipe. The young boy's face fascinated him—the distant, meditative gaze. It was a young face, but there was something ancient about it, as if the boy had been sitting there for centuries, the pipe balanced between his fingers. Martin was entranced by the roses and blues in the painting. The colors looked light and delicate, rich and subtle.

Martin could see a similarity between these two people: his old friend Peter Stoneman, and Picasso's boy. Both bodies looked lean and loose-limbed, both sets of eyes dreamed into the sunlight in the room on Street of the Prophets. There was something in the room that Martin wanted to sink into. It was there in the rose-blue tint of Picasso's brush strokes, there also in Peter Stoneman's loosely draped body, and in the shadows cast by the sun as it danced through the leaves of the trees. It existed in the rich wine hue of the bottles, in the colored wax that had dripped slowly and patiently over the sides of the bottles, the colors encasing the glass.

His friend belonged to the room, Martin kept thinking. He had put it together, and now, he rested inside it, part of it, just as the boy was part of Picasso's painting.

"I really like this room," Martin said sincerely. There was a heavy, dreamy quality to his voice. The words floated out of his mouth. They were dappled like the sunlight.

"There's quite a history to this room," Peter nodded slowly and calmly. "Jesse used to rent it. It's been passed along from friend to friend for years. I was very lucky to get it."

Yes, Martin thought, it was that kind of room, a place with a rare, mellow tone that could be passed from hand to hand, carefully, quietly; and Peter, Martin mused, deserved to be part of it. His eyes were calm enough, his fingers long and loose enough.

"There's just something about it," Martin whispered.

"It almost has a soul, doesn't it?" Peter smiled, lifting a cup of coffee to his lips.

Martin gazed at his friend again. His eyes looked quiet and peaceful. Was Peter really content, Martin wondered, was he really living the calm, Zen-like existence that he and Jesse admired? Had he reached that state of perfection at the young age of twenty-four? The state of being he had heard so much about—being that which you are, and nothing more? He wanted to see it in Peter, to believe in it, that it existed, that it was possible to be as a candle "is", a slim configuration of waxed contours. How far away from the whole thing he felt. He was still striving, struggling with words, with people like Gila, with sounds, with noise, with impressions. He could still hear a cracking noise in his head, the blind man's cane falling on metal, snapping against it.

"Whatever happened between you and Lisa?" Martin asked. He sipped at his coffee, tasting the honey that Peter had spooned into it.

A broad smile wrinkled Peter's face. He began to laugh.

"You know something, I had almost forgotten who got me into that."

Peter's grin flashed across at Martin, and Martin couldn't help but chuckle.

"What a mess," Peter continued. "You know, there were times I was sorry you ever introduced us. She's somewhere in Italy now. Every once in a while I get a letter from her."

Martin gazed into his coffee cup. The steam rose under his chin. He was still curious, but he didn't want to prod and poke. He wanted Peter to continue on his own. Peter let his gaze wander out the window, looking at the leaves and sunlight.

Peter cleared his throat. It sounded like something was stuck inside, and he was trying to loosen it up.

"Well," he sighed, "it was real good in the beginning. But Jesus, did it ever go downhill fast. First, she wanted to get married, then she got pregnant."

"Oh no," Martin grimaced.

"Oh yes," Peter nodded.

"Did she have the baby?" Martin asked, a tone of disbelief in his voice.

Peter covered his mouth with his hand. His eyes looked heavy now, dark and serious. His head bent forward. His whole body looked stiff, and tired.

"It's still a hard thing to talk about."

Martin gazed at the folds in the mauve material covering the coffee table. His eyes were fixed and intent. He didn't want to look into Peter's face.

"No," he murmured, "she got an abortion before she left."

Peter's words sliced into Martin. They jarred and shook him.

"I'm really sorry," Martin half-whispered. "Now I wish I hadn't introduced you."

"That makes two of us," Peter groaned.

The atmosphere in the room had completely changed. The same picture of rose and blue hung on the wall. The same candles on the table. The same bottles encased in colored wax. But everything looked cold now, stiff and unreal.

Peter stretched his legs, and refolded them. He was trying to get into a comfortable position on the floor.

"I was lucky though..." Peter murmured. "Jesse was able to recommend this doctor here in Jerusalem. He was really good. Some of these guys are butchers, but he really knows what he's doing."

Martin thought of Lisa. It was a different person he was seeing in his mind. She had aged. Her eyes were darker now, circled with black lines, her face heavier and wrinkled. How slowly she travelled across northern Italy. She plodded along. There was no one with her, only the wind pushing at her legs.

"I had no other choice," Peter said. "It was either that or get married. We weren't getting along before she got pregnant. No. It wouldn't have worked."

Peter's last words trailed off. Martin sat silently, his fingers gripping his cup, pressing tightly against the sides. The silence grew, as he wanted it to. What more could be said? He was relieved when Peter reached out and placed his hand for a second on his, tapping his skin lightly.

"It wasn't your fault, Martin. How can anybody tell how these things will work out? I went through a lot, but it's over with now. Lisa's letters sound O.K. She'll get along, I'm sure."

Martin didn't reply. The wind blew through the leaves, changing the shadows in the room. They slid across the coffee table, along the pink-blue stones that made up the floor. Peter opened a box that was lying on the table. He took out a stick of incense and lit it. The dreamy scent of sandalwood began to waft through the room. Martin tried to concentrate on it, to calm himself once again, to think of nothing but the fragrance, just the aroma and nothing more. "The Chinese have a saying," Jesse once told him, "when you eat, eat. When you drink, drink. When you sleep, sleep." Jesse's words flowed through him. He concentrated on the sandalwood scent, trying to smell it, and to think of nothing else. Perhaps if he relaxed, it would dispel all thoughts of Lisa, her bare legs, her tired face, moving slowly through the mountains of northern Italy.

There was a knock at Peter's door. It was a light rapping of knuckles.

"Come in," Peter called out; his voice sounded easy and fluid.

The door opened slowly inch by inch. A head peeked through the crack. The eyes glimmered and danced with a benevolent light. In walked Jesse.

"Ah, sandalwood," he said, sniffing the air. "Good morning, boys."

He glanced at Martin. His tone was nonchalant, as if Martin had never left Jerusalem, as if he had talked to him the day before. It was almost a year since Martin had seen his old friend. Yes, Martin thought, he had become part of Jerusalem. Just as the hills had not changed, nor the wind on the backs of leaves, Jesse had remained the same. At least he appeared that way: his eyes still deep-set, glowing inside his bony skull. His lips were twitching, a bemused smile forever playing around the corners of his mouth. In a single motion, an effortless calisthenic, Jesse sat down and folded his legs together into a perfect lotus position.

"It's good to see you, Jesse," Martin said, drifting his hand hesitantly across the table.

Jesse gripped it, shook it, wrung it, and let Martin take it back again.

"We all thought you dropped off the end of the earth," Jesse glimmered.

"It was the same," Martin shot back. "After a year in Tel Aviv, it's like coming back from the dead."

Martin was grateful for the silence that followed. It gave him a chance to relax himself on the floor, to try to adjust to everything that was happening. Peter busied himself around the hot plate, making a coffee for Jesse.

"Well, what can we tell you?" Jesse smiled. "You know what the French say—the more things change, the more they are the same. What is there to say? Lisa's gone to Italy. Peter's probably told you that. I've had three or four young ladies pass through my life. They come and they go. You've probably had an affair or two yourself. And so the world goes on."

And the wind blows outside, Martin thought as Jesse spoke, the leaves shake, the shadows fall, the incense burns, and here we are together once again, the three musketeers. In a way, it was a comforting train of thought, and almost trance-producing. Everything could be seen in this way: how honey had its allotted place in their coffees, and candles were intended to be placed in wine bottles.

"Sure," Martin nodded, "the world goes on. I guess that just about sums it up. Why worry?"

"Are you worried?" Jesse asked, glimmering directly into Martin's face.

"I don't know," Martin shook his head.

A weird heaviness began to ooze in Martin's chest. Was he worried? What did it all mean?—this scent arising from the center of the table, his body seated in a room once again with Jesse and Peter. Was Jesse correct? Had three hundred and sixty-five days gone by without making a single change? Jesse seemed to revel in the thought, to wear it, to be it, to act it. It frightened Martin. Yet it seemed the only way of looking at things. Change. Perhaps it had occurred. But what change, and what did it mean? Wasn't it wiser to dismiss it from his mind? Oh, he thought, if he could only stop thinking, just for a half-hour. Why not? Why not accept Jesse's point of view? The smell of incense, wasn't that the ultimate reality—the particular fragrance at that particular moment? Why search for anything more? And for a second he could rest in it, and allow the leafy shadows to dance across his forehead, and allow the breeze to bathe him.

"The disciple asked the Zen master, 'What is the Buddha?'" Jesse said, curling his mouth around each word. "And the master hit him with a stick. The disciple flinched, but asked the question again. 'Please, master, what is God?' 'Haven't you understood?' the master replied, and he hit the disciple with his shoe. Again the disciple flinched, and again he asked the same question. 'Well,' the master said wearily, 'it seems you have not understood. I will tell you then. God is a string of dry dung.'"

Jesse smiled and glimmered into Martin's face. Peter, now, knelt between them, pouring coffee into Jesse's cup. He poured a fresh coffee into Martin's cup and into his own.

Martin had heard these Zen stories before. Jesse had a storehouse of them. What is water?—the Zen master asked his disciples one day. He was an old Zen master, and the disciple who answered correctly would one day replace him. Each disciple answered in turn. "Water is the essential substance of life." Water is this and water is that. A frown, a disapproving glare never left the Zen master's face. He was dissatisfied with everything that issued from his students' mouths. He gazed forlornly at the pitcher of water he had placed in the center of the room. The cook had been watching the whole thing. He had not taken a single lesson from the master. Suddenly, he walked across the room, and said: "I will tell you what water is." He lifted his foot and kicked over the pitcher. At last the Zen master smiled. And the cook, not even a neophyte, became the next master.

"Do you have enough honey in your coffee?" Peter asked.

Jesse nodded, Martin nodded, both heads bobbing in unison. Yes, there was sufficient honey in the coffee.

The three of them sat together on the floor. It was a dreamy morning, a quiet morning of sunlight, shadows, coffee, and incense. Martin sipped at the caffeine, the honey-warm taste, and thought about the three of them. His mind was an eye looking down from the ceiling. There they sat, the three friends—Jesse, Martin, and Peter. It was an assembly of souls, an interaction that had not taken place in a year. How often had the three of them ever gotten together? No more than a dozen times. Yet this was the place they were supposed to meet in late June of 1963. There was nothing random about it, he thought. And then, his mind switched. No, perhaps it was totally haphazard. A shifting of shadows. The wind blew, the leaves turned, the shadows fell. No sense to the whole thing, he dreamed; but no, wait, wasn't it absolutely harmonious? The coffee—could it taste so sweet on the back of his tongue, if this were chaos?

Jesse, Martin, Peter. Coffee, shadows, sandalwood. Sunlight in the backyard, falling, falling softly, warmly. Wasn't this the room beside the garden of trees and sunlight they were supposed to be sitting in, now and forever? Wasn't this the appointed meeting place? Allotted to the three of them years ago? Twenty-nine Rehov ha Neviim, that's where they will meet in late June of 1963. I will put them there, for I am the God of their fathers, and their fathers' fathers, I am He who put the rod in Moses' hand, who made the rod of such spirit that it whipped from rock a stream of water. I am He who put the stick in Aaron's hand, He who made the bald head of wood sprout flowers.

These three children will grow, for I gave the seed to rest fertile in their fathers, the ova alive in their wives. They will grow, unknown to one another for two score years and a bit. In Jerusalem, on the Street of My Prophets I will prepare a room for them, a room that overlooks the trees, the sunlight and the shadows. When the time is right, when I have prepared their hearts, there in that room of stone they shall meet. Their names I give in secret to the wind: Jesse, Martin, Peter. Their fate I have locked in a hollow of a tree.

Where would they be, Martin wondered, years hence? No, not even years, in two weeks what would befall them? What strange, contorted things? What wonderful shadows would dance across their lives? No, not even two weeks, but in the next half hour?

Martin squirmed around on the floor, trying to find a more comfortable position. It seemed impossible. An ache ran up and down his back, his unsupported back. A pain, dull and eternal, shivered along his spine. Would his back too, like his father's, give way in the years to come? It ran in the family—this tendency for discs to fuse, for innocent curvatures to become pronounced, unwieldy, deformed and painful.

"I have to find a room," Martin finally said. "I have no place to stay tonight."

Jesse stroked his beard. Lightly his fingers twirled through the soft fork of hair. He sipped at his coffee.

"I know a room," he said softly, "if you don't mind living with a family. It's near the Valley of the Cross, in a small cottage. There are a few problems . . . well, who knows, maybe they're not really problems. The room is fairly large."

Jesse sighed, stroked his beard, and continued.

"The landlady's a bit strange. She's a widow and lives there with her two sons."

"It sounds O.K.," Martin said.

"Yes, I used to live in that room," Jesse smiled. "It's not bad at all."

"Do you think I could get it today?" Martin asked, a springy hopefulness in his voice.

"We can try," Jesse replied. "I'll take you down there. I'm still on friendly terms with the old lady."

Jesse lowered his head. His fingers paused inside his beard. He seemed to be thinking. Quietly turning something over in his mind.

"One thing I forgot to mention," he smiled, "the youngest son, Larry, is gay. But I'm sure he won't bother you. Who knows, you might find him cute. He's a dancer, a very outgoing fellow. He's almost a fixture around town. Yes, he's got a nice little ass."

Jesse gave the end of his beard a gentle tug. He smiled, and Martin smiled back at him.

"Why not?" Martin grinned. "As long as he doesn't chase me around my room."

"Oh Larry," Jesse sighed towards the ceiling, "quite a character. So young. So beautiful. But I don't think anything goes on inside his head. No, he wouldn't harm a flea. Actually, he's quite insecure when you get down to it. Always looking in the mirror, shaking his ass. He's a sweet person, though. I'm sure you'll get along with him."

Martin took another sip of coffee. Again he noticed that odd sensation along the left side of his tongue and the inside of his cheek. It felt cool, as if there wasn't any taste or feeling. He remembered standing in Zion Square, watching the people pass, the blind man, the vendors. It was nothing, he said to himself, just an odd sensation. It'll probably go away. Again he dismissed it from his mind, and continued to drink.

The three of them talked together, their voices soft, at times no louder than a whisper. Peter sounded quite enthusiastic about his recent studies in philosophy. He had made friends with one of the professors at the Hebrew University, an authority on Wittgenstein, Hegel, Aristotle, and a host of other thinkers, minds monumental, dealing with thoughts, systems, world-views that swung, danced, melded in air so pure, high, clean, that it made Martin's head dizzy just to listen. "Pure reason," Peter at one point sighed. It sounded pure to Martin, so pure that his mind could not grasp it fully, steady it, or see it. Just as something was beginning to clear, to make sense, another idea, two, three, joined in, and it all became fuzzy once again.

"What a mind he has," Peter frowned and smiled at the same time, describing his sixty-year-old mentor. "He's a very good friend of Buber's."

Jesse smiled benevolently at Peter, as if he were a fledgling brother tasting things that he himself has chewed, devoured, and thoroughly digested years ago.

"We stayed up till three in the morning the other night," Peter continued. "A fascinating guy. I wish I knew half the things he's forgotten over the years."

Jesse nodded knowingly, stroking his beard, leaning back on his hands, tilting his head back to allow the sunlight to caress his forehead. The dappled sunlight moved across his brow, into the crevices of his cheeks, his neck. Peter kept on talking. His hands moved through the air, gesturing and describing.

Martin began to feel a little uneasy. He felt a lot closer to the Zen stories, to the monks in the mountains who took their daily walks and meditated on the slant and color of butterfly wings. Somehow, Jesse and Peter, their minds at least, could manoeuvre equally well through the thoughts of Hegel and the other exponents of "pure reason". Martin had heard long ago that such areas could be a danger, a snag to a writer. He had written poems recently about the kibbutz, about the fumes of Tel Aviv, the glint of sun on office windows, and the smell of salt from the Mediterranean. For a second, he thought his mind was just a little barbaric, perhaps even childish, compared with his friends.

Martin ran the tip of his tongue along the inside of his left cheek. It was still there, the cool, mysterious feeling. What was happening? —he began to wonder. At the same time, he began to notice a tic racing across his forehead, a flicker of feeling in the middle of his brow. Suddenly, his whole mouth seemed stretched, out of shape.

What was happening to him? Whatever it was, it began to interest him. And it began to frighten him a bit. Perhaps it was serious. Perhaps he was taking a small stroke, or worse, going crazy. He interrupted the conversation.

"I'm sorry," he said, his voice trembling. "I'm getting these funny feelings in my face. Can you guys see anything?"

Both sets of eyes fixed upon him. And both sets of eyes widened in amazement.

"There is something wrong," Jesse said.

"That's for sure," Peter agreed. "Take a look at yourself in the mirror."

Peter pointed to the mirror above his dresser.

Martin let a sigh escape from deep inside him. Fuckin' shit, his mind clanged, what the hell was happening now? He got to his feet slowly. His body was trembling with fear and excitement. Slowly, he walked over to the mirror. He lowered his head, and placed his face in front of the glass.

"Oh Christ," Martin groaned.

He couldn't believe what the glass was casting back at him. No, it had not been his imagination. It was as real and physical as anything could be. The whole left side of his face was stretched out of shape, contorted and yanked. His left eye was half shut. He opened his mouth, stretched it wide apart, seeing if he could get his face back to normal. It didn't work. The contorted image kept staring back at him.

"Shit," he snapped, "what the hell is happening?"

Peter and Jesse both rose to their feet, almost simultaneously. They joined Martin in front of the mirror.

"It's not a very pretty sight," Jesse commented.

Peter put a hand on Martin's shoulder.

"Listen, Martin. I know a doctor who lives a few houses away. Just back through the garden. He's retired now, but he sees the odd patient. Listen, go over there, and tell him you're a friend of mine. I'm sure he'll see you. He's a fantastic old guy. His name is Doctor Lowenstein."

Peter's voice was getting more and more excited.

"Martin, this guy used to teach medical history at the Hebrew University. He's a bloody world authority. He's old, but don't let that fool you. He'll be able to help you, I'm sure. It looks bad, but it's probably nothing serious. Go over now, O.K.?"

Martin shook his head up and down. Suddenly, he felt tired, almost exhausted. Tears were forcing their way to his eyes, but he held them back. He just shook his head and he thought: always something, always fucking something. His voice trembled as he spoke.

"Jesse, can you wait here for me? I still have to get that room today."

Now Jesse placed a hand on his other shoulder, and massaged it lightly. His voice was soft and reassuring.

"Sure, Martin. I'll be here. This doctor is good. I've heard of him. Just don't worry about it."

Peter gave him the directions to Dr. Lowenstein's house. He had to go through the garden, past a certain cherry tree, around a hedge, and down a paved walkway. At first, Martin was confused, thinking that the doctor's house was on the Street of the Prophets. Peter gave the directions again. He gave them patiently, softly, whispering them into Martin's ear. No, the house was not on the street, but back of Peter's room through the garden. Martin tried his best to understand. Peter pointed from the window, showing him the exact cherry tree, and the hedge he would have to pass.

"Just ring the bell. His house might look quiet, but he'll be there."

"How old is this guy?" Martin asked.

"About seventy-five or so."

The whole thing began to hit Martin as absolutely ridiculous. A nervous laugh came out of his mouth.

"I feel like Al Capone going off to see the Wizard of Oz."

Peter and Jesse began to laugh. The three of them stood in the sunlit room, chuckling, giggling, and suddenly the laughter increased and all three of them hooted until their stomachs got sore, and they buckled over holding on to them.

*   *   *

Martin stood in front of Dr. Lowenstein's front door. The house, as Peter had warned, looked quiet and deserted. Hesitantly, Martin reached a finger up to ring the bell a second time. Before his fingertip touched the buzzer, he heard a shuffling of footsteps behind the door.

The door creaked open, and before him stood the doctor.

He was a wispy man, Martin thought. Old and fragile-looking. A heavy wind could knock him over. His face smiled at Martin, and every wrinkle around his eyes and his mouth looked like an essential part of the smile. He gazed into Martin's face, then frowned.

"Oh, I see you are having problems," he slightly grimaced; the accent sounded German to Martin. "Come in, please come in, we'll have a closer look."

"Thank you," Martin sighed. "Peter Stoneman told me about you."

"Ah yes, Peter. How is he? Quite a student, that boy."

"He's just fine," Martin answered.

Martin felt relieved. He tried to smile. His face felt twisted and stretched. The smile, he thought, on top of the contortion must look weird.

Dr. Lowenstein led him into a room. It looked more like a study than a doctor's office. Bookcases covered almost every wall. They stretched from floor to ceiling, crammed with books, huge volumes. The books were large, old, and yellowed.

"How did this happen to you?" Dr. Lowenstein asked. His voice, too, was wispy and soft. It hovered between a whisper and a sigh.

"I don't know," Martin shook his head, bewildered. "There wasn't much warning."

"I have a good suspicion what it is," Dr. Lowenstein frowned. "Let me see."

He moved his long, almost bony fingers towards Martin's face. His fingers felt cool. He stretched Martin's cheek to the left and to the right, and gently he tugged at Martin's lips. He shook his head up and down, knowingly.

"Ah yes. It's almost a classic case."

The doctor shook his head back and forth. His grey-blue eyes twinkled, and his mouth just slightly curled into a grimace.

"It's so rare. I haven't seen it in a long time. Not in the last five years."

"What is it?" Martin trembled.

"The name," Dr. Lowenstein frowned, "is Bell's palsy. An affliction of the nerves."

"You mean it's psychological?" Martin asked, his voice amazed and dismayed.

"No, nothing like that," he reassured. "The nerves in the face have been affected."

Martin's head began to feel light and dizzy. Suddenly, he felt like smiling. For a second, he was excited by the whole thing, this rare affliction that had attacked him. His heart beat faster.

"What causes it?" Martin asked, his voice filled with excitement and curiosity.

"First, let us sit down. I will explain it to you."

Dr. Lowenstein pointed to two leather armchairs that were positioned side by side near a window. He placed a hand lightly on Martin's back and guided him across the room.

"It is usually caused by a contrast in temperatures. The person is warm, overheated perhaps. He comes in contact with a cold breeze. The breeze hits the heated area, and the nerves are affected. I know, you might ask yourself this question—why doesn't it happen to everybody? This is unknown. In fact, a mystery. We are still very ignorant. After all these centuries of medicine, we are still like babes."

Dr. Lowenstein gestured towards the bookshelves.

"Were you in such a situation recently?" the doctor asked. His voice sounded soft and gentle to Martin. It was an old voice, a little tired and weary, but his words seemed to caress Martin's ears. "Were you hot and did you happen to place your face into a breeze?"

Martin lowered his head and thought. He thought of Herzl Mountain. It was cold that evening. Was he overheated? No. He searched back and forth, sifting through the events of the last few days. Then he thought of the bus that brought him up to Jerusalem. It was hot inside that day. There had been a breeze gushing through the windows as he sat beside the sleeping soldier.

"Maybe on the bus the other day," Martin said, hesitantly. "I was hot, and there was a cool breeze."

"Yes, that could have been it. The movement. The breeze. The stale air inside a bus. Yes, that could do it," Dr. Lowenstein smiled. "But now young man, we have to do something for you. First, please tell me your name."

"Martin Kanner," Martin whispered. For the first time, he noticed it was getting difficult to form words through his half-paralyzed mouth.

"And you are a student? A friend of Peter's."

"Yes."

"I know him. He's been to me," Dr. Lowenstein smiled, gazing at his bookshelves. "He's a fine young man. It's good that you have such a friend. We've had talks together. He has a rare mind, Peter. He thinks like the students used to think. How should I put it? More European, perhaps. Ah yes, sort of Renaissance, if you know what I mean. He doesn't want to look through a peep-hole. He takes a bit from here, from there. Ah, I have found the word. He's an eclectic. I like to see that, especially nowadays. There's much too much specialization, don't you agree?"

Martin nodded his head in silent agreement.

"Yes, he takes an interest in a lot of subjects," Martin said.

"I hope not too many, though," the doctor sighed. "That, too, can be a fault. The ship must have a rudder. With all those sails and no rudder, that could bring trouble in time. But I have faith in Mr. Stoneman. He seems sensible to me. I don't think he would let that happen to him."

Again, Martin nodded in agreement.

"Anyway, Martin Kanner, let's not get off the track. We have still your problem. Now, I want to tell you that it is going to take some time to get your face back to normal. You must have patience. Come to me each day, and I'm sure we'll be able to do something. I won't be satisfied until you are."

"It won't stay this way?" Martin's voice trembled. "There's no chance of that, is there?"

"No, don't worry yourself with such thoughts. I have all the most recent equipment to treat you. First, we are going to try heat. If that doesn't work, or if it's too slow, we'll go on to something else. Try to whistle for me."

"Whistle?" Martin repeated.

"Yes, through your lips, you know, whistle."

Martin tried to purse his twisted mouth. He did the best he could, and blew. A hiss of air slid out of his mouth. He tried again. Another hiss of rushing air. It was impossible.

"No, you cannot do it. But that is what we are going to aim for. After each treatment you will try to whistle. When you can do it, your face will be back to normal. It will be absolutely the same as before. Every muscle is needed to make this whistling."

Martin nodded. He had understood.

"Now, I will give you a heat treatment today. You must come back tomorrow morning. Will you be able to do that, Mr. Kanner?"

"Yes, definitely," Martin said, shaking his head up and down.

"Good. Let us begin."

After the first heat treatment, Dr. Lowenstein asked Martin to try to whistle once again. He screwed his mouth up the best he could. He had the same miserable results. A hiss and rush of air. Would he ever again be able to make that high, pure note?—Martin asked himself.

His legs felt wobbly, unsure of themselves. But they carried him through Dr. Lowenstein's front door, back into the sunlight. The glare bothered Martin's eyes after the subdued light in the doctor's office. Hundreds of spotlights seemed aimed at him. Through the trees they penetrated. A twisted mouth, they shone upon. A half-closed eye. The glare illuminated his paralysis. He was suffering now, he thought. It was real, miserable, and nobody could deny it.

For some strange reason, he began to think of Beethoven. The tic that shuddered on his forehead made him think of the musical genius. Recently he had read a biography. Deaf he was, and yet created. In fact, created his greatest works, deaf as a doorpost. Suffering, Martin thought—how could anyone create without it?

He walked through the garden, his legs trembling. He was worried, excited, hopeful, despairing—all at the same time. Slowly, head bent, he walked back to Peter's room.

* * *

Walking up the steps to Peter's room, Martin remembered a conversation he once had with Jesse. Martin had been happy that day, an inner joy rushed through him. It flushed his cheeks. He had gotten higher and higher.

"What's wrong with people?" he had shouted and laughed. "They're all so sad. Why can't they feel joy?"

Jesse had turned his head away from Martin. Suddenly, he turned it around again, and looked directly in his eyes. The light in Jesse's pupils jabbed.

"It must be nice," Jesse said, "to be blissfully ignorant."

Joy crumpled inside Martin. His laughter ceased. At the time he had wondered—was he, indeed, nothing more than an ignorant joyful fool? It seemed from that time onward that Martin began to search for this suffering that would purge his ignorance.

Up the steps he hauled himself, the old conversation rolling around inside him. Jesse's rebuttal. His cool, observant denunciation.

Peter greeted him at the door.

"What is it?" he asked excitedly.

"My face is paralyzed. It's called Bell's palsy," Martin said, standing in front of Peter.

Out of the corner of his eye he could see Jesse sitting cross-legged on the floor. Slowly, he pulled himself up, and joined Peter.

"I've heard of it," Jesse said. "Is there any treatment for it?"

"Yes," Martin nodded, "he's going to try heat. And if that doesn't work, there's something else."

Jesse bobbed his head up and down.

"It's a good thing it didn't happen to you a few years ago," Jesse said. "They used to operate—cut the tendons and muscles. Quite a mess. I've seen the results."

A sudden, icy fear cut through Martin. Up to then, the whole thing had seemed like a game, a dream; a new experience, an adventure. But now, he could see a face in front of him hovering. The muscles gone slack. Distorted permanently.

"You don't think . . . " Martin didn't have the strength to finish the sentence.

Peter and Jesse read his thoughts simultaneously.

"No," they both shook their heads.

"That was years ago," Jesse reassured. "Back in Europe. Things have changed."

Peter gripped Martin's shoulder with long, warm fingers. He squeezed it tightly.

"Martin, have faith in this guy. If anybody knows anything, he does. Just do what he says."

"Lowenstein knows what he's doing," Jesse agreed.

"Can we sit down for a few minutes?" Martin asked.

"Sure, come in," Peter smiled. His face looked large and warm. He seemed taller than ever to Martin. "Come in, I'll make some more coffee for us."

"Yes, we'll have some coffee," Jesse breathed softly. "Then I'll take you down to see that room."

"Good," Martin breathed. It was hardly audible. It was becoming an effort to form his words. He glanced at Peter's mirror. For a second, he was tempted to wander across the room and take another look. His legs were jerking him in that direction. He let out a sigh. No, to hell with the mirror. He knew what it looked like. He had seen enough of it in the doctor's office.

CHAPTER 19

Stone Cottage

The cottage which Jesse had led him to was made of stone. Round stones. They looked something like cobblestones or beach stones, rough in texture. The mortar which kept them together could hardly be seen. The cottage sat in the shade of some cypress trees, across the highway from the Valley of the Cross.

It looked hunched to Martin, the cottage, as if it were a little old man picking mushrooms in the woods. There were no houses next to it. In all Jerusalem, Martin had not seen such a cottage. They probably existed, but this was the first he had seen of this type.

On the way down, Jesse talked about the landlady.

"Her husband left her a couple of years ago," he said. "She's quite the old gal. Used to be a belly-dancer in Tel Aviv. You'll probably get along with her. She's Yemenite."

"A belly-dancer," Martin repeated, his voice filled with wonderment.

Jesse laughed.

"Yes, she used to do the night-club circuit on the Dizengoff. You wouldn't know it now, though. She's pretty well gone to flab."

"Too bad," Martin sighed, suddenly thinking of old age, how the skin wrinkles, the muscles go slack, the light dims in the eyes.

On that afternoon, walking with Jesse to what was going to become his home, Martin avoided looking at the people in the streets. He didn't want to see their reaction to his twisted face. It looked grotesque, he thought to himself.

Jesse introduced him to Mrs. Shoshannah, the name meaning "rose" in Hebrew. Martin tried to keep the good half of his face turned towards her.

Jesse and his new landlady exchanged quick greetings with one another in Hebrew. It was a cluck and click of sound to Martin, only the odd phrase had meaning. They laughed and joked for a few minutes.

"She hardly knows a word of English," Jesse half-whispered to Martin. "It's probably better. She'll leave you alone."

"Mah pitom? What are you talking about?" the landlady asked Jesse in Hebrew.

"Just telling my friend about the room," Jesse answered in Hebrew.

Martin smiled, and the flesh twisted near his mouth. It was much easier to frown, or grimace. A frown seemed to fit the paralysis, but a grin went against the contorted outline of his cheek.

Martin was relieved to get the room. Jesse didn't stay long, and Martin was just as glad. It was a relief to shut the door, to lock it, to stretch out on his cot.

The room was spartan, Martin thought, yes, that was the correct word for it. A cot. A stand up closet-dresser. A table with one wooden chair. No pictures on the wall. No mats or carpets on the stone floor. No flowers. No radio. No record player. No candles. No incense. No Boy with Pipe. No coffee table. A bare light bulb dangling from the ceiling.

The essentials, Martin thought. What more did he need? Just close the door, and lie on his cot. The basics, Martin mused, a roof over his head.

On the way to the washroom the next day, Martin met his landlady. She looked at him with large brown eyes. They looked friendly and curious.

"You like the room?" she asked.

"Yes, it's fine."

"Good, good," Mrs. Shoshannah smiled, her gaze travelling up and down Martin's frame. "Nobody bother you. My son Larry, a funny boy. But he no bother you. Very good boy, Larry. Dance, you know. Like his mama."

"Yes," Martin nodded, a little surprised to hear how much English his landlady really knew.

He surveyed the landlady's face. She had quite a heavy growth of hair above her upper lip. Not a full-blown moustache by any means, but definitely the beginnings.

"You have girlfriend?" she asked.

"No," Martin shook his head wearily. His head felt like a heavy ball swinging back and forth, as if it didn't really belong to him.

"When you get," Mrs. Shoshannah smiled, "you bring here. It's O.K. She can stay. All night. No trouble with me. O.K.?"

"Yes, thank you."

Mrs. Shoshannah grimaced.

"Jesse, good boy, Jesse. He tell me about your face. Awful thing. You go doctor, O.K.?"

"Yes," Martin nodded, "I am going to the doctor."

"You don't forget what I tell you. You get nice girl, bring her to room. I know young people," Mrs. Shoshannah grinned, the light dancing in her eyes, "the blood rush so fast."

Martin began to chuckle. Mrs. Shoshannah giggled, covering her mouth. With the other hand she patted down her loose-fitting, flowered skirt. For a second, Martin felt aroused. Come on, he said to himself, she's gotta be fifty if she's a day. Nevertheless, for a quick moment or two, he felt heat nibble at his groin. A tingling sensation, and a rush of blood to his head.

The cot creaked under his weight. He stretched out once again, lying on his back. That morning he had gone to Dr. Lowenstein for his second heat treatment, and another attempt at whistling in front of the mirror. The results were poor, but he knew he had to be patient.

It was quiet throughout the house. Faintly, in the adjoining room, he could hear a rocking chair creak. Outside, Mrs. Shoshannah's chickens clucked. They walked around their wire pen hunting for bits of food. Earlier in the day he had heard the screen door slam and Mrs. Shoshannah talking to them.

"Come. Come. Come," she squealed in Hebrew. "Eat, little pets."

And she clucked, imitating them.

*   *   *

Martin sat in the leather armchair in Dr. Lowenstein's office. It was the fourth day of heat treatments. Faithfully, each morning, he got up at eight o'clock, and with the cool morning air caressing the back of his neck, he walked the half mile from the cottage to Dr. Lowenstein's office. After each treatment he went to visit Peter, to have coffee with him, and to talk.

Dr. Lowenstein circled the room. He paused at the window, gazed into the garden. He walked back to his bookshelves, ran his eyes along the backs of the books.

He shook his head. "No, Martin. The heat is not doing it. It's not getting through to the nerves. Oh yes, perhaps it would work in time, but I want to try something else. If you agree. This I'm certain will do the job. Much faster."

"What is it?" Martin asked, his hands clutching the arms of his chair.

"A small electrical shock applied to the face," Dr. Lowenstein answered.

A shudder trembled through Martin's chest.

"Martin, let me be frank with you. The faster we get this cleared up, the better. I want to make your face look exactly as it did before. Are you willing to give it a try?"

"Yes," Martin nodded, his head a heavy weight.

"I'll explain everything to you step by step," Dr. Lowenstein continued. "Come here, and I'll show you what we're going to use."

Wearily, Martin pushed himself up from the chair, his head dizzy, and his legs wobbling.

Dr. Lowenstein stood in front of a small machine. He held out two metal rods about six inches long and an inch in diameter.

"These are the electrodes. You will hold one of these in each hand, and I will apply a small charge to your face."

With a small bony hand, Dr. Lowenstein patted the table in front of him.

"Now, just get up here, and let's begin."

Martin heaved himself up on the table, and stretched out. He held out his hands, and Dr. Lowenstein placed a shiny, smooth rod inside each one of them. Martin began thinking of his parents. They knew nothing of his condition. What would they think, he wondered, if they could see him now?

Martin gripped the rods. Out of the corner of his eye, he saw Dr. Lowenstein holding a metal prong that was attached to a machine by a twisted wire. It looked a little thicker than a needle. Dr. Lowenstein flicked a switch, and the machine began to hum. It was a low growl and a hiss like a radio between stations.

Slowly the prong arced towards his face. For a second, he was tempted to jerk away from it. To avoid it. What the doctor was doing was necessary, he kept telling himself. The prong touched his skin, and his body jerked violently. His legs shuddered with the jolt of electricity, his chest jumped, and his head tossed. It was just bearable, he thought. Again and again, Dr. Lowenstein touched the prong to his skin. Each time the shudder raced through him. This has to do something, he thought to himself. From the very beginning, he didn't have complete confidence in Dr. Lowenstein's heat treatment. But this was different.

Dr. Lowenstein switched off the machine. Martin let a grateful sigh of relief flow from his mouth. The doctor gripped his shoulder and smiled. He gazed down at him with blue-grey eyes.

"That wasn't so bad, was it?"

Martin grinned. "No . . . there's a lot of power in that thing. I could feel it right from my toes up. That's gotta work."

"Yes, I believe it," Dr. Lowenstein smiled.

Martin gazed at his face. It was old, wrinkled, knowledgeable. Seventy-five winters it had seen, Martin thought. Seventy-five summers and seventy-five springs. Through seventy-five autumns the doctor's face had travelled.

"I can see a change already. Go look in the mirror."

Martin walked over to the mirror. He tilted his head to the left and to the right. Yes, he thought, the contortion looked just slightly altered. How could it be otherwise?—with that repeated jolt snapping through every muscle of his body, every tissue of his face. He was not stone, after all. He was flesh, nerve-ending, blood, sinew, muscle. And this was not mere heat the doctor was using. Not now.

"Thank you," Martin smiled into the doctor's face; "thank you," he repeated.

For a second, he felt his eyes filling with tears; tears of relief and gratitude.

"Come back tomorrow, my friend, and we'll give you another treatment. You'll be well in a week. I promise."

"Thank you," Martin again whispered.

Out in the garden behind Peter's room, Martin paused. He gazed at the leaves above him, their backs shining with the intense light of the sun. How bright the sky was over Jerusalem. Not a single cloud. It looked like the original blue, the first intense splatter of that color. It seemed that all other shades—turquoise, navy, powder—were derived from it.

He sniffed at the earth smells, the flowers, the bark of trees. He stood in front of a rosebush and drew the fragrance deep inside him. Everything smelled fresh that morning. He felt wide awake after his first shock treatment with Dr. Lowenstein.

He didn't want to rush up to Peter's room. Slowly, he ambled through the garden watching the bees go about their business. He watched their black and yellow-ringed bodies as if he had never seen a bee before. He slipped down and sat on the grass. Slowly his eyes caressed and surveyed the things around him. The sky they took in, the sun, the leaves, the flowers. Oh, he thought, what was it like to be a bee? To be a rose petal glistening with morning dew? To be a tree hugged round with bark? What was it like to be seventy-five?

* * *

Peter sat in a chair beside the window in his room. Martin sat cross-legged on the floor in front of the coffee table, gazing up at him. A faint smile of contentment lined Peter's face. The sunlight made his black hair glisten. Again, Martin was struck by the perfect contours of his face.

"How is everything going with Dr. Lowenstein?" Peter asked.

Martin smiled. "He changed the treatment this morning. I think it's going to work. He's hooking me up to this machine, and zapping my face with a good jolt of electricity."

Peter grimaced. He shook his head back and forth. "I'm glad I'm not in your shoes."

"Well, I tell you Peter, it really wakes me up. It's better than coffee, that's for sure."

Peter gazed at him in amazement.

"It sounds like you enjoy it."

"It's not that bad," Martin nodded. "I was expecting a lot worse."

The coffee tasted good to Martin, the rich black caffeine laced with honey. The morning air was cool. It flowed through the trees, into the room, along Peter's back, across the stone floor, and caressed Martin's face. The afternoons were beginning to get hot. The sun was beginning to pounce with all its summer strength on the city. Each day the temperature was notching up a little higher.

* * *

It was hot that same afternoon in his room. Perspiration beaded on his forehead, soaked his armpits. Soon, Martin thought, he would have to get a job somewhere in Jerusalem. Even part-time employment. He reminded himself to talk to Mr. Townley about it.

Martin had left his door open in an attempt to catch any cross-breeze that happened along. Looking toward his window, he could see the heat rising, a light film of air.

He heard a high-pitched, girlish voice greet him from his door.

"Shalom. How are you today? Not doing any writing?"

Martin turned his head. In the doorway stood Larry, Mrs. Shoshannah's youngest son. A hand was placed on his hip, one leg bent. It looked like he was posing, trying to be attractive, even alluring. He stood there in a pair of blue short pants and a sleeveless top. The shorts looked like they were made of a silky material. They shimmered as he moved.

"Excuse me, Martin. I don't wish to bother you."

"That's O.K.," Martin said wearily. His voice was heavy, the words emerged slowly. It was an effort to talk.

"I just came from a lesson," Larry informed him.

"Dancing?" Martin asked.

Larry executed a half-pirouette in the doorway. His eyelashes looked extremely long, his brown eyes extremely bright. It seemed that he was putting something on them or in them: some lubricant or gel to make them look shiny.

"Yes, I have a new instructor. He's from New York. He's just here on holiday."

Another figure appeared behind Larry. It was Gideon, his brother, still wearing his army uniform and boots. He was slightly shorter than Larry.

"Is he bothering you?" Gideon asked. His black moustache danced up and down as he spoke.

"No, it's O.K.," Martin said.

"Don't let him be a pest," Gideon growled. "If you get tired, just tell him to leave."

"Mah pitom!" Larry almost shrieked. "We're talking about art."

Gideon growled something back at him in Hebrew. Larry replied in Hebrew. An argument began, the words snapping back and forth. The words were spat out quickly. Martin couldn't understand. Gideon grabbed Larry from the doorway and forced him down the hall. The fight continued, the voices getting louder. Larry's voice was high-pitched, squeaky, shrill, almost hysterical. Gideon's voice got deeper, it began to boom throughout the small cottage. Martin pulled himself up from the cot and closed his door.

Mrs. Shoshannah joined the fray. They were all gathered in the room beside Martin's, Mrs. Shoshannah's bedroom, where she and Larry slept at night. It was the only other bedroom in the house. When Gideon was on leave, he slept on a flimsy cot in the back porch. Martin could hear furniture scraping across the floor. It sounded like chairs were being heaved. Mrs. Shoshannah's voice alternately growled and squeaked.

"It's not his business," Larry squealed in Hebrew.

Gideon growled and boomed something back. The wall between the two rooms shuddered. Finally a screen door slammed, and for a minute there was silence. Martin pressed his ear to the wall. He could just barely hear Larry and Mrs. Shoshannah whispering to one another.

* * *

His money was dwindling. In the nick of time, he spoke to Mr. Townley, who in turn spoke to Mr. Yahmin, principal of the Y.M.C.A. Mr. Townley had once taught there himself, at the Young Men's Christian Association.

"That's strange, isn't it?" Martin said. "A Y.M.C.A. in the middle of Jerusalem."

Mr. Townley smiled, one leg hooked over the arm of a chair. He was stroking Moog, his angora.

"Yes," Mr. Townley agreed. "It's been there for years. The head of the place is an Arab Christian. But you know something, it's Christian in name only. Ninety-five per cent of the members are Jewish."

Martin chuckled to himself, remembering Y.M.C.A.'s back in Halifax.

"I'll speak to Mr. Yahmin. There's no reason why you can't get a job there."

So it was done. Mr. Townley recommended him highly. And luckily, a teacher was needed.

A routine temporarily developed in Martin's life, for a few weeks anyway. Each morning he got up with the chickens, took his treatment with Dr. Lowenstein, then had coffee with Peter. He returned to the stone cottage, napped, wrote a poem or two, took a shower, and walked to the Y.M.C.A., which was not far from the King David Hotel, about two miles from his room, overlooking old Jerusalem.

For a few weeks his daily life almost seemed ordered. The mornings taken up with Dr. Lowenstein and Peter, followed by a few hours of teaching in the late afternoon.

The shock treatments were beginning to take hold. The jolts of electricity penetrated the paralysed nerves.

A few weeks later, he stood in front of the mirror once again in Dr. Lowenstein's office.

"It looks beautiful," Dr. Lowenstein smiled. "Whistle."

Martin pursed his lips. The old familiar high note came out of his mouth.

Dr. Lowenstein ambled across the room, and stood in front of Martin. He placed a cool, bony hand on each cheek, touching, prodding, stretching the flesh.

"The nerves are alive now. They will look after the rest of the healing."

Martin gazed at the doctor. What an old, wrinkled, beautiful face, he thought. Lines from a Yeats poem flooded his mind. Lines from Lapis Lazuli. "And their eyes mid many wrinkles, their ancient glittering eyes were gay."

Martin lowered his gaze.

"Thank you," he said, "for everything you've done."

"Martin," the doctor asked, "you don't have much money, do you?"

Martin shook his head.

"I know," the doctor sighed. "The life of a student. Never enough. Now, as far as payments go, I am not going to say another word. As far as I'm concerned, your bill is paid."

Martin shook his head back and forth. He had forty lira in his wallet. His first pay from the "Y" was still a week away. He took out twenty-five lira and handed it to Dr. Lowenstein.

"Please take this."

Dr. Lowenstein smiled. He didn't say a word. He took the twenty-five lira and slipped it into his pocket.

"If you ever get ill again, I'll be happy to look after you. My needs are taken care of."

"Thank you," Martin whispered.

He shook the doctor's hand for the last time. The fingers were buried inside Martin's grip.

* * *

In late July when Jerusalem and its inhabitants sweltered, Martin closed the door to his room often. He closed it on Larry, his pirouettes and shimmering blue pants, on Mrs. Shoshannah and her chickens. He hid away from Gideon, his army boots and booming voice.

He saw less and less of Jesse, Peter, Mr. Townley. He was no longer interested in talking with them. He had heard enough about Hegel, Wittgenstein, Huxley, Alan Watts. He had imbibed enough poetics of Hart Crane, Dylan Thomas, Walt Whitman. No longer did he wish to see Jesse's pale face and staring eyes. Nor hear Peter's calm voice trying to ooze strength and confidence.

To hell with it, he thought bitterly to himself.

In the months of July and August a far greater paralysis seized him, a slowing of the blood, a growing desire to sleep, to sleep the clock around. Only in the afternoons did he slip out of his room, clinging to the shadows, skulking down to the "Y" to give his English lessons. The sun continued to glare. He wanted no part of it.

He was looking for something, the same old questions arose, and the answers hadn't come roaring out of the pages of books. They hadn't dropped from Jesse's mouth either. Why did he do things? Who was Martin Kanner? Was there any sense to anything? Jesse had recommended that he drop such vain questionings, and live instead moment by moment. Did the butterfly ask about its colors? Did the trees mutter and sob? There were no answers, Jesse had hinted, only days coming and going, the sun rising, the sun falling again at night. Rocks, sunsets, flowers, bees. But no answers. No connection between what he was yesterday, and what he was today.

And the senseless whirl began to eat at him. Sun like a drop of blood over Herzl Mountain. Chickens clucking in the backyard. Shadows in the Valley of the Cross. Larry giggling. Gideon growling, shouting, slamming doors. Moog, the angora, purring. Peter lighting another stick of incense. Tomatoes on Martin's dinner plate, half-eaten. Scabs on his fingers. Dreams. Nightmares. Fears. Each evening he opened the doors on his stand-up dresser. Was there someone lurking there with knife and maniacal glare?

He tried to sleep longer each day. Ten hours, twelve, fourteen, eighteen. He tried to forget that a world existed, that he existed. Perhaps he was a figment of the wind's imagination. And yet, maybe only he was real, and the rest was a show, part of a test he was being put through. Perhaps there were a million celestial judges gazing down at him, at his sleepy, writhing form.

What was he supposed to do to pass the test? What was expected of him? Shit on it, his mind revolted. I will fail, goddammit, I will fail here in Jerusalem.

His dreams startled him. They were vivid and clear. In one he fought his father, muscle to muscle, arm to arm. And his father broke his arm, snapped it.

In another he was bathing in the sea. He could hear Jesse's voice, soft as wind. "Relax, Martin, just relax in the waves." He relaxed, and the waves grew in size. A giant wave picked up his body, tossed him into the air. He landed, hoping at last to be free, to be in a new country. Instead, a wall stood in front of him, a stone wall so high he could never hope to climb it.

In yet another dream, he was down in a basement. He had a gun in his hand. Men in black masks were chasing him, shooting at him. He fired his gun again and again. He pulled at the trigger. It was useless. He couldn't kill them. The bullets dribbled from his gun and fell on the floor. They fell like tears, like jelly beans, like gumdrops. And the men closed in on him.

One morning he awoke in a sweat, cold beads of perspiration on his forehead. He could see the sun on his windowsill. It looked like an animal creeping into his room, coming towards him, getting ready to devour him completely.

During these days he kept repeating a line from Shakespeare, a line spoken by Mark Antony to Cleopatra. "I am dying, Egypt." Who was this Egypt Martin Kanner was talking to, calling to? O Egypt, I am dying. But Egypt could not help him. Egypt was large, benevolent, caring, but beyond his reach. I am dying, Egypt, here in Jerusalem, so far from my native home. So far from the snows of Halifax.

Jesse came to visit him one evening. He sat curled up on Martin's cot.

"What's wrong with you, Martin?" he asked. "Are you depressed?"

"Depressed?" Martin echoed back.

"Don't you understand that? You're not that far gone, are you?"

"I don't know what's wrong," Martin whispered. "I guess I want to be alone."

Jesse curled his legs beneath himself.

"Nobody sees you any more. Mr. Townley's been asking about you. Peter. What do you do all day?"

Martin closed his eyes.

"I sleep a lot. An awful lot. I go to work."

"That's not life, Martin. You can't shut out the world."

Martin's head drooped.

"I can't do anything else right now. I'm sorry, Jesse."

Martin was relieved when Jesse finally left. He could close his eyes once again, fall asleep, forget, sleep and sleep and sleep.

I am dying, Egypt, dying. O Egypt, where are you, do you hear me? Do you see what is happening to me, your favorite son? Do you see the stone inside me, the heaviness? Do you see the scabs on my fingers? Do you feel how sore my gums are? Do you see how they bleed when I bite into an apple? Can you help me, Egypt, I am dying here in this foreign country, here near the Valley of the Cross.

Do your rich rivers see me, Egypt, your life-giving waters, do they sense the dying of this sparrow? Nothing helps me, Egypt. All that I learned in school has come to nothing. My poems, nothing. My friendships, nothing.

Do you see this sparrow, Egypt?

I know, Egypt, you have skirts of gold, and a golden place of darkness and comfort inside your chest. You have eyes to see everything. Why don't you come and cradle me as you would a sparrow with a broken wing? Are you not tired of my complaints? Egypt. Jesus, Egypt, can't you understand?—I am dying. I have no blood in me, Egypt, not any more. No heart. I am turning to stone. Egypt, O fucking Egypt, why have you abandoned me?

I sing to you, my beloved Egypt. Over the waves I lift my voice, I send my prayer. It travels through the night, my sorrowful song.

During this period, he had conversations with God.

"What is life, God, what is it all about?"

God answered in a whisper. He had to listen carefully. He had to pick the words out of thin air. The chickens clucked. He had to hear the voice through the racket in the backyard. Pick it out, he thought. He had to listen intently. He didn't want to mix it up with the wind.

He had to listen through the arguments in the house. Mrs. Shoshannah screeching at Larry and Gideon.

"Martin, life is totally connected. I have made it this way. Each leaf to each branch. Each branch to each trunk. Each trunk to each root."

It was an answer he expected, but it made his stomach feel woozy.

"It doesn't seem that way to me," he moaned. "I can't make heads or tails out of it."

"You must learn to relax, Martin Kanner. You must be patient. You are young. Look at the sun. Does it rush across the sky? Look at my trees. Look how long it takes to grow them."

God laughed, or was that God?—Martin wondered. Or was that the wind whinnying, or the spring on the screen door squealing?

"Look at the valley across the road. It's not bad to suffer. I have made things that way. In your laughter, a tear hangs. And in your tears, a smile lingers."

"What do my dreams mean, God? My father broke my arm the other night. I attacked him with a can-opener."

God's voice got lower, harder to hear. Now, Martin was having trouble separating the voice from the booming of the blood in his own ear.

"Your dreams are messages."

"Yes, I believe they are. But I can't figure them out. Last night, I was dragged down a well, and the stones were clanging."

"Yes, clanging."

"I kept falling deeper. There seemed no end to this well. I was afraid, God, that I was going to fall forever. I was afraid nobody would ever find me."

"Yes, deeper. Deeper. Deeper," God's voice echoed. "Deeper, Martin Kanner, my child, deeper. So deep you cannot see the sun. So deep you cannot see your face. So deep you cannot think. Deeper."

Martin rolled around on his cot. He fell asleep for a second, awoke with a start.

"God, don't leave me, I am dying."

"I must go, Martin Kanner."

"Are you real, God?" Martin asked. He realized that this was the stupidest question yet.

A laugh echoed back. The chickens clucked in the backyard. The wind blew up the meandering gut of the Valley of the Cross. Mrs. Shoshannah dropped something on the floor. It clanged loudly as it hit the stone floor in the kitchen. She cursed in Hebrew.

One afternoon Martin noticed that Mrs. Shoshannah had bought a basket of sabras. She had left them in the porch beside the washroom. What did a sabra taste like?—Martin wondered. He had never eaten one in his life. He knew it was a cactus fruit. From this fruit the native-born Israelis got their name. Gila was one such sabra. Larry another. And Gideon yet another. The name was symbolic: prickly on the outside, but sweet in the centre. Martin couldn't get them out of his mind, that basket of sabras just across the hall from his room.

He wanted to try one. He just had to. He decided to take one without asking.

Out to the back porch, he skulked. He walked quietly. Mrs. Shoshannah was asleep in her bedroom. He grabbed one and took it back to his room.

Oh fuck, you stupid bastard, he said to himself. Sabras were a cactus and he had forgotten. He soon woke up to the fact. His left hand was covered with short cactus needles. They had imbedded themselves in his skin. He cursed again at himself. How could he do something so stupid? Bare-handed, he had grabbed it. He threw the sabra on the floor in disgust. With a tweezer he spent the rest of the afternoon picking needle after needle from his palm and fingers. There seemed no end to them. His hand was sore, and speckled with tiny drops of blood.

I am dying, Egypt, he whispered under his breath. Don't you understand, dying? I'm going under. Will I ever see you again, my beloved friend?

What was happening to him, he asked repeatedly. He looked in the mirror in the washroom. Martin, he said to himself, this is serious. This isn't a game, Martin. Your personality is changing, Yes, wince. Martin, this could be an irrevocable change. You were always so happy, that's what people said. A happy-go-lucky guy. You laughed easily—in high school, in university. Why shouldn't everyone be happy? What's wrong with them? Just a month ago, you asked Jesse those questions. Now look at yourself. You can't stand talking to people any more. You don't write a word. You sleep in that room day after day. You don't give a shit about your teaching job. Oh yes, you do it, but you don't really care. You are turning into a shadow, Martin. Not an ounce of substance. Yes, frown, it's no laughing matter. There might not be any way back.

He thought again of Hansel and Gretel dropping bread crumbs in the woods. That was their way back, poor kids. Deeper and deeper they walked into the black woods. Into the trees without names. They walked where few had ever gone. The crows came. They ate the bread crumbs.

Look at yourself, Martin. This is not ping-pong you're playing. This isn't a trip to Nogales. This is real, you understand, real as those needles you picked out of your hand. That well you fell down the other night—oh yes, that dream was exciting. You wanted to be dragged down there. Yes, admit it. But Martin, what if there is no bottom, and no way back up?

He went back to his room and stretched out on his cot. He started to think about winters in Halifax. How thick the snow used to be in backyards when he was a child. He thought of the cross on top of Mount Royal in Montreal, the cross burning all night long. He thought of his friends at university, those who first introduced him to the wonder of words and poetry. Friends, old friends, you may never see me again. Jerusalem has swallowed me. I could die, old friends, and be buried in that valley across the road. Poppies will cover me. Wind and poppies.

He began to cry. Shake and cry. He wrapped his arms around himself. He cradled himself and began to rock. Rock-a-bye baby in the tree top, if the wind blows the cradle will rock, and if the bough breaks, the cradle will fall, and smash its wares all over the floor. He smiled to himself, he grinned. He chuckled. Oh, Egypt, you foolish fucking country, I am dying and you can't do a damn thing about it. Egypt, you impotent fool. Egypt, you scarred face. Egypt, you dummy, you thought you could save me. I am going to die in this rocky terrain.

He gazed at his hand. It still hurt. It was a bit swollen, and he was hoping it wouldn't get infected.

Who else dreamed such dreams?—he considered. Hamlet? Oedipus? Freud? Who else ever saw the sun creep over a windowsill, a yellow cur of terror? Martin, he said to himself, be mad. It's only for a season. But was it? What was he fiddling around with? Mrs. Shoshannah knocked at his door. He answered it.

"How are you, Martin?"

"I am fine."

"We don't see you," Mrs. Shoshannah frowned. "You work?"

"Yes," Martin nodded, "I teach."

"Ah, teach," Mrs. Shoshannah exclaimed, rolling her eyes. "What a good job. I wish my Larry was a teacher. Dance, that is all he knows. Like his mama. Gideon—maybe he will teach."

Martin stared at the floor. The chatter bored him. It seemed senseless, standing in the doorway, talking to this woman. Who was she anyway? What bearing did she have on his existence? Yak. Yak. Yak.

"You get girl yet?" she asked, playing with the cotton belt on her loose-fitting dress.

"No. Not yet."

"Not good to be lonely too much," she said, twirling her finger into her scalp. "You go meshugeh, crazy."

Martin laughed.

"No, not funny . . . you like your room?"

"Yes, it's fine."

"Good," Mrs. Shoshannah beamed. "I go feed my chickens now, O.K?"

"Yes, fine," Martin answered vaguely.

He shut the door. He went back to his cot. He let out a sigh of relief. Feed the bloody chickens, he thought to himself.

Martin, an inner voice nagged, your mind is turning into a kaleidoscope of fear. Your hands are becoming shadows. Your heart—a stone.

* * *

One weekend he went to Tel Aviv to visit his family. He was sitting on the sofa beside his father.

"How is everything, Martin?" Lines of worry creased his father's forehead.

Martin didn't answer immediately. He was staring at the wood floor.

"Not too good," he finally choked up the words. "I don't know what's wrong."

His father sighed.

"I don't know what to tell you," he said. "I don't think I can help you, Martin. For once, I don't think I can really help you. I don't think anyone can. You're going through something... what can I say? You just have to go through it."

Martin slumped lower in the sofa.

"Yes," he agreed.

"Just remember one thing," his father continued, "no matter how bad it looks, it will pass. You'll get out of it. Things will change."

It seemed to Martin that they were both trying to talk about something as elusive as the texture of wind. They were circling an intangible hurt together. Their minds were going around and around it—a ball of air. Martin's dreams were locked inside the invisible thing. His fears. His night-time battles with can-openers and pathetic guns.

"Yeah, I'll get out of it."

There was no enthusiasm in his voice.

The weekend dragged on. He raced to the bus terminal on Sunday morning.

* * *

In the stone cottage once again, he stood at his window. He stood absolutely still, yet the sweat dripped from his armpits, and soaked his legs.

He gazed at the heat rising in the valley across the highway. A shadow was moving through the burnt, hard grass. It was carrying a scythe. Was that death, he wondered, barely discernible in the Valley of the Cross? Was that the grinning face the world abhorred? The gaping eye-sockets? The laughing mouth of bones and teeth?

Death, how swiftly you move, Martin dreamed. How stealthy you are, unencumbered by robes and jewellery.

The Christ, he thought, the fish, the man of sorrow, the bent-backed saviour. Walking. Stumbling. Up the dark gut of the valley. Towards the Mount of Olives. O Christ, are you real?

CHAPTER 20

Britta and Jacob

On a hot, sweltering afternoon in mid-August, Martin heard a knock at his bedroom door. It had an unfamiliar rhythm to it. He paused before he pulled himself from his cot. Who could that be?—he wondered. He got very few visits. Mrs. Shoshannah didn't bother with him any more. He hadn't seen Jesse in weeks.

Slowly, he pulled himself up, his limbs heavy with the heat, his head wrapped in the haze of his own stupor. He floated to the door, rubbing his eyes, brushing back his hair.

When he opened the door he was surprised at the two people who stood there. One face was familiar, the other a stranger. In his doorway stood Steven Goldman. It took him a second to remember. Where had he seen those round cheeks before, those brown, dreamy eyes, where, oh where?—he wondered. Slowly, like the pieces of a remembered dream, it came back to him. The Turkish boat, the captain, the hunting-knife, the waves of the Mediterranean, the dolphins, the poetry of Thomas Campion. Piece by piece, conversation by conversation, he remembered.

"Do you remember me?" Steven laughed and smiled.

His face was flushed, not just by the sun, Martin thought. And it didn't look like a momentary excitement. His complexion looked altered.

"Steven?" Martin faltered. "Steven Goldman. Boy, am I ever surprised to see you. Come in, come in. How the hell are you anyway? How did you get my address?"

Steven's expression turned a little more serious. He stood aside, revealing the other person.

"I want you to meet somebody," Steven smiled, "a very good friend of mine. Martin, this is Britta Lystrom."

The girl edged forward. Hesitantly, she reached out a hand. Martin grasped it.

"Glad to meet you," Martin managed to utter. His voice sounded stiff and formal.

"We just came from the kibbutz," Steven continued. "I called your parents in Tel Aviv and they gave me your address. It was a little hard to find."

"Kind of lost in the woods, isn't it?" Martin said, standing back, making room for both of them to enter.

He pointed to the cot on the other side of the room, opposite the one he slept on. It was covered with a bedspread and served as a makeshift sofa.

"You must be tired," Martin grinned. "Please sit down. I have some orange juice in the fridge. Would you like some?"

"Yes," they both said in unison, bobbing their heads.

"This is a fuckin' hot country," Steven added.

Martin walked to the kitchen. His head buzzed with excitement. His fingers were trembling. He was surprised at his own joy. It seemed a very long time since he had felt his body tingle from head to foot, and his face crease with a smile. What a surprise, he kept thinking. He never really expected to see Steven Goldman again. Martin found two clean glasses in the cupboard, not his own, but he decided to use them.

Steven moved closer to Britta on the cot. He folded her hand in his.

"Well," he whispered, "that's Martin. He's a great guy, a poet. How do you like him?"

Britta hesitated.

"I just met him, Steven. He seems nice."

Martin's hands trembled and shook as he poured the orange juice. Take it easy, he said to himself. Why are you so excited? But he couldn't dampen the feelings rushing through him. What a surprise! Steven Goldman. He chuckled to himself, remembering the story about the captain with the moustache, the incident in the washroom.

Martin walked quickly back to the room, balancing the two glasses of orange juice.

"What a surprise!" he repeated. "I never thought I'd see you again."

He gave Steven's shoulder a squeeze and a shake.

"A cool drink," Steven sighed, rolling his eyes. "Well, I just tracked you down, that's all. How has life been treating you anyway?"

Martin sat down on the cot opposite them.

"Lousy, I have to admit. What the hell, though, the summer's almost over. Maybe my luck's going to change."

Steven tilted back his glass.

"We want to stay in Jerusalem for a while," Steven said. He put an arm around Britta, squeezed her for a second, and took his arm away.

"That's great," Martin said enthusiastically. "It's a terrific city, Steven. Hey listen, I don't have to teach this afternoon, I can help you find a room if you want. There's all kinds of them in this area."

Britta sat silently on the sofa. She watched both of them, surprised at their mutual excitement. How fast, she thought, the words poured forth. They talked as if they had known each other for years. She was waiting for an opportunity to break into the rapport.

"Jacob," she finally said, looking at Steven, "I have to use the washroom."

Martin jumped up from the cot.

"Oh, it's just out there."

He opened the door to his room and pointed across the hall.

"Thank you," she whispered.

When Martin heard the door to the washroom click shut, he turned to Steven.

"How come she called you Jacob?"

Steven blushed and smiled.

"Do you like that name?" he asked. "I just wanted something more biblical. Steven's a bit dull anyway. How do you like Jacob?"

"It's fine," Martin nodded.

Steven's eyes got more excited. The color changed to a deeper red in his cheeks and forehead.

"How do you like her?" he asked, half out of breath. "I just found her on the kibbutz. She was just sitting there. I couldn't believe it."

"She's fine," Martin managed to murmur, surprised a little by Steven's excitement and the onslaught of words.

His face got even more animated. The excitement took another leap.

"She's Christian."

Steven mouthed the word. He savored it. He spoke it with a touch of awe in his voice. The word came out as if he were talking about a rare jewel, or a sacred religious ceremony. It was the same reverence he reserved for the poetry of Thomas Campion.

"She's Swedish," he continued. "You should see the excitement she causes. Everywhere she goes. How many blondes do you see like that in Tel Aviv?"

Not too many, Martin had to admit. Not too many at all.

"I wrote to my parents about her." Steven added. "I told them everything. Martin, I feel quite serious about her. But can you imagine?—I come all the way to Israel and fall in love with a Christian girl. I'm just wondering what my parents are going to think. Who knows? Maybe they'll disown me."

Steven chuckled to himself. Martin couldn't keep his eyes from staring at his face. His cheeks seemed to be blazing, a hot red.

"They wouldn't do that," Martin frowned.

"They'll be hot about it," Steven nodded. "Who the fuck cares? I've never met anyone like her. Do you know how old she is?"

Martin shook his head.

"She looks about seventeen, doesn't she? She's three years older than I am. And she's been through all kinds of things. Love affairs. Relationships. She's a woman, Martin, a real woman. I haven't had a chance to live with her. Do you really think you can help us get a room?"

"Sure," Martin nodded. "We can go looking this afternoon. We'll find something."

Steven leaned back against the wall. A smile of contentment and pride lingered on his face.

"That's great. Am I ever glad I found you."

Martin lit a cigarette and sat silently opposite Steven. The lethargy of the last few months began to seep into him again. He could feel his limbs slowly going numb, his mind blanking out. He tried to fight it off. Here was a chance, the thought, of getting out of the sleepy pit he had fallen into. Fight it off, he said to himself.

He tried to center his mind on the problem at hand. Keep it simple, he mused. Find a room somewhere in the area where Steven could take his Swedish girlfriend and set up housekeeping.

Britta came back to the room. She opened the door quietly, not wishing to intrude.

"Are you ready to find a room?" Steven asked.

Britta smiled and nodded. It was a faint smile and it looked a little shy. Martin was thinking of what Steven had just told him—how Britta caused a stir among the men of the country. He thought about her age and her experience. Yet she wasn't hitting Martin this way. He looked at her face. Her eyes appeared faintly tired.

"Well, let's go," Martin said, pulling himself up. "Maybe we'll be able to find a place right around here."

Luck was with them that afternoon. They walked along together, meeting few people, just the three of them—Steven who had changed his name to Jacob, Britta who had travelled all the way from Stockholm, and Martin. They knocked at doors together, Martin using every single Hebrew word he had stored up over the years, or at least it seemed that way. Hunting for a room in the ancient language.

They found something about a block away from the stone cottage, a self-contained apartment with a washroom and cooking facilities. The rent was steep, but this didn't seem to bother Steven. It was not a grand apartment, very simple in fact, but more than Martin could afford.

That evening the three of them sat around together in the new place. They had bought some food at the market earlier. Britta prepared a small supper. She moved slowly around the kitchenette. On pieces of matzah she placed cheese-slices and tomatoes. Martin watched her move, talk, eat. She looked a little dreamy to him. Yes, he thought, there was something different about her, this girl Steven had found on the kibbutz. He couldn't put his finger on it. It wasn't merely her blond hair, her blue eyes, or her unusually pale, creamy complexion. No, it was in the slow way her legs carried her, and in her shyness.

And as his teeth crunched into his matzah, and as they sipped coffee together, the Jerusalem twilight darkening the windows, Martin began to think that Steven was very fortunate to be living with such a woman. He tried to imagine himself in Steven's shoes, alone in the apartment with Britta. What would it be like?—he wondered. It was only a dream he was dreaming, certainly only a dream, for whenever his eyes were about to meet hers, he averted his gaze. And Britta, too, looked the other way.

Around eleven o'clock, he said goodnight to both of them. They thanked him for his help, and Steven made him promise to come see them the next day.

dog was lurking down there, teeth chiseled to a fine sharpness, just waiting for him to slip. It was a world of darkness and shadows, an eternity of screeches and moans.

He could feel it pulling him downward. He could hear it whispering in his ears.

What Britta and Jacob were doing together looked like sanity in comparison. Sleeping in the same bed together, embracing, eating their simple meals of matzah and cheese. Walking together in the Judaean hills. Laughing. Steven laughing with his dark, sensual mouth. Britta's eyes bright and happy, a shy twist to her mouth. Certainly this was sane, healthy, normal. What an unnatural life he had been living cooped up in his room, doors shut to everyone. Cooped up with his mysterious nightmares.

And yet he was still puzzled by them, fascinated. The pieces of a dark puzzle had forced themselves upon him. Waves of the sea tossing him against a wall. What was this wall? Why did it look so high? Why did he believe he could not climb it? He remembered relaxing in the waves. Yes, that was a good feeling, the warm arms of water surrounding him. And, it was a marvellous sensation to be tossed into the air. Yes, there was something positive and free about that part of the dream ... flying through the air with the greatest of ease. But then, the shock of landing against this wall. His head just avoiding the stones. An inch away from getting smashed completely.

What a contrast, he kept thinking, between his night-time adventures and the life Britta and Jacob were enjoying together.

He fought against the darkness. It seemed that it wanted to embrace him, wrap him up, engulf him completely.

A few days later he was speaking with Steven. They were alone in Martin's room. Steven looked agitated. He circled the room. Martin sat still on the cot. Steven's face was flushed with anxiety.

"Shit," he said, "I just got a telegram this morning. My father's flying over. I'm supposed to meet him at the airport in Tel Aviv."

Steven stamped his foot on the floor.

"Just when everything was going so beautiful. I know why he's coming. I must've been crazy to write him about Britta."

"What do you think he wants?" Martin asked, his mind clouded by the old numbness, his head wrapped in a misty haze.

Steven slapped the palm of his hand against the dresser. The thin wood shook. The noise cracked inside Martin's ears.

Back to his room he walked in the darkness, still thinking a\
Steven and Britta, and the small apartment he had found for th\
Steven's words had seeped into his mind. "She's Christian, Mar\
. . . there she was, just sitting there."

In the darkness of his own room he stretched out. Was th\
numbness finally departing? He didn't want to shut his doors or\
Steven and Britta. He didn't want to hide away from them. No, he\
would see them the next day, see how they were getting along.

He began to think of his childhood. How dark his house seemed\
on Christmas Eve without a single light for decoration. He was at the\
dining-room window looking out. Up and down the street the bright\
lights were strung—reds and greens, trees shimmering with bright\
bulbs of color. There was only one dark house on the street—hi\
own. Across the street his girlfriend lived, Cathy Nelson. She ha\
dimples and blue eyes, blond hair and red ribbons. He was seven,\
she was six. Yet they went to the movies together, he remembered,\
hand in hand. Through the snow in the backyards they walked\
down to the Armview Theatre. And in the summertime, they would\
hide themselves beneath a blanket and kiss.

Mrs. Shoshannah's chickens were asleep. The house was still.\
Faintly through the wall, he could hear Larry wheezing in his sleep,\
and Mrs. Shoshannah coughing as she turned in her bed. What a\
long way he had travelled, he dreamed, what a long trip. Was Cathy\
Nelson married? Did she have a couple of kids? What did the stree\
look like now, Macdonald Street, the first street of his childhoo\
years? Had they paved it? Had they filled in the pot-holes and mad\
it smooth for traffic? What a long way they all had travelled: Mr\
Shoshannah, Larry, Steven, Britta.

From his bed he could see the moon hanging over the Valley\
the Cross. It was lean and white. He hoped that Steven and Brit\
were comfortable in their new apartment. Were they asleep no\
locked in each other's arms?—Britta's blond hair falling on Steven s\
chest. Did he have a place in their minds, he wondered, was he a\
flickering image that passed through their dreams?

The next few days passed slowly. After work he would visit\
Steven and Britta. The old numbness and sleepiness would attack\
him, his eyes would grow heavy, his blood would slow down, but he\
tried to shake it off. He didn't want to slip into that pit again. It\
frightened him. Down there inside his depression the stones were\
waiting, the clanging stones and the beat of horses' hooves. A yellow

"Hah!" Steven exclaimed. "I know what he wants. He wants to take me back, that's what he wants. Fuck, Martin, I don't want to go. But the guy's so bloody persuasive. I'm afraid I'll get there, and the next thing I know, I'll be in the plane flying back to Cincinnati."

"Just don't go," Martin wheezed half-heartedly.

"Sure, sure. It looks simple, doesn't it? Just tell him to get lost. Sorry, Dad, I'm staying in Israel. It's not that simple. That's the fuckin' problem."

Steven rolled his eyes towards the ceiling. He stood i the middle of the room looking upward. He was gazing at the if a message might've been written there, a solution to his dilen le slapped his hands together, and walked across the room to Martin. He extended his hand, and Martin grasped it.

"I'm going to shake hands now," he said wearily. "I might no another chance. Listen, Martin, I'm going to try my fucking best stay. I like this city. Things are just starting to go well with Britta. Boy, what a beautiful girl. I don't mean just looks. Her soul is beautiful. There's something pure about her. I know it sounds crazy, but to me she always seems innocent. I know about all the guys she's been with. But it doesn't matter. Here's what I'm trying to say —if I have to go back, I want you to look after her. Just make sure she's getting along okay. I just hate the idea of leaving her all alone here. Will you do that for me?"

"Sure, Steven," Martin nodded. "I like her a lot. Don't worry about it. I know how you feel. Do you really believe you'll have to go back?"

Steven turned away, and began pacing the room again, stopping at the window and absentmindedly looking out.

"I'm going to try my best. There's no way I want to go back. He'll be awfully determined, though. Don't forget, Martin, he left his bloody business to come here. I don't understand it. Flying all the way to Israel just because of that stupid letter I sent him."

Steven shook his head back and forth. Martin sighed to himself, feeling Steven's anguish inside his own stomach.

"Don't worry about Britta," he whispered. "She'll be O.K."

That same afternoon, Steven packed his few belongings and took the bus to Tel Aviv.

That evening after his English lesson, Martin returned to the cottage, entered his room, and closed the door. He wanted to be alone. He couldn't get Steven out of his mind. What was happening at the airport? He tried to imagine the scene. Mr. Goldman stepping off the jet, his eyes determined and his mouth held firmly. Steven walking slowly towards him, head bent. Both of them getting closer to each other. Mr. Goldman in a business suit and wearing a tie. Steven sauntering along, but his legs trembling. Words exchanged between them. A discussion that got mixed up and swallowed in the whir of engines, the flapping of flags in the wind.

Was that the last he was going to see of his friend? It was hard to believe that he would not come back to Jerusalem. Steven had just arrived a few days before, his face flushed with hope and energy.

He thought about Britta alone in the apartment, sitting there, awaiting some word of news. He was tempted to go knock at the door. But no, it was too early for that.

And he had to fight again that evening against his recurring dreams, and the lethargy that was trying to crawl inside him, to occupy his body. He had had enough of it. Enough struggles with his father in nightmares. He could still feel how easily his arm had been snapped and broken. His arm, as if it were nothing more than a toothpick. An image of the can-opener dangled inside his head. What a cold vicious weapon he had chosen in his sleep to fight back with.

Instead of sleeping, instead of dreaming, he tried his best to keep himself awake. He made himself a coffee. When the web of drowsiness surrounded him, he shook it off. He walked to the window. How bright the stars were in this desert country, how brightly they hung over the Valley of the Cross. And there was no missing the moon against the blackness of the sky.

What would happen, he wondered, if Steven didn't come back?

By the time the next evening rolled around, he had still heard nothing. Around seven o'clock he wandered up to Steven's apartment, and found Britta there. She looked sad and downcast. She was sitting on the sofa. Her blue eyes looked hazy and mystified.

"Have you heard from Steven?" Martin asked, taking a seat opposite Britta on a hard kitchen chair.

Britta didn't answer immediately. Absentmindedly, she played with a loose thread on her skirt. Martin was beginning to wonder if she had heard his question.

"He called me this morning on the landlady's phone. He was at the airport."

Britta's voice sounded dreamy. There was a vague softness in each word.

"He went back?" Martin asked. It was an effort to form the words.

Britta nodded. Martin gazed at her face. She wasn't crying, but now he noticed that her eyes were red. She had been crying earlier in the day. Britta shook her head slowly back and forth.

"I don't understand it," she whispered, rubbing the loose thread between her forefinger and thumb. "It doesn't make any sense to me. Everything was going so well between us. I know Steven was happy."

Martin nodded his head in agreement.

"Yes, he was."

"Then, why did he do it?" Britta asked. Her voice sounded shaky. Martin couldn't detect any anger in her words. Her voice sounded tired and puzzled.

"Maybe he didn't have a choice," Martin offered.

Britta shook her head again.

"That's all he talked about on the kibbutz. How we would come to Jerusalem and live together. He was really excited about it. It was the first time he ever lived with anybody."

Martin was a bit surprised by what Britta was telling him. He was sure that Steven had lived with girls before. But he thought about it again. Steven. His father. The airport. Cincinnati. It began to make some sense to him. Perhaps this was the first time Steven had lived outside his parents' home.

"He really cared for you a lot," Martin whispered across the room.

"I know," Britta nodded. "That's why it's so hard to understand."

No more words came out of his mouth. What more could he say? It was hard for him to understand. It had all happened so quickly. One day they were living together, and the next day Steven was gone, out of both their lives. One day he was in Jerusalem just a block away, the next in Cincinnati.

"How are you going to get by?" Martin asked. "Do you have enough money to get food?"

Britta nodded, and laughed to herself. There was a slight bitterness to it.

"I guess his father's well-off," she mused. "Steven told me on the phone that he managed to get some money from him. He wired me three hundred dollars from the airport."

"I'm glad to hear that."

Britta moved her hand from the loose thread on her skirt, and began playing with the ends of her hair.

"Well, I guess it's all over," Britta sighed. "He said on the phone he might come back in a month, but I don't see how he could. He'll probably go back to university this fall."

Martin stared at the floor. He was beginning to feel closer to this girl who was sitting across from him. Her voice sounded soft to him. He had not really noticed her face before—the very faint hint of wrinkles around her eyes. Below her lower lip, he noticed a soft protuberance of flesh. She *was* beautiful, he thought to himself. Steven was right. Somehow he had not fully seen it before. There was something knowing in her eyes, yet an innocence. For a second, he felt a strong desire to put his arms around her, to draw her close, and to comfort her.

But he shook this off. It was far too early to do such a thing. It was as if they were both in mourning for Steven, their mutual friend.

"Are you going to stay in Jerusalem?" Martin asked. His voice sounded hopeful and encouraging.

"I don't know. I'm so mixed up right now. I've even thought of going back home. I'm just tired of the whole thing."

"I really hope you stay, Britta," Martin said, his voice wavering. "I know you'll like Jerusalem. We can be friends."

Britta raised her gaze just a bit. She didn't look directly into his eyes.

"Maybe I'll give it a try. I just don't know what to do. I'll have to look for a job. I need time to think about it."

She shook her head again.

"Everything happened so fast."

"I really hope you find work," Martin added.

Britta lowered her head again. He could sense that she wanted to be alone.

"Well, I'm going now," he said, trying to sound cheerful. "Can I come by tomorrow, and see how everything's going?"

Britta nodded. "Sure. You're always welcome here."

Martin walked slowly through the streets and down the stone path to his room. Everything seemed still. The trees, the houses, the stars. A hush surrounded him, a quiet stillness. Yes, he thought, Steven was right. Britta was beautiful, and she had an innocence and a softness that he liked.

He went to sleep thinking about her.

CHAPTER 21

Blond Stranger

The last dry hot days of August and the beginning of September passed. Britta received a few letters from Steven, postmarked Cincinnati. The first few messages were hopeful and kept Britta that way. He wanted to come back to Jerusalem as soon as possible. There was a good chance of it, he wrote. Slowly, however, his optimism eroded. The letters became cooler in tone, and finally he wrote that he had registered for a full course at university in his hometown. The letters, eventually, stopped altogether. Britta looked drained. Her complexion had become a little too pale, and the skin on her face was drawn too tight.

To make matters worse, the money which Steven had provided was slowly evaporating.

In the center of Jerusalem, a bar existed that catered to men of the press, a few businessmen, and U.N. officers from the peace-keeping force. Mr. Lupo, a Hungarian Jew with a lean face, black darting eyes, and a closely clipped moustache, was the proprietor. It was here that Britta finally found part-time employment as a barmaid. Working from eight p.m. to one in the morning, she would make just enough to keep things going. Just enough to provide for food, shelter, but very few extras.

Martin got into the habit of picking her up at closing time, and walking her back to her apartment. The bar itself puzzled him. It was a dim place with one or two tables, subdued red lighting, and a huge mirror behind the parade of bottles. Customers were few and far between. Rarely did Martin see more than five men in the place at one time. How did it survive?—he wondered. Did Lupo even make a profit out of his night-time venture? Martin couldn't imagine how it could do more than break even, but from Britta he discovered that Mr. Lupo ran a catering service during the day. Sometimes she would make a few extra dollars serving food and liquor at bar mitzvahs and weddings.

In the evenings when he finished his teaching assignment, he came directly back to the stone cottage. He lingered in the darkness alone, waiting for midnight to arrive. Then he would suddenly revive, shake off his stupor, wash his face with cold water, brush his teeth, comb his hair, make himself look somewhat presentable, and walk down to Lupo's bar.

It was becoming part of his routine, this late-evening vigil, his hour at Lupo's waiting for Britta to finish work. He rarely got to sleep before three in the morning, and he was just as glad. He could sleep in until noon or later the next day, and do it with a clear conscience.

He never thought about it much at the time. He took it for granted, but it struck him later. In the months that Britta worked for Lupo, he hardly ever saw another woman in the place. Yet Britta was popular. She coasted behind the curved bar with a smile on her face, pouring the liquor, making cocktails, joking with the customers.

After work, one early morning about two a.m., walking with him down the dark quiet streets, Britta looked unusually agitated.

"Is there something wrong?" Martin finally asked.

Britta plunged her hands into the pockets of her skirt.

"It's that place. It sometimes gets me down. Especially Mr. Lupo."

Martin gazed at his own feet moving along the sidewalk. He was waiting for her to continue.

"I wish he could keep his hands to himself. Every time I bend over, he pinches me. I'm getting tired of it."

"Why don't you tell him to fuck off?" Martin spat, feeling the anger rise inside him like a rope knotted tightly in his throat.

Britta smiled to herself. It was a wistful smile that Martin could see out of the corner of his eye. The moon lit up her face. Was there any woman, he wondered, in all Jerusalem as soft and desirable? It was no damn wonder that Lupo had hired her, and that he followed her so closely behind the bar.

"It's not just him," Britta continued in a soft caressing voice. "It's the whole thing. The other day I met a French businessman. He's about forty years old. Very suave and very rich. He wanted to set me up in my own apartment in Paris. The crazy thing about it, Martin, is that he was absolutely serious. It's a big temptation, you know. I get tired of having so little money."

Martin let his head fall. A tightness formed in his chest, a hardness tinged with anger.

"I can't see you doing something like that, Britta. It's just not you."

Britta stopped walking. She stood still in the middle of the sidewalk.

"No..." she considered, "I've never done anything like that before."

Britta smoothed down her skirt. She was looking away from him. She paused, then began to speak again.

"By the way, Martin, Lupo was complaining tonight. He doesn't think you should be coming down so early to get me."

Now the anger began to seethe inside him.

"That fucking prick!" Martin hissed. "What does he want anyway? I buy a drink or two when I'm there. I should tell him to shove it up his ass."

Britta started walking again. Martin kept pace with her. They were silent now. There wasn't another person on the dark, early-morning streets. The wind moved slowly through the trees, just barely rustling them.

"Britta, I want to talk to you about something," Martin finally said. "Do you know how I feel about you? I don't want to be just friends. I feel a lot more than that."

Britta reached out a hand and gripped his arm for a second, then removed it.

"Yes, I know," she whispered. "And I really like you, Martin. But I'm just tired of relationships. The thing with Steven really took a lot out of me. You know that, yourself. I don't want to go through the same thing all over again. I just want to let it rest for a while. You understand, don't you?"

Martin nodded his head slowly in the darkness.

"Yes, I think so," he murmured. His reply was hardly audible.

"I just want to take it easy for a while," Britta repeated.

They walked slowly together in silence once again. Slowly, over the days, his desire for her had grown. It was beginning to ache inside him, in his stomach and in his groin. Night after night, his eyes had followed her movements behind the bar. Her skirt moving along her legs. He walked her home once again, said goodnight at the door to her apartment, and walked back to his room alone.

He couldn't get her out of his mind. How much he wanted to embrace her, to kiss her, to undo her skirt, and watch it fall to the floor. How much he wanted to sprinkle soft kisses up and down the length of her legs. He imagined his tongue flicking out at her bare skin. He tried to imagine how she smelled. What fragrances lingered between her breasts?—he wondered. In his room alone, drowsy and tired, he thought about Lupo and his bar. If he were Lupo, wouldn't he also be tempted to gaze at her legs as she bent over? Wouldn't he be overcome by the temptation to touch her, just once? And if he were an old Jewish businessman, rich and suave, wouldn't he also offer her an apartment in Paris? A penthouse, if need be. If he were fifty, old and tired and rich, wouldn't he shower her with presents? Perfumes, candies, rings and clothes. Anything she wanted, in fact. How could he really blame them?—Lupo and the others. Wasn't she the most exciting creature walking the streets of Jerusalem? Who else was there? She was young, intelligent, Swedish, and beautiful. She was well-built and sensual. How could he blame anyone for losing their bearings? His own breath choked in his throat when he thought about her.

In the darkness lying on his cot, he smiled to himself, thinking about her. I love you, Britta, I really think I do. He whispered it inside his mouth. He kissed the darkness with his words. How could anyone in this dark, ferocious country not love her? She was like a fresh breeze walking down the street. He had a strong picture of her in his mind walking down King George Road at noon hour. This wasn't a fantasy. He actually saw it happen several times. She was dressed all in white: a white top and white slacks. The sun sparkled off her blond hair. Her complexion looked whiter and creamier than ever. Yemenite women would call after her—"Oh, blondit, oh so pretty, blond one." He actually saw a couple of them reach out dark, bony hands towards her hair. "Oh, blondit, let me touch." Britta would smile, laugh, and toss her head. And little dark Sephardi kids would chase after her, entranced, it seemed, by this strange-looking creature. And men on streetcorners, in bookshops, in cars, would swivel their heads as she passed, trying to get a better look. They'd wink, call to her, whistle hopefully at her swaying figure.

How could he do anything but fall in love with her? He thought about her alone in her apartment. It made him feel uneasy. He was afraid she would fall in love with somebody else, or in a moment of weakness, accept the Frenchman's offer to fly her to Paris. He was agitated. What if she did find somebody else who was more appealing? He'd be sick with jealousy. He would be consumed by it—bitter and broken. Full of despair and hatred.

Every evening, now, he went to sleep with Britta on his mind. Lupo would swirl into view, his eyes darting blackly. Saliva on his lips. And the fat Frenchman would impinge upon his reverie, three expensive rings glistening on his hand. I love you, Britta, he whispered to his four unhearing walls. I've fallen in love with you, and it could be forever. Those were the last words his mouth would form before he fell asleep.

Night after night, he went to Lupo's bar. Where else was there to go? Who else was there to see?—Britta. What else was his life composed of? He was tired of the dark dreams that had assaulted him. He had grown more distant from Jesse and Peter. In Lupo's bar each of his days ended, it seemed, and the next one began. Began in a swirl of cigarette smoke, the sick aroma from expensive cigars, the clinking of glasses, the shifting of ice. Ended in the red lights reflected from the mirror.

A record spun on the turntable. The Russian words filtered through the stale air and chatter. Britta translated them for him. They were crying, moaning, whispering: I thank my heart that it knows how to love. What a simple message. Did his heart know how to love? Was he finally being consumed by it?

The men around the bar all looked the same, though they seemed to change from night to night. Only Lupo stood out, and a Dutch U.N. officer. He was a tall gentile gentleman with a mote in his left eye. He leaned his tall frame against the bar. Somehow, he didn't seem to fit in with Lupo and his friends. Yet he fit perfectly. He talked simply and quietly with the others, giving his opinions about Arab-Jewish relations.

As the evenings passed, Martin grew tenser. He began to despise everyone except the Dutchman. And he hated the look of his own face cast back by the mirror. It was growing thinner and darker. His skin was stretched over the bones. He tried to keep his eyes fastened to Britta.

"A man's got to take it easy in matters of the heart," the Dutchman told him one evening. "It can swallow a person."

Martin nodded knowingly. He could see his head bobbing through the bottles just in front of him in the mirror.

"I want to be swallowed," he confided to the U.N. officer. "I want to feel it in my bones."

The Dutchman leaned away from Martin. A slight tremor flickered across his face.

"She's got everyone on a string," he whispered. "It's not her fault. But it can backfire."

Martin sipped on his beer. It tasted stale, uninteresting. It mixed badly with the taste of cigarettes in his mouth. He was tempted to lift his glass and hurl it at the bottles in front of him.

"I want to break all those strings," he whispered over the lip of his glass.

"Yes, I understand that," the Dutchman intoned. "I've been in love. Just go slowly. I'm telling you that as a friend. I've got no interest in it myself."

It seemed sincere. The U.N. officer could stand aside, Martin mused, tilt back his drinks and watch what was happening.

Night after night, a similar scene took place. The Russian record revolved, playing the same old tune. How tense could he grow before he exploded? He was getting sick of the whole thing. One night he decided to speak to her as soon as he took her home.

It was about two o'clock in the morning when Britta unlocked the door of her apartment. Martin followed her inside.

"Britta, I've got to talk to you."

"O.K., come in." Her voice sounded weary. The perpetual smile she wore down at Lupo's had disappeared.

She stood in the middle of the floor. He walked over, and was standing in front of her.

"Britta, I can't take it any more," he almost shouted.

She looked surprised.

"You know exactly what I'm talking about," he continued. "I'm sick of the whole thing. Picking you up at Lupo's. Walking you here. Going home alone. I don't want to be friends any more. I love you, do you understand? Steven's been gone a month. You can't use that as an excuse. Do you want people like Lupo breathing down your neck forever?"

Britta turned away from him. She walked across the room, and stood with her back to him. Her shoulders looked hunched and tired.

They stood silently. The minutes seemed to drag past. Martin was determined to stand there until morning without saying another word.

She turned around slowly. Her face looked softer and more relaxed.

"I don't know if I love you, Martin," she whispered. "I'm just so tired of everything."

He moved his face towards her and kissed her on the cheek. It was a soft kiss.

"Can we talk about it?" he asked. There was a hopefulness in his voice.

"Yes. Let's sit down. I'll make coffee for us."

He walked slowly towards the sofa, and let his weight drift down into the cushions. He was beginning to feel more relaxed. The skin on his face felt looser. A smile was pressing against the corners of his mouth. Slowly, he let himself sink into the sofa. He stretched out his legs. It was the first evening he hadn't said goodnight at the door.

Britta busied herself around the stove boiling water. He was thinking about the kiss he had given her. He had gotten his face close enough to her mouth to smell her breath. How different it was from the cigar and whiskey smells down at Lupo's. It was a familiar fragrance that lingered on her lips. Something fresh. Something familiar. He tried to remember what it reminded him of. And then, slowly, it came to him. Apples, fresh apples in the autumn, apples in the Annapolis Valley just before they were picked.

They talked together over the coffees. Britta told him about her family in Stockholm. She talked about the mountains in Norway, the fiords, things he had only read about. He kept glancing at her. Her face. Her body. He yearned to know what she looked like with her clothes off.

They talked until the morning light began to filter through the windows. He could hear a cock crowing in the distance. The sun was slowly rising once again over the hills, over the tops of the cypress trees.

"I'm not a complicated person," she said. "Maybe you are. But I'm not. Maybe you're looking for things that are hard to find.

Things you only get out of books. Maybe you have dreams that are hard to capture. I'm not that hard to understand. I want to love somebody and to be loved. That's not so complicated. I want to have a family. Kids are very important to me."

Martin nodded his head as he listened. How he wished things were simple. Perhaps they were after all, but he just couldn't perceive it that way.

"Maybe what I want is the same," he whispered. "You know what I mean—underneath."

How could he expect her to know what he meant? He wasn't sure that he knew himself. He wasn't totally convinced by his own words.

"Things aren't that complicated. I think people make them that way," she continued. "Look, the sun is coming up."

She ran to the window and gazed out.

"Come here, Martin, take a look. It's so beautiful."

Martin got up, walked across the room, and stood beside her at the window. The sun was shedding a red, soft skirt of light over the sky. The hills looked blacker against it. Everything looked new and fresh to him.

"It's just gotta be simple," he sighed.

Britta leaned closer against him. He could feel the heat of her body.

"Let's try, then," she whispered. "I'm willing to try. Undress me, Martin, and we'll make love."

He gazed at her. He couldn't quite believe he was finally hearing those words. He looked at her blue eyes, her blond hair, her soft sensual mouth. He suddenly felt a little tired.

"You're like a beautiful present. So beautiful I don't want to unwrap it."

It was a silly thing to say. He realized that as soon as the words came out.

He kissed her on the mouth for the first time. His tongue flicked out and touched hers. He couldn't get over the freshness of her breath that first morning. He was tasting apples. Gila and Josephine flashed for a second through his mind. Had they tasted like anything?—he wondered. Had he even noticed?

He undressed her, covering her mouth and eyelids with kisses. He got undressed himself. She was lying naked now on the bed-sofa—in the same room they had talked all night in, in the same room she

had shared with Steven. How white her skin looked, he kept thinking. And her legs looked sturdier than he'd expected. They were
short, sturdy legs, and quite muscular. He wanted to kiss every part
of her, to kiss her as he had kissed nobody else.

He moved his mouth down the length of her arms, kissing the soft
skin. Kissing her breasts and nipples. Flicking out his tongue. Her
nipples grew hard under his kisses. He moved his mouth along her
belly, lower and lower, towards the tuft of blond hair between her
legs. He knew where his mouth was heading now, what his tongue
wanted to taste. It was something he'd never done with anyone else.
He had no desire to do it with Gila or Josephine. The thought had
made him feel a little sick. But with Britta it was different. He
wanted to do it and he had to do it. And he was going to do it.

He could feel the short, curly hair tickling against his mouth. For a
second, he wanted to sneeze. He was thankful when this sensation
passed. He was used to making love in the dark, but now he could
see where his mouth was moving. His tongue flicked out and she
tasted just slightly salty. He let his mouth linger, tasting, flicking out
his tongue. And he was pleased to hear Britta sighing above him.
And he was happy to see her legs move, and her body press up
closer to his mouth.

"It feels so good," she sighed above him.

They made love and went to sleep, both of them smiling in the
early-morning light. When they woke up, they made love again. He
was glad that the spell had been broken, and that he could go to
Lupo's that evening without hatred and suspicion jabbing at his
heart.

Martin had an idea of what love, "real love", should be. He had
picked it up from books, from conversations with Jesse and Peter,
from movies. It was a feeling inside him. Up to this point he felt he
had been cheated. With Josephine and Gila it had never been quite
what he imagined it should've been. There had always been something missing. But with Britta, he thought, things could be different.
If he couldn't feel it with her, who would he ever be able to
experience it with? Here was the girl all Jerusalem yearned for. The
blond stranger, the wistful, sensual creature from Sweden. And now
she was in his custody. Not in Lupo's or Steven's or the Frenchman's, but in his.

What was this idea he had? Love should be free, he thought, like the wind. Gay and effortless. Happy and, yes, ecstatic. He wanted to run through the streets with Britta like a couple of kids on holiday. Like that day in June when the school doors are finally flung open, and all the kids pour out, shouting and laughing, dancing down the streets.

The next evening he almost swaggered into Lupo's. He couldn't stop grinning as he walked up the flight of stairs to the old, dingy bar. He could face them now, he thought. He could look Lupo in the eye. He could survey the other customers and smile to himself. The mirror no longer frightened him. When he walked inside, he spotted Britta. She was wearing her usual barmaid's smile that she put on for her working hours. But when she noticed him, her expression changed. There was a warmth in her eyes he hadn't seen before.

He sat down at the bar.

"You're looking happy tonight," Lupo commented, his eyes shifting from the drink he was pouring to Martin's face.

Martin nodded, a warm feeling in his chest, the blood dancing and skipping to his head.

"Why not? It's a great world, don't you think?"

Lupo pursed his thin lips together. His eyes shifted back to the jigger in his hand.

"Well, what's up?" he asked laconically. "Did you win the lottery?"

Martin gazed at Britta. She just glanced at him from the corner of her eye, a little shyly. Lupo went on with his business, pouring the drink, stirring it, swirling the ice cubes. Then Lupo said something that surprised him.

"Give him a drink on the house, Britta. We have to look after our steady customers."

"Thank you," Martin murmured.

He couldn't quite tell if Lupo had heard him. Almost before the words were out, Lupo had swivelled around, the drink in his hand, and he moved off to a table with four customers, all men, and the only table occupied that night. Britta followed closely behind him with two drinks balanced on a small platter.

The Dutch U.N. officer had been standing as usual at the end of the bar. He edged closer to Martin.

"So you did it," he whispered. "I'm happy for you. For the both of you. She needs something steady. I was beginning to worry about her. It was like bees around the honey."

Martin liked the sound of his voice. It was soft and fatherly.

"Just look after her," he continued. "I know what it's like to be a stranger here. She's young. Her head can be turned very easily."

He shook the ice in his drink. "Let's make a toast," the Dutchman smiled.

Martin raised his glass and clinked it lightly against the Dutchman's.

"What shall we toast?" the U.N. officer asked.

"Whatever you like," Martin answered, feeling the warmth in his chest grow.

The Dutchman sucked on his pipe-stem, and gazed for a second towards the ceiling.

"To peace first," he smiled, "and to love. We can't go wrong with that, can we?"

Martin smiled and nodded his head in agreement. "To life," he added. "L'chaim."

When Lupo's bar closed for the night, Martin took Britta's hand and they walked into the darkness, just the two of them. He didn't want to go home immediately. Britta was in a light-hearted mood.

"I just want to run through the streets," she laughed. "You know what I feel like, Martin?—a blade of grass. Just a little green blade of grass."

She began singing and running in front of him. He ran after her.

"I'm a blade of grass," she sang out, running down King George Road, turning a corner, and dancing towards Zion Square.

Martin noticed a police car down by the square. Two policemen sat in the front seat. They were eating falafels and drinking coffees together.

"I'm a blade of grass," Britta sang out to them.

"Yaffa," they shouted in Hebrew. It meant beautiful.

Neither one of them wanted to go back to the apartment that evening. To sleep seemed a waste of time. Blades of grass, Martin thought, didn't worry about such things. And he wondered to himself, was this the beginning of the "real thing"? Was he finally experiencing it?—what he should be feeling. How could he be sure, absolutely certain?

They walked back up the street from Zion Square towards a

restaurant that they knew would still be open. It was the only one still operating in Jerusalem at one-thirty in the morning. Britta had gone there several times with Steven. She liked the person who owned it. He was a swarthy, heavy, round-bellied man from Turkey. He was almost completely bald and in his early fifties. He called himself Tom or some such simple name for the sake of his English-speaking customers.

"He's such a nice man," Britta smiled as they sat down at the bar. Tom sauntered towards them, a smile on his pudgy face.

"Ah, my Swedish sweetheart," he drawled, patting Britta on the head. "Where have you been? I haven't seen you in such a long time. And your friend, where is he?"

"He had to go back," Britta answered, smoothing out her skirt. "Back to America."

"You mean he left you here all alone in Jerusalem? And I thought you two ran off and got married. It just shows you how an old man can be wrong. And you've got a new friend, I see."

Britta smiled and introduced them. Tom gripped Martin's hand. It was a huge hand, Martin thought. Big and beefy and covered with thick, curly hair. The palm was sweaty.

"You're a lucky fellow," he said, "If I were ten years younger . . . " Tom rolled his eyes and let out a sigh.

"Well, Miss Beautiful, what can I get you? The usual?" Britta turned to Martin.

"It's a good drink," she said, "Tom's own recipe. There's no alcohol in it. I think it's made with yogurt. Tom calls it an Istanbul cocktail, do you think you'd like to try one?"

Martin shrugged. "Sure, why not?"

Tom reached out and pinched Britta's cheek.

"Two Istanbul cocktails coming up."

Tom prepared the drinks. He moved around the bar quickly for his size. Britta couldn't stop raving about his drink.

"It's very unusual. I've never tasted anything quite like it."

Tom finally placed the drinks in front of them. He served them in tall, tapered glasses. They looked a little like strawberry sodas to Martin. But the taste lived up to Britta's enthusiasm and his expectations. It was unusual. In fact, he'd never tasted anything quite like it. And what was stranger, after he had the first one, he couldn't get the taste out of his mind. What the hell was the recipe?—he wondered.

"It's great, isn't it?"

Martin had to agree. "I wonder how he makes it."

"He won't tell anybody," Britta said, shaking her head. "He told me that this is the only place in the world that serves Istanbul cocktails."

Tom was busy with other customers. But he kept glancing over at them and smiling. With the huge white apron he wore, he looked a little bit like a sailboat—moving, always on the move, tacking to the left and the right among the tables.

Each night after Lupo's from then on, Martin and Britta went to Tom's place.

Martin couldn't quite understand it—but he actually began to crave Tom's special drink. The day didn't seem complete unless they went there together about two in the morning and ordered one of those pink, sudsy specialties. A couple of times he woke up in the morning beside Britta with those Istanbul cocktails on his mind. What, he wondered, did Tom use in them? And Tom had become imprinted on his brain—the swarthy complexion, the huge, sweaty palms, the belly billowing beneath the white apron.

It always seemed to make Tom happy when Britta and Martin walked in together. "The usual?" he would ask, beaming. "Yes, the usual," they nodded. And Tom would trundle off, grinning.

CHAPTER 22

The Washroom

Even though Britta was still working at Lupo's, she could no longer afford the rent on her apartment. She had to find something cheaper.

She finally found a tiny room on the top floor of a five-storey apartment building. One door in the room led out to the roof. The room had originally been used as a laundry room. There was an iron grate in the middle of the cement floor. Here the sudsy wash-water used to drain off into the pipes and plumbing below.

"You know what this is?" Britta laughed, standing beside Martin in the doorway, holding his hand. "It's a washroom. I don't even believe it's legal to rent a place like this. But at least it's cheap."

Martin surveyed the place. It was odd-looking, he thought. Yet there was something about it that he liked. It seemed to get a lot of light. There was just enough room for a small cot, a dresser, and a tiny refrigerator.

"Where do you go to the bathroom?" he asked, shifting his weight from one foot to the other.

"Well, the landlord lives downstairs on the next floor. I can use his. He gave me a key to his apartment, and he told me if I really had to go, I could use the old drainage hole here."

Martin frowned, the lines bunching up around his nose and forehead.

"Just pee in the middle of the bedroom?"

Britta chuckled to herself and tightened her grip on Martin's hand.

"Well, I guess if you gotta go, you gotta go."

They began living in the old laundry room together. Martin kept paying rent for his room in the stone cottage, but he rarely went there. Once in a while he would stroll down to pick up a piece of clothing, and he would successfully avoid meeting Mrs. Shoshannah or Larry.

Yes, he thought, there was something he liked about living in the laundry room with Britta.

Sometimes he would wake up in the morning, the sun pouring in through the windows. He would rub the sleep from his eyes, shake his head. Slowly, his eyelids would unglue themselves. In front of him he would see Britta in her nightie. She'd be squatting over the iron grate in the middle of the cement floor. She had hiked her nightie up to her waist, and he could hear her pee tinkling. She looked like a little girl, he often thought, caught short in the woods.

"Good morning," he called from the cot. "How's the toilet working?"

"Just wonderful," Britta smiled.

And she would make a motion with her hand, and a noise with her mouth as if she were flushing.

At times, a faint pee stench lingered, but Britta kept a pail of water in the room, some soap, and a scrub brush. When she finished, she would give the grate a good scrubbing with soapy water. Martin, too, would get his turn to use the facilities. He tried his best to aim the stream without splattering too much.

"I had another nightmare last night," Britta sighed against his neck one bright morning.

"What was it about?"

Britta flung a leg over his and drew him closer.

"That's what bothers me. It's always the same. I dreamt that I had three or four babies. I was playing with them. Everything was fine, but suddenly they grew small. Tiny as little marbles. I couldn't hold them any more. They started falling on the floor, rolling all over the place. And there were holes in the floor, Martin, and they went down through the holes, and I couldn't find them . . . "

Britta was shaking. Martin glanced at her face and he could see tears rolling down her cheeks.

"That's awful," he said, squeezing her tightly.

"Martin, I've had the same dream for years. You know, I had a miscarriage once. I was engaged to this boy in Stockholm. I guess we were both too young. He was nineteen and I was only eighteen. Maybe the miscarriage was the best thing that could've happened. Soon after that we broke up."

"Did you love him?" Martin asked. His voice was heavy and thick. He could feel cotton and gauze in his throat.

Britta shrugged in his arms. "I guess I did. It was a long time ago. We were just kids."

Britta began to shake again, and Martin tightened his grip on her.

"Martin?" Britta sighed. Her voice sounded wistful and dreamy. She didn't continue. She was waiting for him to acknowledge that he had heard her speak his name.

"Yes," he replied. He could feel his voice melting and mingling with the streams of sunlight pouring through the window onto the bed.

"Do you want to have a family some day?"

"I guess so," he replied. "Some day. I don't think about it too much."

"Martin," she continued, "we could have one together. I know we'd be happy."

He could feel his body stiffening. His mouth got tight. And then slowly he began to relax again. Would it be that bad—he wondered —married to Britta with a house full of Swedish-Jewish kids?

"I'm too young, Britta. I've got a lot of things I want to do."

"You could still do them, Martin," she whispered, her breath warm and tingly against his skin. "And you're not too young. Do you know what I believe? Marriage and a family can make a person into a man. You've got to accept responsibility some day."

Again Martin could feel his limbs and muscles stiffening. He shook his head back and forth.

"I wish I could think that way, Britta. I honestly do. But I couldn't do it. I'm just not ready."

He could feel her drawing away from him.

"Do you know what you're saying? You're telling me that there's no future in what we're doing together. It's just going to end like all the others. Like Jacob. I don't want that any more. I'm just so tired of things beginning full of hope and love, and the next thing you know, it's over."

Martin could feel himself withdrawing. The skin on his face got tight. His face began to feel like a mask—as if his features were made out of plastic. He was afraid of what Britta was talking about. He could see himself buried in Jerusalem with Britta for the next twenty years. Yet he wanted to believe that happiness could be achieved in this way—a beautiful, sensitive wife, a couple of kids, perhaps a job at the university.

"What would we use for money?" he laughed almost sarcastically. "I can just see you nine months pregnant and still working down at Lupo's."

Britta whispered her reply against his cheek, her lips brushing the skin.

"You don't want to teach English at the 'Y' for the rest of your life, do you? You'd make a fine professor, Martin. Why not take a few courses at the university and build up to it slowly?"

Why not?—he wondered. What Britta was saying seemed so logical and straightforward. She was drawing out the plans for a sane existence: a family, a good job, love and peace.

"What do you want out of life anyway?" she continued.

"Britta, the most important thing to me is writing."

"Where do you think writing comes from?" she shot back. "It doesn't come from words, Martin. It comes from living and loving. And not everything is composed of words. Life is more important. Can't you understand? There's more to it than anything you can write, or anything that's ever been written about it. Do you think you can sum everything up in a poem?"

Again, what she was saying seemed to make sense. He began to think about God's voice ringing out to Job. Can you measure Leviathan? Can you hook him like a fish? Can you weigh and measure him, o foolish man?

He could feel himself begin to tremble.

"Perhaps you're right," he murmured. His voice sounded thin.

She pressed her body closer to his. She began kissing his neck.

"Oh Martin, I know I'm right. You'd make a good father, I just know it. Do you realize that you never stop talking about your baby brother? I can just feel how much love you have for him."

Martin could feel something melting inside him. His bones seemed to be turning into a warm liquid.

"I wish you could meet him, Britta. He's so innocent and free. Just like a chubby little animal. I wish he could stay that way forever, and not feel any pain. You know what? I wish we were all like little babies. Just sit around and chew cookies all day. Britta, let's go to Tel Aviv together some day. I'd like you to meet my family."

He could feel her stretching and pressing against him. Her body seemed to be getting warmer and warmer. She seemed to be melting into him. And he wanted to let himself relax, every inch of his body, every speck of his mind, and melt back into her.

"Martin, let's make a child together."

He could feel an urgency in her voice, and a plea.

"Now?" he asked, his voice shocked.

"Yes, now. Right now, while we're feeling so close. It would be a beautiful baby, Martin. I just know it would. You would love him even more than you do your brother. Let's do it, Martin, please."

A coolness entered him once again. It was a stone in the middle of his chest.

"Britta, let's wait. I want some time to think about it. It's not something I can do on the spur of the moment. We're talking about our entire lives."

He could feel his breath getting short as he talked.

"I just hate putting that thing inside me, Martin. I get to feel so warm towards you, then I have to put that gooey contraption inside me. It turns me cold."

Martin drew himself away from her embrace and fell down again on his back. He wanted to block his ears, close his eyes, forget that she was in the room with him.

"O.K., Martin," she whispered. "Just promise me one thing—that you'll think about it. Don't just forget, please don't do that. Think about it seriously. Will you promise me that?"

He felt exhausted. It seemed that every speck of energy had drained out of him.

"Yes, I promise," he said wearily.

She brushed a hand along his forehead.

"Martin, you do love me, don't you?"

"Yes, Britta, I've never really loved anyone else. It was all game-playing. Fooling around."

"Do you want to make love now?"

"Yes," he replied, turning over, and kissing her softly on the cheek.

"O.K.," she smiled, "I'll go put that stupid thing in. It's so greasy. Yuck."

Britta screwed up her face and smiled. Martin was always surprised at the way she could turn from a serious mood so quickly. He still felt heavy, weighed down, drawn and tired from their conversation. Yet Britta was smiling, her face almost totally transformed. How could she do it?—he wondered. It was a quality that he admired. His own moods lingered, shifted slowly, and they could last for days. He remembered the stone cottage, and a shudder passed through him.

She got out of bed and went looking for her diaphragm. They always took a double precaution—Martin wore a safe. She hunted through the dresser. Martin got up and started searching for his package of prophylactics.

"Do you know what I read the other day?" she said as they looked together. "They're working on a pill right now. It's supposed to be a hundred-per-cent effective. The woman just takes one every morning."

"A pill?" Martin asked, surprised.

"That's all, just a pill."

"Boy, that would make things a lot easier. I hate these damn safes."

"That's another problem," Britta frowned, "they're not very safe at all. And these diaphragms aren't much better."

Martin sighed. "I guess we just have to do the best we can. And keep our fingers crossed."

"Or get married," Britta said, shuffling through a drawer, looking for the box she kept her diaphragm in.

In a few minutes, Britta was sitting on the edge of the bed, the diaphragm in place. Martin sat up, a pillow propped behind his back. The sun was streaming in through the windows. It was dancing on Britta's hair, on her smooth back. She had a faraway, dreamy expression on her face.

"Do you know how the trolls make love?" she asked. Her voice sounded soft, and filled with mystery.

"Who are the trolls?" he asked, reaching out and touching her shoulder.

"Oh, they're very famous, Martin. They're little furry creatures that live in Sweden. Way up in the mountains. They're very shy. Hardly anyone has ever seen a troll."

"What do they look like?" Martin asked. His voice sounded curious.

"They have bushy eyebrows," Britta replied, bunching up her face. "And deep, warm eyes. They're so sensitive that even a falling leaf will frighten them. Sometimes they go inside their little caves and they won't come out for days."

"Very sensitive," Martin repeated with a smile on his face. He was beginning to like Britta's trolls.

"They have a sense of humor too," Britta grinned. "They play tricks on each other and on people. They like pinching bums, especially human bums. But they're so quick, you can't catch them. They just disappear into the trees. And they have a good laugh together."

"And how do they make love?" Martin asked, his curiosity aroused.

"Well," Britta smiled, "like I told you, they're very sensitive. In everything they do. And they have tails, quite long tails, in fact. It's the most sensitive part of their bodies. They do it very gently, very shyly, very slowly."

Each time the word "very" came out, Britta paused and pouted her lips, drawing it out.

"So, how do they do it?" Martin asked, excitement now in his voice.

"Well, they work up to it. It takes them a long time. And finally they twine their tails together."

Martin could see Britta's trolls very clearly—hidden away in the woods, twining their long, sensitive tails together. And he imagined that each little inch of their tails was as sensitive as the very tip of his penis.

"And you know something else," Britta continued, "they're very loyal and faithful. Once a boy troll has twined his tail with a girl troll, they never part. And they live for thousands of years, the same two trolls in love."

"No divorce," Martin quipped.

"No," Britta said emphatically, "not even a spat."

Britta squeezed Martin's knee.

"Wouldn't you like to be a troll?" she asked.

It was the exact fantasy that was now buzzing in his mind.

"And twine my tail with yours?" he smiled.

"And mine with yours," Britta laughed.

Martin felt very warm towards her. She had melted the stone inside him. His insides felt like hot liquid melting. He moved closer and cupped her breasts from behind. He kissed her on the back of the neck, and moved his mouth towards her ear.

Throughout the lovemaking that morning, he could see the shy sensitive trolls behind his closed eyes. Thousands of tails entwined, up in the mountains of Sweden.

She didn't seem as stiff to him. Her thighs were softer. He felt like he was going inside a soft dark forest, and he would never come out again.

*　*　*

The end of the summer of 1963 was a relatively peaceful time in Israel. Every once in a while, a few skirmishes took place. Martin had seen the sandbag barricades that divided the two sectors of Jerusalem. He had even caught glimpses of Arab soldiers with rifles slung over their shoulders as they guarded the Jordanian border. From Gila he had heard about the Syrians in the Golan Heights— how they shot at the kibbutzim near Tiberias. But generally, things had been peaceful during those years he had lived in the country. He could feel the underlying tension, but no major war had occurred in seven years. Not since the Sinai campaign in 1956.

Late one night, Britta and Martin were to discover that the peace was, indeed, fragile.

Earlier that night, around two a.m., they were sitting together in the converted laundry-room. Britta had finished for the evening at Lupo's. They had gone to Tom's together for their usual Istanbul cocktail, and now they were back in the small, cramped room together.

Britta went downstairs to use the landlord's washroom. Martin sat on the cot half-asleep.

Britta's face was flushed with excitement when she came back up. She was out of breath, and could hardly form her words.

"What's wrong?" Martin asked, reviving himself.

"I just met the landlord's son," she gasped.

"So? So what happened?"

"Oh, it's so stupid. I was just walking down the hall, and he came out of his room. He undid his zipper, and took it out and started swinging it in front of me."

"That stupid idiot," Martin hissed.

"He must have something wrong upstairs," Britta gasped. "The guy's about forty."

"So what did you do?"

Britta shook her head back and forth.

"I was very firm with him," she giggled nervously, and choked on her words. "I just told him to put it away. I told him it didn't interest me in the least. And he did it. But if it ever happens again, I'm going to talk to his father."

Martin bit down on his lower lip.

"You should tell him right now!" Martin spat. "Fuck, a guy like that could be dangerous."

Britta picked up a brush from the dresser, and began sweeping it through her hair. The strokes were long and even.

"No, I'll give him one more chance. But that's it. Maybe he just got carried away. And I'll start wearing a housecoat over my nightie when I go down."

Martin nodded and sighed. "You should," he agreed. "I guess the guy's only human."

Britta put down the brush and joined Martin on the bed. Her body was trembling slightly. He wrapped his arms around her. She was still quivering with excitement, but gradually he could feel her beginning to relax.

"I'll make some tea for us," he said.

As he busied himself with the cups and the tea bags, and with boiling up the water, he kept glancing over at Britta. It was difficult to get the landlord's son out of his mind. He could see him unzippering his pants and swinging his cock in Britta's face. But it looked like Britta was recovering from the fright. She took out some embroidery she had been working on. He was glad to see her face becoming calm once again. His own fingers were still trembling, as if he were the person who had been accosted. He was amazed again at how she could take certain things in her stride—much more easily than he could.

Martin's hands were still shaking, and it was difficult to get the cup to his mouth without spilling tea on the bed.

"I can't get that guy out of my mind," he said.

"Just forget about it, Martin," she whispered, sipping at her tea. "I'm sure it's not going to happen again."

"How can you be sure?"

"I could tell by the look on his face, and the way he zipped up so fast and ran back to his room. I think he was more scared than I was."

"Well, I'm glad you can be so sure." Martin was surprised by the tone of his own voice. He was surprised that his words were tinged with anger. He almost resented her coolness.

He decided to forget it, to file it away inside him. If she wasn't going to be upset, why should he? If she was so sure of herself, he wasn't going to tremble in front of her. To hell with it, he thought. I'll drink my tea and shut up.

The minutes passed slowly. Martin poured two more cups of tea. A half hour passed with little conversation between them. She shouldn't be going down there anyway, he thought, in that transparent nightie. He was beginning to feel sorry for the landlord's son. Poor guy, he dreamed. Maybe he's never been with a woman his entire life. Forty years old, and still living with his father. Then night after night, he sees this woman come down in nothing but a nightie. No wonder he went a little nuts. And it was no wonder he ran back to his room.

Martin poured two more cups of tea slowly. He was glad to see his fingers were steady now, and his grip relaxed.

They sat together, yawning, drinking their tea, thinking about going to bed. The house was quiet and still. Then they began to hear a rumbling noise, explosions, cracks of sound. The windows lit up from flashes of light. Martin sat bolt upright on the edge of the bed. Britta put down her embroidery.

"What the hell is that?" Martin muttered.

"Let's go see," Britta said excitedly, and she jumped off the bed, pulling Martin up by the hand.

Britta ran to the door which led to the roof. Martin followed close behind.

Out on the roof, the flashes of light were much brighter. They had a clear view to the Jordanian border and old Jerusalem.

"It's a war, it's a war!" Britta shouted, her words mixed with an excited laugh. "Oh, isn't it great? It's the first war I've ever seen."

Britta was leaping around on the roof, her white nightie flying out behind her. And she was absolutely right. They could see the flares lighting up the King David Hotel, and they could hear the bazookas booming.

So this was what it looked like, Martin thought. The darkness perforated by bright flashes. The silence torn by rifle-cracks.

"Oh, I want to stay out here and watch it. Isn't it the most exciting thing you've ever seen?" Britta shouting and laughed, and she kept skipping around the roof, pointing to the flashes of light.

Martin was not so sure.

"Maybe we should get inside," he suggested hesitantly.

And at the same time, he didn't wish to appear over-anxious or afraid.

"Oh please, Martin, let's just watch for a while. I might never see a war again."

Martin stood in the darkness. He could feel an excitement in his mind and stomach. But he couldn't laugh and joke as Britta was doing. In fact, he felt heavy and somber watching it from the roof.

War, he thought, so this was it—happening before his very eyes. Down there—bullets pierced skulls, people were losing eyes. Britta's excitement disgusted him just a little bit. And yet his own heaviness weighed on him, filled him, made him feel uneasy.

As they stood on the roof together, Martin heard a bullet—he was sure it was a bullet—whizz past, only about twenty feet away. Britta jumped.

"Did you hear that?" he asked.

"What was it?" she asked. Her voice now sounded worried and brittle.

"That was a bullet. I'm sure it was. And it was fucking close. We better get inside, Britta."

Britta clutched Martin's arm. She was pushing him towards the door.

"Let's go back inside," she agreed.

The fight at the border continued until dawn. They sat on the bed together, huddling.

The next morning Martin read about it in the Jerusalem Post, the English-language weekly. He read about the Israeli casualties. A few holes had been blown out of the King David Hotel. What he remembered most vividly, however, was Britta's dance on the rooftop, and the bullet that had chased them both back inside.

For days the same images circled in his mind like painted horses on a merry-go-round. A forty-year-old man unzipping in front of Britta. A whizzing bullet in the darkness. A white nightie on a rooftop. Flashes of light. They mixed together insanely. The washroom. The iron grate on the floor. Britta lifting her nightie early in the morning to have a pee. And more images. Babies turning into marbles. Can-openers. Broken arms. Walls that could not be climbed.

His life, he thought, was just as dark and crazy as any nightmare. They were running into one another—images, images, and more images.

* * *

When fall came to Jerusalem, the change in season wasn't striking. The evenings became cooler, and slowly the days moved towards winter and the rains. Rosh Hashanah, the New Year, came and went. Yom Kippur, the Day of Atonement, made its yearly appearance. On this day, stores throughout the country were sealed tight. The believers flocked to the synagogue, but just as many packed up the car with kids and other members of the family and went off to Tel Aviv beach, or took a trip to Haifa.

Filled with nostalgia, Martin remembered the autumns in Canada. He recalled how the days got cool and nippy, and how the trees blazed with the dying leaves. It used to be a good time of year, he dreamed, to hop in a car and drive to the hills north of Montreal.

Britta had similar memories of her homeland. She told him about how she camped out with her boyfriend in the mountains of northern Norway. They had to huddle together in their sleeping bags, and squeeze their bodies tightly together to keep warm.

Another holiday made its appearance in the autumn. It was called Simchat Torah, the celebration of the law. During this celebration, the Jews rejoiced over the sacred scrolls that they had preserved down through the years. It was a light-hearted observance compared to Rosh Hashanah and the dead-serious Day of Atonement.

One evening during Simchat Torah, Britta and Martin were walking through the religious sector. The street was narrow and cobbled. They came to a small brick synagogue. Light poured out of the tiny windows, and they could hear singing. Britta ran to the window, pulling Martin by the hand. She peeked inside. Martin looked in also, his head pressed against hers.

Rabbis and men of the congregation were dancing around the altar. They carried the beloved torahs, clutching them closely to their chests. The decorative bells jingled. They were singing together in low booming voices. "Yesh ha torah," they sang, "yesh, yesh." Loosely translated, it meant—we have a torah, yes, yes. Or—we have a law, for sure, for sure. Britta was fascinated. Like a young girl, she pressed her face against the windowpane. Her nose was pressed flat and white against the glass.

"Oh look, Martin," she said excitedly, "look at that little boy. Isn't he beautiful? Look, he's sitting on his father's shoulder."

Martin pressed his face closer. And sure enough, one of the men, possibly a rabbi, had a young boy draped around his neck. The man was big and burly.

"Wouldn't you like to have a little boy like that?" Britta asked, squeezing Martin's arm, squeezing it tighter and tighter until it almost pained.

Martin said nothing, nor did he bob his head in agreement.

Britta pulled away from him, and began dancing in front of the synagogue. She jumped from one foot to the other. She held her arms out in a circle, and she pretended that she was carrying a torah, imitating the rabbis. In a low voice, with her mouth screwed up to make herself look old and serious, she boomed out the chant. "Yesh ha torah, yesh, yesh . . . I have a torah," she sang in English, "yes I do."

It was a large torah she was pretending to carry, Martin thought. She could hardly get her arms around it. It was a heavy torah, and she pretended that it was buckling her knees just slightly.

"See," she laughed, "you're not the only ones with a torah. Look how big mine is."

She walked back to the window again. She pressed the side of her face against Martin's cheek. She smelled so fresh that it made him dizzy. She pointed out the boy again, sitting on top of his father's neck.

"They look so happy," she sighed. "I bet you they've had some wine to drink."

And then, almost as an afterthought, she made another comment:

"I wonder where the women are? Can you see any, Martin?"

In the darkness, Martin shook his head.

"They're probably home baking challah," he mumbled under his breath. "Anyway, they wouldn't be allowed to dance with the men, Britta. Not in the synagogue. The Orthodox never do that."

"I don't think that's very fair," she complained.

"Fair or not fair, that's the way it's been for five thousand years."

They stayed by the window together for a few more minutes. The dance continued, and the chanting. We have the law, yes we do. Martin gazed at the young boy on the rabbi's shoulders. His cheeks looked red, his hair was black and curly. He was a chubby little boy with round, dimpled knees, and he made Martin think about his brother.

Sometime around Simchat Torah, Britta missed her period. Don't worry about it, Martin said to himself, these things can happen. In a few days, it will come. It could be emotional stress, he said to himself. It could just be anxiety, or wishfulness on Britta's part. The days slipped by. Each evening he asked her about it. Did you get it today, he enquired. Britta bowed her head, and shook it somberly back and forth.

He began to notice a slight change in her face. The wrinkle lines around her eyes and mouth looked more pronounced. Her face looked softer, older, and more serious. Surely, he thought, the period will come.

"I'm beginning to worry," Britta said, sitting on the bed in the laundry room. "It's been two weeks. I should've gotten it by now."

Martin gazed at the floor. The cement looked darker and colder than ever. His head was swirling.

"Maybe you should go see a doctor."

His voice sounded cool and clinical. He kept his hands close to his sides.

"I'll give it another week. Then I'll have to go."

They sat on the bed together, both lost in their own thoughts, their own worlds whirling inside their heads.

Seven more days went by and nothing happened. Each night Britta repeated the same words: "It hasn't come yet, Martin." And at the end of the week, she finally said, "I'm going to see a doctor tomorrow, Martin. I've got this funny feeling inside me. I just hope I'm wrong."

The next afternoon, Martin was sitting in the laundry room alone. It was about five o'clock, and the light was falling weirdly across the sky. It left the room in semi-darkness. The dresser could be alive, Martin thought to himself, a shadow that would suddenly move, rise, attack him.

Everything looked a little unreal to him: the cement floor swirling, the dresser crouching, and Britta's nightie hanging on a doorknob. Jerusalem, he thought, what am I doing here, living in this room, pissing through the floor? He couldn't get Britta's nightmares out of his mind. Babies slipping through her fingers, tiny as marbles, rolling around, going through cracks in the floor. He could see her—how she would look in her own nightmare. Her face gone white with anxiety, trying to catch just one baby before it was lost forever. He could see her fingers grasping, trembling, frantically digging at the floorboards. He could hear her fingernails scraping against wood. But it was hopeless. Every single marble found an opening, an escape into the darkness below. They had minds of their own, he thought—those marbles.

He shook his head and tried to wake himself from the daydream.

He finally heard footsteps on the staircase. They were moving quickly towards the door of the room. The door swung open and Britta stood before him.

"It's awfully dark in here," she said, taking off her sweater. "Were you asleep?"

"No, I was just sitting here thinking."

Britta switched on the overhead light. Martin closed his eyes, and then began to rub them.

"I'm pregnant," she said without warning.

The word ripped through his chest.

"Oh Christ," he muttered, clutching his forehead. He gripped the flesh, squeezed it, tried to feel the pressure from his hand.

He could feel his teeth grinding together. It was involuntary.

"What the hell are we going to do?" he asked, just barely managing to wrench out the words.

Britta opened a drawer on the dresser. The old wood squealed.

"You make it sound like we just murdered somebody," Britta snapped. "It's a beautiful thing. If only you knew what it felt like."

"That's not quite possible," he said coolly. The chilly tone of his own voice frightened him. It seemed as if his words were knife-blades slicing the air without mercy.

Britta walked across the room, dropped to her knees, and knelt in front of him. She gripped his legs.

"Martin, I want to have this baby so badly. You've told me a million times that you love me. Let's have it together. I just know he's going to be so beautiful."

He was tempted to wrap his arms around her head. He could hear the words she wanted to hear: *Yes, I love you, Britta. We'll get married and have this child. We'll have a wonderful life together.* But did he believe in such a thing?

No such words came out of his mouth. His whole body had gone stiff and cold. His fingers felt like wooden sticks.

"I can't do it, Britta. There's no way."

"You can do it," she moaned, digging her fingers into his trousers. Her fingernails bit into his skin. "You just think you can't do it. You won't even give yourself a chance. You're just closing your mind to it."

"I wish I could, I honestly do. How am I going to support a family?"

"Money's not the issue, and you know it," Britta snapped back. "It's something deeper than that. How can you be afraid of life? Don't you think this was meant to happen?"

Martin drew farther away from her. Her fingers were going limp on his leg.

"What do you mean?" he asked. "You're not going to start giving me a lot of crap about God, are you? And fate!"

"That's your problem," she replied, "you think everything revolves around yourself and your writing. Can't you realize there are bigger things? We're talking about a human life, something that's growing inside me. Something you put there."

Slowly, the coldness inside him was beginning to turn to anger.

"O.K.," he hissed, "I put it there, and I'm telling you to get it out!"

Britta began to tremble. She let her head fall on the cot.

"Oh Martin, you wouldn't, you wouldn't make me have an abortion."

He could feel the heat of his own anger still frothing and rising inside him. But now it was mixed with guilt. It was getting more difficult to reply.

"That's what I'm saying. You've got to do it. There's no other way."

He could hear Britta begin to cry.

"You can't control life that way," she sobbed. "You're just treating life like a horse, and you think you can ride along on top of it. You can't do that, Martin. One of these days it's going to throw you off."

Britta's words clanged inside his head. He could feel the walls closing in on him. He got up from the cot, pulling himself away from her.

"I'm going for a walk," he said, jerking the words up from his tight throat.

"You're not going to leave me, are you? You're coming back."

Her voice sounded tiny and lost.

"No, I'm just going for a walk. I need some fresh air."

Britta reached out, and gripped his hand.

"Don't block your mind to it, Martin."

He turned quickly, and walked out of the room. The stairs seemed to be rolling towards him, waves of wood, and sickness in his stomach.

Outside, it was getting dark and chilly. He wasn't wearing a jacket or sweater, and the cool twilight air nipped at his chest and arms.

He walked towards the center of town. He had no definite goal in mind. He just walked along, feeling the weird shadows of twilight swirl around him. What a mess, he thought. What a mess they were both in.

Britta's words gnawed at him. They swirled inside his head. "You can't control life like a horse." Was he trying to ride the whole thing, his hands tight on the reins? Was he jerking the soft mouth to the left and to the right, the silver bit digging in? And was it going to toss him some day, as she predicted, throw him off, break his back?

He found himself standing in front of Pepe's spaghetti house. Suddenly he realized that he was hungry and cold. He thrust his hands into his pockets, looking for change. But there was nothing inside, not a single agora. He looked through the wide window into Pepe's: a row of men sat on stools, hunched over plates of spaghetti and slices of pizza. It looked warm inside. He cursed at himself for not having enough money to buy a coffee.

And suddenly, everything seemed cold and meaningless to him — the twilight, the weird shadows, the men forking up spaghetti, his empty pockets. Everything seemed ridiculous, and he felt like laughing and crying at the same time.

Unexpectedly, he felt a hand on his shoulder, and he heard a voice behind him.

"Chaver, you look cold. How about if I buy you a coffee?"

He pivoted in a single motion, and Jesse was standing in front of him.

"Hi Jesse," he smiled. "God, am I ever glad to see you."

"C'mon," Jesse said softly, patting Martin on the back, "we'll get ourselves some warm grub."

They walked into Pepe's together. The warm air and bright lights hit Martin in waves. The place was crowded, but they managed to find two empty stools next to each other.

"Well, where have you been, stranger?" Jesse asked, swivelling in his stool to face Martin. "Are you still seeing that Swedish girl? What was her name, anyway?"

"Britta," Martin whispered, lowering his eyes. "Yes, I'm still seeing her. We're living together."

The waiter walked over to them, and Jesse ordered two plates of spaghetti and two coffees. Before the waiter left, Jesse exchanged a few witticisms with him in Hebrew.

"Things aren't going too well between us," Martin continued.

Jesse nodded his head and pursed his lips together. He glanced at the ceiling for a second, his eyes looking deep and pensive.

"Are they really bad?" Jesse asked.

"They're terrible," Martin muttered.

Jesse raised his hand to his mouth, and began squeezing and massaging his lower lip between his forefinger and thumb.

"I hate to say this, Martin, but you two have always reminded me of two spent swimmers clinging to each other."

Martin didn't reply. He allowed Jesse's words to seep into his mind. In a way, he resented Jesse's quick analysis of the situation. How could he sum it up so easily in a single sentence? After all, Jesse had only run into them a couple of times on the street. And yet there seemed to be some truth in what Jesse was saying. It was possible—that they were drowning and clinging to each other, hoping some miracle would save them.

And there was something in Jesse's words, and in his tone of voice that made him relax, that almost relieved him. For what, after all, could be expected of him, if he were truly drowning, and she was no better off? And if he clung to her and she to him, wouldn't they both go down to the bottom?

"Maybe you're right," Martin finally replied. "I just don't know."

The waiter came back and slid two steaming plates of spaghetti in front of them.

"Eat up," Jesse smiled, his eyes bright and glowing. "Things always look worse on an empty stomach."

Martin dug into the spaghetti and meat sauce, trying to forget about everything for a few minutes. He sprinkled some grated cheese on top.

Martin glanced around the room, and he realized there wasn't a single woman present. And it suddenly dawned on him that he had rarely seen a woman in all the times he'd eaten there. Perhaps one or two, he thought, but they always looked a little tough. They wore a bit too much perfume and eye-shadow. Most likely hookers, he concluded, as he tried to savour the long slippery strands of pasta.

"Good stuff, eh?" Jesse commented, sopping up the last dribbles of meat sauce with a crust of bread.

Martin tilted back his coffee. He could feel the warmth travelling down his throat into his stomach. Jesse was right, or partially so. He was beginning to feel a little better, slightly more optimistic with the warm food inside him.

"There's something eating at you, isn't there?" Jesse said, sipping at his coffee.

How long could he keep it inside?—Martin wondered. How long could he clutch it privately? He wanted to handle the thing himself, to keep it between Britta and himself. It should be a private matter, he thought, but his insides felt stretched to the breaking point. He had to tell someone.

"It's Britta, she's pregnant."

"I thought so," Jesse said. "That's exactly what was going on in my mind."

Martin was surprised. "What made you think that?"

"I've seen it happen before," Jesse replied coolly.

Martin stared at the bottom of his cup. A few dregs of brown coffee clung to the white procelain.

"I don't know what to do." His voice was thick and muffled.

"There's only two choices . . . " Jesse said, pausing. "You could get married, you know. That wouldn't be so bad. From what I've seen, Britta seems like a very nice girl."

A warm stream of feeling coursed through him. "She is. She's a wonderful person. But that's a big decision, Jesse. I don't know if I'm ready. I can't just go out and do it on the spur of the moment."

"How does she feel about it?" Jesse asked. He leaned closer to Martin. He seemed quite curious about the reply.

"She wants to have a baby. It's a very important thing to her. She wants to get married."

"And you're not sure."

Martin shook his head.

"You know what the alternative is . . . " Jesse continued.

"Yes, an abortion."

"Yes," Jesse repeated, "an abortion."

Martin sat silently. He twirled his coffee cup—clockwise for half a turn, and then back again. His mind seemed to be falling into the bottom of the cup. It was getting swallowed by the white porcelain and by the brown dregs. He twirled it again—half a turn left, and right. His mind seemed blank, nothing more than a piece of white pottery shifted in one direction and back to the other.

"It seems to me," Jesse said in a contemplative tone, "that you need time to think about the whole business. When did you find out about it, anyway?"

"Just about an hour ago," Martin murmured.

Jesse placed a hand around Martin's back and squeezed his shoulder.

"I'm glad I ran into you," Jesse said warmly. "It's not an easy thing to carry around inside you."

Jesse gave Martin's shoulder another tight squeeze and removed his hand.

"Look, Martin. I have a suggestion. Why don't you think about it? Or better still, just forget about it for a while. Do something different, anything, something totally unrelated. It might help to clear up your feelings. But I want to let you know something—if you decide against it, I know a doctor here in town. There's nobody better, believe me. Lisa went to him, and I had a girlfriend who went through the same business. He's an expert. There'll be absolutely no danger to Britta. The guy charges about two hundred lira, and if you don't have the money I'll lend it to you. You can pay me back later."

Martin felt relieved. It was as if he had been inside a dark tunnel with only one exit, only one bright light shining. The exit was marriage, and a family with Britta. Now Jesse had torn some rocks free, and a new light was shining, another bright path to freedom. It seemed, now, that he had a choice, a clear choice. He had mentioned abortion to Britta, but he'd said it in anger. Now Jesse had made the route appear clear and practical. The doctor existed. He was real. Not only real, but an expert. The fee was not ridiculously high, and the money was almost being handed to him.

Yes, he thought, Lisa had gone through it and survived. Peter had survived. Jesse's girlfriend, whoever she was, had gone through it, and both of them had survived. Thousands of women, he reasoned, must have gone to the same doctor. And a myriad of men, at one time or another, had had to make the same decision that was facing him.

Martin let a sigh flow from his mouth. For months, it seemed, that gush of breath had been locked there. He reached out and squeezed Jesse's shoulder.

"I really feel a lot better, Jesse. Just to know that it's possible. You know what I mean—that there's some other way."

Jesse smiled. "I know exactly what you mean."

The waiter passed in front of them, and Jesse ordered two more coffees.

"You thought it was the end of the world, didn't you? We all go through the same thing. And you know something, Martin?—it's just an illusion. There's always another path."

Martin sipped at his coffee, trying to digest the meal, and to understand what Jesse had just told him.

"By the way," Jesse smiled, "I saw a good friend of yours in Tel Aviv the other day."

"Who was that?" Martin asked. His mind felt vague, and his thoughts hazy.

"Oh, somebody who really thinks a lot of you. An old flame, you might say."

"Josephine," Martin murmured, his mouth twitching with a smile.

"Yes, Josephine," Jesse grinned back.

Martin had forgotten that he'd given Jesse Josephine's address. He was glad that his two old friends had finally met one another. He was curious about what had gone on.

"What did you think of her?" Martin asked, excitement and curiosity in his voice.

"Quite a gal," Jesse glimmered, pursing his lips and nodding his head rhythmically. "And she's not bad in bed, not bad at all."

"Oh, you slept with her."

Martin was surprised. He could picture them discussing and arguing philosophy for hours, but he couldn't quite see them making love.

"Yep," Jesse nodded.

"How is she doing?"

"Well, you know Josephine. She's quite a determined lady. She got herself a raise at work recently..." Jesse paused, "but you know, she's a little worried about you."

"She is?"

Jesse stroked his beard.

"Well, to be frank, she's worried about your emotional life."

"What do you mean?" Martin asked, his forehead wrinkling.

"She said something very interesting," Jesse replied, drawing ends of his beard through his fingers. "She thinks you kind of avoid issues at times, that you hide yourself in your writing. At least you try to."

"I see," Martin said, feeling something inside him buckle and fold.

"But you should realize," Jesse continued, "that you've made quite an impression on her."

Martin turned in his stool, and gazed outside at the darkness. People were walking through the streets. They looked shadowy, hunched over.

"Did you stay overnight?" Martin suddenly asked.

Jesse nodded. "It kind of makes us bedfellows-in-law, doesn't it?" he quipped.

Martin tried to smile. His chest ached. He began thinking of Britta again, alone in the washroom with tears streaming down her cheeks.

"I better be going," Martin said, his voice strained. "I don't want to leave Britta alone too long. Thanks for the meal, Jesse. I really appreciate it."

As Martin got up, Jesse gripped his wrist lightly.

"I hope things work out for you."

"Thanks," Martin murmured under his breath.

"Let me know what you decide," Jesse said seriously. "I'll need some time to arrange things. And don't worry about the money. You don't even have to consider it. And Martin, please give my best to Britta."

"I will, Jesse."

His feet felt heavy as he walked out of Pepe's. Full darkness had descended on the streets. A few people were walking home. Others were standing under a streetlamp waiting for a bus. What dark houses were they going to?—Martin wondered.

He trudged along, head bent. So Jesse had slept with Josephine, he thought.

It seemed to take him a long time to walk the three or four blocks back to the laundry room.

CHAPTER 23

A Succos Party

On the weekend, Martin had an opportunity to do something "un-related" to the problem at hand, just as Jesse had recommended. He and Britta had been invited to a Succos party at Ralph's house in Ramat Rachel.

Ralph was also a poet, a friend of Mr. Townley's. He was an American Jew who had recently arrived in Jerusalem after living a couple of years in Italy. He too was older than Martin, but a year or two younger than Jesse. On the door to his room, a brass plaque was nailed. The words "Il Poeta" were inscribed on it, the same title that was once accorded to Ezra Pound. Ralph had received the plaque from a group of friends as a going-away present. He often gazed at the plaque and talked about Rapallo dreamily.

The party would be a good diversion, Martin thought. Ralph would probably provide wine for his guests. Mr. Townley and a few other aficionados of the arts had been invited.

On Friday evening, the day before the party, Martin met Ralph on King George Road.

"You're coming tomorrow, I hope," Ralph smiled.

"Sure," Martin smiled back, "I wouldn't miss it for anything."

"And you're bringing your girlfriend? . . " Ralph enquired.

Martin nodded.

"Good, good," Ralph nodded in unison.

"Listen," Ralph said, "I have a great idea. Why don't the two of us go camping together tonight? You know what I mean—a sort of warm-up for the party. We can take some wine with us and have a hell of a good time."

Martin had reservations about the idea, but Ralph was very enthusiastic.

"I've got all the equipment we need," he said excitedly, "a couple of sleeping bags, a few pots and pans. We'll go up to the hills near my place. I don't think it'll be too cold tonight. What d'ya think, Martin?"

Martin hesitated with his reply.

"I'll have to see Britta first. Just to let her know where I'm going."

"O.K., that's great. Look, go see your girlfriend, tell her you'll meet her at my place tomorrow. Pick up a sweater for yourself and I'll meet you at my house in about half an hour. How does that sound?"

Martin was still not absolutely sure, but the idea was beginning to appeal to him. Ralph seemed very intent, and excited by the prospect of camping out. He stood on King George Road with a small yarmulke on his head, a little blue beanie he always wore.

"O.K., Ralph, what the hell. Let's do it. We only live once, right? I'll meet you at your house."

Ralph patted Martin on the back.

"You're a true poet," Ralph smiled.

His brown cheeks seemed to gather the afternoon light. His brown eyes darted.

Ralph walked away quickly, down the street, smiling to himself. About a half-block away, he turned around and waved at Martin.

"See you later!" he shouted.

As Martin walked up the short hill to the laundry room, he began to rationalize the upcoming night-time excursion with Ralph. Why not, he reasoned. He needed the break. For weeks he'd been sleeping in the same bed with Britta. Perhaps he could get her condition out of his mind for a few hours.

When he walked into the room, Britta was standing in front of the dresser mirror, getting ready to go shopping for food.

"Britta, do you think you can meet me at Ralph's house tomorrow? I just met him downtown, and he wants me to go camping with him tonight."

"All night?" Britta asked, her voice just a little surprised. "Where are you going to go?"

"I don't know exactly," Martin admitted, his voice dazed. "I guess Ralph knows the area pretty well. It's up in the hills near his house."

"And I've got to sleep alone?"

"It's just for the night, Britta."

Britta pouted a bit in front of the mirror. She opened her mouth and gazed at her teeth, judging their whiteness.

"Have you made any decision?" she asked. "I hope you've been thinking about it."

"How can I help but think about it?"

He bowed his head. "I had a talk with Jesse yesterday."

"Well, what did he have to say?"

"He was very sympathetic. He even said that marriage wouldn't be a bad idea."

Britta's face got red, flushed with anger.

"It's not what he thinks that's important. How do *you* feel about it? Has anything changed?"

Martin gazed down at the floor.

"No," he admitted. He didn't know whether to continue or not. "There's a doctor here in Jerusalem, Britta, a very good doctor."

"What can be good about him?" Britta snapped. "He gets paid for killing babies before they even have a chance to live. Do you know, Martin, that there's always a chance that the woman will never be able to have a kid again? That's what frightens me the most."

Martin could feel a pressure inside his chest, and inside his head. It was a knot of feeling that was tightening inside him, threatening to strangle him completely.

"Listen, Britta, I'll see you at Ralph's tomorrow. I've gotta go. Ralph's probably waiting for me."

"O.K., Martin," Britta sighed. "I just wish I knew a way of getting through to you."

Martin darted his eyes around the room, spotted his sweater, and grabbed it. He brushed his lips against Britta's cheeks. He knew if she began crying that he might not get to Ralph's.

"I'll see you tomorrow," he said. There was a finality in the tone of his voice, and a determination to get out of the room.

He swivelled quickly. And he left the room, almost running down the stairs. His heart was pounding.

Outside, it was still bright. As he walked towards Ramat Rachel, he could hear hammers click nails into wood. People were building small huts all over the city to celebrate Succos, the harvest. Suc-

cahs, the wooden huts were called, wooden structures that were
draped with leaves and grapes and apples and oranges. For almost
a week now, people had been building them—on rooftops, in backyards and alleyways.

Click, bang, click. He could hear the nails plunging into the soft
wood, and every once in a while, he could spot someone with a
hammer in hand feverishly trying to finish the hut before darkness
and the sabbath descended. All work would have to stop at night-
fall.

His own head felt like a nail. Bang, bang, he could hear Britta's
words hammering at his skull, Britta's words, and Jesse's advice.

Slowly, his feet carried him towards Ramat Rachel. It was situated close to the Jordanian border on one side, and on the other a
narrow valley separated it from Mount Zion. He gazed at old Jerusalem, and on top of the Mount of Olives he saw the brassy dome
of the great mosque shining.

Ralph lived in a large room, part of an Arab-styled house. As he
walked towards the front door, he spotted Ralph's succah. He was
surprised at how much care Ralph had taken in building the hut.
The light wooden walls were in place. All the nails had been carefully banged in.

Bunches of grapes, pomegranates, oranges, apples, and squash
adorned the walls. Ralph suddenly emerged from his room. He
held a knapsack in one hand.

"How do you like my succah?" he asked.

"It's great," Martin said, trying to sound enthusiastic. "It must've
taken you some time to build."

Ralph walked slowly towards the wooden hut. He gazed at it as
if he were seeing it for the first time. He reached out a hand and
patted the wood affectionately.

"It's built to order," he grinned. "I don't know if I ever told you,
but I used to be a yeshiva student."

"You were going to be a rabbi?" Martin asked.

Ralph surveyed the succah, a dreamy expression on his face.

"That was quite a few years ago," he sighed. "Before the poetry
bug hit me. Now I string turds together like everyone else."

Martin laughed.

"Well," Ralph said, changing the subject, "are you ready to go
camping? I've got everything ready. Just one thing, though—we've

got to be a careful to stay on the Israeli side of the Jordan River. It's actually just a stream where we're going."

Martin was beginning to feel a little nervous about the camping trip.

"Is it dangerous?" he asked.

"As long as we stay on the Israeli side, we'll be okay," Ralph half-grinned.

They headed out towards the hills together, carrying sleeping bags. Ralph wore his small knapsack on his back. Darkness fell sooner than Martin expected. The sky was unusually black. Slowly the stars appeared.

Ralph pointed out the trickle of water that was supposed to be the Jordan River.

"Are we on the right side?" Martin asked. His mind was swirling with doubt and fear. He looked up at the hills, and imagined soldiers there with rifles pointed at both of them.

Ralph hesitated with his reply.

"It's so fucking dark," he cursed, "I can't really tell."

Unhurriedly, the moon ascended. Martin had seen bright moons and white moons and glaring, almost obscene moons during his years in Israel, but the moon that evening was so bright that it looked unreal.

It looked like the huge thigh-bone of some dead animal.

The light from the moon pounced on both of them. It carved weird shadows on the hills. It made Ralph's face look ghostly white.

"Oh shit!" Ralph suddenly shouted. "We're on the wrong bloody side. C'mon, let's go."

Ralph began running. Martin followed close behind. They got to the stream and Ralph jumped over. Somehow, Martin slipped and one foot fell into the water. He jerked it out, and continued chasing after Ralph.

"Are we on the right side now?" Martin shouted.

"Yes," Ralph replied. He pointed to a hilltop. "You see that hill. We'll camp up there tonight. We'll be able to see everything. We'll start a fire to keep us warm."

Ralph ran towards the hill. Martin wasn't at all sure that they were heading in the right direction. He imagined Jordanian bullets suddenly slamming into his chest and skull. But he followed after Ralph.

Up the hill they ran. It seemed to never end. Loose stones fell behind them.

Finally they reached the top, a tiny mesa of land.

"Let's sleep here," Ralph suggested. "We'll look for some wood and make a fire."

The fire was made, and they crawled into their sleeping bags. It was a cold night. Martin found it difficult to keep warm, and even more difficult to sleep. The wood in the fire crackled.

In his half-sleep, he could see Britta alone in the laundry room clutching her belly.

Ralph was still awake.

"What do you really think of this country?" Ralph asked.

The suddenness of the question took Martin by surprise.

"It's okay," Martin replied non-committally.

"Do you think you'll stay here?" Ralph continued.

Martin shook his head in the darkness.

"I don't know, Ralph. There seems to be something missing. I can't tell you what it is, though. Maybe it's the language. I just can't get used to it. And sometimes I think about . . . well, about small things. It might sound stupid, but I think about water and trees and snow. Things like that."

Martin could hear Ralph chuckling to himself. It was a muffled sound seeping out from under the sleeping bag.

"There's nothing stupid about that," Ralph said softly. "What else do we poets think about? What else is important? I miss New England myself."

For a second, Martin was tempted to tell Ralph about his problem with Britta. But he decided to keep it to himself.

Martin found it difficult to sleep. He would slip off for a few minutes, and then wake with a start. A noise in the darkness. A branch in the fire crackling. Was Ralph having the same problem?—he wondered. Or was he pleasantly snoring away the hours, tucked away, buried in sleep, dreaming of cozy bygone days in Rapallo?

Britta's face floated inside his head. What a tired face she wore. It was larger. Her face had grown. Wrinkles around her eyes and mouth, lines of worry.

He was thankful when the light of dawn began to creep over the horizon. Soon they would be able to get up and continue their journey. He glanced over at Ralph. The poet from Rapallo looked like a small boy. His mouth was half open, sucking in air as he slept.

He wanted to call out to him. "Ralph, Ralph," he wanted to whisper, "let's get up. It's morning, Ralph." Yet he didn't want to disturb him. Ralph turned over, moaning in his sleep.

"Ralph," he finally whispered, "Ralph, let's get up."

Ralph moaned again.

"What's wrong?" Ralph groaned.

"It's morning," Martin replied.

"Oh," he groaned.

"Do you want to get up, Ralph?"

"Yes," he groaned. "I'm hungry. And there's nothing for breakfast."

Sleepily, they dragged themselves out of the sleeping bags. An ache gnawed at Martin's legs. Yawning and shaking themselves, they rolled up the sleeping bags.

Ralph rubbed sleep out of his eyes, and looked around.

"Good," he said. "I know where we are. There's a little road near here that'll take us back."

They began walking together. What was it all about?—Martin wondered. What the hell was he doing out there in the hills with Ralph? Weren't there more important things to do? And to think about?

They found the trail that Ralph had mentioned, a trail of loose pebbles winding through the hills.

"Look over there," Ralph said. "Look at that bush."

They walked towards the bush. On the bush two lonely purple plums hung. Martin was amazed, not at the plums, but at the fact that only two remained. It seemed that all the plums had been picked off the bush by someone. Not only that one bush, but all the neighboring ones. Every single plum had been taken, snatched and harvested.

Martin entertained a crazy thought: those two plums were left there on purpose, part of a grand design. Some great universal mind had ordained the whole thing—that these two poets would awake on the morning of the Succos party, hungry and tired. And suddenly, by some stroke of magic, they would find a message hanging on a bush: two edible plums preserved.

The message was clear, but the meaning as usual escaped Martin.

Ralph plucked them off, and handed one to Martin.

"It tastes good," Martin smiled, sinking his teeth into the skin, into the heart of the fruit.

"I knew we'd find breakfast," Ralph laughed. "You see, it's so simple. All you got to do is have faith."

Yes, faith, Martin thought, why not?

It was a small breakfast, but finding the plums changed their moods.

Yes, something had to be right.

"Do you believe in God?" Ralph asked.

"God," Martin repeated, his voice dreamy.

"It's kind of an old-fashioned idea, isn't it?" Ralph continued, and he spat the plum pit into the bushes.

"Yes," Martin agreed. "But sometimes I wonder."

"Do you believe?" Martin asked.

Ralph adjusted the beanie on top of his head.

"Yes," Ralph whispered, gazing at the hills. He seemed to be thinking about God. Then, something else caught his attention, and he raised his hand and pointed. "You see that building over there. It's Herzliah Hospital. Isn't that an amazing place to have a hospital? Way out here in the wilderness?"

The sun shone on the edifice. It had an awesome number of windows, Martin thought. They were blood-red, reflecting the sun, sparkling back in their eyes.

"Well, let's get back," Ralph encouraged. "We'll have some food and wine before the others arrive. I've gotta take a shower anyway . . ." Ralph paused, then continued. "By the way, Martin, is your girlfriend going to come?"

Martin nodded.

They continued along the trail, leaving Herzliah Hospital behind them.

They walked in silence now. A taste of plum juice lingered in Martin's mouth.

*   *   *

It was about two o'clock in the afternoon. The guests had not begun to arrive. Ralph was inside his white-stucco house taking a shower. Martin sat on a bench in the shade of the succah.

He gazed at Ralph's handiwork—the simple structure of two-by-fours, the thick tropical leaves on the roof, everything put together with care. It reminded him of one of Ralph's poems. It had the same feel of controlled luxuriance. It was almost balanced—neither too wild and frantic, nor too low-key.

The blue autumn sky seemed to be racing above him; there were no clouds to show the movement of wind, but nevertheless the whole sky appeared to be moving quickly, and chattering to Martin that this was indeed autumn, October, harvest-time in the Holy Land.

He was grateful for the cool wind that kept nipping at his cheeks and his neck. It slid cool fingers up his pant-leg, and awakened him. If it were not for this breeze, Martin thought, he would surely fall asleep and miss the party.

How many hours did he sleep in the hills with Ralph? . . . surely no more than two, and perhaps it was just a matter of minutes.

He thought of Britta, what was going on inside her, the live thing beginning to grow. Arms, legs, fingernails, eyes, ears, mouth, all taking form in the darkness. And it would, if nurtured, come yelping out one day, a tiny human, their own.

Ralph had opened a bottle of red wine and left it outside for him. Martin poured a few dribbles into a glass and sipped at it. How fast the sky was racing, he dreamed, how quick the season was shifting. Soon the winter rains would splatter down again, the cold drops falling from Herzl Mountain to Zion Square.

"Hello, Martin," a warm, soft, familiar voice greeted him.

It was Mr. Townley slowly walking towards him. He was relieved. The first guest had arrived.

Martin got up and shook hands with his old professor friend.

"Where's Ralph?" Mr. Townley asked.

"He's just taking a shower. Would you like a little wine?"

"Sure," Mr. Townley nodded, standing in front of the succah.

"He did a fine job on this, didn't he?" Mr. Townley smiled, accepting the glass of wine from Martin.

Mr. Townley reached out a hand and absentmindedly picked up a bunch of grapes attached to the succah by a string. He fondled them between his fingers, then let them fall back to their resting place.

He took a seat with Martin on the bench.

"And how are things with you?" Mr. Townley asked.

Before Martin had a chance to reply, he saw another figure enter the yard. It was Britta. His heart took a sudden leap inside him. He excused himself and walked over to her. He gave her a hug and kissed her on the cheek.

"What a nice little hut," she said, gazing at the succah. "It's just so surprising, all these holidays. Look at that—it's got everything on it. Just look . . . pomegranates, grapes. Did Ralph build this?"

Martin nodded, smiling, and he felt proud of Ralph, his poet-friend. And he felt just a tinge of pride for this holiday they were about to celebrate, and the parade of holidays that fascinated Britta. A feeling of warmth began to grow inside him, a feeling that was linking everything together—Britta and Mr. Townley, Ralph and his succah.

He introduced Britta and Mr. Townley, and the three of them sat on the bench together, Britta squeezed between the two men.

"Do you have a succah?" she suddenly asked Mr. Townley.

"I didn't put one together this year," his voice wavered.

"We don't have one either," Britta sighed. "You know, Martin, we could've built one on the roof. It would've been so nice. Just like camping out. Oh well, maybe next year."

If there was going to be a next year together, Martin thought. He couldn't express the thought. Would he see another season of holidays in this land?

"How do you like our country?" Mr. Townley asked. "Martin tells me you're from Sweden. You're a long way from home."

"I just love it," Britta smiled, sipping at her wine. "It's so different here, especially in Jerusalem. It's kind of mysterious, the whole thing . . . these strange holidays that keep appearing."

"Are you going to stay for a while?"

Britta began playing in the dust with her foot. She had taken off her sandals. Her big toe scraped a line in the dust, and she crossed it over with another line.

"I have no real plans," she answered dreamily. "I just want to take things as they come. It's so useless to have plans, don't you think? They just never seem to work out, and you let yourself in for big disappointments."

Mr. Townley gazed down at the dust, and all three of them were watching Britta's toe making its criss-cross designs over and over again.

"That's not a bad attitude," Mr. Townley almost whispered.

"What will be, will be. I guess we all have to learn to live each day, and not worry too much about the future."

Britta sighed, and for a second, she seemed to be swaying and leaning her weight against Martin, then shifting the other way, pressing herself lightly against Mr. Townley's arm.

The other guests began to arrive. There was Sharon, a painter and student, an overweight Jewish girl from New York. And Neil, her boyfriend, a tall gentile boy who idolized Lawrence of Arabia, and felt almost positive that he was distantly related to the desert warrior. One or two others also came. An English Jew who wrote part-time, and spent his days proofreading the Jerusalem Post, poring over the fresh ink, trying to catch misplaced commas and wayward periods.

And finally Ralph emerged from his room wearing a blue singlet, short pants, sandals, and the blue beanie that always rested on the tip of his skull.

"Ah, the master of ceremonies," Mr. Townley joked, raising his glass to toast Ralph.

Everyone laughed and chortled, and raised their glasses of wine, looking in Ralph's direction.

Ralph beamed and tipped his beanie at everyone. He walked from person to person pouring fresh wine into their glasses. He seemed to enjoy this role as host, and master of ceremonies, and chief architect of succahs.

Martin began drinking quickly, downing glass after glass of sickish-sweet wine.

He could hear pieces of conversation: people talking about movies, paintings, poetry, aesthetics, existentialism, Albert Camus and Jean-Paul Sartre. He found it hard to join in, to be as light and witty as everyone else.

He was quickly getting drunk, and he noticed that Ralph, too, was drinking at a tremendous clip.

Britta had moved, and she was sitting on a bench beside Sharon. How different the two girls looked, Martin thought. Sharon with her thick thighs, her frazzled hair, the curls going every which way.

An hour passed. More wine was drunk. The conversations sounded thinner and thinner to Martin, more distant, and more meaningless. Who really cared, he thought, about all the witty observations that were being made? Who cared about Sartre anyway?

Who cared about France? It was all shit, he thought to himself. What did it all mean, if he couldn't figure out what was going on inside himself and inside Britta? Chatter and more chatter. How could he really give a fuck about painting in Florence when right before his eyes, there in Jerusalem, in a certain backyard in Ramat Rachel, he hadn't the faintest idea of what was going on?

He drank more wine. Shit, it's all shit, he thought to himself. It's all torn foetuses and swollen bellies. He gazed at Mr. Townley and at Ralph. He began to wonder if they had ever gone to bed together. Had Ralph ever nestled his skinny brown body against Mr. Townley's grey-haired chest?

He gazed at Britta again. Her head was bent and she was moving her bare foot through the dust—scraping it along. Martin was beginning to feel lonely, as if nobody was really there in the backyard, just disembodied voices chattering and laughing. He was beginning to feel cold inside.

His brain was reeling with wine, his stomach turning over.

Why was he so cold and alone, he wondered, why couldn't he join in with everyone else and be a little more civilized? Didn't he have a single clever thing to say? Couldn't he dredge up something—some little piece of wit from inside his frozen skull? But no, he thought, what would be the use? It would come out, someone would laugh, and he would be thrown back into his isolation.

He walked over to Britta, and let himself fall down in the dust beside her feet. He hugged her dusty legs. And he brushed his cheek against her calves. He liked the blond curls that grew on her legs, the feel of them against his lips.

He noticed that Mr. Townley was staring at him, and in his grey-blue eyes a flicker of disapproval danced. Martin turned his head away. He began kissing Britta's toes, tasting the dust. He just wanted to bathe her feet with kisses.

"Martin, please," Britta whispered, pushing his head away, "this isn't the place."

He glanced up at her. And although she was pushing at his head, he could see a smile of amusement slipping across her mouth, and a twinkle of excitement in her eyes.

"Aren't I allowed to kiss my beloved?" he asked, his voice childish and faintly tinged with anger.

He began to feel cold again, more lonely than ever. He tried to wrap his arms around her legs tightly, to get rid of the uneasy feeling.

He glanced at Mr. Townley again. Why does he have to look at me that way?—doesn't he realize how cold I feel inside, how much I need to squeeze her legs and kiss her dusty toes?

He spotted Ralph. He was tilting back another glass of wine. Ralph was grinning at him, beaming, chuckling to himself. He seemed to like the vision before him: his friend, Martin, lying in the dust, stoned out of his mind, hugging a pair of legs, dust on his lips.

Ralph suddenly raised his glass, as if he were toasting the sun, the sky, the leaves on the trees.

"I give a toast!" he yelled and laughed. "I salute all lovers and poets."

Everyone raised their glasses.

"To Ralph, our host!" someone shouted.

"To Ralphie," Martin laughed.

Ralph began to dance in front of everyone with his glass held high above his head. He kicked out his skinny brown legs. With his free hand, he took off his blue yarmulke and tossed it high in the air. To Martin's amazement, he was able to catch it again by holding out his wine glass, and letting the beanie fall down on top.

Martin glanced at Mr. Townley. He was smiling faintly, turning his wine glass slowly between his fingers.

"Who wants to dance with me?" Ralph shouted. "We can't let the rabbis have all the fun."

He glanced at Martin, his eyes brown and drunk, his lips wet with wine.

Why not?—Martin thought. Why not get up and dance with Ralph? Why not dance for all of them?—for Mr. Townley, for Sharon, for Neil, and for Britta. Why not show them how it was really done, with his mind reeling wildly and his fingers trembling?

He pushed himself from Britta's legs and crawled to his feet. He poured himself another glass of wine. He needed more alcohol, a little more courage.

"I'll dance with you, Ralph!" he shouted. Wine and dribbles of saliva escaped from the corners of his mouth.

They began to dance together—Greek style, arms around each other's shoulders.

They kicked out their legs together. For a second, Martin felt a little bit like a can-can dancer. One leg out, then the other.

"Hey, who's going to join us?" Ralph shouted. His voice seemed to be daring the guests to get up, to kick out their heels, and spray dust behind them.

Everyone seemed just slightly embarrassed by the two of them. Britta kept her eyes on the ground. Mr. Townley stared into his wine glass. Sharon and Neil kept talking to each other, as if nothing was really happening.

"What's wrong with them?" Ralph whispered in Martin's ear, leaning his cheek and mouth closer.

"They're meditating," Martin whispered back.

"Oh, they're dead, that's what I think," Ralph chortled. "Don't they look funny?"

Ralph started pointing an accusing finger in the direction of his guests.

"Ralph," Martin protested, feeling the heat of embarrassment rise to his cheeks and ears.

They did look a little wooden, Martin thought. Britta heavy, intent on staring at the ground. Mr. Townley not at all wild with drink, his sober grey eyes musing at his wine. Sharon and Neil talking, discussing, drinking, but not allowing the spikes of alcohol to pierce their brains.

Ralph began shouting wildly, and dancing around the succah. Martin followed close behind. They looked like Indians, Martin thought, doing a war dance around a camp-fire.

Suddenly they heard voices, and saw dark faces behind a stone wall that surrounded the backyard. It was a bunch of young Yemenite or Moroccan boys. Guys in their late teens, perhaps younger.

"Shickorim!" they were yelling at Ralph and Martin. "Drunkards, look at the drunkards!"

"Hey!" Ralph yelled. "We can't let them get away with that. Did you hear what they called us? This is fuckin' war!"

Ralph ran towards the stone wall, shouting.

"Shoo, shoo, get away, you're not invited, beat it!"

The brown-faced, curly-haired boys ran off a few yards, and then came charging back again, shouting in chorus:

"Shickorim, shickorim, shickorim!"

"Ah, you want to fight!" Ralph yelled.

Martin was surprised at Ralph's intense reaction. Ralph ran back to the succah and tore a couple of pomegranates from the side of the hut. He gave one to Martin, and threw his at the taunting boys.

Martin handed his pomegranate back to Ralph. He was laughing too hard to throw it. He was buckled over, and his stomach was paining with laughter.

The boys on the other side of the fence retrieved the bruised pomegranates and fired them back at Ralph and Martin.

"See!" Ralph yelled. "They want to fight. Let's really get them."

Martin could feel a gaiety and fever rise quickly inside him. He ran back to the succah with Ralph and tore off a few pomegranates and started firing them wildly at the teenage boys. On the other side of the wall, the Moroccans must've found a pomegranate tree of their own, for the bruised red fruit came back faster than Martin and Ralph were throwing them.

They were hitting the side of Ralph's stone house, splattering the red juice everywhere. It almost looked like blood dripping down the white stone.

Martin couldn't figure out how exactly it happened, but during the fight, the walls of the succah began to tremble. Ralph was pulling squash and grapes from the sides of the flimsy hut, and tossing them over the wall. And somehow, the succah walls shook too much, and the sides separated from the two-by-fours and caved inward. The leafy roof fell inside—a bedraggled heap of leaves and branches.

Mr. Townley, Sharon, Neil and Britta were watching the whole thing. At the beginning, Ralph had encouraged them to join the fight. They all had refused. More than once they had to duck their heads to avoid getting hit by a mushy squash or a bleeding pomegranate.

"Oh, watch out!" Britta yelled as the walls of the succah caved in.

But it was too late. Ralph's handiwork lay in a heap on the ground.

"All things fall and are built again!" Ralph shouted, quoting from Yeats's poem.

Mr. Townley was shaking his head back and forth, as if he couldn't quite understand what had just taken place.

"That poor succah will never be the same," Sharon grinned, her head turned, now, away from Neil.

As soon as the succah clattered to the ground, the Moroccan boys took off, laughing, and patting each other on the shoulder.

"Where are you going, you cowards!" Ralph yelled after them. "Come back and fight. It's not over yet."

But Ralph's shouts were not heeded. They kept running down the dirt road, and were soon out of sight.

A silence descended on the backyard. Ralph began to chatter, but no one responded. He too shut his mouth, and took a seat on the bench beside Mr. Townley. Martin wandered over to Britta, and sat down on the bench beside her.

The backyard was littered with pieces of broken fruit and crushed vegetables. The wine glasses stood half empty on tables and on the ground. No one was lifting a hand to drink.

How forlorn the succah looked, Martin thought. Just ten minutes earlier, it stood proudly in the sun, bedecked and adorned. It had been a good succah, as good as any Martin had seen in Jerusalem.

"Can we go?" Martin whispered to Britta.

Britta leaned her shoulder against him. Her voice sounded tired and sad.

"Do you think he'll build it again?" she asked. "It was such a lovely little hut."

Martin felt dazed. "It sure came down fast, didn't it?"

For a second, a smirk forced itself at the corners of his mouth. It never developed. His face became drawn and tight once again.

"Let's go," Britta whispered. "I feel so depressed."

Martin got up, and walked over to Ralph. He reached down and squeezed his shoulder, thanking him for the wine and the party.

"Come back next year," Ralph grinned up at him.

Neil and Sharon said goodbye quickly to Ralph, and left the backyard before Martin and Britta.

Martin walked slowly out of the backyard holding Britta's hand. He needed to squeeze her hand, and feel the pressure coming back. He glanced back over his shoulder. Mr. Townley and Ralph were sitting alone on the bench. They were talking quietly to one another.

"Shickorim," he could still hear the word ringing out under the bright autumn sky.

"I feel sorry for Ralph," Britta said sadly as they walked through Ramat Rachel back to the center of town. "He seems such a lonely person. I wonder if he's ever had a girlfriend."

"He must've," Martin replied quickly.

"Don't be too sure," Britta sighed, gazing down at her feet moving. "What a mess that backyard is. Maybe we should've helped him clean it up."

Martin shrugged, but he didn't answer.

It was about five-thirty in the afternoon. The sun seemed to be bleeding over the rooftops. Everything looked drenched in blood: the Y.M.C.A. bell tower, the King David Hotel, and all the little stone houses that hid succahs in their backyards.

Slowly, on tired legs, they made their way back to their apartment building. They climbed the staircase together, back up to their home, to the laundry room they knew so well.

CHAPTER 24

The Operation

There wasn't much room to pace in the cramped laundry room, but Martin walked up and down between the dresser and the cot. It was a couple of days after Ralph's party. It was about eleven o'clock in the morning, but he still felt half asleep. His eyes were half closed, and he kept wiping yawns from his mouth.

His thoughts were gradually jerking him awake. Britta was still in bed, half-lying and half-sitting, her back propped up with a pillow.

No, he thought, gazing at her blond hair and blue eyes, at her pouch of belly beneath a sheet. No, he couldn't allow it to go any further. He couldn't just stand back and let it happen. As each day passed, the live thing was growing inside her. It was no time to go to sleep. He couldn't allow the months to slip dreamily past, and wake up one morning and realize it was too damn late.

Only a month had gone by since the doctor told her that she was pregnant. He realized the longer he wavered in making a decision, the harder it would be to tell her. And the operation itself could get sticky and dangerous. At the moment, it was only a small cyst of life inside her, soon it would become a sack of pulsing blood, a fully formed creature kicking at her stomach.

For a second, he imagined himself inside her. It was dark and cramped. He was struggling to catch his breath, fighting to get free. There was a temptation to stop kicking. There was a temptation to just lie back in the darkness and warmth, to just huddle there, and drink whatever came his way.

Again he jerked himself awake, and began pacing faster, his feet clicking on the concrete floor.

"I've made a decision, Britta," he spat suddenly. "I just can't go through with it. You've got to have an abortion. There's no other way."

No words came back at him. Britta sat silently on the bed. It was difficult to look directly at her, to meet her blue eyes. Why doesn't she say something? Out of the corner of his eye, he could see her sitting there, not a word coming forth.

He could sense that she was growing softer. It was a feeling that was coming from her body, her head, even her mind.

How long could she sit there and not say anything? Momentarily, he was afraid that her mouth would suddenly open and an explosion of words and feeling would leap out. All the things he had heard already. How life was sacred. How he was riding roughshod over everything.

Instead, he noticed that her shoulders were trembling. It was a slight movement of her flesh—almost gentle. He moved a little closer to the bed.

He could see the tears slowly welling in her eyes. Her cheeks were getting damp, and one fully formed tear rolled and glistened down the side of her face, hung on her chin, and fell off.

He walked over to the cot and sat down beside her. He wrapped his arms around her. Her body felt warmer than usual, almost hot, and he was amazed at how gently she was crying, how softly the feeling was pressing to the surface.

"I'm sorry, Britta," he whispered against her cheek. He could taste the salt of her tears, and feel the dampness against his skin. "I just wish I could be the person you want me to be."

Inside, he could feel his own tears growing, pressing against his eyes. No, he said to himself, don't cry, not now. He knew very well that if he broke down, he could alter his decision, and that he might promise her anything—things he would later regret and renounce.

"Please say something," he whispered against her cheek.

Britta heaved in his arms.

"I can't argue any more with you, Martin. I can't force you to be what you don't want to be. I still think you're making a mistake, and someday you're going to wake up and regret it."

An image formed in his mind, an image inspired by Britta's words. He was waking up in the morning. He was reaching around to feel her body. There was nothing there beside him, and his fingers were clutching at cold wrinkled sheets.

"Martin, I feel so tired," she whispered. "If that's your final decision, let's do it quickly. You don't know how much I've cried and worried and wished and hoped for things in the last month. I just want to get it over with now. I can't go through any more without breaking."

Martin cleared his throat. A bone, a hard desperate bone seemed to be lodged inside his throat.

"I've got everything arranged," he rasped. "I just have to speak to Jesse. I'll get the name of the doctor and borrow the money from him."

Britta became silent once again. She drew away from his arms and turned her face towards the wall.

"Just leave me, please," she whispered. "Do what you have to do. I need some time by myself."

He squeezed her shoulder tightly before he got up.

He found a sweater and quickly pulled it over his head. Without lingering, he left the laundry room, and walked quickly down the stairs. He needed air, air, air, just some fresh bright air to breathe.

*   *   *

The garden outside the doctor's office looked like a snapshot. It was very still on the day of the operation. As they walked up the cement pathway, Britta turned to him.

"Martin, you can still change your mind. There's still time. I'll just tell him we decided not to."

His feet kept moving him forward. How still the garden was. Not a breeze stirred, and not a single bird ruffled the air with its wings or a song. He shook his head in silence.

No, his mind clanged.

No.

And the "no" was as silent and stony-still as the garden. How thin the trees looked, skinny as saplings. The flowers looked ornamental. They could've been made out of paper, he thought.

And he dreamed of long ago, living on a certain street across from a Catholic university. The bells clanged for mass each morning. They shook in the belfry.

His mother's rhododendrons stood on the front lawn, two of them, one on either side of the front steps. They too looked artificial.

"It's no use, Britta," he muttered.

He wanted to kiss her, to hug her, to rock her in his arms. But how could he do that? How could he do it, walking her to this place where soon the doctor's knife would flick and cut into her soft flesh?

"Then you've made up your mind?" Britta whispered.

His head jerked up and down, a heavy weight on top of his neck, a monstrously heavy weight.

"Leave me here," she said with tears in her voice. "It's going to take about an hour and a half."

She pushed against his arm. He moved his face towards her, but she turned away and walked quickly up the path.

He turned around, and almost raced out of the garden, his shoes clicking on the pavement.

On the street, things looked a bit more normal. He couldn't figure it out. The garden looked dark and deathly still, yet on the street he could see the wind blowing high in the trees. The leaves were turning, catching the sunlight. It was an extraordinarily bright autumn day.

What a day, he kept thinking, what a bright, windswept, blue-sky day for such a thing to be happening. Life was going on as usual: people walking quickly along, doing their shopping, chattering to one another. For an hour, he wanted to melt into them, into the sunlight, and into the wind.

And he could feel pangs of hunger in his stomach, as if he hadn't eaten in weeks. What an awful thing to feel, he mused, on such a day.

He found himself in front of Pepe's spaghetti house. Through the wide front windows, he could see the usual assortment of beefy, hungry men sitting on stools. How could he think of eating?

He took a seat and ordered spaghetti. How hungry he was. He forked up the long strands, and sucked at the tomato sauce. He was beginning to feel ill. On his plate he could see blood and strips of flesh. Yet he continued to eat until his plate was white and empty.

He ordered another coffee and kept glancing at the round-faced clock on the wall. The hands moved slowly, marking off the minutes.

He was depressed about what was going on in the doctor's office, yet he felt free, with the sunlight streaming into Pepe's, the warmth of coffee in his mouth. He remembered playing hooky in grade two, getting on one of those old tramcars, just letting it carry him around Halifax.

It rocked him down Quinpool Road. The sun was shining, and the dark, chubby boy was dreaming out the window. The sun bathed his forehead and eyes. How he hated the smell of ink in glass wells, the smell of the blackboard and chalk. How he despised the scraping of desks. He was only eight, but he played hooky quite often. He bought a single ticket and let the tramcar take him around the city again and again. A policeman caught him one day, and took him back to his grade-two teacher. The teacher was angry. His parents were told. It was the last time he played hooky in the younger grades. And he could remember his father laughing: "I guess he's a rebel already, Dahlia. At least he comes by it honestly."

He shook his head, as if trying to get rid of the daydream. He took another sip of coffee. He felt guilty about eating at Pepe's that morning. It wasn't right. The sunlight shouldn't feel so warm on the back of my neck, he thought.

An hour had slipped by. He glanced at the clock again. It was time to go back, and he knew he would have to go into the doctor's office this time. He would have to face him, he would have to meet Doctor Bluestein, there was no way around it.

The garden outside the doctor's office hadn't changed. If anything, it was quieter and stonier than before. It was like entering another world. He dragged himself into the building. He knocked at the doctor's door and was told to enter.

He spotted Britta immediately. She was sitting on a wooden chair by a window, her eyes blankly gazing at the garden. The skin on her face looked stretched. She turned her head slightly, but did not look at him.

Doctor Bluestein was an Austrian Jew. His eyes were blue-grey, the same color as Mr. Townley's, but they shone more brightly.

"Now, I want you to look after her," he said, smothering Martin with his gaze. "She needs rest. Make sure the sheets on the bed are clean. Feed her—salads, chicken, just some good solid food. Don't eat it all yourself."

Each of the doctor's words thumped against his temples. He bowed his head, and kept nodding as each sentence formed and hit him.

"How long should she be in bed?" he asked.

"For a few days at least," the doctor replied. "She's got to get some color back in her cheeks. It's not a minor operation. She needs to rest."

Martin wanted to walk across the room and touch her, just touch her softly, but his legs wouldn't move. They were rooted to the tile floor in front of Doctor Bluestein.

He glanced at Britta. The operation seemed to have had an effect on the color of her hair. It no longer looked bright and shiny. It had gone darker. At least it looked that way.

Somehow, he managed to walk across the room until he was standing beside her. She was still gazing out the window at the garden.

"Take me home, Martin, please." The words emerged slowly from her mouth. "I just want to get out of this place. I can't take another minute here."

In the background, he could hear Doctor Bluestein on the telephone. He was ordering a taxi to pick them up.

Slowly and stiffly, Britta got to her feet. He was afraid that her legs were going to suddenly give way. He gripped her arm trying to support her. He could hear Dr. Bluestein's voice over his shoulder.

"Remember, young man, food and rest. I don't want to see her back here with nervous exhaustion."

Tears again were beginning to burn up from inside him. He couldn't tell what he was feeling most—hatred for Dr. Bluestein, or sympathy for Britta. The two emotions swirled inside him. He forced the tears back, and his face became just as stony as Britta's, just as drawn and stretched.

He had decided the day before to take her back to his room in the stone cottage rather than the laundry room. The day before, he had cleaned up the room, swept it, dusted it, and put fresh white sheets on the bed. He had tried to make everything as clean and sanitary as possible. And he had bought food, stocked it up in Mrs. Shoshannah's refrigerator.

They were both shaking as they left Dr. Bluestein's office. Again, Martin felt sick to his stomach. A weird thought kept buzzing at him —where did he put the foetus? Did he just wrap it up and throw it in the garbage? And a more grotesque idea assailed him. What if he had offered it to them, a keepsake, as dentists sometimes do with young children—presenting them with a tooth, blood and tissue still clinging to the roots?

The thought sickened him, made his stomach ooze. For a second, he thought he was going to faint or throw up, or do both, right in the middle of the office. Just fall in a heap on the floor.

Shakily, they walked out of the office together. Martin was thankful for the sunshine on the sidewalk, for the brisk air hitting his forehead. Britta still felt stiff and wooden, but she allowed herself to lean against him as they waited for the taxi together.

He wanted to say something to her, something warm and comforting, but anything his mind devised seemed banal. "I'm sorry"—only those two words hovered on his lips, and moved under his tongue. He couldn't say them. Instead, he squeezed his arm tightly around her shoulder.

The taxi arrived. Inside, it had that freshly cleaned look, as if the upholstered back seat had been recently shampooed. It looked almost too clean, too sterile, and reminded Martin of the doctor's office. The taxi moved them quickly down the three or four blocks to the stone cottage. Martin, too, felt like a patient, a sick tormented person in need of care.

Thank God, he thought, as they walked up the path to the cottage, thank God that Mrs. Shoshannah was nowhere in sight. Britta had only been there once before, on the day she arrived with Steven. It seemed many months ago, that August afternoon when he dragged himself out of the cot and answered the door.

He glanced around. Nothing appeared changed. The chickens were still clucking inside their wire pens, just as they did throughout the summer. Thank God, he thought, the house looked empty, quiet and a bit dark. Mrs. Shoshannah was probably doing some shopping, and Larry was most likely at a dancing lesson.

Thank God. He couldn't face them that morning, with Britta hanging on his arm, her face white and drawn. Her eyes looked blank and she stared straight ahead. It frightened him, her face. There was no expression on it. Not a grimace or a frown, nor were her lips curled in anger. That would've been easier to take. Instead, her face was corpse-white, and wooden.

And what did his own face look like?—he wondered. Wasn't it a mirror-image of hers? His skin felt like leather stretched over an understructure of wood. His eyes were gaping holes staring straight ahead.

"I just want to go to sleep, Martin. I can't think about it any more. I just want to fall asleep for a few hours and forget."

"Sure, Britta. I've got everything ready. The bed's ready. I had your nightie cleaned."

Britta didn't reply. He guided her into his room. He was glad, now, that there were two single beds in the room. He too could lie down, and not bother her with his body. He could just let her go to sleep and forget. He knew from the inside this desire — to allow the mind to close down.

"I don't even feel like moving my arms," Britta said.

"That's okay," he replied quickly, "I'll undress you. You don't have to do anything, Britta. Just let me do it for you, please."

She held her arms out, and allowed him to unbutton her blouse, unsnap her brassiere, and slip everything off. She stood there silently, and let him take off her skirt, her panties, her shoes and her socks. He felt as if he were undressing a small, helpless child.

Carefully, he slipped the nightie over her head, making sure not to snag it in her hair.

"Can I get you something?" he asked. "Something to drink?"

"No, Martin. Just let me go to sleep. That's all I want."

He nodded his head in agreement. That was all he wanted, too. He just wanted to sink into sleep, into those soft arms that could make him forget, that quieted his mind. Only nightmares could get him there, and he prayed that none would attack her, or invade his head.

He tucked the white, fresh sheets around her. Very quickly, she sank into sleep. Before he had a chance to kiss her or say another word, her eyelids closed, and she began to breathe heavily and rhythmically. He took off his clothes, and slipped into the cot on the opposite side of the room.

Sleep, he sighed to himself, as he glanced at Britta, at her blond hair splayed on the pillow. Sleep, just sleep, and he wanted his own mind to be still. If he had one wish, he thought, he would close his eyes, fall asleep, a deep sleep, and never wake up again.

For half an hour, pictures rushed through his mind. He could see his mother in a white nightie, the material billowing over her stomach. She was eight months pregnant. He was reaching out a finger to touch. Just faintly, he could feel a tremor, a tiny foot kicking. He could see his father's black, smiling face, his teeth flashing, a row of white . . . his father's proud face as Dr. Goodman shook his hand and told him it was a boy.

As sleep began to overtake him, to sink him down into its soothing arms, the pictures became wilder, more diffuse. A tramcar rocking around the city. His grade-two teacher telling him to stand in the corner until noon-hour. Did he really see a sliver of a grin on her stern old face?

And marbles were falling from the clouds. Hailstones and marbles. He grabbed for them and they melted between his fingers. They turned into liquid.

A conversation took place as he sank deeper into the darkness.

"You've got to learn to whistle," a doctor was advising. "And cook chicken. You've got to make salads. The boat can't go anywhere without a rudder. Don't you know that, young man?"

"A rudder?" he enquired. "Where am I supposed to go?"

The voice chuckled. It sounded soft and faraway.

"The ship knows where it's supposed to go when the captain's at the helm."

Helm. Helm. His mind gurgled the word. Red rudder . . red rudder . . red rover, come over. He remembered the boys playing red rover in grade three. No grass on the playground. Not a single blade, just hard cinders and a few sticks and stones. How roughly they played. Boys with red hair and flushed faces. He stood in the shadow of the huge old schoolhouse and watched. Down they went as they hit the opposing line. Often the cinders ripped through their kneecaps and shins. The flesh was cut open and blood trickled out.

Go to sleep, he said to himself. Where will you get with such pictures inside your head? Please go to sleep. His mind resisted. He glanced for a second at Britta. She looked soft and innocent in her sleep. Her mouth was partly open as she breathed.

He closed his eyes again. Please, God, he whispered, don't destroy her insides. Let her still be able to have babies. She wants them so much. Let her still be open and whole.

And the darkness finally wrapped him up. His mouth hung open and he breathed heavily. They slept together in the same room, in two different beds that morning. "Thank you"—those were the last two words Martin uttered, before his mind blanked out and he was asleep.

Martin woke up first. Britta was still stretched out on the other side of the room, breathing heavily. He listened for Mrs. Shoshannah's slippered footsteps. He listened for her husky voice. The house was still quiet and he was glad. He had a chance, now, to slip out to the kitchen to prepare something for Britta before she woke up, and before Mrs. Shoshannah came back home.

He dressed quietly and slipped out to the kitchen wearing only his socks.

He decided to make her a fruit salad. He had purchased everything the day before. He hoped the dish would be high in vitamins and iron. He hoped that it would help restore her strength.

He had to pay attention to what he was doing. He wanted to get everything right for a change. Slowly, he peeled the apples, oranges, bananas. He cut them into small edible pieces and placed them in a bowl. He paid special attention to the green grapes. He dealt with each grape individually, sucking out the seeds, spitting them into the garbage, and he peeled off the skins. That was the least he could do, he thought—make the salad carefully, put a special effort into it. He mixed the fruit together and covered the salad with sour cream. He hoped it was a good salad. Carefully, he wrapped cellophane over the bowl and placed it in the refrigerator, all ready for the moment when Britta would awake.

Quietly, he slipped back into the room. He gazed at her sleeping form. What had he done to her, his mind clanged, what had he done to this soft, beautiful girl who had travelled to this country all the way from Stockholm? Perhaps she had made a grave error, he thought. Maybe she would've been better off in that apartment in Paris. Or better off alone.

She had trusted him, he thought, put herself in his care, and look how the whole thing had turned out. Steven's face kept sweeping into his memory. Steven's round cheeks, his black sensitive eyes. What a joke, he thought, promising Steven he would take good care of her. He was glad that Steven was thousands of miles away, that he couldn't see what happened that morning.

He watched Britta awake. At first, she was wooden and stiff as she had been before she went to sleep. But then a change began to take place. Her body began to tremble and shake. He knew she was crying. He couldn't hold back his own tears any longer. For days, he had been pressing them back. Back into his chest, until his chest ached. His own face had become wooden, without a trace of feeling.

It was a relief, now, to walk across the room, to lower himself to the cot beside Britta, to embrace her trembling body. Tears flowed from his eyes and he began to feel softer and warmer. As Britta cried and shook in his arms, he could feel her body getting warmer, softer, more alive. And heat was rushing through him, going out to her.

"Oh Martin," Britta sobbed against his chest. "What did we do? What did we do? It was ours and it was alive."

Martin couldn't say anything to her. He wrapped himself tighter around her trembling, hot body. He was sorry, but the words seemed meaningless.

"You know what it's like, Martin? It's like we owe the world something. We owe the world a human life."

The thought made him shudder, but it drew him closer to her, made his tears flow even more, and his body heat up.

"Martin, I know this is going to sound crazy to you, after what happened this morning. But I would do it again with you. I would have your baby if you thought you could go through with it."

He found it hard to believe—what he was hearing. It created a mad turmoil of feeling inside him. It frightened him, yet it drew him close to her. It made him feel like melting into her hot, tearful body. Perhaps he was crazy too, he thought, but he was tempted to go through the thing again, and not make her have an abortion. He was tempted to marry her, to raise kids with her. When he thought of leaving her, a lonely, empty feeling invaded him. What was there outside? Who was there? He kept thinking of the bare Judaean hills on rainy winter nights—how cold and frightening they were. And soon the winter rains would come again. He would have to live through them again, and how would he manage without her?

"I want to say 'yes' so much, Britta. I still love you. Maybe I have no right to say that after what you went through this morning. But I still do."

Britta continued to cry softly. It was the gentleness of her suffering that moved him, and made him feel close to her. It was like a light rain on a summer evening—soft and caressing.

"I made a salad for you," he finally said, smiling through his tears.

He was smiling and tasting the salty wetness trickle between his lips. It was an odd sensation, he thought. It was like the sun pushing out through the clouds after a rainstorm. He had almost a triumphant feeling inside his chest, as if they had gotten through something together.

"What kind of salad?" she smiled back, licking tears off her lips. "I hope it's a good one."

"It's great," he grinned. "Just wait till you see it and taste it. It's got everything in it."

Now they were smiling and grinning together, and crying. What a powerfully warm feeling he had inside his chest, and he knew that Britta was experiencing the same. Certainly they had gotten through something together, he thought, and it all seemed worthwhile now, with those flames of gentleness and warmth licking at the inside of him.

They only received one visit during those two or three days when they were both recuperating, holed up in the stone cottage together. Martin had successfully avoided running into Mrs. Shoshannah. He would only slip out of the room to use the washroom or kitchen when he was sure she was nowhere around. Britta hadn't encouraged her either. It was just as well, Martin thought. He still felt guilty about Britta, and he didn't want his landlady to find out about the abortion.

When Frank Laskey finally showed up, it was good to see a familiar face, and to talk to another human being. Frank was in his final year of M.A. studies at the Hebrew University. He was another Jewish exile from the diaspora, an American, and a good friend of Mr. Townley's. He too was part of that small community of English-speaking intellectuals and artists, that tiny side-society that existed in Jerusalem in the early sixties.

Frank and Martin had been friends for about a year. Quite often, they would run into each other on campus, or on the street, or in one of the restaurants they both frequented. Both their faces lit up when they met each other, and they would shake hands warmly. They would gossip with each other about mutual friends, talk about books, and once in a while, Martin would read Frank something he had recently dashed down on paper. Although Frank didn't write himself, he always listened attentively, a smile on his lips.

Martin was impressed by Frank's life. He was almost forty years old. In the forties, just after the Second World War, Frank had organized workers in Texas, and in other parts of the States. He still clung to his socialist beliefs. In '48 he immigrated to Israel, and he fought in the War of Independence. What a life, Martin kept thinking. It seemed exciting to him. He could picture Frank standing in front of a crowd of laborers in Texas, exhorting them to unite, to join their sweaty hands together, and to throw off the yoke of their capitalist masters. It was a romantic vision that he had of Frank. How tough he looked in his mind's eye—muscular and lean, fearless and humane.

He could see him fighting in Israel's first struggle for survival—his friend, Frank Laskey, in the forefront of battle, his brown eyes keen and sharp. Martin was proud and happy that Frank liked him. He had done so little in comparison—worked on a kibbutz, gone to university, written a few poems. It seemed that Frank had immersed himself in the rigors of "real" life. What courage, Martin often thought, it must've taken to stand before that beefy, clamorous crowd of tough men in Texas.

One evening about a month before Britta's operation, he had been talking to Frank on King George Road. During the conversation, Martin had mentioned Britta. He was surprised by Frank's enthusiasm.

"She's really Swedish?" Frank said excitedly. "That's great, Martin. I'm crazy about Scandinavian girls. There's just something about them. About a year ago I was engaged to this girl from Norway. What a beautiful girl! Intelligent. Sexy. God, she had everything. I'm still trying to figure out why it didn't work. Anyway, to make a long story short, I lost her. She went back to Norway. I've received a few letters, but I guess it's pretty well over."

Frank looked down at the sidewalk. His mood had changed. Martin could feel a heaviness inside Frank, and a weariness in his own chest. He could feel remorse in Frank's mood, regret, nostalgia, and a sense of loss.

"That's too bad, Frank," Martin said, looking down at the sidewalk also. "It sounds like she meant a lot to you."

Frank bit down on his lower lip. For a second, he met Martin's gaze, and then turned his eyes away.

"Well, old buddy," Frank smiled, slapping Martin on the shoulder, "who knows, maybe we'll get together again. Christ, you can't give up. But I'll tell you something, just between you and me. Every once in a while I'll get up in the morning and take a long look at myself in the mirror. And you know what I say? I'll tell you, Martin. Frank, I say, you old stupid bastard, you aren't getting any younger. You're going to be forty soon, and what do you have to show for it? Precious little, that's what. No wife, no family, not a single fuckin' hope for the future."

Martin was moved by what Frank was revealing on King George Road. His words moved through Martin's bloodstream. It gave him a slightly altered picture of his friend. Martin sighed to himself. There were other things, he thought. Other things that were important, no matter how many men were organized, no matter how many wars were won.

"Were you ever married?" Martin asked.

Frank shook his head in the darkness.

"No, I guess I've just never met the right girl. In the early days, I never thought about it much. I was involved in politics. Then I came to Israel, got involved in kibbutz life. But now I'm beginning to feel it. It's a feeling of emptiness right in the middle of my gut. Almost a feeling of waste, as if I've missed the boat altogether."

Martin gritted his teeth. His molars were twisting down upon each other. He could feel a tiny ache along his jawline.

"You still have time, Frank," he said weakly. "Christ, you're still young. There's no way you look forty."

Frank's dark eyes lit up once again. He patted his stomach, sucking it in, throwing out his chest. He had a good body, Martin thought. His muscles looked toned and defined, and his neck looked thick and strong.

"Well, what the hell," Frank gleamed, "that's the least I can do for myself, just try to keep in shape. I think if I ever went to flab, I'd just lie down and call it quits."

That evening, Martin took Frank up to Lupo's and introduced him to Britta. It was a casual meeting, with smiles exchanged between them. Frank seemed content to sit on the stool beside Martin and talk with Britta about the small Norwegian town his girlfriend had come from. Did Britta know the place, he enquired. Britta nodded, and she began to describe the hills, the trees, the way the sunlight fell on the snow in winter. Yes, she had been to the town. Yes, it was a beautiful place, small but very enchanting.

Frank looked serene. Martin was happy to see him that way. The furrows in his forehead had smoothed out. His mouth looked more relaxed. He seemed to be bathing in Britta's words and her good-natured smiles.

"It sounds like you really miss her," Britta whispered across the bar.

Frank nodded and knocked back another beer. As the evening progressed, and headed towards closing time, Frank's speech became a bit slurred. He was perfectly understandable, yet his words seemed to run into one another. Britta kept nodding, talking, reassuring, and Martin listened, smiling to himself.

In the street, after Lupo's shut down for the evening, Frank walked beside Martin with his arm around Martin's shoulder and his fingers grazing Britta's back. He began singing "Solidarity Forever", his voice loud and booming, echoing through the near-empty streets. Britta was laughing gaily, enjoying herself. They joined Frank in the chorus. And Martin wanted to feel that it wasn't merely a song. He wanted to feel that something joined the three of them—something that broke down all barriers of age and background. How he wished that that something was real—that it was in the blood, that it was essential, and that it was good.

Frank sang a slew of union songs. He taught them to Britta and Martin as they walked home together. "I dreamed I saw Joe Hill last night, alive as he could be." And he sang "Union Maid", and it seemed that he bellowed out every working-man song that he could remember.

And Martin wanted to believe it—that they were all working people, underdogs.

Half the songs, he had never heard before, but they touched something inside him. Together, he thought, yes, he just wanted to be together with Frank and Britta, with Joe Hill, with the poor people of the world. He wanted all the barriers to come crashing down and to melt away.

Martin was pleased to see Frank Laskey at the stone cottage three days after Britta's operation. He looked almost shy when he entered the room. He was carrying something in a brown paper bag.

"I just picked this up," he smiled, looking at Britta, then at Martin. "I thought you might enjoy some peaches."

He handed the bag to Britta. She was sitting on her bed in a housecoat.

"That's terrific," she smiled. "I don't think I've had canned peaches since I left Stockholm."

It was a nice gift, Martin thought. Canned peaches, he mused. In Israel, it was almost indulgent to spend money on such things.

And yet, it seemed a strange gift, an unusual offering. There it sat in Britta's lap, supported lightly by her pale-white fingers.

"Thank you, Frank," Britta murmured.

"And how are you two doing?" Frank asked, sitting on the other cot beside Martin.

"We're fine," Britta smiled.

Frank hesitated before forming the next sentence. He looked shy, and just a bit embarrassed.

"Did everything go okay?" he enquired.

Britta lowered her eyes. Her fingers caressed the can of peaches.

"Yes," she nodded. Her reply was just barely audible.

Frank changed the subject, trying to sound cheerful.

"Oh, by the way, I saw Lupo the other day. He was asking about you. They really miss you down at the bar. I've been in there a few times—just to have a beer and shoot the breeze. They all wanted to know when you were coming back."

Frank chuckled to himself.

"It looks like you have a lot of admirers down there."

Britta raised her head and her face and hair caught the sunlight streaming into the room. She had a smile on her face, and her skin was glowing.

Pains were shooting through Martin's chest—guilt and remorse. He made up his mind never to enter Lupo's again. He would have to meet Britta outside at closing time. The idea of facing Lupo and his friends sent shudders through him.

Frank was beginning to feel uneasy. He shifted his weight back and forth on the cot.

"Well, I don't want to overstay my welcome. Just wanted to drop by and say hello. Just see how you were doing."

He patted Martin on the back.

"Good to see you, old buddy."

"Good to see you, Frank," Martin murmured. The words caught in his throat. The sounds came out raspy and broken.

"Thanks again for the peaches," Britta smiled up at him, as Frank stood by the door.

For a second, Martin thought that Frank was going to cross the room and kiss her on the forehead. Instead, he rocked and swayed, and opened the door.

"Be good," he said, and he left the room quickly.

For a few minutes, there was absolute silence in the room. Britta gazed at the can in her lap. Martin stared at the floor. Finally, he had the urge to speak.

"What a great guy he is," Martin blurted.

Britta nodded.

"I think that Norwegian girl was crazy," she said. There was a heavy tone to her voice. A feeling of regret.

Silence crept in again between them. Through the window Martin could see the sun beginning to set near the Valley of the Cross. It was huge, fiery, and red. Slowly it was going down like a huge tear rolling down someone's cheek.

CHAPTER 25

Another Chance

About a week later, Britta moved back to the laundry room. She began working again at Lupo's. As usual, Martin made his way to the Y.M.C.A. every evening and taught his lessons in conversational English.

The routine of their two existences started up once more, almost the same as before, as if nothing had happened.

On a Friday morning, another bright chilly day, Martin left the laundry room early and just walked along the streets. Yes, they were both working, he thought, life was going on, but something was missing. Inside, he felt a vacuum, an empty region that was always cold and barren. He gazed at the blue sky. He shuffled his feet on the sidewalk.

Suddenly, he felt tired of everything—his job, the country, the people passing him in the street. It had been a long time since he had seen his mother and father in Ramat Aviv. How were they getting along?—he wondered. How was his father's back, his business, his nerves? How was Darrell doing? Was he walking yet? Was he growing chubbier, rounder, more lovable?

During Britta's trouble, he had avoided thinking about them altogether. It was simply too painful. What would they think of what he had put her through, this lovely soft girl from Sweden? Certainly they would've been shocked, he mused.

In the past, he had told them about his adventures with a certain pride in his voice. This, however, was different. It was not something he wanted to shout from the rooftops. He wanted, if possible, to forget it completely, to sweep it away.

Why not, he thought, take Britta to Tel Aviv to meet his parents? Not long ago he'd promised her that very thing. In the sunlight as he walked down King George Road, the idea began to grow and develop. Yes, it wasn't a bad idea. He had never introduced any of his girlfriends to his parents, and certainly never brought one home.

He was beginning to get excited now, and the sunlight felt warm and refreshing on his cheeks. It would be good for Britta, he dreamed, perhaps it would even repair the rift and emptiness he felt inside. And Britta too was probably feeling empty and cold. How could she get any satisfaction out of her job now?—in dingy Lupo's night after night. She knew the records by heart: the heavy, sentimental Eastern European love-dirges.

Yes, he thought with growing excitement, he wanted to take her to his parents' home. He wanted her to taste some of his mother's cooking, to meet his father, and to see Darrell. It could change things between them, he hoped and dreamed. Perhaps that was what was missing all along. Perhaps that was the reason for their loneliness.

I do love her, he thought. He no longer had doubts about the meaning of the word. Britta was Britta, and he loved her, it was as simple as that. When he thought about her, his chest tingled warmly. He could see her face, the shy way she held her mouth, her blue eyes, dreamy-looking, tired at times, and her full lips. Maybe they would get a whole new feeling for their relationship just by going there. It would be wonderful, he thought, if the visit would patch things up between them, and give their love a brand-new life. Perhaps they would return and start everything again on a fresh basis.

He felt hopeful on King George Road. It was a beautiful day, he hummed to himself. Sunny and warm, cool and invigorating. His chest was warm, yet his skin was cool from the breeze.

He decided to go back immediately while he was feeling so positive, and suggest the trip to Britta.

"Look, we can go tomorrow," he said to her in the laundry room. "We can go by *sherut*. I'm sure they run on Saturdays. I know you'll enjoy it, Britta. Mom's a great cook, and you'll probably love my father—most women do."

Britta gazed up at him from the cot.

"Do you think they'll like me?"

"Of course they will. They'll treat you just like a member of the family. Just wait till you meet my mother—I know she's going to find you attractive."

"And your father?"

"Oh, don't worry about him. He's a great guy. We're very close, you know, Britta. Well, how about it? You'll be able to see Darrell too."

"Okay," Britta nodded.

"That's great," Martin said, shaking his head up and down. "I just want to get out of this town for a while. Even Mrs. Shoshannah's giving me trouble. I don't know what's got into her. About a day ago, my light-bulb burnt out, and I asked her for a new one. She shook her head and started getting angry—over a stupid light-bulb! And then later, I heard her yelling and screaming and telling Larry that I was a Nazi."

"Maybe she was mad about me being there those days," Britta suggested.

Martin shook his head, a bewildered expression on his face.

"I don't know," he stammered. "At one time, she was all hot about me getting a girlfriend. And you're the only one I've ever taken there. I don't know what's wrong with the old bitch. Maybe she's going a bit senile."

"Do you think she knew about my operation?"

Martin frowned and shook his head.

"It's hard to say. Unless Jesse told her. Anyway, let's just forget it. I think I'll try to get another room."

Britta reached out and touched his fingers, caressing them warmly. He bent down and kissed her on the forehead. His eyes were closed and he was thinking about his parents, the familiar living-room, and the mahogany dining-room table where they would soon all be gathered together to enjoy one of his mother's tasty meals.

*   *   *

That evening when Britta was alone, she stood before the mirror in the cramped room. She wished there was more light in the room so that she could get a better look at herself. I should clean that glass, she thought. The mirror was smudged with powder prints and dust.

She stood there naked, gazing at her body—the round hill of her belly, the small drooping breasts, the sturdy legs. Her legs, she thought, were almost too thick around her thighs. She leaned her head forward to get a better look at her face. Was it still a young face—she wondered—or did it show, the tiredness she was feeling inside? How old she felt at times, like one of those wrinkled ladies in the market. Would Martin's mother like her and find her attractive?

Hesitantly, she moved her hand to her belly, and began to massage it. In there, she thought, that's where he shoved his instruments and knives. She could remember the morning vividly—the grey-blue eyes staring down at her.

"I'm not going to put you to sleep, Miss Lystrom," he intoned above her. "I just don't believe in it. I only do it in extreme cases. I'll use a local anesthetic—is that okay with you?"

"Yes," she had replied. And she thought to herself—just get it over with, do it, do what you have to do, and let me out of here.

She hadn't felt too much pain, but she could feel the pressure of the instruments against her bare flesh. The doctor chattered on during the whole thing. She was getting sick of his voice.

"Believe me, Miss Lystrom. I don't enjoy this type of thing. I'd much rather see you young girls married and settled down. But who knows—maybe I'm preventing a lot of unhappiness. I do what I have to, the thing I do well—what more can be said? And believe me, Miss Lystrom, I do it well."

Britta patted her belly, massaged it, stood in front of the mirror, and gazed at the tuft of blond hair between her legs. It almost looks like a nest, she thought to herself, a nest of straw and withered grass. She remembered the conversation with Dr. Bluestein, just before the operation.

"Doctor," she said hesitantly, trying to form her words, and not let them get away from her. She didn't want to break down in front of him. "Is there any chance that I won't be able to have children again? I've heard that it can happen."

"I won't lie to you," he said, screwing up his mouth tightly. "It happens in about fifteen per cent of cases. But those are usually older women. And of course, in cases where it's left to the fourth or fifth month. But you're young, Miss Lystrom, young and healthy, and we've caught it at the best possible time. I won't promise you the world, young lady, but I personally believe you will bear children."

Standing in front of the mirror, Britta could still hear his voice. It had a German accent. It was a monotonous voice that droned on and on.

She cupped her belly gently. If only I could see inside, she thought, below the skin. If only I could tell for sure that everything was okay.

When she had returned to Dr. Bluestein three days after the operation, he had examined her thoroughly.

"Everything looks fine," he had reassured. "The uterus, the womb, everything."

But he was only human, she thought. How could he know for certain—with his instruments and lights and machines? He couldn't see into the darkness beneath the layers of skin any better than she could. Deep down inside, that was where the truth was hiding.

She tried to smile at herself in the mirror. It was an effort. It came out more like a grimace, like an infant experiencing gas-pains. Come on, she encouraged herself, smile. How could she go to Martin's family looking old and haggard, nervous and drawn? That would ruin everything.

She looked at her belly again. There's only one way to tell, she said to herself. She thought of Martin again. How nervous he looked, the last couple of days. He couldn't stand still for a minute, always pacing up and down. It was as if something was chasing him, and he had to keep moving out of its reach. He just had to stay a step ahead of it. How she wished she could figure the whole thing out. What did he really want? She was sure family life would be good for him. And she still loved him, even after what had happened.

A picture formed in her mind—a new Martin sitting in an armchair. He had aged slightly, he had even gotten slightly pudgy in the cheeks. But his face looked softer, more relaxed. His eyes didn't have that nervous, haunted look. And she saw a child playing on the floor near his feet, a small gurgling toddler. He bent down and chucked the chubby child under the chin. She could see herself coming into the room. She looked almost radiant. She had aged, but there was a more mature beauty to her face. She was perfumed, glowing, smiling—she was wearing a dress and passing him a cup of coffee.

"Are you happy, Martin?" she was asking.

He smiled up at her.

"Yes, happier than I've been in my whole life."

Tears were coming to her eyes. She couldn't hold them back any longer. Now she looked like a blur in the mirror, all her features running together.

Memories of Stockholm began to swirl in her mind. Soon it would be Christmas, she thought, and she would probably spend it in Israel. It would be the first Christmas away from home. Something good just had to happen before December. How could she spend Christmas alone?

She remembered her father talking to her on the day before she left for Israel.

"So, you're off tomorrow, missy," he said with a twinkle in his grey eyes.

"Yes, Dad."

"And you're going to try one of those farms in Israel?"

"Yes," she nodded again.

She wanted him to kiss her before she left, to kiss her warmly. But she knew it wasn't going to happen and her chest ached.

"Take care of yourself," he added. He bent down and brushed his lips against her forehead.

She wanted to throw her arms around him, and force him close. She wanted to hug him until she found the hidden heat of his being. Instead, she kissed him back on the tip of his chin.

In the mirror her body looked like it was shimmering. Stockholm seemed a million miles away, a settlement on another planet. She imagined Martin and her father side by side. What a contrast! Her father long and lean, impeccably dressed, his features fine and chiseled. And Martin looked so soft and warm, a bit rough in comparison.

Why didn't Martin kiss her more often? She knew he had that warmth inside him. Why did he guard it so much, why did he keep it hidden? Why did he always back away at the last minute? Everything would be perfect—all he had to do was let it out, bathe her with his warmth.

She wanted things to change between them. Just give it another chance, she thought.

She glanced in the mirror again. She was beginning to feel chilly, standing in the middle of the room without a stitch of clothes on. Something in her life had to be resolved by Christmas. It just had to. She turned from the mirror, and began dressing.

*   *   *

The weekend in Tel Aviv came and went quickly. Martin remembered sitting in the living room surrounded by his family. Across the room, Britta was sitting on the sofa, holding Darrell in her lap. She was bouncing him on her knee.

He couldn't get over how good she looked. Her blue eyes sparkled. Her skin was glowing. Who could've imagined what she went through just a week or so before? The transformation shocked Martin, but it made him feel good. No, he thought, as he watched her bounce Darrell up and down, no, he hadn't destroyed her. There she was—Britta, twenty-three, still beautiful, still alive, still hopeful. What would it be like, he wondered, if they were in their own living room together, and instead of Darrell, Britta was hugging their own son, their own flesh and blood?

"Things are going pretty good in Sweden these days," he could hear his father saying. "I understand they have a very stable living standard."

Britta flashed a smile across the room at Mr. Kanner. It was a quick, intense smile.

"It's very middle class. Yes, you might say people are happy."

Martin grinned at Britta's quick reply. It sent a warmth plunging down into his stomach. He was beaming.

"Yes, middle class," his father said somberly. "Don't tell me you're one of these rebel-artists like my son here."

"No," Britta beamed, kissing Darrell on the cheek. "Actually I'm a very simple person. Give me a warm house, and good friends, and I'm satisfied."

Martin was surprised at how withdrawn his father had become. It seemed that the more Britta laughed and smiled and hugged Darrell, the heavier his father was becoming. Soon he picked up a copy of Time and began reading it.

"What a beautiful baby," Britta laughed. "Did Martin look like this? I can just see him."

Dahlia reached over and patted Darrell on the head. The back of her hand brushed Britta's chin.

"Martin was a very unusual baby. Almost too good to be true. He was extremely quiet."

Britta glanced at Martin. Debrah was sitting on the sofa beside her mother. Dahlia and Debrah were gazing at Britta. They seemed fascinated by her creamy complexion and blond hair.

"I wish he were mine," Britta whispered to both of them. "He's just so lovable. He just looks at me with those big brown eyes and I almost melt."

His mother nudged closer to Britta, and Debrah wriggled closer to her mother.

"Oh yes, that's Martin all over again," Dahlia smiled.

Martin couldn't take his eyes off Britta and Darrell, his sister and mother—the four of them on the sofa together.

And Martin's mind was whirling. Before they took the trip, he thought Britta and his father would talk a lot more than they were doing. He hadn't imagined his father getting quite so quiet. From time to time, he could hear the pages on the magazine rustle.

"Can I steal you?" Britta was asking Darrell. "Do you think I could take you back to Jerusalem with us?"

Darrell gurgled and clapped his hands together.

Those were the main impressions he retained from the weekend. Britta was undoubtedly the center of attention. Darrell looked absolutely right on her knee. He seemed to belong there, taking his horsey rides.

He had never seen his father so uncommunicative and withdrawn. At the beginning, his wit was as sharp as usual, but after a few hours, it petered out. Martin talked with him very little. Attention was focused on Darrell, Britta and his mother.

"You seem to be enjoying yourself, Martin," his mother said, glancing over at him. "What are you thinking about?"

Martin realized that he had been sitting there for almost half an hour. He hadn't said very much, but he could feel himself smiling.

"Oh, just dreaming," he replied. "Just taking it easy."

"Doesn't he look happy, Jake?" his mother asked.

Jake grunted his assent. He glanced over the top of the magazine for a second, then turned his eyes back down. What was wrong with him?—Martin wondered. He glanced over at his father and he could see the skin moving up and down near his ear. He was grinding his teeth together.

On Sunday morning, they said their goodbyes and took the bus down to the depot.

"What a nice family you have," Britta smiled on the bus. She was half-turned to the window. Soon they would be back in Jerusalem. "I can't get over your mother. She looks so young. I think she could pass for thirty-two if she wanted to."

Martin was pleased, but he wanted to know Britta's feelings about his father. He asked her quietly, trying not to make it sound like a big issue.

"He seems like a nice man," Britta said, tapping her knuckles against the window. "I wish he had said more, though. You told me so much about him, Martin. Actually I was a bit disappointed. Maybe he felt a little hemmed in or something."

"Yeah, that could be," Martin nodded. He felt puzzled himself. "Usually we're yakking at each other all the time. And he has a good sense of humor. Maybe he had business on his mind. Things haven't been going that great for him."

They both became quiet. The flatlands swished past. The farms, the orange groves, the vineyards. The bus climbed the curved road to Jerusalem. They both gazed at the rusty tanks by the roadside. The air as usual got cooler as they neared the city.

*　　*　　*

About a week later, they both changed rooms. Britta had become tired of the laundry room. It was just too small, and it seemed to reek of bad memories—the arguments with Martin. They had had good times together there, but the arguments seemed to coat everything: the concrete floor, the walls, and the ceiling.

Martin felt he could no longer stay in the stone cottage. The tension between Mrs. Shoshannah and himself increased. Every time he saw her, she had a scowl on her face. Why don't you leave, she seemed to be saying with her round hard eyes. He decided to look for another place.

On King George Road he met Jesse.

"Guess what?" Jesse gleamed. "Peter's getting married."

"You're kidding. To Bonita?"

"Yes," Jesse nodded. "He's going to do it. And they're going back to Canada together."

"God, that was quick!" Martin said, shaking his head. "How long has he known her—a couple of months?"

"If that," Jesse said with a quick shrug of his shoulders.

Martin stood there thinking about Bonita and Peter together. They were both fine-looking people. Bonita was a sabra. She had long black hair and eyes that flashed brightly. She was a dancer, and her legs looked long and lithe. She had small breasts and a boyish body.

He remembered Peter telling him about meeting her on the campus of the Hebrew University.

"I was in a funny mood that day," Peter grinned. "She was standing by the wishing well. I just went up to her and said, 'Boy, I'd like to fuck you.' It sounds pretty coarse, but I was so sick of beating around the bush with these broads. Do you know what she said? She looked me right in the eye. She said, 'I'd like to fuck you too.' Martin, it almost blew my brains out. I could've dropped right there on the spot."

Excitement and pleasure choked together in Martin's throat.

"Wow! It's just so bloody straightforward. That's fantastic, Peter."

Peter shook his head back and forth, as if he too had a hard time believing it had actually happened that way.

"She's a tremendous person, Martin. She can dance, paint. She even does a little writing. I want you to show her some of your stuff some day . . . "

About a week later, Peter introduced him to Bonita. She lived up to Peter's enthusiasm. Her whole face seemed charged with vitality.

"I'm going to miss that guy," Jesse said, jerking Martin out of his remembering. "When he goes, this place just won't be the same."

Jesse hunched his shoulders again.

"I hope he's doing the right thing," Jesse continued. "He's only twenty-five. It seems awfully young to get hitched. And it happened so fast."

Jesse hesitated. He seemed to be thinking, pondering over something.

"What do you really think about it, Martin? I mean this whole marriage business. Do you think it'll be good for him?"

Martin didn't have a quick reply. He tried to think of Peter, what kind of person he was. He tried to consider the whole thing in an objective manner. He was almost positive he couldn't take that step himself. Yet Peter *was* three years older. He was a different person.

"I don't really know for sure, Jesse. Who can? I don't know what's going on in Peter's head. But I have this feeling about it. It just seems that he's taking a step ahead. I guess he's making a real commitment, that's all."

Jesse pursed his lips together.

"Well, I hope you're right. I'd hate to see the guy make any wrong moves."

Was he right?—Martin wondered. He wasn't sure himself about the words he had just uttered. Was he just trying to reassure Jesse and himself? Was he just being hopeful, looking for something positive and meaningful in someone else's life?

The conversation ended between them. Jesse had to go to work down at the translation bureau. He walked away slowly with his hands in his pockets. Martin watched him. His shoulders looked more hunched than usual. It seemed that he was carrying a weight on his back.

Martin decided to go visit Peter on the Street of the Prophets.

When he arrived, Peter was alone, sitting on his bed, reading a thin volume of philosophy. It was a hard-cover edition.

"Congratulations," Martin smiled, extending a hand. "Jesse just told me the news."

Peter beamed. He placed the book gently on the floor.

"And you're going back to Canada. When do you think that will be?"

"Two weeks, Martin."

"Two weeks!" Martin repeated, amazed. "Now we see you, now we don't. And Bonita's going with you?"

Peter crooked his knee and began massaging it.

"I want to get back and get settled. I'll probably start classes at U. of T. in January. We'll be living with my parents for a while."

Martin lowered his head. He could feel a nostalgia mixed with sadness sweep over him. Peter was one of his closest friends in Jerusalem. When he left, a piece of his life would be broken off. Jesse, he knew, was taking it a lot harder. Jesse and Peter had been seeing each other on almost a daily basis for three or four years.

"Fuck, this place isn't going to be the same, Stoneman."

Peter gazed at the ceiling. His face was becoming contemplative and smooth.

"I really feel I need a change, Martin. It's hard to explain. I feel like I'm part of this city. Not the country actually, but Jerusalem. I feel I could just go along here ad infinitum as I've been doing. But that scares me a bit. It's like a dream I didn't want to wake up from. Yet, there's just something here that's not completely real for me. Maybe I'm hooked on the snow back home—something stupid like that. Anyway, it's been good here while it lasted."

Peter's words sent a rush of remembrance sweeping over Martin. As he spoke, Martin could see Toronto, the corner of Bathurst and Eglinton in winter. His feet were slipping on the ice. The wind was pushing through a tunnel. The trucks were grinding the snow into slush, and he could hear their motors on the concrete walls of the underpass.

"I think I know what you mean," Martin said, letting out a long sigh. "Sometimes I think I've been over here too long myself. You get kind of out of touch."

Peter nodded. His eyes looked calm, almost determined.

"I know I won't be here forever," Martin continued. "I just have to find the right time to leave. Does that make any sense to you?"

Peter smiled warmly. He was gazing affectionately at Martin, caressing him with his eyes. And suddenly, Martin could see Jesse walking down to the translation bureau. He was shuffling along, head bent.

"Do you think Jesse will ever leave?" Martin asked.

Peter grinned.

"Oh, you know Jesse. He's been talking about it for years. Going to California, living by the sea. He might surprise me, Martin, but I don't think he's going to make the move. It's different for him. We're going back to something we know, something we grew up with. What the hell does Jesse know about California?"

Martin had to agree with Peter. He couldn't imagine Jesse in San Francisco or in Toronto. It was hard to imagine him in any other place but Jerusalem. In fact, he travelled very little inside Israel. Perhaps once or twice a year he would go to Tel Aviv, or Tiberias. But that was it.

"I think you're right, Peter," Martin said, furrows beginning to line his forehead. "You know, he's really going to miss you. He was very quiet about it this morning."

Peter glanced down at the book lying on the floor.

"He's been a bloody important part of my life," Peter murmured.

"When I first met him, I was just a kid. He opened up a lot of things for me."

Peter hesitated.

"But recently, Martin, to be truthful, we haven't been as close. I don't know what it is. Jesse's pretty set in his ways."

Martin was beginning to feel warmer towards Peter. He had never heard him talk so candidly about Jesse before. And there was a slight guilt in Martin—a feeling that they might be betraying their mutual friend. But inside, he felt relieved. He had noticed these things about Jesse, but he'd never had anyone to share it with. It seemed that Jesse was no longer saying new things. Peter was right. He could hear Jesse's voice—"The more things change, the more they are the same." That was one of his favorite quotes. But how did it help to repeat it over and over again?

Martin gazed at the stone floor.

"I've noticed that too," Martin said forlornly. "I guess he's satisfied with the things he's doing. He's got his work, and his reading. I don't like to judge the guy."

The atmosphere was beginning to get heavy and thick in the room.

It was almost a relief when the door swung open and Bonita appeared. She came into the room quickly. Martin had seen her enter this way before. She came in as if she had just stepped out of a hurricane. Her black eyes were flashing, and as usual, she was excited.

"What a beautiful day! I was just down on the square. You guys should go out for a while. It's really refreshing."

She danced over to Peter and threw her arms around him. She was wearing black slacks and a red cape. She threw the cape over Peter's head.

"Now I've got you," she laughed.

They began kissing each other in front of Martin. It always embarrassed him a bit to see this display. He didn't know where to look or what to do with his hands. Yet, it was something he yearned to do himself with Britta—to kiss her in the street, to even fondle her. But he always held back and only showed his affection when they were absolutely alone with the doors closed.

"How are you, Martin?" Bonita asked between kisses, glancing over her shoulder. "Did you hear the good news? We're going to

Canada together. As soon as I get there I'm going to make a snow-man. I swear it. And I'm going to throw ice down Peter's neck, just like this."

Bonita plunged her hands down the back of his shirt, making him squirm.

There was something Martin liked about their playfulness. He was wishing he could be the same way with Britta. And then he thought —perhaps they were that way together in the beginning when Britta used to run through the streets at two in the morning. "I'm a blade of grass!" she shouted. He could still see her in white slacks and top down by Zion Square.

After a minute or so, Bonita excused herself, left the room, and went downstairs to use the washroom. It was situated off the bal-cony, just beside the landlady's apartment.

"Peter," Martin said softly, "I've gotta get out of that room. Have you promised yours to anyone?"

Peter smiled benevolently and shook his head.

"I'd like you to have this room, Martin. I was just thinking about it last night. We have to keep the tradition going, don't we?"

Martin remembered that the room had always been passed down from friend to friend. It had a special significance to him because of this. He glanced around the room. His gaze fell on the bed, the purple-cloth-covered coffee table, and Picasso's Boy with Pipe on the wall behind him.

The furnishings were Peter's. Without them, the room would look cold and bare.

"Are you going to sell the furniture?"

Peter shook his head.

"No, I thought about that too. You can have everything, Martin— the bed, the dresser, even the coffee table."

"That's fine," Martin smiled. "I just don't have the money to buy that stuff."

There was one thing that Peter hadn't mentioned. Martin was hesitant about bringing it up. Peter was already being very generous.

"Peter, I hate to ask you, but can you leave that Picasso print?"

"The Boy with Pipe?" he grinned. "Sure, you can have it, Martin. It goes with the room. You've gotten attached to that painting, haven't you?"

Martin grinned back at him.

The room, he thought, might be bearable now, with Peter's things still in it. It was a beautiful room, but whenever Martin had thought about sleeping there alone, a cold feeling swept through him. He knew at night that the wind, especially the winter wind, would rush under the door, and rattle through the cracks at the windowsill. Now, with the rose-and-blue Picasso, the coffee table, and perhaps a candle or two, he would be able to bed down comfortably.

It would be different, he thought, from living at Mrs. Shoshannah's. In the stone cottage he was living with a family. Here, the room was self-contained. He wouldn't hear any familiar footsteps padding along the floors—only the wind, and the branches of trees groaning.

Martin got up, and shook hands once again with Peter.

"I'll probably see you again before you leave."

"Sure," Peter nodded. "I'll tell the landlady you'll be taking the room."

Martin gazed at Peter's face. He was looking at Peter as if he might not ever see him again.

On the way out, he didn't run into Bonita. The wind was blowing hard, and sunlight was flashing off the leaves as they spun.

Britta's new room was also self-contained. It had its own washroom and small stove. It was darker in atmosphere than the laundry room, but generally an improvement.

Martin spent a lot of time there with her. He found himself wishing that there was more light. A single bare bulb dangled from the ceiling. There was no other source of light—no lamps or wall-fixtures.

One evening, about a week after visiting his parents, they were lying in bed, huddled closely to keep warm. Britta was wearing a cotton nightie, and Martin was naked. He pulled the covers over his ears. He wrapped himself around her, trying to get warmed up from her body heat.

Martin was thinking about Peter and Jesse, his two best friends. Soon, Peter would be gone. And Jesse, what was happening between him and Jesse? They talked to each other less and less. There seemed to be little to say when they got together. Jesse would ask about Britta, how she was doing, etc. Martin would ask Jesse about his job. And that would be the extent of it. What a difference, he thought, from two years ago when they first met. He remembered the marathon conversations they had together—how they would talk excitedly all through the night, and they wouldn't quit until the sun was high in the sky.

Once in a while, a tremendous feeling of loneliness attacked him. He was alone, he thought. Who did he really have but Britta? He nestled his head into her armpit.

Britta was also feeling sad. She couldn't get Martin's brother out of her mind. How warm she had felt with him on her knee—warm and secure and happy. What was she doing in this country?—she wondered. Soon it would be Christmas, and she was thousands of miles from home. She imagined her mother shopping in downtown Stockholm. She could hear bells ringing. She could see her father sitting in an armchair near the tree. He was smoking a pipe. She could see it so clearly—his face lean, almost rugged, but his eyes were gentle. The little boy in him, she thought, always came out in his eyes, and sometimes, in the way he would smile.

She could feel Martin hugging her. It was so intense, the way he was doing it, pushing his head into her armpit, burrowing into her warmth. What did he really want?—she wondered. What would really make him happy, and satisfy the both of them?

"You're not feeling good, are you?" Britta whispered, hugging him closer.

"I feel rotten," he admitted.

"I know," she said, rocking him in her arms. "I can always tell."

Martin could smell her skin beneath the nightie.

"Peter Stoneman's leaving the country. He's going back to Canada."

"That's too bad," Britta whispered.

She kept rocking him, hugging him, drawing him closer.

"Martin," she said softly, "I want to make a baby with you. It would be different this time. This time it wouldn't be an accident. It would be something we planned, something we did because we love each other. It was so stupid before. The safe broke. The diaphragm didn't work. How could we feel right about it? That's no way to start a family together. I want us to do it in the open this time . . . with both of us knowing exactly what we're doing."

Her words seemed to be dripping softly into him. They were making him feel warm, and closer to her. He found it hard to believe that this was happening. Perhaps, he thought, that was what he really wanted all along—Britta and a family. A cozy room with all of them together. She seemed to be tapping into his hidden wishes.

"You make it sound so good," he whispered into her armpit. "And yet, it frightens me a bit."

"Of course it does. It's not a little step that you'd be taking. It's a big responsibility, Martin."

He could feel his blood beginning to pulse and beat. His head was beginning to feel dizzy. And yet his body was getting warmed. The center of his chest was heating up, and his insides were turning to liquid.

When the next words came out, he almost found it hard to believe that he had spoken them.

"Britta, let's do it, let's make a child together."

He could hear her laughing gently above him. She was squeezing him tighter and rocking him in her arms.

How deep Britta felt that night when they made love without taking precautions. In the past, she had often felt stiff. That evening, her vagina was a warm well of feeling wrapped around him. Deeper and deeper, he was plunging and falling into her. There seemed no limit to how deep he could go. He imagined his seed travelling past the uterus, his million-headed seed seeking her ova.

Softly she hugged and rocked him, whispering in his ear. Oh Martin, it's going to be so good. Our baby, just think, our own baby. It was a lullaby she was singing and chanting against his cheek, an old lullaby.

Britta was giving her body as she had never given it before. She was laying it open for him, spreading it, making it a soft, enveloping tunnel of flesh. Please, she was thinking, as she wrapped her arms around his back, make me pregnant. Shoot your love into my womb.

He came with a long sigh on his mouth. As usual, he found it difficult to tell if Britta had had an orgasm. It annoyed him a bit. Why couldn't she really let him know, one way or the other?

Only five minutes after the lovemaking, his mind began to whir. His chest ached. What the hell am I doing? I must be crazy, he thought. Let her go through an abortion, and only a few weeks later, try to get her pregnant again. He shook his head in the darkness. What the fuckin' Jesus am I trying to prove?

He was angry with himself. He decided there and then that he would never do it again, enter her with his bare flesh.

About two weeks later, Britta was late with her period. He couldn't believe it was happening. Not again, he shuddered. And this time, there would be no escape. It would mean marriage. He was sure of that. To even think about another abortion made him feel sick.

Two or three days passed, and Britta didn't get her period. He could feel himself slipping into a depression. Again, his cheeks were getting wooden. He wanted to go to sleep forever and forget. What kind of fuckin' animal am I?—to do such a thing.

Britta came back to her room about seven o'clock one evening. Martin was waiting for her, sitting on the bed, reading a book of poetry. Her head was bent. And her face looked drained of color. She took off her sweater and laid it over the chair.

"My period came today, Martin. You'll probably be happy to hear that."

Oxygen and joy shot to his head. He couldn't control himself. He jumped off the bed and began dancing around the room. He clenched his hands together and raised them above his head.

"Oh, God, thank you, thank you, thank you. Oh Jesus, I was so scared."

He tried to embrace her and to kiss her. She turned her body away and her face.

"You don't have to be so demonstrative about it," she said bitterly. There was a harsh and sad quality to her voice.

"I'm happy," he shouted. He could no longer control what he was saying. "I'm sorry, Britta, but I'm so fucking happy. And you should be too. You didn't want to have another abortion, did you?"

And he crumpled up into a small ball, and fell down by the side of the bed. He buried his face in the blankets.

"Thank you, God. Oh, thank you."

He could hear Britta's footsteps on the stone floor. He could hear her words raining down on him.

"You know, Martin, I never realized till just now how scared you were. I wanted your baby so much, but now I'm relieved too. It wouldn't have worked. I can see that."

He hung on to the bed. He was drained—of feeling, of energy, of thoughts. They had all flowed out of him. He felt like a lifeless sack, but he was glad for this tired sensation.

"No, it wouldn't have worked," he whispered back.

Did the words even reach her?—he wondered. Or were they muffled completely in the blanket his lips were pressed against?

For the rest of the evening, they were lost in their own thoughts. Britta was trying to think of the future, but no clear image emerged. Again, Martin had the urge to go to Tel Aviv for a few days—just to change the scene. He felt he needed a change in atmosphere.

No clear image formed in Britta's mind. When she looked forward, the days seemed blank and cold, swirling in darkness.

"I'm going to Tel Aviv this weekend," he said. "I have a few things to do there."

What things? He didn't know himself, but he couldn't stand the thought of staying in their room with only the bare light bulb dangling down. And he was still not used to the idea of staying alone in the room on Street of the Prophets. He imagined Tel Aviv drenched in sunlight. It was bright, almost too bright, but at least it would give him a chance to clear his head.

What things?—Britta wondered. Why did he talk so vaguely at times? It was vague, yet when he said "things", his tone of voice gave them an aura of importance, almost necessity.

It was just as well, she thought. She needed time alone. How could they keep going on this way? Martin pulling in one direction, she in the opposite.

"It's just as well," she sighed, repeating her own thoughts. "I think we've been living too close together. After all, it is a small room."

Martin nodded his agreement.

CHAPTER 26

One Red Rose

That weekend he went back to Tel Aviv alone. He didn't know, himself, why exactly he was going there.

Early Friday evening, he was sitting in the living room with his father. His mother and sister were out, doing some last-minute shopping before the sabbath darkness fell. Darrell was sleeping peacefully in his parents' bedroom.

Why they began to reminisce together, he didn't know. But they began to talk about the old days in Halifax. They were talking about the various houses they had lived in—the first one on Macdonald Street, and the huge mansion they occupied on Bloomingdale Terrace when Martin was a teenager. It had fourteen rooms, and his father employed a man to look after the grounds.

"I need this place," his father used to say, walking around the grounds with Martin. "I need a place I can spread out in. A lot of people are going to say I'm crazy—that the upkeep's too expensive. Let them say what they want. What do you think of it, Martin?—it's gotta be one of the largest houses in the city. Do you think your old man's flipped his lid?"

In those days, Martin smiled at his father's antics. Why not have a huge house, he used to think to himself. If he can afford it, why not?

Just a year before, around the time of his bar mitzvah, his father had gone broke. They lived in a cramped apartment, an old building where the mice bred in the garbage sheds outside.

Just a year later, his father had made an amazing recovery.

"It's a great house, Dad," Martin had smiled back at his father.

"Of course it is," his father continued. "And do you know who lives across the street—in that house with the pillars? For Chrissakes, a bloody senator lives over there. No, this street has class. We've got some old established families for neighbours. I'll tell you, Martin old boy, we're living right at the top."

It was twilight in Ramat Aviv, not quite dark yet, and the light that filtered into the living room had a soft hue. His father continued talking and Martin was swimming in memories. Houses they had lived in, streets, old neighbours, childhood friends.

How it happened, he didn't know exactly, but they began talking about the maids that used to live in some of these houses and help his mother with the housework.

"Do you remember Sally Grant?" his father asked.

"Sure," Martin smiled, "on Robie Street."

Sally Grant. He had a vivid picture of her in his mind. He was nine years old and they were living in the south end of the city, across from a Catholic university. Sally was eighteen, a farm girl from the Annapolis Valley.

She used to play baseball out in the backyard with Martin and his sister. And Martin remembered the man she eventually married. He came to the house a couple of times when his parents were out. He was a tall man, as Martin remembered, and Sally had told them proudly that he was a minister.

"Didn't she marry a minister?" Martin asked, just to check up on his memory.

"That's right, a very fine guy. What the hell was his name anyway?"

His father rubbed his chin, trying to concentrate.

"What the hell was that guy's name? . . . It's just on the tip of my tongue. Anyway, he was a minister. In fact, your mother and I went to the wedding."

His father leaned back in the sofa. He slipped out a cigarette and lit it. The light was still soft in the room, but it was beginning to fall at strange angles. At times, Martin was getting an eerie feeling. He remembered nightmares he used to have on Robie Street, bogeymen and shadows curling themselves around his bed.

Martin noticed a peculiar smile that had crept into his father's face. His eyes began to dart blackly. It made Martin curious. He knew the smile well.

"What are you smiling about?" Martin asked, a frown creasing the skin on his face.

His father continued to grin, and he bobbed his foot up and down. He took a long drag from his cigarette and blew the smoke towards the ceiling.

"I've never told anybody about this—not a bloody soul. In fact, I don't know if I should tell you. But I guess you're old enough to understand."

His father's grin broadened.

"Okay, go ahead, tell me." Martin's voice sounded curious, but it was tinged, now, with a bit of annoyance.

"Well, it's not such a big deal," his father shrugged. "But before Sally Grant left to marry her minister friend, I fucked her."

Jake grinned directly into Martin's face, then turned his head away.

Martin was at a loss for words. What was he supposed to say?—he wondered. Congratulations, Dad? Did you really? Anything like that would have sounded foolish.

Why had his father even bothered telling him? It was years ago, Sally Grant and Robie Street. What did it have to do with anything?

It was getting darker in the living room. Soon, his mother and sister would arrive from their shopping.

The next day, in the afternoon, Martin found himself alone once again with his father. Martin had almost forgotten the conversation of the day before. Jake was talking about politics in a rather vague manner. Martin waited for an opportunity to change the subject.

Finally, there was a lull, as Jake repositioned himself on the sofa. His back was still giving him problems. Jake winced, trying to find a more comfortable spot.

"What did you think of Britta?" Martin finally managed to ask.

Jake frowned, then managed to smooth and calm his face.

"She seemed to be a pleasant young girl," he said non-committally.

"She's attractive, don't you think?"

His father frowned again.

"Yes . . ." he considered. "I wouldn't say she's a raving beauty, but she's attractive."

His father flashed a quick, knowing smile at Martin.

An anger began to slowly rise inside Martin. Didn't his father realize that she was important to him? How could he talk about her as if she were one girl in a long line-up? His father's coolness gnawed at his insides.

"She's a very nice person," Martin said, trying to make his father understand. The tone of his voice was strained.

Jake got up from the sofa and began pacing the room.

"I don't doubt that, Martin. But don't forget—I just met the girl. How can I really say anything? A month ago, I didn't know her any better than I know the Queen of England. What I'm trying to say is that she's a stranger."

Martin got up and began pacing the living room with his father. They were walking in opposite directions. Occasionally, Martin would stop, look at his father and say a few words.

"We've been through a lot together," Martin almost whispered. "I've even thought of marrying her."

Jake stuck his thumbs into his belt and continued to pace.

"And how did you think you would support her?"

"We could get by."

"Just live off the land," his father chuckled. "It's no joke, believe me, to bring up a family. I suppose you'd just throw your college plans out the window and get some hack job."

Martin slapped his own thigh. The skin burned under his trousers.

"It'll probably never happen," he said, with the words rasping out of his throat. "I think the whole thing's fucked up."

Jake stopped by the dining-room table. He stood there with his fingers grazing the mahogany surface. Martin was walking towards him. He stopped a few feet away.

"It's probably just as well," his father said coolly. "There'll be other girls. You'll meet somebody when you're ready to."

Martin could feel his anger seething just below the surface. How could he make him understand that Britta wasn't just another girl?

Martin glanced at his father. Again Jake had that peculiar smile on his face. Martin decided that he wasn't going to be drawn into it. He clenched his teeth together.

"Last year it was what's her name . . . Josephine, the psychic. The year before that, someone else. Christ, in two weeks, you could forget all about this Swedish girl, and be off with another. I know you, Martin."

It angered him that his father thought that he had all the answers. Martin stared at the floor and shook his head. He could feel his whole body trembling. Tears were beginning to well in his eyes. They were beginning to sting in the corners. He forced them back down. He wasn't going to break down in front of him.

"Britta had an abortion," he finally choked up.

For a second there was silence in the room. Martin was hoping that at last his father had understood.

There was a slight grin on his father's face when he looked up.

"Well," his father said, "you know what they say—girls that play must pay."

Jake's words stunned him. Then he began to feel his fists curl into tight knots. The heat of his anger jabbed at his insides. For the first time in his life, he wanted to smash his father in the face. He wanted to break his jaw and send him reeling across the table. If he says another word, Martin thought, just one more word, I'm going to smash him, and splatter his nose across his face.

Martin couldn't believe the feelings rushing through him—that he was actually on the brink of hitting his own father.

Jake, now, had a puzzled expression.

"That was a fuckin' stupid thing to say," Martin hissed. "It was stupid, do you understand—you fuckin' asshole! And if you say another word, I'm going to smash you."

Martin couldn't believe the words that were gushing from his mouth. He was completely out of control. His legs were shaking and his palms were clammy with sweat.

Jake backed away a foot. He lowered his head. He no longer had a grin on his face.

Martin stood there waiting, but his father wasn't speaking. Jake had a guilty expression around his mouth.

"Martin, it was stupid of me. I had no right . . . I'm sorry."

Martin wheeled around looking for his jacket, speaking at the same time.

"Just forget it. It's no use, just forget it—everything. There's no fucking use. I'm going out. I'll probably not be back tonight. Just tell Mom not to worry."

Jake made a motion towards Martin, just to place a hand on his shoulder—but he stifled it, and drew back.

Quickly, with his eyes burning and his whole body shaking uncontrollably, Martin grabbed his jacket and walked out the door. He walked towards the bus-stop, crying.

* * *

On Friday evening of the same weekend, Frank Laskey decided to walk up the hill and visit Martin and Britta. It had been over a month since he had seen them.

He had been trying to do some work on his M.A. thesis, but the words that came out seemed wooden and lifeless. He sat down at his typewriter, tapped at a few keys, got up, walked around, and sat down again.

His apartment seemed larger than usual, and cooler. It had an empty feeling, despite the familiar books on their shelves and the few plants he was cultivating.

The evening before, he had dreamed about Ingrid, the Norwegian girl he almost married. She was walking through the woods beckoning to him, laughing, tossing her head. He saw mountain peaks behind her, snow-clad—beautiful and ominous.

And he woke up not thinking about Ingrid, but of Britta.

Where was his life heading?—he wondered. Would he wind up in a basement apartment as Mr. Townley had, taking his lovers in on weekends and watching them shuffle off on Monday mornings?

In a few months he would be teaching full-time at the university, making a good salary by Israeli standards. He glanced up at the poster over his work desk. Che Guevara stared down at him, and the large letters burned into his mind. *Viva el 26 de Julio.* Was it all a cop-out, he wondered, this course in English literature—Walt Whitman, John Donne, Shakespeare? What did it really have to do with the workers' movement and the International?

Yet he felt tired. He walked into the bathroom and looked into the mirror. He was going bald, slowly it had started a few years back. The bare flesh was marching back over his forehead.

Staring into his own brown eyes, he tried to imagine a woman in his apartment, and a couple of kids prancing around, yelling, shouting, tossing toys at each other. And amid the turmoil, he could see Che staring at him. "My friend," he was saying, "viva la revolución."

What revolution?—he thought with a twist of irony in his mind. In '48 with the kibbutz movement, it looked like the whole country would swing to the left—kids brought up communally, working together, equals in every respect. Now, the Dizengoff existed. Israel had joined the world, and the Jews could boast of their very own pimps, hookers, and black marketeers. The Dizengoff—he had been there a few times, outdoor cafes that served creamy coffees in tapered glasses just as they did in Paris or Vienna. Burlesque shows. Striptease queens. Men in pointed shoes and striped three-piece suits. Was this what his friends died for in '48?

He walked back to the living room. Che was still staring out into the middle of the emptiness, his tam at a rakish angle, his eyes black and burning. "Viva, my friend, viva." Frank picked up a bottle of brandy that was sitting beside his typewriter. He gulped it back, the hot liquid scorching his throat and warming the lining of his gut.

He raised the bottle in Che's direction, downed a few more ounces. "I give you a toast, Che," he muttered through his wet lips. "To the women of the north." He drank again. And again. It was going to his head fast.

In the fresh air outside, he tried to sober up. The chill air was hitting his forehead, but his forehead felt wooden. He reached out and tapped it, remembering what a friend had told him once—you're not stoned until you can't feel your forehead. Yes, he thought, he could feel it, the skull-bones white and hard under the thin covering of skin.

At first he thought that nobody was in at Britta's new room. He hoped that Martin had given him the right address. The place looked dark. Just be there, he thought, I need some company, chaverim. Not a single light was glimmering through the curtains.

He knocked at the door, rapping his knuckles against the wood. Come on, Frank, he said to himself, that's much too loud, you could wake up a fucking corpse pounding like that. For Chrissakes, sober up.

Britta answered the door wearing a nightie and rubbing sleep from her eyes.

"I'm sorry," Frank said, backing away a step or two, "I didn't think anyone was in."

"That's okay," Britta answered, recognizing him and remembering the can of peaches at the same time. "Come in, I'll turn on a light, and put on a housecoat."

"Where's Martin?" Frank asked before he moved forward.

"He had to go to Tel Aviv. Come in, I'll make you a coffee."

The warmth inside the room wrapped itself around him. He could smell the heat of Britta's body, and the aroma of sleep. He sat down in an armchair beside Britta's bed and watched her spread a coverlet over the crumpled sheets.

He sank into the armchair. Waves of warmth rushed through his chest, and he could still feel the brandy burning inside him. He picked up a pencil from a small table beside the armchair and began rolling it between his fingers.

"When do you think Martin will be back?" he asked, watching Britta bend over the gas stove.

Britta was still wearing her long cotton nightgown that came down to her calves. She hadn't bothered putting on her housecoat. It was frayed anyway, she thought. For a second she remembered the laundry room and the landlord's son.

"I think he's gone until Sunday." She lit the stove and put on a pot of water. Her back was turned to Frank, but she could feel him watching her. It wasn't an unpleasant feeling. Ripples of warmth fell across her shoulders and travelled down her back and down her thighs.

"I feel a little funny about being here," he continued. "You know, I consider Martin a good friend."

Britta was silent. It was only a few minutes, but it seemed like hours before she said anything.

"Things haven't been going well between us, Frank. We just seem to want different things out of life. I want a family, and Martin's just scared to death of the idea."

Frank gave the pencil a few more turns between his fingers, and put it back on the table. He folded his hands and rested them on his stomach.

"I can't picture Martin married," Frank said, staring at his hands. "Not now. I think he has to swing around for awhile. Sometimes he gives the impression that he's a lot older than he really is. After all, he's only twenty or so. Maybe he's just trying too much at times."

Britta could feel her chest stinging and tears forcing themselves against her eyes. Her words came out muffled and a bit shaky.

"I think you're right, Frank. I really do. And I guess I've been pushing him . . . trying to make him into something he isn't. I'm just tired of trying. I guess it's just not fair to either of us."

Her back was still turned to him. The water was already in the pot, but she lingered by the stove, trying to get a grip on herself.

She liked the sound of Frank's voice. It had a deep, rich tone, a peaceful resonance that made her feel comfortable and secure. What he was saying seemed to make sense. Not just in Martin's case, but also in Jacob's. They were both three years younger than herself. Hadn't she just tried too much with both of them?

Britta walked across the room and sat down on the edge of the bed, facing Frank. She looked at his face and it seemed as if she had been looking at it for years—the high cheekbones that the light seemed to give a polished glow to, the dark intense eyes under thick brows, the mouth loose and gentle, but with a hidden strength to it. When he talked, a slip of saliva would collect in the corners of his lips. She was melting into his face, almost mesmerized by it. This, too, wasn't a bad feeling. It was like jumping into warm water and just allowing herself to sink to the bottom with the bubbles of warmth rushing past her ears.

Frank was beginning to feel a new strength surge through him, a sense of well-being that he hadn't experienced for over a year, not since Ingrid was with him. They were similar—Britta and Ingrid. It was the way Britta was looking at him. Ingrid would do the same thing occasionally, kind of look at him as if he were taller than he actually was. But the outlines of Ingrid's face had been harder, the bones almost jutting from her chin and cheekbones.

"What are you thinking about?" Britta finally asked.

"Oh, a girl I used to know."

Britta smiled, she could feel a stronger warmth course through her.

"The Norwegian girl?" she asked hopefully, bathing his face with her smile.

Frank nodded and began rubbing the palms of his hands along the arms of his chair. It was a rhythmic movement, and he was rocking slightly back and forth.

"Are you sorry you didn't marry her?"

Frank stared at the wall behind Britta. "It was my own bloody fault. She wanted me to, and I just kept fiddling around. I was just starting my M.A. and I guess I thought I might wreck it."

Britta was surprised herself at what she did next. It happened quickly, involuntarily, but there was something natural about it. She reached out, and put her hand on top of Frank's hand.

It had been a long time since Frank had been with a woman.

Britta's warmth travelled up his arm. He could feel it in his chest burning. His groin began to ache and tingle. He wanted her right there and then. He wanted to smother her with kisses, to stroke her breasts, to hold her close, to smell her body, to breathe in her hair.

But Martin kept pushing himself into his thoughts. He had a strange picture of Martin in his mind—his hair was wind-blown, his cheeks were flushed red, a slight chubbiness to them. Martin's expression was bewildered, and his shoulders were hunched as if he were protecting himself from an icy gale.

He put his free hand on top of Britta's, and pressed her hand tightly.

"God, I want you, Britta. But I keep thinking we're doing all of this behind Martin's back."

For a second Britta stiffened. She could feel her arms going rigid. And suddenly she felt that her whole body was composed of sticks. She turned her gaze away from Frank. She was beginning to cry, gently.

"Have you ever had something with another person, it's still there, but all the pieces are broken? You can remember what it was like in the beginning, and you still love what it used to be. He's still inside me, Frank, and I'm still inside him, but we can't help each other any more."

Frank nodded. His head felt heavy and tired.

Again he could feel the warmth from her hand travelling through him.

"Do you think we want the same things?" Britta asked.

Frank knew what Britta was talking about. It was as clear to his mind as if she had drawn a picture for him. She wanted to be settled, to be secure, not to be blown around any more from experience to experience. Didn't he want the same thing? Wasn't he sick of going back to the concrete walls of his Arab-style house? Wasn't he sick of walking along the street, looking hopefully into every female face for some response, some flicker of feeling and recognition? Wasn't he tired of the days marching and flashing by, and just a little scared of how fast they were disappearing? Wasn't he tired of going to bed alone and lying there coldly staring into the darkness?

"Do you think Martin will understand?" he asked, pressing her hand again. "I mean, really understand."

Britta moved her face closer, and grazed Frank's cheek with her lips. Then she drew back.

"You might think this sounds sentimental," she replied, "but I really believe that Martin loves both of us. He's talked a lot about you. He admires you, Frank, he really does."

Frank's face brightened and a smile formed. He could feel rivulets of warmth rushing up and down his chest. He shook his head back and forth as if he were a little surprised.

"I know he likes me, but I never knew he looked up to me in any way. You know what I mean—I've never really thought about it."

Frank moved his face closer, and Britta moved to meet his lips.

They made love that evening, and it seemed that a whole year of yearning, perhaps several years, was pouring out of Frank's body. The first time, he came too quickly, but later he began to settle into her warmth. It was as if he could feel every pore in her skin, and he was breathing in this person, a scent behind her ears, a different scent in the creases of her neck.

Britta was happy. Her whole body was glowing from the warmth of his hands. It was only after they had made love the first time that she realized they'd taken no precautions. Not a single word had been mentioned about pregnancy.

Frank left about nine in the morning to do a few hours' work. He came back around noon-hour with a gift. Britta unwrapped the crinkly tissue excitedly. It was a single red rose in a slim turquoise vase. She sniffed at it, danced around the small room, and threw her arms around Frank.

"Let's stay at my place tonight," he smiled. "I want you to get used to it."

Britta placed the rose on a small table. She was still wearing her cotton nightgown. She wrapped herself around him, clinging to him, pressing, it seemed, every inch of her body against his.

"I'm falling in love with you. Do you know that?" Britta asked, her words bubbling out, mixed with laughter and excitement.

They walked down to Frank's place together in the afternoon. It was a bright day and the sun seemed to be pouring down at them, going right through them.

"Can I put curtains up?" Britta teased, walking around the large living room. "And little chintzy things on your shelves. Do you think he would approve?"

Britta was looking up at the poster of Che Guevara and smiling. Frank glanced at the poster, just for a second, and kissed her on the back of the neck, burrowing his lips into her light, blond hair.

*   *   *

On the bus from Ramat Aviv to the center of Tel Aviv, Martin could see his father's face, a lewd grin stuck to it, and he could hear his words about girls playing and paying. Play, pay, play, pay, the huge rubber wheels slapped the rhythm against the pavement. If you play, you must pay. He could almost visualize his father's distorted picture of Britta—a lipsticked broad in the slums of Halifax wagging her finger wantonly at passers-by. Was that the image his father had gathered from their weekend visit, when Britta bounced Darrell on her knee? Impossible, Martin thought. For some reason his father had twisted it, pulled it out of shape.

He kept thinking of Sally Grant. Sally Grant and Britta Lystrom. Sally, freckled and fresh-skinned from the Annapolis Valley. Britta, blond and fair from the northern climes of Sweden. They were both floating through his mind, both girls smiling and dancing and talking. Between them, among them, and around them, Jake's blocky body moved.

He was glad to find Josephine at home. She answered the door with a familiar wrinkled smile on her face. Her eyes glimmered.

"You look tired," Josephine said rather seriously, sitting down on a chair opposite him. "And you look a bit worn out, and a bit older. I hope you don't mind me telling you, Martin."

She paused, looking into his face. She was searching for a reaction. Then she continued.

"Yet your face has a lot of character. And it's going to get better as you get older. It's just that kind of face."

Martin smiled. His insides were warming up.

"So . . . " Josephine continued. "Tell me what's been happening to you."

It was a difficult thing to do—to summarize the last six months for her. How could he ever convey it all? Steven, Britta, Gila, Peter, his father, the abortion, Lupo's. She would end up getting a bare schematic like those drawings that describe the guts of radios and television sets. A skeleton, a cold bony representation. Yet he wanted to tell her about it, to just tell it all to another person.

She questioned him about Gila—was he still seeing her? He described it quickly, too quickly. He was rushing forward, swamping her with words. And when he came to Britta, he found it very difficult to speak.

"Well, you are young," she interjected, "for babies and responsibilities like that . . . and you mean you actually tried again?"

Josephine shook her head and clucked her tongue.

"Oh Martin, I don't know what's going to become of you. What if she'd become pregnant again? I guess you never thought of that."

Martin lowered his head. He didn't want to meet her bright, inquisitive eyes. He had no way of explaining it to her. How could he? He hardly understood it himself—what he wanted, what he was trying to do.

"Are you still writing?" she asked. "I hope you haven't just thrown it all out the window. That would be a shame, Martin, it really would."

"I've done a few things," he nodded. "Some poems, and I've tried a couple of stories."

Josephine brightened when she heard that he was dabbling around with prose. She still read a great deal, Each month, she borrowed five or six books from the library, mostly novels.

"I read a good book the other day," she grinned. "It was written by one of your countrymen. A fellow called Lawrence Hart. Now what was the name of it? Oh, yes, I remember. *The Longest Swing*. It was one of the best books I've read in years. In fact, I went back and took out some of his poetry."

Josephine's words revived old memories in him. He was a bit surprised to hear that Lawrence Hart had written a novel. He never knew Hart during his days at McGill in Montreal, but he was good friends with a band of young Jewish writers who idolized Jake Manning, and considered Hart a spiritual offshoot.

"I think I still have the novel lying around. I must lend it to you."

In his mind Martin could see the snow packed high on Sherbrooke Street, and the huge stone portals of McGill that led to the Arts building. The street was filled with people wrapped in scarves and wearing floppy galoshes.

It all seemed miles away, years and aeons distant—Canada, Montreal, Halifax. Would he ever be able to pull himself away from Israel and go back? He wondered about it.

"Well, do you think you're going to marry her? You must know that much."

The question came at him, it seemed, out of nowhere. He was still buried in remembering: snow, snowflakes, bare trees in autumn, lecture halls, a certain Hungarian restaurant.

Martin shook his head. He felt dazed. His head felt wrapped in thick cotton gauze.

What was going to happen? All he could remember vividly was Britta giving him the news that her period had come. And then he saw himself leap from the bed, laughing, shouting, clapping his hands together. What a relief it had been.

"I'm not sure," he sighed, "but I think it was the last straw. For Britta, I mean. When I got so excited about her getting her period."

Josephine nodded knowingly, smiling to herself.

"I can appreciate that. It must've been a bit like pouring a bucket of ice-water over her."

Josephine lit a cigarette and dragged deeply.

"You know, Martin, I still haven't given up the idea myself. I'm going to have a baby yet. Husband or no husband. If I had been Britta, I'd never have agreed to an abortion. You could've gone your merry way. But . . . I guess that's the difference between me and her."

Martin could feel himself growing tense, a pressure building in his chest and head. The atmosphere in the room had become almost brittle. He wanted to change the subject, to forget about Britta and babies for a while.

"Hey," he said, trying to sound cheerful, "Jesse told me that he came up and saw you. What did you think of him anyway?"

Josephine was anything but enthusiastic. A sardonic smile twitched at the corners of her mouth.

"Jesse. Oh yes, Jesse. God, Martin, I don't know why you were so impressed by that guy. You had me all built up. I was really expecting someone special. What a let-down! He didn't have that much to say, and what he said was puerile, just plain adolescent crap! As far as I'm concerned, he's a little boy."

Martin sat there dazed. He hadn't expected this onslaught. He, too, recently had been having doubts about Jesse, but he never pushed it as far as Josephine was doing.

"It sounds almost like you didn't like him or something."

"You might say that," Josephine said curtly, her eyes flashing.

Martin remembered the conversation with Jesse at Pepe's a couple of months earlier.

"But you slept with him," Martin said, trying not to grin, and feeling bewildered at the same time.

Josephine looked shocked. Her eyes got larger, and they seemed to be burning with a mixture of disgust and hatred.

"I did what?!" she almost shouted. "Did he tell you that?"

Martin sat there with a puzzled look, and he nodded.

"You didn't?" he asked.

"Of course I didn't. That little pipsqueak liar. I wouldn't sleep with Jesse if he were the last man on earth. Listen, Martin—I draw the line somewhere. And Jesse's so far on the other side it isn't funny."

"He lied," Martin said, repeating the thought, as if this would help him come to grips with it.

He had a weird feeling inside him. It was as if something expensive and rare had been dropped on the floor and smashed beyond repair. And yet there was a queer sensation of relief.

He glanced at Josephine and he was surprised to see that she was quivering and on the brink of tears.

"That makes me so angry, Martin."

He reached out and lightly gripped her arm.

"I'm sorry. I didn't know. I never thought Jesse would lie about something like that."

"It was a lie," Josephine said. Her voice was quavering and trembling. "It was a goddamn mean little lie."

It was silent now between them. Martin stared at his feet. He tried to think about Jesse, but the picture he had of him was watery. It wouldn't stand still. In his mind Jesse's beard looked like strands of limp grass. His eyes were bulbous, big and gaping as a fish's. His features ran into one another: forehead with nose, cheekbone with chin.

Had anything Jesse told him been true? Was it all lie built on lie? —the dancing boys in Jerusalem, the girls, the whole bit about mysticism and the perennial philosophy. Some of it had to be true, Martin thought, it just had to.

This bothered him more than anything—not knowing what part was true and what was fabricated, and the proportion between them. Why did he make up that story about Josephine? How many others had he concocted? Martin was sure that Josephine was telling the truth. He had no doubts about that.

"I guess it comes as a shock to you," Josephine said. Her head was bent and she was staring blankly at the coffee table. Her voice sounded a bit calmer. "I know how much you believed in him."

Martin let out a sigh. It was filled with weariness.

"I don't know, Josephine. We haven't been so close recently, but I never expected something like this."

A short nervous laugh came out of Martin's chest.

"Oh Christ, let's forget about him for now," Josephine said in a high-pitched voice. "That's all we've been talking about—Britta and Jesse. Let's forget about them."

Josephine placed her hand on Martin's knee. She began rubbing it, and moved her hand slowly up his thigh.

Martin glanced out the window. The sky was bright as usual over Tel Aviv. And at the same time it was so blue it looked impenetrable. The concrete heads of buildings appeared jumbled. Building after building under a hard blue sky. What a mess, he thought. The city, the sky, the buildings—everything hard and mixed together. What a mess his feelings were in—everything jumbled together, nothing clear or defined. For a second he felt like screeching, just going completely crazy, just letting himself explode. He had felt that from time to time in Tel Aviv—that he had a bomb inside him. And that some day he would explode and blow himself and everything else to smithereens.

He shook his head wearily back and forth. How completely exhausted he felt! It seemed that all vitality was dripping out of him.

He could feel Josephine's tiny hand massaging his leg, creeping slowly towards his groin.

"Can we make love?" he asked. "I just feel I want to be close to you."

Josephine smiled. It was an old familiar smile. It looked like it could turn into tears at any moment.

They made love. It wasn't a great comfort to either of them, but it seemed to help. I've known this woman almost three years, Martin kept thinking as he kissed her eyelids. Josephine used to tell him that she believed they had a bond of friendship together that would never be destroyed. Martin hoped that she was right. He didn't want to feel that everything was changing, shattering, falling apart.

He spent the rest of the weekend at Josephine's. Late Sunday afternoon he went down to the bus depot and bought a ticket for Jerusalem. He used a pay-phone to let his parents know he was going back. Was he imagining it?—or did his father's voice sound just as tired and lifeless as his own?

* * *

It was dark when he got back to Jerusalem. He went directly to Britta's, wondering if anything would be different between them.

As soon as he got inside the room he could feel something unfamiliar. The room looked the same—the dangling light bulb, the small bed, Britta walking around in her nightgown. Yet he could feel something strange and altered in the surroundings.

Finally, he spotted one red rose in a slim vase.

"Where did you get that?" he asked immediately.

"A friend," Britta answered, turning her head away from him.

Her voice sounded heavy, almost mysterious. The word "friend" seemed to open up, spread out, become large, and almost dark in tone.

"A friend?" he repeated. "Did some man give you that, Britta?"

"It was just a friend," she said, lying down on top of the bed.

Martin started pacing around the room. He knew there was a lot more to it, and he wanted everything to come out. It agitated him, made him feel angry, this darkness and sense of mystery in Britta's voice.

"It was a man, wasn't it?"

A feeling of jealousy began to burn in his chest, catch in his throat.

He gazed down at her. For a second he had the feeling that he was putting her on trial, interrogating her, shooting words at her, and shining bright blinding lights in her face.

"Just tell me," he said, gritting his teeth, grinding them together. "Just tell me. Listen, I know it was a guy."

Britta's voice sounded weary. "Okay, Martin, it was a guy."

"Did you sleep with him?" Martin shot back.

Britta didn't answer. He could see her begin to shake and tremble on top of the bed. Martin forgot about the question he had just asked.

"Who was it, Britta? I just want to know who it was."

He continued pacing, stopped for a second near the bed, and started pacing again.

"I can't tell you that." Her voice was trembling. "What difference does it make?"

Suddenly, he felt tired again, exhausted. He walked to the bed and sat down on the edge of it. He reached out and put his hand on top of hers. He could feel her hand contracting, the muscles stiffening. The skin was cold. He took his hand away.

What guys did she know? He thought of the men down at Lupo's, the worn-out puffy fat businessmen; who the hell could it be? He could feel his skin begin to crawl with a sensation of disgust. What if it was one of those fat men with rings on his fingers? The thought caught in his throat, and he began to feel sick to his stomach.

No, he thought, it just couldn't be one of them. Then a picture slowly formed in his mind. It was Frank Laskey handing her a can of peaches in a brown paper bag. Frank smiling. Frank a little drunk and singing Solidarity Forever at one o'clock in the morning. Frank with bits of saliva caught in the corners of his lips, getting worked and dry as he talked. Frank Laskey yakking to her about that town in Norway, about the snows and the winds, and the high cool airs of his ex-girlfriend's hometown.

"Was it Frank Laskey?" he murmured.

"Oh Martin."

"Was it?"

He glanced down at her, and saw tears in her eyes.

"It was Frank, wasn't it?"

He was straining to hear her voice.

"Yes." Her reply was muffled, and he could just barely see her nod her head.

Martin got off the bed, and began pacing again. He walked over to the table where the rose was standing in the turquoise vase. He picked it out of the vase. He was tempted to crush it, to break the stem and pull off the petals, and to toss the crumpled mess on Britta's bed. Instead, he raised it to his nose, sniffed it quickly, and slipped it back into its resting place.

"Good old Frank," he muttered loud enough for Britta to hear. "I go away for a bloody weekend, and he's in there like a fucking dirty shirt."

"It wasn't his fault, Martin. I encouraged him. If you want to blame someone, blame me. Frank wouldn't have done anything on his own. He thinks too much of you."

His legs seemed to be buckling again. He walked to the bed and let himself down. What could he say? Hadn't he just come out of Josephine's bed? What right did he have to judge her? He could see himself again leaping from the bed, yelling and shouting his joy, just a few days before.

"Do you love him?" he heard himself asking. He was listening to his own voice, and it sounded like it was coming up from the bottom of a huge canyon.

"I do love him, Martin. I'm sorry, but I do. How can I explain it to you? We just need each other. Frank wants to settle down and have a family. I can't stand the thought of having another bad experience. I just go crazy when I think about it."

Something inside Martin was folding—a hardness crumbling, melting away. He was moved by what Britta was saying. Didn't he want her to be happy? How could he keep on hurting her, withdrawing from her, not giving her what she wanted? How could he just keep on thinking about himself?

And yet he was still burning with jealousy.

Half-heartedly, he tried to embrace her again, hold her in his arms. A quick thought shot through him. Perhaps he could make love to her and change her mind.

"Can't we make love just once more, Britta, just one last time?"

There was a plea in his voice. It sounded shaky and tearful.

He could feel her body stiffening and drawing away from him.

"I'm sorry, Martin. I can't. I just wouldn't feel right about it. Not now. It's too late."

He knew he had to go to the room on Street of the Prophets alone that night. But he kept fighting against it. He had never slept there alone, in Peter's old room. Never had he bedded down in solitude beneath Picasso's Boy with Pipe. It scared him—the stone walls and the stone floor, the wind shooting cold tentacles under the door and through the cracks of the windows.

He had to face up to it. How could he stay near Britta, begging for a tiny niche in her life?—how could he keep crying for something that no longer existed?

"I'll go," he said wearily, dragging himself up from the bed.

Far below, it seemed, miles away, he could hear her voice.

"I'm sorry, Martin. Please be friends with us. We both like you."

Words, he kept thinking, meaningless words. They were rising up from a canyon, strokes of wind against rock.

He gathered a few of his belongings together, and kissed her on the forehead before he left.

"I still love you," he whispered against her cheek. He could hear his own words melting away, losing their texture and meaning.

The room was cold at 29 Rehov ha Neviim, cold and barren-looking, just as he'd expected. This time of year, near the beginning of December, he should've had a gas heater going. It was windy that night. Walking to the room, he had hunched up, trying to protect himself. The chill air slid down the front of his shirt.

What a cold windy night, he thought, to leave everything behind. The long-stemmed rose was imprinted on his memory. He could see it standing a little forlorn-looking, and a little proudly in its turquoise vase.

An old sleeping bag was lying on Peter's bed. At first he was tempted to crawl into it fully clothed. How could he possibly keep warm stripped down to his underwear? He could hear the wind beating against the windowpane. It was creaking the branches of trees out in the garden where Dr. Lowenstein lived. With a strange smile forming on his face, he remembered the fragile old doctor. Whistle. Whistle. You will be cured when you learn how to whistle. He was tempted to whistle, to imitate the wind.

No, he thought, don't do anything crazy. Keep a grip on yourself, or you'll slip down into something, and maybe that something will be madness. From time to time he had that fear—of going completely insane, slipping into a dark region where nobody would ever be able to reach him.

"Oh God, I'm so cold," he whispered to himself, getting into his sleeping bag with only his underwear on. The insides of the sleeping bag felt sandy to him, and was it his imagination, or could he feel the stuffing coming out, gobs of old cloth and fur?

"I love you, Britta," he muttered out loud. "I still love you." His words were rising to the ceiling mixed with the cool ghosts of his breath. The wind was devouring the syllables, chewing them up and spitting them back at him. Could the stone walls hear him, was there a speck of understanding, was anything hearing him?

For a moment he imagined himself going down to Frank's house, finding Britta, slapping her, hitting her hard across the face and dragging her away. He slammed his fist into Frank's gut, crumpled him, made him gasp for his breath.

No, he thought, it's not possible. I couldn't do anything like that. No. No. No.

He fell asleep for minutes at a time, woke up. His skin crawled with tingles of fear. The wind seemed to be laughing at him. It was a cruel beast, he thought, without any mercy. It laughed hysterically, gloated, grinned lewdly through the trees. "I love you, Britta," he whispered each time he awoke. And each time, his voice got weaker and thinner.

Wind, wind, wind, he kept thinking. His mind was spinning him slowly into sleep. Slowly the darkness covered him, made his eyelids heavy—two heavy coins he could no longer budge. "Britta"—he could barely say her name. Britta. Britta... Brit... ta... tah... tah...

When he awoke the next morning it was a bright day. The wind was still blowing, but it blew slivers of light through the windows and under the cracks of the door. He still felt cold and barren, as if his arms had been nibbled away, and now and forever he would have to get along with the rounded stumps.

The people in his life marched through his thoughts. Jesse, his father, Frank, and particularly Britta. How distant they all seemed. They were drifting away from him. They went to their separate cubicles and rooms.

He was tempted to laugh out loud at everything—at the sun, and the bright slivers of light. At Britta and his father and Jesse. But again he said to himself—be careful, Martin, you'll go mad: you'll end up like a windowpane staring from an empty building.

Martin gazed around the room. So this was the place, he thought, that had been passed from friend to friend. What had Peter called it? —oh yes, he remembered: a tradition. So, he thought, I'm lying here in this rotten sleeping bag smack in the middle of a tradition. The thought made him want to open the window and shout curses into the backyard. Perhaps old Dr. Lowenstein would hear him and rush to his room. And then again, perhaps he wouldn't. He was a frail doctor, after all, wispy and fragile from years of delving into the history of medicine.

Isn't there anyone I can talk to? And again he thought, don't cry, you miserable thing; think of Jeremiah when Jerusalem fell—how he wandered around the empty streets. Yes, Jeremiah in rags, his black eyes vacant and wild.

So here I am, he considered, living on the Street of the Prophets. Shouldn't I clap my hands and celebrate, grow a beard and learn how to sense the future? Steven Goldman impinged on his musings. How fast he had left the country.

And what was Britta doing this morning? Was she wrapped snugly in Frank's arms? I hate both of them, he thought bitterly. What were they after all?—that he should envy them. Frank a teacher and broken-down socialist. Britta a barmaid and mommy-to-be. Didn't he have greater things to accomplish?

He lay in bed a long time hugging himself inside the sleeping bag, trying to keep warm. He could feel his feet and toes prodding at the old wool; gobs of it came out, fell to the bottom. What a miserable life he was leading, he thought—teaching two hours a day to make his miserable fifty lira. Only Britta had kept him fully sane; now she was gone, gone, sucked into a vacuum where he couldn't touch her. If only I could write, he thought, two or three hours a day. He had read accounts of this—Thomas Mann arose in the morning, took his shower, and his black coffee and wieners, sat at his desk until noon hour. And in the afternoon he was back at it, reading, writing, or doing revisions. Yes, he thought, if I could find the key to the secret —how did they do it?—Faulkner, Hemingway, Lawrence, Kafka. How did they keep their noses to the grindstone?

Suddenly, tears rushed to his eyes and his chest began to ache. He was thinking of Britta after the operation eating his humble fruit salad. How soft and warm and loving she had been.

He was a bit startled when he heard the knock at his door. "Just a sec!" he shouted out. Hurriedly, he pulled on his trousers, shirt and sweater. Who could that be? Probably the landlady. He didn't want to get his hopes up. He needed to see a friend badly that first morning away from Britta, but he didn't want to hope for too much.

"Hi, old buddy," the tanned face said as he opened the door.

In front of him Frank Laskey stood smiling broadly.

"Can you have lunch with me?" he asked. "We'll go up to the market and have some shish-kabob."

Rivulets of warmth streamed through Martin. He no longer wanted to smash this man in the gut. His own feelings surprised him. Shouldn't he be angry, he thought, shouldn't he turn a cold shoulder to him, and shuffle him out the door?

"Sure, Frank."

Frank placed a hand on Martin's shoulder and squeezed.

"I owe you an apology," he said, looking down at the floor. Then he raised his eyes and looked into Martin's face. "I should never have done it while you were out of town. The least I could've done was spoken to you first, explained things to you."

Martin's shoulders hunched up. He seemed to be contracting into a ball of flesh, shrugging at the same time.

"I want to marry her, Martin. I don't want you to get the wrong idea. It's not just a fling or a piece of ass. I couldn't do something like that to a friend."

Martin nodded. Words were trying to form themselves inside his mouth. It was difficult to speak, to make a sentence come out, to say something that made sense.

"She needs that," he finally whispered. "I've known that all along. I just can't do it . . ."

Martin could feel tears coming to his eyes, welling up, and burning in his chest.

"Are we still friends?" Frank asked. He moved his hand from Martin's shoulder and gripped his hand.

Martin nodded. His hand gripped Frank's, squeezed it, shook it, lingered on the warm flesh.

Frank began smiling again. His black eyes danced with light.

"C'mon," he grinned, "let's go to the market and get ourselves a good meal."

Outside, the sun was shining brightly. It was pouring shafts of light into the trees, into the cement, into the buildings. The rains were coming. Martin could feel it in the brisk December wind. Soon the black drops would be falling again. Another winter, soon it would be here—the rain would turn up mud in the Valley of the Cross. Ping, ping, ping. He could almost hear it as he walked with Frank along the bright sunlit street.

Where was it going to lead, Martin was thinking, this third winter in Israel? What was it going to be like without Britta?—without Britta's blond hair on the pillow beside him, without Britta telling him about the trolls in the mountains of Sweden, how they twined their wonderfully sensitive tails together? What would it be like? A shudder passed through him, a cold shiver of foreboding. No, he couldn't do it, he thought, he would end up freezing, and crying, and talking to the raindrops on his windowpane.

He could see himself as a child. He had few friends when he was nine years old. His family had just moved to a new street. How often he stood in front of the window on rainy days imagining that each raindrop was a person. Down they would slide, down to the bottom of the windowpane where they seemed to melt and die forever. What a short life they had, he used to think. He could see them forming at the top, becoming round and full, but it was a quick journey to the bottom. Sometimes he imagined them racing each other. Don't race too fast, little raindrop, there's nothing at the bottom—you're going to die, melt away, you only have one chance, and it's such a quick slide down the slippery glass.

Martin was glad the sun was shining, that the winter rains hadn't begun. He was trying to sniff the sunlight into his chest, and to feel every speck of warmth on the back of his neck.

"It's a beautiful day, Frank," he murmured. There was a sadness in his voice.

Quickly they sprang along, walking up Jaffa Street towards the outdoor market. He could see old women from Iraq wrapped in black shawls. What kind of life did they live, he wondered, sitting on their mats, selling spices all day long? He was suddenly glad that he wasn't an old toothless woman from Iraq.

They ate their shish-kabob together. Martin was trying not to think of Britta. But he kept seeing her in the laundry room squatting over a grate in the floor. Her nightie was hiked up over her knees. How smooth and creamy and white her legs were. He remembered his lips kissing her legs, brushing against the blond curls of hair.

Frank looked relaxed sitting on the chair opposite him, tilting back a beer. He was leaning back, letting the sun fall on his face and shoulders.

Martin was thinking of the picture of Britta he had inside his wallet. Her face looked slightly plump. On the back of the photo she had written a short message . . . To Martin, memory of a troll, summer 1963, Jerusalem. Love, Britta.

Soon the rains would come, he kept thinking. They would race down his windowpane and die at the bottom. Soon black clouds would cover the city, and it would be winter once again. He would get sick, he thought, if he didn't buy a heater and put it in his room. How could he spend the winter without a girl?—without a warm body to snuggle up to?

They finished their meal and shook hands once again.

"Come down and visit us, Martin. Don't hide away from us."

Martin promised to visit.

What a bright day, he kept thinking as he walked back to his room alone. He could still taste the shish-kabob in the back of his throat. The spices he had dipped the gobs of meat in lingered and burned.

PART FOUR

CHAPTER 27

Be Thou as Brave

What were those final months like?—Martin often thought years later—the last days in Israel, the whirl of people and events from December to July? There was Helen Tannenbaum, Jerry Duke, Roger Stanton and his sidekick Jean Paul, rushing upon him, peopling the streets of Jerusalem, appearing suddenly like ducks popping up at a shooting gallery.

There was Fernando de Lopa who changed his name from Green, and his wife Gene who lost all her teeth at the young age of twenty-three.

There was hashish, a haze of smoke, and pot cookies and hash tea. Henny Penny—he sometimes thought of that old nursery-story character. The sky is falling, the sky is falling—Henny Penny, the harried chicken, cried. Somebody told me the sky is falling. Of course they put down and scorned the poor hysterical little bird; how could the sky possibly fall? The scorners, of course, were right. Everyone could see it. The sky was in place—look!—blue sky from horizon to horizon. What a ridiculous notion! What could anyone expect from a cold pebbly-skinned frightened fowl?

But it seemed to Martin in those last months that the sky was indeed crumbling, and the Valley of Judgement near Mount Zion was heaving up the bones of ghosts.

The witch's warning to Macbeth buzzed through him—a man not born of woman, and until the forests move. How the fuck could the forests move, and a man spring to life but through that narrow passageway? And Christ's riddle riddled him—you must be born again, die and be born fresh as a daisy all over again.

Poor Macbeth. He thought he had it in the bag. What a devilish little trick! Safe on two counts: forest moving, ridiculous; sky falling, absurd. Man coming into life in any other way but between a tense

pair of thighs. If I were truly evil, Martin thought, and if I had a
Lady like Madam Macbeth, wouldn't I forge ahead?—scrap the
world and shoot the works. He remembered telling Mr. Townley
once: there can't be any halfway measures in life or writing. It's one
shot to the end. He had an image of a great shot-put artist. He
heaved the lead one day—amazing, a record; it would stand for
centuries. "You did it! You did it!" they yelled in his ears. "Congratulations!" He just barely heard the applause. Then suddenly, something snapped inside him, something exploded—the brawny man
buckled and clutched his chest. A heart attack—a lovely painful
relaxing heart attack, and he died smiling and blubbering among his
admirers.

There was only one week between the break with Britta and
meeting Helen Tannenbaum. It was ironic and somehow just that
Frank Laskey invited Martin to that party in the outskirts of Jerusalem. An old friend of Frank's was throwing a party.

The night was dark when Martin got off the bus. Where the hell
was he? He didn't know if he was in the north or south of the city.
Everything looked a little weird. The houses appeared thrown together like army barracks. It was as if a strong blow could come up,
a hurricane or cyclone, and send the tattered structures flying: wood,
plaster, paint, wallpaper, furniture, bits of wood, flying, flying, torn,
raped, smashed completely.

He had had a few drinks before he arrived. The hot liquor
wormed through his gut. He was trying to forget his loneliness, to
loosen up, to smile, to be optimistic. One shot to the end, he kept
thinking. Open up, you fuckin' tight bastard, open your eyes, your
ears, your skin. Open up your bloody pores. To what?—he thought.
To everything, you fool, to everything, to every single possibility.
Booze, that would help, he thought; it would loosen his tongue, it
would make him smile, just long enough to be amenable—long
enough to meet some woman.

He met Frank at the party. Frank had also been drinking. It was a
bit surprising to see Frank alone at the party, half-corked already.
Where was Britta? They had only been together a week, and here
was Frank, quickly getting stoned, thoroughly pissed, acting as if he
were a free agent. Perhaps Britta was working, Martin reasoned.

"You see that girl over there," Frank slurred at him, slinging his arm around his shoulder. "You can probably fuck her if you want. I think she's the type that goes."

The girl was wearing black leotards and a black skirt, a red sweater, and her long black hair, straight and combed back without any adornments, fell past her shoulders. It was a crude way of putting things, Martin mused—you can probably fuck her if you want; but the girl did look just a bit seductive. And Martin did want to sleep with somebody that winter, perhaps even love somebody, although now those four letters, L-O-V-E, were more mysterious than ever. Jesse had introduced Martin to the writings of Henry Miller. He remembered Miller's acute analysis and summation of one character's problems—he's not in love, that's all he talks about, but he's definitely not in love, he's cunt-struck, that's what he is.

Miller's writings often seemed like a bright beam of light that shone into Martin's face, seared his eyes, and pierced through the retinas to the murk and mist that lay behind. He felt accused when Henry Miller derided the worshippers of LOVE—those who idealized, fantasized, and danced around the concept as if it were a god, the newest golden calf. They all want a piece of ass, Henry wrote, they moan and groan and roll their eyes towards heaven, and moan some more while they remain celibate for years, and they talk about love through their pinched lips, and all they really want is a good lay. Why don't they go out and get it, the fools, Miller wrote, get a good juicy piece, and they'd feel a hell of a lot better.

In those days, it never crossed Martin's mind that Henry Miller himself was sometimes a worshipper of the fantasy, and only years later he discovered that Miller had imagined himself into a good number of beds.

Why not loosen up, Martin mused, as the author of the Tropics suggested? What was wrong with it after all?—to take things at their face value. Girl equals cunt, boy equals cock, they meet, and have a good time with their god-given attributes. Henry Miller—he had immersed himself in all his books, Capricorn and Cancer, The Rosy Crucifixion; he swam through Miller's ragged, steaming back alleys, through Paris and New York.

As it turned out, Helen Tannenbaum was from New York City, from Greenwich Village in fact, and she had been living in Jerusalem for a year or so. Not only that, she was an artist, working on crude stones, unprecious gems, polishing them, shaping them, breaking them, and joining them into jewellery. They danced a few dances together, and talked about writing and art. And was Martin imagining it, or could he feel a lovely delicious heat rising from beneath her skirt and leotards? Was she really pressing and molding her pelvis against his as they swayed together? He had drunk a little too much whiskey to be absolutely sure.

The light at the party was dim. Everyone was a stranger except Frank. Who were these other people? He had never laid eyes on them before. They looked shadowy and distant. As he drank more they seemed to recede into their chairs, almost into the texture of the nondescript walls. He could hear chatter all around him, lining the room, a dull mix of voices and laughter. Only Frank Laskey appeared real, Frank and Helen Tannenbaum.

Suddenly, he could hear someone shouting and yelling, piercing the smoke and chatter with tormented screams. It was Frank. What the hell was he doing? He was on all fours in front of the fireplace, rocking back and forth, and he was banging his head against the brick chimney.

"You weren't there. None of you were there. You don't understand!" he was screaming and yelling, his face red and contorted. "I saw my buddies blown up. Blood, blood, blood! No face, no arms, no hands. Just blood. Can't I make you see it? Blood for a nose, blood for eyes, blood for a chin. No features. Nothing. You're all too fucking young to understand."

"What's he talking about?" Martin whispered to Helen, dazed by drink and smoke, and Frank's sudden outburst.

"The war," Helen whispered back. "I think he's talking about '48."

Of course. Of course. Of course. Wheels were jamming through Martin's head.

"I want you to see it!" Frank screamed. The room was silent except for Frank's voice. And he was beginning to blubber and cry. Tears were rolling down his cheeks and his lips were twisted. "I'm going to make you see it," Frank gasped, trying to catch his breath. "You've got to see it. I had a friend. He was a whole person, just like you and me. Arms, legs, eyes, nose. He had a father, he had a mother, he had a girlfriend. And he was blown apart. He was running beside me, my friend, my buddy, he was running beside me, I could touch his hand. Oh fuck, it was awful, it was horrible, oh it was so fuckin' horrible. He wasn't there any more. He was mush and bones and blood. Why didn't I get it too? Don't you understand? Can't I make you see? Why am I still here? Can you tell me that? Can you? Can you? Tell me, tell me!"

Frank was trying to get to his feet. He was screaming louder than ever, pointing at everyone in the room. Then he fell back to the floor again, rolled over, hugging himself, rocking back and forth, lying on his back.

Martin walked quickly across the room and knelt down beside him. Others followed. Martin could sense Helen standing behind him, then she knelt too. Martin gripped his shoulder, and bent down and whispered in Frank's ear.

"Frank, take it easy. We understand, we really understand. Take it easy, Frank, please."

"Let's put him up on the sofa." It was a low gravelly man's voice. Martin could hear it falling from behind him.

Martin, two other men, and Helen lifted Frank from the floor. Frank had gone completely limp. A dead weight—Martin was thinking. In gym class in grade nine, a fellow student, a tall muscular athletic boy, had called Martin that. "Move," he had commanded, "I can't carry you." (They were doing exercises together.) "Oh, c'mon, get some life into you, you're a bloody dead weight."

All four strained around Frank's arms, back and legs, supporting him, heaving him, lifting him onto the sofa.

"Oh, I can see it!" Frank began to scream again, rolling around on the sofa. He covered his eyes with his hands as if this would block out what he was seeing. "I can see it inside my head. Explosions. Darkness all around us. It's so dark and cold. My buddy gets it. His blood is splattering everywhere. It's so dark out there. I'm all alone."

"It's okay, Frank," Martin was whispering softly above him, gripping his shoulder. "We're all here. You're not alone, Frank. Just take it easy."

Frank's hand wrapped itself around Martin's knee. He was leaning his face closer to Martin so that only Martin could hear.

"Thank you, old buddy. Thank you. Thank you. It's so cold out there—dark as shit, and cold as ice. There's no one, no one, no one at all. Please hold me."

Martin tightened his grip around Frank's shoulder. For a second he was feeling twinges of embarrassment. C'mon, he said to himself, he's practically having a seizure. He needs you. There's nothing to be embarrassed about.

"Martin, you're not angry at me," Frank was whispering. "You don't hate me, do you? I know how much you loved her. I promise you, old buddy, I'll take good care of her. Don't hate me, Martin, please. I like you an awful lot, don't hate me."

Martin could feel his mind whirling, his heart beating faster.

"I don't hate you, Frank," he whispered back. "I just want you and Britta to be happy. Something's got to work right. Something's got to be fucking right."

Frank began to chuckle a little hysterically. Sobs and cries punctuated the short gasps of laughter coming out of his throat.

"Just a speck of fucking rightness," Frank giggled. "One tiny inch of it."

"Frank," Martin interrupted, "why don't you just lie back and maybe try to get a little sleep? Just forget about everything."

"Okay, okay," Frank murmured and nodded.

It was a relief when Frank let his head fall back against the cushion. It seemed as if he were gradually relaxing, and Martin was hoping that he would go to sleep. His breathing was beginning to come in even strokes. Frank's hand fell limply from Martin's knee. Martin waited a few minutes. When he was sure that Frank had slipped into a light sleep, he eased himself from the sofa, and walked backwards slowly. A hand reached out and gripped his hand from behind. He glanced around. It was Helen Tannenbaum smiling at him.

"The poor guy," she whispered, "I could just see what he was describing. It must've been horrible. What was he saying to you anyway?"

Martin shrugged. "Oh, nothing important. Just something between us. I hope he gets some sleep now."

Helen glanced over at the sofa. Frank was beginning to sob again. It was difficult to tell if he was doing it in a dream, or if he was waking up. Helen walked over to the sofa and placed a hand on his forehead, leaving Martin standing alone. Frank cried in short bursts, then became silent. Martin watched Helen massaging his temples.

Martin walked over and stood behind her. He whispered in her ear.

"He's already got someone to take care of him."

Martin's words startled her a bit. She withdrew her hand.

As soon as the words were out of Martin's mouth, he regretted saying them. What a small mean thing to utter, his mind chastised. But now, there was no taking them back.

Frank was slowly dropping off into a deeper sleep. The sobs came farther apart and sounded fainter.

The host came up to Martin. As soon as he spoke, Martin recognized the low gravelly voice that had suggested putting Frank up on the sofa.

"Listen," he said, "don't worry about him. He can sleep here and I'll give him a ride home in the morning, or whenever he wakes up."

"Good, good," Martin whispered. "He needs to rest."

Soon after the party Martin began seeing Helen Tannenbaum regularly—in fact, he was practically living with her in her small basement room on Street of the Steps. What a cramped little room— it was about fourteen feet long and seven feet wide. But Helen had done her best with it. She had covered the narrow bed with a gold-red blanket. On the walls various prints hung: Chagall, Modigliani, etc. To Martin, however, the most interesting thing on the wall was a square of cardboard with the words, "Be Thou as Brave as the Rhinoceros". Above the commandment, Helen had drawn and colored bluish-grey a fat, determined, content-looking rhino. The beast's head was bent. It was musing at the water weeds growing between its steely toes.

Was Helen as brave as a rhinoceros?—Martin wondered. He questioned her about the origin of this eleventh commandment. It turned out that she got the idea from an old boyfriend in Greenwich Village, a Jew who had started off as an artist and then switched to psychology.

"Do you like it?" Helen asked, leaning her slim breasts and bony pelvis against his back and bum.

"It's great," he said. "What could be braver than a rhinoceros?"

"That's it, that's exactly it," she purred in his ear, rolling and squeezing her crotch against his backside. "Can you imagine how fantastically brave they are? Grunt, I eat. Grunt, grunt, the sun's out today."

It would be wonderful, Martin thought, to be rid of the mind's proddings. Just grow a skin with a thousand grey wrinkles. Develop eyes that could pierce into the blackness of rivers.

"I would like to be that brave," he grinned.

"You can be," Helen purred, her breath licking at his earlobes. "All it takes is faith."

Martin stared at the small square of cardboard. Over the next several months, he never tired of looking at it, gazing at it, glancing at it as he crossed its path. The eyes of the rhino never varied in hue. The skin never lost a single fold or wrinkle.

At the beginning Helen and Martin made love often, even in the first week of their acquaintance. One evening about a week after the party, they had just finished wrapping themselves together, heaving and gasping and coming. They were up in Martin's room on Street of the Prophets. Martin noticed that Helen's mood had taken a turn for the worse.

"Is there something wrong?" he asked, placing a hand on her bony hip.

"I don't know," she said, shaking her head wearily. "Sometimes I think that all this amounts to is a whole bunch of fucking. What does it mean anyway, you and me?"

Helen's words surprised him. The tone was cool and the words sliced through him.

"What's it supposed to mean?" he asked.

"A lot more than fuck, fuck, fuck," she said, her voice tinged with anger and desperation.

"Is that all you think it is?" he asked.

Helen hung her head down. Absentmindedly, she was playing with the zipper on the sleeping bag.

"I don't know, Martin, I just don't know. Why don't you go outside for a few minutes and think about it? Just think about it. I'm a person, don't forget."

"Okay," Martin said sadly.

He slipped on his clothes quickly and left the room. Outside on the balcony it was chilly. What a silly thing to be doing, he thought, standing here all alone contemplating Helen's question. Henry Miller swished through his mind. Why didn't he cover this in his books? Martin gazed at the black night sky.

What a cold winter it would be, alone in that room. It was a critical few moments, he realized. Was he going to let her slip away? Yet he knew it was within his power to convince her that more than fucking was involved. Was there more, though? Could he answer that question himself? Who was this Helen Tannenbaum anyway?

Was it completely arbitrary that he was with her now, and not with one of a million other girls?

Bang, the thoughts were shooting through him. Each question unfolded into a new one. What did he know about anything? He wished he could look up at the black sky and suddenly see just one answer writing itself across the darkness. Just one bloody answer, he thought bitterly.

What did he know? He knew for sure it would be a cold, lonely winter without Helen. He knew for certain he was not a rhinoceros, nor as brave as they were reputed to be. Alone that winter, he would be shaking and quivering in Peter's old room, fighting off nightmares, checking under his bed for bogey-men. No, definitely not, he didn't want to be alone. Was Helen right? Was it just a lot of fucking? Fuck and fuck, and fuck some more. Was she just an object to stick himself into, and warm his body against?

He went back inside the room.

"Helen," he whispered, putting his arm around her slim shoulders. "You're you. If I just wanted a bunch of sex, why wouldn't I be with someone else?"

"Do you love me?" she asked, looking into his face. "That's important, you know. We can't toss everything out the window."

He lowered his head so that his lips were touching her shoulders. On her white cool skin he murmured his reply.

"Yes, I love you, Helen."

He could feel her mood changing. Swiftly, it was beginning to turn. She kissed him on the chin.

"I'm sorry about what I said before," she whispered. "It was an awful cold thing to say. Let's forget it was ever mentioned, okay?"

"Okay," Martin echoed back.

He could feel stirrings in his groin again, more powerful and urgent than before. Again they wrapped their bodies together. Cleaved to each other, sucked and licked and slapped themselves together. Was it just fucking? He couldn't forget her question. How could she ask him to forget it? It was as if the question, once uttered, had become a real thing with a life of its own. There was no cancelling it out or forgetting it.

They didn't stay long that night on Street of the Prophets. Helen's question seemed to hover on the bare stone walls. The room was colder than ever in Martin's mind. Soon after the fucking or lovemaking or whatever it was, they got on their clothes and went back to Helen's room, her basement cave on Street of the Steps. It was a cave, Martin mused, a small underground catacomb, but at least it was brightly lit and cheerily decorated, and Helen owned a small gas heater which was almost constantly on the go, the blue-yellow flames licking upward, staving off the chill winds of December in the high hills of Jerusalem.

In the beginning they had friends. Helen had a small group of acquaintances, mostly painters and musicians who had come to Israel from English-speaking countries. Martin saw Britta and Frank, and Mr. Townley occasionally. Slowly, however, their friends faded —or did they fade, or rather did Martin and Helen withdraw into the small room together, the underground cloister?

Before this happened, Martin remembered going to the house of one of Helen's friends near the Street of the Prophets. The host was a stonemason and painter. He was a short, plump, cherubic-looking man, his thin blondish hair fading. He looked almost gentile, Martin remembered thinking, but it turned out that he too was one of the "tribe". The gathering took place about five days before Christmas. Everyone in the room, everyone gathered around the huge stone fireplace was, in fact, Jewish.

A sing-along began with two guitars and somebody shaking a tambourine. And for the first time in three years, since Martin had arrived in Israel, he heard the melodious strains of O Come All Ye Faithful, and a medley of other carols. What was happening, he wondered: all these Jews from London, New York, San Francisco, and other scattered outposts of the diaspora sitting together and singing with the vigor and enthusiasm of the Salvation Army? The songs swept over him, into him, through him. They seemed to be lifting him up, taking him back, back to Canada and the snows of yesteryear, back to Halifax, where as a small boy he would gaze out of his dark window on Christmas Eve. How beautiful the houses looked to this young child, the houses decorated with lights and spruce and illuminated St. Nicks. These houses, the houses of his childhood friends, were just across the street, yet they seemed distant, and he often wondered what it was like inside one of those houses on Christmas Eve. What was it like to lie inside a mound of presents, to watch the lights on the tree twinkle on and off?

The cherubic, balding host was singing in a booming, yet soft voice. His face was flushed with enthusiasm. Helen Tannenbaum swayed and hummed and leaned against Martin. Had she too cried for a Christmas tree when she was little?—Martin wondered.

Near the end they threw in a few Israeli folk songs, perhaps for good luck, Martin was thinking. And the gathering ended with punch served, and yet another chorus of O Come All Ye Faithful.

After this Christmas get-together they saw less and less of their friends. Helen went to work for three hours in the morning at a print shop, returned to the room at noon-hour, and went to jewellery classes in the afternoon. Martin rarely left the room, except for two or three hours around suppertime to take his daily walk to the Y.M.C.A. and teach his classes in conversational English.

Martin was amazed himself at how much they were making love, screwing around, exploring the "world of fuck", as Henry Miller so neatly put it. It seemed that Helen knew all the angles and tricks. She encouraged him to enter her vagina from behind. "You really go into me deep that way," she said in a throaty voice. It seemed that she could clamp every muscle in her ass around him, every muscle of her cunt, clamp, squeeze, and suck. She encouraged him to make love when she was wet and running with her period. "I don't know why," she said, "but it's best this time of month. Maybe because I don't have to use my diaphragm." He felt a little squeamish about every new suggestion, but when he finally got down to doing it, it wasn't as disgusting as he imagined it might be. In fact, most of it was enjoyable.

Into her anus, she encouraged him to go. They fucked this way once or twice, but it always left Martin feeling weak, as if they were taking things just a bit too far.

"You've got the biggest cock I've ever seen," Helen would often tell him, licking her lips, smiling, her grey eyes going misty and soft.

Then one day she came up with another suggestion.

"Martin, you know what I'd like to do, I know it might embarrass you a bit, but I'd really like to measure you. I'm just curious, that's all."

"Do you have a ruler?" Martin asked.

Helen nodded. "Uh-huh," she grinned mischievously. "I brought one home from work."

Martin shook his head. He could feel red blushes, hot and tingly, creeping up his neck into his cheeks and forehead. He began to snicker and giggle.

"You are embarrassed, aren't you?" Helen laughed, sticking a finger into his bare stomach.

"No," he snickered, shaking his head. "But listen, if you're going to do this measuring, you've got to wait until it's really up."

Martin could sense that this wouldn't be a problem. The idea had already begun to arouse him. Blood was pumping vigorously through his groin, and he could feel his cock beginning to bob up and down.

As Helen searched for the ruler, Martin kept chuckling to himself. He had never been measured before, and he'd never gotten out a ruler himself. The idea had just never occurred to him. He was just as curious as Helen was.

The ruler that Helen had borrowed from work was ridiculously long. It was the kind used on drawing boards, or in classrooms.

"You should fit into this somewhere," Helen giggled, slapping him on the ass with the long rigid piece of wood.

Martin kept losing his erection during the measuring process, but finally Helen, who was kneeling on the floor to get an accurate measurement, came up with a figure.

"It looks like eight or nine inches," she smiled, pinching his knee. "I guess it would depend."

There was a let-down after the whole thing was done. It was as if to be measured, to be put into inches, summed the whole thing up, and closed the book on the case, so to speak.

"You look down," Helen observed.

"Aw, it's nothing."

"I still have a few minutes before I go to my jewellery class," Helen gleamed.

"Good," Martin smiled back.

Helen quickly slipped out of her clothes and they were at it once again. It always amazed him: how quick and effortlessly Helen could undress and be ready. It seemed that her skirt, leotards, sweater and bra came off in one piece, something like a small animal sloughing its skin in the spring.

Who are you, Jerry Duke? Are you a liar? Are you a psychopath?

Are you completely mad? Are you really a lawyer on the skids? These were questions that Martin soon found himself asking, questions that bothered him more and more as the winter wore on.

Helen and Martin met him one evening just after twilight on King George Road. It was a chilly evening. The wind was tunnelling down the street. It rose off Mount Zion, slid off Mount Herzl, jabbed through their clothes and bit at their skin.

Jerry Duke came up to them and asked them for directions. He was wearing a gaberdine coat that came down to his knees. It was a frayed-looking thing, threadbare, patched and torn. He appeared lonely to Martin and Helen. His right arm was in a cast. "Fell off my bike," he explained. "Down near Beersheva. Don't know what happened. Guess the sun got in my eyes. I hit an oil slick." The cast was covered with names, slogans, mottos, and pieces of wit. "Will you sign it for me? I know I just met you, but I kind of like you two. You're my kind of people."

Jerry gazed at them. He was six-foot-three at least, with a considerable stoop to his shoulders, and he gazed at them as if tears might come to his eyes if they refused.

That same evening Helen and Martin invited him down to their small room to have a coffee and share some of their meagre food supply. There was never enough food. Martin was noticing this more and more. Between them they made about one hundred lira a week, but it never seemed enough to buy decent meals. They were existing on matzah, tomatoes, pieces of salami when they could afford it. Occasionally, they would buy oranges. Helen was already skinny, her body honed down to a thin covering of skin over bone. Martin was losing weight, and at times his gums ached, and when he ate his oranges he would notice a thread of blood on the rind.

"Christ, it's good to find some real human beings," Jerry said. He was leaning his chair back, his feet propped up on Helen's bed.

He had taken off his boots, and Martin could detect the sickish stench of dirty socks.

"I was beginning to wonder if there were any left," he continued. You know what I think? I think we're all turning into machines. We're losing our hearts, that's what's fucking happening. It makes me feel so bad sometimes."

Jerry hung his head forward. He cupped his bearded chin.

Martin was beginning to feel a strange kinship with Jerry. Didn't he know exactly what Jerry was talking about? Wasn't it a cold, lonely world with everyone marching to work, marching back again, keeping their noses to the grindstone, their eyes on the pavement?

Jerry's words made him feel warm inside. It was good to be recognized as a "real human being". And yet at the same time, there was a small grey section of Martin's mind that suspected him. Was he just telling them all this to make them feel good, as sort of payment for the meal, and for future meals, and for their friendship?

"Do you know that just two years ago I had a law practise? I had one of the finest law firms in New York State. Did a lot of criminal law, defence cases mostly. You've heard of Melvin Belli, haven't you? Well, old Mel was a good friend of mine. Quite a sharp cookie, that guy . . . the best defence lawyer since Clarence Darrow."

As he talked, Jerry peppered his monologue with questions, but never waited for a reply. A stream of words continued from his mouth. Where was it all coming from?—Martin wondered. From somewhere inside it travelled up, and emanated through strands of his matted, scraggly beard.

"I'm still trying to recover," Jerry continued, "from the shock."

There was a pause. Martin was just about to ask the normal question, "What shock?", when Jerry started up again.

"I came home from my office one afternoon around suppertime. It was an average afternoon. I was to have supper with my wife as usual, maybe take her to a movie. I had a wonderful son too. He was about three years old at the time. God, that little guy was smart. Probably a genius, in fact. At three he was playing chess, and almost whipping his old man's ass. And I'm not fuckin' shooting the bull either . . . Oh Christ."

Jerry let out a deep sigh. He allowed his chair to rock forward, took out a dirty handkerchief and began wiping perspiration from his forehead.

"I just walked up the front path. But I could sense something was wrong, even before I saw the two cops standing at the door. 'Are you Mr. Duke?' they asked. Then they told me there'd been an accident out on the highway. 'There's two bodies,' they said, 'but they're very badly charred.' The car had gone over a cliff, smashed through a guard-rail. I knew already, but I didn't want to believe it. Have you ever seen burnt meat? That's all that was left of my life— two pieces of burnt meat."

Jerry coughed, tried to clear his throat. It seemed that he was choking on the memory.

"You probably know the rest," he coughed, tears coming to his eyes. "You've probably guessed it already...I started drinking. What the hell was there to live for? I let the practise go all to hell."

Jerry snorted ironically.

"Two years ago I was wearing Brooks Brothers suits. Just look at me now. Been on the road now for a year and a half. Where the hell am I supposed to begin? Can you tell me that?"

Jerry glanced at Helen and Martin, then let his gaze fall. He was wiping his eyes and trying to blow his nose.

Helen and Martin sat on the bed opposite Jerry. They were both silent, and feeling uneasy. Was this all true?—Martin wondered. If it wasn't, then he and Helen were the biggest suckers in the world, and Jerry the damnedest liar in creation. Yet what if it were all true, right down to the last detail: the little boy who played chess at three years old, the wife who was turned by fate into a piece of smoldering flesh. The law firm. The expensive clothes. The drinking, the slide, the downward skid. What if it were true? All true? If they didn't show some sympathy, wouldn't they be the coldest, most unfeeling beings in the universe?

Jerry bowed his head. He was silent, and seemed to be waiting for a response. Martin could almost visualize the small car crashing through the guard-rail with Jerry's son and wife aboard. He could smell human hair burning, flesh being roasted, he could hear muffled cries and shouts and screams that never got beyond the windows of the car. What a horrible thing!—Martin was thinking—for Jerry, for his wife, for his son. The story just had to be true, Martin decided. What kind of person would fabricate such a morbid tragedy?

"Jesus," Martin almost gasped, still smelling the charred flesh. "I'm really sorry, Jerry."

He wanted to say more, but he let his head fall forward and remained silent. What more could be said?

"It's just something that can't be rubbed out," Helen added. She shook her head back and forth, as if she too could smell the bodies burning.

It was quiet in the room, stony-still. Martin was almost wishing that Jerry would begin talking again, just say something to break the dead silence. Minutes were slipping past. All three mouths were shut, and all three heads drooped.

Out of the corner of his eye Martin could see the plaque of cardboard above the head of Helen's bed. Old rhino, brave and tough, was standing his ground. The skin was heavy and grey. It looked pleated like the suits of armour on knights of years gone by. Be thou as brave, he kept thinking, what else was there to do? Brave as a sturdy rhino staring at his feet. The water weeds kept growing, growing.

Finally, thank God, Jerry started up again. And once he opened his mouth this time, the stories poured out non-stop. He told them about his marine training, his years in Korea, battles, victories, losses, heroics. He told them about his travels in India, Nepal, Thailand, and other far-flung corners of the planet. It was never merely a travelogue, or a documentary re-accounting of war, no, never only that, but in each story Jerry Duke was rounded, formed, and created into a full-fledged character equal to any that Martin had ever encountered in the world of fiction.

How could he do all these things?—Martin was beginning to wonder. How old was he? He couldn't be much over twenty-eight or so. How could he fit it all in? If he truly did everything he said he had done, it seemed to Martin that he would have to be at least forty. How could he have possibly fit all these things into ten years of adult life?

Jerry was rocking and squeaking Martin's mind. Martin found himself thinking about the car accident, the original, grand, tragic story that had begun the evening. If he had doubts about these later tales, how could he be sure about the first one? Who was this person they had invited back to their small cubicle? Was he a bundle of energy, adrenalin, a firing-range of tension, and a mouth that vented all this—a kind of oracle that kept spewing forth, a crack in volcanic rock, spewing and tossing its magma up, its stories and answers and questions and riddles, even when no one was asking it anything?

Story after story after story. Each one seemed to get wilder than the one before—more elaborate, zanier, with a harder punch-line. Martin's head was swimming. There were so many that they no longer made any sense. Martin was getting dizzy, his whole soul and being was floating along on this man's voice, tossed to the left and the right, plunged to the murky center, expelled again to the surface —onward, forward, downward without a stop, or break for rest.

Jesus, Martin was beginning to think, is there no end to it? He found himself wishing that Jerry would just shut up. He wanted to throw up his hands and yell—enough, enough, I give up, I've had enough, please stop. Yet he remained silent and even tried to look interested. There were so many stories that contour and feeling disappeared. Words and more words poured up from the mat of hair on Jerry Duke's face.

Finally the words stopped, the mouth grew silent. What a relief! What a blessed relief. Beautiful silence, the quiet world of an old wise rhino contemplating flies and the summer breeze. Martin let out a long sigh. He was hoping that Jerry had heard it, and understood what it meant.

Helen was fidgeting around on the bed. She was just going to put on coffee when Jerry opened his mouth again. This time a question emerged.

"What d'ya think of everything I've told you?" Jerry asked, eyeing both of them through his glasses. His eyes looked black and marbly, almost beady, and intense.

The question, to Martin, seemed almost like a challenge. Perhaps Jerry was just testing both of them to see how gullible they were, and if they came back with the wrong answer, he would get up and laugh in their faces. Martin decided to be frank and honest, even a little tough with his reply. He considered long and hard before he spoke.

"Well, Jerry," Martin finally said, toughening his mouth and mind simultaneously, "here's how I see it. I want to be as truthful as I can. You're either a great story-teller, a psychopathic liar, or everything you've said is absolutely true."

For a second, or just split half-second, Jerry was taken aback. Then he snapped his fingers, and grinned directly into Martin's face.

"Good!" he almost shouted. "That's what I like to see. A guy with guts. But you know, I'm not going to tell you, or try to convince you about the things I've been through. I'm going to let you figure the whole thing out for yourself. Life would be the shits without a few puzzles, wouldn't it?"

Jerry leaned back in his chair, smiling to himself. He wriggled his shoeless feet on top of Helen's bed. He looked satisfied with his reply to Martin's statement. It was as if he had been playing chess with Martin, and he had just moved his queen into a formidable position on the board.

Jerry sat there a few minutes nodding his head, a smile hovering around his lips. Then he seemed to grow restless.

"Hey, listen, do you guys smoke?" he asked, reaching into his back pocket and dragging out a crumpled plastic bag. "Got some great hash here. Lebanese stuff. Black Lebanese. Let's do some up. What d'ya think?"

Martin glanced at Helen. Helen looked at Martin and shrugged.

"Sure, let's have some," she said in a tiny voice.

"Sure," Martin nodded. "Why not?"

Jerry rubbed his hands together. His eyes were getting harder, brighter, almost excited.

"Good, good. I'll just get this stuff ready. Get me a knife and a flat piece of cardboard and we'll be in business ... Gotta pay you guys back somehow for the nice meal ... a little smoke, a little coffee, good company, what more could a guy ask for? Right, Martin? Right, Helen?"

He was looking into their eyes again imploringly. Let's be friends, his wistful, puppy-dog gaze seemed to be saying.

"Haven't had hash in a long time," Martin smiled, trying to be as warm and friendly as he could.

Jerry heated the knife over the gas burner, then the hash, cut the brown lump into fine slivers. He looked intent on what he was doing, cool and intent. He conducted the whole thing as if it were a scientific experiment; everything had to be done exactly right—at least he was communicating this feeling to Martin and Helen.

"I don't mess around with this stuff," Jerry said coolly, looking down at the knife, then over the top of his glasses at Martin and Helen. "Why not do it right?"

Martin had seen hash prepared before on one or two occasions. The tone was always a little ceremonious and religious. Not so with Jerry Duke. Martin had the feeling he was watching a delicate operation, an expert surgeon going through his moves.

And yet there was something incongruous, off-kilter, about the whole thing. The surgeon in this case was wearing a cast. His beard was matted with dust and grime. And out of a hole in one of his stinking socks, a big toe protruded.

That was the beginning of a lot of hash-smoking for Martin. Once Jerry opened it up, there seemed to be a supply of great black Lebanese stuff everywhere. Martin never paid for it. It was always offered, and by people who had an endless supply of it.

Fernando Green, the painter, alias de Lopa, toked up with them every time they went down to his house, or he came up to theirs. He made it into tea and cookies, placed it in an ornate pipe of woven silver.

"You just taste this," Fernando would say, giving them cups of hash tea. "You'll hear the jungle birds talking."

Jungle birds, Martin thought, yes, jungle birds, great speckled red and green-feathered birds of Africa, yes he could hear them singing and clucking to each other high in the trees. Weren't they all jungle birds?—Gene, Fernando's wife, who wrote stories for children, tales about monks in monasteries who talked to the sunlight, talked to the bells, far-away dreamy revelations for all the kiddies all over the world; and Fernando himself, skinny, pale-skinned Fernando who originated somewhere in Peru. Fernando de Lopa, who told them about the gringo journalist who came to Peru and fell in love with the Sun God.

"Ah yes," Fernando sang, "he went up to the temple where the Sun God lives. He stood there on a balcony. The sun came up. The Sun God was shining on the stone floor below him."

Fernando began to chuckle.

"He jumped, yes, he jumped into the Sun God's arms. What I mean is—they found him dead the next morning on the floor of the temple."

Martin found this story much harder to take than the jungle bird fantasy. Especially when he was stoned. He could see it so clearly—that crazy journalist jumping into his loved-one's arms. Flesh met concrete; bones and nose, forehead and chin smashed into fragments, blood everywhere.

In Helen's room, Martin often slept until noon hour. In the morning he would vaguely hear her getting ready to go to work. He turned over, grunted, pulled the blanket over his head, buried himself in the darkness once again.

Sometimes around eleven o'clock he'd hear a loud knock at the door. It was too loud, he thought. It pounded through his sleep, startled him, frightened him a bit. Yawning, he would get out of bed, throw on some clothes, and open the door. In would walk Jerry Duke.

"Are you still in bed, Martin? What the hell's wrong with you? You're missing the best part of the day. Look!"

Jerry walked in as if he owned the place, strode to the curtains, and flung them apart. Bright, harsh shafts of sunlight flooded the room.

"What d'ya do here all the time?" he snapped, glaring at Martin with beady eyes. "You're going to sleep your fuckin' life away. I was up at seven this morning. Had a shower, toked up a bit, fucked around the market..."

He paused for a second as if considering.

"Are you still scribbling those poems? Christ, you can't be doing that all day. Did you see the one Helen wrote?"

Martin vaguely remembered. "The one about her work?" he mumbled. "The ticky-tocky men or something."

"Yeah, that's the one," Jerry gleamed. "I hate to tell you this, old friend, but in my opinion it's a little bit better than what you've been doing. You know why? She's out there, she's not hiding away. You get what I mean?"

Martin shook his head. It was just too early in the day to guard against Jerry's onslaught.

"Maybe you're right..." Martin replied vaguely.

"I know I'm right... But what are you going to do about it?"

Martin shrugged.

Jerry walked across the room and put his hand on Martin's shoulder.

"Aw, you'll come around," he said with a fatherly softness to his voice. "Just keep scribbling, do what you have to. Who the fuck am I to say? Christ, for all I know, you might be a bloody genius. Wouldn't that be something? Yeah, I can just see it. I'd be tellin' everyone—yeah, I used to toke up with that guy."

Martin found himself grinning, rubbing sleep from his eyes, and grinning.

"Listen, man," Jerry continued, "I just got booted out of my room. Can I use yours for a while, just a night or two until I find something? You're never there anyway."

Martin was too tired and shell-shocked and blinded by the sunlight to give it much thought.

"Yeah, go ahead. But listen, Jerry, find a place of your own. Please. I might need that room sometime."

"Just don't worry your fuckin' head. I'll get myself a broad pretty soon. I'm just not looking right now. Do you know how many cunts I've been into in the last two years? You probably won't believe this, but I'm not shittin' you—one hundred and thirty-three. I've got 'em all marked down somewhere too. Man, I've had so many pussies, it'd make you fuckin' dizzy. What the hell, though? In my books, a cunt's a cunt. If you've had one, you've had 'em all. You know what I mean?... After my wife died I just decided that was it—no more of this love-shit. So I'm trying to get to three hundred. A little game I'm playing—that's all."

Martin eased himself down onto the bed. The words kept raining down on him, Jerry's sentences, rhetorical questions, bits of philosophy. It was just too early in the day to defend against them. Martin sat on the bed, trying not to hear most of it. But once Jerry got started, it was a relentless stream, pounding and pushing at his eardrums and brain.

The winter wore on. Once or twice Martin walked down to Frank and Britta's by himself. They had already set a date for the marriage.

"And Martin, I have some good news," Britta whispered, her face radiant. "We're going to have a child by next September."

"That's great, I'm happy for you," Martin murmured.

The visits weren't long. Martin soon left, returned to Helen's room, and waited for her to get back from work. How many times a week did they make love together? They were jumping into bed at every opportunity. They screwed around in the morning, at noon-hour, after supper. Three times a day. Three times seven is twenty-one. Four times twenty-one is eighty-four. Eighty-four times a month, and over a thousand times a year—flesh against flesh, love juices mingling, sperm and vaginal fluids. Wasn't it losing all meaning like Jerry Duke's stories, this incessant fucking?

Helen would often put him in her mouth, wrap her long black hair around his erection—tingle him with her tongue, graze him with the sharp edges of her teeth. Bring him to a climax with her lips, swallow what was going between her lips.

"Does it taste bad?" Martin asked.

"No, not really," Helen answered contemplatively, gazing at the ceiling. "It's a little salty, that's all. Haven't you ever tasted it?"

Martin was surprised by the question.

"What do you mean?" he asked, his face wrinkling with a mixture of surprise and disgust.

"I just thought you might've," Helen answered dreamily. "Just out of curiosity, you know what I mean, when you were alone."

It took Martin a long time to understand. Sure. Now it was clear. She didn't mean that some guy had shot off in his mouth. No, not that. She was merely talking about masturbation, and being curious, and perhaps just for a second tasting the tips of his fingers.

"No, I never have," he said. His voice sounded serious and puzzled.

Did guys do that, he wondered, after they had masturbated? Did they sometimes, just out of curiosity, take a quick lick at their fingers? No, he wasn't going to do it, he decided. The thought sickened him. What could be more disgusting than to taste his own sperm? He could almost taste it in his mouth—that sour, sickish-sweet and salty taste. He could feel it choking in his throat.

"No," he repeated, "I've never done that."

The winter seemed to go on forever. Long chilly wet days of January and February and early March.

Just as he feared, Jerry Duke took over his room at Street of the Prophets. Martin would sometimes get him to leave, but Jerry would get in again somehow.

Jerry's stories got a touch more unbelievable as the winter continued. Terry Southern's novel *Candy* was very popular that winter in Jerusalem. Jerry spent hours trying to convince Martin and Helen that he himself was the author of *Candy*, and Terry Southern was a pseudonym he had cooked up back in New York City. It was a wild story, the hardest one yet to swallow, but for moments Jerry made it believable. He had all the facts at his fingertips: how the story came to him, where it was written, etc.

Day after day the routine continued: screwing around with Helen twenty-one times a week, sleeping until noon hour, trying to scribble poems, even stories. Smoking up became part of the winter weariness, and listening to Jerry. Yak. Yak. Yak. New stories, old ones revamped.

Why doesn't the weather change?—Martin wondered. Wouldn't that make a difference, just to see some bright sunny days once again?

Even books began to lose their interest. What was the use, he thought, of re-reading Dostoyevsky and Flaubert? There was only one book that winter that seized his interest. It was James Baldwin's *Another Country*. Now there was a book, Martin thought. How he yearned to write like that himself. Baldwin seemed to be writing about a whole world, not just a fantasy inside his head, but about a world that existed for others as well. Black people, white, Irish people, homosexuals, couples, Brooklyn Bridge, the dark skyline, rain, seagulls squawking. And what a beginning to the book—the tragedy of Rufus. Martin could see the cornered black man. Where was there to go? What escape was there? Rufus dove off the bridge—what a powerful scene, his shoes sucked off his feet by the plunge, and his words echoing and dying over New York harbour: Here I come, you motherfuckin' God, here I come.

What warmth Baldwin injected into that scene between Eric and the Irishman, that love scene between those two cold lonely men. What warmth, feeling, beauty. It was a great book, Martin decided. He was sure of it. No professor had told him. He had decided for himself. *Another Country* was a great novel, as good as anything ever written.

How could he, Martin Kanner, develop that same compassion that James Baldwin possessed? Would he ever be able to create a Rufus and an Eric, make them live, breathe, suffer, love, even die? Make the rain fall, the bridge creak, the seagulls whimper. What was the meaning to his life if he couldn't do that?

What was the meaning?

Was he going to live in a small cramped room forever, making love eighty-four times a month, listening to Jerry Duke pump stories through his brain? Was he going to end up scribbling nonsense? Baldwin, he wondered, how did you do it? How did you learn to breathe out those people? How could you give them so much life? How, how, how the hell was it done?

CHAPTER 28

Valley of the Cross

A smell of spring on Street of the Steps—perhaps it was the three-thousand-year-old stone, or the wash of Yemenite and Moroccan women, or something wafted by the breeze up from the Valley of the Cross or down from Mount Zion. It was a cloistered smell, but bright with hope, specks of hope, pieces of straw blown by the wind.

A smell that entered Helen's room when she threw back the curtains in April, and heaved open the window. Was there yet another chance, Martin dreamed, of making a fresh beginning in this country? Was there something that he'd missed? A neglected song, perhaps, that he hadn't sung?

Outside, he raised his head, rubbing sunlight and sleep from his eyes. Ropes were strung across the narrow street from window to neighboring window. On these the dark women hung their wash: bright sweaters, sheets, pantaloons. Red, green, blue, yellow garments flapped in the wind.

"Have you seen the poppies yet?" Helen asked one bright morning after they'd finished making love. And the lovemaking that time seemed special, as if the new fresh winds, the specks of hope, had entered their limbs during sleep, and loosened them up. Martin came, and came, and came, holding nothing back, it seemed. Riding on top of Helen's thighs that morning seemed like a trip down bubbling currents, just letting himself go, go, go, his arms and legs and head and feet far looser than they usually were.

"What poppies?" he asked, still clutching her bony body to him, his lips loose and relaxed on her shoulder blade.

"In the Valley of the Cross," she smiled. "The whole valley's covered with them. Poppies everywhere. Let's go down this afternoon. Maybe we can take a little picnic. Okay?"

"Sure, let's go. I've never been down there. Isn't that crazy? I've seen that valley now for three years, and I've never walked around it. Yeah, let's go, Helen, it sounds like fun. We can take some bread and cheese with us, and a blanket."

Martin's enthusiasm was growing. He remembered Jesse in the darkness whispering: "That's the place where they cut the cross. Right there, Martin, just in front of us. And do you see that building? It's a monastery. Monks still live there. They make very good wine, I'm told."

Wasn't it a wonderful thing, Martin thought, smiling to himself, to be able to wake up in spring, make love, come as he never came before in his entire life, then just pick up and go to that place, that famous place of long ago, that valley where they found a tree to cut, to make into a huge cross-beam of wood, a cross that would some day find itself reproduced in miniature from Athens to Atlantic City, from Jerusalem to Singapore, from Vancouver to Halifax? Little crosses all over the world—hanging from people's necks, silver and gold, jade and ruby; crosses that shone in the night above the beds of teenage girls. Giant glowing crosses—like the one in Montreal burning through the blackness of winter nights, beckoning to the faithful to come and adore.

It all began, he mused, just a few blocks away from Helen's room on Street of the Steps.

And wasn't it just about the same time of year, around Passover, April, Eliot's cruelest month, when the Saviour of the gentiles, a Galilean Jew, was made to walk through that valley?

Helen was right, absolutely correct. Martin wasn't disappointed. The entire valley was blanketed with poppies, bright red heads bobbing in the breeze.

"Let's roll around in them," Martin laughed.

He let his legs buckle, his tired, winter-stiff knees. They cracked as he fell to the ground. The earth was still damp from the winter rains. Around and around in the poppies they rolled together, burying themselves, sniffing, snorting in the fresh smell of wet earth and new grass.

"What a place to die," Martin laughed. "Helen, I feel so good today, I could die. Isn't that stupid? But that's how I feel. Somebody could come along right now and snuff me out. I wouldn't mind. I really wouldn't. Just close my eyes and sleep forever in the sunlight."

"What are you talking about?" Helen asked, her face pinched and flushed a bit with annoyance.

"Death, death, death. That's what I'm talking about, Helen. I'd just like to go sometimes. Don't get mad. What's there to get mad about? Haven't you been so happy that all you wanted to do is die? Maybe I don't want to wake up from today. You know, start over again."

Helen rolled her head over on top of his chest. She was trying to snuggle her face under his chin.

"Why wake up?" she whispered, her warm breath licking and tickling his skin. "Can't every day be like this? You know what I think, Martin? I think you have to learn how to receive."

"What do you mean? I've been receiving all my life. I always had everything. You should've seen it when I was a kid. Cars, clothes, toys, anything I wanted. All I had to do was ask for it. I have to learn how to give, don't you think?"

Helen shook her head.

"No. I don't agree. You don't let yourself receive. Not enough. You're learning to, I guess. But you don't let enough in. Just when it's getting through to you, you close up. That mind of yours starts working again. It's like shutters on a window. You shut them tight, and nothing can get through."

Martin turned over on his stomach. He began running a fingertip along the red-soft petal of a poppy. Receive, he mused, receive. He couldn't understand what Helen was advising. It didn't make any sense to him, yet he couldn't get the idea out of his mind.

They spent the whole afternoon there in the valley, striding up and down it, running, laughing, rolling around in the thousand red flowers of spring. They gazed at the monastery—the yellow brick, a thousand years old, bright in the sunlight. Not a single monk was in sight. Martin was hoping to see one. He imagined he would look something like Friar Tuck, Robin Hood's famous chaplain, a pudgy monk in brown sackcloth with a belt of rope around his midriff.

Were they inside at this very moment?—Martin wondered. Lighting candles to their Saviour? Were they singing in Latin, chanting, rolling the holy words around their mouths? Were they down in the basement making wine?—adding just the right amount of yeast to crushed grapes? Were they down on their knees on the hard cobblestone? Were they scraping their knees on purpose, afflicting themselves, drawing blood, opening up old scabs again and again? Were they receiving? Did they know the secret of what Helen had whispered under his chin?

And did they ever feel how he felt that afternoon?—what a wonderful thing it would be to let his eyelids shut forever, to let his heart stop its jagged pumping, to let the brain rest. It wouldn't be so bad, he thought, to go to sleep under all these poppies. Forever and forever. Never to think about writing again, or love, or his parents, or his baby brother. Never to whimper again. Never. Never.

"It's getting chilly," Helen whispered, wrapping the blanket around her shoulders. Martin could hear her teeth chatter.

Her words woke him up, and he could feel the chill sliding down the back of his neck.

"Do you want to go?" he asked. "I guess we better. It'll soon be dark."

Shadows were beginning to lengthen on the monastery. Shadows of the hills, and long shadows from the cypress trees. It was beginning to get dark quickly. Soon the poppies would tuck and fold their petals inward, bunch themselves up into tight little knots for the night.

"Boy, it is getting cold," Martin agreed.

He no longer felt like dying. For the time being, the dream had passed. He just wanted to get back to Helen's room, light the gas burner once again. He wanted to warm his hands and his feet.

On a bright Saturday afternoon about a week later, they decided to go up to Mount Zion together, just the two of them again. April— he could smell it, it was fresher than ever, it seemed to be blowing across the bare heads of the Judaean hills. Yes, he was still thinking, maybe it was possible to wake up to something really new.

"I've never been up there, Helen."

Helen looked at him, a flicker of surprise crossing her face.

"Oh Martin, wait till you see it. It's really special. I can't put it into words. Just the atmosphere. It's kind of old and holy. King David's buried up there, you know."

"Still there?" Martin asked in a daze. His mind was whirling somewhere, into darkness and free space. The question came from a black pit inside him.

"Yes," Helen chuckled. "He's still there."

Mount Zion was situated on the other side of town, near Ramat Rachel where Ralph the poet lived.

A narrow road led up to the mountain. The road split a valley in two. Walking towards Mount Zion, the right side of this valley was inhabited. The houses looked poor, some no larger than huts. But grapes were growing outside the huts, wash was hung on the lines, children were playing, yelling, laughing, chasing each other: little brown children who probably originated in Aden, Iraq, Morocco, and Yemen.

The left side of the valley looked desolate. It was composed of jagged rocks, outcroppings of hard flint. There was not a single house or vineyard there, just on the other side of the road, and not a single child playing.

"That's funny," Martin said, thinking out loud. "Why aren't there any houses over there?"

Helen smiled, but her voice was low and serious. "Over there, where all the huts are—that's the Valley of the Saved. The other one is the Valley of the Damned. And d'ya know what's going to happen? On Judgement Day all the saved will be gathered together, and the damned will be tossed over to the other side. They'll slide down through the cracks in the rocks and go to hell."

The idea sent shivers through Martin's chest. Yes, the valley on the left looked like it could be the entrance to hell.

Martin chuckled, trying to relieve the pressure in his chest.

"Where do you think you're going to go?" he asked, staring over her head at the black jagged floor of the Valley of the Damned.

Helen shook her long black hair out and frowned.

"All artists will be saved. We'll all have little vineyards to look after."

"Well," Martin announced, his voice hardening, "just for the hell of it, I'm going to go the other way. Even if I wind up among the saved, I'm going to jump over the road, and slide through the rocks."

"And leave me behind?" Helen smiled.

"You can come with me, if you want," he grinned back.

There were sets of steps built into the mountain at various angles. Up these Helen and Martin walked. Martin was surprised to see so many trees, mostly tall cypresses, offering shade. Nowhere else in all Israel, it seemed, were there so many trees, tall trees bending in the wind, deflecting the sunlight.

"Can you feel it?" Helen asked, tugging at his hand. "Isn't there just a fantastic holy atmosphere? It's almost like you can listen to the sunlight. Look over there—can you see that priest?"

Sure enough, Martin spotted a priest in a long black robe walking slowly up the steps with a bunch of beads wrapped around his hand.

"Where do you think he's going?" Martin asked.

"There's a monastery up top. There's a little room up there. It's very holy to the Christians. It's where Christ was supposed to've eaten the last supper. Just before he was crucified. It's kind of weird, isn't it? King David's Tomb and The Last Supper side by side. And you know something else? The place is holy for the Moslems too. Mohammed was supposed to have done something here. Isn't it wonderful? All these holy men walking around peacefully together. Rabbis and priests, and who knows what else. And just over the other side of the mountain there's barbed wire and sandbags. What a crazy world!"

Crazy, Martin mused. Yes, it was crazy. He remembered the night he and Britta saw the Israeli bazookas flare, and heard the Arab shells pounding into the King David Hotel. He recalled also the story Gila told him: her brother shot from a tractor as he worked in the fields. And a strong picture came to his mind—Frank Laskey's contorted face, his screams, his description of blood and death.

Holy, holy, holy he thought. What the fuck did it mean, with all the carnage going on? How could anyone live in vineyards? Wasn't there only one place to go?—into the jagged rocks until his own skin bled, until his flesh was ripped so hard he could feel what Frank was screaming about.

"It's sickening, Helen. That's what it is. All these people with their bloody beads and prayers."

Helen shrugged. "It's not their fault."

Martin kicked his foot against a stone step.

"Maybe you're right. Who knows? Something's screwed up. That's all I know. The world's in a fucking mess."

Finally they reached the top of Mount Zion. There was a soft atmosphere that seemed to be descending with the sunlight, and sliding off the branches of the tall dark trees. Martin spotted a few tourists walking around, cameras dangling from their shoulders. And he spotted a sign. It was made out of rickety wood; the words were painted in black. The sign looked a little haphazard, as if somebody had decided to put it up on the spur of the moment. "Chamber of Horrors", it read, and an arrow pointed downward to a set of steps.

"Let's go down," Helen said, tugging at his hand. Her fingers felt bony and tight against his skin.

"Down there?" Martin asked, looking at the sign again. "It sounds like a side-show or something."

"Don't let that bother you. It's just for the tourists. Don't you want to see King David's Tomb?"

Something was not making sense to him. King David's Tomb and the chamber of horrors—why were they down the same set of steps? And what was the chamber of horrors anyway?

"Sure, let's go down," he finally agreed.

They walked down the steps together and along a dark passageway. He could smell candles, and the only light down there came from the flickering flames. He could see shadows on the wall, shadows of men and women walking around slowly, talking to each other in hushed voices.

"It's over here," Helen whispered, and she pointed to a block of stone with Hebrew writing on it.

Around the walls, and on the slab of stone itself, the monument to King David, numerous candles were placed. Their flames licked upwards and cast shadows against the dank stone walls. And around the slab of stone a crowd of men stood praying, *davening*, rocking back and forth on their heels. A few tourists stood among them, but most of the men were Chassidic Jews, probably from Mea She'arim, Martin mused. Their faces looked pale and drawn, as if they hadn't seen too much sun. But wasn't his own face a little white, lacking color?—Martin thought.

"His bones," Helen whispered, "King David's bones are supposed to be lying underneath that block of concrete. Can you imagine? Still there after all these centuries. Doesn't it give you the willies? It makes my stomach feel a little funny."

The smell of wax burning, and the sound of the men *davening* in Hebrew, and the dank darkness of the place, began to bother him.

"C'mon Helen. Let's get out of here. Let's go back outside. I just can't take it any more. C'mon, let's go."

He began walking towards a sign that read EXIT. Helen followed closely on his heels. Up a narrow corridor they walked. Halfway to the end, he could see flashes of light. They got closer. It was a group of tourists taking pictures. What the hell were they looking at?—he wondered. Then he saw some glass cases with objects inside. They got closer to take a look.

There wasn't that much to see, but what he saw disgusted him and made his stomach churn. It was a display of shirts made from the holy sheepskins of torahs. Each shirt had a black star of David painted on it. In the center of the star the German word Jude was engraved. Now it became clear to him. Down there inside the catacombs, they had set up a small display testifying to the holocaust. The "Chamber of Horrors"—he remembered the sign outside.

"C'mon Helen, let's get out of here. I've seen enough. Let's go. They can keep their fucking chamber of horrors."

"What's wrong? Why are you so upset?" Her words were echoing behind him as he raced up the steps, heading for a shaft of sunlight at the top.

He didn't bother to answer Helen. Her words were like loose stones falling behind, and he was going upward, clawing his way up like a person digging feet into a slippery hillside. Up, up the long dark corridor towards the square of light at the end, the patch of sun and fresh air.

What disgusted him more?—he wondered. What was aching and turning in his gut? Was it the Nazis, or those who devised the underground cavern to keep the memory of bones and death alive? How pale the Chassidic Jews looked. They smelled of snuffed candles, and old bits of dried food. He had to get up to the sunlight. And he was thinking of his own face, still white and pale and drawn from the weeks of sleeping until noon-hour down in Helen's room.

When he got to the top he took in gulps of air.

"What's wrong with you?" Helen asked, catching up with him. Her voice was burning with annoyance.

"Nothing." He shook his head and looked away from her and gazed at the trees, the long spindly branches at the top.

She put one hand on her hip and scraped at the dust with her right foot.

"Why do you have to spoil everything?" she asked. Her face was drawn tight with anger, the skin pinched around the bones of her chin and cheeks.

"I got claustrophobic. That's all. I needed some fresh air. For a second I thought I was going to faint. I'm sorry."

"You do look kind of pale, Martin."

Helen swished her flowered dress and began walking around, looking here and there. She came back to him again.

"Let's forget it," she smiled. "Maybe it wasn't a good idea. It was awful close down there."

They spent the next hour or so walking around the garden on top of Mount Zion. Helen pointed out the great mosque to him on top of the Mount of Olives. The gold leaf of the dome glittered in the sun. He was glad when they finally decided to leave.

During these days he spent a lot of time thinking of what spring was like in Canada. He remembered how it came as a sudden shock of warmth in Montreal. Almost suddenly, people put away their heavy winter coats, their galoshes, their mittens, and bared their skins to the sunlight rushing down from the sky above Mount Royal.

"It comes very quickly," he told Helen. "One week we're freezing and then it's spring."

He could imagine women walking along Sherbrooke Street, French girls in skirts, their legs bare. And he remembered driving with a good friend up to St. Adele in the Laurentian hills. They celebrated spring that year with two Havana cigars, the smoke twirling and dancing out the open windows of his friend's small car. What a relief after all those months of heavy snow, ice, slush, what a relief to see the green buds appearing.

He began to yearn to hear English. His friends, of course, spoke English, but it didn't seem enough. He had a dream about walking into a drug store and hearing a customer ask for a prescription. They were talking English, simple, everyday, common English. And he realized that it was this he missed—street English, "what do you think of the weather" English, and he realized that he was tired of hearing the Hebrew tongue; sick of hearing it on buses, in stores, on street corners; tired of its opaque, guttural sounds. How little he had picked up in three years. It was almost amazing how he had avoided it so successfully. Even by a simple process of osmosis he should've known more. "Toda raba", thank you. "Bivakasha", you're welcome. "Ani rotzeh", I want. "Ani medaber Ivrit", I speak Hebrew. A few phrases, yes, a few heavy gutturals, but that was all he really knew, all he wanted to know.

"I just wish I could see some of my old friends," he told Helen. "Somebody from Canada."

He was thinking of fellow students at McGill in Montreal. Perhaps they had all changed. Why not? Hadn't he? Perhaps they had all gone their own ways. Perhaps they would have nothing to say to each other. He was thinking particularly of a group of friends at university. Three years ago they were all aspiring writers; poets, they all wanted to be. Even back then Martin had thought—if all of us get our wish, there's going to be a hell of a lot of poetry floating around.

He wanted to talk to one of his old friends once again. He wanted to find out what had happened to that person. It was a long time, it seemed, those three years. Had anyone travelled down a similar road? Was there someone, someone he used to know, who had met people like Jesse, Josephine, Britta and Helen? Was there someone out there, he wondered, someone he could compare notes with?

He remembered about a year earlier getting a letter from Roger Stanton, a gentile friend and poet, who was brought up in a fine house in Westmount, an upper-class adjunct to Montreal. He received the letter just before he took his short trip to Istanbul and Greece. In it Roger had talked about life and poetry, about how it was important to stay awake and aware of what was going on. One line in particular shafted its way into Martin's psyche—"Just be careful," Roger warned, "not to atrophy." He had to look up that poisonous-sounding word in the dictionary. Atrophy—to dry up and wither away; to die from lack of nourishment. How could he possibly have known when he received Roger's letter, that his friend had written the warning just as much for himself as for Martin?

He began talking to Helen about his friends, Roger Stanton in particular. The words came out in streams, as if the memory was letting loose a blocked river inside him, a pent-up source of inspiration.

"You know what this guy Roger Stanton once did?" he said to Helen. "Well, first of all you gotta get a picture of him. He came from an upper-class family. You know what I mean—they had money for years. Roger's great-grandfather founded a huge steamship line or something. Anyway, his uncle, who's a very respected lawyer in Montreal, gets Roger a job on a pleasure-boat for the summer. The boat travelled up and down the St. Lawrence between Montreal and Gaspé. So there's Roger. He's got this summer job, right? Now the people on this boat are the bloody elite—lawyers, doctors, priests, nuns, mother superiors—who knows what else? Back then Roger had really gotten into Nietzsche. He idolized him.

"Anyway, one day during the summer, there was a religious convention aboard—bishops, priests, nuns, etc. And you know what Roger does? Before they leave from Montreal he gets about a thousand Nietzschean tracts printed up. You know the kind of stuff—God is dead, priests are a blight on humanity—that kind of thing.

"As the boat's heading up the river, one night around midnight, Roger sneaks out of the servant-quarters and slips these bloody tracts under everyone's door. Can you imagine the uproar in the morning? The captain, believe it or not, orders a search of the ship. And don't they find those leaflets in Roger's room?"

"You're kidding," Helen laughed. "So what happened?"

"Well, they haul Roger up in front of the captain, then interrogate him just like a trial or a court-martial. I can't remember exactly, but I think they got an apology from him and let him keep his job. I guess because of his family they couldn't do too much else."

Martin felt a warmth burning inside his chest as he told Helen the story. Roger Stanton, he thought. Wouldn't it be great to see him again, or one of his other friends—just to get a little bit of news about Montreal? Martin shook his head. He had really cut himself off in the last couple of years. The letter-writing had long ago stopped. Wasn't there any connection with that old life? How could it have been chopped away from him completely? Yet it seemed that way.

Just after finishing the story about Roger, they heard a loud knock at the door, someone pounding with the heel of the fist, and then rapping with the knuckles.

"Anyone home!?" a gruff voice yelled. "Is anyone in there?"

"Just a second!" Helen shouted back. "We're here."

Helen opened the door, and Jerry Duke walked in holding up his right arm.

"Got that bloody cast off today," he announced. "Now you'll see the old Duke operate. How the hell are you two? Hiding away as usual?"

"Hi, Jerry," Martin mumbled from the bed.

Jerry's voice was splitting apart the dreamy, nostalgic mood he'd slipped into.

Jerry took his usual chair, flung off his army boots, hoisted his smelly feet up on Helen's bed. Then he turned to Helen, who was still standing at the door.

"What's wrong with this bloody guy anyway?" he asked, tossing his head in Martin's direction. "He sleeps to fuckin' noon hour. Gets up and scribbles some of his usual shit. I never see him downtown. Christ, he's worse than the fuckin' rabbis in Mea She'arim."

Helen kept smiling. She leaned her shoulder against the wall and tilted her head in that direction.

Jerry picked up one of the army boots off the floor. He turned it over, examining the sole thoughtfully. He gave it a few raps with his knuckles.

"Guess they'll hold out," he declared. "You know that march they have every year—that fifty-miler? I'm going to walk with them. Give 'em a little idea of what an ex-marine can do."

Jerry was talking about the annual walk marathon from Tel Aviv to Jerusalem. It was held to commemorate independence. Old men, young, sabras, tourists, girls and even camels took part in it.

"Why don't you come with me?" Jerry asked, eyeing Martin, and slapping the boot against Martin's knee. "Do you some good. You could use the fuckin' exercise."

Martin stared at the floor and shook his head silently.

"Well, how about you, Helen? You could do it."

Helen smiled, and moved her weight from one foot to the other.

"I have to work, Jerry."

"Well, at least you've got a valid excuse."

Jerry creaked his weight around in the chair, and allowed the boot to fall on the floor.

"So, what've you guys been up to?" he asked, changing the subject.

"Nothing much," Martin answered, his words coming out heavily.

"Seen any good movies lately?" Jerry asked.

Helen and Martin shook their heads in unison.

"Listen, if you want to see some of my work, there's a movie playing in town right now. Dr. Strangelove, with Peter Sellers and George C. Scott. Go take a look at it. I wrote the screenplay about a year ago. Well, not the whole thing really. Just some of the funnier parts."

"You're kidding," Martin said in a daze. This bit of information sounded wild, but he didn't know what to believe any more. What if everything Jerry had told them was as true as gospel? What if he were Terry Southern? It was hard to swallow, but then anything, Martin mused, was possible.

"No," Jerry said, screwing up his mouth into a tight knot, his eyes getting hard and marbly behind the glint of his glasses. "I'm not kiddin'. Go see it. It's a great movie."

Silence reigned again—only the sound of Jerry scratching his big toe.

After a few minutes Jerry got restless.

"How about doing some hash with me?" he asked, searching his gaberdine pockets for the plastic bag he kept it in.

"Not tonight, Jerry," Helen answered. "I've gotta get up early tomorrow."

"Well, how about you, Martin? We'll just let Helen get her beauty rest, and we'll fuck down to your room. What d'ya say?"

Martin wasn't in the mood. And the idea made him feel a bit uneasy—to go with Jerry in the middle of the night down to that bare room on Street of the Prophets.

"Not tonight, Jerry."

"Okay, I can see when I'm not wanted," Jerry said mock-seriously, putting on a boot at the same time. "Maybe you wanna ball. Go right ahead. Ball your lives away if you wanna. See if I care."

Then he broke into a smile, an almost warm and friendly expression on his face.

"You guys take it easy. I'll catch you some other night. Okay?"

His voice was slightly plaintive.

"Sure, Jerry," Martin responded, trying to sound a little warmer towards him.

"Yes," Helen agreed, smiling. "Come back some other night. We're just a little tired from the weekend."

After Jerry left and Martin was sure he was not hanging around outside the door trying to listen (Martin often got the feeling that Jerry would've given anything to hear what they said about him in private), after Martin checked through the keyhole, he whispered to Helen:

"I think he's really lonely."

"Yeah, I think so," Helen nodded, frowning. "But what can we do?"

"I don't know," Martin said, shaking his head. "After a while he just starts getting through to me. Just his voice. It's like a buzz-saw or something. Guess that's why he's lonely. No one can take it."

Helen bowed her head. "Yeah, you're probably right."

"And yet," Martin said, his eyes looking puzzled, "there's something I like about the guy . . . even if he turns out to be a liar. There's just something about him. At least he tells you what's on his mind. No beating around the bush, maybe that's it."

"Maybe . . ." Helen whispered. Her voice sounded dreamy and wistful.

That evening Martin had a dream. He was down in the Valley of the Cross once again. The valley looked longer and wider than it really was. The poppies were everywhere. It was getting dark, and he was searching for Helen. "Where is she?" he wondered, getting a bit upset. He was beginning to feel cold and alone. The sun had started to set behind the trees. And he saw a shadow over by the monastery. He ran towards it. Perhaps that was Helen, he had found her at last . . .

He got closer. The shadow took form, human form. It wasn't Helen at all. It was a man. It looked like Jerry Duke, Jesse, and Frank Laskey all rolled up into the same person. The shadow was beckoning to him to come closer. The fingers looked bony as he approached. And suddenly he began to shudder. The figure had turned into a skeleton. He woke up, moaning and sweating, with an eerie feeling in his chest. His whole body was tingling with fear.

Helen woke up beside him.

"What's wrong?" she asked.

"It's okay, Helen, go back to sleep. I'm sorry. I just had a bad dream, that's all."

Helen turned her back towards him, hugged her pillow tightly, and she was soon asleep once again.

Martin sat bolt-upright for a few minutes, perhaps longer, casting his eyes around the darkness of the room. Had anyone crept in while he was sleeping? Was there someone there, ready to plunge a knife into his heart as soon as his eyelids got heavy and he couldn't defend himself?

That's nonsense, don't think that way, he kept saying to himself. Take a few deep breaths and go back to sleep. Oh let me go back to sleep, he whispered into the darkness.

Slowly, his thoughts gave way. They melted, melted, became as soft as running water. He fell asleep beside Helen, nestling his face against her back.

CHAPTER 29

New Blood

Who could've imagined such a thing?—just two or three days later Martin was walking down King George Road towards the Y.M.C.A. The sun was still shining brightly around five o'clock.

He passed a small group of guys wearing knapsacks. He seemed to recognize one of them—the face looked familiar. The guy was tanned; he was smiling and laughing.

Could it be?—he wondered. Could that actually be Roger Stanton standing on King George Road, just standing there, big as life? No, his mind recoiled, look very carefully, you probably want it to be Roger Stanton, and your mind has created an illusion—a mirage, like a sheet of fresh water in a desert.

He approached the group slowly, eyeing the tall, lean boy with the big white teeth and brown face. He circled for a second, then he spoke.

"Roger Stanton?" he asked.

The guy turned around rather quickly.

"Kanner. Martin Kanner," he said, then paused. "Kanner, you're looking respectable these days."

The remark shook Martin up. It seemed a little cool. Was that the way you greeted a friend after not seeing him for three years, and then suddenly, mysteriously, almost miraculously running across him on a street eight thousand miles from home?

"What a surprise!" Martin gasped. "I just can't believe it. Where are you coming from?"

Roger shifted the knapsack around on his back, perching it higher on his shoulders.

"We just got off the march," he smiled, motioning his head towards his friends. "This is Jean Paul, and you remember Danny Lester, don't you? He was at McGill with us. We just met Danny on the march."

Martin glanced at Roger's two friends. They smiled back at him. But no, he couldn't remember Danny Lester. Perhaps Roger was mistaken, perhaps Martin had never run across him during the old days in Montreal.

"Where are you guys staying?" Martin asked. "Do you have a place?"

Jean Paul snickered and said something to Roger in French.

"No, we just blew in," Roger shrugged.

"Listen," Martin said excitedly, "I've got this room. I'm pretty sure it's empty right now... there was a guy staying there... but I think he's gone. You guys can have it if you want. You can stay there, no problem."

There was an animated conversation in French between Roger and Jean Paul... Roger explaining to his French friend Martin's offer.

Jean Paul's eyes widened with surprise.

"Ah, gude, une chambre."

Jean Paul kissed the tips of his own fingers, and smacked his lips, showing his pleasure.

"Oui, oui," he continued, "that's gude, we need a chambre. Certainement."

Jean Paul gazed at Martin with a smile on his face. He seemed to be coating Martin with friendliness.

"Good," Martin smiled back, "you can have my room."

"Where are you staying?" Roger asked.

"Oh I've got this girlfriend," Martin grinned. "I stay down at her place."

Jean Paul smacked his lips against his fingertips again. He seemed to have understood what Martin had said.

"That's gude, Marteen. Une femme. A piece—eh? A gude piece."

He began to giggle slightly and Roger joined in. Martin glanced at Danny Lester. What a dazed-looking guy, Martin thought. It was something about the way he held his mouth, or didn't hold it. His lips looked thick, almost livery, and his mouth hung open.

"Marteen," Jean Paul said a little more seriously, "can you show us this chambre? We are très fatigués. Like dogs, oh my pauvre feet."

"Sure," Martin laughed, amused by Jean Paul's speech, and his facial expressions that seemed to match the pidgin English. "It's just a few blocks away. C'mon, I'll take you there. I have a few minutes before I go to my class."

The four of them trooped down the street together. It was an odd-looking group—three guys dusty and grimy in short pants with knapsacks on their backs, and Martin leading the way still wearing his knee-length overcoat. The days were getting warmer, but Martin could still feel the winter chill inside him.

The others looked warm, almost flushed. For three days they had been marching towards Jerusalem. Up the long curved highway they had walked, part of the annual march, the fifty-miler Jerry Duke had spoken of.

So these were added to the last months: Roger Stanton, looking tanned, Jean Paul his travelling companion, Danny Lester who wrote poetry; and to these were added Roger Stanton's girlfriend Paula, a heavy dark-eyed girl whose family was from Iraq (Roger had met both her and Jean Paul in Italy), and Isolde, a Swiss girl of Jewish descent.

The next day, Martin was telling Roger and Jean Paul a little about Jerry Duke.

"I think we saw that guy on the march," Roger said excitedly, his face suddenly flooded with light. "Hey, Jean Paul, you remember this guy Jerry Duke?"

Roger was speaking to Jean Paul in French, but Martin could get the gist of it.

"No. Jerry!" Jean Paul laughed, slapping his bony knees. "The bastard with the tea. Oh yes. The soldier. Oui!"

What was going on?—Martin wondered.

"Quite a shmuck, that guy," Roger nodded, forming his mouth into a tight knot.

"A grand *mamser*," Jean Paul laughed. "This Jerry is a great bastard."

"Do you think we're talking about the same guy?" Martin asked.

"I'm sure," Roger Stanton nodded with an air of authority. "A tall guy, right? Scraggly beard, wears glasses, beady-looking eyes."

Yes, Martin had to admit, it sounded like none other than Jerry Duke.

"We remember him," Roger nodded, twinkling at Jean Paul. "We couldn't forget this guy. When we first saw him he was wearing a G.I. uniform. He came on real strong. Started telling us about his father, how he owned a thousand-acre ranch in Texas. Then he starts bragging about Korea. As if we gave a shit. Guess he thought he was going to impress us or something."

"What was this about tea?" Martin interrupted.

"Oh, the tea," Jean Paul laughed. "Roger, tell Marteen about the tea. Oh please."

"Well," Roger smiled coolly. "On the second day of the march, this guy kept dropping behind. He kept taking off his boots and massaging his feet. He wanted some hot water to bathe his feet in. So he goes up to the cook and starts bugging him for water. It was the only hot water around, but it was the tea-water."

Martin hung his head down.

Jean Paul began tapping a finger against his own head.

"The guy, I think, a bit cuckoo. Don't you believe that? Not complètement sain. Uh, Roger?"

Roger nodded.

"Yes," Roger mused, "I think he's a bit flipped out. Anyway, the damn guy didn't even finish the march. It was ridiculous really. He was coming on with all this marine shit, and he pooped out on the second day. And there were lots of girls who finished it."

Roger leaned back, supporting himself with his hands. They were sitting together, the three of them, in the room on Street of the Prophets. Danny Lester had gone back to Tel Aviv for a week or so. Paula, Roger's girlfriend, was supposed to arrive in Jerusalem the next day.

"How come he was staying here?" Roger asked, his voice a little mystified.

"Well," Martin shrugged. "The guy didn't have a room, and I wasn't using this one."

Martin paused.

"He's not a bad guy really," Martin continued. "If you can just ignore the lying."

"Maybe we'll see him again," Roger shrugged. "Do you think he'll be back here?"

"Probably. Yeah, most likely. He'll come back."

Martin was sure he hadn't seen the last of Jerry Duke.

"What if he wants the room?" Roger asked, his eyes wrinkling with doubt and a slight hint of worry."

"Just tell him to get lost," Martin said, biting down on his words, and clenching a fist together. "Tell him I gave you the room, and that's it. If he gives you an argument, just tell him to fuck off. I mean, after all, it is my room."

"Okay," Roger grimaced slightly. "That might not be so easy, though. Maybe he thinks he has a claim to it. You know ... sort of like squatters' rights."

Martin shook his head and waved his hand at the same time.

"Don't let him bug you, that's all."

Around midnight Martin said goodbye for the evening and walked back to Helen's place alone. He had already told her about the miraculous appearance of his old friend Roger Stanton.

"I was just talking about the guy a few days ago," he had said excitedly. "Can you imagine the shock I got when I saw him just standing there on King George Road? You know, Helen, he's changed quite a bit. Back at McGill he was really pale, up to his neck in books and ideas. Now you should see him—he's got this tan, he's travelled all over Europe. It's amazing how people change."

Helen smiled. She seemed to be happy that Martin had gotten his wish.

"It must've been telepathy," she said, "meeting him like that. Listen, Martin, why don't you invite him down here? I'd like to meet him."

"Sure," Martin agreed, "that'd be great. Maybe I'll get him to come down some night."

What a good thing that these new people had hit town, Martin was thinking as he walked back down to Helen's room. They showed up just at the right time—just when everything was looking hopeless and bleak, when Jerry Duke was getting on his nerves, and when it seemed that he didn't have a person in the world to talk with other than Helen.

He could feel a lightness inside himself. It was a feeling of rejuvenation and new hope. That's what the town needed, he grinned to himself, some new blood.

He lay in the darkness that evening beside Helen thinking of his friend Roger Stanton. Helen was already asleep. He could hear her breathing heavily beside him.

It was Roger who had introduced him to the poetry of Wallace Stevens, and the fine, soft lines of Li Po and other Chinese poets. Back at McGill, four or five years before, they used to have lunch at a small Hungarian restaurant on Stanley Street. What amazed and fascinated Martin just as much as the poetry was the way Roger handled the books. They looked well read. And it seemed that Roger had caressed the pages lovingly, leaving his fingerprints here and there. It was as if Martin could see Roger's dark eyes on the actual page, his gaze and feelings imprinted on the creases of the book.

And there were a few poems written by Roger himself that had a mysteriously soft, dark quality. One poem ended with a guy standing on a bridge over the St. Lawrence, shouting his poems down the thousand-mile river. What an image! Martin could never quite forget it—the river dark and winding, going on for a thousand miles, and perhaps forever, and someone shouting above it, and into it, and down it, lines of his own conception.

Once or twice Martin had gone out to Roger's house in Westmount. It was a huge dark house, Victorian in style, set on a small hill. There, he had met Roger's mother, a woman who looked bony and padded, sensual and determined, all at the same time. And Roger's father—he frightened Martin a bit, the tall lean man in a conservative suit with cool grey eyes. Was he looking at Martin with suspicion, perhaps with a tremor of revulsion, or was that merely Martin's imagination?

Martin was used to entering gentile homes. He had visited his gentile friends in Halifax often when he was a child, and later as a teenager. But Roger's home was different. It was the house of a long-established Anglo-Saxon family, and the walls seemed coated with British tradition.

Roger Stanton, Martin thought in his half-wakefulness, you've really changed in the last couple of years. It amazed Martin that Roger had been able to take off for Europe alone, travel through Germany, Italy, and along the way dump all his books, or just leave them behind. And along the way, somewhere in Rome, on a sunlit piazza, he met Jean Paul and later his girlfriend Paula. It must've taken courage, Martin was thinking, more than he himself was able to muster . . . He remembered the short-lived trip to Turkey and Greece.

"I know," Roger had told Martin privately, "Jean Paul must seem like a bit of a clown. But don't let him fool you. He's a solid guy. There's lots going on inside him. He might seem to be smiling and assing around, but he sees everything."

"Yeah," Martin agreed. "I like the guy. He seems to take everything in his stride."

"He's a good painter too," Roger added. "Not great stuff, but he has this light touch. That's how I met him. He was making a few bucks doing sidewalk sketches in Rome."

"On the sidewalk?" Martin asked, a little surprised.

"Yeah, chalk-drawings. He'd attract quite a crowd with them."

Suddenly, Martin had a vision of the rains descending on the Italian capital, and Jean Paul's handiwork getting washed away forever into the Tiber.

The next day around noon hour, they were all gathered together in the room on Street of the Prophets—Roger, Martin, Jean Paul, Danny Lester and Isolde. Paula hadn't gotten into Jerusalem yet.

Isolde and Jean Paul had bought some pastry on Zion Square. There seemed yards and yards of the stuff: cherry strudel.

They were all sitting around munching away. The atmosphere seemed light and easy-going, almost joyful; there wasn't a drop of liquor or speck of hash, yet everyone was in tremendously high spirits.

"Munch, munch, munch," Isolde said, mimicking an animal.

"Ah, it's gude," Jean Paul laughed. "This cherry strudel. What is la vie? Eat, munch, munch, enjoy."

Roger was loosening up more than ever. Martin had never seen him this relaxed, uncaring, letting himself go. He was buckled over laughing at Isolde's antics and Jean Paul's comments.

Martin himself couldn't stop laughing. What was so funny about it? Yet he didn't care—sunlight, cherry strudel, Jean Paul and Roger. What was there to worry about?

"I am going to eat my way to the end of the world," Isolde rasped, imitating an old man or an ogre.

"You are a chicken-face," Danny Lester told her, as if this were the final, the absolutely final comment on her character.

"I am the great chicken," Isolde laughed, buckling over, spewing bits of strudel out of her mouth.

Jean Paul got to his feet, hunched over, began flapping his arms as if they were wings.

"Cluck, cluck, cluckety-cluck," Jean Paul grunted.

Roger was leaning back on his elbows, pointing at Jean Paul, streams of laughter coming out of his mouth.

There were chunks of cherry strudel everywhere, it seemed: on the floor, on the bed, on the windowsills.

"How much of this stuff did you buy?" Roger asked.

Jean Paul threw up his hands. "Just one, two bags. I don't know."

"It was a special," Isolde grinned. "The special of the year. No one wants cherry strudel. They had piles of it."

"Oh, oui!" Jean Paul agreed. "Regarde—it was in big montagnes. A montagne here, a montagne there. Nobody was looking at it."

"Maybe there's something wrong with it," Isolde grimaced, screwing up her face. "Martin, does it taste okay? Maybe it has bugs or something."

Martin felt a wave of disgust in his stomach. He turned the hunk of strudel over in his hands, examining it closely.

"Look!" Isolde laughed, slapping her thick, fleshy thighs. "He's worried about the bugs."

"It's gude, Marteen. A few bugs. Ah, oui. I can taste those nice bugs," Jean Paul grinned.

The gathering stuck in Martin's mind. He didn't know what was happening up in the room that noon-hour. Were they a bunch of maniacs? Yet it was good to laugh, to laugh until his stomach pained, to let it all come out, to watch Roger Stanton giggle and imitate a chicken himself. It was good, and he remembered afterwards how soft the sunlight felt as it streamed through the bare trees into the room. Sunlight on Jean Paul's delicate French face, sunlight on Isolde's thick, sensual thighs, sunlight on Danny Lester's livery mouth that continually hung open as if he were in an eternal state of awe, sunlight on Roger's long, horsey face, on his long eyelashes, on his black hair that was crawling over his ears. And sunlight on Martin's face, warming his lips, his cheeks, his nose, warming them, heating them up, dispelling the chill of the winter he had just gone through.

CHAPTER 30

On the Beach at Eilat

Roger, Jean Paul, Paula, Isolde, Danny Lester and Martin took a trip together down to Eilat, hitch-hiking through the Negev until they arrived at the port on the Red Sea. Marie, a Dutch-gentile girl and friend of Paula's, made the trip with them.

It was about a week after Passover, and the weather was really beginning to warm up, and they noticed this especially as they headed south through the long, dry stretches of desert. Martin was glad for the opportunity to get away from Helen for a few days, to just hit the road with his friends and allow things to happen.

Things did happen, piecemeal and disjointed. On the way down, they all stayed overnight at Roger and Jean Paul's kibbutz just outside of Beersheva. When the sleeping arrangements were finally organized and settled, Martin found himself in a room alone with Isolde. Secretly, he had been hoping things would turn out this way, because he was beginning to find Isolde's "chicken-face" attractive in a cute sort of way.

Was Isolde warming up to him? It was difficult to say, for Isolde seemed chummy with everyone. She would brush Jean Paul's hair for him, smile enticingly at Roger, and even pinch Danny Lester on the backside occasionally.

When the lights went out, Martin crept in the darkness over to Isolde's cot. She was lying on top of the bed in a white nightie, her juicy thighs just glimmering in the bit of moonlight that was nudging into the room.

"May I kiss you?" he asked, bending down, then kneeling so that his mouth was close to her face.

Isolde shrugged. "It doesn't matter. If you want."

Martin laughed nervously. "You don't sound enthusiastic about it."

Isolde shrugged again.

Martin pressed his lips against her cheek, then her mouth, but her lips felt strangely lifeless. He manoeuvred his body on top of hers, balancing himself on her thick thighs. He tried to massage her breasts, but she kept moving them away. He just lay there, and he could feel his own enthusiasm and interest begin to wane.

"You don't want to, do you?" he murmured.

Isolde didn't answer. Her eyes were shut and she was breathing heavily. Had she really gone to sleep while he was lying on top of her, or was she just pretending? He sighed to himself and went back to his own cot for the night.

It was a Friday night when they got into Eilat. It was just beginning to get dark. They were all thankful that evening had arrived, and it was beginning to dispel the intense desert heat. No stores were open, since it was the sabbath. They had no food with them.

On the beach at Eilat it was beginning to get chilly. Jean Paul wandered off on his own, and returned to the group with something in his hand.

"Mes amis, look here," he grinned and twinkled, and he held up a box of matzahs for everyone to see.

"Must be left over from Passover," Paula laughed. "There's nothing I'd like more, now, than a good stale matzah."

Jean Paul shrugged.

"Food is food, oui? We mange this matzah, maybe we not so hungry. Eh Roger?"

Roger agreed. "Sure. Why not? It looks okay. The box isn't damaged. It hasn't been opened. Sure, let's try some."

Paula turned her back on them as Jean Paul and Roger dug into the matzahs. The cold seemed to be affecting her the most. She stood in the moonlight on the beach with a blanket wrapped around her wide shoulders.

Martin was also shivering, but he didn't want to let on that the chill night air was bothering him.

"It's so cold," Paula shivered.

"Yeah," Roger commented, munching on a matzah. "And tomorrow it'll be hot, and you'll be complaining about that."

It was a little surprising to Martin to see this tenseness between Roger and Paula, which he had been sensing, come to the surface.

Jean Paul, Marie and Isolde seemed more accustomed to it. They went about their business, spreading blankets on the sand, getting ready to bed down for the night, and paid it little attention. It was early for sleep, but what else was there to do on a Friday night in Eilat with everyone almost penniless?

Roger was correct. Tomorrow would be hot. Forty-three degrees Celsius had been forecast.

But for the moment, on the chill beach under the moonlight, with the stars glinting in a black sky above the Gulf of Aqaba, it was difficult to imagine the heat of the next day.

There were other people on the beach. All of them seemed to have tents, or sheets rigged up on poles to make lean-tos against wind and sun. This larger group, Martin and his friends, had nothing so elaborate. They were going to bed down in sleeping bags and under blankets, with nothing between them and the wind and the sand kicked up along the beach, but a layer of cotton and wool.

This was the way it was, Martin thought; so he was going to shut up and bear it with the rest. He didn't want Roger to shove him into the "complainer" category along with Paula. But the truth was—it was chilly that evening, sandy and gritty, and they were hungry, and there was nothing to do but close the eyes and pray for sleep to come.

"The life, it's gude, eh Roger?" Jean Paul piped up from his sleeping bag.

"Sure," Roger drawled. "We've got all this fresh air."

"There's something a little funny about you guys," Danny Lester interjected. He had been quiet for a long time, but it seemed, now, a pronouncement was on its way. "You know what you remind me of? Mutt and Jeff, yeh, that's it, I got it. *Mutt aaand Jeff.*"

Danny was lying between two blankets, a huge grin on his livery lips. He felt satisfied with what he had just said.

"And who are you?" Roger asked, his voice tinged with annoyance. "The Cisco Kid?"

"No," Danny Lester said quite seriously, "I know who I am."

"Sure you do," Isolde mocked from her covers.

"You shut up, chicken-face!" Danny whipped back. "We didn't ask you for any of your shit."

"Danny!" Paula exclaimed. "Please!"

Isolde began laughing to herself, a high-pitched whinny that sounded a little hysterical.

"I think the only sane people here," Paula pronounced, "are Marie and Martin. They just keep quiet and mind their own business. The rest of you, so help me, sound like a bunch of kindergarten kids."

"Yes, Mom," Danny mocked. "You tell us."

"I give up," Paula groaned.

"You asked for that one," Roger said with a bite to his voice.

Under the covers Martin was grinning to himself. What else was there to do? All these voices jamming together. A cross-fire, he kept thinking, but much more complicated than the good guys versus the bad, or the Arabs against the Jews.

There were three girls and four guys on the beach that evening, but only one couple, Roger and Paula, lying together. It seemed strange, everyone needed to be warm, but they all slept apart except for Roger and his girlfriend. What was wrong?—Martin kept thinking. Why couldn't it just happen—the guys getting together with Marie and Isolde? Then he thought of Isolde on the kibbutz, her lifeless body beneath his. And Marie seemed to cling pretty close to Paula, and not communicate too much with the others.

"Is everyone asleep?" Isolde whinnied.

There was silence.

"I'm not," Marie answered.

It was good to hear Marie's voice. It was one of the rare occasions when it could be heard coming out clear and alone.

More silence.

"Hey, Isolde, why don't you come over here?" Martin whispered loudly.

"What for?"

"You know what for," Martin said sarcastically and a little bitterly.

"Oh go to sleep," Isolde clucked.

Martin could hear bodies turning over on top of the sand, shifting their weight this way and that, trying to find a comfortable hollow to go to sleep in.

"Good night, my friends," Jean Paul yawned.

"Good night," Martin murmured.

Before he fell asleep, Martin could hear Roger and Paula whispering to one another. He tried to make out the words, but it wasn't possible. And before he finally went to sleep, he could hear people breathing heavily, snoring, and he could hear the waves of the Red Sea lapping up against the beach.

Danny Lester's comment the next morning seemed to define the tone for most of the stay at Eilat beach.

They all started stirring about six in the morning, wiping sand off their bodies, folding blankets, trying to awake. Danny was one of the first to his feet. He stood there surveying the small tents and lean-tos. Bodies could be seen rustling and moving under canvas and sheets. Backs, legs, arms.

"What's happening?" Roger asked Danny. "What's everyone doing?"

"Oh, nothing much," Danny answered. "Just flapping off and getting ready for breakfast."

Roger began laughing. He found this an amazingly acute summation of what was going on. Enthusiastically, he repeated Danny's remark to Martin.

Flapping off and getting ready for breakfast, Martin thought. It was a somewhat clever statement, but Martin found it difficult to get that excited about it. What a chilly world-view, so lean and cold. Did it really come down to that?—everyone pulling their wires, and cracking eggs at the same time?

Martin gazed along the beach. What a weird color in the sky, a blackish blue. And the waves of the Red Sea looked chilly. It looked like a winter's day could be just beginning at six-thirty in the morning. Yet soon the sun would rise, and the sky would turn paler, washed with its rays. Soon the heat of the day would pounce on all of them. What then would there be to do at eleven o'clock in the morning without a single white sheet to protect them against the sun?

It did get hot, just as everyone expected. The sun rose higher, and with its ascent the heat came, jabbing at them, prickling their skins, roasting their blood.

"Look, mes amis," Jean Paul said, "we are crazy. We have this water, all this water. Let us swim—no?"

"Yes," Martin agreed, "let's go."

It was the best idea he had heard so far.

"Roger," Jean Paul encouraged, "we swim, oui? We take some nice water and put it on our bodies. Nice cold water, eh Roger?"

Roger was gazing at the sand, drawing a squiggly line with one foot.

"I don't know, Jean Paul. I don't like the water. I can't swim, you know."

"Oh, come on, Roger, don't worry," Paula said, patting Roger on the shoulder. "We'll give you a swimming lesson... Jean Paul, écoute, we must show Roger how to swim."

Jean Paul grinned.

"Mais oui, certainement. Oh Roger, you will see. What nice water. Come, let us go everybody. Merde! What heat! It is worse than the hell, I'm sure."

They all got into their swimming suits except Roger. He hadn't expected to go swimming.

"It's okay; who cares?" Paula exclaimed. "Just wear your underwear, no one will notice."

"Listen, Paula," Roger said rather seriously, "I'll give this thing a try—okay? But don't push it. I'm going to stay close to the shore."

"Don't worry," she laughed, "we're not going to let you drown."

"Who says?" Isolde teased. "I am going to come under him like a monster. And then, I shall pull him into his watery rest."

Paula laughed and Roger shuddered just noticeably.

Martin was left with a vivid picture of Roger that morning. The others, Danny Lester included, could crawl like the Australians, swim on their backs, breast-stroke, side-stroke, duck-dive, and generally cut through the blue-black waves. Or float, or just relax, allowing the water to cradle them, cool them off, revive them.

But Roger went no deeper than his waist. He allowed Paula to stand above him and support him, her thick, strong hands under his chest and stomach.

Martin kept thinking—yes, it would be good for Roger to learn to swim, to get over this fear. It was difficult for Martin to understand Roger's phobic reaction to water. It was just as intense as his own fear of high places. Yes, he could understand what Roger was going through—that sickening feeling in the stomach, that panic that made one breathe too hard; but the actual element water, how was it possible to really get in a panic over it? It seemed so innocuous—that wet stuff.

"Just relax, Roger," Paula whispered so that the others couldn't hear. "I won't let go of you, and it's not that deep. Just move your hands and kick your feet a bit."

Jean Paul swam in close to the pair.

"Eh, Roger? You like this water?"

Roger shook his head.

"No, Jean Paul. They can baptize all the whores in Italy with it. I don't like it. What is there to like? Can you tell me that?"

Roger's teeth were chattering. His arms and legs were goose-pimply.

"Ah, but the heat, my friend. It takes it away."

"No," Roger shook his head, "I've had enough water. I'm going up to the beach and dry out."

"But you were doing so well..." Paula protested. "You can swim, I know you can."

Roger shook his head again. "Tomorrow. Maybe tomorrow we'll give it another try."

"Okay," Paula agreed. "I'm going to stay in a while with the others."

They all swam another fifteen minutes or so, sucking in the water, spewing it out again. Martin dove a couple of times towards Isolde, trying to snatch a quick feel of her crotch under the waves.

On the beach he could see Roger Stanton standing alone with a white towel over his shoulders. He still looked cold, watching the waves, surveying his friends. And suddenly, Martin recalled a teen-age friend back in Halifax. Jim Cogswell was his name. And his nickname was Patch. He was dubbed Patch because of a blanket his mother had made for him out of bits and pieces of material. It was a multi-colored, raggedy cloak. Patch often wore it around the house, or out at Queensland on the beach. He too got the shivers and goosebumps often.

What was the point to it all?—Martin wondered—this trip to the Gulf of Aqaba. It was hotter than hell. They had little money for food. At night it was chilly, and hard to find a comfortable spot on the rough sand.

Yet they all continued on for a couple of days, putting their few agorot together to buy bread and tomatoes, and the odd piece of cheese.

Danny Lester spent a lot of time standing in front of the ice cream cooler in a local supermarket, or "supermarketa", as it was called in Hebrew.

"This is the best bloody place in town," Danny declared.

He held his hands over the deep-freeze, and leaned his face towards the chilly air.

Danny also spent a few hours at the local airport watching the piper cubs take off and land. He had a fascination with this sort of thing: tramcars, trains, boats, planes, anything that moved. It seemed that he saw them all as part of his private collection.

Isolde fooled around with some of the local teenage boys, but they soon lost interest, discovering that she wasn't serious about love or sex.

Paula continued to complain: the heat, the lack of food, the chilly nights, the sand in her hair. She wasn't afraid to voice what the others were feeling. She told Roger that she thought Martin would make a good father some day—once he settled down and got a grip on himself.

Marie stayed close to Paula as usual, and she said little about the weather or the lack of food. In fact, it was rare to hear words come out of her.

Jean Paul joked around, quipped, and to Martin's amazement, he picked butts off the road and smoked them.

"Why not?" Roger said in his defence. "The heat has probably sterilized them."

"Why not?" Martin shrugged, but inside he felt revulsion. There were lots of reasons why not. Maybe the last guy to smoke the bloody thing had TB, or worse, syphilis of the mouth.

Martin wanted a smoke, but he couldn't bring himself to pick up a butt and try it.

On the way back to Jerusalem, they all stayed overnight at a kibbutz in the Negev just twenty miles north of Eilat. It was a rich kibbutz. How did it make its money?—Martin enquired. They specialized, he was told, in strawberries. When strawberries were out of season up north, they made a good profit selling the crop to restaurants and stores in Tel Aviv and Haifa.

Martin was hesitant about using the outhouse on the kibbutz, fearing an encounter with a Negev scorpion. What a horrible thing —to be sitting there with his pants down, and one of these scorpions suddenly striking at a bare leg. He expressed this fear to Danny Lester.

Danny Lester proceeded to tell him a rabbinical parable:

"A certain rabbi was a very fearful man. One day a fly flew up his nose. He couldn't stop worrying about the fly. It was on his mind night and day. Eventually the rabbi died. They did an autopsy, opened his skull, and looked in. You know what they saw, Martin? The fly that flew up his nose twenty years earlier had turned into an eagle with claws. And the claws were fastened to the rabbi's brain."

Danny Lester licked his lips and eyed Martin.

"It's just a little warning," he grinned, showing all his white teeth. "That's what fear can do to you."

Martin didn't reply, nor did he use the outhouse that evening.

In the morning they all began hitch-hiking back. They broke off into small groups. Finally, Martin found himself alone in the desert. He found one bare tree that gave a minimum of shade. He remembered Rick, the English boy, and his case of heat prostration. And he remembered Danny Lester's little story about fear. Was there an eagle growing inside his head with claws of steel?

Luckily, in a half hour or so, a van stopped and gave him a lift back to Jerusalem.

CHAPTER 31

The Sky Is Falling

It was good to feel Helen's body once again. She was under him, above him, beside him. She wrapped her black hair around him, cooed, and sucked, swallowed the sperm. The lovemaking or fucking started up where it had left off.

Roger and Paula rented a room on Street of the Prophets about two blocks away from Martin's room. Jean Paul found a place to stay. So did Danny Lester.

And Jerry Duke moved back into Martin's room. Martin didn't particularly want him there, but it seemed impossible to keep him out. Martin visited the room one morning. The place was a mess. No one was there, but he could feel Jerry Duke's presence everywhere.

The first thing he noticed was a broken window off the balcony. It looked like it had been smashed on purpose. Beside the bed, on a chair, Jerry had left an assortment of hash pipes, Black Lebanese scrapings, a knife, and four or five booklets of matches. His clothes were everywhere: old shirts lying on the bed, underwear on the floor, boots on the coffee table.

"What a fuckin' mess," Martin muttered to himself. He noticed that the candles had burnt down to the lips of the wine bottles, and they hadn't been replaced. Jerry was using the purple tablecloth as a bed cover. Picasso's Boy with Pipe was still on the wall, but it hung there all askew. Martin tried to straighten it out, but for some reason it always swung back to a tilt. "What a bloody mess," he muttered again. "What the hell's the guy doing?"

He remembered the way Peter used to keep the room—everything in its place. What would Peter think if he could see it now? Martin grimaced thinking about it.

He heard the door swing open behind him.

"Hey man, what d'ya say?" Jerry grunted. "Where the hell have you been? I thought you blew this fuckin' town. Couldn't find you down at Helen's. Where the fuck have you been?"

"Eilat," Martin muttered, still peeved about the window and the condition of the room. "Listen Jerry, did you break that window?"

Jerry was kneeling on the floor, fidgeting around with the straps on a knapsack.

"I'm not going to fuckin' lie to ya. Yeah, I broke it. But what was I supposed to do? I come here one night. It's colder than a bitch out. Really, it was colder than a witch's tit. I don't have a key, you know that. What was I supposed to do—just stand around and freeze my nuts off? You tell me."

What was he supposed to tell him?—Martin wondered. It seemed useless to argue with him.

"Okay, okay," Martin muttered. "But can you get the bloody thing fixed?"

"Sure," Jerry nodded, giving the strap on the knapsack an extra hard yank. It looked like he was trying to throttle a chicken. "Sure, I will ... when I get the bread."

Martin let his shoulders slump. What was the bloody use of arguing with him? He decided then and there that the room was a lost cause. Aw, just relax, he said to himself, let him have the room. If you start worrying about it, you'll go nuts.

Martin glanced over at the chair beside the bed.

"Hey man," Jerry grunted, "you wanna toke up?"

"This early in the morning? It's only ten o'clock."

Jerry frowned, looking a bit put off.

"So what? As soon as I wake up, I toke. What the hell. You see, that's the difference between you and me. You always gotta think five fuckin' times before you fart. You gotta move your ass, man. Come on, have a toke with your old buddy."

Jerry's eyes had turned suddenly soft and plaintive.

Martin shrugged. "Okay, why not?"

Jerry began going through the regular routine of cutting and heating the small brown lump of hashish.

"Hey, by the way," he grinned, "met that friend of yours the other day, and his Frenchie pal. They came by to pick up their stuff."

"Oh, Roger?" Martin said in a daze.

"Guess that's his name," Jerry grunted, concentrating on the hash and rolling it into joints. He seemed to be thinking, gauging his next remarks.

"What kind of guy is he anyway?" Jerry asked. "Doesn't say much, does he? Asked him to toke up, but he didn't want any. He seemed like kind of a queer duck to me ... "

"He's a good friend," Martin mumbled. "We used to go to university together. Back in Montreal."

"Oh shit! Don't tell me. Not another fuckin' writer."

"Yeah, he writes a bit."

Jerry began blowing through one of the pipes, cleaning it out with gushes of breath. Flakes of ash shot up from the bowl.

"You guys make me laugh. You always have the same story. I write a bit. I write a bit. Why don't you fuckin' well get down to it? You can make a buck off it, you know. Fuck, you and me would make a good team. I've got the experience, you like to scratch, we could write a great book together. Make a bloody bundle. All you gotta do is have plenty of sex, and make it funny. People don't like to read a whole bunch of depressing shit ... so what d'ya say?"

Martin frowned, thinking about it.

"Yeah, maybe we could."

"No fuckin' maybes about it. You just think about it. I've got this fantastic plot brewin' around in my head."

Jerry finished rolling the joints. They began smoking together, sucking it in, holding it down. Martin choked and spluttered with the effort. He didn't want any to escape from his lungs unused. Jerry was cooler about it. He was holding it down for just as long, and his eyes got big, but he wasn't choking or turning red in the face.

"There's enough here to keep you high for three fuckin' days," Jerry said seriously. "When I make joints, I don't mess around."

Jerry paused. Something else seemed to be buzzing through his mind.

"Met that broad Isolde the other day too. You know, the one that laughs like a chicken with a hernia. She's not bad. Not fuckin' bad at all. Good set of tits on her. Nice ass if you like 'em meaty. One of these days, I'm going to throw a fuck into her. You just wait and see. When I get finished, she's going to know what fucking's all about."

Jerry choked just a bit, and he rolled back on the bed laughing to himself.

The hash was making Martin dizzy, and a bit paranoid. The walls seemed to be shimmering, rolling inward on him. He glanced at the knife on the chair beside the bed. Was that brown hash on the blade? Or was that his own blood? Who was this guy, anyway, with the beady nervous eyes? Perhaps he was a maniac. What could prevent him from grabbing the knife suddenly, and plunging it through his chest?

Martin decided he had to leave soon, get out of Jerry Duke's company. The thoughts going through his head were just too insane.

"Hey," Jerry laughed. His mouth looked contorted, twisted out of shape. "I met your pal's girlfriend too. I forget her name. That's a good fuckin' ass too. Bet she's good in bed. What d'ya think, Martin?"

"Don't know." Martin shook his head.

"Wouldn't you like to fuck her? Come on, tell the truth. I won't squawk it to your pal. Wouldn't you like to throw a fuck into her?"

No, Martin thought, thinking of Paula. She didn't appeal to him—with her black, frizzy hair, her pudgy brown cheeks.

"Not really," he replied.

Jerry sat up on the bed. He raised his shoulders, taking in a deep breath of air.

"What d'ya think, Martin? D'ya think your old pal gives her enough? Do you think he satisfies her in bed? . . . Come on now, tell the truth . . . "

Martin sat there a bit stunned, the hash high going through him in waves. Why the hell had he smoked so much?

"I think she's itchin' for it," Jerry sneered. "That's what I think. You know what?—I could see her eyein' my cock the other day. She's a horny bitch—that one. You better believe it. I'd like to pin her fat ass for her. Yes siree."

Jerry's voice was marching through his head. Each word seemed like a heavy army boot, stomping, stomping. It was relentless.

"I think I'm going to take a walk," Martin finally said, trying to get to his feet.

"What if I go with you? We'll trip around a bit together. What d'ya say?"

Martin shook his head. The stone floor was rolling beneath his feet.

"No, Jerry, I've gotta try to straighten out a bit. Whew! I've got to teach this afternoon. God, I shouldn't've toked so much."

"Aw, don't worry about it," Jerry said, waving a hand at him. "You'll probably give 'em a hell of a lesson. This stuff's great, man. It increases your bloody concentration. No fuckin' shit. They've fuckin' proved it in lab tests. You know those fuckin' tennis pros— half of 'em toke up before a game. Slows up that bloody ball, man. Just look at how slow the time's going. How long you think we've been here?—a half hour, an hour? . . ."

Martin shrugged.

Jerry glanced at his watch.

"Three fuckin' hours, that's how long."

Three hours, Martin thought. It was hard to believe. He had a few more hours before he had to teach down at the "Y". But at this rate, would he ever make it?

Jerry collapsed again on the bed. Martin aimed himself towards the door. It seemed a good chance to get away.

"I'm going," Martin whispered.

"Yeah, okay. Catch you later, man. Have a good high."

What a wash of sunlight out on the street! What a long time it took him to get there! He had to navigate the stone staircase that led from his room down to the Street of the Prophets. Watch your step, take it easy, he kept whispering to himself. Your perception is fucked up. He kept thinking of tennis pros toking up. Did it really slow down the ball? What a crazy thought! He could see a white ball floating over a net, slow as a hand waving. Crash!—the racket in slow motion whacking it back. Into the slot it went—another victory for the hash-heads.

Sunlight, his head rolling, his feet plodding along, taking giant dreamy steps. Were there cops watching him, ready to seize him, to question him, to make him cough up the truth? *Who gave you this stuff? Where's the stash?* How the hell would they say it in Hebrew? What would they look like? Would they be wearing badges? Or dressed in plain grey suits?

No, he would never tell, he decided. They could flash bright lights into his eyes. They could manacle him, but he'd try not to give Jerry away.

It seemed that Jerry was right. He stayed high for the next three days. Somehow—he couldn't figure it out—when it came time to teach his lesson in conversational English, he was able to shake his head, remove the clouds, wake up. He had no idea whether the lessons were up to scratch. But he got through them. It was amazing, he thought. Each evening, he came down, talked to Helen reasonably, made love with her, but in the morning when he woke up, he was high again. Three days in a row, just as Jerry had predicted.

On the third day it was beginning to worry him. When was it going to go away? He couldn't wake up stoned every morning for the rest of his life. A terrifying thought ripped through his head. What if he had altered his brain waves? What if there was no way down?

He was grateful when the high wore off. He made himself a promise—to never toke that much again. He was happy and relieved to see things fall into their usual places. Yes, the sidewalk, yes, the normal passage of time, yes, the trees as they were supposed to look. Thank you, he whispered into the air, as if he were thanking some invisible force. Thank you for letting me off that merry-go-round.

In May of '64 a movie came to town—The Great Escape. Martin went off to see it with Helen. He wasn't expecting much, another movie about the Second World War. He had seen dozens of them. The plot was simple—soldiers in a concentration camp in Germany trying to get free.

A couple of hours of the movie were spent underground, the soldiers digging a tunnel to the surface. It had to be long enough to bring them out outside the gestapo walls. Martin found himself quite involved.

They were digging in the darkness with everything possible—jack-knives, spoons, forks, old pots, broken shovels. They scraped at the black muck and the hard rock. Inch by inch. Foot by foot. What a long, dark way it was up to the surface. Their faces were grimy with muck, sweat and dust mixed. Their fingernails were splintered and broken.

"This is a good movie," Martin whispered to Helen in the darkness of the theatre.

"Mmmm," Helen answered. She wasn't enthusiastic.

And what a relief when they finally made their way up, when they finally broke through the last crust of black earth, and they could see the sunlight pouring down through the trees. Had they calculated correctly? Yes, they were outside the walls.

What happened next amazed Martin. The soldiers went crazy with their new freedom. They ran into the woods and got lost. Some stole motorbikes, whipped them into a frenzy of speed, smashed them into walls and trees. Some were recaptured as they wandered dazed inside the forest. And a few, perhaps only one or two, made it past the German border into Switzerland.

Martin felt drained after the movie, but when he came out of the darkness of the theatre with Helen, he had a smile on his face. It was as if he had spent a couple of weeks clawing and scraping with the soldiers, tearing at the muck, splintering the stones.

"Did you see that guy on the motorcycle?" he asked Helen. "Wasn't that beautiful? So fuckin' happy!"

"Yeah," Helen said, a tone of reservation in her voice, "and did you see what happened to him? He wound up right back in the camp again."

Martin nodded as they walked along King George Road together.

"But those few minutes of freedom," he sighed. "Did you see the expression on the guy's face?"

They walked silently along together. The movie was still glowing and burning in Martin's stomach. There had to be a message there, he thought, for it to have hit him so deeply. Wasn't the whole movie a symbol? An emblem? A warning? Claw, he thought, claw and scrape through the darkness, dig for the light, scrape and sweat to get out of the muck.

"You know, Helen," he whispered, "sometimes I wish things were that simple. Do you know what I mean? I wish I knew the enemy, just like they did. There they are—clear as anything. The gestapo—soldiers with guns ready to shoot you. I just wish I knew what I had to do... Do you know what I'm saying? If I only knew—there's the ground you have to dig through, there's the prison walls, and outside is freedom. Fuck, Helen, I could do it then. I'd just throw myself into it and get out."

He could hear Helen sighing to herself.

"Yes... I think I know what you're saying. But don't you think the answer's inside you somewhere... that you just have to find it?"

Martin looked down at the sidewalk.

"Yeah, it must be. It just fuckin' must be. Yet everything seems so dark and mixed up. Who is the gestapo? Where are the walls? Which way is there to go?"

The next evening when he saw Roger Stanton, Martin told him about the movie.

"I don't know if it's art, Roger, but that movie really got through to me."

"It was just about a prison camp?"

Roger looked surprised. Martin could sense Roger's mind turning over, calculating, adjusting, trying to decipher what he had just said.

"Yeah," Martin nodded, "that's all it was . . . Maybe if you saw it, you'd know what I mean. It was just the way they got free, and what happened to them afterwards."

"Maybe I'll go with Paula," Roger murmured.

How could he explain it, Martin thought, how could he transmit those feelings that had just gone through him?

That evening he had another dream. Somebody had sprinkled hash into the city's water supply—tons of it. Everyone was stoned: the cops, the vendors, Martin, Roger, Helen, Jean Paul, the principal of the Y.M.C.A., Mr. Townley, Jesse, the soldiers at the border, the Israelis, the Arabs, all stoned, and grinning, walking around in a daze. He could hear people laughing up on Mount Zion. Rabbis and priests laughing to each other. He could hear laughter in the vineyards in the Valley of the Saved. Even the children were high.

He woke up beside Helen in a sweat. He was clawing at his pillow. His fingers were gnarled and cramped.

* * *

Was this going too far?—Martin wondered. Jerry Duke was slipping barbiturates into Isolde's coffee. The three of them had toked up together in the room on Street of the Prophets. Isolde was lying on the bed, her head against the wall. She looked half-asleep, in a daze.

"This is going to knock her out," Jerry whispered to Martin. "Listen, once she's out, I'm going to fuck the ass off her. You take off and come back later. Then you can ball her."

Martin felt his stomach turn over, a mixture of disgust and too much hash.

"Look," Jerry hissed, "she's almost out already."

Martin glanced at Isolde. Her head was hanging to one side. She reminded him of a limp rag-doll. Martin was getting nervous.

"Listen Jerry, for Chrissakes, don't put too many pills in her coffee. You'll kill her."

Jerry looked annoyed.

"Don't fuckin' worry. I know what I'm fuckin' doing. Go take a walk. I wanna get into this broad. Don't forget to come back. Then you can take a shot at it."

Martin glanced at Isolde. She had a silly grin on her face. Her eyes rolled open, then shut again.

"Hey, where's my coffee?" she suddenly shouted.

"Coming up," Jerry said cheerfully. Then he whispered behind his hand to Martin. "She's going to get more than coffee. About ten fuckin' inches more."

"Why's it taking so long?" Isolde moaned.

Then Isolde began to giggle to herself.

Martin's head was spinning once again. Should he stay around, he wondered, just to see if Isolde would be okay? He was getting higher. No, he decided, I'll just take a little walk out in the sunlight, have a look at the trees and the buildings.

"Catch you later," Jerry snorted.

Down the stone staircase he thumped once again. Why worry?— he thought to himself. What the hell was wrong with it?—Jerry and Isolde tearing off a bit of ass. Martin decided to relax.

It was about two o'clock in the afternoon. Would Isolde still be there when he got back? He walked along dreamily, the hash moving around inside him. What was going on up in his room? Was Jerry throwing one into her? Was Isolde squealing with pleasure, or was she out completely, just a hunk of dead meat?

About an hour later he returned to the room. He was almost afraid to open the door. He couldn't hear a sound coming from inside. The silence seemed to be drifting outside, and it wrapped him up. He was getting a bit nervous. What if Jerry had given her an overdose, and poor Isolde had expired completely?

Nervously, he opened the door, inch by inch. Isolde was lying on the bed. A blanket was slung across her legs, but it just covered he calves and feet. She only had a pair of white panties on. Martin shoc his head. Guess Jerry did what he said he was going to do, Martin thought to himself. He was glad to hear Isolde snoring. At least she was still alive. That worry was over.

Martin inched his way closer to the bed. He could hear Jerry's words ringing in his ears. "You can come back later and take a shot at it." Now what was he supposed to do?—undress himself, take off Isolde's panties, and screw her while she slept? Or was he supposed to slap her cheeks a bit, pour some cold water on her face, try to revive her, and then convince her it would be a good thing if they got it on together? He remembered the evening on Roger Stanton's kibbutz outside Beersheva.

For a quick second he bent down and embraced her.

"Isolde," he whispered.

"Whaa, ah, umm," she mumbled, tossing her head away from him.

He straightened himself out and stood above her, gazing downward. Oh, poor Isolde, he thought. You look so cold lying there in just your panties. He reached down and drew the blanket up, and covered her body with it.

"Have a good sleep," he whispered.

He was sure she couldn't hear him, but it felt good to say it anyway.

"Have a good sleep, Isolde," he whispered again into the silence.

Quickly, he spun around on the stone floor and left the room. It was getting late. He was still a bit stoned, and in an hour or so he had to show up at the "Y" and teach another lesson in conversational English.

In June he could hear Henny Penny's warning clucking and ringing in his ear. The sky, dear sirs, is falling. The sky is falling, falling, falling down. And it seemed that way . . . things seemed to be splintering, breaking up, pieces of his life crumbling. The ice breaking. A glass cracking, a singer hitting that note that finds the thin fissure of no resistance. An opera singer screeching, reaching, and a lovely wine glass atop a polished piano splintering.

Events came one upon the other. Bad news. Sickness. Etc.

He found out that Roger and Jean Paul were not going to stay in ᵃael forever. In a couple of months they were going to head for

Africa—Addis Ababa, Ethiopia, and later Kenya, perhaps. This was probably the worst news of all. What was he supposed to do when they were gone? Hide away once again in Helen's basement room? Cavort with Jerry Duke, fight him off, wake each morning with the sound of his knuckles cracking against the door to Helen's room?

From Jerry Duke he caught the crabs. He saw Jerry scratching himself one day in the room on Street of the Prophets. "Jerry, do you have the crabs?" he asked directly and bluntly.

"C'mon, Martin. Do you think I'd do something like that to a friend?" Jerry whined back.

Yes, he would, Martin soon found out. He discovered the small beady parasites moving through his pubic hair and clawing around his belly-button.

Helen got some sort of intestinal amoeba. The sickness sucked the color out of her cheeks. She was losing weight. She became bonier.

What a mess, what a mess, what a mess, Martin kept thinking.

"You know, Helen," he said one afternoon down in her dark basement apartment. "I think I've just about had it."

"What do you mean?" Helen looked puzzled, almost afraid.

"Had it! You know, had it!" he almost screeched, feeling waves of frustration choking him. "Had it with this fucking country, that's what I mean. Nothing's going right any more. Roger's leaving for Africa soon. When I heard that ... I don't know ... it was just the last straw."

"What about your job? Your writing? Us?" Helen's voice was thin and high-pitched. The amoebic infection was still working inside her.

"Helen, I can't live here any more. Am I going to teach those lessons two hours a day for the rest of my life? I'm thinking about going back to Canada ... maybe I'll get into university again. Finish off my B.A."

Helen's eyes were narrowing. Her face looked pinched now, the cheeks hollowed out, her lips thin and anemic.

"University!" she almost shouted. "And what are you going to write about there? Or maybe you're thinking of giving that up too."

His head drooped forward.

"No, Helen. I'm going to go back. I've had it!"

The conversation ended. It dribbled off, and he left the room quickly, happy to be outside once again, out of the darkness, up on the Street of the Steps where the sun was pouring down and the sky was blue and the wash of Yemenite women flapped in the wind.

There was a small café on the Street of the Prophets. Here, Roger and Martin met quite often in the last days of June. The owner was an elderly woman, a beefy, wrinkled person with a thin thatch of moustache curling above her lips. She sat at the cash and eyed the waitresses and customers.

"I think she's looking at us again," Roger often whispered across the table, between the cups of cappuccino and various flaky pastries and the odd strudel.

"Aw, let her look," Martin said, a bit of disgust clotting in his throat. "She's just an old battle-ax."

Then Roger would lean back in his chair for a second, and notice something else about the café.

"Did you ever count the locks in this place?" he asked.

Martin glanced around at the various doors. The front door, the back, the doors which led to the back garden. He had never counted them; in fact, never noticed, till Roger brought it up, just how many bolts and locks there were—and a variety, some that slid with brass devices, padlocks, and combinations.

"I just counted them," Roger grinned, sipping the creamy foam off his coffee, leaning closer to Martin so that the beefy owner wouldn't hear him. "There's thirteen of them."

"You're kidding!" Martin exclaimed, a devilish grin curling his lips.

And he would begin counting. He would get up to eleven or twelve, but never quite finish the task. Roger straightened him out. He would point to the one that was down by the floor, or the one hidden behind a plant.

From the corner of his eye, Martin glanced at the owner. She seemed to hover over the cash register, guarding it, tapping on the keys. What a life, he kept thinking, trying to imagine her existence. What would it be like to be an old woman with varicose veins, a moustache, an old woman deathly afraid of thieves?

"Is she looking at us?" Roger asked.

"Nah, just counting her money."

It was about eleven o'clock in the morning at the small café where they used to meet quite often during Martin's last days in Jerusalem.

It seemed the only place, now, where Martin could relax. Jerry Duke had taken over his room completely. Helen's room was just too dark and cramped.

The sun fell softly through the windows, and crawled through the open front door.

"What are you going to do in Africa?" Martin asked. A thought had crossed his mind. Perhaps he could sail across the Red Sea with Roger and Jean Paul, explore Africa with them. But when he really considered it, the idea frightened him. What would he do in that tangle of jungle, all alone with Roger and Jean Paul? It wasn't a real possibility—just another far-fetched dream.

"I don't know. We'll knock around a bit. There's gotta be something new about it. Africa! How many people really go there?"

"Are you going to take Paula with you?"

Roger shook his head.

"Well, things are pretty tense between us. And I don't think Paula could hack it. Maybe we'll meet her again back here, or in Greece."

Martin was letting himself drift into the sunlight. He was trying to block out the sound of the cash register ringing and clicking, and the scraping noise that the drawer made as it was slid open and shut again.

"I'm thinking of going back to Canada," he said softly and dreamily. "There are things I miss. I'm sick of all this heat, and the sand. I keep thinking of trees in Nova Scotia, and all that water. Maybe I'll get back into university. I only have a year left for my B.A."

Roger twirled the coffee cup slowly between his long fingers. He was looking into it, and over the edge of it.

"Why not?" he finally whispered. "I'll probably go back eventually. Who knows? But I'm not ready yet, that's for sure. Things were pretty bad before I left. The last year in Montreal was a bloody disaster."

Martin was glad that he was getting Roger's approval. Roger's old warning about the danger of atrophy still gnawed inside him.

"I think I'm ready," Martin said, shaking his head. "I don't know, it just seems that all the doors are closing over here. I just want a change."

Roger nodded. "Yeah. I guess I know what you mean. I got that sort of feeling back in Germany. It was horrible there, so cold and mechanical. As soon as I got to Rome—what a difference!—the sun, the people, a hell of a lot more relaxing and alive."

Martin nodded slowly and took another sip of coffee. He lit a cigarette, an El Al, named after the Israeli airline. He could vaguely remember the taste of Canadian cigarettes. It was often said that Israeli cigarettes tasted like camel-shit. Martin sucked the smoke back. They were dry, these cigarettes made in the Holy Land, dry and coarse-tasting.

Roger was fidgeting a bit in his chair, moving around, trying to find a more comfortable position.

"Martin," he finally said, "it doesn't really matter to me, I'm just curious. Did you screw Isolde that day Jerry Duke got her stoned?"

Martin was a bit surprised and embarrassed by the question.

"Oh," he laughed nervously, "you heard about that."

"Yeah, the story went the rounds . . . Paula was a bit upset about the whole thing. She kept calling Jerry an animal, and she said if you were in on it, you weren't much better. I just laughed about it myself. Well . . . it was a bit heavy, but no one got hurt."

"Yeah," Martin agreed, "it was a bit much. I went back afterwards. Isolde was conked right out. I couldn't do it. She was just lying there. I guess I thought about it."

"So what did you do?" Roger's eyes looked vaguely excited.

"I just put a blanket over her, that's all. I thought it was best to let her sleep it off. I stayed a few minutes, then I left."

Martin could feel that Roger was relieved.

"Jerry's really too much sometimes," Roger said with his eyes narrowing. "He takes things just a little bit too far."

"Yeah, I know," Martin agreed. "Sometimes I wonder if he's completely nuts."

Martin was glad when the conversation shifted, and they began talking more generally once again.

* * *

Jean Paul got terrific attacks of asthma. It was a side of him Martin had never expected to see. But there he was quite often — lying on his back, in Roger and Paula's room, or on the ground, and out would come a small rubber bulb. He squirted the atomizer mist down his throat, gasping for air and for breath. His delicate, light-hearted face was turning red, getting twisted. Just a breath, he seemed to be screeching, just an ounce of oxygen in my lungs. It was awful to see him writhing around, squeezing the black bulb desperately.

Watching him, Martin was dragged back to childhood, and reminded of his bronchial attacks—the days he spent away from school, and the horrible smell of the hot vapor that kept him breathing. And yet when he was eight years old, those were days of relief as well as pain. True, he had that awful hacking in his chest, that tossing and turning at night, that desperate lunging for a breath of air. But those were also days he could escape from the chalk squealing down blackboards, from gym class, from cold dank showers, from snapping towels, days that he spent at home with his mother, reading Hardy Boy mysteries, listening to Maggie Muggins on the radio, learning to knit, playing canasta or gin rummy with his mother.

He would often be three weeks or a month confined to his house, and it was just as well, he used to think. He looked out the window —snow everywhere, driving sleet, ice, hail, slush in the gutters. Wasn't it better to be inside, to just relax, to read his comic books? And didn't he have a right to rest in the middle of January? For the first week he would stay in bed, drawing the covers around himself, listening to his faithful radio, or just sleeping. Slowly he would get braver, stronger, more confident. He'd pad around the house in soft slippers, and a warm kimono that fell below his knees.

In the last days of June in Jerusalem, Martin got headaches quite often, and dizzy spells. He complained to Helen about them.

"Why don't you get glasses?" Helen suggested. "I'm pretty sure your eyes are bad."

He remembered getting his eyes tested six years before, when he was sixteen. Even back then, the optometrist had suggested glasses. But Martin had put it off. It just didn't fit the picture he had of himself. He didn't want to look like a bookworm.

He began to compare his vision with Helen's. Could she see this, could she see that? What was she seeing? No, things were blurred, there was no doubt about it.

"It might open a whole new world to you," Helen encouraged. "You're not seeing half of what's going on."

Yes, he thought, perhaps she was right. He was feeling drowsy, out of touch, as if he were walking around in a blurred dream, or living underwater.

He got himself a pair of glasses. He had been missing a lot, and he was amazed at just how much. He decided to walk down Jaffa Street and just take a look at the people and the stores.

He was seeing better, but now everything seemed to be leaping out at him: men with bulbous noses, warts on cheeks, broken teeth. The faces came at him; more and more came in his direction, grinning and grimacing, leering. He took off the glasses and slipped them back into their plastic case. Once in a while he would take them out again, slip them over his nose.

"Did you get them?" Helen asked, vaguely excited.

"Yes."

"Why aren't you wearing them?"

Martin screwed his face up.

"It's too much."

"What do you mean—too much?" Helen asked, her lips sneering.

"I don't need it," he said angrily, trying to close the discussion. "It's an ugly world, that's what I mean."

"But you spent good money on them. Why don't you put them on just for a second, let me see what you look like?"

Slowly, his arms feeling heavy, Martin took them out of the case, and slipped them over his nose. Helen's pinched face leaped at him.

"They're not so bad. Makes you look kind of dignified."

He could feel anger rising in him once again. He snapped the glasses off his face, and shoved them back into the case.

"You gotta give it a chance," Helen whined. "What do you expect? It's a new thing."

"Just drop it, Helen! Okay? I don't want to talk about it."

The discussion ended. Helen looked offended and a bit hurt.

Why was he thinking of Canada so much?—he wondered. It came to him as pictures, and the pictures brought feelings that stirred and moved inside his chest. He could feel new forces moving inside him, and a new optimism.

Pictures, and the pictures brought smells, and the smells and sounds and memories began to move through his body, charge his mind with hope.

Criah, criah, wide-winged seagulls, dirty old birds with long black-yellow beaks diving near the wharves of Halifax harbour. And he could smell the rotting timbers of the wharves on rainy days, and the smell of mackerel, herring, cod, tuna. A big black tuna he remembered. It was caught at sea off Queensland when he was on vacation with his mother—down on a wharf one afternoon fishing with Jim Cogswell. It weighed almost a thousand pounds, the young boys were told, this huge shiny black citadel of flesh.

Queensland, the Sea Breeze Hotel, mountainous waves forming deep in the throat of the cove, building, mounting, riding high with caps of white foam, plunging forward towards the beach, washing over the heads of swimmers, crashing down, sweeping up the sandy shore, throwing tons of black water-weight against the rocks.

Why shouldn't he think about it, and think about it seriously, he mused, as he walked up the steep road towards the room on Street of the Prophets. Wasn't that the place where it all began twenty and some odd years ago? Halifax—that citadel of rock clinging to the sides of the Atlantic.

When he entered the room, Jerry Duke was there. He looked different, more subdued. His face was curiously pale. It seemed that he'd gotten a haircut or a trim. He was wearing a white shirt, a light summer sports jacket and grey slacks. The room was still in its usual state of disorder and chaos, but Jerry was sitting quietly, looking contemplative, almost serious.

Martin didn't say a word. He didn't want to be the first to talk. The crabs he caught from Jerry were still bothering him, and he was still putting on blue ointment, trying to get rid of the pests that bit and itched in the dark creases between his thighs.

Jerry was the first to speak.

"Hi, old buddy," he almost moaned. "Guess you notice something different about me."

Martin shrugged.

"I don't want you to laugh," he continued, "I'm absolutely serious about this. It means a lot to me. I'm thinking of becoming a rabbi and living down in Mea She'arim."

Martin was a bit shocked. He realized suddenly that Jerry was wearing a small black beanie, a kipah as it was called in Hebrew, or yarmulke in Yiddish. It was the same color as Jerry's hair. He had missed it completely when he first came into the room.

He was tempted to laugh, or if not to laugh outright, to snicker, to release the nervous sensation in his chest. But Jerry looked so wan and pale and drawn and serious that he stifled it in his throat.

"I've fucked up my life, man. I've gotta do something with myself.

Everyone's got something. You and Roger have your writing. Maybe it won't amount to much, but at least you have it. Even the old ladies in the market got something. Do you get what I'm saying?"

Martin lowered his head and nodded. Jerry was dragging him into his mood.

"It's not easy, you know, becoming a rabbi. You should see the things you have to do. There's about a hundred and forty-four laws you have to follow. They have laws about everything—food, drink, sex, clothes. Nothing's missed, man."

Jerry looked down at the floor. His pale, serious face looked resolute and determined.

"I'd have to give up this stuff," Jerry suddenly blurted, waving a hand towards his hash pipes.

Martin was looking out the broken window that Jerry had smashed. He could see the sunlight and shadows moving through the trees. He found himself thinking about Dr. Lowenstein, that old, wrinkled man. Was he still there, seated in a leather chair among his huge collection of books?

"Maybe it's a good thing," Martin suddenly said. "What've you got to lose?"

"Yeah," Jerry nodded, "if I can give up this pot . . . There's a few other things that bother me. They're funny about sex down there, you know. They never take their clothes off. Can you imagine that? Trying to get off a piece of ass with all your clothes on? I guess they just poke it through their zipper or something. And I guess the women do it in those black skirts they wear. Oh fuck, who knows? Guess I just have to buckle down, and do as the Romans do. Christ, everything has its sacrifices. Look at yourself. You're poor as a fuckin' dormouse. You probably won't make a buck for years. Who knows if you'll ever make it?"

Martin was getting depressed once again. Jerry's heaviness and forecast of gloom was beginning to sink its claws into his heart and brain.

"Aw, perk up," Jerry almost commanded. "So, we're down now. So what? Everyone's down. Maybe we'll get together ten years from now. In New York or somewhere. Maybe we'll both be famous by then, and we'll look back at all this and have a good laugh. Can't you just see us?—famous! rich! on top of the fuckin' world, Kanner and Duke, the famous writers. Jerusalem—we'll be laughing together about it. I can just hear you. Duke, you'll be saying, do you remember those crazy days in Jerusalem?"

A feeling of warmth was now streaming through Martin's chest. What a crazy bastard he is, he kept thinking. A rabbi, he wants to be, and the next minute he's talking about riches and fame. Why fight him?—Martin thought. Why not just relax, don't take a word too seriously, just drift along on Jerry's fantasies?

At the beginning of June, Martin had spoken to his parents about going back, taking a course at Dalhousie University in Halifax. Maybe he could get his life back on the right track, he reasoned with his father. He explained the language problem he was experiencing.

"You feel cut off—is that what you're trying to say?" his father asked, his eyes narrowing, trying to understand, his skin wrinkling with a hint of worry.

"Yes," Martin nodded.

"What makes you think things are going to be any better over there? You know what Halifax is like as well as I do. Provincial, small, narrow-minded. And it hasn't changed much, believe me. We had a visit from Jack Coleman, remember him? So help me, all the guy could talk about was the number of bloody units he was buying up. That's his world—units. That's what they call it in real estate these days. I got a pain in my gut listening to him. He kept telling me how great Halifax was nowadays. But I don't buy it, not for a minute . . . Listen, all I'm trying to say is this—don't go there with any illusions. Maybe you have a rosy picture of the place. Don't forget, you were only a teenager when you left . . . Listen, I'll tell you what I'll do. I'll write a letter to my father. Ask him when the courses are beginning. How's that?"

"Good, that's fine," Martin nodded.

It was a difficult letter for Jake Kanner to write. He had to make it sound serious, yet not too serious. He didn't want to alarm his parents.

This was part of the letter: "Father, I'm sorry to have to write this, but the truth is that Martin is not having an easy time over here. I am beginning to fear for his health and general well-being. We've slowly watched him go downhill in the last several months. He's underweight. I don't believe he's eating properly. For the last year or so, he's been very depressed. Please *don't* get alarmed. I'm sure all he needs is a change in atmosphere. If he could get back into university, I'm sure a lot of his problems would clear up. To be frank with you, I just can't afford to send him. He has mentioned Halifax a few times. Can you make a few inquiries at Dalhousie, and let me know when courses begin? . . . "

The letter that came back didn't surprise Martin's father. Jake knew he had worded his own letter absolutely right, with the exact amount of pathos necessary. Martin's grandfather, who had done extremely well in real estate, was willing to send the price of a plane-ticket, and to pay tuition, food and board, and whatever else was needed once Martin arrived. There was only one stipulation: it had to be Halifax, where he personally could keep an eye on him. He wasn't going to put out good money, and "watch it go down the drain in Montreal or Toronto". It's an investment, Jake's father wrote, and I want to make sure it works out.

Martin's grandfather also wrote that the summer course was beginning in the second week of July. The letter arrived in Ramat Aviv, with plane-ticket money included, on the twenty-third of June.

On the twenty-fifth of June a letter from Martin's father arrived in Jerusalem: "How fast do you think you can clear things up there? If you need some help, I'll drive down. You can pack your stuff in the car. Give us a phone-call and let us know."

Martin's mind was in a whirl. He was excited by the possibility. In just a week or so, he could be back in Halifax. He was walking down to the "Y", his heart pounding with excitement. Yeah, he thought, what a relief to get out of this country. Just leave behind Jerry Duke and his crabs, Helen and her amoeba, Jean Paul and his asthma. How sick he was of the whole scene—the barbed-wire fence at the border, the heat, the soreness in his gums, the itching in his crotch. And yet, there was something in him that was growing sad. What a lot of things had happened to him in the last three years. People crossed his mind like bright shadows—Josephine and Jesse, Peter Stoneman, Britta and Steven, Mr. Townley, Roger Stanton and Jean Paul, Helen Tannenbaum.

He was going to leave a whole world behind, just disengage himself, board a plane, and in a few hours land on a different continent.

Time was running out, he kept thinking . . . It was Wednesday, the twenty-sixth of June. In just two weeks the course began. No, he thought, he just couldn't stand the idea of spending another summer in Israel. He had to get back, and register, do it fast. His head felt light. He was smiling to himself. Just fly the coop. Vamoose. Scram. Get out. Hop a jet. Go. Leave. Take off! Yes, take off!

His fingers trembling, his mind whirling, he called his father at his office in Tel Aviv. I can come down on Saturday, his father told him. I don't want to hang around, just have everything ready. Sure, Saturday, Martin agreed. Yes, he'd have everything all set. He'd throw it in the car and that would be it. No delays, he promised.

Saturday, Martin thought. He counted off the days on his fingers. Recounted them, made sure he was right. Saturday the twenty-ninth of June. And classes began on the eighth of July. Time, yes, the time was going by fast. He preferred it this way. What was the use of a long-drawn-out plan? Could he make it, though? Get to Tel Aviv, arrange for a flight, get back in Halifax in time to register? Sure, why not? His grandfather had written to Montreal for his university records. He was in contact with the administration building at Dalhousie. Everything was being set up.

Faster, his mind whirled and spun. He spent the next few days saying good-bye--to Roger, Helen, Jean Paul. He met Jesse on King George Road.

"How can you do such a thing?" Jesse twinkled and grinned. "Our Jerusalem . . . just think, Martin, maybe you'll never see it again."

Then Jesse turned serious. "No . . . go, if you have to. We all wish you luck. There's going to be a lot of people around here that'll miss you."

Martin shook his hand. It was as slim as ever, light-fingered yet bony. His eyes seemed darker that day. It was as if Martin were gazing into a well, and he couldn't see the bottom, only a dark light that kept plunging.

And down in the basement room on Friday night, he made love with Helen for the last time.

"Can I write to you?" she asked.

"Sure."

He wrote out his grandparents' address.

"Please write me, Martin. We shouldn't lose contact."

He could feel tears coming to his eyes. How pale she looked, drawn and pallid. He felt guilty. Here he was, taking off and leaving her behind. She'd have to fight it out alone with the amoebas. He wished he could somehow touch her with a magic wand, bring the color back to her cheeks, make her strong and healthy. Then his mind laughed ironically. The sick, he thought, the sick healing the sick. As soon as he got back, he thought, he'd have to see a dentist. His gums were rotting—he was absolutely sure of that.

The next morning the rush continued. He jumped out of bed at eight, kissed Helen, and between the kisses said good-bye. He kissed her again and again, on her bony cheeks, her forehead, her eyelashes. And between his kisses he apologized, said he just had to go.

He rushed out of her room. His father was scheduled to arrive at ten. Or was it noon? He'd forgotten. Up the Street of the Steps he strode, hopped, and ran. Britta and Frank Laskey were racing through his mind. He didn't get a chance to say good-bye to them. On Thursday night he had gone down to their house. It was dark and empty-looking. He rapped at the door. Pound, pound, pound. No answer. No one at home. And that was it . . . there was nothing he could do . . . no time to try again.

He raced down King George Road. People, people, people, he kept thinking, goodbye, goodbye, goodbye. Pepe's spaghetti house. Lupo's bar. Zion Square. Gotta get my things ready. Good-bye, everyone . . . going back to Canada . . . taking a jet; soon, oh yes, soon . . . good-bye, shalom, adios. He looked into the sky, that same old blue sky over Jerusalem, and he realized how few birds he'd ever seen there. Maybe he hadn't looked at the sky often enough. Maybe he hadn't searched for them. Few birds, hardly any, not many . . . his mind was revolving, knocking, racing . . . no time for stupid thoughts . . . gotta do what I have to do.

Good, good, good, he thought when he entered his room. Jerry Duke wasn't there. That's the last thing he wanted—Jerry Duke and his father meeting. O Christ, not that. Stay away, Jerry, just stay away for a few hours. Give me this chance to get out.

He fumbled through clothes in the room. Jerry's dirty clothes, his own, all mixed together. Heaps on the floor. Mounds of dirty clothes in the dresser. Jerry's socks, his socks. What a jumbled mess! He tried to figure it out . . . get his own stuff . . . throw it into sheets . . . wrap it up. T shirts, a pair of jeans, underwear. He had to have clothes. Something to wear back in Halifax. In only six days he would be there.

He finished the job, slumped back into a chair, let out a sigh, tried to relax. Take it easy, he whispered to himself. You're going to get out.

He checked his watch and smiled to himself. It was an old watch, growing older each year, and now it was nine years old . . . a Westbury with jewel movement, seventeen jewels. What did that mean?—he wondered. Seventeen jewels. He didn't know anything about the insides of watches. Were there rubies and diamonds inside spinning and revolving, helping his old friend to keep time?

Yes, he mused, they were growing older together. He and his Westbury that was given to him for his bar mitzvah. An expensive gift, he dreamed. And it hadn't come from a relative. Mr. Cohen, his father's business partner, had bestowed it upon him back in Halifax nine years ago. It was the only bar mitzvah gift that remained . . . cameras, wallets, photo albums, all gone, into the garbage heap, chewed up and destroyed. And Mr. Cohen himself was gone, and he went the same way as Danny Berlman went. His heart gave way in 1958. Stopped, folded, ceased its pumping. Yes, he died, Martin dreamed, just a couple of months before his father and the rest of the family moved away to Montreal.

Martin shook his head, looked at his watch again . . . five minutes to ten . . . no time for dreaming. His father would be there soon, he'd pull up his small blue Ford. Gotta get down to the street and wait for him . . . don't want him to come up to the room. No, not that. It's just too much, this room. I'll wait for him down in the street.

His father arrived almost on the dot of ten, punctual, just as he said he would.

"Just stay here, okay? I'll get everything. It'll only take me a minute. The room's pretty messy."

His father had that old grin on his face, ironic and bemused.

"It's that bad, is it?"

"Yeah," Martin nodded, "it's a mess."

"Okay, get your stuff. I'm just going to get out and stretch my legs."

His heart pounding, Martin dashed towards the front steps, and started up them, taking them two at a time. His room was paid for up to the end of the month, but he hadn't notified the landlady of his departure.

A few bags—that was all he had—a few bags of dirty clothes. He was leaving Peter's furnishings behind. And Picasso's print. Travel light, he kept thinking—why not? He bundled everything together. Good, he could take it all in one load.

He took a quick look around the room, as if he were taking a mental snapshot, storing it, an indelible print on the brain's soft tissue. Window, yes, window by the bed. Stone floor. Stand-up dresser. Peter's room on Rehov ha Neviim. Candles. Purple table-cloth. The last time to see it, the very last time. Who would get it now?—he wondered. He hadn't passed it on to a friend, not in any orderly fashion. Jerry Duke? No, he was going to become a rabbi and live down in Mea She'arim. In two days, the landlord would ask somebody for the rent.

He came down, his arms loaded with bags of dirty laundry. His father was standing on the sidewalk in a white shirt and black trousers. He had rolled up the sleeves of his shirt to his elbows.

"I'll just throw all this in the back seat," Martin gasped, trying to catch his breath. Sweat was beading on his forehead and rolling from his armpits down his sides.

"Is that it?" his father asked, still grinning.

"Yeah, that's it."

"Good. Let's go, then. Maybe we can make it back by noon."

And down the hills the blue Ford rolled, down the curved high-way, his father hunched, but still confident behind the wheel. Martin remembered an old Mayflower his father used to own back in Nova Scotia. It was years ago. The Mayflower was small, even a bit tinny-looking, but his father used to jam the accelerator to the floor, pass everything on the country roads. And they came through a few narrow escapes together, when his father would take it out into the passing lane.

"Dad!" Martin remembered shouting, "there's a car coming."

He remembered his little boy's eyes big with excitement and fear.

"I got enough room. Just relax, Martin," his father used to say.

Miraculously, he would push it, stomp it, wheel it into the right lane again.

Who could drive like his father?—Martin used to think, his young boy's heart pounding with excitement and pride. Who in the whole world had such nerves of steel?

"I guess you'll miss your friends," his father said, one hand on the wheel, bringing the car lighter up to a cigarette with the other.

Martin watched the cigarette ignite, then fastened his eyes to the road.

"Yeah, I will," Martin answered. "It seems funny, leaving."

They drove by the rusted trucks, the small farms, the irrigation pipes, and just as his father had predicted, they arrived back in Tel Aviv around noon-hour.

CHAPTER 32

The Last Argument

His brother was now fourteen months old. What a chubby little thing, Martin thought, as he watched him in his playpen. He hung on to the top with wrinkled chubby fingers. He pulled himself up, shook the playpen, lowered himself again, or just let himself fall on the thick cushion of his diapers and backside.

Just a little animal, Martin kept thinking. He began to wish that people didn't have to grow up, that they didn't have to eventually feel the squeeze and war of thoughts charging through the brain.

Martin was still scratching between his legs and smearing his crotch with blue ointment. No, he thought, he couldn't bring these crabs into the house and not tell anybody. Wouldn't it be a horrible thing if his mother caught them, his father, his sister, or worst of all, if they somehow attacked Darrell?

"Mom," he said, "I want to tell you something. I'm awfully sorry about this."

They were standing in the hall together outside his mother and father's bedroom. Martin paused, and looked at the floor. His mother already looked worried. Oh God, he thought, why is there always something?

"What is it, Martin?"

Martin screwed up his mouth and shook his head. If he looked really guilty, he thought, really sorry, really distressed, maybe it would lighten her reaction.

"Do you know what crabs are?"

His mother broke out into a smile. What the hell was happening, he wondered.

"You have them?" she nodded.

"Yes."

And her next words surprised and relieved him.

"It's okay. Don't worry about it. Your sister had them about a month ago. It's not your fault. They're very common over here."

Martin began to smile. What a relief, what a blessed relief.

"O God," he sighed, wiping his forehead. "I was so worried about telling you. You mean Debrah had them too? I'm just so glad you know about them."

His mother reached out and put a hand on his shoulder.

"Are you using the ointment?" she smiled.

"Yes," he nodded vigorously. "Blue ointment. I've got it. I'm using it all the time."

He let out another sigh. It was his second day back in Ramat Aviv, Sunday, June 30th. He just couldn't tell anybody the day before. Now it was out, and he'd gotten the best possible reaction.

"Boy, does that ever take a load off my shoulders."

"I can see that, Martin," his mother smiled, reaching up her mouth and kissing him on the cheek.

He walked back to the living room, smiling to himself, and he felt lighter, easier, just as if he had been constipated for days and finally the wonderful relief had come.

He had to get his passport ready, get a few new clothes, make arrangements. On Monday he booked a flight for July 4th. Yes, he thought again, time was running out. Just four or five days, and that would be it. And he began thinking about his parents, his sister Debrah, and his baby brother. Would he ever see them again? It could be years. There was nothing unrealistic about that thought. He wasn't being sentimental or melodramatic. In a few days he was going to fly away, and he was going to put eight thousand miles of ocean and sea between himself and them.

Yes, it was a big step, he kept thinking. No longer would he be able to hop a bus and visit them on weekends. Nor would he be able to ring them up on the telephone. He had an image in his mind of the long gut of the Mediterranean, and the vast mountains of Atlantic brine. All that would be between them, all that endless, lonely, cold wash of water and salt. And yet, he felt exhilarated, excited by it all. He was going to step out on his own finally, cut the umbilical cord, and there'd be no more discussions, arguments, talks with his father. No more cabbage soup from his mother. That would be it.

His blood was pulsing inside him—excitement mixed with a hint of fear. What if he needed them? For something. Absolutely needed them? No, he couldn't think that way. He'd have to get by, that's all, no matter what the circumstances. He'd have to do it on his own, that's all there was to it. He remembered his depression in Jerusalem, the stone cottage, the terrible weeks of nightmares, numbness and sleep. Hadn't he come out of that by himself? He remembered his father's words: "What can I say, Martin? For the first time, I really don't think I can help you."

Yes, yes, he thought to himself, wasn't it time to be brave? He'd just have to come through in any situation without their help. He'd have to find an opening, a crack in the darkness, a space he could get through. That's all there was to it, his mind buzzed.

The movie, The Great Escape, was going through his mind. He could see it clearly, very vividly once again. The men, yes, he could see them: dusty, muddy, sweating. He could see them clawing with broken fingernails, with rusted cans, tearing their way through rock and mud. And he could see a crack of light appearing, a thin fissure of hope and freedom. He was sitting in the apartment in Ramat Aviv, and he was reliving those wild moments of joy at the end of the movie when they finally emerged. Sky, forest, water. Outdoor smells. Free, at last.

He took a bus down to Sholom Aleichem Street to say goodbye to Josephine.

The apartment had not changed, he thought, nor Josephine. She was still surrounded by books and the odd plant, living alone as usual. She still had the same scissory movement of feet, her high heels clicking along the floor.

"So you're going back," Josephine said, glimmering at him through her contact lenses. "There's only one thing that worries me, Martin. And you should think about it seriously. I hope you're not taking the easy way out. You have a tendency to do that."

Martin was a little upset, even angry.

"So what if it's the easy way? Maybe it is. But why should I take a less fertile route?"

Josephine lit a cigarette. She looked a bit distressed.

"Let's not argue, Martin. We might never see each other again. I guess you just have to do what you believe is right."

Martin smiled. Good, he thought. She was dropping it. He didn't want to argue with her. He just wanted to remember the good times they had had together, and forget the others.

They began talking again. Josephine told him that she still wanted to have a baby, but she had reconsidered, and realized that she needed a husband, because she didn't want to bring an illegitimate child into the world.

"I looked into it," Josephine said, her eyes narrowing. "Illegitimate kids don't have any rights. It's a stigma, that's what it is."

Martin could feel Josephine's desire for a baby, just as if it were inside his own stomach.

"Why don't I marry you?" he said bravely. "What would it matter? I'm going back to Canada. It would be all legal, and then you could do what you wanted."

Josephine's face lit up with warmth and feeling. He was glad to see her smile, glad that his words had moved her.

"That's one of the nicest things you've ever said to me, Martin. In fact, one of the nicest things anybody has ever said to me. But no . . . I couldn't do that. It wouldn't be fair to you. What if you found the girl of your dreams and you really wanted to get married? You never know, Martin, it could happen."

Martin was smiling back at her. Yes, this was how he wanted to remember her. This was how he wanted it to end. What a warmth he was feeling inside his chest, and he knew that Josephine was feeling the same way. It was as if their insides just for a second had been joined.

He decided there and then not to make love with her on this last visit, and not to delay too long. He didn't want anything to spoil it.

He said goodbye for the very last time, and kissed her on the forehead. It was a brotherly kiss, he thought; there was almost something chaste and saintly about it. If only he could leave now, he thought, without the mood changing.

"Good luck," Josephine whispered under his chin.

When Martin got home he looked at his bookshelves, searching for the bible that Josephine had given him. He found it finally and took it down. Josephine had given it to him two years before. It was a modest-looking bible with a light-blue cover. He had no idea how old it was. Perhaps Josephine had carried it with her all the way from South Africa. It made him think of her ex-husband, the Catholic guy who used to beat her with a strap, the fellow she eventually divorced. And, Martin remembered, he had become a priest after Josephine swore and fibbed that they had never had intercourse together, never consummated the marriage.

He fondled the bible lovingly. Inside, there were a few illustrations, almost childlike in tone. Biblical scenes, little sketches of camels, doves flittering here and there, dark ominous wooden crosses. What a lovely gift, he kept thinking. He wasn't planning to take many books back to Canada with him, just one or two at the most. But this would have to be one of them, he decided.

He flipped through the bible again, stopping now and then when a certain passage caught his eyes. The Song of Songs: all that camphire, all those rubies, and the eyes of doves. Jeremiah lamenting the fall of Jerusalem. That particular illustration seemed to fascinate him the most. It was a small sketch—Jeremiah in rags, and he was hugging the stones of the fallen city.

Another thing often puzzled him about this bible, this gift from Josephine. The New Testament was included, all four gospels, the letters of St. Paul, everything, right down to the last book, the divine vision of St. John.

As he dreamed on the sofa, the bible in his hand, he remembered what Helen had told him once. Her words had startled him, but he liked what she had said:

"You know, Martin, there's something about you that's priest-like."

"Really?" he smiled. "What do you mean?"

"I don't know how to put it into words," Helen hesitated. "It's a hard, almost lonely quality."

"It sounds like it bothers you."

Helen pinched her lips tightly together.

"Yes and no," she replied. "It just hits me like a fortress sometimes. And I can't get through. And yet, it's that very thing that makes you attractive."

Martin smiled to himself, remembering the conversation down in Helen's basement room on the Street of the Steps. What was wrong, he thought, with being a fortress?—if he could live with it, if he could find some value in it. And he remembered sometimes down there in her room he used to sing a verse of Shma Yisroel in Hebrew. In a deep booming voice he used to sing it, gazing into the light bulb dangling from the ceiling. Shma Yisroel, Adonai Elohenu, Adonai Achad. Listen, O Israel, for the Lord is God, and the Lord is One.

Yes, he decided, he would carry this bible, Josephine's gift, back to his hometown with him.

It was Tuesday, the 2nd of July, and in two days he was leaving, hopping a jet, taking off forever. The prospect seemed to open his mind, make him feel light, easy, reflective. He walked out to the balcony often, just stood there, and looked at the city sprawled out before him. Miles of apartment buildings, small houses, smoke from the odd factory, and the sun was pouring down early in the morning.

His thoughts travelled back to Jerusalem. He was glad he was there no longer. It seemed old to him now, the city, old and worn out, as if the buildings he knew had become shells, stone and wood, and inside, everything had folded, dried up, and evaporated. Jerry Duke, he shuddered, no, in his present mood he wouldn't be able to talk to him. Images flashed through his mind. Jerry Duke in various guises—riding a motorcycle with his arm in a cast, cutting up hash, giving Isolde an overdose of barbiturates, and finally Jerry Duke repentant, wan and pale, talking of his rabbinical future.

Later that day he was padding around the apartment. He stopped for a while and looked at the bookshelf. He was going to leave most of it behind, his collection of novels and poetry. D. H. Lawrence, Dostoyevsky, Thomas Wolfe, John Steinbeck. He liked the parade of colors almost as much as the contents. Paperbacks, most of them. Red jackets, yellow, blue, orange, two-tone grey and black.

It was about five o'clock in the afternoon. His sister Debrah had just come home from work. He could hear her high heels clicking through the apartment. She had a good job now, working as a secretary. She was very fluent in Hebrew. Martin was amazed at how quickly and easily she'd picked up the language. Most of her friends were sabras. And in the past, Martin had seen his sister and a group of her friends together. They were all yakking together in Hebrew, switching occasionally to English, and there was Debrah, rattling off sentence after sentence in the old biblical tongue.

He was almost proud of her for this linguistic ease. He realized, of course, that her choice of boyfriend had helped. He was a sabra through and through. Chaim was his name, a slim, muscular Yemenite, nineteen years old with bright blue eyes. God, his eyes were startling, Martin often thought. So unexpected. The skin dark, almost black, and those two blue orbs dancing and shining out of his skull.

He stood before the bookshelf, his eyes travelling along the titles. Lovingly, he took a book down, flipped through the pages, let his eyes fall on a paragraph, reading it, savoring it once again. He put the book back up, and his eyes began their travels back and forth until another hit him, interested him enough to pull it from its resting place.

He took John Steinbeck's *Of Mice and Men* off the shelf. It wasn't a huge weighty thing, just a slim two hundred pages or so, perhaps less. What a wonderful book, he kept thinking. The story came back to him—Lenny, big Lenny with his huge heart of feeling, and George his intellectual friend. What a sense of life Steinbeck had, he thought. He made everything so real—the flowers, the animals, the people. The way they talked—it amazed him: so simply, just ordinary language, yet it was packed with so much feeling and meaning. It was a language, Martin thought, you could hear on the street, in a hotel, in a barber shop. Ordinary street-English, something he missed during his years in Israel.

Yes, he dreamed, Lenny and George. Weren't they wonderful creations? He could visualize Lenny, big and tongue-tied, unable to express himself, and what was that pet he had? Was it a mouse or a rabbit? He'd forgotten. Some little animal. And Lenny didn't even realize his own strength. Did he actually crush the poor animal, his beloved pet, crush him to death? Martin had forgotten.

And there was a girl, Martin remembered. And didn't Lenny desire her, think she was beautiful, just like his pet mouse or rabbit? Didn't he try to fondle her one day? Didn't she protest? And didn't he unwittingly crush her too, kill her by mistake?

He remembered the last scene—George and Lenny on the run together. The police closing in. What a powerful scene! Weren't they in the woods together, on a high hill somewhere above the town? Wasn't George crying, but hiding his tears from Lenny? And he remembered the feeling between these two men, the love, these two beings so different on the surface. George—brainy, philosophical, understanding. Lenny forever tongue-tied and slow. How was Steinbeck able to do it? To create two people so real, so believable, and yet so different, worlds apart from each other. Yet something joined them. Wasn't that the whole point of the story? There was something deeper beating between them than most of the world could fathom or understand.

And the final scene—Martin felt his skin tingle and his heart beat faster as he thought about it. George realized the jig was up, and soon Lenny would be in the hands of the police, at the mercy of the townspeople. No, not Lenny, George thought, they'd make him crumple up and die slowly. How would he ever understand their questions, their jibes, their taunts? And George's next step surprised Martin, shocked him, and yet it was right. In spare, lean language Steinbeck described it: George took out his revolver, and shot Lenny from behind without saying a word.

The ending thudded inside Martin's head, yet how else could it end? There was no magical solution. Yes, it was right.

He was still fondling the book, Steinbeck's masterpiece, when Debrah walked into the living room. She had gotten out of her tight-fitting clothes that she wore to work—the black skirt, the blouse, the high heels. She was wearing a brightly colored caftan that fell in light folds down to her heels.

"What are you looking at?" she asked.

Martin was in a bit of a daze. Her voice jerked him back out of the book, out of Lenny and George's world.

"A book by Steinbeck. *Of Mice and Men*. Have you ever read it?"

He could see her face getting pinched, a frown, her eyes narrowing, her lips almost sneering.

"Yeah, I read it," she frowned. "What do you see in a book like that? It left me cold. It was horrible."

"Horrible?" Martin gasped, amazed and bewildered. How could somebody think of it as horrible? "What do you mean?"

Debrah shook back her hair.

"What's it about anyway?" she sneered. "These two guys running around together. One a big dumb lummox. And the other guy was creepy."

Martin could feel himself getting angry. His chest was beginning to pain with the pressure of his own anger. And his head was swirling.

"You didn't understand a fucking thing about that book, Debrah. Is that all you got from it? Couldn't you feel what was going on between them?"

Now Debrah's face was getting red and flushed. She hated when her brother talked down to her, when he used that awful school-teacher voice. No, she decided, she wasn't going to let him get away with it. Not this time, not just two days before he was going to leave. She was going to stand up to him. He wasn't so smart anyway, she thought. Sure, he read a lot of books. He went to university. But he hadn't even learned Hebrew, and she had. And she was making good money at her job.

"You know what I think, Martin," she spat. "Those two guys in that book—they're just a couple of fairies, that's all they are. A couple of homos. And the guy who wrote about them was probably a queer too."

These unexpected words left him speechless. He was stunned by them. He stood in front of her shocked, almost too shocked to feel anger. But it was there, inside him, choking him, pounding at the sides of his head. Did she know what she was saying?

Debrah's eyes were still burning. She was trembling with anger. Good, she thought, I've finally shut him up.

"Debrah," he said in a shaky voice. He was feeling weak now, almost sick. "What you just said is crazy. You're talking about a great book. You're talking about something that's beautiful. How can you say something like that?"

"I don't care!" she snapped. "That's what I believe. You can take it or leave it. Digest it or dump it."

She didn't wait for any response. She turned around quickly and left the living room.

Martin stood beside the bookshelf. *Of Mice and Men* hung limply from his hands. His insides seemed to be turning watery, a sick, weak feeling. He couldn't get her words out of his head. They scraped inside him. Homos, fairies, queers. What was she talking about? How could she see George and Lenny's friendship like that? It made him feel like crying or just lying down and giving up.

He tried to dismiss it. Why let it bother him?—he thought. What did she know anyway? What could she know—clacking at a typewriter all day long, still living at home? What had she ever experienced in life? He reasoned, and reasoned, and reasoned some more, but still he could hear her voice, those horrible words, and the hatred that had gone along with them.

What a horrible feeling inside him. It was watery and cold, as if everything solid inside his chest was breaking up, and turning into liquid. It made him feel alone and lonely. He felt as if he were standing high on a mountain peak, and there was no one there except the ghosts of Lenny and George, and Steinbeck's words swirling around like fog. How could he and Debrah be living in two such different worlds? It frightened him and made him feel uneasy. What he loved, adored, and revered, she despised. It didn't make any sense to him. And yet he knew somebody had to be right, and somebody had to be wrong. It couldn't just rest with that rift, that jagged rift.

He still had Steinbeck's book in his hand. In two days, he thought, he'd be out of this apartment, he'd be on his way, and soon thousands of miles away. Perhaps it was all for the best. He walked slowly over to the sofa and let himself fall on it. He was still clutching the book. Just go to sleep, he said to himself, forget about it, forget the whole thing. What did she know? How could she know anything? He fell asleep for an hour with his cheek resting against the book.

That evening at supper, a black mood hung over the dining-room table. Martin couldn't taste his mother's cooking. The meat seemed flavorless. He was hardly noticing what was going inside his mouth. He was chewing it mechanically, swallowing lump after lump of roast beef. He kept his eyes on the plate, on the white porcelain, and on the chunks of food. Debrah was sitting across the table from him. He didn't want to look at her. His short sleep on the sofa hadn't erased his anger, or his bewilderment.

Debrah, too, was silent. Good, she was thinking, I've made my point. And yet she felt a tightness inside her chest, an uneasiness. Somewhere inside, she knew she hadn't heard the end of it. She'd seen her brother in these dark moods before, these long heavy silences. Something was probably working inside him, churning around, and he was just waiting his chance to bring it out. When did she ever get the last word?

Jake Kanner wiped away the grease from around his mouth with a napkin. He looked tired and a bit drained. Supper was almost over, and hardly anything had been said.

"Can somebody please tell me what's going on?" he asked a bit angrily. "I come home for supper and it's like a bloody morgue. What's going on?"

Martin remained silent. He was looking at the bottom of his glass of water.

"It's silly," Debrah said in a grating voice. "Martin and I had an argument over a stupid book. I don't know why he's taking it so seriously."

Words were beginning to jerk up from Martin's throat.

"First of all, Debrah," he said, his voice trembling slightly, "the book is not stupid. And it is serious."

Jake Kanner's eyes narrowed. "Okay, okay. For Chrissakes, stop the arguing for a second. What the hell book was it anyway?"

"*Of Mice and Men*," Martin answered in a low serious voice. "Steinbeck's novel."

Martin's father looked puzzled. "Yeah, *Of Mice and Men*—so what? I know the book. What the hell was there to argue about? To cause all this?"

Martin dropped back into his silence. As far as he was concerned, it was up to Debrah to tell him. It was her brilliant remarks that had started the whole thing. Let her tell him.

"I didn't like the book, that's all," she said in a high-pitched voice.

"That is not all, Debrah, and you know it," Martin snapped back at her. "Tell him the truth. Tell him exactly what you said."

Debrah could feel a pressure inside her stomach, pressing against her, making her feel tired and angry. Why did he have to always yell at her like that?

"Those two men in the book," she began, her voice quavering, "I said they were fairies, and I don't care. That's all they are. I don't care what Martin thinks. I don't care how smart he is. I don't care what any of you think. They're fairies, fairies, fairies."

Debrah burst into tears. She scraped her chair back quickly and ran out of the room and down the hall to her bedroom.

"Look what you've done, Martin," his mother snapped. "All over a stupid book. You should know better than to talk about books with her."

Dahlia Kanner got up from the table and left the dining room. She walked quickly down the hallway and into Debrah's room. Martin could hear the door slamming shut.

Jake Kanner looked tired and drained, as if the wind had been knocked out of him. He was massaging his scalp with forefinger and thumb. Martin watched from the corner of his eye—his father's fingertips rotating near the temples. Soon he would speak, Martin thought. He'd seen this kind of build-up before.

"Your mother's got a point," he finally said. "You can't talk to Debrah like you talk to your friends, and expect to get the answers you're looking for. You should know that by now."

Martin pinched his lower lip between his fingertips, massaging it, squeezing it together, and letting the flesh relax again. He let out a heavy sigh.

"Yeah, I guess you're right. I just couldn't believe what she said, that's all. There was so much hatred in her remarks."

A tiny grin was beginning to crease his father's cheeks. And then it disappeared, as it if were completely involuntary.

"But she was right about one thing, Martin. She has a healthy hatred for queers. In that respect, she was right. I've always been disgusted by them. Something in my stomach turns over when I think of homos. They're very sick people. Dangerous, in fact."

Dangerous. Sick. Disgusted. His father's words beat inside his head. Martin was thinking of Mr. Townley in Jerusalem, his professor friend, and his cat, Moog. He was thinking of Larry Shoshannah in his shimmering blue shorts. He was thinking of Jesse's flip side, the boys he described.

"I don't agree with you, Dad, I'm sorry. I had some good friends down in Jerusalem who were gay. They weren't any more dangerous than anybody else. In fact, they were quite warm and intelligent."

His father's eyes darkened. They were shot through, now, with a black darting light.

"Very nice people! Are you kidding, Martin? How well did you know these people? As far as I'm concerned they're among the lowliest forms of life. If it were up to me, I'd have them all incarcerated, and the keys thrown away."

His father's words were hard to believe. Martin looked at him, directly into his face. There wasn't a hint of frivolity. His father was absolutely serious, sober and grim.

"I knew these people very well," Martin said slowly and deliberately. "They were good friends of mine. You remember me telling you about Professor Townley? He's gay. I've stayed at his house. He's read my writing. He got me that job at the "Y". He's made me meals and introduced me to people. He's one of the nicest people I've ever met."

His father was rubbing his eyes now, covering them, hiding them away. Martin was looking into his face.

"That's the side you saw, perhaps. Don't kid yourself, Martin. Did you ever see the little boys he brought down to his place? They're notorious for that."

His father scraped his chair back and got up, turning his back to Martin.

"No, they thoroughly sicken me. I still maintain my original position. Throw them all into the can. I don't believe they can be rehabilitated. Not from my experience, anyway."

"Have you ever known any?" Martin asked, a bite and thrust to his question. Martin got up from his chair and followed his father into the living room. He was determined not to let the discussion end this way.

"I've seen enough, Martin, believe me. Yeah, I've met the odd queer. I haven't exactly lived in a cocoon. I've seen it—their mincing and prancing. It turns my stomach just to think about it."

His father lit a cigarette and began to cough. He was choking and spluttering, his face going red as a brick furnace. It was one of the worst coughing fits Martin had seen him take. His father was doubled over, tears coming to his eyes. He seemed to be having a hard time catching his breath.

Martin walked over and placed a hand on his father's shoulder, pressing, trying to steady him.

"Are you okay, Dad?" His voice sounded soft and worried.

His father convulsed some more.

"Yeah, yeah, I'm okay," his father managed to reply, out of breath. "Thank you, I'm okay."

Still hunched over and coughing, his father walked over to the sofa and let himself fall into it, sitting down, his head falling back against a cushion.

"Oh Christ," he wheezed, "these fuckin' things are going to do me in some day."

Jake Kanner sat on the sofa wiping his forehead. He'd broken out into a sweat. He took a handkerchief out of his pocket and dabbed his forehead with it, then rubbed it more vigorously around the back of his neck.

Martin sat down at the other end of the sofa. His father's remarks were still going through him. One of his father's pet phrases kept swirling inside him. "Stand up and be counted," his father used to say. "That's the problem with a lot of people, Martin, I've seen it time and again. They might believe in something, but when it comes down to the crunch, they never stand up and get counted. They fold, cower away in their corners. There are times in your life you just have to do it, Martin—stand up, and be counted."

How many times, Martin wondered, had he heard his father tell him this when he was a young boy, and later as a teenager? Now, the words came back at him. Years later, they were still inside him, still important to him.

Martin was tempted to let the discussion drop. His father still looked weak sitting on the sofa, trying to recover from his fit of coughing. The sweat was still beading on his forehead and he was still rubbing it away with his white handkerchief. But how could he leave things this way? In two days he'd be leaving. No, he wanted to take a stand, just as his father used to advise. How he used to admire that phrase as a young boy, and admire the man who spoke it. He wanted to stand up that evening, stand up on that issue, and he wanted his father to count him, to know with absolute certainty where he stood, and that nothing would make him alter his position.

"Dad," he began again, "I don't believe they're sick people. But even if they were, what good would it do to throw them in prison? Does that really make any sense? Would they change there? And besides, they're not hurting anybody, not any more than you are or I am."

His father wiped away some sweat from above his upper lip.

"I don't care what you say, Martin. They're sick people, and you'll never convince me otherwise. Their lives are twisted. Their sense of values."

"I'm not talking about that!" Martin snapped back. "Look—I don't believe they're sick. They have a different thing about sex, that's all. But that's not the issue. You're talking about taking a whole group of people and throwing them in jail. Is that any different from what Hitler did to the Jews? It's insane, that's what it is."

Jake Kanner was feeling a pressure building in his chest, tightening around his head. Was he being logical?—he wondered. There was a feeling of truth in Martin's words that was beginning to gnaw at him. Queers *were* sick and twisted, he thought. Martin could talk till doomsday—he would never change his opinion on that. But prison? Was Martin right? Was he taking the whole thing too far?

"Okay, maybe I went overboard, Martin. Maybe I did get carried away. Maybe prison isn't the right place for them. Maybe some of them aren't criminals. How am I expected to know? That's a job for trained psychologists. Okay—I can see your point. But I still don't like the idea of them roaming the streets. Let them be rehabilitated— just like any other nut case. Does that satisfy you?"

Martin got up from the sofa shaking his head.

"No, Dad, it doesn't satisfy me. I'm sorry, it just doesn't. They're not nut cases. They're not any crazier than you or me. You believe *me* this time—I've met them, and I don't believe you have. I really don't think you have."

Martin started pacing the living room, walking up and down it, his heels clicking against the fake wood floor. He moved towards the balcony, turned around, crossed in front of his father, looked directly at him, into his face, paced towards the bookcase, glanced at the books, spun around again, and headed for the balcony.

He felt a new energy inside him. It added a springiness to his legs; it buzzed in his chest—a heat that massaged him. He walked to the balcony and looked down at the city—Ramat Aviv, Tel Aviv, the night was sprinkled with light from houses. And inside some of those houses, he thought, there were people like Mr. Townley, like Larry Shoshannah, men who talked to each other, kissed each other, danced together, and men who went to bed together, hugged each other, and there was nothing wrong with it. They had every right to do it. They were not crazy. If only his father could meet Mr. Townley, get to know him, then meet Jerry Duke. If only he could make the comparison for himself.

But that was the problem, Martin thought, that was the problem. What did his father know about his life down in Jerusalem? What could he ever know about it? How could he explain it to him, show it to him, make him feel it the way he had experienced it? There was no way—even if they talked for two days straight, or two weeks, or two months. Mere talk would never do it. His father would have to go there, live there, meet the same people, and lie on his back for a month in the stone cottage fearing madness and death. And what was even more impossible, a ridiculous thought, his father would have to become Martin; he would have to give up Jake the computer specialist, Jake the husband of Dahlia; he would have to make the written word his first love. How else could this transformation occur?

Jake Kanner lit another cigarette. He tried to drag on it slowly and evenly. He didn't want to take another coughing fit; he was still weak from the last one. He watched his son pace in front of him. A fear gnawed at him. What if Martin was not just arguing abstractly, what it he had actually done it himself? That was what worried him most. What if his own son was turning that way, the very thing that sickened him the most, that nauseated his whole being?

Jake Kanner wanted to speak, but he didn't know how to phrase it, to make it sound diplomatic.

"Martin... " he began, "I respect your ideas on this matter... you're entitled to them... I don't know how to put this." Jake paused, trying to order his thoughts. "Let me put it this way. I just hope for your sake, for your well-being, that they are just ideas. Do you know what I'm saying?" Jake paused again. "It would be a horrible life, Martin."

His father's words made him stop his pacing. Yes, he knew exactly what his father was saying. Martin looked directly at him once again, into his face.

"No, Dad," he shook his head wearily, "I haven't turned gay. But it's not just ideas either. I have a feeling for these people... there's something warm about them, and open. Can we just leave it go at that?"

Martin could see his father nodding in the darkness; the tip of his cigarette bobbed up and down.

"Still a rebel, aren't you?" his father grinned.

"Yeah, I guess so," Martin smiled. "I guess you could put it that way."

Martin was glad that the tension had broken between them. They spent a half hour talking together. They kept the conversation general, trying to skirt subjects that were potentially volatile.

Martin's mother joined them.

"Where is Debrah?" Jake asked.

"She went to sleep. She was pretty tired out from work. The poor kid's really trying her best."

"I'm sorry I argued with her," Martin said softly. "I'll apologize in the morning."

"Will you do that, Martin?" his mother asked imploringly. "Please, for me. She looks up to you, Martin. She really does. She doesn't want you to leave with bad feelings."

"Yeah... I'll make peace with her."

"Good," his mother smiled, rubbing his shoulder.

The three of them talked together. They reminisced about Halifax,

the different houses they'd lived in together when Martin was growing up. They talked about the movie theatres, about Queensland on
the South Shore Road.

Martin could almost smell Halifax on a rainy day. It was a vivid
memory. In the downtown area, where his father used to have his
office, on a rainy day it smelled like it was raining particles of fish.
Cod and haddock, mackerel, and there was a softness when it
rained, when it mixed with the fog, as if the whole town were
wrapped in a soft hand.

And in his mind he could see Barrington Street on such a rainy,
fish-smelling day. The trolleys were rocking through the streets.
They swayed from side to side like huge whales.

CHAPTER 33

Departure

The El Al jet was on the runway and the huge motors were tuning up.

It was about five-thirty in the afternoon, Thursday, July 4th. Martin Kanner could see the first glimmerings of sunset. The outer rim of the sun had a rosy tinge. He remembered a childhood rhyme: salmon sky in the morning, sailor's warning; salmon sky at night, sailor's delight.

He was sitting beside the window looking out. In the crowd of onlookers who stood beside a chain-link fence, he could see his mother, father, and sister waving. His father looked small and hunched. He wasn't waving as vigorously or as often as the others. Almost shyly, he raised his hand once or twice and tilted it in Martin's direction.

He could feel the motors winding up—the whole plane rattled, and the windowpanes vibrated. There was an excitement in his stomach that seemed to match the low growl and whine of the engines roaring.

The plane taxied down the runway, made a complete U turn, and rolled back slowly past the relatives and friends in the crowd. Everyone was waving now, a flurry of hands and handkerchiefs.

Martin was thinking of that Hebrew word "aliyah"—going up. He smiled to himself. Technically, he was going down. Anyone who left Israel was not on aliyah, but its opposite—*yoridah*. He flipped the word over in his mouth, Yoridah, yoridah, yoridah. He could feel the "r" in the word crinkling his tongue.

He waved back at his parents one last time as the plane began to taxi faster. It rolled past the onlookers and headed for the end of the runway. The motors buzzed and roared. They reached a high-pitched whine.

He settled back into the cushioned seat, the belt fastened around his stomach.

He could feel the plane rising, taking off; it was going up at a 45-degree angle, and he could feel himself being tilted back.

Goodbye, he was thinking. Shalom. He could see faces of friends in his mind: Britta in white slacks dancing down King George Road, and she was singing about being a blade of grass. Jesse near the Valley of the Cross explaining about the cross and how it was cut centuries before from a tree that lived in the blackness of the valley. Jesse stroking his beard and talking about the ballet dancers that he once knew. How young they were, and agile. Josephine slipping out her contact lenses, slipping them back in again. And then he saw just a crowd of faces—Jesse, Josephine, Britta, Helen, Jerry Duke, Roger Stanton, and he was beginning to feel a little sad. Everything, he thought, was being erased as the jet rose higher and levelled off.

But how could they ever be removed?—he wondered—they were so fresh in his mind.

He looked out his window. They were heading into a sunset. In five hours they would land at London airport, just five hours. He would sleep overnight in a motel beside the airport, and the next day board another plane for Halifax.

He settled back into the cushioned seat, took out a cigarette, and lit it.

He looked out the window again. The rest of the passengers were looking and murmuring, whispering to one another, and some were exclaiming. The sun was setting behind huge mountains of clouds. The clouds looked like enormous, red-orange cliffs drenched in the sun's dying light.

Martin smiled. It was an amazing sight—a sunset taking place twenty thousand feet above the ground.

As they headed towards England, going west, the sunset continued. The plane was going through time changes, and it was keeping up with the sun dropping out of the sky.

Martin lit another cigarette.

Israel, he kept thinking, shalom. Shalom, shalom, shalom. He said the word so many times it began to lose meaning, and to sound a little ridiculous, nonsensical; the syllables slid together.

He opened a small blue flight-bag, and looked for the Time magazine he had bought at the airport. He spotted a gift his father had given him, just before he left. The gift puzzled him. It was a clothes-brush. He picked it up and revolved it slowly in his left hand. It had black bristles, and there were tiny yellow-red flowers painted on the back of it. What a strange gift, he kept thinking. His father knew very well that he went around in jeans and T-shirts most of the time. When would he ever use it? Yet he liked the look of the thing, especially the soft, mellow tones in those delicate flowers. How small they were, those tiny buds of petals. What kind of flower was it?—he wondered. Certainly, it must have a name. But he was never good at this kind of thing—remembering the names of flowers, or unusual colors.

He slipped the brush back down, wedged it securely between a couple of books.

When they arrived in England it was just getting dark. The sun had finally gone down.

Toronto, 1978

Glossary

Note: The *ch* sound in Hebrew words is similar to the *ch* sound in the word "loch", or in "Bach".

aliyah (Hebrew) 1. a going up. 2. immigration to Israel.

bubah (Yiddish) grandmother.

challah (Hebrew) egg bread, usually eaten on the sabbath.

chaver(im) (Hebrew) friend(s), comrade(s).

daven (Yiddish) to pray.

eretz (Hebrew) land, nation, country, or the country (Israel).

gelt (Yiddish) money.

Histadrut (Hebrew) Israel's central labor organization.

maftir (Hebrew) a reading from the Prophets.

mah pitom? (Hebrew) what now? so what? what's this all of a sudden?

mamser (Hebrew) bastard, scoundrel.

Mapai (Hebrew) governing political party under Ben Gurion, slightly left of centre.

Mea She'arim (Hebrew) main area of residence of Orthodox Jews in Jerusalem.

sabra (Hebrew) 1. a prickly pear. 2. a native-born Israeli.

Sephardi(m) (Hebrew) Jew(s) from Africa and the Middle East.

sherut shared taxi service, used in Middle East.

shmatah (Yiddish) rag, kerchief.

ulpan (Hebrew) adult school for learning Hebrew.

vilders (Yiddish) wild men, savages.

Yehudim (Hebrew) Hebrews, Jews.

yoridah (Hebrew) 1. a descent, a going down. 2. emigration from Israel.

zeyde (Yiddish) grandfather.